Soulflame

THE DRAGON SINGER CHRONICLES | BOOK 3

MICHELLE M. BRUHN

SONGWEAVER
MEDIA

Cover by Kirk DouPonce, www.DogEaredDesign.com
Map by Soraya Corcoran, www.SorayaCorcoran.com
Edited by Katie Phillips, www.KatiePhillipsCreative.com

ISBN 978-1-7349925-6-4 (paperback)
ISBN 978-1-7349925-7-1 (ebook)

For the lost and confused,
And those who cling no matter the cost.

TABLE OF CONTENTS

ARRAN
F'renn's Mnt
Rorenth's Mnt
Kannin
Parrin
Azron
Serpent's Fangs
L'rang
Western Hill Country
Southlands
@SorayaCorcoran

Belin
Sea
Eastern Forests
Nissen River
Twi-Peak
Meran
Soren
Cherrin
N. Russig
E. Russig
Russig Lake
S. Russig
Fool's Landing
Tsamen & Paili's Mnt

PRONUNCIATIONS & DEFINITIONS

A'dem (ah-DEHM) - *the planet*

Alísa (ah-LEE-suh) - *slayer, Dragon Singer, daughter of Karn & Hanah, Illuminated to Sesína*

Allara (ah-LAH-ruh) - *(deceased) slayer, Dragon Singer, daughter of Namor & Tenza, mother of Kallar & R'lann*

An'reik (AHN-rayk) - *"sold-soul", mortals who have given their souls to the Nameless Ones in exchange for power*

Anam (ah-NAHM) - *"soul"*

Aravi (EHR-uh-vee) - *ice dragoness, daughter of Saynan & Aree*

Aree (ah-REE) - *dragoness, mate of Saynan*

Arran (eh-RAN) - *the continent*

Bodhrán (BOW-rahn) - *a wide, flat drum played by mallet or hand*

Branni (BRAH-nee) - *the Eldra of warriors and slayers*

Bria (BREE-uh) - *the Eldra of Dragon Singers, was once a mortal woman*

Briek (breek) - *slayer, Alísa's human second-in-command, former Eastern wayfarer*

Céilí (KAY-lee) - *a dance for two or more partners where steps are called; also a social gathering with music, dancing, and story-telling*

Chrí¹ (chree) - *(deceased) drek, mate of Rann, mother of Rís & Chrí²*

Chrí² (chree) - *drek, daughter of Chrí¹ & Rann, sister of Rís*

Crakil (crah-KIHL) - *dragon, alpha, Sesína's father*

D'tohm (dih-TOHM) - *the Eldra of wind & spirit*

Dezra (DEZ-rah) - *dragoness, Illuminated to Rassím*

Drek (drehk) - *small, dragon-shaped creature that lives in the forests; plural form: dreki (DREH-kee)*

Eldra (EHL-druh) - *an angelic being given stewardship over specific aspects of A'dem; plural form: Eldír (EHL-deer)*

Faern (fayrn) - *(deceased) dragon, father of Komi*

Falier (fah-LEER) - *slayer, son of Parsen & Kat, brother of Selene, mind-kin to Graydonn*

Farren (FEHR-ehn) - *normal, songweaver of Karn's clan, Alísa's musical mentor*

Gia (JEE-ah) - *slayer, mother of Tobin, stepmother of Kallar*

Graydonn (GRAY-don) - *dragon, son of Koriana, mind-kin to Falier*

Hanah (HA-nuh) - *normal, wife of Karn, mother of Alísa*

Harazím (hehr-ah-ZEEM) - *dragon, alpha with a peace treaty with Alísa*

Harenn (HEHR-ehn) - *dragon, son of Tsamen & Paili*

Hwinn (hwihn) - *dragon, Illuminated to Selene*

Iila (EE-luh) - *dragoness, initially of Rorenth's clan*

Illumination - *the sharing of minds at a dragonet's hatching which binds their mind to their chosen parent*

Iompróir Anam (YOHM-proh-ihr ah-NAHM) - *"soul-bearer"*

Isarra (ih-SAR-uh) - *an'reik, controls dark mists that can become solid, amplifies other an'reik powers, facilitates possession*

Jossen (JAH-sehn) - *slayer, Karns-man*

Kallar (ka-LAHR) - *slayer, Karn's apprentice, Dragon Singer, son of Allara, brother of R'lann*

Karn (kahrn) - *slayer, chief, husband of Hanah, father of Alísa*

Kat (kat) - *normal, holder, wife of Parsen, mother of Selene & Falier*

Komi (KOH-mee) - *dragoness, mind-kin to Trísse*

Koriana (kohr-ee-AN-uh) - *dragoness, mother of Graydonn*

Korin (KOHR-ihn) - *dragon, mate of Rayna, initially of Rorenth's clan*

L'non (luh-NON) - *slayer, brother of Karn, father of Levan & Taer*

Laen (layn) - *drek, Selene's friend*

Lellani (leh-LAH-nee) — *dragoness, subjected to an an'reik alpha*

Levan (LEH-vehn) - *slayer, son of L'non, twin brother of Taer*

Lorin (LOHR- ehn) - *slayer, chief of Bezin*

The Maker - *creator deity*

Marizarr (MAHR-ih-zahr) - *an'reik, fire-manipulator, Isarra's second*

Me'ran (meh-RAN) - *Falier's home village*

Mennáli (meh-NAH-lee) - *dragoness, volunteers to work with riders in Alísa's army*

N'ravi (nuh-RAH-vee) - *slayer, chief of Eskann*

Nahne (NAH-nee) - *the Eldra of those whose work cares for people*

Nameless Ones - *Eldír who turned against the Maker and were stripped of their names and stewardships*

Namor (NAY-mohr) - *(deceased) slayer, husband of Tenza, father of Allara*

Nissen (NEE-sihn) - *river dividing the hill country from the forests*

P'raenn (puh-RAY-ehn) - *dragon, volunteers to work with riders in Alísa's army*

Paili (PAY-lee) - *(deceased) dragoness, mate of Tsamen, mother of Harenn, Allara's bane*

Parsen (PAR-sehn) - *normal, holder, husband of Kat, father of Selene & Falier*

Prilunes (PRIH-loons) - *mountains dividing Arran's north and south lands*

Q'rill (kuh-RIHL) - *dragon, son of Tora, initially of Rorenth's clan*

R'lann (ruh-LAN) — *slayer, son of Allara, Kallar's younger brother*

Radharc Anam (RAD-hark ah-NAHM) - *"soul-seer"*

Rann (ran) - *drek, mate of Chrí[1], father of Rís & Chrí[2]*

Rassi (RAH-see) - *slayer, Trísse's younger brother*

Rassím (rah-SEEM) - *slayer, radharc anam, initially from the Southlands, Illuminated to Dezra*

Rayna (RAY-nuh) - *dragoness, mate of Korin, initially of Rorenth's clan*

Rís (rees) - *drek, son of Rann & Chrí[1], brother of Chrí[2]*

Rorenth (ROHR-enth) - *(deceased) dragon, an'reik alpha*

Sareth (SEHR-eth) - *(deceased) dragon, of Rorenth's clan but turned to Alísa's*

Saynan (SAY-nehn) - *ice dragon, mate of Aree, father of Aravi*

Selene (seh-LEEN) - *slayer, daughter of Parsen & Kat, sister of Falier, Illuminated to Hwinn*

Sesína (seh-SEE-nuh) - *dragoness, Illuminated to Alísa*

Ska - *drek, Falier's friend*

T'kan (tuh-KAN) - *slayer, chief of Vennia*

Taer (tayr) - *slayer, son of L'non, twin brother of Levan*

Taz - *slayer, Selene's pursuer, Harenn's rider*

Tella (TEH-luh) - *slayer, chief of a western wayfaring clan*

Tenza (TEHN-zuh) - *slayer, wife of Namor, mother of Allara (deceased)*

Tern (turn) - *slayer, Trísse's pursuer, Kallar's best friend*

Tobin (TOH-bihn) - *slayer, Kallar's stepbrother, son of Gia*

Tora (TOHR-uh) - *dragoness, mother of Q'rill, initially of Rorenth's clan*

Toronn (TOHR-ahn) - *slayer, chief of Azron (Alísa's home village)*

Trísse (treeS) - *slayer, mind-kin to Komi*

Tsamen (TSAH-mehn) - *dragon, mate of Paili (deceased), father of Harenn*

Varek (VEHR-ehk) - *slayer, Karns-man*

Yarlan (YAR-len) - *(deceased) slayer, Alísa's tormentor in Me'ran*

AUTHOR'S NOTE:

Dear readers and songweavers,

Thank you for coming on this adventure with me and my dear character children. Before you embark on this last leg of the journey, I will warn you that this book is the darkest in Alísa's trilogy. Amidst the friendship, growth, and banter there is also pain, torture, and grief. My promise to you, dear readers, for this book and every book I will ever write, is that though sorrows may last through the night, joy comes in the morning. (Psalm 30:5)

With eyes ever lifted,
~ Michelle M. Bruhn

Trigger Warning: suicidal thoughts, demon possession, death

A HISTORY OF ALÍSA DRAGON-SINGER

Transcribed and edited by Songweaver Farren
from a speech by Sesína Singer-Bound

Alísa Dragon-Singer was not always the great alpha-chief you see before you today. Like everyone, her story began in a much humbler place. Or, as humble as it can be when one's father is chief of the north-central wayfaring slayers.

As a child, she developed a vocal stammer that severely marred her confidence. Warriors do not take kindly to weakness, whether true or merely perceived. After years of hoping it would mend, Alísa's father Karn took on an apprentice to lead the wayfarers after him instead of her. Kallar, who would years later become known as Allaras-son, was everything Alísa was not— confident, a talented swordsman, and a dragon-hater.

The daughter of Karn was *not* a dragon-hater, you ask? She wanted to be. She knew she should be. But her vocal stammer was not her only weakness. As her empathic powers developed, she and her father learned a terrible secret— her empathy uncontrollably connected to dragons. She couldn't block it out or overpower it by focusing on human emotions instead. She felt every emotion and pain of the dragons within her empathic range, and with it came a care for the 'evil beasts' that no slayer should have. And she hated herself for it.

But those encounters with dragons were solely during killing ceremonies, full of sorrow, fear, and rage. When she finally encountered something else, her entire world changed. On an excursion from camp, she saw two dragons flying overhead—a father and son training in flight—and Alísa felt their joy. A joy so deep and true, and not over destroying villages or killing or fighting, simply in flight and family. Could any truly evil creature feel joy for such a reason, she asked herself?

But tragedy struck. Karn and Kallar saw the dragons near their beloved Alísa and attacked. They killed the father dragon and captured the son for a killing ceremony for the following day. As they tied him down, the young dragon heard Alísa's protests and the power in her voice. He petitioned her for help, calling her 'Singer' for the first time, and she knew his name. Graydonn.

That night, she tricked her uncle into leaving Graydonn alone with her, and she released him. He told her she belonged with the dragons and begged her to come with him. When she would not leave her family, he prayed for her safety among the enemy and respected her wishes, flying away without her.

When Alísa's treachery was discovered, she argued for Graydonn's goodness, but none would listen to her. In fact, her father and his apprentice began acting strangely, speaking of things Alísa didn't know and refusing to explain. So she made a choice, one that would reshape the world. She left her family and went in search of Graydonn.

She found among the dragons the secret Karn and Kallar had hidden from her—she was a Dragon Singer, able to empower or destroy dragons with her songs. Desperate to bring the war to an end and protect both her slayer family and new dragon clan, she trained to use her powers to bring peace to humans and dragons alike. Along the way, she made many friends:

Koriana, Graydonn's mother and a fierce warrior.

Falier, a holder hiding slayer powers, who bonded to Graydonn as mind-kin.

Selene, his sister, who saw both sound and telepathy dancing in the air.

Chrí, Laen, and other dreki—tiny creatures who join minds to become strong.

Namor, a slayer who gave his life to protect hers.

Saynan, an ice dragon who held both wisdom and battle prowess.

Briek, a slayer chief who led his clan to befriend Alísa's dragons.

Bria, the former Dragon Singer who, upon her physical death, became an Eldra.

And, of course, Sesína—a dragoness Alísa hatched and bonded deeply to. A dragoness full of hope, humor, and awesomeness. A fabulous beta. And—you'll just have to experience the rest for yourself.

Alongside these, Alísa defeated the an'reik alpha Rorenth and set the land free from his tyranny. She protected the village of Me'ran from dragon and slayer attacks alike. And she built a clan worthy of pride.

But not all accepted peace. The slayer Yarlan rallied slayers and normals against Alísa's clan, nearly destroying them and Me'ran. Amid his many attacks, Alísa came to her lowest point and became certain that humanity would never listen to her. But through Eldra Bria's guidance, Alísa began to face the lies she had always believed about herself, growing in confidence as a leader.

During this time, she also developed a romantic relationship with Falier. But this isn't the time or place to go into all that mushy stuff.

As Alísa worked in the eastern forests, her father Karn searched for his beloved daughter. Songweaver Farren, Alísa's musical mentor, crafted a song about her plight and that of the previous Dragon Singers Bria and Allara, hoping to soften hearts and gain allies who would help bring Alísa home. The word spread, and as they waited, dark visitors came to their camp. While the an'reik alpha Rorenth tried to snuff out Alísa's light, the human an'reik took a different approach, coaxing Karn to trade his soul for the ability to find and save Alísa. The great chief rejected them, and only a fire-manipulator and a woman who commanded dark mists escaped his wrath. Soon after, Yarlan came with news of Alísa's location. Karn allied with Chief Tella and her wayfarers, marching toward Me'ran to free Alísa and the villagers from the dragons' clutches.

Fearing for her friends' lives, Alísa surrendered herself to her father. Risking everything, she showed her family her memories, begged before Tella, and sang to her former clanmates, hoping that some would end their war against the dragons. Another clan of dragons, however, heard her among their enemies and attacked, lest the slayers use the Singer against them. It was then that Alísa's own clan fought to stand between the two armies. Much happened that day— from Harenn finally accepting his rider Taz, to Alísa's friend Trísse receiving a sudden mind-kin bond to Komi, to Kallar revealing he was the son of the Dragon Singer Allara and discovering his own identity as a Singer.

As the battle ended, Alísa brought the chiefs and alphas into parley. Through her song, she showed them the partnerships she had grown between humans and dragons—the Illumination bonds that fostered deep knowing like hers and Sesína's, the mind-kin bonds that revealed purposes aligned like Falier and Graydonn's, and the unbonded friendships between dragons, slayers, normals, and dreki. Through memory and action, she proved that good and evil exist in every race, and that war to exterminate any was wrong. And at her song, the battle ended.

That day, Alísa secured peace treaties from Chief Tella and Alpha Tsamen, as well as an alliance with her father. Tella and Tsamen went their separate ways, but Alísa and Karn developed a plan to continue bringing peace to the war-torn western hill country. They would not discover until later that the warriors who deserted Karn and Tella in protest would encounter the same an'reik Karn had refused. Had they known, they might have been better prepared for what came next...

PROLOGUE

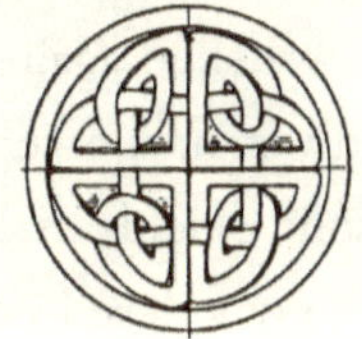

How quickly the world could change.

Tern pulled his horse to a halt as his commander and fellow slayers stopped at the crest of a hill. Grass yellowed by the long summer waved in the breeze, pointing toward the village in the valley below.

The mining village of L'rang was one Tern had visited many times as one of Karn's wayfarers. Though dangerously close to the Serpent's Fangs mountain range, it was among his favorite villages. Slayers here were hard and capable, like wayfarers, rather than softened by village life. He also never needed to stay in his tent in L'rang. Kallar's family lived here, and Kallar always preferred company when under his father's and stepmother's roof.

Kallar would have made a better leader than Harrík, who Tern's group of deserters currently followed. For the hundredth time since leaving Karn's wayfarers under the cover of night, Tern wondered what on A'dem had gotten into Kallar. He should have been the first to leave following their chief's alliance with the Dragon Singer. Instead, Kallar had stayed among the traitors of humanity. Tern had left many friends behind, including his beloved Trísse, who had somehow become bound to one of Alísa's beasts. Could he have saved her if he had remained?

Tern dismissed the thoughts and returned his focus to the front of the group, where Harrík surveyed L'rang. Tern should be there too, searching for signs of whether all was well. But he couldn't focus on the quiet morning routines of the villagers. All he could see was *her*. Sitting tall on a stallion with a second an'reik riding at her side, their guide Isarra demanded attention.

Dark braids circled Isarra's head like a crown. Her garments draped her in earthy greens and browns, making the unnaturally bright green of her eyes more startling. The stallion she rode was aggressive toward other horses when pastured, yet it stood docile under her command. Some of Tern's fellows spoke of her power over it with awe. It made his own heart shudder.

Only a couple weeks ago, Tern would never have dreamed he and his fellows would listen to an an'reik witch. The an'reik, *sold-souls*, worshiped the Nameless Ones—Eldír who had rebelled against the Maker long ago—and in exchange for their souls received various powers. Tern had seen Isarra control dark mists, shaping them into solid shields or bindings as she pleased. Seeing how the others deferred to her, he wondered whether she could do more.

Tern started, suddenly aware of Isarra's too-green eyes on him. Chiding himself, he held her gaze. He was a slayer—he had faced and killed many dragons. Surely he could stare down a single an'reik woman.

Isarra's lips curved ever so slightly, and Tern released his breath as she returned her gaze to Harrík.

"You will not get your answers from the outside, friend." She nodded toward L'rang. "You will find everything as I said. We have only a peaceful presence here. The village chief and chief slayer are amenable to us, as is their songweaver."

Harrík looked at her. "One songweaver? L'rang has two."

"The chiefs dismissed the other because he would not abide by peace. He left their presence disgraced but unharmed." Isarra smiled. "You can ask to be sure. We would join you in the fight against dragons and the Singer. The only humans we've interest in fighting are those aligned with her."

Apparently satisfied, Harrík kicked his horse forward, leading them down to the village. Tern fought not to glance back at Isarra as she stayed behind. Theoretically, the an'reik were not their enemy. The dragons were—those beasts who burned villages, devoured child and warrior alike, and ensnared the weak-minded. Isarra and her band had been nothing but amiable toward Tern's small clan. He had witnessed no blood-drinking or human sacrifices like the legends described. No fits of madness, just people with strange powers. Somewhat creepy people, but not his enemies.

Assuming, of course, that Isarra told the truth. That was the mission today—investigate L'rang and ensure that the an'reik within had brought no harm. If they found it so, Isarra and her band would be invaluable allies against Alísa's dragons.

Hoofbeats changed from plods to sharp clops as the long grasses gave way to stone pathways. Just before reaching the village, Harrík turned his horse to look back at them.

"I sensed no lies in Isarra, but we must be sure. Karn has sided with the dragons. It is up to us to protect the villages he has abandoned. Stay in pairs and speak with the villagers. Find out if the an'reik presence is truly peaceful. I'll go to the chiefs."

With that, Harrík pushed toward the center of the village, the rest following his instructions. Tern glanced around, skimming over the shops. Kallar's family would be a reliable source of information.

Tern aimed for the slayers' quarter, clicking his horse forward. Another slayer did the same, coming alongside. Alsum, a former Tellas-man with olive skin and a scout's sharp eyes.

"You seem to know where you're going," Alsum said. "Mind if I join you?"

Tern grunted his assent. They rode in silence for a time, nodding to villagers as they passed. Shopkeepers stood with their wares before stone buildings, the most affluent ones under awnings made of dragon scales dulled by the sun. Living only a few miles from the foot of the Serpent's Fangs required everything to be fireproof. Village-bound slayers patrolled the streets fully armored, ready should dragons attack.

Were they more on guard compared to Tern's last visit? Or was he merely projecting his own wariness onto them?

An'reik also wandered openly, marked by ragged-edged cloaks and an air of power even most warriors didn't possess. One stood at the baker's shop as Tern passed it, giving coin for his bread as any normal human might.

Tern grabbed his water-skin from the saddle horn and caught his partner's eye. Rather than wary, Alsum appeared calm and assured. Alsum had refused Isarra at first, had even attacked her. Another Tellas-man named Yarlan and a Karns-woman had joined him, but Isarra had subdued them all. After a private talk, Alsum returned with Isarra while the other two went free. Apparently, what she said had convinced him completely.

A flash of movement caught Tern's eye. A hooded figure, about five feet in stature, ducked through an alleyway between shops, carrying a small bundle. Though the behavior might speak 'thief' to some, Tern hesitated. The figure's gait seemed familiar, and something inside pulled him toward them.

"Hold on," Tern told Alsum, pulling his horse to a stop and swinging down. Moving swiftly, he ducked into the alleyway after the figure, his partner shadowing him.

A shushing sound came from around the corner, sounding like a child's voice. Hand on his sword, Tern rounded the corner and found a dagger inches from his chest.

Instinct took over. Tern swiped his arm through the space between him and his attacker, his dragon-scale bracer protecting him from the blade as he pushed his opponent's arm across their body. The force of his movement caused his smaller opponent to turn from him, and he easily got one arm around their neck and grabbed their wrist to prevent a second attempt.

The child's voice returned—this time a fear-filled "Mamá!"—and Tern looked beyond his attacker. Two boys huddled in the shadows behind an older man. The man's fine tunic was torn at the shoulder, right where a pin might have fastened a sash. All three seemed familiar.

The cloaked attacker struggled in his grip, the voice desperate and feminine. "Let us go! By Maker's light and all things holy, leave us alone!"

The woman's tone and the fear in the children's eyes tightened Tern's chest. "I'm not going to hurt you. Drop the dagger and I'll release you."

She struggled all the more, stamping her foot and making Tern dance back. Alsum forced the weapon from her hand, drawing a small whimper. Tern let go. He was a warrior trained to kill dragons, not frighten mothers and children.

The woman whirled to face him, arms out to shield the boys from view. Tern recognized her. Yarlan's wife. She had fled with their sons before Yarlan and Alsum attacked Isarra.

"Essie? What are you doing, sneaking around and pulling a knife on us?"

Essie tensed as he took a step forward, baring her teeth. "You won't have my children, too!"

Tern lifted his palms in a gesture of peace. "I just want to know what's going on. Where's Yarlan?"

At her husband's name, the fire in Essie's eyes dimmed. "You don't know, then." The blaze returned. "What happened when you sheep followed the Maker's enemies? Did you truly believe they would let him go?!"

"Hush." The older man placed a hand on her shoulder. "Don't let the others discover you."

"They did let him go," Tern assured. "Alsum was there. He just hasn't found you yet." After three days. That was an awfully long time.

Tern shook his doubts away. "Tell her, Alsum."

"It's true," his partner said. "Yarlan refused and went free. Are you sure he isn't waiting for you elsewhere?"

Essie's eyes turned to daggers. "I went back, serpent. I found his body."

Pieces fell into place in Tern's mind, filling him with equal parts horror and rage. Alsum had lied. In the space of a second, he looked from Essie's raging tears, to the boys huddled in fear behind her, to the man he now recognized as one of L'rang's songweavers, disgraced without his advisor's sash and pin.

Tern grabbed for his sword and whirled to face Alsum. His opponent's weapon was already ringing from its sheath. Tern blocked, steel colliding as they pressed blades.

Alsum gave a crazed grin. "I never was as good a liar as the mistress."

Tern brought his sword into a defensive position. "Essie, get out of here!"

He stumbled as Alsum sprang forward, blocking just in time. Alsum pressed another attack, then another, eyes wild. Tern fell back two steps, feinted, then pushed his own attack. He slashed at Alsum's middle. Alsum twisted away and got close again. Tern wasn't fast enough. Fiery pain ripped through him as Alsum cut deep into the bicep of his shield arm.

Tern cried out, arm hanging limp at his side. That would throw off his balance, and Alsum was already larger and stronger than him.

He could not win this fight.

But losing now would mean leaving Essie and her boys at the mercy of the an'reik. They needed more time.

Tern dodged right.

What would Kallar do?

Pain zinged up his arm as he blocked.

Use his pain.

He stumbled against the wall.

Break the slayers' code.

Tern gritted his teeth. He grasped onto the pain in his arm and pulled it forward, forming it into a telepathic spear. He had only ever mind-speared dragons—the thought of using his powers against another human sickened him. But not so much as failing Essie and the boys would.

Alsum swung again. Tern blocked, releasing his mind-spear with the clang of their weapons. Alsum roared with pain and fell back a step. Tern formed another spear and shot it at him like he would a dragon. This time, however, his telepathy struck something solid, then ricocheted back into himself.

Tern screamed, sliding down the wall as his knees gave out. Another shock came as Alsum retaliated with a psychic attack that made Tern's vision white. Sight returned just as Alsum raised his sword above his head.

Thunk.

Hot blood spattered over Tern as an arrow lodged in Alsum's stomach. He rolled before Alsum's sword could fall, arm protesting every jolt and bit of dirt. Looking up, he found Essie sitting atop his horse and nocking another of his arrows. She shot Alsum again in the chest, then a third time as he fell. The traitor didn't move, face in the dirt.

L'rang's songweaver rushed from holding Alsum's horse with the two boys to help Tern up. "Do you know a village untouched by an'reik?"

"Yes," Tern said without thinking. His ears still rang from the telepathic attack. And how much blood had he lost?

"Good. Take them, protect them." The songweaver nodded to Yarlan's family. "We've been trying to find a quiet way to get them out past the an'reik for days, but it seems you now need an expedient escape rather than a silent one."

Tern sheathed his sword and placed a hand on his throbbing head. "But my clan—they need—to know."

"I will do what I can. What I cannot do is protect this family in the wilds." He grimaced as his eyes fell on Tern's arm, then pasted on a grim smile. "Even wounded, you can do better."

The sound of ripping cloth drew Tern's eyes to Essie. She passed a piece from the bottom of her skirt to the songweaver. "Bind above the wound to stop the bleeding. I'll clean it when we are safe. Please." Her eyes implored. "Help me get my children away from them."

Tern swallowed, then nodded. He ground his teeth as the songweaver pulled the cloth too tight, then approached the horse carrying the boys. Tern knew this territory and chiefs who would never bow to the Nameless Ones.

Then again, he had once thought Karn would never bow to the Dragon Singer. That Trisse would never yield her mind to a dragon. That Kallar would never capitulate to the beasts.

After the songweaver transferred the trembling younger boy to sit in front of his mother, Tern sat behind the older. Giving a word of encouragement to his own horse, he kicked Alsum's forward, trotting them through the alleyways until they could run.

How quickly the world could fall apart.

1

————

IN THE GAP

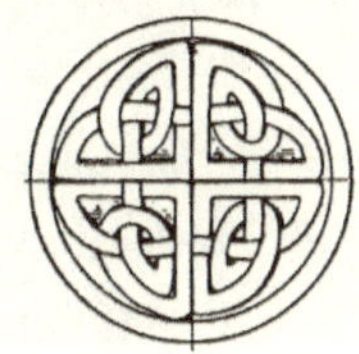

Fire flashed on the mountain, marking the place Alísa's clan would be tested once more. She tightened her hold on Sesína's spine as the dragoness banked toward the battle, their hearts racing with a mixture of anxiety and excitement that was wholly them.

Thirteen dragon-rider pairs flew with them, some well-versed in standing in the gap between warring clans, while others were on their first mission. All were ready for battle with an eagerness Alísa didn't have. She belonged in the sky with them, but she would never relish the fight.

Sesína entered Alísa's mind via their Illumination bond—the deep telepathic connection dragons formed with a parent upon hatching.

"Nor should you relish it. You're built to bring peace." A bit of mischief flavored the dragoness' thoughts. *"I, on the other hand, am a fire-breathing, enemy-humbling, aerobatic ball of battle-prowess. And awesomeness—don't forget awesomeness."*

Alísa shook her head, though her lips curved upward. *"That's a bit much, even for you."*

"Anything to make the alpha smile."

Alísa patted Sesína's ebony scales. Pulling an errant mahogany curl from her face, she set her eyes on Alanti, the blue dragoness flying far ahead of them. Alísa had formed a peace treaty with Alanti's alpha only two days prior. She intended to go to the nearby village of Bezin with her father in three days, when Karn arrived with his clan. Their clans had worked together this way for the past month since forming their alliance.

Three days shouldn't have mattered. Village-bound slayers almost never attacked caves. Yet this morning, Alanti had appeared at Alísa's cave with news of an attack on her clan. Something had changed.

"Connect me to Alanti," Alísa said.

Sesína did as she asked, establishing a telepathic link. Alanti's fear and determination caused Alísa's heart to race. She breathed against her pounding dragon empathy, then spoke.

"Can you reach your clan, Alanti? How goes the battle?"

"The slayers are close to the caves," Alanti said, a growl in her voice. *"Many dragons have landed to block them and now face swords and spears."*

Alísa's thoughts raced. Ahead, black smoke billowed from the mountainside. How much was fueled by the bodies of fallen slayers—her people? Yet the slayers attacked unprovoked. She preferred not to arm either side, but non-combatants were at risk. Hatchlings. She couldn't let harm come to them.

"Connect to your alpha," Alísa ordered. *"Since I can reach you telepathically and you can reach them, I will channel my strength song to them through you."*

Alanti's fear lessened. *"By Maker's wings. Thank you, Singer."*

The thread of their communication opened wider, allowing in the frantic thoughts and emotions of battle. Alísa gritted her teeth against the influx of pain—slashed legs, ripped wings, a blinded eye—then released it in a long, desperate note.

At the sound of her cry, the dragons and riders of her clan began connecting to her. Their presence bolstered her. Among them, she felt Koriana's fortitude, Graydonn's steadiness, Falier's belief. Their emotions wove into her song, refilling her as she poured out her strength to them and their allies.

> This war has brought us hearts of stone
> Full of winter's icy chill
> Its fire fills our aching bones
> Burning as our blood we spill
>
> Now hear my song and feel the cool
> Abandon heart for lung and limb
> Renew your strength, while fire pools
> Within your hearts, new life within

Alísa stopped singing once her dragons flew at their maximum speed. The song's effects would last a few minutes, and she needed to conserve her voice.

"Alanti—"

But Alanti cut off her communication to Sesína just as Alísa started speaking. The sapphire dragoness speared into the fray, her flight buoyed by the Singer's power and love for her clan. There would be no help from her to calm the dragons.

Alísa spoke to her warriors. *"Koriana, Briek—you and your squad focus on the dragons still in the air. Keep them back so the slayers don't have to watch the sky. Tora and T'lan, your squad will follow me to stand between the armies on the ground. Ensure the dragons do not attack. My squad will face the slayers."*

Nearly at the mountain, the acrid scent of smoke tickled Alísa's throat. Dragons roared, men shouted, and fire crackled over what brush settled on the rocky slopes. A rush of wind revealed the spot where the dragons stood their ground, desperate to protect their caves.

Alísa took a steadying breath. *"Move."*

Sesína trumpeted a battle-cry. The rest of the clan, dragon and rider alike, joined her call, drawing the combatants' attention. Koriana veered away, her squad of four dragon-rider pairs following her to circle the dragons in the air. Sesína dove for the battle-lines before the cave, aiming for the space between the two armies.

Alísa shout-sang as Sesína landed, announcing to all that the Dragon Singer had arrived. Sesína flared her wings and thrashed her tail as Alísa slid to the sloped ground. Slayers fell back, wide-eyed at their sudden appearance. Behind her, Alanti's clan roared their battle-readiness, until Alísa's dragons blocked their way.

Despite the haze of the smoke, Alísa soon found the face she sought. Lorin, the chief slayer of Bezin, led his men with rage in his eyes. Sweat plastered his black hair to his neck, and his tanned skin was even darker with dirt and ash.

How she wished her father were here already—he had a good rapport with Lorin. She was just Karn's quiet daughter to the slayers of Bezin. But she could remain so no longer.

"Lorin." She lifted her hands in a peaceful gesture. "You must stop this. These d—d—dragons are under my p-p-protection, and they mean no harm t—t-to you and yours."

"So it's true, then." Chief Lorin spat on the ground. "Your father told me you'd been captured. Asked my help to find and save you. Now here you are, siding with them."

"I fight to p-protect the Maker's *iompróir anam*." A few slayers balked at the claim, but Alísa pressed on. "Skinned or scaled, it makes no d—difference."

As if on cue, riders slid to the ground and stepped forward to show their allegiance. She threw a glance at them, meeting the eyes of Rassím, Trísse, and others.

"We would tell you much," she said. "Stories of friendship and heroism, if you and your men would listen."

Jaws snapped at the air behind her, and Alísa pivoted to see the emerald alpha Harazím flaring his wings. *"You call this alliance, Singer? They attack us, and you offer them words of comfort?!"*

Alísa let out a quiet breath. The slayers raised their swords, unable to hear the dragon because of the shields around their minds.

"Alpha Harazím asks why I g—give a chance for p—p—p-p—" —*Ignore the smirks and stares. Breathe.*— "for p-peace to those who attack my allies. I d—d—do so because we were all like you, once. We have all k-k-k-killed and been k-killed for a lie."

She returned to Harazím. "W—war brings many evils, and it will never end until all p-p-p-parties have both truth and the chance t—to act on it. As the daughter of Karn, I know your c-c-clan has attacked villages before, and not merely slayers who attacked you first."

Alísa's boots crunched on rock as she faced Lorin again. "But Harazím's clan has vowed not to attack villages anymore, j—just as multiple village-bound clans have vowed not to storm caves. Dragons are not soulless beasts any more than slayers are heartless monsters. We have all b—b—believed lies, but my allies have p-p-proven the t-truth."

She held out her hand to the chief. "I will defend these dragons, but first I would give you the same chance I have g—given them. End this madness."

The battlefield was silent but for crackling flames. Alísa released her empathy, letting its misty power flow out to feel the surrounding emotions. She ignored her clanmates' firm courage and focused in front of her, on the chief with loosening shoulders. Curiosity lapped at the edges of her powers— curiosity that was overtaking his anger.

She had him!

Lorin stepped forward, the tip of his sword low to the ground. Then another man wearing the yellow paint of a second reached for his arm and halted him.

"Tsorr said this would happen." The second gripped his weapon tighter. "Her power is in her voice—lulling us to sleep like a serpent."

A strange humor washed through Alísa, out of place while standing between two armies. No one had ever attributed power to her *speaking* voice.

"M—my power is in my songs. I am not t-t-t-trying to trick you."

A shadow flew over the mountain, and the buzz of connection to her clan shifted as more minds entered. Saynan—an ice dragon and one of her betas— had finally arrived with his riders. Dragons made room for him to land, but Bezin's slayers reacted with fear. Chief Lorin fell back like a spooked horse.

"Yet you bring more against us! How can we trust you?"

"Trust me," a familiar voice asserted.

Boots hit the ground, and Karn strode forward, leaving behind Saynan and his rider. Karn's brown eyes softened as they met Alísa's, then returned to those of a wayfaring chief. He strode past her to stand before Lorin in his full armor made of leather and red dragon scales.

"Alísa speaks the truth. She and her clan have proven themselves repeatedly by protecting both races. You would do well to listen."

Lorin scoffed. "I hardly think that the word of her father is proof. You would be the easiest for her to turn."

"One would think," Karn chuckled, a hint of regret lacing the edges. "You know my zeal and stubbornness. If you need more proof, know that Tella, too, has accepted peace. The villages of Annakím and Vennia have heard us, as have dragon clans throughout the region."

Lorin's second sneered. "We know all this. Tsorr warned us of your treachery, warned that we would be next. Many may believe a lie—it does not mean we should as well!"

"Who is Tsorr?" Alísa stepped forward. She knew the names of Bezin's leadership. This must be someone new.

"A messenger who told us of the Dragon Singer," Lorin said, though he addressed Karn rather than her. "News beyond that of your clan's song. He raises many questions I would have answered."

"Then we shall speak with him," Karn said. "Return home, Lorin. Vow to leave these dragons alone until we have answered your questions. It will take a day to return to your village?"

Lorin grunted affirmation.

"Then we will come in two." Karn looked back at Alísa. "Is this acceptable?"

Alísa nodded, glad to let him take the lead here.

Karn returned to Lorin. "We shall see you then."

The second's brow raised in question. After a moment of scrutiny, Lorin sheathed his sword.

"Move out. We are finished here—for now."

With that, Lorin pushed through his men and marched down the mountain. Some immediately followed his example. Others looked to his second, uncertain. With a loud grunt, he shoved his weapon into its sheath and slunk after his chief, the rest following behind.

Questions wafted through the clan's mind-link, prompting Alísa's attention. While she didn't expect Lorin and his slayers to return, she also couldn't simply trust that they wouldn't. She grasped onto the Illumination bond.

"Sesína, please make sure Harazím can hear me as I speak to the clan."

Sesína had it done before Alísa completed her sentence. Alísa found the clan's mind-link next and pushed her words through it.

"Well done, all. With Harazím's leave, three dragon-rider pairs will remain here in case Lorin does not keep his word."

Harazím sent a mental affirmative, and Alísa continued. *"I have two riders versed in healing. They have helped dragons before, stitching wounds closed and applying salves of mixed herbs that speed recovery. Would you like their help?"*

Harazím rumbled in his chest. *"That would be acceptable. Thank you, Singer."*

Alísa assigned Rassím and Trísse to check the wounded and three pairs to stay with the clan until her meeting with the slayers. Sesína trotted off with the healers to facilitate, as she had done before. When she toned down her sass, she was quite good at ensuring understanding between parties.

"Please. My sass is charming."

Assured all was in hand, Alísa returned to her father. Karn had watched as she worked with the dragons, his expression a mixture of pride and the confused interest that always rose when she communicated telepathically. Despite being a telepath, he was hesitant to join the mind-link. The slayers' code taught never to use one's powers on another human—they even frowned on simple communication links. Their code was his, and he hadn't been around dragons long enough to contemplate change.

Alísa hugged him. "Thank you for coming so quickly."

"Darrin said it was urgent." He kissed the top of her head. "I don't know how your riders do it—I thought I might fall with how fast the dragon flew."

"Saynan," she supplied. This was more important for her father to learn than telepathic communication. Dragons had names, and with that came the reminder of their status as *iompróir anam*—soul-bearers.

"Saynan," Karn repeated, giving her a knowing look. "I will remember to thank him by name when he takes me back. And, speaking of" —he backed away a step— "I should speak to the clan. We must move more quickly to reach Bezin in two days' time."

Alísa smiled sweetly. "I can always send dragons for you again."

Karn chuckled. "I do not think Kallar is ready to ride a dragon."

Alísa's heart shriveled as thoughts of Kallar filled her. Her father didn't know that Kallar, too, was a Dragon Singer. Nor did he know how much Kallar resented Alísa for helping unlock the power, which now forced him to feel dragon emotions. Not that their relationship had ever been good.

She pushed the thoughts away. "Thank you again for your help, Papá."

"Always, my Lísa."

With that, Karn headed for Saynan and Darrin.

"You let your father take over again."

Alísa tried not to let her mental sigh travel the communication line, but was sure she failed. Koriana approached her, Briek almost jogging at her side to keep pace.

"You and your squad did well," Alísa told them both. *"Thank you."*

"Alísa-Dragon-Singer." Koriana growled softly. *"You do not need him."*

"I thought she balanced it well enough," Briek said. The beads at the ends of his many warrior's braids rattled as he came to a stop in front of her. *"The point of having allied chiefs and alphas is to have their help in communicating to their respective races. It's the only reason I'm here."*

His dark eyes sparkled with his last sentence, making Alísa chuckle. Koriana, however, was not amused.

"I do not dispute that, but a dragoness does not allow other alphas to decide for her clan. You should not have let your father dictate the terms."

"But he said exactly what I wanted."

"And established himself as the leader in the other chief's eyes."

Alísa shook her head. *"What was I supposed to do? Come up with an entirely different plan? Or tell him, 'No, actually,' then say the same thing?"*

"You could have asserted yourself before he gave his plan."

Alísa pinched the bridge of her nose. She would never get Koriana to understand the struggle of her stammer, nor how preferable it was to let someone she trusted do the talking. She and Papá had a rhythm now, and he had stuck to it today. That was good enough for her.

"Headache, Líse?"

Frustration gave way to a smile, and Alísa turned to find Falier and Graydonn. The pair walked toward her side-by-side over the rocky slope. Graydonn's talons gripped the rock with ease, while Falier walked uphill of him with a hand on the dragon's green withers.

"J—just thinking." Alísa waved goodbye to Koriana and Briek, then closed the distance to Graydonn and Falier. Reaching for Falier, she laced her fingers with his. "You two make it through unscathed?"

"One of the airborne dragons flamed at us before she figured out who we were," Graydonn said, amber eyes brightening with humor. *"But we were quick and avoided burns."*

"He says 'we' like I had any part in the reaction time." Falier grinned. "You were brilliant with the chief."

"Thank you." Alísa pushed up on her tiptoes and kissed his bearded cheek. It still made her happy, seeing his formerly clean-shaven face now sporting a close-trimmed beard, all because she had told him she liked it.

"I think you got through to him even before your father showed up."

"Most certainly," Graydonn agreed.

"I just hope Tsorr, whoever he is, is as open t—to new ideas."

Alísa hoped her smile didn't look as forced as it was. Her worst defeats were never on the battlefield. They were within villages, where the eyes of those judging her made her feel like a cornered animal. But her friends were right, she was coming into her own, and her allies were strong and growing in number.

For the first time in her life, it seemed peace was finally within reach.

2

THE MESSENGER

Alísa led her dragons to land a ten-minute walk from the village of Bezin, where their approach would be less threatening. Despite the coarse grasses, the dragons settled comfortably on their bellies. They would wait here while the humans faced the scrutiny of the villagers.

Nearby, Karn dismounted his horse alongside his people—Alísa's mother Hanah, and Karn's apprentice Kallar. Patting Sesína's neck in goodbye, Alísa headed for them. Her human representatives accompanied her—Falier with his hand in hers and a carefree mask covering his nerves, Briek with powerful strides tamed to their pace, and Tenza with her quiet confidence.

Alísa's clan had shifted since facing Karn and Tella's combined wayfaring clans. With her decision to remain in the west, some of Briek's slayers declared that they, too, would remain. Briek in turn swore himself to Alísa's leadership and now acted as one of her betas.

When her dragons took warriors back to Me'ran, they returned with the families of the slayers who remained with Alísa. Tenza came as well, largely due to Alísa's message that Kallar was her grandson. Looking at them, Alísa could see a slight resemblance. Tenza's hair, though lightened with gray, bore the same black base and thick texture as Kallar's. His eyes were a brighter blue than Namor's, but they held a bit of Tenza's almond shape.

Kallar's stance turned rigid the moment he noticed his grandmother. Rather than meet Tenza's gaze or stare her down, he looked away. He hadn't spoken to her once, ignoring her or leaving whenever she tried to communicate with him.

It made Alísa's blood boil. Kallar knew who she was to him, had seen her honor and sorrows through Alísa's memories, yet he remained hostile. All

Tenza wanted was to connect with one of the few remaining pieces of her daughter, the late Dragon Singer Allara. Maybe someday, Alísa could take Tenza to L'rang to visit Kallar's younger brother R'lann. R'lann would accept her without hesitation.

Falier squeezed her hand and a buzz of telepathic connection entered her mind. *"You're angry. What's going on?"*

Alísa sighed. *"I'm sorry. It's just—why can't he even try for Tenza?"*

"Did you expect him to?" Falier's distaste flowed through their connection. *"You can't focus there. Not right now."*

"I know. Sorry."

He shook his head with a light humor, then nodded at the village. *"No more apologies, alpha-chief. Eyes up. You've got minds to change."*

Alísa straightened. He was right. She closed the distance between her and her father's party. Her arms ached to hug her parents, but with people coming out to greet them, now wasn't the time. Instead, she gave a little wave, then came alongside her father as they continued on to Bezin.

Grass gave way to dirt and gravel, the greenery cleared away long ago in hopes of stopping dragon-fire. For the same reason, they built every building of stone or brick. Though Alísa had known such constructions all her life, she had gotten used to the warm welcome of the east's wooden structures. How strange this must be for Falier, villages full of dead buildings.

Bezin itself, however, was very much alive. The cobblestone paths held many people, all hurrying toward the center of town. Would the entire village attend? The thought made Alísa's breath shake. How was it she could face angry dragons, yet crowds of villagers terrified her?

But I'm done running. I was made for this.

Sesína's pride washed through her. *"That's my alpha."*

Alísa and her companions stopped at the edge of the village, where Chief Lorin, his second, and the village chief awaited their arrival. Lorin clasped arms with Karn, appearing the least wary of the three. The second glared at Alísa, while the normal chief, a younger man with pale skin and blond hair, looked how Alísa felt—nervous, yet ready to play his part.

"Come, old friend." Lorin gestured into the village. "You shall make your case in the square. We shall see if your answers are sufficient, or if next time we meet will be at the end of our blades."

He said it so cavalierly, yet he kept his emotions locked tight behind a telepathic shield. Did he use humor to hide his fear, or was this just a show? She couldn't read him.

Sesína chuckled. *"Imagine if you weren't an empath and could only read tone, expression, and body language. You'd be lost."*

Alísa hid her smirk as she followed Lorin. *"How do normals function?"*

Sesína snickered, then returned to her silence, allowing Alísa time to gather her thoughts. Two holders met them just within the village to take the horses to a guest stable. A few minutes later, they entered the square, where all Bezin gathered to listen. Slayers stood armored among the normals, weapons at their sides. Falier tensed at the sight.

"Does that mean trouble?"

Alísa returned a negative. *"It's a show of their strength. If they expected trouble, there wouldn't be civilians here."*

She scanned the crowd and most of them stared back. The rest instead watched a man in the center of the square. He wore the blues and whites of a messenger—noncombatant colors, though he also wore a knife strap across his chest like Rassím. Over his tunic lay a brown cloak with ragged edges that appeared more stylized than ripped. His pale skin was slightly sun-kissed and his hawkish eyes a hazel-brown.

The man smiled and spoke smoothly. "And so our opponent enters."

Alísa stared at him, trying to decipher what she sensed. The crowd held a mixture of fear and something akin to calm that she couldn't quite place. Calm felt green with peaceful life to her, while this was more akin to tent leathers pulled tight to avoid wrinkles. The same almost-calm held strong in her 'opponent.'

Lorin looked to the people. "The Dragon Singer and her allies come to answer Tsorr's accusations. Make your case, Karns-daughter."

Alísa breathed deeply as Lorin took his place between her and Tsorr. That was her cue.

Eldra Bria, give me words.

"Some of you know me. You've s—seen me at my father's side as he worked t—to protect your village. Many of you have heard the tale of how I t-t-t-turned to the d—dragons and empowered them with my songs. What you don't know is what happened in between."

She paused, taking a moment to breathe past the nerves building up inside her.

"Like all of you, I g—grew up in fear of the dragons. I looked at them and saw only b—beasts who had sold their souls to evil. I knew the stories of d—d—demonic voices and hearts that only found joy in destruction. Worst of all, my empathy c-c-c-c" —*breathe*— "c-connected to them, bringing me to tears as I watched hatchlings fight in the ceremony circle. My greatest shame as the d—daughter of a slayer."

Alísa's throat was tight. The longer she spoke, the more pronounced her stammer became. If only she could pause longer, breathe deeply for a few seconds, but such silence might invite someone else to interject. She settled for a quick swallow.

"B—but then I met a dragon. I felt his joy in simple flight, saw the honor in his actions t-t-t-toward me, and heard his voice that p-p-prayed to the Maker for my safety. Here wasn't a b—bloodthirsty beast or soulless demon, but a fellow *anam*. A t-t-terrible, life-changing t-truth—one that my family was not yet ready for."

She smiled gently at her parents, hoping to show she was not shaming them. Karn had agreed that his initial refusal was a truth that needed to be shared. The villagers needed to know that he had not believed her solely because she was his daughter.

"And so I went to the d—dragons and lived among them. I learned to see them t-truly, as individuals who m—make choices for good and for evil j—just as we humans do. As I did, I discovered the w—war between our k-k-k-kinds is not a holy one fought against soulless monsters, but one that hurts *iomproír anam* on both sides."

She lifted her hands to the crowd in entreaty. "We needn't be at war. Already, my c-c-clan of dragons and slayers have protected p-peoples of both races and won p-p-peace for them. The d—dragons in the nearby mountain have vowed to stand down. I urge you to do the same. End the violence between our p-peoples. Join me in seeking peace."

Her speech finally over, Alísa lowered her hands. She focused on loosening the tension in her throat. She would have to speak again soon.

Tsorr clapped a slow, mocking applause. His voice was smooth and rippled through the air like a gentle stream. "Well, that sounded difficult. Congratulations, you've aired your lies beautifully. Didn't she do a splendid job?"

The people seemed at a loss. A few smirked, others frowned, and some politely clapped, all more embarrassing than helpful. Alísa did her best to stand firm and keep her hands still rather than worry the fabric of her skirt. His first blow was one she had taken many times, yet she had never truly been able to block it.

"So refreshing to hear the ideas of the young," Tsorr said in his charismatic tone. "They invent the most engaging stories. Monsters as allies. Who could have imagined it but someone unburdened by experience?"

'Unburdened'? Alísa gritted her teeth. As if she hadn't grown up among slayers and witnessed the aftermath of countless battles!

A surge of determination and—Compassion? It felt wrong.—filled the air as Tsorr pointed to someone in the crowd.

"E'mun, you spoke to me of your father's death by dragon-fire." He pointed to another. "K'hanne, your injury—was it created by man, or by beast? Zapharr, how many livestock have you lost to them?" Finally, he looked at Lorin. "You have not forgotten your people's woes simply because of a child's fantasies?"

Nods and agreeing murmurs spread through the people. Chief Lorin, too, seemed swayed as his agreement wafted through the astral plane. Irritatingly, Alísa found her own heart wavering at Tsorr's arguments. And was that one of her own allies behind her also agreeing? Kallar? No, his shield would be up—

Sesína pressed encouragement to Alísa. *"Don't focus there. You know what you speak is true. Keep going."*

Alísa shook herself and pulled her empathy in tight against the distraction. She chose her words carefully, hoping to avoid those that would make her stumble.

"Is it fantasy that my dragons and slayers have fought to defend both races? Ask any behind me and they will t-t-tell you it is so."

"Yet you yourself told us your empathy connects to dragons uncontrollably." Again, Alísa's heart wavered as Tsorr spoke. "They gained your mind, poisoned you against your own kind, and manipulated you until their lies became your truth. A 'truth' with which you have infected other weak-minded individuals."

'Weak-minded'? Alísa almost wanted to laugh. None of her party could be described so. She opened her mouth to speak in defense of her people, but her father spoke first.

"The *dragons* prey on the weak-minded?" Karn's voice held a dangerous quiet as he stalked past Alísa toward Tsorr. "You dare accuse while attempting the same?"

Alísa's heart beat faster. What was he doing? This wasn't the plan!

Chief Lorin placed himself between Karn and Tsorr. "Get back in your place, Karn. What are you about?"

Karn didn't move. "When we met, Lorin, your telepathic shield was up. Tell me, is it still? Or has it fallen as your friend here spread his venom?"

Alísa looked at Lorin. He *had* let his guard down at some point. She had sensed his slow agreement with Tsorr's arguments, and now she felt his confusion.

"Or the rest of you slayers," Karn continued. "Has your hold slipped inexplicably during the last few minutes?"

Tsorr squinted at Karn. A change flowed over the astral plane—that strange not-calm again. The pull against wrinkles rather than the gentle call to peace.

Multiple slayers in the crowd shifted, some shaking their heads to clear them. Lorin muttered something, then spoke as though waking from a dream.

"Yes, there is something—"

A surge of protection collided with Alísa as her mother grabbed her arm and pulled her back, nearly throwing her into Falier. Alísa made to ask for an explanation, but her father spoke again.

"I've met this power once before," Karn growled. "One that opens minds to manipulation and breaks down even a slayer's telepathic shield. Your 'friend' is an 'reik!"

Alísa's heart trembled at the declaration, visions of dark clouds and a giant, brutish dragon filling her mind's eye. Across the distance, Sesína went on high alert, her growl filling Alísa's mind. The crowd shifted with gasps and exclamations of outrage. His people divided, Chief Lorin spoke.

"Tsorr has been nothing but affable, and I have sensed no influence before today—when your daughter, whose power is in her voice, spoke to us. You had better be able to prove this claim!"

A new voice entered the fray, growling and reluctant. "Then ask yourself who you're being influenced toward." Kallar came to Karn's side. "Besides, her power only works when she sings."

Karn glared at Tsorr. "If you need proof, Lorin, check the astral plane."

Tsorr chuckled and lifted his hands in a sign of peace. "No need. I will admit our dragon-loving friend is correct. I do hold power, given by an Eldra stripped of her name simply because she desired to give humanity the ability to stand against dragons. I even used this power—a heightened form of empathy— as I spoke to you. My only wish was for you to hear the truth instead of her lies."

Karn laid a hand on his sword. "Lorin, allow me to rid your village of this serpent."

"Ask yourself this," Tsorr said, "who has harmed Bezin in the past— an'reik, or dragons?"

His words soothed in Alísa's ear and mind. She pushed her empathy against the manipulation and prayed others would do the same.

Tsorr gestured to Alísa. "Will you believe those aligned with dangerous beasts over those who ally with great spiritual beings?"

Lorin crossed his arms. "The Maker and his Eldír are the only spiritual beings from whom I accept counsel."

"Bah. They won't protect you from the dragons. Only—"

A sword rang from its sheath, drawing all eyes as Kallar lunged past Lorin and plunged his blade into Tsorr's stomach. Tsorr's eyes widened, then rolled back in death as Kallar yanked out his weapon. Tsorr's body fell to the ground.

No one moved. Alísa could barely breathe as Lorin's face turned red with fury.

"How dare you! Attacking an unarmed man under my hospitality. Even Karn himself did not dare touch him!"

Kallar matched Lorin's glare. "You were just going to keep talking while his empathy affected the people? He admitted it with his own mouth. If you won't protect them, I will."

Lorin drew himself up, affronted, but Karn stepped in.

"The deed is done. Regardless of how, Tsorr's threat to your village is no more. In our recent encounter with an'reik, they attacked my clan with powers of speed, hellflames, and dark mists. Who knows how else Tsorr might have harmed them? Kallar's act was right—forgive any fault of impropriety, or else place it on me. He did as I should have."

Alísa watched, tense. Her father's gentler words did not escalate Lorin further, but they didn't placate him either. How could she salvage this?

Calm assurance wafted from her mother as she stepped past Alísa to approach Lorin. Her voice was impossibly even.

"Chief Lorin, despite Tsorr's manipulations, you brought us here. You proved that even the powers of the Nameless cannot sway a man seeking truth. Let us begin again, without the stench of the Dark One in our midst. The Dragon Singer has proven that peace is achievable. You witnessed it two days ago, when she protected not only the dragons, but you as well. Search your heart, ask your own questions, and believe."

The tension dissipated as Alísa's mother spoke. All knew Hanah. Throughout her years of wayfaring, she had proven herself to the people of each village as she lived and worked among them while Karn marched on the mountains. As the villagers relaxed, Alísa wished she could change how she had behaved within the villages growing up. Introverted and ashamed of her stammer, Alísa had always hidden in the shadows, helping but never connecting. Perhaps if she had acted differently, Bezin would be more receptive now.

Lorin gave one last look at Kallar and Tsorr's body. Closing his eyes, he breathed out and returned to Hanah. "There is wisdom in your words. Very well. Let us begin again."

3

BLESSING

Falier hated feeling redundant, even—perhaps especially—in the wake of success. The talks in Bezin went far more smoothly with Tsorr gone. Lorin and the chief of the village both agreed to peace soon after. There, Falier was content to support Alísa through his presence.

Here, though, sitting amid Alísa and Karn's leadership at the outskirts of the wayfarers' camp, Falier found himself drumming his fingers on his thighs as his mind wandered. They spoke of an'reik and wanted him here since he had witnessed Tsorr, but he didn't truly have anything to say on the matter, nor did anyone invite him to speak.

"I don't like it," Alísa's uncle L'non said. "An'reik are supposed to keep to the shadows, waiting in the wilderness for some poor soul to run afoul of them. But this marks our second encounter with them in only a few months."

Karn rubbed his beard. "Not to mention word of more in the south."

Koriana rumbled in her chest. *"That is an oddity among your kind?"*

L'non nodded curtly. After a silent moment, Alísa elaborated.

"I d—don't think any of us have encountered an'reik until now. Besides Rorenth."

Falier held back a shudder. He could still remember that brute's power slashing and biting at his own as he, Graydonn, and the dreki fought to mind-choke him together.

Koriana clicked in her throat thoughtfully. *"Though I am sure some an'reik dragons hide within clans with decent alphas, many of them flock to clans like Rorenth's as vultures to a carcass."*

Falier whispered to Graydonn through their bond so the others wouldn't hear. *"Then, we probably fought more than one an'reik that day?"*

Graydonn kept his eyes trained on the meeting. *"I did not notice any besides him, but they might have been fighting the slayers, or else their powers were not easily detectable."*

"Powers like what?"

"Shouldn't we be paying attention?"

Falier shrugged. *"They don't seem to need us."*

"And so we don't need them? This information might be important."

Falier let out a breath and listened. Karn was speaking again, wondering aloud if they would find more an'reik as his and Alísa's clans continued west.

"—We must be vigilant on our way to Azron, even if it makes our journey longer."

Falier looked at Alísa. Azron was her and Karn's home village. Karn felt confident he could persuade its influential slayer chief, Toronn. Alísa reached for her necklace, but she caught herself and straightened.

"I agree. I w—wonder, though, where Tsorr was headed? Lorin said he came from the north. Was he going from village to village with his message as we are? Or d—did he have another goal?"

A few eyes shot to Kallar, who crossed his arms. "What? You truly think a man powered by the Nameless would have given us anything?"

Alísa's response was gentler than Falier expected. "No, I agree. We would have gained nothing from Tsorr. However, he may have slipped with someone else before t—t-t-today."

Karn agreed and continued the conversation. Falier caught himself smiling. Alísa was doing so well! Looking at her and her father right now, it was easy to forget they were child and parent. They were just two chiefs, making decisions that would affect their clans and, hopefully, the whole western hill country. Yes, there were times Alísa remained quiet, but when she needed to speak, she did so without apology. She had come so far, and, Maker above, did he love her.

I only hope I can stand as tall when I talk to Karn and Hanah tonight. And that sent his mind twisting away again into words and phrasing.

After a bit more discussion, the meeting finally ended. The clans would continue their course toward Azron, but ask about Tsorr and any other word of an'reik in the area. If they heard more, they would reevaluate.

Falier stood with Graydonn as the rest of the leadership broke for supper.

His eyes landed on Karn and Hanah as they passed him. *Not yet. Wait for after food, when their minds aren't on an'reik and their stomachs are full.*

"Kallar, wait." Tenza's voice drew Falier's attention. "I would speak…"

Her words fell off as Kallar stomped away. He glared at Falier as he passed within arm's reach.

"Why were you even here?"

Falier bristled, fists forming at his sides while Graydonn growled. Kallar, however, kept walking. Honestly, that was worse. If Kallar had railed against him, Falier could brush it off as just the hot-head's temper. Just that simple, pointed question, though…

"Hey." Alísa touched his arm. "What did he say to you?"

Falier shook his head and relaxed his hands. "Nothing. Doesn't matter." He pulled her into a side-hug. "Let's get supper. I'm starved."

"Falier…"

"I promise, it's nothing. Just jibes that aren't worth repeating."

She leaned into him and rubbed a hand over his back. That was nice.

"Okay, but if you ever decide it *is* worth telling me, I'll listen. I understand what it's like to be mocked."

He kissed her temple. "I know. Thank you."

Supper was delicious, expertly seasoned as Selene worked alongside Karn's people. Even Hwinn—Selene's Illuminated hatchling—helped. The tawny adolescent, now four feet tall at the withers, stood behind a serving table and ensured everyone only took one piece of flatbread. Some of Karn's wayfarers still tensed having a dragon so close, even a young one like Hwinn, but others were starting to grow accustomed.

Falier and Alísa ate in a small group composed of both clans. On his shoulder sat Ska, the drek with sapphire mane, eyes, and wing-baubles who loved Falier's drumming. He knew music would come soon, and he occasionally thumped his tail against Falier's neck to remind him he was waiting. Falier offered pieces of meat in exchange for the drek's patience.

Sesína, too, sat with their group, interacting as she could with the slayers who relaxed their telepathic shields. Graydonn lay at the camp's edge with most of the other dragons. A few riders stood with them instead of Karn's people, even though Alísa had practically ordered them to integrate for the meal. Alísa didn't seem keen on admonishing them for it, however. The dragons needed interaction beyond themselves, and it couldn't hurt for Karn's clan to see fellow slayers getting along with their former enemies.

This circle of people was relatively quiet as they ate. A couple of Karnswomen engaged with Alísa about Rís, the adolescent drek preening his ruby mane on her shoulder. One rider commented on the high quality of the venison and received various agreements. Whenever Falier tried to start a conversation, it was met with less-than-enthusiastic responses from the rest. Perhaps it was the presence of a dragon and various fluttering dreki that kept the Karns-men reserved, but Falier couldn't help but remember Kallar's taunt. Did these men hold the same thoughts?

I do belong here.

In the back of his mind, Graydonn rumbled his agreement. The dragons accepted him, and Alísa's slayers treated him as one of them. He just needed to convince Karn's people.

Hopefully not Karn himself.

Maybe tonight wasn't ideal for this…

"I wouldn't mind you waiting."

Graydonn. Falier focused on their bond. *"He won't kill me. I think. Alísa's ma likes me, at least."*

"I would prefer you be sure before putting yourself at his mercy."

"Putting myself—I'm asking to marry his daughter, not challenging him to a duel."

"His only *daughter."*

Falier forced his eyebrow not to raise. Random facial expressions would *not* help his relating to Karn's clanmates. *"More time won't change that."*

"I don't understand why you need this. You and Alísa have already committed to each other—in dragon culture, you're practically mates. All that remains is to declare it to your clan. Why humans insist on ceremony rather than bonds that are already there is beyond me."

Fear lingered in that statement, the same Graydonn always felt when he saw Karn. Falier should have caught it sooner.

"He won't hurt me for asking."

Graydonn's growl rumbled in Falier's head. *"I know."*

"I'm still going to talk to him."

"I know."

Falier hesitated, then offered, *"You can listen in if you need to."*

The dragon could have done that anyway—Falier wasn't strong enough to block him—but permission would put Graydonn at ease.

Graydonn didn't answer in words, but his fear eased a little before he backed away from the communication line. Falier sighed, then turned his attention back to his group of slayers. Beside him, Alísa answered a question about dragon body language, a joy-filled grin on her face. She was doing what she loved, bringing the races together, and it was beautiful.

And oh, how he wanted that beauty, that strength, that deep caring, at his side forever.

Well, that settles it.

When it finally came time for music, Falier excused himself from the group. Songweaver Farren sat on a weathered wooden bench near the largest of the campfires, lute in hand. Across the way, Selene and Taz approached with their instruments, Taz limping along with his walking cane. He and Harenn had both taken terrible injuries in the last battle, but they were slowly recovering.

Besides her flute, Selene also carried Falier's bodhrán. The thought of the goat-skin beneath his fingers, responding with the exact sounds he desired, set something right inside him.

Ska, too, came alive at the sight of the drum, leaping off Falier's shoulder and heading for Selene.

"Hey!" Falier laughed. "I'm still the one who's going to play it!"

A few other dreki joined Ska in flocking to Selene and Taz, twirling around them with eager chitters. Karn's people eyed the tiny dragon-shaped creatures with caution. Hopefully the dreki's dancing would soon put the slayers at ease.

Arriving at the fire and taking his instrument from Selene, Falier settled next to Farren. A fiddle and a bodhrán sat at the songweaver's feet, his drum smaller and less ornate than Falier's. The thought of playing with a second drummer reminded Falier of Me'ran's céilís.

By Farren's suggestion, they began with a simple instrumental piece while their clanmates continued conversing. Then, as some of Alísa's people rose to dance, Selene selected a lively jig she hoped would call more to follow. Behind Falier, the wing-beats of the dreki dancing around the fire added to his percussion like an unruly drum-partner who couldn't quite keep a steady beat, or else like the storm rains he had learned to make music within long ago.

Slowly, more people rose to dance. The easterners moved through traditional céilí steps learned in Me'ran. As for Karn's people, a few men twirled their partners and one couple tried to copy the céilí steps, but beyond that, they simply moved to the beat. Maybe one day they would allow him and Selene to teach them steps.

They ran through a fast reel that brought in a few more people, then Farren led them in a song Falier didn't recognize. Karn's clan all knew it, however, and they sang along with him. The repeated chorus was simple, allowing Falier to harmonize on the second round. He smiled, seeing others pick it up too. By the end, the slayers sang together, the dreki danced and chirped, and even the dragons tapped their talons and growled with the low notes.

Happiness swelled in Falier's chest, and with a flourishing beat, he convinced Farren to lead them through the chorus once more. Falier had found camaraderie in many forms—flying with the clan, or over shared meals with excellent conversation. But nothing brought unity quite like a shared song with voices lifted as one. It was enough to make him forget his insufficiencies and feelings of separation amid slayers. Ultimately, they were all the same.

With those thoughts bolstering him, he took the applause of the crowd and excused himself from the musicians. Karn and Hanah stood off to the side— a perfect opportunity to speak with them privately.

Selene grabbed his arm as he walked past, turning him toward her. "Good luck."

Falier blinked, then quirked a smile. Of course she knew what he was doing. Selene *always* knew. It was an annoying part of being an older sibling, apparently.

"Thanks."

Turning back to his mission, Falier headed for Karn and Hanah. Briek and his wife stood with them, the four quietly conversing as the next song began. Falier waited, wiping sweaty palms on his trousers.

Be bold. Bold, but respectful. Respectful and firm. No, not firm—confident?

"Do you need Karn, or me, Falier?" Briek asked.

"Uh, Karn," Falier said, voice faltering as Alísa's parents turned to him. He cleared his throat. "And Hanah. But you can finish talking. I can wait."

Briek nodded toward the dancers. "I promised my wife a dance. We'll take our leave."

With polite farewells, Briek and his wife departed, leaving Falier with Karn and Hanah. Hanah bore a ready smile, while Karn had—it wasn't *quite* a frown.

"This celebration was an excellent idea," Hanah said. "I'm glad you and your sister thought of it."

"Thank you. I'm glad they're enjoying it." Falier drummed his fingers on his thigh. "Could I pull you two away to speak privately?"

Hanah leaned a bit into Karn, as if she were subtly trying to get him to answer. Karn raised a brow that said she wasn't subtle at all, then nodded at Falier.

"Come."

Without another word, the chief led them from the gathering toward a spot clear of both tents and dragons. They stopped at the place where the next of the endless rolling hills began sloping up. The firelight was dim here, and the stars shone like a million tiny witnesses.

"All right," Karn said, fixing chiefly eyes on Falier. "We're alone."

Falier caught himself before rubbing his neck. He glanced at Hanah, but in another not-so-subtle move, her eyes directed him back to Karn.

Falier cleared his throat. "Thank you, sir. I—"

He stopped. The speech—where did it go? How did it fall out of his head between dinner and here? He remembered the general direction of it, but the words he'd crafted—

Gone.

"Breathe," Graydonn ordered in his mind. *"You're making me nervous."*

"You're nervous?!"

Sucking in a breath, Falier forced his attention back to the most important man in Alísa's life. He was doing this for her.

"I think you both know that I love your daughter." *Don't cringe at the terrible wording, just keep going.* "I admire her strength and courage, I believe in her mission, and making her smile is the greatest feeling in the world. And, well, I know our relationship started—unconventionally. But I'd like to end it—no, not end, uh, continue. I'd like to continue it correctly, on a path with her family."

Karn's face betrayed nothing. No 'yes', no 'no', no indifference. And

Hanah's patient smile didn't help him interpret at all.

"I want to ask her to marry me. And I'd like to ask for your blessing."

Again, Karn remained expressionless. The silence pounded in Falier's ears—he wanted to fill it. Was this a test? Could he stay quiet longer than the chief?

As Karn scrutinized him, Falier tried to hold himself with the same confidence and fortitude Karn's people possessed. And, though he hated to recognize it right now, as Kallar would. The man Karn had initially chosen for his daughter.

Releasing his breath, Karn seemed to shrink a bit. "Your request does not surprise me. I have dreaded it since the day I walked in Alísa's memories and saw how quickly she fell in love with you."

Falier swallowed. 'Dread' wasn't a promising word.

"It was always my intention she marry a warrior," Karn continued. "One who could shield a woman with dragon empathy from humans who despise her and dragons who desire her."

Karn stepped past Falier, toward the gathering of clans. Falier looked from him to Hanah in question. Hanah merely nodded his attention back to Karn.

"Such threats proved far different than I imagined," Karn said, watching the dancers. "But they still exist. My desire will always be for her safety. Yet" —he glanced at Falier, eyes softer now— "safety is not all she needs, is it?"

Silence stretched until Falier realized he was expected to answer. Swallowing his nerves, he stepped up to Karn's side.

"No, sir. Her mission, her dream, isn't safe. I would protect her as best I can, but we've already faced moments that required sacrifice and I—I had to let her go, because I believe in her. That's something I can give her without reservation. I will encourage her, champion her cause, and strengthen her when she falls. I'll do that the rest of my life, if she'll have me."

Karn hummed, then looked behind them. "And what do you say?"

"You know what I say." Hanah's eyes twinkled as she considered Falier. "I'm honestly surprised you waited this long to speak with us."

Falier rubbed his neck before he could stop himself. "This is the first time I've seen you when we weren't strategizing peace talks or otherwise busy."

Hanah looked at Karn expectantly. After a moment, the chief exhaled.

"I've seen you care for Alísa in sun and shadow. Even watching through her memories and all their rose-colored tints, I know your love for her is true, as is hers for you." He came forward and clapped a heavy hand on Falier's shoulder. "Very well. If Alísa agrees, you have our blessing."

A grin spread across Falier's face, overtaking the wince at the weight of Karn's clap. "Thank you, sir. Hanah."

Just standing felt awkward—he needed to do something. Return Karn's gesture? Hugging him seemed out of the question.

Thankfully, Hanah was already on her way and Karn moved. She gave his arms a quick squeeze.

"I'd wish you luck, but I don't think you need it." She stepped back. "When will you ask her, and how?"

"Soon. I've been thinking about it, but not in detail. I wanted to have this conversation first."

Hanah nodded her approval. Behind her, Karn turned his attention to the gathered clans. He held a vigilance honed by years on the battlefield, taking in everything with unblinking eyes. Hanah clasped her hands in front of her in a dignified waiting pose as she watched her husband. She apparently knew Karn wasn't finished. The silence stretched a long while before he finally spoke.

"Your road will not be easy, young slayer." His voice was quiet, making Falier focus past the music and chatter. "If Alísa agrees to marry you, you will take up a leadership role beyond what you currently hold. You will have authority over warriors, but they will not easily give their respect to a holder, even if he holds the title of tiern."

'Tiern.' Falier glanced at Hanah. The title was like her title of lady of the clan. He returned to Karn.

"I have earned their respect."

"From Alísa's clan, perhaps," Karn said. "But what of others? If you had spoken to Lorin today instead of me, would he have heard you? Will my people hear you?"

Falier swallowed. Back in Me'ran, when Briek and his men were learning to ride dragons, his connection to Graydonn had earned their respect. Every other slayer clan, however—Segenn's, Tella's, and now Karn's—tended to dismiss him.

Karn continued. "In hiding your true nature, your family made your journey harder." With a start, Falier made to defend his parents, but Karn stopped him with a hand. "I don't say this to shame them. Maker knows I held Alísa back to protect her. And your parents' choice formed you into who my Lísa needs. Nevertheless, you have far to go to catch up to your slayer brothers."

Falier forced his shoulders to relax. "What do you suggest I do?"

Finally, Karn looked at him, his expression gentler than before. "As I said, your family's actions made you who you need to be. Others would have fought me, yet you answer with humility. That will serve you well, for you will be learning basics where your peers carry years of experience. Devote yourself to three things: the sword, multitasking between physical and psychic planes, and the confidence to speak in gatherings."

The last point hit harder than it would have yesterday. "Even if my opinions have already been voiced, or everyone else holds more experience than me?"

Karn scrutinized him. "My Lísa does not love you because you are like everyone else. Learn your strengths, form your opinions, and do not let another speak them for you. A leader may come in many forms, but none will follow someone they do not know."

"I concur," Hanah said, coming up on Karn's other side. "As tiern, there will be times to remain silent in deference to your chief, but your people must also know you are not merely following her submissively. You must actively support her in your own words and with your own ideas if they are to trust you as they do her."

Karn offered his arm to her, which she took as he continued. "It is a hard road to walk, for you are not only marrying Alísa, but the clan itself. Can you accept the choices and sacrifices which accompany that?"

The sword. Psychic mastery. Confidence. Essentially, become a slayer. That *was* what Falier had been working toward since the day he realized he would leave Me'ran. He had trained minimally in sword-play, and Graydonn and Alísa both had taught him much of telepathy. But Karn was right—he had a long way to go. And if he was going to stand beside Alísa as she called the slayer clans to heel, he needed to be someone they could respect.

Falier met Karn's eyes. "I can."

The corner of Karn's lips lifted, just slightly. "Good man. I know Alísa's clan has a weapons trainer, but I recommend you also work with my brother, L'non. There is none better with the sword."

Graydonn grumbled in the back of Falier's mind. *"I hate it when you fight with swords."*

"It will just be training swords, though, made of wood or else dulled metal blades."

"You fight psychically. I'm supposed to do the physical fighting."

"But if it makes slayers respect me more…"

Graydonn left out a huff of steam that Falier could *feel*. *"Sword-prowess shouldn't matter when it comes to respect."*

"And yet it does." Falier said it as firmly as he could. This wasn't the first time Graydonn had objected to his weapons training. Anxiety always accompanied it, like Graydonn feared he would be harmed. Touching, but the lack of confidence it displayed also hurt.

"Thank you," Falier said, refocusing on Karn. "I would like that."

"Then I will speak to L'non in the morning. Until then" —Karn nodded toward the celebration— "we should get back to our peoples."

Falier agreed, and as he walked alongside Alísa's parents, one thought dominated his mind—he had a new calling now, one he should have been about all along.

Tonight was his last night as a holder.

4

APPRENTICE

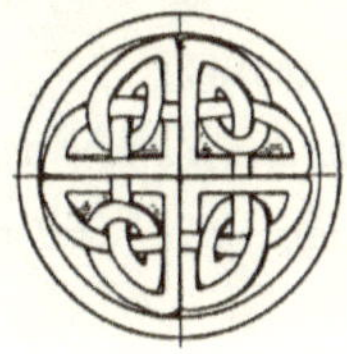

Dragons. So many flaming dragons.

Power pounded in Kallar's skull as he stalked through camp, held captive by his own telepathy. The afternoon sun lit his way, yet his vision blurred every few throbs, a weakness only *just* more tolerable than the dragon emotions he shielded against.

It wasn't right. Home should be a sanctuary, a place he could let his guard down. Especially since the pounding headache aggravated everything else, including his still-healing shield arm. Instead, Alísa brought her flaming dragon lieutenants to meetings he was required to attend. And, rather than leave when the conference ended, they just stood there visiting.

The situation made his blood boil. He never asked to be a Dragon Singer. Never asked for this accursed connection to the enemy. Never asked for his mission to change from protecting humanity into also protecting monsters. But Karn, his chief and master, had bought into Alísa's so-called calling, and so the clan followed as well.

Kallar gritted his teeth and kept walking. *I should have deserted with Tern.*

But he had said no when Tern entered his tent that night—the night Alísa won peace between Karn, Tella, and the dragons lurking in the Serpent's Fangs. Kallar was no traitor. Even two days later, when Karn had given permission for clanmates who disagreed with the alliance to leave without repercussions, Kallar stayed. He didn't run when things got hard—he powered through.

And look where that's gotten me.

Telepathy battered the inside of Kallar's head, begging him to release it. Though he used a similar shield in battle, there he would relieve the pressure with mind-spears. Holding everything in was excruciating. But he would not relax, not with dragons nearby.

"Kallar."

No. No no no, he would not face that voice. Yet another of Alísa's unnecessary visitors, this one human, but perhaps even more unwelcome.

Tenza of Me'ran. Technically, his grandmother. Practically, Alísa's ally.

Truthfully, his mother's betrayer.

She thinks she can just show up and act like none of it happened? Like she and her husband had supported Ma in her pain or allowed her a shred of control over her own life?!

He and R'lann wouldn't be alive if Tenza had gotten her way. Allara would still be in Me'ran, kept from fighting the dragons, from her lover, from ever passing on her curse.

Perhaps that last part would have been a blessing. Had R'lann inherited the power, too? Was it sitting dormant inside him back in L'rang, waiting for him to discover that monsters had souls so it could punish him for the knowledge too?

Kallar pressed past tent after sun-bleached tent, weaving out of sight of Tenza before ducking into his own. As soon as the flap closed and the glaring sunlight filtered yellow through the leather walls, he relaxed his shield. He fought not to gasp in a breath of relief, lest she hear. He held as she stopped beside his tent. As she called his name again. As her footsteps faded and he was finally alone.

Rounding his trunk, Kallar yanked the buckle of his sword-belt and threw the weapon onto his unmade bed. What was she even doing here? What Eldra saw fit to sport with him by bringing her and Alísa together so she could torment him?

He lowered to the dusty deerskin mat. The pounding in his head had nearly subsided, and the throbbing in his arm was gone. He flexed his fingers, feeling his muscles press against the splint and wrappings. The healer said he could start working strength back into it within the week. Until then, it was useless.

Just like him.

A slayer forbidden from slaying.

An apprentice who no longer believed in his master's purpose.

Once betrothed, now cast aside.

The last one didn't sting so much anymore. He and Alísa had never gotten along—it would have been a miserable marriage. Still, fire filled his veins every time he saw that damned holder…

"Kallar?"

He fixed his eyes on the tent flap. That wasn't Tenza.

"What?"

Songweaver Farren took on an authoritative air. "I need to speak with you."

Kallar growled to himself. "Fine."

Sunlight pierced the shadows as Farren entered. The commanding manner lived solely in his voice. His demeanor was kind and his eyes soft. Pitying.

Kallar huffed. "What do you want?"

Farren lowered to the ground cross-legged, his movement smooth as he kept those eyes on Kallar. This conversation would be incredibly irritating if that didn't let up.

"To check on you." Farren scanned him up and down. "You're not yourself. Haven't been for a month now. I had hoped to leave you alone as you would desire, but—"

Farren gestured to Kallar, as though that conveyed everything.

"You're right." Kallar made eye-contact. "I do want to be left alone."

"Show me you can handle that, and I'll go."

Kallar scoffed. "What is it you want to see? You want me to be happy? To embrace this like centuries of bloodshed never happened? Like I haven't given up everything to keep humanity safe from those monsters?"

"We've all sacrificed much."

I've sacrificed more.

But Farren would refute that, and the problem wasn't what Kallar had given up—he had done it gladly. "And now we're supposed to get all friendly? Sing a little song together and forget what happened? Is that what you think, Songweaver?"

Farren shook his head. "I think you don't care what I think. So we shall proceed with facts. Fact one" —he began counting on his fingers— "your tent is a mess."

Kallar averted his gaze, brushing the shorn side of his hair. "And?"

"And after our planning sessions for that blasted song we're now cleaning up after, I know how you keep it. Everything in order, easy to grab at a moment's notice. Yet now, with dragons roaming about our camp, your trunk is open in the middle of your space, suggesting you merely threw it inside. And you've just tossed your weapon on the furs rather than placing it at your side where it belongs."

Farren indicated the next finger. "Fact two—you are no stranger to pain, so the problem isn't your arm or the headaches you've been getting. Don't give me that look. You haven't hidden them well."

Kallar's arm throbbed, alerting him to the tension in his body. He kept it, not wanting Farren to see he was hitting the right nerves.

"Fact three" —this time, curiosity wafted through the astral plane— "you did not desert. You follow your master, even though you disagree with him."

Farren regarded him, awaiting an explanation. Kallar didn't have one.

"So? Tell me your grand conclusion, Songweaver. Where do these oh-so-interesting facts lead you?"

The pitying eyes again. "You are floundering, Kallar. The truth challenges your life's foundation, and you don't know how to move forward. You cling to what you've lost so tightly that you cannot see what might be gained. Is it not strength to admit when you err, pick up the pieces, and continue on?"

Kallar stood. "We're done here."

"Isn't that what you did when your arm burned? Or again when it was broken?"

Kallar stormed out. He could have insisted Farren leave instead, but he had no patience left for talk. He needed to move, to fight, to punch something!

Movement caught his eye. L'non, training the boys in swordplay.

Including that flaming holder boy.

Falier had been working with L'non every time Alísa visited camp. As if he could ever amount to anything. He managed to make the minimal leather armor appear clunky—he hadn't been born in it like everyone else here. The holder moved through a single strike over and over, moving in tandem with the clan's young teens. The weight of the wooden waster sword was obviously getting to the holder, after what could only have been ten minutes of work after the meeting.

Pathetic.

Kallar stalked forward, stopping next to the chest full of more wasters. A foreign anxiety filled him and he growled, rebuilding his mental shield to block out Graydonn. *Hellflames!* He hated that he knew the dragon's name.

Pulse pounding, Kallar reached for a waster of his own. "Let's see how long you last with an *actual* opponent—"

"No."

A hand gripped Kallar's shoulder, causing him to whirl around on whoever—

Karn stood there, his expression quiet. Shame weighed Kallar's heart, a bucket of cold water on his anger. What was he thinking, about to challenge essentially a child to a duel? Then to be caught by Karn himself…

Karn looked him over, surely seeing his shame. Stooping, the chief pulled two wasters. He reached one out to Kallar.

"You'll fight me instead."

Kallar looked at the wooden sword, unmoving until Karn pushed it into his chest. He took the weapon and raised an eyebrow. Karn met his gaze, then inclined his head toward the outskirts of camp.

"Come."

Gripping the waster, Kallar followed. Was this a rebuke for what he nearly did? Mere redirection? Or something else? Karn gave no indication as he crossed camp. They passed all the living tents, the kitchen tent bustling with women, and a small gathering of people around Alísa and Ses—the black dragon. Tenza was there too, the sight of her reigniting Kallar's anger. Good. That would help as he sparred.

Karn didn't stop until they stood a decent distance from camp. No spectators here.

"Set yourself," Karn said as he picked his spot and got into his own ready stance. He held his waster in a two-handed grip, tip up and toward Kallar. His expression was still unreadable.

Kallar picked a one-handed grip, his still-splinted arm not allowing for more. Despite preferring two hands, he had plenty of practice with one. He needed it to hold a shield when fighting dragons.

But that didn't matter anymore, did it? No more slaying. Everything— *everything*—Kallar had worked for, *everything* that made him who he was, was gone.

And Karn had allowed it all.

Teeth gritted, Kallar moved. He skipped the circling and testing—they needed no such formality anymore. He simply advanced and struck.

Karn deflected easily, taking controlled steps backward as Kallar attacked. Each meeting of weapons was a sharp crack in the air, like rams butting heads. Kallar preferred the ringing of metal blades, how they sang with the spirit of true battle even when dulled for sparring. Karn met every blow with a calm assurance that made Kallar push harder.

"Did you only bring me here to toy with me?" Slash. Thrust. "To make me expend energy so I can't do it elsewhere?"

Karn blocked and pressed his weapon against Kallar's. "Is it working?"

"It was a dumb mistake. Won't happen again." Kallar shoved him off and dropped the waster. "If that's all you want, we're done here."

Kallar turned back toward camp and began walking. As he did, however, he heard Karn's footfalls behind him—fast and light.

Left side.

Kallar dodged right as Karn's weapon swiped through the space he had just occupied.

"What the—"

Karn smiled. "When did I ever teach you to turn your back on an opponent?"

"I said we're done."

Kallar pressed on toward camp, but Karn blocked his path after only a few steps, sword raised.

"You said we were finished if I merely challenged you to make you leave Falier alone. Your assumption is incorrect, *apprentice*. Pick up your weapon" — he lunged, causing Kallar to stumble back— "or face the consequences."

Karn's goading grin unlocked memories of better times. Kallar pushed them aside. A part of him still wanted to refuse, to not give Karn what he sought. The rest of him...

Kallar bolted for his discarded waster. Karn gave chase, his heavier footfalls a warning as Kallar approached the weapon. If he stooped to grab it, Karn would knock him down and claim the match. Instead, Kallar dove for the waster, snatching it with the hand of his bad arm and using his good arm to tuck and roll. A clumsy execution, but the wooden weapon wouldn't punish him for it. Kallar's roll brought him to one knee just in time to block Karn's strike. Bracing with his good arm, he ensured only a slight jolt reached his injured one.

Karn didn't press, hesitating as he noticed Kallar's splint. That was an opening. With a shout, Kallar sprang to his feet in a lunge Karn parried. Kallar changed his grip and attacked. This time, Karn fought back.

Thrust. Parry. Block.

"I've missed this," Karn said between blows. "I haven't sparred in Maker knows how long."

Kallar didn't respond. Talking took focus from the fight. And he needed to *fight*!

Lunge. Duck. Swipe.

"There hasn't been time," Karn continued. "Sometimes I feel the world has been upended and I'm left trying to walk upside down."

Kallar leapt at Karn, pressing swords as best he could with only one hand. Karn tried to hook his leg and send him to the ground, but Kallar leapt back. Sweat forming, he surged forward again.

Slash. Block. Thrust.

"I still start when I see one of her dragons out of the corner of my eye. My battle instinct flares."

Kallar ducked a swipe and rolled to get behind Karn. He swung but couldn't catch Karn before he blocked. The wooden crack sent his bad arm throbbing.

"I don't know how her riders have gotten past that. Perhaps it's because they went through it together." Karn gave a pointed look, confirming the inkling building in Kallar's mind. Karn wasn't talking about himself.

Kallar slashed toward Karn's chest and the chief blocked and slid his blade up to catch Kallar's weapon against his cross guard. Kallar glared as Karn pressed swords with him.

"I'm fine," Kallar said through clenched teeth.

Karn raised a skeptical brow. "Glad to hear it, because a lot of us aren't. Perhaps they would all be 'fine' if I didn't hide my own struggles. Perhaps I left them feeling like they were alone in theirs."

Kallar shoved him back. "*Perhaps* they don't want you or nosy songweavers butting in."

"*Perhaps* it's my responsibility. I took them from their homes and families. I led them into..." Karn faltered, the point of his sword lowering. "Into a lie. And now we all must wrestle with the truth."

Anger pulsed through Kallar's veins. He tightened his grip and swung. *Don't you give up!*

Startled, Karn blocked, parried, and returned the attack. He finally stopped talking and just moved. It was like he had kept an untapped reserve of energy, adding speed to his skill. Kallar could only beat Karn four times out of ten, but anyone could beat a more skilled foe. All it took was to be ready the very moment one's opponent made a mistake.

Still, Kallar fought to keep up. Strike. Parry. Lunge. Block. Dodge. Swipe—

Karn stepped back rather than blocking the attack, then got close as Kallar sloppily twisted with the momentum of his swing. He tried to hit Karn with the pommel of his waster, but Karn had already hooked his leg. With a pull, he sent Kallar to the ground. The point of Karn's weapon was at Kallar's throat a second later.

"Well fought," Karn said. His brow glistened with sweat and his breaths were heavy. Even with a loss, Kallar couldn't be too upset when Karn breathed harder than he did.

"Glad you finally decided to *start* fighting." Kallar pushed away the waster at his neck and stood. "Was your plan just to wear me down with all that half-assed sword-waving first, or to lull me to sleep with talk?"

Karn grunted a laugh. "Neither."

They returned to camp in silence. The breeze cooled Kallar's neck, arms, and the shorn side of his head. The hair there was over an inch long now. He'd have to get someone to cut it down again.

Kallar dropped his waster into the chest of training weapons, not allowing himself to glance at the holder boy continuing to practice. Just thinking of him threatened to kill the scrap of a good mood Kallar had found. As he turned back toward the tents, the sight of Alísa, Trísse, and their bonded dragons off to the side killed it anyway. He had never really liked Trísse, but he had always known her to be sensible. How had a dragon gotten its claws into her mind?

Karn came alongside him, walking between Kallar and the dragons. He kept his eyes ahead as he spoke quietly.

"What would you suggest I do for those of us who aren't 'fine?'"

Kallar raised an eyebrow at him. "You're the chief. If you don't know your men, who can?"

Karn gave Kallar a pointed look. "All right. Tell me truly, if I offered the chance to leave again, would you stay?"

"Would you want me to?" Kallar shot back.

Karn's brow creased. That drew blood. "You think I wouldn't?"

"You have Alísa back. Strong, confident, and perfect in your eyes. You have a new son-to-be, and we aren't even fighting dragons anymore." Heart pulsing in his head, Kallar grabbed the flap at the entry to his tent. "I'm irrelevant."

Kallar made to duck inside, but Karn seized his shoulder and pulled him back around. The chief's eyes narrowed.

"It was not Alísa who stopped the an'reik in Bezin. My men do not look to Falier in times of uncertainty, and though we no longer hunt dragons, I am confident we are not done fighting. If you wish to leave, I give you that right, but don't you dare tell me that you are irrelevant!"

Karn paused, his grip relaxing from its near-bruising weight. His voice lowered. "Or that I don't want you here. Because Maker knows I do."

Stunned, Kallar met Karn's eyes and forced a breath.

"All right, then. I'll stay."

The lines on Karn's face disappeared, smoothed by relief. "I'm glad to hear it. And, if you need to talk—"

"I'm fine." It sounded false even to Kallar's ears.

Karn simply nodded and let go of Kallar's shoulder. The chief's eyes flitted behind him and a sad smile formed.

"Tidy your space, son."

With that, Karn turned back toward the field. Back toward Alísa and her little black dragon. Kallar shoved his way inside, half expecting Farren to still be there. But the songweaver was gone and Kallar was alone. He stared at the floor, then grabbed his trunk and heaved, shoving it into its spot by the door.

5

BONDS

The sun always seemed warmer when flying, even with the air rushing around him. It lighted on Falier's skin and held him like an embrace, welcoming a creature made for the ground but dreaming of the sky.

"Hwinn, Dezra, form up behind Komi," Alísa ordered. Underneath her, Sesína banked to better watch the students. *"You'll practice wing-dragon positions while your riders train psychically."*

The adolescents did as commanded, each zipping toward the much larger brown dragoness. They were three months old now, the age Sesína was when she fought her first battle. Dezra proved the hardest to spot with her light-blue scales. She moved gracefully, twisting and banking while Rassím leaned into her movements.

Then there was Selene and Hwinn. What a pair. All Falier's life, his sister had been a steady river—strong, gentle, and unexpectedly powerful. Who could have guessed that her Illuminated dragon would be so flighty and energetic? Their first flight resulted in Selene taking an unexpected dip in the lake they practiced over. That instance scared Hwinn straight, however, and he hadn't thrown her since.

Once the youngest dragons found their positions behind Komi, Alísa instructed her to lead them through maneuvers. Then she turned her attention to the riders.

"Today, we'll continue our work on mind-sharing. Selene, since you've already achieved this, I want you to focus on channeling Hwinn's power to enhance your empathy. If it works, pull away from the others so they aren't caught in the emotion you're pressing. The rest of you, start your push-and-pulls and ease toward a mind-share."

Falier closed his eyes and began the familiar pattern. His psychic power was like a forest creek, while Graydonn's was like the rushing Nissen river. He had accessed it quickly in many a battle, but today he went slowly, focusing on the basics as L'non and Darrin both had him doing in swordplay. Breathing deeply, he widened his connection to Graydonn and let the dragon's power pour through. He marveled at just how much Graydonn's mind held. How did he contain it all?

As Falier took in Graydonn's power, it quickly became too much. Before Falier accepted the bond, he had to release the power at this point, sending a barely controlled bolt of psychic energy into the sky. Now that their bond was sure, however, Falier instead began pressing telepathy back toward Graydonn. Here the water analogies didn't quite work, as Graydonn's energy continued pouring in while Falier also allowed it to flow out. Equilibrium. Push-and-pull.

Eyes still closed, Falier checked the astral plane, where the world was dark except for the minds of living beings. Before him, Graydonn's head and neck were glowing outlines the same amber as his eyes. Further out, the rest of the dragons and riders were similarly outlined. And between his fellow trainees lived shining lines of psychic connection. Some were merely telepathic communication, but each bonded pair also had a bright line that was the bond itself. The only partners in the sky today without a bond were Taz and Harenn. They wouldn't join this exercise, instead working to rebuild their strength after weeks of recovery.

Falier brought his attention back. *"You ready to try again?"*

Graydonn rumbled an affirmative, straightening into a forward glide. They had gotten so close to a mind-share last time—surely today they would succeed!

Breathing deeply, Falier reached across the mind-kin bond. Graydonn's emotions were full here—curiosity, the joy of flight, and an undercurrent of worry flowed around Falier's consciousness.

"You all right? You seem anxious."

The dragon blew out steam and relaxed his mind. *"Not about this. Keep going."*

"If you're sure."

In response, Graydonn's end of the bond opened wider. Falier continued reaching out, remembering Alísa's instructions. *"Try to feel the wind rushing over Graydonn's scales and the leather of his wings."*

Falier pressed into Graydonn's joy of flight, following its path further down into Graydonn's mind. He tried to find the sensations, but despite his ability to follow Graydonn's emotions, Falier once again found an unyielding barrier. It felt different from last time, though. Here, Falier discovered a new emotion from Graydonn—sorrow. It mingled with the undercurrent of anxiety, inseparable.

Distantly, Graydonn also hit a barrier. When the dragon pressed, Falier realized the emotions swimming at the bottom of his own mind. Fear and striving.

With an unspoken agreement, they each pulled back into themselves.

Falier shook his head, his brain buzzing. *"Not today, then."*

Graydonn rumbled a gentle growl. *"Not today. I'm sorry."*

Eyes still closed, Falier observed Selene and Hwinn. The two of them glowed in a mixture of Selene's brown and Hwinn's sapphire—a new, unique color. Rassím and Dezra also seemed to be close, their colors nearer to matching than their last few attempts.

Falier opened his eyes. *"Maybe it's because we're mind-kin and not Illuminated. Our bonds work differently."*

"This is achievable by mind-kin," Graydonn insisted. He looked at Komi and Trísse, who also had not joined, and his amber eyes dimmed. *"But perhaps the difference makes it harder."*

They continued flying, following Sesína's orders for flight-patterns. Selene and Hwinn flew alone, practicing with empathy like Alísa had told them. Falier checked once and saw an empathic cloud that surpassed any Selene had created prior. Falier smiled. The cloud was bright blue, the color of joy.

After only half an hour of training, Alísa called the end—she had meetings to attend to at the cave. She was always running to and from meetings nowadays. The trappings of being chief.

Komi pulled up alongside Graydonn as the dragons aimed for the mountain. Trísse stretched her arms over her head, then reached one across her chest and held it there, looking down at Taz and Rassím.

"Anyone up for some sparring?"

Komi looked back at her. *"You're going from one training straight into another?"*

Trísse switched arms. *"There's a big difference between training the mind and training the body. Besides, I'm getting antsy just sitting on your back. I need to do something."*

Falier wasn't sure he agreed. Training his mind felt just as strenuous as his body most days. But then, Trísse's lifelong training had encompassed both mind and body. Something Falier had missed out on as a holder.

Karn is right, I have a lot to catch up on.

Graydonn grumbled beneath him, but said nothing. Probably more objections to Falier using a sword.

"I could do with some sparring," Rassím said.

"Same here," Taz agreed. *"Just, you know, don't kill me. I'm practically an invalid."*

Falier could feel Selene roll her eyes. *"Oh please, you barely need your cane anymore. Trísse, you have my full permission to push him."*

Taz sent mock hurt through the psychic connection. *"I thought you were on my side!"*

"I am," Selene said. *"I need you back in shape so I don't have to worry about you fighting."*

Taz huffed. *"You should worry about me if Trísse is my sparring partner."*

"You could be mine," Falier suggested. *"I'm not ready to spar with Trísse or Rassím yet, but an invalid…"*

Taz grinned up at him. *"And if the invalid defeats you? What'll you give me?"*

"Bragging rights for life."

"Nah, I'd take that anyway. How about you take my next armor-laundering duty?"

Falier fake-gagged as though smelling the sweaty leather armor. *"Fine, if you reciprocate."*

"Deal!"

Graydonn, Komi, and Harenn pulled into a circling pattern as Sesína, Hwinn, and Dezra approached the main entrance. Though it and its landing platform were large, only two adult dragons could land simultaneously. When it was Graydonn's turn, he landed with barely a scrape of talons. He quickly shuffled clear for Harenn and Komi, following the others down a ramp of rock to the floor.

The main cave was enormous—big enough to fit perhaps six houses lengthwise and five along its width. It also reached up, up, up into the mountain, its walls pocked with alcoves and tunnels leading to other caves. Unfortunately, there were few humans could access without draconic help. While a dragon clan would have used the spacious cave for meetings and community, the slayers needed it to live. Though Alísa wanted to find ways to give them space and reclaim the main cave for its proper use, her energy was focused on her missions of peace.

Falier walked beside Graydonn along the perimeter of the living tents, careful not to trip on ropes pounded into cracks in the floor or tied to stalagmites to keep the canvas upright. Further down, sounds of wood cracking against wood already echoed from the training cave. Falier, Graydonn, and the others followed the sounds into a tunnel winding down to it. Alísa and Selene didn't follow, Alísa hurrying off toward Koriana while Selene kissed Taz on the cheek and then went to help prepare supper. Even though she trained with Hwinn, Selene seemed perfectly at ease being a holder rather than a slayer.

Falier kept a hand on Graydonn's wither as the tunnel darkened, trusting the dragon's eyesight. Normally, a torch sat outside, but those already inside had taken it. Falier would have ask Briek about buying another with the resources from Rorenth's horde.

Finally, firelight appeared and they emerged into a new cave, smaller and squatter than the main one. Three chests full of weapons and leather practice armor sat near the tunnel, which Trísse, Rassím, and Taz all approached. Further in, Darrin, a man with pale skin and shaggy brown hair, watched the clan's two young teenage boys as they sparred with wooden wasters.

"Hold," Darrin said. The boys obeyed, separating and panting. Darrin approached Falier and the others. He had been the primary trainer in Briek's former wayfaring clan and was skilled with many weapons. He typically rode Saynan, their teaching ways complimenting each other well.

Darrin looked straight at Falier as he spoke. "I'm afraid I'll be working with the boys for another hour, so you'll have to wait before I can facilitate your matches."

Falier drummed his fingers on his thigh. An hour was an awfully long wait. "Can't I switch in?"

Darrin shook his head. "I'm teaching them something you're not ready for. Taz, you'll need to wait, too. You're likely to hurt yourself without supervision. Trísse and Rassím, you may spar on the opposite side of the cave as the boys."

Taz made to protest, but then his eyes flicked to Falier and he stopped. "Guess we can spar after, then."

"All right," Falier said. "I can still learn by watching in the meantime."

A light smirk played at Darrin's lips. "Oh, you won't be watching."

Falier slumped, realizing what was coming. Darrin pointed to two wooden buckets beside the larger barrel of water.

"Strength training. Fill the barrel to the brim. It's only half-empty, so I'm giving you a thousand heartbeats. Take longer and I'll have more tasks for you before you can spar. Taz, make yourself useful and count for me. I'll know if you cheat. Go."

Pulling in a breath, Falier snatched up the buckets and jogged to the tunnel. Without Graydonn, he had to move slowly until he reached the main cave. He headed for the back, where a stream flowed with cold, fresh water. No one knew whether it was melted ice that had slowly found its way here or a spring bubbling up from underground. All they knew, thanks to the dragons' excellent senses of smell and taste, was the water was pure and safe.

As Falier pressed on, he caught relief pulsing from Graydonn. Annoyed, Falier pushed it away. He needed to learn the sword. Even if he only fought as a dragon rider, other riders used swords to slash at enemy dragons who came too close. And if he was going to earn the respect of other slayer clans, he needed to become someone they couldn't push around without consequences.

Thinking to shave some time off his run, Falier slowed a bit to weave between tents. This path was more direct, but as he stopped to avoid running into a woman chasing her child, then a man charging out of his tent, Falier wondered at the wisdom of his choice. Surely there were ways to improve this. People needed space, not tents crammed together. Also, the kitchen should be closer to the water source, not beyond the living spaces.

Falier slid to a stop at the stream and dunked his buckets in. Dreki currently occupied this cooler section of the cave, fluttering around a tunnel about five feet off the ground. One-by-one, they phased into the right base of the tunnel and emerged on the left. Falier was just in time to witness the stone crack, creating the beginnings of a step. Apparently, phasing through an object enough times weakened its structure, so with concerted effort, dreki could carve into stone. The process was slow, but the dreki seemed eager to help give humans access to the lower caves and tunnels. They also enjoyed sowing flowers and vines into the walls, beautifying certain sections with impossible plant-life kept alive by some power none but the dreki understood.

Falier returned his focus to his task. Now came the hard part. He pulled the buckets back out, each filled to the brim. If he ran, they would splash, requiring more trips. If he didn't make it on time, Darrin would probably have him fill the kitchen barrels next. Or haul stones from one end of the sparring cave to the other.

Falier skirted the tents this time, walking as quickly as he could. He would use Taz's count to figure out if he should try running. It would take at least three trips, maybe four.

On his third trip back, heart pounding with exertion, he spotted Alísa conversing with Briek and Koriana. Alísa caught sight of him and waved. He could only return her smile and keep going. Much as he knew he needed strength and sword training, Falier couldn't help but be jealous. He should be like Briek, a strong warrior always at Alísa's side, sharing in decisions and helping her carry them out.

I need to talk to her about Karn's suggestion that I take part in leadership meetings. He passed back into the tunnel. *Once we're engaged. Let's not get ahead of ourselves.*

Returning to the barrel, Falier dumped the last of the water, a minimal amount splashing over as it reached the brim.

"Nine-hundred forty-six," Taz announced. He raised a hand for a high-five, which Falier could barely meet. His biceps ached and his legs wanted to give out.

"Excellent," Darrin said, pausing the boys. "Grab your leathers, Falier and Taz. It's your turn."

Falier stared at him. "But you said you weren't available for an hour. It's only been a quarter of that!"

"Come, Falier, you must learn not to take everything your trainer says at face-value. There will be many battles where your hope for rest is cruelly snatched away. Now let's move!" He clapped his hands for emphasis.

Falier let out a long, tired breath, then fetched his armor. Behind him, Graydonn growled.

"That's not right. You barely know how to hold the weapon and he expects you to fight in this condition?"

Falier drew himself up. *"I can do it, and I will."* He grabbed a leather greave and began strapping it on. *"I am a slayer."*

6

CRAKIL'S CLAN

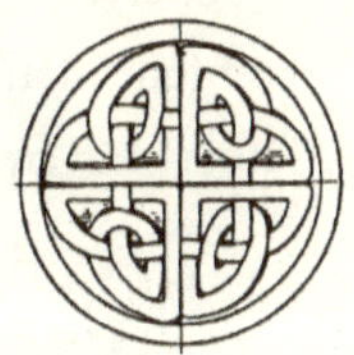

Alísa shivered as Sesína ascended the mountain on the winds. Ahead, the scouts of another clan led them toward their cave, where Alísa would make her case to an alpha who had once tried to hold her captive. To her left flew Koriana, the dragoness level with Sesína rather than in her typical spot behind her.

"Crakil will try to intimidate you," Koriana cautioned. *"He will not have forgotten your last meeting."*

Sesína's eyes brightened. *"But this time, you'll have far more support."*

Alísa looked back at her entourage—six dragons and their riders, plus a few dreki. Definitely a better situation than when she escaped with Koriana and Graydonn all those months ago.

One of the highest peaks in Karn's wayfaring territory, Crakil's mountain held caves made of both stone and ice. Here at the beginning of autumn, the ice had diminished drastically, leaving some caves uninhabitable. Graydonn spoke with melancholy of the summer months when he and his family would move into the main cave. Living with other hatchlings and adolescents was nice, but proximity to the alphas often brought his parents strife. Apparently, Graydonn's father D'lann had a 'nasty habit' of teaching hatchlings that humans were neither vermin nor all evil, which the former alpha F'renn did not appreciate. That didn't bode well for this meeting. Neither did the fact that F'renn died at Rorenth's talons while chasing down Alísa.

"Who knows," Sesína said, *"maybe F'renn was awful and they'll all be grateful that your actions put Crakil in charge."*

Alísa shuddered, remembering Crakil's attempt to compel her to jump off Koriana's back and into his talons. *"I somehow doubt that."*

Sesína's mood dampened as she shared Alísa's memory. *"Yeah. I guess he's not so great either. Do you think he'll recognize me?"*

A mixture of hope and anxiety swirled in Sesína. Alísa considered her reply, trying to decide what would help Sesína more in her confusion.

"He might figure it out, but you were only an egg then."

Sesína snorted. *"An egg with personality."*

Alísa let the half-hearted statement stand. They had spoken before of Sesína's lack of desire to meet her father, but hypotheticals were often different from the real thing.

Ahead, the scouts swooped into the largest cave mouth. Here, Koriana took the lead, diving through its maw. Sesína followed, the darkness engulfing them. As Alísa's vision adjusted, colored pinpricks of glowing dragon eyes soon became visible, sprinkled throughout the cave. The clan was perhaps twenty-five dragons strong.

Alísa felt her slayers tense. Though Crakil knew they were coming, he hadn't provided a fire to light their way as a courtesy. A fine start to their little talk, but one Koriana had predicted. A rush of wings passed Alísa and the sharp clops of dropping firewood echoed in the space. With a blast of her breath, Koriana lit the wood Saynan laid down, illuminating the cavern and all its crevices.

Dragons clung to the cave walls and lounged in side caverns, all facing the great black dragon on the ground. Curiosity rose from Sesína as she landed fifty feet away, but she kept her emotions tied back so no one else would sense it.

Crakil's flame-orange eyes flashed as the rest of Alísa's dragons settled. Koriana landed last after lighting the fire. She sliced her tail through the air in a sign of authoritative displeasure.

"Crakil. I present to you Alísa-Dragon-Singer."

Crakil snapped his jaws, his creaking voice entering the clan's link. *"I know who she is, deserter. We've met before."*

"We have not." Alísa slid to the floor and stepped forward. As she moved, dreki fluttered to their perches among her warriors. Chrí's son Rís alighted on her shoulder. *"You met a terrified girl who understood nothing. Before you stands an alpha who has not only defeated dragon and slayer alike, but has brought them together as allies."*

Rumbles echoed through the chamber, some holding more ire than others. Sesína kept Alísa in a light mind-choke to keep the actual emotions from bombarding her. Alísa only heard the alpha's words through Sesína's own connection to him.

"The true Dragon Singer, Bria, never stooped to fraternize with slayers. You are a mere hatchling who could not leave the safety of her father's wings." Crakil's gaze lifted to Koriana. *"The Koriana I once knew would have kept the Singer on the correct currents. I see now that your mate's teachings have corrupted you."*

Graydonn growled, and Koriana snapped her jaws. Alísa rushed to speak before either could rise further to the antagonizing comment.

"Is it weak to choose peace rather than war?" Alísa indicated those behind her. *"These brave souls prove——"*

"It is weakness to let one's enemy live," Crakil countered. *"The slayers murder, yet they stand among you as equals while you destroy dragon clans. I know how you destroyed all but a remnant of Rorenth's clan, how you decimated Tsamen's. Even as a scared hatchling, you brought F'renn to his doom. You are no friend of dragonkind, slayer wench!"*

Rís hissed as jaws snapped at the air and tails thudded against the ground in agreement. Alísa's heart pounded in her chest as she stepped forward to claim authority.

"Segenn. Tella. Karn. Lorin. I stood for dragons against each of these chiefs and their clans. Ask those behind me if I extended to Rorenth's and Tsamen's clans the same choice I gave the slayers. All who vowed to leave innocents alone have been protected."

"And assimilated," Crakil growled. *"I will not give up my clan to you, Dragon Singer. Nor will I allow you to steal any away, as Koriana did my daughter."*

Sesína started, her mind-choke around Alísa faltering as Crakil's eyes landed on her. Alísa pushed peace, resisting the urge to place a hand on her scales. Neither of them could show weakness here.

Crakil swiped his tail through the air, staring at Koriana. *"I gave her to you to Illuminate and guide in the loss of her mother. You betrayed me, taking her away and allowing a human to Illuminate her! What life has she known? What would the Singer impose upon us if we ally with her?"*

Sesína snapped her jaws. *"I'm right here. Ask me yourself!"*

The alpha dragon's eyes dimmed marginally as his gaze returned to her. *"Sesína."* He seemed to taste the name as he caught it in her telepathic connection. *"Speak, daughter."*

Sesína stepped up alongside Alísa, wings raised slightly to make herself look bigger and more authoritative. *"I have known a life of wonder. They say the Dragon Singer is a dragon's soul in a human body. Illuminated by a human, I am the other side of the coin. Err"* —she stopped, searching for a more draconic metaphor— *"other side of the mountain? You know, the opposite."*

Sesína clawed at the rocky cave floor, recomposing herself. *"I have seen the souls of humankind in a way other dragons cannot. And though I faced challenges growing up without a dragon's Illumination, I have also seen dragonkind with fresher eyes than any hatchling. I see the beauties and horrors of both races, and I stand by Alísa-Dragon-Singer in the belief that we are stronger together than alone."*

Hearing the finality in Sesína's tone, Alísa spoke again. *"I do not wish to absorb your clan. I seek allies who will help us defend the innocent of both races."*

Alísa let the silence stretch as she finished. For a few seconds, not even a rumble of thought reached Alísa's ears. Then Crakil growled.

"Of course, Sesína would speak as she has—she knows no better and loves her kidnapper as her mother."

Sesína pulled her head back as though slapped, eyes dimming. Alísa gritted her teeth in anger, again resisting the urge to reach out and comfort her physically.

"We have heard enough," Crakil said, a growl in his throat. *"Leave now. Sesína may stay if she wishes to be free—the rest of you are not welcome here."*

Alísa nodded curtly, her disappointment overwhelmed by her ire. *"Then understand this. Clans may operate as they wish, but if you attack any of my allies— human or dragon—you will face our combined wrath."*

Crakil's wings rose like hackles on a wolf. *"We do not attack villages unless attacked first. It is beneath us."*

"Then we have no quarrel." Alísa turned to Sesína, allowing her eyes to soften. She reached through their private connection. *"You were amazing."*

Sesína rumbled in her chest. *"I felt some of them respond. Not all of them are like him."*

Crakil roared. *"No quarrel? You've taken my daughter, using her as a pack animal and coercing other dragons to act the same. You will stay out of our territory if you know what's good for you!"*

Alísa ignored him, pulling herself into place on Sesína's back. *"I know a bit about stubborn fathers."*

"Somehow, I don't think this situation will turn out the same."

Koriana growled at Crakil. *"You could have Illuminated your daughter upon your mate's death. Instead, you gave her up to a family of dragons you did not particularly like. Do not huff smoke now about your care for her."*

Alísa looked from dragon to dragon in the cave. Many of them displayed hostile postures similar to their alpha, but a few simply watched with light rumblings. They would follow Crakil, but they weren't nearly as upset as he. Perhaps one day she could convince some of them to join her.

But not today.

Catching Alísa's desire, Sesína took off toward the entrance, the others behind her. Koriana was the last to leave. Her tail lashed as she leapt into the air, but Alísa felt satisfaction emanating from her. Catharsis, perhaps. At least someone had gotten something positive from this meeting.

Two of Crakil's scouts followed Alísa out of the cave—escorts to ensure she left the territory. Not wanting to report a complete failure to her father, Alísa made a gamble.

"Sesína, connect me to the scouts, please."

Sesína reached out to them with her telepathy, allowing Alísa to speak.

"I have heard tales of the effectiveness of your clan's scout network," Alísa said, treading carefully. Koriana had been the one to set it up. *"I wonder if you can help me. In our visits to villages, we've recently encountered an an'reik. We are trying to discover his origin or destination. Have you noticed anything?"*

The dragons did not respond immediately. The lead scout and her young wing-dragon rumbled at each other. After a minute of bickering, the older dragoness spoke.

"We do not pay heed to the lives of humans. It is beneath us."

Alísa felt herself slump. *"Of course."*

Koriana growled. *"But…"* When the others remained quiet, she snapped her jaws. *"You did not just argue about nothing. I know Carrási is* radharc. *Did she see something?"*

Alísa struggled to keep up. *Radharc anam* was someone like Rassím, a soul-seer who could see an Eldra's touch on a mortal. Was this Carrási one of Crakil's scouts?

The lead scout kept quiet, but after a moment her wing-dragon spoke. *"Yes. She reported seeing a human an'reik at the southern border of our territory a week ago. Riding west to east."*

Alísa straightened. *"Can you show me where?"*

The lead scout snapped her jaws at the younger dragon. *"Koriana knows our border. Figure it out for yourself, traitors."*

Alísa would, once she got back to the cave and her maps. Direction wouldn't reveal much, but it was better than—

Wait. *"Did you say a week ago? Singular?"*

The lead scout roared. *"Leave!"*

Koriana quickened her pace to come alongside Sesína. *"We mustn't try their patience anymore, else Crakil sends his warriors to fight. They did say a single week. If you encountered Tsorr further east one week ago—"*

"Then there's another an'reik headed in the same direction Tsorr was." Alísa clutched Sesína's spine tighter. *"Koriana, take the rest of the squad home. Sesína and I will go to my father."*

For once, Koriana didn't argue at the mere mention of Karn. She blinked slowly and sped ahead. Sesína veered south. Alísa wasn't sure yet what they could do with this knowledge, but she certainly wouldn't leave her former clan in the dark. Perhaps it was coincidence, but with so many an'reik encounters in such a short time, she wouldn't take any chances.

7

THE RETURN

Kallar's dagger was in his hand before he knew he was awake. Mind flaring with the knowledge of someone else's proximity, he twisted from beneath his deerskin furs and thrust the blade between himself and the intruder. Moonlight poured through the open tent-flap, painting a shadowy silhouette. The shadow raised its hands as the opening closed behind it.

"Peace, Kallar. It's me."

Tern? Kallar relaxed only a fraction. Had Tern changed his mind after deserting? Or was he here to try again to convince Kallar to leave?

Or to end the threat of those allied with the Dragon Singer?

Kallar stood, dagger arm loose to feign lowering his guard. "What are you doing here?"

He could practically hear Tern's eye-roll. "I missed you too."

"I'm not the one who deserted."

He walked past Tern, mind wide open to sense any attack before it happened, and peered outside. The full moon aided him as he scanned camp. No shadows moved amidst the tents. No sounds of slayers turned assassins— nothing but snores from the tent next to his and the crackle of flames from the night watchmen's campfire.

Kallar pulled back inside. "Who else is with you?"

"No one. I had to leave them behind." It sounded like a confession. "I can't stay. I can't trust Karn but—I had to tell you. About L'rang."

Kallar's blood turned to ice. Thoughts of dragons descending from the Fangs and razing everything to the ground rushed through his mind, irrational though they might be. It took everything within him to wait instead of demanding information.

"There are an'reik in L'rang. Both chiefs have welcomed them."

"What?!" Kallar grabbed Tern's shoulders, images of his father and younger brother flashing behind his eyes. "What do you mean, 'welcomed'? They're just wandering the streets, performing their blood magic and dark ceremonies? The chiefs are too smart for that. They have to be. They would never let—could never be…"

He backed off as his stomach roiled, a far less welcome emotion coursing through him. If the chiefs welcomed an'reik, what would it mean for the slayers who would rather fight? Pa wouldn't roll over and allow an'reik to walk the streets, spreading whatever dark magic they pleased and sacrificing to bloodthirsty fallen Eldír.

Tern gripped Kallar's newly healed arm. "I didn't witness any dark ceremonies. The an'reik are just there, appearing ordinary and claiming to want to fight dragons. Nothing seemed wrong until I caught one attempting to murder a family in a back alley. That's when I retreated. Took them to Azron, then came here."

Kallar looked up. "You went to Azron first? How long ago was this?"

"I left L'rang a month ago." Tern jumped back as Kallar advanced toward him. "The family had no one—I needed to make them my priority. Toronn was the only chief I knew wouldn't fall to either an'reik or the Dragon Singer. I swear, I came looking for you as soon as I got them to safety. It isn't exactly easy to find you now that Karn's got the wayfarers off-course."

A month. Kallar ground his teeth. His father wouldn't stand by for an entire month. Had he opposed them? Pushed them back? Or, without the slayer chief's support, would he have fled and gotten his family out of harm's way?

"Karn." Kallar met Tern's concerned gaze. "You need to tell him what you've told me."

Tern's eyes hardened. "Do what you must, but I won't stand before that traitor again."

"Idiot. Karn isn't the traitor here. Think!" Kallar slapped his hands together for emphasis. "The an'reik claim they want to fight dragons—dragons who should be their *allies* if the stories are true that all dragons belong to the Nameless." Bile rose with the admission, but he wouldn't stand by and wait for his family to be slaughtered. "I've seen an'reik oppose Alísa and Karn. One party is lying, and you've already caught the an'reik in their lies. You've deserted the wrong side."

"Or they're *both* the enemy, and we're caught in the middle."

"Wake up! Alísa's clan saved our hides that day, even before Karn agreed to peace."

"You agree with her?" Tern scoffed. "You, who would have happily bathed in dragon blood if it meant their evil was gone? Now you side with the flaming Dragon Singer?!"

Tern's questions echoed Kallar's own. He didn't want to fight this fight, couldn't make himself argue further for the goodness of some dragons. So he switched tactics.

"Look. If they are both the enemy, we are hopelessly outnumbered. Our best bet is to help one take out the other. Now, would you rather fight alongside those who have allied with dark Eldír, or the misguided daughter of the chief?"

"And her dragons, that also follow the Nameless."

Kallar shook his head. "I saw her memories. Much as I hate to admit, Alísa has found some…tolerable dragons. At least, ones that won't raze villages to the ground. They certainly won't eat someone's soul like a Nameless would."

Tern clenched his fists. "What about Trísse? One of those monsters bound her to itself! Morning, she was herself; evening, she was choosing it over me. Over her family! What does that sound like to you?"

Tern's frustration coiled in the astral plane, ready to turn to anger and strike. They had both lost their women to the dragons, but Tern had gotten the worst of it. He and Trísse actually loved each other.

Kallar needed a softer touch. Forget his anger and fear—reach his former sword-partner.

He looked Tern in the eye. "I don't know why Trísse did it, but I can tell you she's okay. She's been around camp, acting like herself, visiting with family. Alísa would never let anyone harm her."

Tern averted his gaze, but the astral plane shifted. Kallar almost had him. He placed a hand on Tern's shoulder.

"I've been able to avoid the dragons for the most part. You can too. We'll go to Karn and make a plan to fight the an'reik. Once the primary threat is gone, we'll figure out the rest."

A moment of hesitation. "Will he even listen? I deserted. What is the punishment for that?"

Kallar didn't know. No one had ever deserted before. Karn wasn't terribly hard, and Tern brought important information. But desertion dishonored both a man and his former chief.

Still, better that Tern stay with us than walk alone.

Kallar squeezed Tern's shoulder. "I've stood beside you against dragons—do you think I would waver before men?"

The astral plane shifted as Tern tested the emotions running through it. He would find no lies. Finally, Tern reached up to grip Kallar's arm and nodded resolutely.

Victory.

"—I took the family to a safe village far away from L'rang. Then I returned to you, great chief."

Tern barely met Karn's eyes throughout the story, often glancing at Kallar for reassurance. The campfire backlit Karn's face, shadowing his expression. Hanah, L'non, and head scout Drennar stood with him, each at varying stages of alertness after the midnight awakening. With anything else, Kallar would have approached them in the morning. With his family possibly at the mercy of an'reik, however, Kallar could not wait.

In Karn's silence, Tern shifted. He appeared genuinely remorseful—no longer combative, as in Kallar's tent. Standing before his former chief, perhaps he had remembered just how great was the man he had betrayed.

Karn looked at Kallar. "You believe his words?"

"We've trained, fought, and bled together for years," Kallar said. "I know when he's bluffing."

Scrutiny filled Karn's eyes, and Kallar braced himself for the question that would come next. Was he certain that fear for his family and home village was not clouding his judgment?

But Karn didn't ask, instead turning to L'non and the others.

"Nomadic an'reik attack camp. Rumors of more turning in the south. Tsorr in Lorin's village. A dragon scout spotting another heading east. Now this? An'reik gathering openly in a major town?"

L'non nodded gravely. "If I had to guess, I'd say Tsorr and this second an'reik Alísa spoke of were heading to L'rang as well."

Karn returned to Tern, tone sharp. "How many were there, boy?"

Tern startled, then recomposed. "I've seen nine or ten—"

Drennar scoffed. "That would hardly overrun a village with a slayer population as large as L'rang's."

"It's not just the an'reik themselves," Tern rushed to finish. "They are winning over slayers. Good men and women are placing themselves under their command. A couple of them even spoke of becoming an'reik themselves. We have to save them from their lies."

A shadow passed over Karn's face, the chief still uncertain in Tern's report. Kallar couldn't let that be—he needed to hear from his family.

"You know what they'll do, Karn," Kallar said. "We've always known they are more dangerous than even the dragons."

Calculations ran through Karn's eyes. Calculations that would certainly include things Kallar didn't care about, such as the Maker and his Eldír. Kallar wanted to eradicate the an'reik in order to physically protect humanity. Blood magic, dark deals, people who cared for nothing but their own goals—all would destroy the lives of many innocent people. This was all Kallar cared about.

But for most of the clan, including Karn, the conflict held spiritual weight. The an'reik advocated turning away from the Maker and his Eldír, something Karn viewed as inherently evil. Kallar did his best not to judge his master for it, but in Kallar's estimation, the Maker cared for humanity just as little as the Nameless did.

The slightest relaxing of Karn's shoulders declared Kallar's victory. "L'non, take Tern to the watchmen to be kept under guard. We will discuss how to handle this news."

Tern stiffened and Kallar shook his head, remembering his promise. "Tern was there. We'll need his insight."

"We're sending our own scouts before we do anything," Karn said. "I will not entrust my men's well-being to a deserter's word."

L'non moved to grab Tern, but Kallar got between them. "I will take responsibility for him. He can help us, Karn, both with his knowledge of the situation and with his sword. He will prove himself again."

Karn's eyes narrowed, shifting between Tern and Kallar. Kallar remained tall at Tern's side, as he did on every battlefield. They were sword-partners. Yes, Tern had abandoned him in a desperate moment, but he returned. That counted for something.

Finally, Karn relented. "Very well. He will stay under your watch. But if his presence harms anyone, understand that is your responsibility as well."

Kallar nodded curtly. "I understand."

The matter settled, Karn turned his attention to Drennar. "We need a team of scouts, fast and stealthy, to assess the state of the village and enemy numbers. Keep the team small enough to avoid the temptation to engage on their own." Karn looked at Kallar. "I know your family is there. Can I trust you to recognize whether it is safe to extract them? Can I entrust my men's safety to your leadership?"

"Yes."

Karn scrutinized him, but he would find no lie in Kallar's promise. He knew the men and their capabilities. If it wasn't safe, Kallar would send the scouts away and stay behind alone to get his family out.

"Good. Drennar, pick the men. Tell them to be ready to leave at sunrise. While they are gone, the clan will also move toward L'rang to be nearby when they return. Alísa will find us easily enough from the sky, and we will request her help clearing the village."

Dragons descending on L'rang. Keeping the village-bound slayers from attacking Alísa's clan would be difficult, at best. L'rang's slayers were more than used to dragon attacks due to the proximity of the Fangs. But they would ford that river when they came to it.

And should a few dragons fall in the chaos—

Kallar shook his head. He couldn't think like that anymore. Besides, that would kill riders too. No, he had a new quarry now.

Karn dismissed the leadership with orders to ensure the clan would be ready to move in the morning. Kallar caught Tern's attention and nodded toward his tent. They started forward together, but Karn clapped a hand on Kallar's shoulder. With the others gone, the chief now displayed both fatigue and concern.

"Are you alright?"

"I will be, when I know my family is safe." He paused a moment before adding. "Thank you for sending me instead of Drennar."

"You have done enough sitting down this last month. You were made to move." Karn squeezed his shoulder. "Do not make me regret this choice."

"I won't. In and out, then the battle."

"Good man." Karn released him. "Get some sleep, if you can. You'll be no help to your family without it."

Kallar pulled his fist to his heart, affirming the order, then returned to the darkness of his tent. He wasn't sure he could rest with his fear for his family and eagerness for the task ahead, but he provided Tern with extra furs and laid down.

Tomorrow, it was time—finally time—to move.

8

TRUST

For the tenth time since waking up, Falier checked his pocket.

Still there.

"And it will continue to be there." Graydonn poked Falier in the shoulder with his muzzle. *"You're quite nervous for a man who is sure she'll accept."*

Falier rubbed the back of his neck, surveying the main cave as it slowly woke. *"Any chance you could just"* —he sucked in a sharp breath to illustrate— *"the anxiety out of me?"*

Graydonn wove around a tent. *"No. I could push calm to you, but where's the fun in that? I prefer to tease."*

"Thanks. Really feeling your support here."

Falier shoved Graydonn's shoulder, glad for someone to joke with amid his nerves. The action, though, made his muscles remind him just how hard he had been working them. He stretched his arm across his chest as Graydonn thrummed his good mood. No arguments today. No *training* today. Today had a different goal entirely.

They stopped at the kitchen area, where crates of food were stacked high, cauldrons hung over fire-pits, and a dreki-carved hole in the wall became a makeshift oven. Selene and another woman already stood behind a flat stone surface, prepping the day's breakfast.

A bit of envy ran through Falier. He missed working the kitchens and serving the clan. But no. He shook the thoughts away. As tiern, he would still serve them, just differently.

Selene pulled out a loaf of sweetbread wrapped in a cloth. "As requested."

Falier took the proffered food. "Thank you. It's her favorite."

"I know. You told me three times already." Selene chuckled as she came around the platform and hugged him. "Have fun. I'd say good luck, but you don't need it."

Falier forced himself to slump into the hug and release the tension in his body. "I just want it to go perfectly."

"Hey, if it doesn't, you'll have something to laugh about later." Selene stepped back with a wink. "Now go, wake the poor girl from her slumber."

Falier shook his head. "Thanks for the food."

Alísa's tent was only a hundred paces away, backed up against a wall with ropes tied to stalagmites and a nail pounded into the stone. Smaller than most tents, it had only one chamber, like his own. Sesína lay just outside the entrance, her tail and neck curled up under a wing. The dragoness' snout peeked out, revealing sharp teeth as she snored faintly.

Graydonn reached out to Sesína. *"It's time. Are you awake?"*

Falier could have sworn he heard a mental yawn. *"'er-mean. Fi-mor-minutes."*

Falier looked at Graydonn. *"I didn't know telepathic speech could slur."*

"Only when we want it to." Graydonn thrummed. *"Wake her, Sesína, or Falier will die of nerves."*

Falier glared at him. *"I'm not that bad."*

Sesína grumbled, shifting to reveal a glowing emerald eye. *"You got the things?"*

"Yes." Falier resisted the urge to check again. He had wrapped the pieces in a silk cloth and placed them in a buttoned pocket. Even with all the flying they planned to do, it couldn't fall out.

The dragoness uncurled and stretched her long neck, her spine popping several times. Then she stuck her head through the tent opening and, guessing by her motions, began prodding Alísa with her snout. Alísa moaned within, followed by an "oof!" as Sesína jabbed her harder.

"Wake up, birthday girl," Sesína said. *"One should always pay attention when being kidnapped."*

Alísa's part of the telepathic link buzzed to alertness. *"Kidnapped? What are you—"*

"I'm under duress." Sesína's voice dripped with sarcasm. *"There's a slayer out here, and a dragon, both with cruel timing. They've threatened to keep waking me up at this horrible hour for the rest of my life if I don't get you up."*

Rustling came from inside the tent and Alísa emerged, her bed-clothes covered by her cloak. She looked between Falier and Graydonn, curiosity sparking.

"What is she talking about?"

Falier winked at Alísa. *"You're coming with us. No arguments, no complaints."*

"And no responsibilities," Graydonn added.

Falier grinned. *"Happy birthday!"*

Alísa's smile formed, then dropped. *"I have duties today. Briek, Koriana, and I were——"*

"Moved to tomorrow," Sesína said, pulling from the tent. *"What did he say about arguing?"*

"But Laen and the dreki need——"

"Taken care of."

"But——"

Sesína snorted steam in Alísa's face. *"Do you know how difficult it is to clear your schedule without you noticing? Don't undo all my sneakiness!"*

Alísa glanced at Falier and Graydonn, her eyes silently begging for confirmation.

Falier held up his pack. *"You aren't going to let Selene's blackberry sweetbread go to waste, are you?"*

Alísa shrugged. *"I'm sure you'd find someone to take it off your hands."*

Falier glanced behind him. *"Should I start looking?"*

"No!" Alísa hurried forward, a playful smile on her face as she grabbed for the bag. Falier twisted and pinned her to his side with his free arm.

"Caught you."

He pressed a kiss to her lips, which she returned eagerly, wrapping her arms around him.

Or, rather, *reaching* around him, to grab for the pack.

"Hey!" He pulled back, grinning. *"No food till the kidnapping is complete. Sesína, get her dressed more warmly. Graydonn and I will be waiting at the landing platform. With the bread, in case she gets any more ideas."*

Alísa giggled. *"No please, I'll do whatever you say—just don't take the sweetbread!"*

Sesína rolled her eyes and draped a wing over Alísa's shoulder to pull her away. *"So dramatic."*

Falier chuckled and climbed onto Graydonn, trying not to wince at the soreness in his legs. Phase one complete. On to phase two!

Chilly morning air whisked Falier's breath away as Graydonn and Sesína raced down the mountainside. Each twist and turn made his stomach flip with exhilaration. How Graydonn and Sesína could keep this up for over an hour astounded him. Alísa's songs helped, but she only sang a few times. The rest was pure draconic energy and muscle.

Black scales darted past them. The sound of Alísa's song was barely audible over the wind, and nothing poured into Graydonn's mind.

Graydonn trumpeted a playful note. *"No fair, only giving Sesína the strength song!"*

Sesína called back to him with a wolf-like bay, her tone high with elation.

Graydonn flapped his wings with increasing intensity as he chased her, the two dragons soaring higher into the sky. Just as fatigue began edging Graydonn's mind, Alísa's power filtered into him as well. Her strength coursed through the mind-kin bond and filled Falier with its echoes. It didn't make him physically stronger as it did for Graydonn, but it bolstered him with something akin to hope or confidence.

Of course, he might feel that simply because Alísa, his beloved, was exuding such joy. When she sang it felt like his insides both melted and became stronger. How the two feelings mingled together he could not explain. It was just—love.

Graydonn thrummed. *"Careful. If Sesína catches that thought, she'll gag."*

"Don't worry, I'll save the rest for when both of you are elsewhere."

The mind-link widened as Graydonn caught up to Sesína, allowing the dragons to dance in swirling patterns. They weren't as graceful as the dreki, but the communication link helped them anticipate each other's movements and avoid collisions. Sometimes the whole clan danced like this in a show of camaraderie, their massive bodies becoming light as the air itself.

Falier leaned into Graydonn's movements as wind, gravity, and momentum all pulled him in different directions. His eyes met Alísa's as Sesína flipped upside-down over Graydonn. An inkling ran through the shared mind-link, calling Sesína to flip over them again. When Sesína passed over, Falier and Alísa reached toward each other for a mid-air high-five. His palm stung from the force of it, but he joined the others in their exclamations of delight.

With the group's spirits soaring, Falier decided it was time for phase three. He directed the dragons up the mountain they currently flew around. It wasn't their home peak, just another within their territory, and it had a small flat section near the top.

Talons scraped against stone as the dragons landed. The section was too cramped with everyone, but became the perfect size after Graydonn and Sesína departed.

Falier took the bag off his shoulder and touched his pocket. Still there. Alísa, meanwhile, swept her gaze over the land below, with its green hills, winding rivers, and jagged mountains in the distance. The wind blew through her hair, cloak, and skirt, adding an ethereal tone to her beauty.

Falier stepped up beside her and tried to see what she did. Their mountain range stretched to the south and northwest, most peaks taller and therefore colder and harsher than this one. To the east of the range was Tella's portion of the hill country, and beyond it the forests where Falier had grown up. To the west lay Karn's land, less lush than Tella's, but more vast. Alísa's eyes fixed there. She loved this land—had walked every hill, splashed in every river, visited every village. It was as much a part of her as her songs were.

Falier wrapped an arm around her shoulders. She swiped at her cheek before leaning into him.

"Thank you," she said. "First the flying, now the q—quiet. And the view. I haven't taken the t-time to just look recently. It's—"

A whistling wind yanked her words away. Chuckling, Falier connected them telepathically.

"Say again?"

"It's different on dragon-back, when everything is rushing by"—Alísa grinned—*"like that wind."*

"True." It was probably better they were speaking telepathically, anyway. She would feel more comfortable answering his question. He motioned out at Karn's land. *"Tell me about this hill country. Why do you love it?"*

Alísa snuggled closer as a sharper breeze cut across the mountaintop, wrapping both arms around his ribs and setting her head on his shoulder. *"How could anyone not?"*

"I've seen so little, most while flying."

Alísa pondered a moment. *"I love the wind. Especially when it gives you an* excuse to hold me."

Falier laughed. *"I like that too. But seriously——tell me about your homeland."*

She gave him a curious look, then motioned at the hills. *"It's freedom. Everything is so vast and open. I love the way the land dips and curves, giving each piece its own personality, and how the winds flow through them as though calling me to dance. I love how green prevails——even when summer washes it out to yellows and browns, green still thrives in the valleys. And in the springtime, the wildflowers grace the hills with their joy and vitality."*

She turned her smile to him, full of happiness that overwhelmed their connection. *"And the sky, so unimpeded——at least until it reaches the mountains. But even the mountains, once considered omens of death, are now full of beauty. Then there's the stars, close enough to touch. The small patches of trees that provide shelter. Don't ask me to pick a favorite——I could go on forever."*

Falier smiled back. *"I know. The way your face lights up, I couldn't miss it if I tried."* He fiddled with his pocket. Here went nothing. *"I hope everyone sees that on me when I look at you."*

She looked down, bashful, though her emotions said she was pleased. He continued, pairing bits and pieces of her speech to the words he had planned.

"I love how kind and open you are, how you give others freedom to be themselves and to grow around you. I love your musicianship and that one of my first memories with you is of dancing. In wind or rain, you're my favorite person to dance with."

Alísa looked at him again, her self-consciousness growing. *"You too. I——"*

Falier placed a gentle finger on her lips, which stopped her despite their using mind-speech. *"Let me finish?"*

Alísa pressed her lips together and nodded.

"I love your strength in the face of adversity, like the greens that refuse to die in summer's heat. Seeing you grow in that has been an encouragement and a joy. Your smiles are as precious as the wildflowers, your laughter as the stars. The way you found beauty in the mountains astounds me. Your eyes, blue like a storm, fill me with hope and music. Don't ask me to pick a favorite attribute——I could go on forever."

Her eyes lowered, then returned to his. Her emotions wavered between pleasure, embarrassment, and happiness. *"I don't think I can handle much more."*

"Only two more words, then." Falier pulled from her embrace, the mountain's chill filling the space between them. Taking her hands in his, he fell to one knee. *"Marry me, Líse?"*

A wide grin. *"That's three."*

Falier chuckled. *"I hope you don't love me for my brains, then."*

Alísa lowered to her knees in front of him, eyes soft. *"Brains, heart—all."*

She kissed him—*really* kissed him. Fingers in his hair, body pressed to his, lips longing. He wrapped his arms around her and twisted like a dip at the end of a dance. Falier's heart sang and ached, rejoicing in her obvious answer and longing for more. More would come, but later. He pulled back.

"Does that mean yes?"

Alísa giggled. *"Yes! I will marry you."*

Falier grinned and straightened them both upright. Pressing his forehead to hers, he whispered aloud. "I got something for you."

He unbuttoned his pocket and pulled out the silk cloth, lumpy with its contents. Unfolding it, he drew out a necklace. A silversmith at one of their allied villages had jewelry of many kinds, each exquisite piece crafted into shapes of nature and knotted symbols. He had exchanged five days of work at the village Hold for the money, each day disguised as a scouting venture or training flight with Graydonn.

Alísa gasped when he held it up—a delicate tree with roots that twisted together into the knot that symbolized trust.

"I thought of you the moment I saw this," he said. "Of days we spent walking and training in the forest after you entrusted me with your story. Of dancing in the storm with the rain making music in the leaves. There's no better foundation than trust, and I trust you completely."

"And I you," she said, reaching up to loosen her blue dragon scale necklace. She went to place it in her skirt pocket, but Falier held out his hand for it. Alísa hesitated.

Falier winked. "Trust me."

Chuckling, Alísa placed her beloved necklace in his palm. Then she took up Falier's gift and put it on. She fingered it, then looked up at him.

"I love it."

"I'm glad." He pulled the second part of his gift out of the silk cloth—a thick leather bracelet with knotted etchings for family, chiefdom, and protection. "And since I know you'd be lost without your pa's scale…"

He showed Alísa a dug out portion in the leather, shaped like Karn's dragon scale with two small holes on one side. Her head tilted in curiosity, making his smile widen. Pulling the sapphire pendant free of its chain, he bent the leather bracelet just enough to reveal the lip at the edges of the dug out portion. The scale's edges slid beneath the lip until the top where the hole for the chain remained. Recalling the leatherworker's instructions, Falier threaded a thin strap through the holes in both the bracelet and scale, tying it off with a neat knot to hold everything together.

He offered the piece to Alísa, who just stared at it.

"That fits p—perfectly. How—?"

"Sesína is sneakier than anyone gives her credit for." He fastened the bracelet around Alísa's wrist. "She stole the necklace while you were sleeping so I could take measurements."

Alísa's laugh was musical. "I'll have t-t-to be more c-careful with my jewelry."

"Please do," he said, releasing her newly clad wrist. "Silver isn't as hardy as a dragon's scale."

She hummed, looking at the bracelet while fingering her betrothal necklace. "It's perfect. Everything's perfect." She hugged him again, shivering as a blast of wind hit them. "The only way to make it more p-p-perfect is a thicker cloak."

Falier reached into his bag. "Got you covered."

He pulled out a wool blanket to wrap over their shoulders, but jumped as a drek tumbled out too. Rís gave a high-pitch squeal as he thumped to the ground. His ruby mane rippled down his neck and back as he shook himself and barked at Falier.

What had Selene said about something to laugh at?

"Rís!" Alísa leaned down to scoop up the drek. "What are you doing here?"

Rís let out a pitiful whimper. *"Warm."*

Alísa stroked Rís' mane with two fingers. "Does your papá know you're here?"

The little drek's ruby eyes and wing-baubles glowed for a second, like they always did when joining minds. Then he dimmed and gave a satisfied trill. *"Now."*

Leaping into the air, Rís swirled and chirped gleefully, as if the last few seconds hadn't happened.

"D—don't get too far," Alísa said. "It's a long flight home on wings small as yours."

Rís growled—more cute than menacing—and twisted away, content to play now that his nap was through.

Shaking his head, Falier returned to the bag. "I hope he didn't—aha! Nope." He pulled out the cloth-wrapped sweetbread. "Looks intact. Want some?"

Alísa drew the blanket around herself and nodded eagerly. He broke the small loaf and handed her half, then settled next to her as she draped one end of the blanket over his shoulders.

They ate in silence, gazing over the land. Falier tried to focus there, but his mind raced with joy. She said yes! This beautiful, musical, heart-filled woman he loved so much would soon be his wife!

He needed to send a message to Ma and Pa. Could they assign a dragon-rider pair as messengers, to make delivery faster? Or perhaps he and Alísa could take two days and tell them in-person. Briek and Koriana could manage the clan for a bit. Or were thoughts of leaving irresponsible? Especially given all the talk of an'reik activity.

Why was his mind racing so—

A trumpet of alarm rang out and shuddered through the mind-kin bond. Falier shot up with Alísa.

"Graydonn! What—"

"It's an attack!" Graydonn said. "Dragons are attacking a village!"

A second later, Sesína flew into view, veering toward their mountaintop. She provided a village name Falier didn't know but Alísa did. Falier caught sight of smoke to the southwest. Dropping the remnants of her food, Alísa ran to the edge of the mountain to meet Sesína. The dragoness' talons scraped against rock, her wings wide in alarm.

"We're closer than the rest of the clan," she said. "If you sing for us, I'm sure we can fend them off!"

Skepticism passed through Graydonn's mind. "First sing for the clan. Call them to our aid. We don't know the number of attackers."

Barks rang out over the wind as Rís returned and dove for Alísa's belt-pouch. He slipped inside as Alísa jumped onto Sesína's back. They took off, allowing Graydonn room to land and collect Falier. Leaving his blanket and bag, Falier climbed on and they launched after Sesína.

9

LYING LOGIC

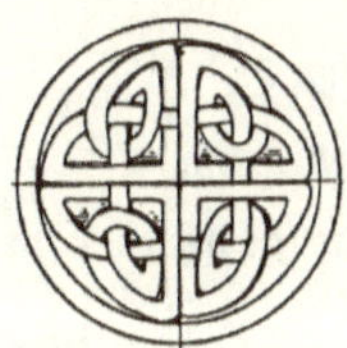

Alísa cursed her terrible luck. Of course, dragons would attack during her one chance to be alone with Falier in weeks. Of course, she would only get half an hour to enjoy being betrothed before disaster yanked her away.

She shoved the thoughts aside and fixed her eyes on the rising smoke. She couldn't afford self-pity now. It was ten minutes to the village at the rate Sesína flew, the dragoness' limbs already tired from all the exercise of the morning. She and Graydonn would both require strength.

But first, Alísa needed to summon the clan. Focusing on their urgent need, she filled her lungs and sang.

> Dragons, dreki, hear my call
> Come quickly now to aid my fight
> Alert the riders, one and all
> Your chief faces a deadly plight
>
> For everywhere the war burns on
> And innocents cry for release
> Come stand with me, fight for the dawn
> To show them all the way to peace

Power poured from her, stretching for the cave. In her bag, Rís chirped, harmonizing with certain notes. His head poked out to reveal glowing eyes. He, too, reached out to the cave. Could the dreki connect from this distance?

"Alísa, the smoke is getting worse!" Sesína growled beneath her. *"We need your help, now!"*

Alísa shifted her melody into her most familiar strength song—one she could sing without thinking. *"How many attackers?"*

"Eight." She said it matter-of-factly, like counting the shiny stones of her collection. *"We can take them!"*

"I would suggest a more careful approach," Graydonn said. *"We might do better if we wait for reinforcements."*

Sesína snarled. *"People are dying!"*

"And how will our own deaths help them?"

"We won't need to consider that if I get them to stop," Alísa said. Battle was now only two minutes away. Time to sway the dragons. She reached out to them in song.

On and on
Must this bloodshed rage upon
Our land and leave us cold and wan?
Or can we change?

On and on
May my——

Alísa gasped and cried out as sharp pain ripped through her mind, accompanied by an unholy screech like talons against a metal shield. Sesína faltered, dipping to one side as the stabs infected her as well.

"Líse!"

Falier locked a shield around her and Sesína's minds, shutting out the barrage. Alísa breathed hard, hand to her head as the remnants of the attack throbbed in her skull.

Sesína hissed as she righted herself. *"What was that?"*

"I don't know. Something——isn't right. The dragons attacked me, but with a power I've never felt before."

"Um, Líse. I think you got their attention."

Alísa looked up to see three giant dragons bearing down on them. She gritted her teeth.

"We're faster than them. Bank around the village and ascend to where their slayers can't reach you. Evade while Falier and I fight psychically. Stay together. Go!"

Sesína banked and Graydonn took wing-position. Pain still shuddered through Alísa's mind, like prickling drek claws skittering over it. She forced herself to sing again and push out strength to Sesína and Graydonn as the three enemy dragons gave chase.

Flames and smoke shot up from multiple buildings as Sesína circled the village. People ran for the underground dragon shelters while slayers stood along their path to protect them. Two dragons stood in the square, a black one fighting slayers on the ground while a blue breathed fire into homes and——

Alísa's stomach churned as the dragon pounced on someone emerging from the house. Its snout glistened red with blood. Her veins chilled, then ran hot with fury.

Man-eater. Only an'reik dragons ate *iompróir anam*.

Sesína swerved and ascended, calling Alísa's attention away. A quick plan crossed between Sesína and Graydonn and they aimed for a copper dragon. Sesína banked hard for its underbelly. Alísa gripped the spine in front of her, bracing herself. Power shot through the astral plane as Falier mind-speared the copper just as Sesína slammed into its stomach.

The copper roared in outrage, sparks dripping from its mouth. Alísa clung to a spine as Sesína ripped at the tough but scaleless skin with her talons, then pushed off it. Meanwhile, Graydonn attacked its wings, tearing them with a ferocity that belied the dragon's typical demeanor. With surprise on their side, the enemy dragon fell quickly.

A roar shook the air, terrible and mighty. Alísa looked down, catching sight of the massive sapphire man-eater on the ground. Its snout pointed at Graydonn.

"Falier, shield!"

The psychic attack hit just as Falier complied. He cried out as his shield shattered on impact, but Graydonn was unimpeded. Fire gushed from another dragon and Graydonn dove under the blaze.

The blue dragon stared at Graydonn and Falier, power gathering for a second mind-spear. Falier's portion of the link fuzzed with pain. He wouldn't be ready.

Alísa released her strength song and shout-sang at the enemy dragon. "Bind!"

Her power slammed into the dragon's mind and spread. Lightning crackled in Alísa's heart at the contact——burning, biting, and cold. She gasped and silenced her song, yanking her mind back.

"Duck!"

Alísa followed Sesína's command without thought, cringing as blazing heat rushed through the air above her. Sesína banked hard, away from the fire and toward Graydonn to regroup. Two dragons speared for them, eyes blazing with hate. Then, from nowhere, a pulse rocked the astral plane. Nausea rippled through Sesína's mind and body and filtered into Alísa.

Another pulse.

The dragon chasing Graydonn veered away.

Another.

Rís growled from within Alísa's belt pouch.

Another.

Sesína groaned, listing to one side. *"Graydonn, do you feel that?"*

Graydonn tossed his head like an aggravated horse. *"It's so...dark."*

Falier stretched his power over Graydonn while Alísa whispered a shielding song over Sesína and Rís. The psychic ripples continued, chasing the enemy dragons toward the mountains. Over and over, the feelings washed against Alísa's shield until, suddenly, they stopped.

Sesína banked in a wide arc over a field south of the village. *"What was that?"*

Alísa pressed a hand to her head. *"I don't know, but whatever it was saved us."*

Falier motioned to the burning buildings. *"Should we check on them? Find out if we can help?"*

Graydonn hummed a warning. *"They don't know us yet."*

Alísa blew out a breath. *"But they know me as Karns-daughter. And the slayers would have seen us fighting their attackers. We'll go carefully."*

Sesína and Graydonn landed at the top of a hill outside the village. The dragons hid behind the hill as Alísa and Falier descended into the chaos of villagers beating down flames with blankets. A crowd gathered at the well, carrying buckets and large pots to be filled with water and tossed on fires. Like most western villages, the buildings were primarily stone and brick, but many had smoke pouring out through windows as curtains and furniture inside burned. Multiple dragons must have landed and shot fire through the small openings.

A slayer with a drawn sword stepped into Alísa's path. "Who are you?"

Alísa swallowed back her anxieties. "Alísa, d—daughter of K-K-Karn. I'm here t-t-to help."

"The Dragon Singer?" He tightened the grip on his weapon. "You did this?!"

Alísa held up peaceful hands as more slayers turned their attention to her. "N—no. You saw the t-t-t-two smaller dragons f—fighting the attackers? That was us."

"There's a dead copper dragon on the eastern side of the village." Falier stepped up. "You'll see talon marks on the stomach and ripped wings that made it fall to its death. We're on your side, and we're here to help."

"Help?" A tall man with dark skin and a shaved head approached, the red sash of a slayer chief draped across his chest. Chief R'gan. Another man, this one pale and freckled, walked close behind him. The slayers parted for them, now ignoring the villagers' commotion as they worked to extinguish the flames. "And yet the famous Dragon Singer, who supposedly commands the beasts, was not who rescued us today."

R'gan indicated the man behind him and spoke more to his people than Alísa. "It was Moraggan, not Karns-daughter, who sent the monsters away. We had imprisoned him for his heresy, but as the dragons descended, he claimed to be able to stop them. In our dire situation, I knew we had nothing to lose."

Alísa's stomach clenched. 'Heresy.' Claiming power to stop dragons. The strange pulses Graydonn called dark. All painted a picture Alísa prayed she saw incorrectly.

"I set Moraggan free," the chief continued, "and he fulfilled his word. I now declare him a friend to our village. He may walk freely and speak his message when the disaster has ended and we have mourned the lost."

Moraggan bowed his head. "Thank you, my friend. I only wish I could have helped sooner, but the power given me requires line-of-sight." He looked at Alísa. "You are right when you say the Dragon Singer commands the creatures. One can only wonder why she, who was present before my release, did not send them away herself."

Alísa clenched her fists. His words, 'the power given me', all but confirmed he was an'reik too. Perhaps the one Carrási had seen. Another messenger sent to deceive the villages and turn them from the peace she offered.

"I d—do command dragons, b—but I do not control them. Each is *iompróir anam*, free to choose j—j—just—"

"*Iompróir anam!*" Moraggan scoffed. "Did you hear that? She equates the monsters with us!"

"Speak for yourself, sold-soul," a slayer growled, earning a glare from his chief.

Moraggan ignored the man. "Daughter of slayers and blessed with a powerful gift, she should have been the one to send the monsters retreating. Instead, she is too blinded by love for the beasts to do her job. Look at her, bringing more dragons to your village now!"

Alísa followed his pointed finger to see growing dots in the sky. Her clan. *"Sesína—"*

"I'll get them to back off. Tell me when you're ready for me to come bite off his head!"

"That's our clan," Falier said in Alísa's silence. "Coming to fight for you. They were further away than we were, but we came despite being outnumbered. We are on your side."

"And yet you did not deliver us from the attackers," R'gan said.

"She already told you!" Falier said, exasperated. "Her powers can't force dragons to obey. They call to a dragon's heart. If they don't align, the dragons will continue in their own way."

"Did she even have time to call?" The slayer who had spoken against Moraggan spoke again. "It looked to me like she jumped in as quickly as she could to help us, rather than bandy words with our attackers."

Slayers near him grumbled, and the chief sent him another silencing glare.

"At least some of those d—d—dragons were an'reik." Alísa forced herself to meet Moraggan's eyes. "Why do you fight your own kind?"

Moraggan smirked. "And how do you know this? Did you take the time to talk to your precious dragons as they attacked? Hear their life-stories when you could have aided these people sooner?"

"Only an'reik dragons would d—dare anger the Maker by eating *iompróir anam.*"

Moraggan's eyes narrowed. "And I suppose one of your dragons told you this? Another lie to make you believe they themselves have souls?"

"If you are on our side," R'gan stepped in, "why do you care who saved us? Why not celebrate the victory and help the wounded?"

Falier stiffened beside her. "That's what we—"

"It seems she opposes anyone with the strength to match her." Moraggan tsked. "Now, why might that be?"

Slayers pressed in around Alísa and Falier, crowding the astral plane with their anger. Alísa pulled her empathy close to avoid being overwhelmed, though ire sparked in her own soul. Moraggan twisted everything she said, as Yarlan once had. His shackles of shame no longer held her captive, but she still possessed no skill in untwisting hateful lies.

"I'll tell you why," Moraggan continued. "This Singer's sole aim is the well-being of dragons. She wants you on her side, speaking words of peace that will turn into dragons ruling over us! Well, the an'reik see through her." A pulse like the ones earlier rocked the astral plane. "And we're here to stop her."

Alarm rushed through the Illumination bond, followed by Sesína's nausea and vertigo. Whatever Moraggan's power was, it affected dragons far more than it did humans.

Falier grabbed Alísa's hand, his fear shuddering through their skin contact. Slayers pressed in, their anger boring into Alísa. She stepped back, but Falier stopped her. There were slayers behind them now, too.

R'gan went for his sword. "Then it ends here."

Barking furiously, Rís leapt from Alísa's pack. He flew at the chief, eyes and wings aglow. Wide-eyed, R'gan pulled his sword, swinging at the drek. Rís phased through the metal and dove straight through the slayer's chest. R'gan stiffened, mouth open as though to cry out, but no sound came.

Heart in her throat, Alísa gripped Falier's hand. "Shield yourself."

She reached out to Sesína, latching onto the vertigo coursing through her and shoving it out into the crowd. Slayers put hands to heads and stomachs as her empathy rushed through them. Two men tried to reach her, but collided due to dizziness.

One slayer looked Alísa in the eye as he bent with nausea. The one who had spoken against Moraggan. He stepped aside, leaving a gap. "Go."

Falier pulled Alísa into a run, Rís coming alongside to dive through another man's chest. Sesína and Graydonn rushed to aid them, flying low over the village and garnering shouts from frightened normals. A mass of dreki flew alongside them, glowing and raging.

Graydonn and Sesína skidded into a landing as another pulse hit. Sesína wobbled as she set down, the misstep sending pain through one of her paws and into Alísa. Sesína growled, shaking her head.

"Get on!"

Dreki shot past Alísa and Falier, Rís joining them as they speared toward Moraggan. Another pulse rocked the astral plane, but it was different this time. Nausea didn't hit Sesína—instead, the dreki chittered and moaned. The group scattered as another pulse surged, lights blinking in and out as though they could no longer join minds. With Sesína's help, Alísa reached out to them.

"Fall back! Get out of here!"

Rann—Rís and baby Chrí's father—sent an image of Sesína and Graydonn flying away with Alísa and Falier on their backs. *"Distract!"*

"He is right," Graydonn said, lifting his wings. *"Moraggan's power only affects one species at a time—we need to leave while he's focused on the dreki."*

Alísa fought back her instincts to protect her clanmates and pulled herself onto Sesína. *"Go!"*

Without a word, Sesína launched into the sky—pain shooting through her sprained paw as she took off. Graydonn and Falier followed behind, the dragons spearing for where the rest of the clan circled. For a fleeting moment, Alísa considered sending them all to the village to destroy Moraggan. But how many slayers would fall as they fought to defend their new ally? How would such a fight further harm the normals?

No, she couldn't order an attack.

Alísa looked back, seeing the dreki following behind. She caught a last glimpse of Moraggan and shivered. Despite the distance, she felt his cold gaze. He had won. By pretty words and lying logic, R'gan's village was his.

10

BROTHERS

The shadow of the Serpent's Fangs loomed over Kallar and his band of five scouts. So near the group of mountains, he could easily spot which of his men believed Alísa. They all heard that the dragons in the Fangs were Alísa's allies and had sworn to cease attacking villages. Those who believed might look warily at the mountains, but they left their swords strapped to their saddles and wore comfortable clothing.

Kallar wore his armor.

The scouts halted at the last hill before L'rang—a spot Kallar knew intimately from many childhood excursions. He and his friends came here with their wasters, taken out from under the nose of their trainer, and imagined themselves hardened wayfarers. Together they faced not only dragons, but highwaymen and an'reik as they sparred. Few of them had actually entered that life, and of them, only Kallar remained.

Kallar and his men stripped themselves of anything that would mark them as slayers. Armor went into packs, shields were piled, and braids were undone. The swords stayed, but became less obvious underneath dusty cloaks.

"Remember," Kallar said, checking his sword belt, "some deserters might still be within the village. Tread carefully and make sure you aren't recognized. We'll meet at the Hold at suppertime and determine our course of action."

Three scouts mounted their horses with Kallar, posing as nomads with a large pack on an extra horse. Tern and one other remained, instructed to go back to Karn should Kallar's team fail to return by noon the following day. A contingency Kallar did not expect to need, but important nonetheless.

From the top of the hill, L'rang appeared unchanged. People moved through the streets, shopping and selling wares. West of the village, warriors sparred with sword and mind in the arena. To the north, mules pulled carts of mining equipment toward the Fangs, miners alongside and slayers at the front and rear to watch for dragon attacks. Pulling stone and precious metals from the mountains was perilous work. To L'rang, however, it was just life.

Perhaps he should ask whether there had been any attacks recently—see if Alísa's friends held to their word.

Kallar pulled his hood up as he neared the village, being sure it shadowed his eyes. Karn might have told him to stay behind to avoid being recognized by his former neighbors, but Kallar couldn't leave anything to chance. He slouched in the saddle, weary and lowly, and pushed into the street. He needed to see for himself that R'lann was safe.

His men broke off, two entering the market and one heading for the Hold. As Kallar's horse clopped over the cobblestone streets, he noted many unfamiliar faces. Some were shopkeepers, obviously living in L'rang and just new to him.

Other strangers, though... Some walked with a slayer's confident swagger, yet carried no weapons. Others skulked about, hoping to avoid detection, though Kallar couldn't discern their motives—whether it was for safety or mischief. Empathy might reveal their intent, but other slayers might notice such use of it. Knowing deserters could lurk nearby, Kallar kept his shield tight.

Finally, he reached his father's house. It was built with large stones crafted to fit together just right. Small openings, less than a foot square, acted as windows, providing natural light while staying small enough to avoid most dragon-fire. Twisted knots symbolizing strength and other virtues were chiseled in various places in the walls. At one dark time in Kallar's life, dirt and lichen gathered in those knots. Then Gia had swooped in. Everything had to be neat, clean, and orderly with her. Even the flat rock covering the entrance to their underground dragon shelter had barely any road dust on it. Kallar only allowed his eyes to skim the shelter, not daring to dwell on the memories.

Kallar tied his horse to the post outside the house and approached the door. He steeled himself, pulling the low breaths he took before battle, and knocked.

After a moment, the door cracked, revealing a man Kallar's age with sandy blond hair in warrior's braids. Kallar could vaguely recall a happier time when they were friends, before Pa betrayed Mamá's memory.

Kallar lifted his head so the shadows of his hood no longer covered his face. "Tobin."

"Kallar?" His stepbrother's eyes widened, then narrowed again in annoyance. "What are you doing here?"

"Kal?" A hand grasped the edge of the door and drew it open, revealing Gia. Her hair was a shade lighter than her son's, pulled back in a low bun with wisps hanging around her face. Her creased brow and the dark circles under her eyes made her look older than her forty years. She beckoned. "Quickly."

The open door revealed Tobin's drawn sword, which he shoved into its sheath before backing up to let Kallar enter. A single candle lit the main room, but Kallar remembered the space well. Furs, dragon skins, and crocheted decor hung on every wall to soften the cold stone. The scent of cinnamon rose from a dried bundle tied with a decorative bow on the mantle. A wood carving of a mountain bear rested beside it—likely Tobin's latest piece. Five chairs crafted of eastern pine surrounded a bear-skin rug. A wall obscured the kitchen, but the dining table was just visible. A vase sat on the table, its floral arrangement drooping with age.

The sight made Kallar stop. Gia didn't allow things like that. Something wasn't right.

"You're here," Gia said, voice low. "Praise the Maker. Is Karn here too? To set us free from these blackguards?"

Disdain rolled through Kallar. The Maker had nothing to do with his arrival.

"Where are Pa and R'lann?"

Gia and Tobin looked at each other. When Gia's eyes returned to Kallar, they were misty.

"They took R'lann."

Fire ran through Kallar, clashing with the ache in his stomach. He fought to keep from lashing out at the obviously distressed woman. Save it for the thrice-damned an'reik who stole his little brother.

"What happened?" he bit out.

Gia gripped the back of Pa's chair. "They came for him three weeks ago. Your father gathered a band of slayers willing to defy the chiefs' orders and go after him, but we haven't heard from them since."

It took Kallar a moment to realize he wasn't breathing. Not just R'lann, but Pa too. *Damn Tern for taking so long to bring the news. Damn Alísa for making Tern too scared to come sooner. Damn it all!*

But that did no good. He needed a plan. Information.

"Why?" he demanded, looking between Gia and Tobin. "Why did they take R'lann? Have they taken others?"

Gia shook her head. "They wanted a child of Allara, to call to their dragon allies."

What? Kallar grasped the edge of a chair to keep from shaking. Allara's children. No one had ever searched for them. None had known to—no one knew Allara's story.

Not until Kallar had given it to Farren for the song to bring Alísa home. He had expected consequences, but not—

The memory of a blood-red dragon bearing down on his mother flashed through his mind. Kallar closed his eyes.

Hellflames. I put R'lann in danger, again.

"We told them it's not genetic," Gia continued, "that R'lann has shown no signs of the Singer's power, but they wouldn't listen and took him anyway."

'Not genetic.' That was only partly true. Which would be worse—if R'lann knew dragons were *iompróir anam* and held the Singer's power, or if he didn't?

"Now that you're here, they might return." Tobin grabbed Kallar's arm, calling him from his reverie. "You need to leave, now."

Kallar wrenched his arm from Tobin's grasp. "And why are you still here? Why didn't you go to rescue R'lann? All that talk about brotherhood not being blood, yet you abandon him?!"

"Kallar!"

Gia's sharp tone made Kallar wince. She strode to him, fire in her eyes.

"Shame on you. It took everything your father had to hold Tobin back and ensure I would have a protector." Her eyes clouded again. "Even when I told Paern I didn't need it, he wouldn't let Tobin go with him. You know how stubborn he is."

She stepped away, no longer between him and Tobin. "Now, apologize to your brother."

Tobin's eyes held an anger Kallar understood all too well. He looked away.

"Sorry."

Tobin grunted. "I still think you need to leave."

Kallar crossed his arms. "No one knows I'm here. That's the point of scouting. I need information if I'm going to rescue R'lann, Pa, and the others."

He wouldn't admit out loud that Pa and the rest could be dead. They might just be captives. They might still be alive.

"Can I count on you," he asked, looking between Gia and Tobin, "or should I find someone else?"

A silent understanding passed between Tobin and Gia. Kallar let down his psychic shield, hoping to catch some emotion to help interpret their secret language. Before he could sense anything, Tobin turned his gaze to Kallar.

"I've been watching since they arrived," he said, "and I can get more information than you. I know who hasn't yet turned to those damned sold-souls. You may have arrived unseen, but the 'great apprentice of Karn'" —he rolled his eyes— "can't escape notice in the village he grew up in much longer. One condition."

"Condition?" Kallar growled. "Seriously?"

"I'm coming with you."

Just what he needed—a village-bound boy to protect.

Still, I'll need village-bound slayers if I'm going to attack the an'reik. The five scouts with me won't be enough.

"Fine. If you can keep up."

Tobin ignored the jab. "What do you need to know?"

11

THE ALPHA'S CALL

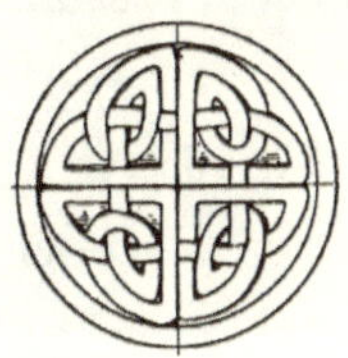

Hours after her confrontation with Moraggan, Alísa's heart still felt caught in her throat. If human an'reik were opposing her to the villages, how would it affect her mission to bring peace between the races? And now an'reik dragons? Which was worse? Should she pause her current plans in order to track them down and destroy them? Could her clan even oppose them all?

Those questions in mind, Alísa and Sesína called a special meeting in one of the small high caves. Koriana and Briek stood with them as war-advisors, Rassím as *radharc anam*, and Falier and Graydonn as fellow witnesses of the battle. A small fire lit the cave for the humans' benefit, and on the other side lay five dragons, all formerly of Rorenth's clan. If anyone held answers to dealing with an'reik dragons, it would be those who once lived under the terrible alpha.

"I understand that recalling this is painful," Alísa said, *"but my knowledge of an'reik is limited and mostly relates to humans. I must know what to expect when we encounter them again. What powers do they have? What are their weaknesses? Are there any ways of finding them, or avoiding them?"*

The dragons exchanged glances, wondering who should speak first. All except Q'rill. The large male dragon had many scars along his ruby-scaled hide—accumulated over a lifetime of attacks. His mother, Tora, had once told Alísa of the clan's cruelty toward him. Though physically an adult, Q'rill's mind was like a hatchling's, and Rorenth had encouraged his clan to 'grow him up' through violence.

"One's fire was hotter than normal and burned through scales," Q'rill said. *"And two of them had spines and horns that grew longer and had bones sticking out between them. I don't know the other two powers, but others said they were an'reik. I think they were right, because those were the meanest. Mother?"*

Tora's eyes were dim. As the silence stretched on, Rayna filled the gap instead.

"One had talons that never dulled or broke," she said, emerald scales glittering in the firelight. *"Those scale-tearers killed many a dragon. Then there was Rorenth. He had an enhanced alpha's call and the ability to multitask between the physical and psychic planes."*

Alísa blinked. *"Alpha's call? What does that mean?"*

Surprise flowed from the dragons. Koriana looked at Briek.

"I do not know what you name it. The inclination within a clan to obey the chief's orders."

Briek glanced at Alísa. "Loyalty?"

"Honor?" Rassím suggested.

"No. The tugging at one's mind."

Briek shook his head. *"I have no idea what you're talking about."*

"Mother"—Graydonn turned from Falier to face her—*"I don't think humans have it. Falier doesn't know it."*

Koriana let out a puff of smoke. *"Humans. Everything has to be difficult."* She lowered her head to Alísa's level, wisdom glowing in her yellow eyes. *"Dragon clans are a bond. They are not simply groups of dragons who have decided they wish to live together. When a dragon joins a clan, lives among them and communicates mind-to-mind daily, they are binding themselves to their shared alpha. The alpha, then, has a certain power over them—what we refer to as 'the alpha's call'. When they give an order, there is an inclination to follow the command deep within each dragon."*

"You mean you're forced to obey me?" Alísa's mind whirled. *"That's awful! Can I make it stop?"*

Koriana's eyes softened. *"No, dear Alísa. No one is forced into obedience. We can resist the impulse. A dragon's heart and mind are merely called to uphold their clan by inclining to their alpha's commands. However, if something more important to a dragon arises, they may disobey the alpha's call. Or the beta's call."*

Sesína perked up. *"Betas have this too?"*

Graydonn thrummed. *"Why else would we listen to you?"*

She grinned, showing all her teeth. *"All right, then. I order you to shut up."*

"For the sake of the clan, I will not."

Koriana groaned. *"There is a difference between an order and a whim, Sesína. But yes, every alpha and beta possesses that power. It is built into the minds of each clanmate when they choose to follow."* She eyed Briek. *"Each* draconic *member, anyway."*

Briek crossed his arms. "Humans are loyal to their chief without need for this—impulse."

"What an'reik alphas have is akin to what you feared, Singer," Rayna said, shifting. *"The Nameless grant them not only a special power, but an enhanced alpha's call that is more compulsion than inclination. Fighting their orders is like fighting your own mind."*

"And even if you can break free, they will likely kill you for it." Rayna's mate Korin growled, his ebony scales seeming to suck in the light. *"Rayna and I had been working to leave for months before you called us, Singer. Complying, showing loyalty, and biding our time until a day we might escape."*

Falier lifted a finger. *"Question. Your clan had only five an'reik, but the clan was huge. Why weren't there more an'reik? If Rorenth could compel you to obey, wouldn't he have made you all swear to the Nameless?"*

"You cannot be forced to give your own soul, young slayer," Tora said, sending everyone else into reverent silence. Her voice grew stronger as she spoke, as though the words themselves gave her courage. *"It must be given freely, whether to dark Eldír or the Maker himself. That was my only solace living as one of Rorenth's mates. He could take everything from me, force anything on me, but he and his dark masters could not touch my soul."*

Alísa's heart shriveled as Tora gazed at the ceiling with eyes aglow in memory. She hadn't known Tora was Rorenth's mate. Did that mean Q'rill—?

But now wasn't the time for such thoughts and questions.

"You asked about weaknesses," Tora said, returning to the present. *"All an'reik are arrogant in their power, and arrogance always leaves blind spots. If their talons are glorious, they will fight primarily with those and forget that, in doing so, they expose their underbelly more often. If their fire is hot, they will use it, forgetting that tail-spines and talons are better at close-range. I never found a weakness in Rorenth. Yet, Graydonn and Falier brought him down alongside the dreki, proving even he could be defeated."*

Alísa nodded deeply, closing her eyes as she did in the dragons' way of respect. *"Thank you, Tora. What about finding them or telling who they are? I know many are larger and some have more obvious gifts. Are there other ways?"*

Alísa caught Iila's eye. As expected, the adolescent remained silent. She hatched only a couple of weeks before Rorenth's defeat, though Alísa hoped her Illuminated memory might provide something. Iila merely looked away, eyes dim.

"They were rather secretive," Rayna finally said. *"And we avoided them as much as we could. They would occasionally leave to meet with an'reik of other clans, or loners."*

Other clans. Koriana had mentioned they existed, but none had bordered with her former clan, so she didn't know who they were for certain. *"Is there another clan with an an'reik alpha nearby?"*

"I am not aware of one, Singer," Rayna said. *"As I understood it, the others hid within their clans, either unknown or unacknowledged as an'reik by their alphas. I know nothing more."*

The others said much the same. After thanking and dismissing them, Alísa turned to those remaining.

"I had hoped to glean more information than that. A path to follow." She glanced at Rassím. *"Any insight from you?"*

Rassím displayed empty hands. "I'm afraid I don't know much. I've never experienced dragon an'reik, and the only human ones I've seen were in the Southlands. Long ago. I'm sorry—I'm a poor excuse for a *radharc*."

"Well, if you remember anything or if the Maker sends you a dream, tell me."

Rassím looked embarrassed. "No dreams either. Ever. I told you—poor excuse."

Alísa smiled reassuringly, then glanced at the others. *"What do you think? Should we keep pressing west, toward Azron and the influence we'll find over villages there? Or should we focus instead on finding and stopping the an'reik dragons?"*

As she spoke the options, she realized which she favored. What did it mean that she would rather face man-eating an'reik dragons than her former chief in Azron?

"Abandoning our current route to tromp directionless through the brush seems foolhardy to me," Briek said. "But leaving villages vulnerable to man-eaters doesn't sit well, either."

"You forget, we are not alone," Koriana said. *"We have allies now—warriors we can call upon."*

Alísa pressed her lips together. *"Most agreed only to peace, not alliance."*

Koriana shifted her wings. *"True. Yet telling them of a problem and pressing for information falls within the bounds of our agreements. The dragons especially may have knowledge of clans in the area who harbor an'reik."*

"And perhaps treaties can become more," Falier said. "If we can convince them that this problem affects them as well, they might offer aid."

"Yes," Briek said. "And Karn would surely assist us if we find where they are hiding."

The emotions of the mind-link chilled at the mention of Karn. Koriana and Graydonn's eyes dimmed, but Alísa only saw it because she watched for it. Briek didn't seem to notice.

He had an excellent point. Papá would help her fight the an'reik dragons. Assuming she found them.

"All right. Have the next rotation of scouts carry messages to those we've already made peace with. I'll speak to my father in the morning and get his advice on how best to alert the villages. We'll continue reaching out to new clans as planned until we find the an'reik. And Rassím" —Alísa looked to him— *"you should join all such excursions. Insight or no, your ability to recognize an'reik on sight will be most valuable."*

Rassím thumped a fist over his heart. "At the very least, Dezra will enjoy seeing more of the country."

Alísa nodded sharply. *"Thank you all. You're dismissed."*

The dragons slapped their tails on the ground and Briek copied Rassím's gesture. As the men climbed onto Koriana's back for a ride, the Illumination bond lit up.

"Good call. Rassím can give any an'reik a knife to the eye before we can think!"

Alísa grimaced at the image, but she couldn't help but chuckle at Sesína's enthusiasm.

"Some end to the day, huh?" Falier said, rubbing his neck absently. "Not that there would ever be a good time for this. Still, I'd hoped to make your birthday worry-free."

Alísa smiled gently. Dear Falier, always wanting to lift others' burdens away, and always disappointed if he couldn't. She took his hand and squeezed.

"We're stopping a war, love. D—did you think it would be easy?"

He gave a humorless chuckle. "No. I suppose not. Still, one day to breathe and enjoy life doesn't seem much to ask."

"We can never choose what each day will b—bring, no matter how hard we t-t-try." She pushed up on her toes to kiss his cheek. "But when I think of you, I am happy."

12

DARK MISTS

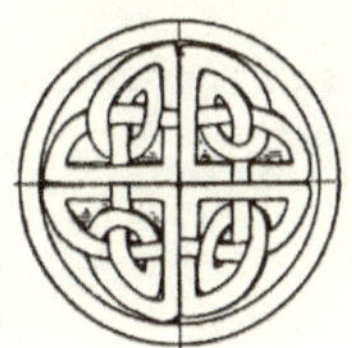

Morning's chill coursed through Kallar's veins with each breath—pure and vitalizing. Mists obscured the hills and muffled the sounds of fastening armor. Horses pranced in place, invigorated by the energy of the warriors—ready to charge the enemy at their masters' whims.

This was where Kallar belonged. Not making friends with beasts. Not wandering from village to village speaking peace. Here, on soil about to run red with the blood of his enemies. Here they would draw the line between innocents and those who would harm them. Sword in hand, warriors gathered around him waiting for orders. He was made for this.

Sixteen hardy slayers of L'rang—men and women—joined Kallar and his scouts. Through the scouts, they discovered an increase in an'reik numbers— eighteen total now, with more arriving every few days. That didn't include the warriors who had joined them. Those apparently kept their own second camp. Kallar's troop needed to be swift against the an'reik, before these reinforced them.

L'rang's holders had also provided valuable information. The village chief required they bring food to the an'reik camp and, like the compliant little holders they were, they did so. One told of a tent with walls dyed black to block out the sunlight and two guards posted in front of it. That would be where they kept their prisoners.

Quietly, Kallar reminded the others of his strategies to face each known power. Maintain telepathic shields to protect against psychic manipulation. Only use mind-spears when the opponent was unshielded, as it could rebound. Fight in pairs against enemies with increased speed and strength, and target their legs. Archers should prioritize attacking fire-manipulators and those speaking incantations.

"There may be other powers we haven't seen," Kallar concluded. "Stay alert, stay smart, stay together. Arrows first. Two volleys, then riders swoop into the confusion to kill as many as possible and reveal their abilities. Ground troops last."

Kallar looked toward the sun. Mist still lay across the land, but it was burning away.

"Move out."

As Kallar approached his horse, he heard Tobin's voice behind him.

"Maker's hand be with us."

Many responded with the traditional 'Maker's hand and Branni's strength,' each with varying conviction. Kallar swung into his saddle, silent. *Whatever gives you courage.*

The riders mounted. Ideally, all would be on horseback, but L'rang didn't have war horses. Against unpredictable powers, a skittish horse would be worse than fighting on foot.

Kallar led them to the crest of the hill separating them from the an'reik. He gripped his reins tighter as the archers crouched to spy the enemy. Tern looked back and gave him a thumbs up. He had spotted the prison tent.

I'm coming, R'lann.

Archers rose to their knees at their commander's signal. Nocked their arrows. Took aim. And fired.

A cry rose from the camp as his archers pulled their second arrows from their quivers. Kallar's horse pranced in place. At the next volley, Kallar kicked it forward. It leapt at his command, charging down the hill, the other riders behind. Below, three men lay dead or dying, arrows in their chests. Two others fled for cover from the cooking fire, while more stormed from their tents—

Fully armored?

Had they known? Was there a traitor in his ranks?

Kallar gritted his teeth and drew his weapon. He had faced worse.

His horse dove into the camp, making to trample an an'reik wielding a sword. Kallar slashed at a man as they passed, his broadsword deflected by a bronze shield. He wheeled around, noting a flash of fire on the opposite side of the camp. Arrows whizzed through the air as Kallar sliced at the an'reik's sword-arm. The enemy spun just in time to save himself.

With a shout and pull at the reins, Kallar made his horse rear, the animal lashing out with its hooves. It hit the an'reik's shield and threw him to the ground under its weight. Kallar pushed forward to trample the man and went after the next an'reik in his path.

Something moved in the astral plane, pounding against Kallar's shield. His horse screamed and bucked, the sudden move almost throwing him. Kallar tightened his legs and grabbed for the beast's mane.

What on A'dem?

The horse bucked again, others now shrieking along with it. Kallar made to break down his psychic shield and send calming empathy into the animal, but caught a flash in the corner of his eye. He dove from the horse's back as hellflames engulfed the terrified beast. Rolling from the pounding hooves and searing heat, Kallar's heart shuddered in horror at his horse's death cries.

He forced himself up and away. He couldn't save the animal, and now a fierce anger burned inside that needed to be unleashed. Kallar ran for another an'reik who stood over a fallen slayer. As the an'reik pulled his sword back to finish the man, Kallar slashed through his unprotected calf. His enemy cried out and sank to a knee, bringing his neck to the perfect height. Kallar dispatched him, then helped the slayer to his feet, now recognizing Tobin. His stepbrother's eyes were wide as he looked around in panic.

"My horse—it—it just—"

"I know," Kallar said, grabbing Tobin's shoulder to make him look at him. On a hunch, he let down his telepathic guard and felt the disoriented panic. Tobin had lost his grip on his telepathy. Kallar pulsed courage through the astral plane and watched his stepbrother's eyes clear.

"Shield up," he ordered. "Stay with me, and stay alert."

Tobin gripped his sword tighter and confirmed. "Branni's strength."

Together, they turned and sought their next opponent. A memory surfaced of training together years ago, before Pa and Gia. Before the world had changed.

A flash of fire brought screams of pain.

Where are the archers? Kallar looked to the hill. His breath caught. Swords and axes clashed on the rise, with multiple slayers on the ground. No an'reik in sight.

His mind raced. There *were* traitors, among the archers!

And one was taking aim.

Kallar dove into Tobin, slamming them both down as an arrow whizzed overhead. A loyal archer—Tern, Kallar thought—ran at the traitor, sword in hand. Another slayer rushed toward him and Tobin, murder in his eyes.

Kallar rolled into a crouch and thrust toward the slayer's gut. The traitor sidestepped and chopped down with his ax, aiming for Kallar's arm. Kallar lifted his weapon to meet the attack near the base, where his blade was strongest. The ax-head hooked on Kallar's sword and his opponent pulled, yanking it from Kallar's hand. It clanged to the dirt as the traitorous slayer drew back for another blow.

Kallar leapt forward, bowling into the ax-wielder. He took him to the ground, pulled his dagger, and slashed through the traitor's neck. As the man's lifeblood poured out, Kallar's stomach clenched. An'reik were one thing, but this was a fellow slayer. This wasn't what he wanted.

He forced himself to breathe and take in the battle. The stench of burnt flesh. The lack of arrows flying. The subtly quieter din of battle. The slayer bodies littering the ground.

They had lost.

"Kallar, behind you!"

At Tobin's call, Kallar rolled off the dead slayer and stood to face his opponent—a sword-wielding an'reik. Holding the dagger between them, Kallar circled toward his fallen sword. He might not survive, but perhaps some of his slayers would.

"Retreat!" The word left an acrid taste on his tongue. The an'reik swung and Kallar dove for his sword. "Retreat!"

Inhumanly fast, his opponent attacked just as Kallar grabbed the hilt. The clang of metal rang out as Tobin met the monster's strike.

"Get up," Tobin growled.

Their opponent moved, returning another blow. Tobin jumped back to avoid being sliced in two. Kallar stood and blocked the next attack. The an'reik's strength threatened to wrench his shoulder out of place.

"Tobin, go!" Dodge. Swipe.

"I can't leave—"

"Your ma needs you." Block. Thrust. "Get her out of here!"

After a moment's hesitation, Tobin ran. The an'reik growled and rounded

Kallar to stop his retreat. Kallar pulled his dagger and slammed it into his side as he passed, drawing a cry of pain. Kallar leapt back, yanking the blade out and allowing the blood to flow.

"We're not done yet," Kallar spat, gripping both weapons as he positioned himself between the an'reik and Tobin.

The monster shook his head. "Fool."

In a blur, the enemy was on him, sword flashing in the morning light. Kallar matched each blow, muscles burning at the pace. Dodge. Parry. Jump. Swing. Step. Block. Thrust. Leap. He could manage only a few attacks.

But if he's fighting me, he's not fighting my men. Vaguely, Kallar noted at least two slayers retreating with Tobin.

Block. Dodge.

I'm sorry, Karn. I said I'd protect them.

Parry. Jump. Block.

I'm sorry, R'lann.

Dodge.

Kallar's foot landed too low—a dip in the ground. He stumbled, and when he blocked the next blow, his sword flew from his grip.

One last trick. I'm taking you with me!

Kallar lunged under the an'reik's blade, dagger outstretched. But his opponent was too fast. With his free hand, he caught Kallar by the throat and squeezed. Kallar jabbed the knife up into his attacker's forearm, making him let go. Falling face-first, Kallar righted himself just in time to see the approaching sword.

"Halt!"

A woman's voice stopped the world. The an'reik's blade hovered only a foot above Kallar's chest. The sounds of fighting ceased. Even the wind seemed silent.

Kallar rolled out from under the sword and crouched. His weapons were gone—the dagger still in his opponent's arm—but he would fight until his last breath.

"You too."

Dark mists struck Kallar as he turned toward the voice. He grunted as the mist became ropes wrapping around him. They pinned his arms to his sides and tied his legs together.

He found her among the fighters, weaving across the bloody soil in a flowing tan dress. Her unnatural green eyes marked her as the same witch who attacked Karn's clan a few months back. Isarra, Tern called her.

Kallar struggled against the bindings, but only made them tighter. He longed to throw a psychic spear into her mind, but the astral plane revealed her shield.

Isarra looked him over, bored. Her gaze shifted away.

"Gather the living," she said. "We must give them their final chance."

The an'reik Kallar had been fighting pulled the dagger from his forearm with a pained grunt, then sheathed his sword. He glowered at Kallar.

"I really hope she lets me be the one to kill you. I'll make it nice and slow."

With that, he grabbed Kallar—wounded arm showing no signs of weakness—and slung him over his shoulder. Torn between dignity and making as much trouble as he could, Kallar struggled, despite knowing the bindings would not fall off.

Within minutes, Kallar was on his knees with six other survivors, each bound by shadows. None were Karns-men. Hopefully, some had escaped to return to the clan.

Did the wayfarers stand any chance here?

Perhaps. They wouldn't have a traitor in their midst.

How had he missed that? Tobin had trusted them all, and he couldn't have been in on it. No one so devoted to the Maker as Gia's son would ally with these thrice-damned an'reik.

Isarra looked impassively on the survivors. "Each of you deserves death for what you've done. Attacking while we slept. Killing my warriors, some of them once your own neighbors. But I am not without mercy."

She walked the line of slayers, her eyes softening. "I understand your fear of my kind. I was once like you—convinced by fanciful tales spun by clever tongues that the Nameless Ones are humanity's enemy. Every word is a lie. Where the Maker and his Eldír claim to desire to help humanity, the Nameless actively do so. They give powers the Maker would never grant, all to protect us from enemies too strong for us, such as the dragons and fae-kind. Now, as the Dragon Singer rises, so do we. Though our allegiance to the Nameless brings hatred upon us, we emerge from the shadows to fight the monsters she would have rule over us."

She crouched in front of Kallar at the end of the line. "I would think slayers, of all people, would understand we are your allies."

Kallar glared at her, forcing every ounce of hatred he possessed into the expression. Isarra didn't react to his loathing gaze. Only glanced back down the line, rose, and began walking again.

"I will give you one chance, for I cannot allow you to continue killing us. We are humanity's only hope against the Singer and her allies. Join us. Become an'reik. Swear yourself to the Nameless and gain the power you need to defeat her. You've seen for yourselves what you will gain. Who would claim this power for themselves?"

The survivors were silent.

Isarra scowled. "Such a waste——"

"I will."

Shock ran through Kallar. He struggled against the misty ropes to see the speaker. Two slayers down, a man gazed earnestly at Isarra.

"I will swear to them, if it means I can better fight the dragons."

The witch smiled. "Yes. If killing dragons is your desire, you shall be granted the power to do it."

She snapped her fingers and the man's bindings released. He barely caught himself with his hands as he fell forward. Isarra went to him and offered her hand, lifting him to his feet.

Traitor. Was there no end to it? Even Kallar, who cared nothing for the Maker and his Eldír, knew not to trust their opposites.

"Prepare him for the ceremony." As another an'reik took the capitulating slayer, Isarra looked over the others. "Anyone else? There is always room in our ranks."

"Hellflames take you," the only woman in the line of survivors spat.

Isarra's smile turned cruel. "We'll see who they take."

She placed her palm over the eyes of the first slayer. He struggled and cried out in pain, then slumped forward, suspended by the dark bindings. The only thing marking him as alive was a slight rising as he breathed. Isarra shook her head and signaled a man standing behind the prisoners.

With a sadistic grin, the man formed a ball of fire between his hands and threw it at the unconscious slayer. Kallar couldn't help a wordless cry as the slayer burned.

Soon only ashes remained and the dark mists which had held the slayer aloft flowed to Isarra's hand, forming into an undulating ball.

Isarra looked down the line. "You see? The Maker you cling to so tightly has abandoned you. No one will save you—not him or any of his so-called benevolent Eldír. You are alone."

Kallar squinted at the witch. What was her game? Why bring up the Maker now? Would their despair simply please her more?

The next man spat at her feet. "Death is no sign of abandonment. We go to his Halls, where death has no seat at the table."

Isarra's face was blank. "Then, by all means, go."

Flames consumed him, and the slayer screamed in agony. His cries reverberated across the hills until the slayer became nothing more than a breath of smoke. Kallar's heart pounded as memories of his arm on fire rushed over him. He forced himself straighter.

Dignity. He would die with dignity.

The an'reik beside Isarra shook his head. "We really must try with them all."

Isarra glared at him. "I know what I'm doing."

Without another word, Isarra grabbed the woman. The slayer writhed under her touch, groaned, then—stopped. The dark bindings disappeared, seeping into the woman's skin.

"Well, no hellflames for either of us," Isarra chuckled. "Go. Stand with your new people."

The slayer obeyed, walking past the witch she had hated only a moment ago and settling among the an'reik.

Suddenly, it made sense. Possession. Isarra was working magic on them to take over their minds, thus growing her ranks.

The next survivor squirmed as Isarra touched him—squirmed until he stopped abruptly and the mist entered his body.

Kallar took in a steadying breath. He knew this man. A first generation slayer, his telepathy weak. Of course he wouldn't be able to fight possession.

The next man—last before Kallar, and a strong psychic—struggled against Isarra until he slumped unconscious from the effort. He had won, and he would burn. Kallar braced himself as the heat poured over him, traumatic memories stirring. But burning was preferable to being controlled.

Kallar was strong. He would fight it, he would win, and he would die with honor. Perhaps the Maker's halls did exist and he would see Ma and lost friends. Perhaps they didn't. Nothingness didn't sound so bad.

Isarra stood before him now, the acrid taste of burnt flesh in the air. He glared up at her.

"Do your worst, witch."

Isarra blinked. She tilted her head, studying him.

"What is your name, slayer?"

He stared back, forming his psychic shield. She shrugged, straightening to her full height, and set her hand over his eyes.

It burned.

Kallar winced, unable to keep from writhing. Pain seared against his shield, burning a hole through it.

No! It will not end this way!

Kallar formed a spear and shot it at Isarra, only for the attack to ricochet back into him. He cried out, then grabbed his pain and pulled it close. He rammed the feeling against the force trying to invade him, pounding it again and again like a sledgehammer.

You. Won't. Win! I. Won't. Let. You!

The foreign entity wrapped around his mind, squeezing like a serpent. Kallar tried to pull away, but it only held tighter. Forming telepathic spikes, he stabbed the wrapping mass, but it felt no pain. It squeezed tighter. Tighter.

Kallar felt his body spasm from lack of oxygen—he was forgetting to breathe, all energy focused inside.

The power rose, a serpent's head amidst its coils. As glowing yellow-white eyes stared into his soul, Kallar forced himself to stare back, now fully within his own mind and unaware of anything outside. He strove against the coils again—stabbing, pressing, spearing, biting, anything he could do to fight it off.

Then it struck, the head slamming into him and taking hold.

"Mine."

The world turned black.

13

PROTECT

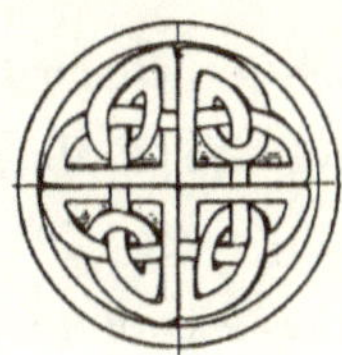

"Shouldn't we be there by now?"

Falier blinked, Graydonn's question pulling him from his conversation with Alísa. He looked over the dragon's side and searched the grassy hills for signs of Karn's wayfarers. Alísa did the same, her anxiety growing with every second.

"You're right," she said, leaning out over Sesína. *"Papá was supposed to make camp in that grove last night, but I can't see them anywhere. Something must have changed. Oh great Maker, don't let it be the an'reik!"*

Falier was fairly confident her last sentence wasn't meant to be heard. He grabbed onto Graydonn's power and tried to push calm to her. The power wavered, then trickled in. That had happened yesterday too, during the fight against the an'reik dragons. He needed to ask Graydonn about that.

Sesína clicked thoughtfully. *"There are no scorch marks anywhere, and I don't smell smoke. A battle between slayers and dragons, even one that ended hours ago, would be easy to spot."*

"I didn't mean to frighten you, Alísa," Graydonn said. *"Perhaps the wayfarers are moving slower than normal. Let's fly back over their planned path. They can't be far off."*

Alísa looked east. *"But we would have seen them."*

Sesína banked, following Graydonn's instructions. *"We're all distracted. We could have missed them. Or maybe they had to alter course."*

Sure enough, ten minutes later, Alísa caught sight of the clan, far south of where they should be. Sesína and Graydonn flew low to the ground so the wayfarers could spot their riders and know not to attack. They landed a distance away, and Falier and Alísa slid down to walk. As Falier landed, his sword bounced against his hip. He should have been holding it steady. It was still so new to him, but he wouldn't be caught without it again. Not like yesterday, when R'gan's slayers surrounded them.

While Alísa's worry relaxed at the sight of Karn's camp, Graydonn's elevated. Falier touched the dragon's shoulder and whispered through their bond.

"I can stay back with you, if you like. Alísa will just be relaying the plan."

Graydonn snorted a negative. *"She'll also tell them about your proposal. You should be there for that."*

"Only if you're sure. They already knew it was coming. I don't need to—"

The dragon gave a small growl. *"I will be fine."*

Falier took his hand from Graydonn, surprised at his forcefulness. *"Okay."*

He returned his attention to the rest of the group just as Rís and Chrí phased through Alísa's bag to flutter on the wind. They chittered and trilled, looping around each other and racing over Sesína as she limped through the grass.

"Not a care in the world," Alísa said, smiling as she watched them.

Falier took Alísa's hand. "Did you know dreki could attack someone like Rís did yesterday? By phasing through them?"

Alísa shook her head. "I once t-touched Chrí—*Mamá* Chrí—when she was insubstantial. It shocked me at first. Only my fingertip. I wonder if it's worse with greater c-c-c—contact."

Falier shuddered. "Maybe. I'd never considered what a drek passing through a person might do."

"There are stories," Graydonn said, his tone now his normal calm. *"Tales of dragons going too deep into fae territory and their minds being torn apart as the creatures pass through them in droves."*

Sesína shook her head violently as Rís and Chrí passed in front of her face. *"I'm glad the little twerps are on our side."*

"No kidding." Falier eyed the dreki. "If it's the mind being attacked, could a telepathic shield keep it from hurting you?"

Graydonn's wings shifted. *"Your guess is as good as mine. I'm not even sure what I've heard is true. And I certainly don't want to ask them to let me see if it works."*

Rís landed on Graydonn's head. *"Test?"*

"I just said no." Graydonn snorted steam and Rís chittered, the sound like laughter.

Sesína cough-laughed. *"Twerp."*

Ahead, Alísa's parents approached from the camp. She hurried to meet them, pulling Falier along while the dreki rushed like swallows on the wind.

"You're in the wrong p-p-place," she said, letting go of Falier's hand to hug her mother. "Did something happen?"

Hanah nodded. "We received worrisome news. An'reik in L'rang."

Falier stiffened. "More of them?"

"L'rang?" Alísa said simultaneously. "What of K—Kallar's family?"

Karn rested a hand on his sword. "He's gone on ahead with some scouts, hoping to retrieve them and gain information. It's bigger this time. A contingency—likely where Tsorr was headed. Perhaps if we eliminate this group, the rest will crawl back into their caves."

Graydonn growled, bristling at the draconic imagery. Falier might have missed the parallel if he weren't connected to the dragon. His stomach clenched, but despite his desire for Karn's approval, his friendship with Graydonn was more important.

"Don't—" Falier cleared his throat. "Don't use those terms. An'reik and dragons aren't the same. Sir."

Everyone turned to him. Alísa looked confused for a moment, then her eyes widened and she nodded firmly.

"He's right."

Karn squinted in thought, then dipped his head to Graydonn and Sesína. "That is not how I meant the words, but I see how it sounded. Forgive me."

Sesína, who apparently hadn't noticed anything wrong either, blinked slowly. Graydonn growled low, so low that Falier only knew because of their bond. The dragon flicked his tail in a more authoritative show of agreement.

"They forgive you," Alísa translated, watching Graydonn a second more. Then she returned to her father as he continued.

"I plan to hold council with N'ravi of Eskann, then march together to free L'rang. I would ask for your aid as well. I'm uncertain what you can do from the air without harming the village itself—perhaps fly the perimeter and catch enemies trying to escape. Regardless of what you do, however, the people will notice you fighting alongside us." Karn glanced at the dragons. "That will greatly assist in the cause of peace between our kinds."

Sesína hit the ground with her tail, talons clawing at the dirt. Graydonn, too, thumped his tail, but the sound was dull. Falier sent a pulse of peace.

"Of c-c-course we will help you free L'rang," Alísa said. "But there's another p-problem. Yesterday, a group of an'reik d—dragons attacked a village. We've no idea where they've gone."

Karn's eyes widened. "Which village? Are there survivors?"

Alísa relayed the story, ending with how Moraggan had won R'gan over by fending off the dragons. She left out the part where the chief had ordered her death, which Falier understood. He wouldn't talk about that in front of his mother, either.

"So the an'reik are fighting each other?" Hanah asked.

"If I recall," Karn said, "the legends speak of the different races of an'reik not getting along with each other. Their goals differ too greatly, Maker be praised."

"Yes," Alísa said. "I have my scouts letting our neighboring dragon c-c-clans know about the threat and asking for any information they c—can give. I hope to g—gain help from them to fight the threat. Can I c-c-count on you as well?"

Karn's brow furrowed. "We will do everything possible, of course. But our ability to reach the battle depends on the dragons' whereabouts. As we progress toward L'rang, we march further away from where the attack occurred. We cannot move as quickly as you."

"It would be faster if you rode dragonback."

Karn gave a wry smile. "I do not believe we are ready for that, my Lísa. We do not know your ways. It is better to fight with a dagger one knows than an unfamiliar sword."

She shook her head. "Just riding t-t-t-to the battlefield would m—make a statement."

He considered that. "That still may be a battle itself."

"An alliance has to work both ways."

Falier nearly jumped at Graydonn's voice, so firm and authoritative. The others started and looked at him. His wings lifted slightly off his back, making him look bigger.

"We are coming to your aid in L'rang to prove to humans that dragons can be trusted, but we need proof of your trustworthiness as well. Mere words will not clear your name, nor your clan's."

Falier's emotions tore him in two directions—worry for Karn's reaction, and pride for Graydonn's courage. Graydonn's own feelings vacillated between anger and fear as Karn held his gaze. Finally, Karn grunted thoughtfully.

"You are right, of course. If I ride, my men will follow." He faced Alísa. "When you find the an'reik, send for us."

"Thank you."

Alísa fell into step with her parents as they trudged toward camp. Falier and Sesína joined Graydonn behind them. Sesína nudged his cheek with her muzzle.

"You were fabulous."

Graydonn growled softly. *"It needed to be said."*

Falier pushed pride, but said nothing. Graydonn wanted to move on.

Ahead of them, Alísa continued with her father. "Considering everything, p—perhaps I should send a daily scout to you. We can k-k-k-keep each other updated on progress or p-p-problems we encounter."

Karn looked down at her. "It would be good to stay apprised of each other's situation, if you can spare a scouting pair for such a task."

"Task?" Rís fluttered to Alísa's shoulder. *"Task!"*

Karn stared at the drek. "Such curious creatures."

"You have n—no idea." Alísa winced as Rís' wing batted her face. "What is it?"

Rís glowed, the light from his wing-baubles flickering over Alísa. *"Task."*

That wasn't Rís' voice. It was his sister's.

Alísa stopped, looking around. "W—where's Chrí?"

Rís chittered a laugh and sent an image of Chrí sitting on Karn's shoulder. *"Task!"*

Chrí's displeasure ran through the link and another image entered their minds, this time of Chrí on L'non. *"Task."*

Falier shook his head to clear it. Chrí's tone held an odd quality—muffled, almost.

Graydonn lifted his muzzle toward the tents. *"I sense Chrí at the far end of the wayfarers' camp. Her voice is being channeled through Rís. I think he's saying they can be our messengers."*

Rís chittered, turning three quick circles around Graydonn's head. *"Task!"*

Alísa looked to camp and back. "Rís, the d—distance between our cave and here is much larger. I d—don't think—"

Rís barked, glowing again. *"Pa!"*

Falier and the others watched him hover in the air until, a couple of seconds later, a new voice entered their heads.

"Rís." Rann's tone was reproving as he responded to his son.

A flurry of images and not-words flew between the two of them, making Falier's head spin.

"Well, that answers the distance question." Sesína thrummed, amused.

"He did that on the mountain yesterday," Falier recalled. "But this reaches farther than even an Illumination bond."

"I wonder how far it can reach," Graydonn mused, eyes bright for the first time since landing.

"Alísa!"

Falier whirled to see L'non striding from camp. The slayer flinched as Chrí spun happy circles around him. She dove to settle on his shoulder and rubbed her cheek against his, only to be pushed off. Undeterred, Chrí whirled through the air again, trilling brightly.

"Task!"

L'non looked exasperated as Chrí perched on his other shoulder. "Can you please explain this creature to me? I have done" —he shoved Chrí off again, garnering more joyful chirps— "absolutely nothing to win or maintain her affections, and yet—"

Chrí landed on his forearm this time, her tiny talons gripping his leather gauntlets. He dropped his arm to his side and she clung on, looking up at him with adoration as her tail wrapped around his wrist for balance. L'non gestured to her as though that was the end of his statement. Falier held back his laughter, but Alísa felt no such restraint, giggling as she spoke.

"Chrí, let him be."

Chrí barked at her. *"Friend!"*

"Task!" Rís trilled and dove for his sister. *"Task!"*

Chrí leapt into the air, twirling with him in a gust. *"Task!"*

L'non rubbed his arm absentmindedly. "What on A'dem is going on?"

Alísa grinned at Falier and the dragons. "I think the d—d—dreki have a solution to our c-c-c-communication p-problem. Can I leave a drek or two stationed here with you, Papá?"

"*Me!*" Chrí squealed, circling Alísa, then swinging past Karn and Hanah to return to L'non. "*Task!*"

"They can c-c-communicate over long distances," Alísa said. "We'll know immediately if something happens."

Karn eyed the dancing creatures. "Can they relay our words? Or only theirs?"

Rís sent an image of glowing dreki eyes, then one of human eyes and the intense knowledge that they were very decidedly not glowing.

"Only dreki," Alísa translated. "Still, it's b—better than nothing."

"Assuming we can even understand them." L'non's head seemed on a swivel as he followed the little ones' movements.

Karn grinned with a wicked air Falier had never seen in him before. "Seeing as you've already gained a good relationship with the purple one, I think I've found just the man to learn the language."

L'non's eyes snapped to Karn. "You can't be serious."

"*Friend!*" Chrí trilled with glee, gracefully fluttering to his shoulder. She pulled her paws close together as she sat and curled her tail around herself, looking quite proper as her wings settled against her back. "*Task.*"

L'non looked between the dreki and the chief as though waiting for Karn to admit it was a poor joke. Instead, Karn nodded expectantly at Chrí.

L'non rubbed the bridge of his nose. "I knew one day I would regret joining my brother's wayfarers."

"And, seeing as our trainer is occupied" —Karn turned to Falier— "how about a friendly sparring match?"

Falier's heart dropped into his stomach. "Uh—"

"You came to train, did you not?"

Falier's eyes darted to Alísa before he could stop himself. He forced them back on Karn. This wasn't some twisted reprimand for calling the chief out, was it?

"I don't know that I'm ready to spar with someone of your abilities, sir."

Karn held up a hand. "Come. I want to see how you're progressing."

Alísa went to her father, concerned. "Papá—"

He whispered something to her, placing a reassuring hand on her arm. The motion should probably reassure Falier too, but welts and bruises were all he could imagine. Graydonn's emotions didn't help either, pulsing with anxiety as they were. Gone was the light air of confidence the dragon possessed a few moments ago.

Alísa backed away from her father with a resigned sigh, only to stop when his eyes landed on her betrothal necklace. She tapped it with the hand garbed with the scale bracelet. She whispered something to him as he took in both pieces. Reaching out to her again, he kissed the top of her head. Hanah, too, pulled her into an embrace once Karn released her. Karn turned to Falier, studying him before speaking.

"Welcome to the family, son."

The words sounded awkward, but Karn wouldn't say what he didn't mean. Falier allowed himself a smile that felt just as awkward.

"Does this mean I can skip sparring?"

Karn barked a laugh. "Nice try."

He opened an arm, gesturing for Falier to walk with him. Well, Karn probably wouldn't kill him, at least. Falier went with him, returning a grin to Hanah as they passed the women. Were they going to watch as Karn soundly defeated him? The thought of Alísa witnessing this formed a rock in his stomach.

Of course, maybe her presence would remind Karn not to hurt him too badly.

He followed Karn to a cart just outside the camp and recognized the chests it carried as training supplies. Throwing one open, Karn pulled out a heavy leather tunic and began putting it on. Falier took off his sword-belt and did the same, pulling out a pair of thick bracers along with it.

Once garbed, Karn passed Falier a waster and indicated an area outside camp. Nerves tightened Falier's stomach, but he followed Karn, passing Alísa, Hanah, and the dragons. The grasses were long and untrampled, but the ground was mostly flat. Graydonn tried to push calm to him, but the dragon's own anxiety overwhelmed it.

Karn held his sword in one hand and began to circle. Falier chose a two-handed grip and did the same, watching Karn's eyes. Darrin had instructed to look for weaknesses here—a hesitation in one's step or favoring of an arm—but the chief displayed nothing but strength.

Karn stepped in with a testing swipe. Falier met it easily, the sharp wooden clack traveling up his arms. The chief moved back into position and continued to circle. It should be Falier's turn, yet he couldn't quite bring himself to get closer to this opponent. Karn struck again, then swung a second time after Falier parried. Falier grunted as he blocked, surprised at the extra hit.

Well, I guess if I missed my step in a dance, he would have to take the lead. I can't miss the next.

As soon as Karn took another step in their circle, Falier made his own testing swing. He went for Karn's empty shield-arm to test his defense of that side. Karn met his strike from underneath, pushing Falier's blade up and around. The chief was powerful. If Falier had been using a one-handed grip, he might have dropped the sword. Keeping two hands, then.

Karn followed Falier as he stepped back, sword swinging. Surprised at the aggressive move, Falier could barely meet each of his three strikes.

"Testing my weak side first only displays your lack of confidence," Karn said, watching him. "Especially after forfeiting your first move. If you're going to do that, at least hold yourself like you think the testing blows beneath you."

Falier swung in a three-stroke pattern L'non taught him. Karn blocked each one, ending in a press.

"Good strength, but I know that move. Try again."

Karn pushed Falier off and swiped at his legs. Falier jumped back and continued retreating as Karn came after him with multiple strikes. Falier blocked each one, forcing himself to breathe.

"Your footwork is good," Karn said, taking up a guard position. "I haven't been able to unbalance you yet."

Falier lunged at Karn's middle, bracing himself for the parry. He tried one of Darrin's patterns, hoping Karn wouldn't know it. If he had more time to consider, he would have realized it was a foolish hope. Karn easily blocked them all.

"I can tell you're a musician. You attack with rhythm. It makes you predictable."

Rhythm? Falier hadn't considered that. It wasn't like he was fighting to a song in his head.

Karn circled toward Falier's weak side. Falier turned to keep his chest parallel with Karn's. *How do I fight without rhythm if I'm not even thinking about that?*

Karn moved, his blade a blur. Falier blocked once, twice, thrice. He jumped back to miss the fourth swing, but Karn advanced again. His blows were unrelenting now, and all Falier could do was defend. His arms ached with each parry, his blocks becoming worse and worse as Karn struck seemingly randomly. If this were an actual fight…

Finally, Karn ended his assault. "That," he said, breathing only a little heavier than normal, "is attacking without rhythm. Predictability will only get you killed."

Falier huffed his breaths, unable to reply. His side ached with a stitch and his arms trembled. He was right—he definitely wasn't ready to spar with Karn.

Karn lunged again, and Falier yanked his sword up in a panic. He hadn't even realized he lowered it.

"Don't assume the battle is over until your opponent is down or retreating," Karn said between blows.

Falier leapt backward and circled toward Karn's weak side. Karn kept coming.

"Falling back isn't always an option. Stand firm."

I can't. Much more and his arms would break off. He backed up again.

"The one you are protecting is right behind you," Karn growled. "Now stand firm!"

Falier forced himself to block, every muscle burning and Graydonn's fear shuddering in his mind. As Karn's attacks persisted, Falier made a choice. He blocked and grabbed onto Graydonn's power. It came reluctantly, then gushed into him once Graydonn realized what he was doing. Falier shot a psychic arrow. It hit Karn's telepathic shield and shattered it, drawing a cry of surprise.

The blows stopped. Falier pulled the power back into a shield and kept his hold tight on his waster, tip up and between them. Karn didn't move, staring with narrowed eyes.

"We don't use telepathy against humans," Karn said, his voice low and menacing. "It's the slayers' code."

Falier swallowed, puffing. "With all due respect, sir, you said the person I was protecting was behind me. If I'm fighting to protect, I won't care about the code. I will use everything I have."

He forced himself to hold Karn's gaze. He may have made the wrong choice, but his words were true. Whether Alísa, Graydonn, Selene, or anyone else he loved, he would never hesitate to use telepathy to defend them. Even after accidentally killing with it, even with that slayer's face seared into his nightmares, it was the truth.

Karn's hard expression faltered just slightly as he considered. Finally, he sighed.

"Well spoken."

Falier gripped his sword tighter, ready for another blow. But Karn only lowered his weapon.

"The match is over."

Falier let his shoulders slump, the tip of his waster lowering to the ground. His breaths came heavily, and he desperately wanted to take off the armor and feel the breeze over his sweat-drenched body. He had never sparred for so long, or against a master. He had so far to go.

Falling into step with Karn, he kept a small distance between them in case the chief pulled any surprises.

"You did well," Karn said. "Better than I expected. Both here and—earlier. When I told you to speak up with authority before other leaders, I did not expect you to manage it so soon with me. That took guts."

Falier glanced at him, unsure what to say. "Yes, sir."

"Karn," the chief said meaningfully.

The tension in Falier's shoulders released. "Karn."

Karn nodded sharply. "It would do you good to continue sparring with me and my men."

Falier's and Graydonn's anxiety spiked simultaneously. "You—think I'm ready for that?"

"No. You will lose, badly and many times. But under L'non's supervision, you will learn far more quickly than just fighting the boys and working on technique. You'll still need the latter, of course, but in sparring with us you'll learn to think like a slayer. That will help when you are called to lead."

Falier's heart pounded. Sparring just now had taken everything out of him. Doing that repeatedly didn't appeal at all.

"Then say no," Graydonn said. *"He respected when you contradicted him—do it now."*

And yet, he needed to learn.

"No, you don't," Graydonn growled. *"You don't have to become one of them. Alisa already said yes, and even this man gave you his blessing without conditions. You*

don't need this."

Falier looked at the dragon. *"Why do you hate this? Other riders use swords, and Karn's right—slayers outside Alísa's clan don't respect me. I need them to if I'm going to support her mission."*

"They're learning to respect her, and she doesn't use a sword either."

"That's different. Female slayers aren't expected to fight, but men are. Whether or not it's right, I can't ignore that."

Falier returned to Karn. "I'll do it."

Karn nodded once, then turned to the carts and began taking off his armor. Falier deposited his waster and leathers in their respective chests, uncomfortably aware of Graydonn's ire. This would just have to be something they disagreed on. He was trying his best for the good of the clan. Couldn't Graydonn support him anyway?

Falier reached for his sword-belt to put it back on, only to stop as Karn stared at it.

"Let me see your weapon."

Falier handed it over, belt and all. Karn drew the blade and held it up with a discerning eye. As he scrutinized it, Falier felt the need to speak.

"I've had it for years. Trained with it when I turned fourteen, like the rest of the boys in my village. I hadn't touched it since, but—"

Falier jumped back as Karn swung the sword, even though the blade was nowhere near him. The chief tested the balance as he spoke.

"This is a decent weapon, but too short for someone of your stature. Sentimental value?"

"Uh, none. Not really."

Karn slipped the sword back into its sheath and laid it on the cart. Then, taking a key from his belt-pouch, Karn unlocked and opened a more ornate chest than the rest. The brass on the corners shone like it had been polished recently, and the wooden sides bore no notches.

"When a slayer falls in battle," Karn said, removing a sword, "his weapons are returned to his family. But, sometimes, there is no one. An old warrior who devoted himself to the fight above all else. A lad whose parents disowned him for fear of his telepathy. A man who fell to flames alongside his wife and unborn child."

Falier's chest tightened as Karn reverently placed three weapons on the edge of the cart. Each sword was of slightly different length and each hilt had a unique design.

"When this happens, the clan keeps their weapons until a new warrior comes to claim them." Karn pulled one from its sheath, tested its weight, then swung it in a quick pattern of three strikes. Nodding to himself, he turned the hilt to Falier. "Try this one."

Falier looked between the sword and Karn. After that list of departed warriors, Falier wasn't sure he was ready to hold such a weapon. Yet, he would not refuse. He took the hilt, holding it carefully as Karn removed his hands from the blade. Plain leather wrapped the handle, just worn enough to be comfortable in Falier's hand. The pommel was diamond-shaped. He tried not to consider what slamming that into an opponent might do.

The sword was long, yet not much heavier than his. He felt foolish as Karn watched him swing it, even though he knew he was moving correctly. Good balance, at least as far as Falier understood the concept. He liked the idea of the greater length as well. He stood an inch taller than Karn—longer arms paired with a longer sword would be an advantage.

"I like it."

"Then it's yours."

Falier looked up. "Really?"

Maker above, he sounded like a child.

A hint of a smile showed. "Wear it always, prepared to protect as its prior wielder was."

Falier rubbed a thumb over the dark leather, pride filling him. "I will. Thank you."

14

FANGS

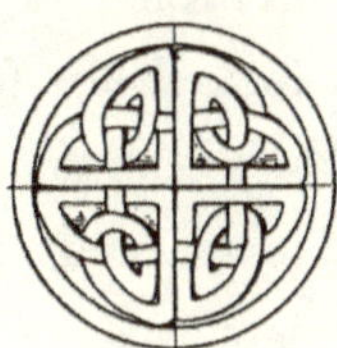

Consciousness returned like a punch to the gut. Kallar jolted upright and twisted to take in his surroundings. Mist swirled around him in a valley between hills. Mountains as high as the Prilunes encircled the land, creating a boundary in the far distance.

Where am I? The sun set beyond the unfamiliar peaks, turning the land blue with twilight. The only other source of light lay behind him.

Turning, Kallar found a large, glowing oval floating several inches off the ground, as tall as he was and twice as wide. In it, like a painting in a frame, was a familiar scene.

The an'reik camp!

Kallar stood to inspect the hovering image. It moved forward with a gentle up-and-down rhythm, strolling through the camp. Indistinct conversations flowed nearby as the scene followed Isarra and a couple of other an'reik. Some people in the scene bore the dragon-scale armor of slayers.

The traitors. Kallar seethed at the memory. They had ruined his plans. Killed his men! Left him at the mercy of—

Kallar stepped away, head swiveling to take in his surroundings again. If that floating oval showed the camp… Was he dreaming? Or was this something else?

A shadow moved on the opposite side of the frame. Shuffling back, Kallar went for his sword.

It was gone.

So was his dagger.

No weapons. None except his telepathy. That should be enough.

Kallar gathered his energies, then stopped in shock as the mists warped around him. Lightly tinged with colors, they swirled toward him as though to seep into his skin. Memory surged, his heart pounding as he remembered Isarra's black mists coming at him.

And the thing. The creature that clawed at his mind.

The shadow stepped out from behind the floating image, revealing a hazy human shape with growths that looked like four wings on its back. Beyond those, it held no distinctive markings—no facial features or clothing details. It appeared as though a shadow had manifested a physical body. The only color it possessed were glowing yellow-white eyes.

Fear surged through Kallar as the eyes fixed on him. Instinctually, he grabbed the emotion and pulled it to himself for a psychic attack. The mists changed to orange-gold and sank into him before he could pull away. Despite the strangeness, they provided the power he needed.

Kallar shot a mind-spear at the shadow. The spear—more a javelin—manifested before him, shooting from his head in the same orange-gold color as fear in the astral plane.

The arrow hit the monster, but flew back at Kallar too fast for him to dodge. Pain coursed through him, pounding through his skull down as the projectile sunk into his body. He doubled over.

Ricochet. Just like with the an'reik.

Pieces flew together for Kallar. This was his mind, and the shadow was what Isarra sent to possess him. He had thought the dark mists were part of her, but now he sensed a difference. This thing was distinct from Isarra, and powerful.

"I wondered when you would awaken."

The shadow's voice was neither male nor female. It slid like oozing mud deep enough to swallow someone whole. Kallar couldn't help but shiver at it, and he hated himself for it.

Gritting his teeth, he tried a different tactic. Pressing through the pain, he gathered his telepathy into one blast and hurled it toward the enemy. At the last moment, he spread his power wide, entrapping the shadow in a mind-choke. This time, it didn't ricochet.

Perfect.

Pouring out his telepathy, Kallar rushed to seal the gaps. The thing merely watched the choke close over it. No struggle, just a strange amusement, like the shadow knew something Kallar didn't.

With gaps sealed, Kallar crept to the window to the outside. It called to him, and without thinking, Kallar reached out and touched it. At the contact, the mind-world disappeared, and the physical rushed to meet him.

Kallar gasped in a breath, battle-tinged air filling his lungs. He was in the camp, in control of his body again. His limbs felt heavy—it took all his strength not to topple. As he fought gravity, the shadow shifted against his mind-choke. He had to choose—hold the choke, or stand.

He fortified the choke, falling to his hands and knees as he battled to keep the thing in his mind locked up. He gasped another breath, then held back a cough at the smell of smoke. He hadn't been unconscious long. The winds hadn't yet cleared the air.

Another possessed man stopped following Isarra to look down at Kallar, eyebrow raised.

Huffing in a few breaths, Kallar pushed to his feet, fighting to keep the mind-choke tight. The shadow—whatever it was—didn't move this time.

Kallar studied the watching man. Was he fighting too? Could they somehow help each other?

The man looked away, resuming his march. Kallar watched him. He could try to run—escape and warn Karn. But if the energy it took to maintain the mind-choke *and* stand were any indicators, the shadow would reclaim his body as soon as he started running. Best to play along until he came up with a plan.

"Clever little slayer," the shadow's voice reverberated in his head. *"We're going to have fun, you and I."*

The voice pierced Kallar's ears, even though it carried no aural sound. He gritted his teeth, following the witch and her new minions.

He rounded a tent and stopped in his tracks, heart in his throat. The prison tent stood before him, its blackened walls stark amidst the other tents, and in front of it—

R'lann!

His sixteen-year-old brother knelt in the dirt, the meaty hand of an an'reik on his shoulder, holding him down. R'lann's black hair was tangled and unwashed. He looked at the ground, but his swollen eye was obvious.

Rage swirled in Kallar's stomach. They would pay. He didn't know how, but he would make them pay!

The hair at the back of Kallar's neck prickled. He turned to see Isarra looking directly at him. A self-satisfied smirk rose on her lips.

"So, your keeper let you out. Like what you see?"

Let out. Somehow, she knew the shadow wasn't in control. But she thought it was the shadow's doing—she didn't know that Kallar held it at bay. He should keep it that way.

Isarra waved off the two an'reik beside her. "Take the others to the slayer camp, where they can work on getting their brothers to join us. I'm keeping this one."

A sharp inhale drew Kallar's eyes. R'lann was looking at him now, wavering between hope and fear.

That did it. Kallar's cover was already blown. He stepped forward, his body so slow as he tried to reach his brother.

"Stay." Isarra commanded.

Kallar attempted another step, but the exertion proved too much. The shadow pierced through his mind-choke, tearing through it like a serrated knife. Kallar cried out as the world began slipping away.

Raging, he grabbed onto his pain and shoved it back at the monster in his mind, trying to choke it again. His knees jarred against the ground and his hand scraped on a rock as he caught himself. Closing his eyes, he struggled to seal the gaps, but the last few minutes had left him depleted. Shoved aside by the shadow, he fell back into the mind-world.

Kallar shivered with exhaustion. He tried to sit up, but only managed to roll to his side. The shadowy figure stood at the window to the physical world, its back to him as it watched and, presumably, controlled. The mists around Kallar were bright with the orange-gold of fear and burning white of rage, but his mind was too weak to command them.

Outside, he saw the creature push his body to its feet. R'lann stared in horror. Then his eyes narrowed as he looked at Isarra.

"What did you do to him?"

The window shifted to look at Isarra. She smiled, leaning down with hands on her knees to condescend to the teenager.

"Just gave him a keeper to ensure he stays in line. I told you I would have one of Allara's children in my ranks and, lucky me, this one's powers are already awakened."

A shock ran through Kallar as unwelcome memories coursed over him. Alísa's dragons around him in conference with Karn. An intense knowing that they were souls. Tightening his telepathic shield to block out their emotions and words. The shadow—the *keeper*—growled like a panther enjoying a meal.

"He also has valuable information," Isarra said. "All slayers here know Karn's apprentice. If Karn has sent forces ahead, the rest will come soon. So, little Singer, tell me your master's plans."

Kallar stared at the keeper. What was Isarra playing at? If she recognized when he was in control, she should recognize it wasn't him now, right?

The keeper moved, one of its dark wings stretching long and thin until it became a tendril of black mists. They plunged into the ground at Kallar's feet, blurring his world into memory. Standing at the campfire alongside Tern. Karn and the clan leadership facing them. Making plans. The next morning with Karn's last instructions.

"They're on their way with the full camp."

Kallar shuddered with revulsion. That was *his* voice. The keeper was speaking with *his* voice!

"Karn approaches Eskann, where he will recruit local slayers. He also hopes Alísa and her dragons will join him."

Isarra's eyes narrowed. "How many?"

Kallar launched himself at the keeper. He couldn't let it reveal anything more!

A wing slapped him away, sending him sprawling across the ground as his voice reported numbers.

Isarra looked thoughtful. "I expect another contingency of an'reik in three days' time. That will still leave us short, I fear." Her lower lip stuck out in a pout. "If only I had means of summoning more warriors. Ones Karn and his allies wouldn't expect. Oh, wait."

Her violently green eyes pinned on Kallar, seemingly penetrating the window.

"Call the dragons."

Dragons? Kallar sat up, his exhausted astral body protesting. *What—*

The mists shifted around Kallar in shades of confusion, fear, and anger. In their midst, the keeper turned glowing eyes on him. The anger spiraled toward its outstretched hand, causing a pulling sensation deep inside Kallar. It felt like a warhorse trying to drag his heart from his chest.

Kallar shouted with effort as he tried to pull back. The mists were his, not the keeper's! But as his cry left his mouth, a cord of white power escaped through his lips. The force on his heart ceased as the power twisted toward the physical world, leaving behind a sense of foreboding.

What in flames—

The keeper placed its outstretched hand in the path of the white power, letting the anger mists mix into it as it speared out the window. Outside, Kallar's voice rose once more, this time in song. Dread and fear collided within him as the poorly conceived lyrics took hold.

An'reik dragons. It's calling for an'reik dragons!

Gathering his strength, Kallar pulled the leftover mists toward him. Exhaustion threatened to sink him to the ground again, but he couldn't let it have him. He couldn't let Isarra gain dragons to her side! He forced the mists into a long stretch of canvas and launched it at the keeper.

The creature turned to face him just before it hit, shadowy arms outstretched to ward it off. Blackness formed at the edges of Kallar's vision as he wrestled the mind-choke around the keeper. It grasped and pulled at the inside of the makeshift confines, but, like before, it didn't stop Kallar from closing the gaps.

Kallar stumbled back into his body. His own weight threw him to the ground, his stomach lurching as he landed on hands and knees. He coughed, the exertion of his fight with the keeper forcing him to expel what little he'd eaten. Already he could feel his mind-choke weakening within, even though the keeper wasn't struggling.

A hand settled on his shoulder, making Kallar start. He yanked away before recognizing it was R'lann.

"Kal? Is it you right now?"

Kallar nodded. "C—can't let her call them."

"I'm quite impressed," Isarra said, looking down with a smug smile. "I've never met anyone who could overpower their keeper."

Inside the choke, the keeper chuckled. 'We're going to have fun,' it had said. They both *liked* someone they couldn't fully control? Well, he would give them the time of their lives. As soon as he discovered how to choke the thrice-damned keeper without falling into exhaustion.

Isarra turned to another of the an'reik. "Go to the slayers' camp. Inform them of our alliance with a Singer who views dragons as tools rather than equals. With the dragons enthralled, the slayers can easily kill them once the conflict ends. Embellish as needed to placate them. I will see to the dragons."

Kallar watched as the man ran south toward the encampment of slayers. Did it take so little to turn them into allies of the Nameless Ones? A message they wanted to hear in order to make them swallow underlying horrors?

A roar sounded in the distance. One of the an'reik dragons? Had he been too late stopping the song?

"Are you done with him?" A man gestured at R'lann. "You have a Singer now."

Isarra pressed a finger to her cheek in thought. "I suppose we would be wasting resources. I already have what I want."

Kallar tensed, ready to move. The keeper might break free again as soon as he sprang to R'lann's defense, but he would not—*would not*—let them hurt his brother.

But Isarra kept talking. "No, devout as he is, he'd probably welcome death. It's no fun when they don't squirm."

She crouched beside R'lann. He kept his eyes resolutely in front of him.

Good lad. Show no fear.

"Perhaps Kallar's pain will be enough to show you the truth of my words." Isarra's voice lowered to a soothing tone. "The Maker and his Eldír have abandoned you. They give you nothing for your devotion. The Nameless care for humanity and generously reward their servants."

"By the blood of the innocent," R'lann spat.

Isarra shrugged. "Innocence is relative. But you, little slayer—the Nameless have a special fondness for you. They are offering you every chance, will give you everything. All you need do is renounce your unrequited devotion to the Maker and you will be given power even greater than mine."

R'lann gave no answer. Pride filled Kallar. R'lann had faced this pressure and abuse for weeks, and he had not broken.

Isarra scowled. "And still you refuse to acknowledge you have been abandoned."

R'lann looked her full in the face, his jaw set. "I am not alone."

Another roar, closer this time.

"We'll see." Isarra straightened, examining the sky. "Our honored guests arrive. Gather close—they can be testy, especially when hungry."

R'lann's courage fled as he looked up. Kallar followed his gaze, his whole body tensing as dragons descended from the clouds. He counted six of the beasts so far, all monstrously large. R'lann crawled to Kallar's side, both of them kneeling on the ground as the other an'reik gathered near Isarra. She began chanting something unintelligible, and dark mists swirled around her hand. They grew to encircle everyone as the dragons' glowing eyes landed on them.

Kallar's heart raced, his hand itching for his sword. On instinct, he formed his telepathic shield, realizing too late that the action released the keeper from his choke. Kallar gasped, bracing to fall back inside his mind, but nothing happened. The keeper just—waited.

What—

"Your fear response pleases me," it said. *"Please, continue."*

Kallar fought back a shudder. No fear. He was a slayer. He had faced pain and death and loss and had always made it through.

The ground shook as the first dragon landed—a copper brute with flame-red eyes. A tent toppled in the wind of its massive wings and another fell prey to its slashing tail.

"Vermin!" The dragon snarled, its hot breath coursing over them. *"Which of you have the masters given power over us? Face us, if you dare!"*

As the dragon's rage rushed through him, Kallar wrestled with the desire to form his shield again. More dragons landed, their emotions compounding in his mind. But if he blocked them out, he would miss important information. He needed any advantage to keep R'lann alive.

Isarra stepped forward, her dark mists lowering from her hand to create a ring around the group of humans. "I'm afraid the masters still haven't seen fit to grant us the ability to control your race."

"You lie!" A blue dragon chomped at the air directly in front of Isarra. *"You always lie. We felt the power pull us toward you!"*

Isarra didn't flinch. "I do not lie to my allies."

"Yet another." The copper dragon thrummed with dark humor. *"Why should we ally with humans? Even those vermin the masters have chosen are beneath us."*

"And likely taste as good as anyone else," said a creaking female voice.

R'lann shuddered, and again, Kallar's fingers itched for his sword.

"The Nameless did not grant this power," Isarra said. "We just happen to have a Dragon Singer in our ranks."

"Singer?!" The copper dragon's eyes narrowed. *"The whelp who slew Rorenth has joined you?"*

"No," Isarra stepped aside and gestured at Kallar. "We have our own, who will work with you in exchange for your partnership."

"What need have we of a Singer?" Another dragon snapped at the air. *"Particularly one so pathetic as that bile-dripping creature?"*

Kallar unconsciously swiped at his mouth, chagrined.

"I'm sure even you can imagine the possibilities if you added his strength to yours." Isarra raised her hands to indicate the other humans. "Rorenth's slayer cannot stand against our combined might. And you and your kind will no longer need to hide amidst your clans."

The copper dragon looked at his fellows, his telepathic line cutting off from Kallar and presumably the others. R'lann glanced at Kallar, anxiety rippling off him.

"You're like Ma," he whispered.

Kallar hesitated before nodding.

"Can you keep that—thing from using your voice again?"

"I'll do what I can." Kallar paused, then added, "I'll get us out of this. Be ready."

"Did you see Gia?"

Kallar grunted. "And Tobin. He came with me. I think he got away."

R'lann didn't look at him. "Pa didn't."

Kallar swallowed. He had known it deep down when Gia said he never returned. "Possessed?"

R'lann shook his head. "He never gave up. Not like you."

Kallar started. "I'm not giving up. I'm going to keep—"

"Very well," the copper dragon said, his presence returning. *"We shall play the game with you."*

"Good." Isarra pointed at the Fangs. "I happen to know that a dragon clan recently moved into those caves. They are weakened from fighting the wayfaring clans, and they have allied themselves with Rorenth's slayer."

Growls and snarls rose from the dragons. R'lann flinched under their ire, while foreboding filled Kallar. Tsamen's clan.

The copper roared a command and together the nine an'reik dragons launched, spearing for the Fangs.

"We should help them along," the keeper hissed. *"Do you want to do it, or shall I?"*

Kallar gathered his telepathy to choke the keeper once more, but the exertion of the morning had taken its toll. The keeper easily took control. With a terrible jolt, Kallar fell back into his own mind, where sickly green mists of dread were his only company.

15

WINDS OF CHANGE

"Begin!"

Alísa caught Falier's flinch as her uncle called out the start of the first sparring match. He already wore his leathers, physically ready for his coming bout even if he wasn't there mentally. They stood on the edge of the crowd, Graydonn and Sesína with them and Rís off playing with his sister amid the wayfarers' tents. Sesína talked with Graydonn in the background of Alísa's mind, trying to keep him at-ease, but the dragon's anxiety nearly drowned out even Falier's. Alísa left Graydonn to Sesína and took Falier's hand.

"You're going to be fine," she whispered. "I know the man you'll be sparring with. Jossen won't let you win, but he won't try to humiliate you either."

Falier smiled ruefully, watching the fighters. "I can humiliate myself on my own just fine."

"You don't have to—"

"I want to. I do." He looked down at her. "If I'm going to be your tiern, I have to prove I can handle myself with other slayers."

Alísa let out a breath. She couldn't argue with that. "J—just know you don't need to do this for me. I fell in love with the holder brave enough to b— befriend a dragon. I need nothing more."

He lifted their clasped hands to his lips, kissing her knuckles. "I know. Thank you."

When L'non called his name, Falier squeezed her hand. "You don't have to stay. You could go see your ma or cousins, if you'd like."

"No, it's all right. I'll stay."

Falier's first match passed as Alísa expected—longer than Jossen's skill should have allowed, but ending with Falier on the ground and the blunt end of a waster at his throat. Jossen helped him back to his feet and walked him to the water barrel as the next pair set themselves.

On a typical day, sparring was less formal. Slayers could spar whenever they pleased, so long as a spotter was available. Some would fight many rounds until satisfied with their exercise. Today, however, L'non had the entire camp in on the action in a tournament-style match, including extra fights for those who lost early on.

When Falier returned, Alísa and the dragons escorted him to the secondary sparring area. Drennar, Karn's head scout, quickly pitted Falier against the man who had lost the first round. This slayer was less kind. He attacked with rapid, precise strikes, each aiming for a quick victory. Falier kept his feet under him with a dancer's balance, but couldn't match the ferocity and soon succumbed to a stab to the heart.

Alísa winced. Wasters didn't have pointed ends, but such a blow would surely bruise even with the protective leathers.

"That stab was unnecessarily hard." Graydonn let out a low growl, thrashing his tail. *"All of this is unnecessary."*

Alísa set a hand on Graydonn's neck, pushing peace. *"He's okay. Look."*

Falier rubbed at his chest and said something with a smile. His opponent just walked away, giving Alísa a pointed look before returning to Drennar.

Sesína cocked her head. *"What was that for?"*

Alísa watched the slayer. *"I'm not sure."*

Falier stopped for water before heading back toward her, still rubbing his chest.

"You all right?"

"Yeah. I—" Falier paused, lowering his hand and looking behind her. "Morning, Karn."

Alísa spun to greet her father. Graydonn turned as well, his stance guarded, unwilling to give his back to the slayer chief. Sesína came around to stand beside him, touching wings in support.

"Morning, Falier. Lísa." Karn opened an arm to Alísa and gave her a quick hug. He returned to Falier. "So, you made it."

Falier nodded. "Two matches so far."

"Good. I mean to keep everyone sparring today. We must be ready."

Falier chuckled. "They all seem ready to me. But maybe I'm not the best judge."

Karn smiled wryly. "Remember, though, they've spent most of their lives fighting dragons. True, we've fought bands of highwaymen and the like, but such battles are rare. Everyone must refresh their skills before we face the an'reik."

"Falier!" Drennar called from behind. "Get back over here! Chief wants you in fighting condition, and I—"

Drennar stopped as the group turned to him and he spotted Karn. "Sorry, chief."

Karn waved it off and glanced at Falier. "He's right. Probably wants to give you some two-against-one training."

Falier's eyes widened. "I can barely fight one person! Two—"

"You'll be on the advantaged side." Karn patted Falier's shoulder, his tone turning teasing. "At least for the first bout."

Falier didn't appear convinced.

"In the meantime, Alísa," Karn said, offering his arm, "I'd like to borrow you for a bit."

Alísa looked at Falier. "I was going to stay and—"

"It's all right." Falier held up a hand. "*I'll* be all right."

"You're sure?"

He nodded firmly. "I'll see you later." Then he turned and jogged off to join Drennar. Graydonn followed, stopping a respectful distance away from the slayers and sitting on his haunches.

Karn nodded toward camp. "Let's give him space. It's hard enough to lose badly and repeatedly—don't make him do so with his lady watching."

Alísa blinked. That hadn't occurred to her. "I want him to know I support him."

"I'm sure he knows. Come." When Alísa took his arm, he spoke a little louder. "You too, Sesína."

The dragoness came to attention, her head perking higher. *"I'm not the one he's pursuing."*

"But you can spy for her. Let the boy save some dignity."

Sesína huffed steam, then rose to follow. Karn led them around the outskirts of camp in silence at first, then spoke as they caught sight of Rís and

Chrí dancing in the sky.

"Curious creatures, these dreki. I must admit, I expected Chrí to become a nuisance, but she seems to reserve that only for L'non. She's curious, but the most mischief she's made is popping in and out of tents at random times. You're sure these tiny dragons are the fairies of legend?"

Sesína swished her tail. *"Those twerps are not dragons. They're far too annoying."*

Karn gave her a dubious look and Alísa clarified. "Yes, Koriana confirmed they are fae. Not d—dragons, just slightly dragon-shaped."

Karn hummed. "Legends say they have magic. I remember seeing them join minds and phase through things in your memories, but not much else."

Alísa pondered a moment. "They can create illusions. During a funeral, they c-c-created images in the air of their lost loved ones. They can also make plants grow out of mountain stone."

"Fascinating." He rubbed his beard. "And you've never noticed them making illusions in battle? I could see some applications there."

Alísa shook her head. The only battle tactics she had seen were joining minds to become strong and phasing through their opponents.

They went silent again, nodding to a few wayfaring women at the kitchen tent as they cooked a hearty meal for the sparring warriors. The wind rustled the grasses, attempting to resurrect the trampled blades. A particularly hard blast rattled the tents, drawing Karn's and Alísa's eyes. Nothing collapsed—wayfarers were too practiced to let anything but a storm do that—but the embroidered symbols of protection, strength, and honor distorted as the wind ran its course.

Her father looked at the tents longer than she did, contemplation in his gaze. "Have you considered what an end to the human-dragon war will bring for slayers? What we'll do when we no longer have to travel clearing caves or worry about attacks on villages?"

Alísa shook her head. She dreamed of peace, but pursuing it left little room for considering what happened next. "What do you see?"

Her father's eyes drifted from the tents to the hills beyond. "The end of an era, of the wayfarers. Some will remain nomadic for love of the wilds, yet many will choose the stability of village life. Ironically, settling down will bring about more young slayers to fight battles that no longer exist."

Alísa chuckled. "It will be good, giving them m—more choice. P—perhaps the chiefs who impose rules about slayers only marrying slayers will have no more ground t-t-t-t-to stand on."

"Perhaps. Or normals will impose it themselves—or something worse—for fear of our power spreading. They may think they have no need of us if dragons no longer pose a threat."

A shiver ran through Alísa. With a war, the races were united within themselves. Certainly there were humans who harmed other humans, dragon clans who engaged in territorial battles, but for the most part humanity stood together, as did dragonkind. Would normals rise against slayers when the dragons were no longer a threat? Would slayers attempt to overpower normals because they were more evolved?

"Slayers were created as a gift to normals," Sesína said. *"A protection. To then turn and harm them—"* She didn't finish with words, growling instead.

Karn continued, his eyes distant. "The absence of war will leave warriors without an outlet. Consider men like Kallar, born to fight and protect. Some will be content to guard villages, ready to defend against rogue dragons. Some may choose to patrol the wilderness and face an'reik and highwaymen. But some might choose to become highwaymen themselves."

Alísa's thoughts continued to whirl. How would peace affect those created for war? The Maker made such men, and her father was one—their purpose couldn't be inherently bad. Surely something could be done for them.

"I'm sorry," Karn said, shaking his head and returning his attention to her. "I'm borrowing trouble from the future. All this is a long way off. It will take many years before the country understands it is safe from war. Maker willing, you and I will not live to see such troubles. But I cannot help but wonder."

Alísa let out her breath and the swirling thoughts with it. Her father's expression made it clear that he couldn't move on so easily. She leaned into him.

"You are a warrior. You were created to search out the next battle."

"Yes." He placed his free hand on hers. "But you, my Lísa, were created to bring peace, and I shall endeavor to live for it."

16

REPLACEMENT

Falier shuffled backward, parrying at a speed he might have been proud of, if he didn't feel like he was about to die. His third day of heavy sparring with Karn's people, yet his breaths still heaved and sweat still dripped from every pore like he hadn't learned a thing. Between the slickness of his hands and the burning in his muscles, he didn't know how he retained his grip on his waster.

Jossen persisted. The wayfarer was of medium build, so though he kept his blows lighter than others did, they also came faster.

I have to break his pattern somehow.

Falier's thoughts flicked toward telepathy, but echoes of Karn sternly reminded him it wasn't appropriate against a fellow slayer. In an actual battle, he wouldn't hesitate. Here, trying to prove he was one of them, telepathy wouldn't help.

Stand firm!

Falier stopped backing up, and when the next blow came, he pressed blades with Jossen. A dangerous position—Darrin and L'non both warned of opponents leveraging your weight against you—but the moment to breathe gave him an idea.

Falier pushed off and circled to Jossen's weaker side. As the older slayer followed, Falier kept dancing away, staying just out of reach. After a few evasions, Jossen chuckled, a smile pulling across his tan face.

"You'll never beat your opponent by avoiding them, young Falier."

"Beat? Nah." It was supposed to sound nonchalant, but his huffing breaths dampened the effect. "I'm just testing to see if you'll make a good dance partner."

"Don't let Alísa hear you say that."

Jossen advanced and Falier scuttled to the side again, this time lunging for the slayer's scale-clad ribs. Jossen twisted away and swiped, hitting Falier's left arm. A glancing blow, not enough to decide the winner, but it required him to fight one-handed—a simulation of true wounds. So restricted, Falier couldn't resist Jossen's strength advantage. The next strike sent his waster flying as he stumbled and landed on his backside.

Jossen pointed his weapon at Falier's throat. "So, am I a sufficient dance partner?"

"We'll need to work on your footwork."

Pressing closer, Jossen grinned. "That didn't sound like a yield."

Falier chuckled. "I mean, you're a natural!"

Jossen pulled back, reaching down. "Better."

Taking the proffered hand, Falier hoisted himself up. Though the fourth loss today, Falier came away lighter than before. He had gotten Jossen to joke with him! Yes, it was technically about Falier being a holder, but he took what he could get.

They went together to the water barrel, where many others congregated. Though today was cooler than the last few, Falier still wanted to dump water over himself. How did people survive prolonged battle without completely overheating?

Falier refrained from drenching himself, simply downing a ladle-full and passing the utensil to Jossen. He could have another when his sparring partner finished.

"Fancy footwork out there, holder boy."

Falier fought not to tense. Varek was a slayer who had kept him and Alísa captive in the battle between Karn, Tsamen, and Tella's clans. Tall as Falier himself, but with the muscles of a lifelong slayer, Varek made an imposing figure, especially with that predatory grin.

"I wish I could fall with half as much grace as you."

How to respond, how to respond, how to respond? "Thanks. I've had lots of practice—falling, and getting up again."

Varek smirked. "I'm sure."

Falier winced inwardly as a few of the others chuckled. So that *wasn't* the good comeback he'd hoped. He forced himself to smile as though in on the joke.

Trísse's younger brother Rassi, who had her sharp brown eyes but lacked her sharp wit, laughed the loudest. Perhaps a year younger than Falier, he seemed just as desperate to fit in——only Rassi had the advantage, having lived among them for years.

"Maybe we should call you 'Fall'-ier." When Rassi got barely a smirk from the others, he continued. "Because he falls so much. You know."

Falier held back a smile. At least the wayfarers wouldn't take *every* opportunity to sneer at him. Only the good ones.

Jossen slapped a hand on Rassi's shoulder. "Adolescents shouldn't bark so loud when they've only just found their feet."

That earned a couple of chuckles, especially after Rassi shrugged the hand away. Falier wasn't sure whether to join them for camaraderie's sake, or to hold back for Rassi's. Despite the young man's attempt, he seemed a more likely candidate for friendship than the older slayers more set in their ways.

Why is socializing here just as difficult as the swordplay? In Me'ran or among the dragons, connecting with other souls had always been Falier's strength.

Metal struck metal in the field, making Falier turn. The next two sparring partners——L'non and Drennar——used dulled swords rather than the wooden wasters. Wasters were crafted to be as heavy as a metal blade, but they were also more forgiving if they hit. The clang of the swords rang in Falier's ears and lingered. He preferred the clacking of the wood, but he should probably try to get used to the metal sounds.

He looked to another slayer. "So, how long before L'non makes me use one of those?"

The man ignored him completely, while another merely shook his head. Neither even took it as an opportunity to mock him.

Another zing of metal in his ears had Falier pulling away. He *should* grow accustomed to it, but opted for a walk to clear his head. In the back of his mind, he caught impressions of Graydonn's flight. Good. Let the dragon focus on something besides how much he hated Falier's training. Not that Harenn and Sesína's bickering would do much for his attitude.

Falier chided himself. Graydonn simply didn't want him hurt. Friends were supposed to wish good and not ill. Graydonn's well-wishing was just very annoying.

As Falier wandered the wayfarer camp, he found Taz, Selene, and Hwinn sitting on the edge, watching the other dragons fly. Hwinn lay on his belly, wings and tail splayed out in his exhaustion. As the wayfarers continued their trek toward L'rang, the distance between Alísa's cave and Karn's camp grew wider and wider. It had taken five hours of straight flying to reach it today. The flight was easy for Graydonn and Sesína, especially with Alísa's strength song. It was harder for Harenn, but he had recovered enough that he intended to fight at L'rang in a week. For Hwinn, barely an adolescent, five hours was almost too much. A relief, as it meant Hwinn was not ready for battle.

Falier approached Selene. "If I sit with you for a bit, will you promise not to gross me out by kissing him?"

Selene smirked. "You're one to talk. Alísa's gotten a lot less shy about smooching you in front of people recently." She patted the ground. "How goes the sparring?"

Falier shrugged, kneeling and trying to ensure his sheathed sword didn't catch in the grasses. "Fine."

Taz leaned forward to look at Falier around Selene. "Oh, come now. For ten hours of flight, you'd better have a better answer than that! What are you even doing over here?"

"I—needed to clear my mind."

Hwinn cocked his head. *"What happened, Uncle Falier?"*

The corner of Falier's mouth twitch upward. A dragon calling him 'uncle' would never get old. "I'm having a hard time connecting. The other slayers tolerate my presence, and that's it."

Taz sniffed. "Finally your turn, eh?"

Falier blinked. "I've seen the way Briek's people treat you. You're a part of them."

"Yeah, but it took months to become so. Years, for some." Taz pulled at some grass, ripping the tops off and twisting them between his fingers. "They're family. They have a lifetime of camaraderie between them. Then someone new is placed in the shield line beside them, and they're told to trust this person not to fall back and expose them to dragon-fire. How can they trust someone who hasn't seen battle?"

"But I *have* seen battle! You know this."

Taz scooted out of line with Selene and faced Falier. "Yeah, I do. But on dragon-back, where you just hang on while they fight." Taz held up a hand to stop Falier's protest, tapping his scarred leg. "We know the truth, but they see slayers too scared to fight on the ground among them. They may never understand."

Falier rubbed his neck and looked up at Graydonn and the others flying patterns in the sky. "So the only way to gain their acceptance is join them on the ground?"

"No, merely the fastest."

Selene shifted. "Don't even think about it. We need you and Graydonn together up there."

"I'm not. Just thinking about how much work I have to do to compensate."

"I'm sorry," Taz said. "I don't want to discourage you. Just know every new wayfarer faces this."

Hwinn pawed the ground. *"You could play them music again. They liked that."*

Falier shook his head. "They liked the music, Hwinn, but I don't think they like me better for making it."

Taz tossed the twisted blades of grass he was playing with and grabbed up some new ones. "It doesn't help that they're probably comparing you to their beloved leader."

An image of Falier standing next to Karn filled his mind. Though Karn was a bit shorter than Falier, his bulk, his stance, his expression all seemed to tower over him.

"Yeah, I don't think I could ever live up to Karn."

Taz barked a laugh. "Not Karn, idiot. The one whose girl you stole."

Falier started. "I don't *want* to live up to him."

"Yeah, he doesn't seem like much fun." Taz let his grin drop, taking on a more earnest expression. "You can do this. You're more intuitive with people and social situations than I am. It'll still take time before they accept you, but they will. Eventually."

Hwinn thumped his tail against the ground in agreement. *"I still think music will help."*

Falier smiled at the dragon, then at Taz. "Thank you. I guess I should get back to it."

He pushed to his feet, wiping bits of dirt from his pants as he did. As he returned to the sparring grounds, he watched Graydonn circling with the others in the distance. Part of him wanted to check in, but decided against it. Better to let him enjoy his flight than make him think about Falier's training.

Reaching the slayers gathered around the water barrel, Falier drew in a breath. Back into the fray.

Varek eyed him. "Thought better of running away, did you?"

"You actually missed me, Varek?" Falier allowed a smirk, trying to emulate the teasing relationships many of the warriors seemed to have. "Didn't know you cared so much."

Varek's eyes narrowed and he muttered something to the slayer on his other side, leaving Falier unsure whether he had made the right choice. Varek was probably the wrong person to try joking with, anyway.

He watched the fighters, paying attention to when the others exclaimed in surprise or cheered approval. Did they do this during his matches? He was always so focused on not dying that he hadn't noticed.

The match ended explosively—one slayer twisted the other's sword from his hand, then the disarmed slayer dove for it, turned it on his attacker, and 'stabbed' him in the stomach just before the killing blow. Falier didn't need the others' applause to know the turnabout deserved cheers.

A man named Senarr—who had guarded Falier and Alísa in the battle alongside Varek—leaned closer to him. "Don't get any ideas. Diving for a dropped sword while your opponent is that close will likely be your last mistake."

Falier looked at him, trying to hide his surprise. Senarr had never been antagonistic, but he hadn't been kind or welcoming either. Best way to encourage this was…

"What would you suggest instead?"

"Besides surrender? Dagger, or any other weapon on your person. It's still risky, but better to face your opponent than turn your back."

Falier nodded respectfully. "Thank you."

Senarr gave a half-shrug and looked away. Falier grasped for something to keep the conversation going. Remembering Hwinn, he ventured, "So, do you guys have any marching songs I should learn?"

Senarr eyed him and muttered. "Holders. Everything's about fun and entertainment with you."

Falier took on a facetious tone. "Well, I figured your songs would be boring or morose. We certainly can't enjoy being slayers, after all. Just blood, sweat, and monotony."

That actually earned a smile. Short-lived, but definitely a smile. "I'm the wrong person to ask. My wife says I couldn't carry a tune if I tied it in my pack."

That gained laughter from a few others. So they were listening, huh? Maybe this would work.

A hand landed heavily on Falier's shoulder. "You're up," L'non said. "You too, Rassi."

Trísse's brother, standing a few slayers away, deflated. Falier shared the feeling, but for a very different reason. Couldn't L'non have let him continue building a rapport? Or at least picked Senarr for his opponent instead of Rassi?

He didn't allow his disappointment to show, however. Merely stepped forward, grabbed a waster of the right length, and walked onto the trampled grasses of the sparring ground. Rassi joined him, cool indifference on his face.

"Don't think I'll go easy on you."

Falier eyed him. "I was going to say the same."

Rassi's eyes narrowed. "This isn't a joke, holder. We're been doing this our whole lives, and you just show up and try to take Kallar's place?"

The name sent a jolt through Falier. So Taz was right.

"I'm not here to replace anyone, simply to learn and catch up." He set himself, the end of his waster high between him and Rassi. "So, let's see what you have to teach me."

Rassi's eyes searched, then hardened.

Falier fought.

17

REQUIEM

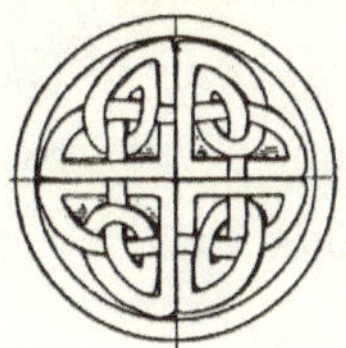

"Singer!"

A trilling screech jolted Alísa from her slumber. She sat up, throwing Rís off her chest before she realized he was there. His glowing red eyes and wing-baubles lit up her tent leathers.

"Rís, w—what is it?" Her heart pounded. "Is it Papá?"

"Chrí!" Rís fluttered in a panic around Alísa's head while the bluebells associated with Chrí's name flashed through her mind. *"Sad!"*

Sesína pushed her nose inside, growling. *"Slow down, twerp. What's happening?"*

Another trill came close. *"Calm."*

Rann, Rís and Chrí's father, zipped through the tent flap. His own red lights shone in the darkness as he pressed his forehead to Rís'. The smaller drek's wing-strokes quieted, but adrenaline still pulsed through Alísa. It took everything within her not to demand an answer as Rann calmed his son.

Sad. What did sad mean? Was Chrí sad? Was Rís sad because Chrí was hurt, or worse?

Rann pulled back from Rís and flew to Alísa. *"Message."*

The word came with an image of many glowing dreki surrounding Alísa and the feeling of asking permission. Having only the barest idea what he was asking, Alísa nodded.

"Yes."

"Follow."

Rann whisked through the tent opening, Rís directly behind. Alísa grabbed her cloak from beside her bed-mat as she stood, covering her nightclothes before rushing out.

Dreki hovered all around, illuminating Sesína and a few other waking dragons and humans. Rann floated in the center before her, his eyes, wing-baubles, and swirling designs on his wings all aglow. Alísa waited as he came closer and brushed her cheek with his muzzle.

Or, he would have brushed her, if he were corporeal. A zap of energy ran through Alísa and turned the world white. The dreki collective pulled her in, their shared thoughts all-consuming as Alísa swam through their depths.

"What's happening?" Alísa asked the dreki, now all floating lights adding to the brightness. *"What message did Chrí send?"*

Chrí. As Alísa mentioned her, she found the adolescent drek among the collective, both a part of them and distinctly her. From her flitted feelings of sorrow and loss. A flurry of images and feelings swirled around Alísa.

Slayers on horseback. The Serpent's Fangs. Light clashing with darkness. Death. Kallar and others of her father's clan. Karn grieving. Dark clouds blotting out the sun. Gia and Tobin entering camp behind Tern.

"Grief."

Alísa gasped in a breath as Rann pulled away, her head swimming like she hadn't breathed the entire time. One image stood out among the rest—her father grasping at his chest, eyes shut against tears.

"Does that mean what I think?" Sesína whispered.

Alísa's heart shriveled. *"I need to go to him."*

As her vision cleared, she recognized an audience of dragons and slayers beyond the glowing dreki. Briek stepped forward.

"Orders, chief?"

Alísa rubbed her face. "I b—believe Karn's scouts were k-k-killed." Her throat closed, and she breathed deep and low to counter it. "I'm going t-t-t-to verify."

"The wayfarers are eight hours away," Briek said. "Perhaps waiting for the war council in two days—"

"No." Alísa caught herself rocking as tension built up inside her. That would not reassure her people. She looked from beta to beta as she found them amidst the crowd. "No, I m—must go now. You keep to the p-p-plan. Lead the warriors to Eskann for me. I'll c-call through the dreki if anything changes."

Her betas acknowledged with blinking eyes and fists to hearts, then Briek set about sending everyone back to bed. The crowd dispersed, leaving Alísa to lean on Sesína. The warmth of her presence helped Alísa breathe through the sorrow, though it could not drown it out.

"Singer?" A contrite Rís fluttered to her. He sent an image of himself in panic, then one of Alísa being confused. *"Sorry."*

Alísa reached out to pet his mane. "It's okay, Rís. You were scared."

Rís trilled and sent a question with a picture of him riding in her bag.

"Yes," she said. Despite the siblings' ability to speak across the distance, they should be together after this scare.

Behind her, footsteps announced Falier's approach. Somewhere along their journey, she had learned to recognize the sound of his stride.

"Do you want more company?"

Alísa waited, torn. She did want him near, yet her emotions were strange and raw. She wasn't sure she could explain them.

"I'm going to P-P-Papá. I'll be okay if you'd rather stay here."

Falier paused, looking her over in the light of Sesína's and Graydonn's eyes. Then he stepped closer and kissed her forehead. The move was so tender it nearly made her drop the tears she was holding back. Whether he caught the shimmer, read her emotions, or simply decided, resolve flowed from him.

"I'm coming."

"I am, too."

Startled, Alísa looked to the dragons and saw Tenza with them. As usual, Tenza held her empathic powers so close to herself that Alísa couldn't sense her. Her expression was impassive.

"We don't know what's happened," Alísa said.

"I must know," Tenza said, "regardless of the answer."

Alísa pressed her lips together. Tenza had already lost her husband and her daughter. If Kallar was also gone…

"We can take her," Trísse said, coming up with Komi.

Komi blinked slowly. *"I can carry two."*

Alísa sighed, resigned. Tern was with the scouts, too. Trísse needed answers just as much as Tenza.

"Okay."

They were ready to leave within a half-hour, dragons laden with riders and packs. Night's chill cut through Alísa's heavy clothing as Sesína set a quick pace. The dragoness was certain she could make the journey in seven hours instead of eight. Regardless, the flight would be long and difficult as everyone attempted to stay awake.

Of course, with how jumbled Alísa's thoughts were, she couldn't have fallen asleep even snuggled in her furs. The scouts were gone. The more she mulled over the dreki's images, the more sure she became. Men she had known, warriors she had grown up among, were dead. Even without deep relationships to them, the memories of their faces wore on her heart. Especially Kallar's.

She had failed him. Only she knew he was a Dragon Singer and the extent of his struggle. Yet, instead of finding a way past his barriers, she had left him to suffer alone. Waiting for him to come to her now seemed an empty excuse. He would never have requested her help.

"Doesn't it follow, then, that he wouldn't have accepted it if you had *gone to him?"* Sesína said.

"I don't know. Perhaps."

"Alísa," Tenza's voice entered her mind, borne by Komi. *"You mentioned before that Kallar is from L'rang. He has family there, then?"*

The present-tense words tore Alísa's wound deeper. Tenza still hung onto hope, but she hadn't witnessed the dreki's message.

"Yes. His father and blood-brother live there, as do his stepmother and stepbrother."

Alísa pulled images of each person to the forefront of her mind, recalling the dinners Gia hosted for Alísa's family. Alísa had never connected with Kallar's father or stepbrother. Tobin was basically another Kallar—same age and similar temperament. Their constant clashes annoyed Alísa to no end. Gia and R'lann were easier to talk to, for what little Alísa spoke during those dinners. Gia was much like a holder, a gracious host with a ready smile. R'lann, though training as a warrior like his brothers, was more likely to admonish his older siblings for their competition than join in.

The images from the dreki only showed Gia and Tobin. Was R'lann gone too? Paern?

"You know his family well?"

Alísa started. Hadn't she—

No. She had told Tenza that Kallar was her father's apprentice. She hadn't elaborated on her own relationship to him, nor did she want to now. But if Tenza sought his family, it would come out. Tenza wouldn't appreciate such a secret.

"Yes. I was expected to marry Kallar."

Shock rang through the mind-link before Tenza remastered herself. *"You were betrothed?"*

Alísa fingered Falier's necklace. *"Not officially, but that was the expectation. It was decided that I couldn't lead the clan. I was to become the next lady and he the chief."*

Understanding rose. *"I suppose I should have guessed that, knowing what I do of your story."*

She said no more, and Alísa didn't wish to reply. After a moment, Sesína broke off the mind-link, allowing Alísa to return to her scattered thoughts.

Alísa sang a shield for the dragons as they approached Karn's camp in the morning light. Even as she slid off Sesína's back, the watchmen seemed jumpy. As she ran to the one closest to her, Rís phased through Alísa's bag. He darted for his sister, who came to meet them. The siblings danced around each other, but their movements held sobriety.

Alísa addressed the watchman. "The s—scouts. Is it t-t-t-true?"

The slayer appeared surprised only a moment. His shoulders slumped with the weight of his words.

"Tern returned with a few of L'rang's slayers. He was the only one."

Alísa's heart clenched. "D—dead?"

He nodded. "Tern's report indicates so. The enemy was too strong for them."

Alísa looked down, grieved. Trísse hurried past her, presumably to find Tern. Alísa needed to follow—to be with her father in the wake of this terrible loss—but she returned to the others. She could barely look at Tenza, who had already lost so much. Sorrow creased her eyes as she searched camp. Looking for—

"The L'rangian slayers." Alísa addressed the watchman again. "Was K-Kallar's family with them?"

"I didn't see any resemblance among them."

No R'lann, then. But Kallar's father was blond and didn't look much like him, nor did his stepfamily. Chrí had sent an image of Gia and Tobin. They at least had to be here.

Alísa's heart felt torn in two. She wanted to find Papá, but abandoning Tenza—

"Go," Sesína said. *"We've got her."*

Alísa didn't hesitate any longer. She ran for the center of camp, searching for the symbols her mother had embroidered into their family's tent. Sorrow permeated the space, suffocating her as she dove deeper. When she found her parent's dwelling, she threw open the flap. Sunlight passed through the leathers, turning the inside a soft yellow, like a dream.

Hanah gasped, whirling around and placing a hand over her heart as she recognized Alísa. Karn was nowhere in sight.

"W—where—"

"He left," Hanah said, voice tired. "He wanted to be alone."

"Which way?"

Hanah sighed. "He walked southward, but I doubt you will find him. He took off about an hour ago."

"Thank you," Alísa whispered. Retreating, she looked back in the direction she came. Komi was still outside camp, as was Graydonn.

She put fingers to her temple as she hurried, signaling Graydonn to connect with her telepathically. As soon as she heard the buzz of connection, she spoke.

"I need your help. I have to find Papá."

She must have exuded more urgency than she knew, because he immediately rose. *"Do you know which way he—"*

"South."

"Climb on."

It took only a couple minutes' flight to spot him. He stood atop a hill perhaps a mile from camp, looking further south. Toward L'rang.

Graydonn dropped her off a hundred feet from the slayer chief, then flew back at her request. She crossed her arms against the chill of the wind and silently approached her father. Though he didn't look her way, his stance shifted enough to show he knew she was there. She stood beside him, staring in the same direction. Eskann was barely visible along the winding path through the country. L'rang was too distant to see.

"The little one's message reached you, then."

Alísa breathed against the rising tears. His voice was so soft, so fragile. No longer the strong chief, but a heartbroken friend, mentor, father.

"Yes."

The breeze tugged at her skirts, but today it wasn't her dance partner. Today, it reminded her of the other half of Eldra D'tohm's stewardship. The Eldra who shepherded the winds, who called them to play in the grasses or tear tent-pegs from the ground, also ferried souls to the Maker's halls upon death.

Were Kallar and his fallen warriors there now? Welcomed despite their crimes against dragonkind? Rewarded for their protection of humanity and their valiant deaths against the an'reik? Tradition declared it so, but more and more it seemed hollow platitude. Men were dead at the hands of monsters. Where was the Maker in that?

"I wish I could tell you it gets easier, my Lísa." Karn's voice was barely audible over the winds. "I still feel every death as though it were my first loss. Today we will celebrate their lives as we always do, but my heart will not be in it. Not when my fool of an apprentice brought it on them all."

Alísa rested a comforting hand on his arm. "P-Papá—"

"No. He was a fool." His hands became fists as he glared across the distance. "I told him not to engage the enemy under any circumstances. Told him to report back so we could fight them together. But that brash, arrogant, over-confident boy! These were not dragons! Not something he knew how to fight, but dark powers we don't understand! And he—"

Karn stopped, a hitch in his breath. "And *I* should never have sent him. I should have known the idiot boy would get himself killed."

Karn's stiff stance melted. Before Alísa's eyes, the great chief became small, collapsing with grief for the man he loved like a son. His mental shield, too, came down as his chest spasmed with sobs.

Alísa threw her arms around him, his sorrow adding to hers as they sank to the ground. She cried with him. Cried for the dead, for the family they left behind, for lost opportunities. For Kallar—the man she never wanted, who endlessly frustrated her, who refused all reason regarding dragons. She shouldn't feel this grief, this loss. Yet a hole tore open inside of her all the same.

Maker, rest his soul. May he somehow find his way to your Halls.

18

TOOTH & TALON

Following Alísa through the warriors' camp, Falier couldn't help but feel the gap between himself and the slayers. Socially, it wasn't as bad as it could have been. Living among Karn's clan these last three days had done some good on that front. Apparently, seeing him support Alísa's family in their grief was enough to quell any outright hatred. No, the distance here was attitude.

Around him, whetstones slid against metal, horses pranced with anticipation, and warriors spoke quietly as they fastened bracers and greaves. Eskann's village-bound slayers intermingled with Karn's men, both clans standing tall in their dragon-scale armor. Despite his recent training, Falier still felt ready to suffocate in his leathers.

Even Alísa seemed confident, weaving through the small war-camp with ease. With her hair braided, leather armor tight around her torso and arms, and a crown of red war-paint across her brow, she looked like a warrior woman of lore.

Falier straightened, trying to match her. He had faced battle before, and he wouldn't be on the ground amidst the slayers. He would be in the sky, wielding telepathy—a weapon far more familiar than his sword. Ironic, considering he had been held back from slayer life because of his weak powers.

"Hey, Falier."

Falier fought back a cringe, turning to acknowledge Varek. The man's smile was laced with mockery as he slid a whetstone over his blade. At least he had stopped just calling him 'holder boy.'

"Varek."

"Shouldn't you be armored up by now? Leather alone won't protect you." He straightened, putting on an air of remembrance. "Oh yes, I suppose you don't need more, considering you'll be far above the danger. My mistake."

Falier saw Alísa tense, her anger rising. Though the wayfarers and Eskann's warriors wore the traditional dragon-scale armor, her people wore thick leathers out of respect for their dragon clanmates. Though they weren't fireproof, they were fire-resistant and, as Varek so eloquently put it, riders were far less likely to encounter flames in this battle.

Falier hurried to speak before Alísa, affecting the tone of good-natured mockery so many Karns-men employed. "Just leaving it to the masters, Varek. But maybe save one an'reik for me and Graydonn, so we feel good about ourselves."

Varek chuckled and shook his head, saying no more. Alísa eyed Falier a moment, as though asking if that interaction was truly okay. He smiled an assurance and continued walking, coming alongside as they searched out her father and N'ravi, the slayer chief of Eskann.

But while Alísa seemed content to let it go, Graydonn grumbled. *"Why would you say that? The slayers already think little of us. Your joke makes it sound like we add nothing to this fight."*

"Of course we add something, but arguing that point won't make Varek respect either of us. Let him see us in action."

Graydonn growled from his spot in Alísa's ranks, separate from Karn's and Eskann's. *"You could have walked away. What does it matter if Karn's men respect you?"*

Well, Graydonn was in rare form today. *"I don't want to argue about this. I can't take back what I said—let's just focus on the mission."*

Hurt radiated from Graydonn, leaving Falier with a pit in his stomach.

"I'm sorry. You are a great fighter and we make an incredible team. I didn't mean to imply otherwise, only to get out of a conversation I couldn't win."

Graydonn's pain lessened, though it was more swallowed than gone. *"I know. I know you didn't mean it. Just, please don't joke like that again. Not to them."*

Falier nodded. *"I won't."*

He pulled back from the conversation, his mind feeling as achingly empty as the rest of him. He took Alísa's hand, seeking connection. Brow creasing, she looked from their clasped hands to his face.

"What's wrong?" she whispered.

Falier chided himself. Skin contact with an empath had been a bad idea.

"Nothing. Graydonn and I are just agitated about the upcoming fight." Not the whole truth, but this wasn't the time to regale her with their problems.

Alísa pressed her lips together. "I'm worried, too. I just have to keep telling myself that we aren't alone. We have the numbers needed to defeat the an'reik, even with what little our dreki scouts could confirm."

The darkness surrounding the an'reik camp was so great the dreki couldn't approach. They complained of sickness whenever they drew near it, though the slayers' camp further south posed no problem. Hopefully, Karn's scouts would have better luck.

Alísa continued. "Once the an'reik fall, we may have to face their slayer allies, but Papá and I trust we can talk them down. We've had plenty of practice."

Falier took the words in with a low breath and a prayer. *Eldra Branni, help me believe it. Give me strength.*

It still felt odd to pray to the Eldra for warriors rather than Eldra Nahne, who claimed holders among her people. Thinking of her brought his family to mind. Ma and Pa were oblivious to everything happening here in the war-torn west. As for Selene, she wouldn't fight today—Hwinn was too young. Instead, she waited outside Eskann with Karn's non-combatants and the other two young dragons—Dezra and Aravi. His family was safe.

Falier and Alísa soon found Karn and N'ravi, both garbed and ready for battle.

"My scouts have returned," Karn said. "If we attack swiftly and finish before the slayer camp hears of the fight, we will outnumber the enemy three-to-one. Or two-to-one if you count dragon-rider pairs as a single unit."

Something loosened in Falier's chest. Those were better odds than previous battles. This would be fine.

"Good," Alísa said. "I will ready my people."

Stepping forward, Karn reached out his arm. Pride rippled from Alísa as she moved to clasp it, then N'ravi's. Falier's own pride in her swelled. She was an alpha-chief in her own right—acknowledged not only by her father, but by another, separate chief.

Alísa-Dragon-Singer had proved them all wrong. If she could change so drastically, perhaps he could, too.

Keeping a mask of confidence proved far easier on Graydonn's back. Amid his own clanmates, nervous energy and loneliness gave way to camaraderie. Even his prior argument with Graydonn seemed insignificant as the dragon emanated his readiness to fight as one. Graydonn's shifting muscles beneath Falier were a comfort as they waited a mile from the enemy camp. Separate from them, Karn's wayfarers and the slayers of Eskann gathered on horseback.

Graydonn stood between Komi and Harenn. Trísse sat confident on Komi's back. Alísa had been helping her and Selene both learn to use empathy in a fight, but it was difficult to do without also affecting allies. Trísse also carried a sword, ready to help if a dragon descended on them or if Komi got into a grapple. Falier carried his own weapon, but felt far less sure it would help him here. Not when he still dropped his waster on occasion.

Alísa and Sesína headed for their lines, returning from their final conference with the other chiefs. The astral plane shifted as dragons and slayers formed a mind-link between the full clan. Alísa rode tall on Sesína, both seemingly devoid of nerves. They stopped before the troops, then directed everyone's attention to Farren. The songweaver stood between the groups of warriors, hands lifted to the sky. Closing his eyes, Falier breathed in the blessing.

By Branni, may your hearts be strong
With justice hard as mountain stones.
By Sachi, may your muscles move
With mem'ry stored within your bones.

By Adne, may your fires burn
And purge the land of darkest dross.
By Níla, may your wounds be bound
Protecting us from death and loss.

By Veni, may we seek the truth
With wisdom's light to know our way.
By Maker's breath, we march as one
Guide our swords and might, we pray.

As Farren's last notes faded, Falier grasped onto the words. *We march as one.* As they fought the enemies of the Maker, he and his Eldír would surely be with them. What was there to fear?

If only knowing something in one's head meant that one's heart would fully believe it.

Karn's voice rang out as he spoke to the ground troops. It sounded like a rallying cry. Simultaneously, Alísa's words traveled through the clan-link, firm and sure.

"My warriors. Today, once more, we fly into battle. I can think of no others I would rather fight beside—brave dragons, slayers, and dreki who fight as one. By protecting L'rang from this evil, we will show all of Arran that we are stronger together!"

Around Falier, dragons growled in anticipation. Scales shifted beneath him as Graydonn pawed the ground.

"Though the world quakes before this enemy, we shall not. Together, we shall give the an'reik something to fear!"

Briek called out in agreement, the other slayers taking up the call after him. The desire to roar built up inside Graydonn, but the dragon held it down, knowing that their attack required stealth. He snarled with the other dragons, smoke pouring from his mouth while the dreki flared glowing wings. Falier remained silent, but the surrounding emotions sounded in his chest, his heart pounding a new rhythm.

Fight. Fight. Fight.

The ground troops moved. Sword drawn, Karn led them up and over the southern hill on horseback. A single mile remained between them and the enemy. Strengthened by the Dragon Singer, the dragons would easily overtake the slayers for the first assault.

Power built up in the astral plane as Alísa sang her strength song. Graydonn's mind and body drank it in, psychic energy building on his end of their bond. Falier opened his mind, letting the power flow in and back out in push-and-pulls. It came slowly at first, its current growing from a creek to a river as Graydonn relaxed his hold.

Graydonn growled. *"Ready, my friend?"*

Falier's body tensed as though he were the one about to launch them into the sky. *"Ready."*

Alísa's song ended and Sesína shot into the air. Graydonn's muscles bunched as Alísa's squad of four dragons followed her. The glowing dreki accompanied them, silent as the night sky as they passed through the winds unhindered. Koriana rose next, and with her, Graydonn sprung into flight with their squad of three. Behind them, Saynan and his four brought up the rear.

The land spread out before Falier—the Serpent's Fangs to their left, spreading hills on their right, and soon L'rang and the enemy camps before them. The sight of the an'reik camp made Falier's heart pound again. They would have a watchman on duty. No going back now.

Dragons roared from the Fangs, sending a wave of shock through the clan-link. A moment later, emotions cooled as Alísa's voice came through.

"Tsamen must have heard my song and come to join us!"

The clan exulted in the news, the energy pulsing through Falier. But another voice rose. Harenn.

"My father wasn't among them, Singer. Something isn't right—the alpha's roar should be the loudest."

From the Fangs, black shapes formed against the sunrise. Their flight was quick, some even faster than Alísa's song could make a dragon fly. Below, Karn's slayers galloped toward the an'reik, expecting Alísa's dragons to rain down fire on the camp just before they reached it.

"Koriana, Saynan," Alísa said, *"what do you suggest?"*

Saynan's calm tones filled the link. *"Continue the attack. I will take my squad to investigate."*

Upon Koriana's agreement, Alísa gave the order. Saynan broke off toward the interlopers as Sesína dove for the enemy camp. Her squad followed, eyes ablaze with inner fire, mouths open to release their flames.

Falier adjusted his grip on Graydonn's spine. They were next.

"Wait!" Rassím called. *"Those dragons, they're glowing dark!"*

A draconic scream rang through the clan-link just as Rassím's warning ended.

Saynan!

Alísa's squad wavered as fear filled the link, some of their fires sputtering as they descended.

Falier searched the sky, panic pounding in his chest. Saynan fell, sapphire eyes dark. None of the approaching dragons were close enough to have struck him physically—what happened?!

An attacking dragon followed Saynan, mouth ablaze to snuff out Darrin as he clutched to Saynan's spine. Their squad dove after them, one dragon latching onto the attacker's tail while Aree went to catch her falling mate. Three attacking dragons descended on them while another seven speared past, heading for the an'reik camp.

The buzz of the clan-link changed as Saynan woke, his tenor voice filled with rage.

"An'reik! These dragons are an'reik!"

Shock and fear coursed through the link, sending Falier's connected mind into a flurry of thoughts.

An'reik! So this is where they were hiding!

Why are they helping each other?

What about Tsamen?

We're outnumbered now!

What's the plan?

Alísa's voice rang out with orders. *"Koriana, Laen, take your squads and intercept them. We'll make another pass at the camp and join you. We can't let them reach our slayers!"*

Koriana's affirmative filled the link with such force that all thoughts besides obedience fled from Graydonn—the beta's call, Falier recognized. He grabbed for Graydonn's power, only to find it had diminished to a creek again.

"Graydonn, I can't access—"

"I'm sorry," Graydonn said, forcing his mind to relax and let the power flow.

"Is it one of the an'reik's powers? Something that—"

"No, I was just distracted. Hit them, now!"

Pushing aside his fears, Falier shot a lightning bolt of energy at a massive blue brute. A screech filled Falier's mind as it hit, one that made him want to cover his ears. The dragon seized and tumbled from the sky.

"Graydonn, Harenn, after him," Koriana ordered.

Graydonn dove, Harenn behind. The an'reik dragon's eye-lights faded in and out as it fell. Graydonn pushed faster as Alísa's song poured into him. They needed to reach the dragon before it—

The dragon's eyes popped open. It spread its wings, catching itself a mere fifty feet from the ground. Graydonn speared for it and Falier shot another psychic bolt. The dragon's shield formed just as the lightning hit, shattering on impact but sending part of the attack ricochetting back at Falier's mind. Falier cried out as heat and thunder ran through him, and he pulled for more of Graydonn's power on instinct to press against the pain. It came slowly, Graydonn having to relax again.

What was going on? They never had this problem before!

Having to focus on the psychic realm, Graydonn missed a bank as the an'reik dragon tried to evade them. Harenn, however, swerved in time, slamming into the creature's back. He clawed at the base of its wings while Graydonn caught up. He took the opposite wing, the two adolescents ripping at the small scales to reach the leather underneath.

Closing his eyes, Falier checked the astral plane. The monster's shield was still firm—if he attacked, he would hurt himself more than the dragon.

The an'reik lurched, spinning to throw the smaller dragons from its back. Graydonn clung on, talons deep in the leather while Harenn dipped under. As the enemy spun and tried to throw Graydonn, its shield faded, unable to multitask between the physical and psychic planes.

Falier shot another telepathic bolt. Graydonn lurched downward as the dragon fell unconscious again, taking them with it in gravity's hold. Graydonn released his grip while Harenn dove for the an'reik's head. As Harenn snapped his jaws around the enemy's neck, Taz pulled his sword and stabbed down into the dragon's skull. After a twist, Taz removed the blade and Harenn let go, letting the dragon crash to the ground, dead.

Dragons screamed and bled above, while slayers cried out in both victory and pain amidst the blazing tents. Falier's chest caved. This wasn't the plan. Even Alísa's song wavered with confusion and horror, tainting its effects.

Despite everything, Graydonn roared their victory. Harenn and Taz joined him. They knew where their minds had to stay. Here and now. Anything else would get them killed.

As Graydonn and Harenn rose back toward the main fray, Falier forced himself to roar with them.

There is another power here
I feel it clash against my song
With lyrics untamed
Unrhymed
Unreal
For with it comes a name——

Kallar.

19

DAGGER

Kallar choked and sputtered as the keeper released him into the physical world. The song. The keeper had used the flaming song again, strengthening the an'reik dragons beyond what their Nameless masters already gave them!

Dragons roared and screamed far above camp, and on the ground—chaos. Fire consumed multiple tents and flashed over the grasses. The prison tent, too, was ablaze, but they had moved R'lann last night to prepare for Karn and Alísa's assault. Between the keeper using Kallar's memories and Isarra claiming divination from a powerful source, they had learned days ago when this attack would occur.

A shock of pain ran from Kallar's head down into his feet. He fumbled to keep from dropping his sword.

"Move. Fight."

The keeper's words resonated through his mind. Kallar breathed through the pain and made to sheathe his weapon.

Another shock, like lightning coursing through his bones.

"Fight."

Kallar clenched his teeth. *"I'd rather burn."*

Ahead, Karn's slayers rode into camp, swords drawn and battle-cries on their lips. The more melee-focused an'reik met them, fire flashing from outstretched palms while those with enhanced speed and strength charged forward.

A pulse rang through the astral plane at Kallar's back, followed by the screams of horses. Slayers scrambled to control their mounts as the creatures reared and bucked. Kallar caught one of the an'reik staring at them, a hand to his temple. Another pulse rocked the air, hitting Kallar with no effect but bringing another round of distressed calls from the horses.

I'll fight. Kallar gripped his sword tighter. *Him.*

Another strike of lightning ran through his veins. His heart skipped two beats before he could gasp in a breath. He clutched at his chest while the keeper growled like a mountain bear.

"You will fight Karn's men." Another bolt. *"Now."*

Kallar's thoughts raced, spurred by pain and rage. How much more could he take? Why wasn't the keeper controlling him? Was there a time-limit? In the last few days, it had only taken control in bursts. Maybe it had used up its energy on the song and now needed to rely on Kallar himself.

Another jolt forced a strangled cry and sent him to his knees. If he was correct, he had two choices. Refuse and die, or fight half-heartedly and hope Karn's men defeated the an'reik and rescued him and R'lann.

"Fine," Kallar gritted out, rising. "I'll play your game."

The keeper practically purred, sending disgust roiling through Kallar's stomach. Holding R'lann firmly in his mind, he headed for the battle. The pulses of the an'reik behind him had left Karn's warriors on foot. Kallar stalked forward, hoping the slow movement would let him stall without setting off shocks again.

The keeper didn't move. A minor victory.

He scanned the field for familiar faces. Karn fought the largest of the strength-increased an'reik, L'non at his side. Tern and Rassi dodged flames with their bronze shields high, just like they would fight a dragon. Another slayer fell too quickly for Kallar to recognize. A speed-increased an'reik stood over the fallen man. Kallar moved, running to defend him.

An intense shock of pain set fire to his bones, sending him sprawling. He gasped in a breath and fought to rise, but the slayer was already dead. Kallar shouted in frustration, pounding the dirt with his fist.

"You will fight Karn's men." The voice rang in his head, echoing several times at a volume that made Kallar cringe. It pulled at his muscles, as though the keeper tried to control him again, but couldn't.

Pain gone, Kallar rose. *Play the game. For R'lann.*

"Kallar?" Kallar looked up to see Varek running toward him. "It is you! We thought you dead—"

"Fight him."

Gritting his teeth, Kallar lifted his sword in a defensive stance. Varek skidded to a stop, eyes widening.

"It's me. Varek."

I know who you are, idiot. Kallar tried to say the words, but choked. It felt like a fist closed around his vocal cords, keeping sounds from forming. His hand moved to his throat.

"Don't talk. Fight."

The keeper's voice echoed in his mind, incessant. *Fight. Fight. Fight.* Kallar could barely hear Varek's continued platitudes.

"This week must have been hell, but it's over."

"Fight!"

Kallar swung his sword, being sure to telegraph his movement. Varek blocked and stepped back.

"What are you—"

Kallar followed him, his attempts half-hearted as he struggled to free his voice. The keeper had never controlled only one piece of his body before.

I must be right. Kallar swiped again, always careful to aim where Varek could easily block. *It requires energy to control me, and it used most of its strength for the song. Now it can only command a piece of me, and I own the rest. And it doesn't seem to care how I follow its demands, so long as I do.*

Kallar parried as Varek made his first blow. *That's one more weapon I can use against it.*

"Traitor!" Varek spoke through his teeth. "You fight for them?!"

Kallar blocked a flurry of blows. *No, idiot! Can't you see I'm not even trying?!*

Varek advanced, backing him up against a tent. Kallar hated to let him win—Varek only bested him three times out of ten—but what other choice did he have?

Use your brain, Varek. Something's wrong with me—figure it out!

The keeper laughed. *"Your old friends are indeed idiots."*

Kallar blocked and Varek pressed, their swords locked between them. Hatred flared in Varek's eyes.

"How could you betray us? Betray Karn?!"

I haven't!

Kallar pushed him off, shaking his head to try to communicate. Varek didn't notice, attacking again. If only he could speak telepathically, but Varek's shield would require Kallar to break it first. Even without that, the keeper's presence might make telepathy unsafe.

"Finish it."

Kallar gritted his teeth as the words echoed and his muscles pulled. He was stronger than that. He swiped in a too-wide arc, leaving an opening he would never allow. Varek struck as Kallar stepped back and deflected.

This isn't me. Figure it out!

"Kallar!"

Both combatants stopped and faced the voice. Karn, clothing stained with the blood of his enemies, stood there, stance wide as though bracing himself. Shock, betrayal, all of it written on his face. The keeper purred at the sight.

"Nevermind. Kill him."

Kallar tried to will away the echoes. *Never.*

Karn waved Varek back toward the main fray with its shouts and clashing metal. "Leave us."

Varek glanced between them, hatred still in his eyes as he looked at Kallar. Then he gripped his sword tighter and ran for the main fray, leaving Kallar alone with his master.

"What have you done?" Kallar barely heard Karn over the sounds of battle. "I never thought you, of all people, would bow to them."

I haven't. Kallar tried to form the words, but the fist around his voice tightened. He couldn't even move his mouth so Karn would know he was attempting to respond.

"Fight him."

Kallar swallowed against the feeling and took a defensive stance. Karn was smarter than the others and sparred against Kallar frequently. If anyone could figure out something was wrong through combat, it would be him.

"Was it the dragons?" Karn came forward, sword at the ready. "Was that what pushed you to betray your brothers?"

Kallar shook his head, swiping a hand through the air to indicate 'no.' But though Karn noticed the gesture, he didn't seem to understand. He had just witnessed Kallar fighting another wayfarer—it would take more than gestures to convince him something was wrong.

Kallar circled as though this were a sparring match. If he pulled Karn into routine, he would more easily notice something off. He would find a way to rid

Kallar of this flaming keeper!

Karn's eyes hardened. "I gave you space to adjust, told you I would listen, and you said nothing!"

Kallar's heart beat in his throat. The betrayal in Karn's eyes didn't belong there. Not for him. He made the first move, a clumsy swipe at Karn's chest, easily blocked.

"Oh come," the keeper hissed. *"You can do better than that."*

Karn followed Kallar back. "I trusted my men to you!"

A part of Kallar told him to let Karn hit him—that would show him something was wrong—but his instincts kicked in too quickly. He parried the blow and stumbled backward.

Come on, Karn. This weakness isn't me!

Karn didn't step back, striking once, twice. "I made you family. Gave you everything!"

Kallar backed away, completely on the defensive. He *never* went on the defensive. Why didn't Karn see it?

The keeper's voice took on a warning tone. *"I'm getting bored."*

In the instant that Karn disengaged from his attack, the keeper sent a shock through Kallar's system. This time, his stumble wasn't forced as the pain coursed through him.

"Fight harder."

Karn's sword came down toward Kallar's shield-arm. Kallar twisted, his body reacting to the danger before he could think. That strike would have taken his arm off. Karn was truly fighting.

"Speak for yourself!" Karn boomed.

Kallar struggled to talk again, blocking two more blows, but nothing came. Karn struck faster. Not trying wasn't an option anymore. Kallar defended, evading each blow. He wouldn't attack, only defend, but he wouldn't let Karn severely injure him, either.

"I warned you," the keeper growled.

His muscles moved of their own accord—or, rather, the keeper's. It swung for Karn's chest. The chief parried, then stepped in for another blow. Kallar grasped at the keeper while dodging, but he was so occupied with staying alive that the thing slithered from his grip. It pulled at his arms again, thrusting toward Karn's middle.

Kallar threw himself backward, the dual movement throwing him off-balance. He hit the ground on his left side, his newly healed arm protesting the landing.

Karn's expression changed to confusion and worry. Finally, he saw something was off!

"Kill him!" the keeper shrilled.

"I've had enough of you."

Taking advantage of Karn's hesitation, Kallar turned his attention inward, wrestling to pull a choke around the keeper. It didn't put up much fight, lending credence to Kallar's conclusion that it was weak. Why hadn't he choked it earlier? He might have regained his voice sooner! As the choke sealed, Kallar opened his mouth—

PAIN!

The keeper lashed out with a thousand blades, turning the mind-choke to dust. With a snap like a broken bone, Kallar fell from the physical world. His mind felt torn apart as he laid in the everlasting dusk of the mind-world. He struggled to rise, weighed down by exhaustion. The mists swirled around him, most hemorrhaging from him. Colors of rage, pain, and dread.

Why dread? Why—

Karn.

Kallar rose, his astral body protesting. Searching for the window to outside, he found it a hundred feet away. The keeper had thrown him far.

He scrambled toward the window, sickly green dread mists changing to an orange fear. The keeper stared out at the scene as light poured into it from the ground, feeding it something. Before it, Kallar saw Karn's sword flashing, keeping up blow for blow with Kallar's body. The keeper moved with practiced speed, striking over and over.

"No! Stop!"

Kallar flung himself onto the thing's winged back, trying to get an arm around its neck. The light feeding the keeper fell over Kallar as he hung on, sending memories coursing through him. The memories weren't visual—they were movements, practiced and sure. Muscle memory. It was accessing his body's ability to fight!

The keeper looked at him, smug. Spikes formed over its back and neck, spearing through Kallar with a burning cold. He screamed and dropped to the ground. Emotion mists bled from every hole, pooling around him.

What could he do? He had to stop it. He tried to push up, but felt like his body—his mind—would rip apart. The holes were closing, but slowly. He grabbed onto the mists, his mind on fire. Pressing hard, he attempted to form another choke, but they barely responded to his commands, growing thicker but not shaping.

His gaze fell on the outside world. The sweat on Karn's brow. The determination in his eyes. The dragons battling in the sky, closer than before. He heard the keeper's breaths in his stolen body, heavy but even. The roaring of fire. The screams of dying men.

The fight continued in a frenzied dance. Thrust and parry. Slash and side-step. Swipe and block. Hack and dodge. Karn met the keeper blow for blow, no longer questioning or accusing. Gone was the betrayal and sorrow, replaced by an intense focus seen only on the battlefield.

Cold ran through Kallar—a mixture of fear and, oddly, relief. Karn was going to kill him. End this misery.

The window's image shook violently as the keeper rolled from an attack, coming up on Karn's side. The chief whirled on him, slashing a cut on Kallar's arm. Flinching, the keeper reached a wing toward Kallar. The appendage lengthened into a tendril of mists, then lashed around him. Pain lanced through him, landing in his astral arm right where Karn's blow landed. Just beyond it, he sensed the keeper's relief, like it had channeled all the pain out of itself and into him. It wanted all of his strength and none of his weakness.

Kallar's sword blocked an attack, then swung high. Karn met the slash, swinging in a circular motion to push Kallar's sword out and leave his torso exposed. Karn stepped in, free hand going for his dagger.

That was it. Kallar braced himself for the killing stroke.

The keeper purred. *"Fool."*

Kallar's body twisted, taking the blow in the left side while dropping his sword. Pain seared through Kallar as the blade met bone, the attack deflected by his ribs. The keeper head-butted Karn while grabbing Kallar's dagger with his sword-hand. Karn fell back, dazed. Undeterred by pain, the keeper stepped in and plunged the dagger through Karn's heart.

"NO!"

Kallar screamed and writhed in the keeper's grip, only to be thrust back into his body. The dagger was in his hand. Sapped of strength and flamed with pain, Kallar could only fall to his knees, taking the weapon with him. Karn stumbled, hand pressed to his chest as blood squeezed between his fingers.

No. Karn!

Kallar's voice still wouldn't work, the keeper's fist tight around it. Karn fell a second later, crumpling to the ground. Dropping the dagger, Kallar crawled to him, agony pulsing in his marrow with each jerky movement. As he grabbed Karn's hand, the keeper's hold became stronger, spreading into his face, untwisting the anguish away. Karn wouldn't see. Wouldn't know the utter despair he felt. The keeper's pleasure at the thought writhed through him, churning his stomach.

Karn's eyes clouded as he met Kallar's. Gone were the looks of betrayal and rage, replaced by an overwhelming sorrow that shook Kallar to the core.

I'm sorry. I'm sorry, I'm so sorry!

Karn's gaze turned to the sky as his shield broke down, connecting with someone above.

His hand went limp in Kallar's. The astral plane rocked as a cry of despair sent coursing waves of energy. Alísa. Kallar's heart echoed her scream, but though he tried, no sound would come. No release of the agony. No witness to the tearing of his heart except the monster who fed on his grief.

20

BETRAYAL

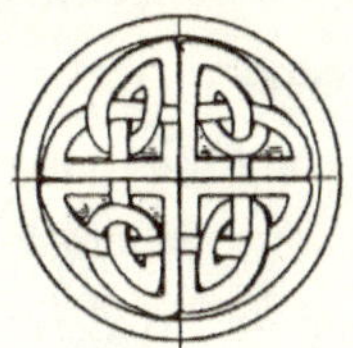

"Get our people to safety."

Trust had accompanied her father's last words. Trust in her, alongside terrible sorrow. Betrayal.

Kallar.

As her scream of rage and grief tore through the astral plane, Alísa could only hope that it hurt him as much as it did the an'reik dragons. The enemy fell around her and Sesína, some scrambling to stay in flight, others with darkened eyes. The sight might have encouraged her to continue attacking, but with so many dead, especially on the ground among her father's men—the price was too high.

She forced grief to the back of her mind. *"Saynan, Laen—kill any you can, then follow. My squad and Koriana's will cover the humans' retreat. Move!"*

Sesína dove for the camp with a roar, their three remaining squad-mates behind her. Below, the slayers fought valiantly amidst the flames, but their dead outnumbered those of the an'reik.

"Retreat!" she cried as Sesína swept over the battle. "Retreat!"

Sesína aimed for a wayfarer caught between two an'reik. Her breath rattled as she filled her chamber of inner fire. The slayer ducked on instinct, recognizing the sound. His opponents possessed no such instincts. Sesína released a torrent over one and smacked the other with her tail as she passed.

Alísa sent quick directions to her squad as Sesína lifted back into the air. Komi attacked the other an'reik, who rolled away from the flames with his enhanced speed. Tora and Q'rill did the same for another slayer, attacking his foe to aid his retreat.

Alísa's dragons continued the pattern, but the enemy knew what to expect on the second pass. They turned their attention to the dragons, blasting fire back at them or throwing javelins. Flames assailed Alísa's mind as Rayna screamed, caught in grasping black mists that slammed her to the ground. The dragoness and her rider fell in a heap of broken bones, their pain snuffed quickly as a fire-manipulator burned through scales and flesh. Rayna's mate Korin roared his grief and rage, and Alísa's heart echoed.

Enemy dragons streaked through the sky, some diving for Alísa's dragons, while others went after the retreating slayers. Sesína led their squad toward the slayers. Behind them, Q'rill trumpeted in alarm and flipped sideways to grapple an attacking dragon. Tora's motherly instincts flared in the clan-link as she banked to assist.

Below, their ground troops continued running. Only about twenty remained—half of their ground forces. So many dead. Human enemies chased them with arrows and flames, while dragons shot fire from above. The horses had all fled because of an an'reik power like Moraggan's, leaving the slayers slow and vulnerable.

"Komi," Alísa ordered, *"help us make a wall."*

Sesína swerved, Komi behind her. Alísa sang as they dove, renewing her strength song. She ducked low as an'reik aimed their arrows, but Sesína and Komi proved too fast. They sprayed the ground with flames, creating a wall between the human sold-souls and the slayers.

Sending instructions to the clan, Alísa directed Sesína and Komi back toward the slayers. Many had their telepathic shields up in defense, keeping Sesína from relaying directions to them. Fire from the enemy dragons sliced across the grasses in long lines, sending smoke into the air. They would have to be fast.

Pain shot through the Illumination bond as one fearful slayer mistook Sesína for an an'reik on their approach. Sesína trumpeted, shaking her head and flapping hard to course-correct her landing. Alísa waved her arms to reveal herself as a rider, raising her voice as Sesína touched the ground.

"Get on!" She coughed at the smoke. "One at a t-t-t-t-time. W—we're flying out of here!"

The men hesitated, some watching the sky rather than her. Despite their fear, none would be the first to abandon the others.

L'non grabbed Rassi, the smallest of the remaining warriors. "Go with

Alísa." He snagged Tern next. "With Trísse. Be quick!"

Sesína shifted, stretching her wings as Rassi approached. Blood spattered the young man's face and chest, and he had a nasty cut on his arm. Alísa reached and pulled him up behind her. She guided his good arm around her waist.

"Hang on. Watch the astral p-p-p-plane" —she coughed— "and spear any an'reik w—without a shield."

Sesína launched, wings straining against gravity. The effort weighed in Alísa's arms as though she were the one carrying two people. Alísa sang again, using her easiest strength song. They needed to keep the an'reik dragons away as the rest of the slayers mounted.

Rassi's grip tightened as Sesína swerved around a massive beast, knocking Alísa's breath from her lungs. The enemy banked after them, its dark power lending it speed. Alísa pushed harder, her voice cracking as she poured every ounce of strength into her song. Her vision began turning black at the edges. Sesína wove and dipped, changing her course each second.

"I think I'm going to be sick," Rassi moaned.

Sesína dove. *"Tell him to aim his sick at the other dragon, not me!"*

The dragon chasing them roared as Komi swooped in to grapple. While Komi kept one of its wings plastered against its side, Trísse drew her short sword and stabbed just above its hind leg. Their opponent bleated its pain and tore away, dipping as it worked to open its wing again. Komi swerved into wing-dragon position behind Sesína.

Alísa raised a fist to Trísse. Rassi, too, seemed bolstered by his sister's move. An arm left Alísa's waist as he drew his sword. He spoke, but the wind carried his words away.

"Telepathy!" Alísa shouted to him. "I c-c-c-c-can't hear—"

The buzz of the clan's mind-link changed as he connected to her. *"Tell your dragon to get underneath one."*

"I'm not going anywhere near those talons, dummy," Sesína said. *"Let's try for a wing."*

Scales slid beneath Alísa as Sesína banked hard, aiming for a dragon chasing Graydonn and Harenn. The flight-partners worked well together, swerving in unison, then breaking apart so their pursuer had to choose who to follow. The longer they kept the brute occupied, the more time they gave the slayers on the ground.

Alísa sent them Sesína's intentions, and they split, Graydonn diving and Harenn flipping over backward, Taz hanging on expertly. The enemy dragon swerved after Harenn, but was too large to keep up. It saw Sesína too late. She zipped just above his wing and banked so that Rassi's sword-arm could reach. He slashed a bloody hole through the middle, drawing a pained cry.

"*Singer!*" Saynan's voice came through the link. "*We've loaded the last one. Where do we go?*"

"*North,*" Alísa said, noting the many slayers who were also connected. "*Slayers, keep spearing the an'reik dragons. Hopefully, we can lose them before we reach Eskann!*"

Alísa's voice cracked in and out as she tried to continue strengthening everyone. Around them, her dragons pulled out of pursuits and grapples to follow her instructions. Their wounds and protesting wings pounded in Alísa's head, blurring her vision.

Sesína dodged a dragon's talons and Rassi clutched at Alísa, nearly falling. His arm touched hers and he yelped at the pain, yanking away as soon as he righted himself.

"What in flames?!"

Alísa couldn't respond, too focused on staying awake. She pulled power from Sesína, but Sesína was fading as well. It was all too much. They would fall.

Like her father.

The clan flew, slayers keeping attackers off their backs with mind-spears and chokes. After a few miles and an an'reik death, the enemy finally gave up their pursuit. Though her dragons were slow with extra riders, the slayers' psychic power proved too concentrated for them.

"*They had a Singer,*" Koriana said. "*How? Can the Nameless produce this power? Tora?*"

"*I don't know human an'reik any better than you,*" Tora said. "*We never interacted with them.*"

"*Did anyone see him?*"

Alísa trembled as grief and rage collided. "*It was Kallar.*"

Shock took the mind-link, and Tern's voice rose. "*Kallar's alive?*"

"*And a Dragon Singer?!*" Kallar's stepbrother Tobin's disbelief surpassed everyone else's. "*I would know——*"

"*He is,*" Alísa cut him off. "*And he killed Karn.*"

L'non's voice faltered as emotion tried to consume him. *"Are you sure?"*

Rassi pulled away from her. *"Kallar would never—"*

"He did!" Alísa glared back at Rassi. *"I was in Karn's mind as he died. I felt every frantic emotion as his lifeblood poured out! Kallar betrayed him—betrayed us all!"*

Alísa faced forward again. Peace flowed from multiple individuals in the clan-link—Sesína, Falier, Graydonn, even Koriana. Alísa pushed against them all. There was no peace here. Only anger and pain and terrible, terrible sorrow.

After a long moment of sullen silence, Briek spoke. *"What do you want to do?"*

Alísa's breath shuddered. Her father's last words echoed in her mind so loudly the others surely heard them.

Get our people to safety.

Eskann would not be safe. It was a half-hour's flight and a couple hours' ride on horseback from L'rang. Assuming the an'reik had horses. Otherwise, it was a one-day march. No matter which, Eskann needed to be evacuated.

No time to mourn. Not today. Not for her, for Korin, for the widows and children left fatherless, for a clan bereft of their chief. She couldn't get caught up in grief yet, no matter how sharply it bit at her heart.

Alísa drew herself up. *"We will fall back to a safer location until we can plan our next attack. L'non, Chief N'ravi, I will need your help to evacuate Eskann."*

Upon landing, N'ravi ran to prepare his people. Despite being small, Eskann would take hours to evacuate. Villagers would begin on foot, guarded by slayers, while the dragons ferried non-combatants as quickly as they could, all heading for Vennia, a village halfway between L'rang and Alísa's cave. There, Alísa and the chiefs would begin preparations for war.

Alísa slid from Sesína's back. In the flurry of movement, she sought only one person. As the wayfarers ran out to meet them, Alísa locked eyes with her mother. With a single glance, she watched her mother's world crash around her.

Alísa tried to speak, but grief choked her attempts, denying her even her mother's name. Hanah rushed to her with arms crushing and comforting. Hand on Alísa's head, she took Alísa's tears on her shoulder as her own spilled.

"My girl. My brave, brave girl."

Alísa choked on sobs. "He—he—he's—"

Her mother shushed her gently. "I know." A shuddering breath. "I know."

She held Alísa as the rest of the world rushed around them. In the back of her mind, Sesína, Graydonn, and Falier checked on her, but she had no words for them. She had felt the moment her father slipped from her—here one second, then mercilessly snatched. She could still feel the emptiness.

Hanah shifted, grasping Alísa's arms and locking eyes with her—shining, wet, yet determined eyes. "Alísa, my love, we must move now."

The words brought on a fresh wave of tears. "I—I c-c-c-can't."

"You can," Hanah assured, cupping her face. "You are his daughter, and there is so much strength in you. We will continue to grieve, but we mustn't lose our people in the process. They look to us now."

Get our people to safety.

Her mother was right. It wasn't fair, and it sure as hellflames wouldn't be easy. But it was right.

Alísa swiped her hands over her cheeks, sniffling back her sorrows. More tears fell. She couldn't stop them.

Hanah took her hand. "Walk with me until you are ready. The tears will slow as you focus on the living."

Sniffling again, Alísa nodded. So many depended on her. Grief wouldn't change that. This was the cost of being the alpha, the chief, the leader in the war for peace—now the war against the an'reik.

Hanah squeezed her arm and, as one, they moved to take care of their peoples.

21

THE KEEPER'S GAME

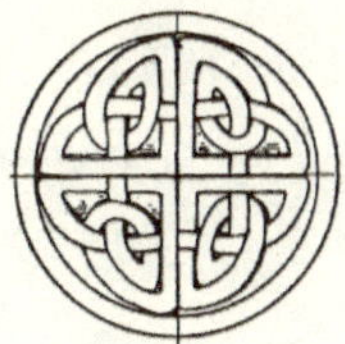

Kallar didn't look up as the an'reik dragons returned. Couldn't look up. He could only stare at his master's lifeless face.

What had he done?

No, it was the keeper.

Not me.

Not.

Me.

The shadow laughed. *"It makes no difference. He saw only you."*

Kallar's breath shook. The betrayal in Karn's eyes as they fought, as his dagger plunged into him, as he fell—all of it agreed with the keeper. Even Karn hadn't been able to figure out something was wrong. Even Karn thought Kallar could betray him.

"Rise, my little Singer."

Isarra's voice set Kallar's teeth on edge. She practically floated across camp toward the dragons, passing the bodies of the dead. She raised an eyebrow at him.

"Rise."

Kallar shuddered as the keeper moved. It waited a moment, then reached through his limbs to force him up. He struggled against the muscles moving without his consent, but nothing stopped the madness. He rose and stepped into place beside Isarra, the cuts on his arm and side protesting.

"This is better than merely forcing you back," the keeper mused. *"I wish I had thought of it before, so you could feel muscle and bone give way beneath our might."*

Kallar pulled at his telepathy, trying to choke the shadow in his mind. The keeper slapped it away, stinging like a thousand wasps. Again, he couldn't cry out or roar his frustration. The keeper had stripped away all control. All he could do was follow Isarra as she approached the angry dragons.

The copper brute growled at her. *"You lie again, vermin. You claimed your Singer would give us victory, but Rorenth's slayer lives, as do many of her people!"*

Isarra shook her head dismissively. "I did not expect her cowardly retreat, yet it serves my point. The girl's combination of dragons and riders is quite effective. You cannot face them alone, as you've discovered, and neither can we."

The copper lashed his tail. *"Any of your vermin who attempt to ride us shall quickly discover the error of their ways. I will not bow as her sniveling dragon clanmates have."*

"The thought never crossed my mind," Isarra said. "I don't doubt such an attempt would end in disaster for both parties. Yet, as we discovered today, we need each other."

The copper lashed out, snapping his jaws mere feet from them. *"We need nothing from you!"*

"Overgrown hatchling. Your tantrums are embarrassing." Isarra looked at her fingernails. "You need more dragons, and my dear Dragon Singer here is how you'll get them."

Smoke poured as the copper growled. The others tensed, waiting for the word to strike. Kallar went for his sword, only to find it missing. The keeper had dropped it before—

A fresh wave of grief hit him, unwelcome as an'reik surrounded him. Perhaps it didn't matter. Better to let the dragons kill him and be done with it.

The copper's tail lashed. *"How would you use him?"*

Isarra picked a piece of dirt from a nail, then looked up. "Two of you are alphas. Three, if you count the heap of scales." She pointed to a dead green dragon on a rise. "The masters' strength has amplified your alpha's call, yet some of your clanmates still fight you every step of the way. Even futile attempts can become tiresome. Think of these, and of those nearly convinced to swear fealty to the masters themselves. With my Singer's power amplifying you, your clans will fall to your whims and become stronger. Perhaps even immune to Alísa's cries for their freedom."

"And what stops us from simply killing you and taking this Singer for ourselves?"

"Dragons do not control Dragon Singers. But I do."

Kallar jerked away as she ran a finger down his cheek. The freedom of movement shocked him, then moved him to action. He grabbed the sword of a man standing next to him, yanking it free of its scabbard and swinging around to Isarra. She met him with a grin and black mist. The blade struck the mist like a brick wall, sending vibrations shuddering up both his arms.

Something else, then.

He closed his eyes, calling the astral plane to his vision. The copper dragon's shield was down for communication. He threw a psychic spear into it. The dragon roared in outrage, flames gushing from its maw as it shook its head against the pain. Isarra's dark shield rose to protect the living, while bodies of dead an'reik and slayers burned up.

"Again with the tantrums," Isarra tsked.

Kallar looked at another dragon. This one was smaller. If he—

"That's enough."

At Isarra's order, the keeper took control. It pulled and scraped, like another skeleton fitting itself under Kallar's skin. It clamped around his mind, flinging him back into the twilit astral world.

No. Not again!

Kallar flung himself at the shadow, but spikes emerged to impale him. He fell from the monster's back, emotion mists hemorrhaging from his wounds. Outside, Isarra continued speaking to the dragons, but the keeper turned its attention to Kallar.

"And still you try."

Kallar struggled to sit up. He was so—so tired. Shades of rage and grief spread out from him. The keeper walked through them, its white eyes lighting further as it absorbed the emotions.

Kallar spat at it. *"I'll never stop. I've defeated you before, and I'll do it again!"*

"Fool!" The keeper threw itself at him, its shadowy form pinning his arms and body down. Kallar twisted and kicked, but the monster was stronger. *"Can you truly not see it?"*

Its predatory stare sent a shock of fear through Kallar. He couldn't move, like when he was eight and the dragoness Paili bore down on him. But this time, there was no Ma to stand between him and his attacker.

Move! He commanded his astral body. *You can beat it. Move!*

"You honestly think you, a mortal made of dirt, can oppose even a piece of an Eldra?" The keeper chuckled wryly. *"That of everyone we have possessed over the ages, you are the only one strong enough to overpower their keeper?"*

Memories flashed before Kallar's eyes. Isarra's words. She said his ability impressed her, that he did something she had never seen before. Now those words held a new meaning. The copper dragon said she always lied.

"We have been playing with you," the monster growled, *"and what a delightful toy you've been! The pride in yourself as I let you choke me. As you fought your former clanmates, thinking you could keep me at bay. And even now, after I made you kill your chief, you still think you can fight me and win?"*

The keeper sat up and breathed in deep. The emotion mists flocked to it, disappearing within the dark void of its body. *"Well, I've enjoyed your pride, but I'm ready for a fresh meal. Now I'll take your grief."*

It stood, yanking Kallar up by an astral arm, and threw him at the window.

Kallar landed back in the physical world, barely able to keep himself standing. The talk was over, human an'reik turning their backs on the dragons, unafraid. They must have come to an accord.

Isarra gave him a knowing glance as she passed. "You understand now. A pity. I would have played the game a bit longer." The sickening sound of crunching bones made her grimace. "Ugh, do that if you must, but do it somewhere else."

Movement further in camp set Kallar's heart racing. A black dragon, approaching Karn's body. With a burst of energy he shouldn't have, he ran. Gathering his psychic power, he shouted, making the dragon shrink back. Kallar slid to a stop between it and Karn, growling.

"Leave him."

Smoke curled from the dragon's maw as its anger poured over Kallar. The emotion only fueled his own.

"Now!"

Again, the dragon shrunk at his command, this time slinking off to find its meal elsewhere. Around camp, dragons took to the air, the dead in their mouths and talons. Kallar forced himself to look away. Some would be the bodies of his friends, but as his strength waned, he knew he couldn't save all of them. A body without its soul was just a shell. He would have to find comfort in that teaching.

"A teaching from the same people who taught you dragons lack souls," the keeper reminded. *"Shaky ground indeed."*

Kallar shuddered against the echoes of its voice, then turned to Karn. His master's lifeless eyes watched the sky—a reminder of his constant vigilance in the war against the dragons.

"Or how he searched for comfort from his daughter because the man he loved like a son betrayed him."

Kallar gritted his teeth, but it did nothing to ease the ache of the keeper's words. They were true. Karn hadn't seen through the keeper. He had only seen Kallar raging against him, turning against everything, stabbing him through the heart.

He sank to the ground beside Karn, choking back his sorrow. The keeper wanted this—to feast on his grief. He couldn't let it.

Reaching, he shut Karn's eyes. His master's skin was cold to the touch, his soul long gone from his body. If the Maker's Halls were real, he was surely there now. Would he know what actually happened? That it wasn't Kallar who held the knife? Would Karn even care?

"No one else will," the keeper hissed, shoving more memories at him. The feeling of the dagger in Karn's chest. Alísa's terrible scream. The men falling as they retreated. *"You are the face of their enemy. Hated. Alone. They will rise against you, and they will fall just as he did."*

More images, but these unfamiliar. Strengthened an'reik dragons descending on those with riders. L'non and the men falling to flames. Another scream from Alísa, this of pain and death.

Kallar trembled. "No. I won't let it happen!"

"You can do nothing."

R'lann with a knife in his chest, just like with Karn.

"No!"

Kallar lunged for Karn's dagger, yanking it from its sheath and turning it on himself. *No blade for R'lann. Only for me.*

His arms seized just as the weapon's tip pierced the armor over his heart. Kallar ground his teeth, straining against the keeper's hold. His heart pounded, still beating where it had no right.

"You can do" —the keeper purred— *"nothing."*

Kallar dropped the dagger, the blade thudding to the dirt. He didn't know whether the keeper forced him to drop it or he did of his own accord. His chest shuddered and spasmed until hot tears fell over his cheeks. He sagged over Karn's body, gasping for breath against the sobs that wanted release.

His scream of anguish put Alísa's to shame. And the keeper smiled.

22

A SLAYER'S STRENGTH

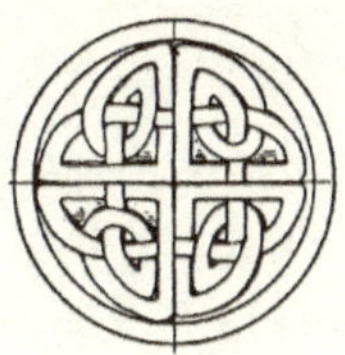

Fatigue draped over Falier, pulling at his eyelids as Graydonn completed their third trip to the village of Vennia. The flight in one direction typically took four hours. Overladen with riders as the dragons were, however, they needed to take more frequent stops to rest.

Graydonn's extra passenger immediately behind Falier still clung to him as tightly as when they first launched. Eleven-year-old Missy's tears stuck his shirt to his skin—tears for a father who would never come home. Behind her rode Alísa's cousin, Levan. For his previous passengers, Falier had distracted them by pointing out landmarks below. This trip, however, had mostly been in the dark. The land was only beginning to brighten with the sun's rise.

Graydonn landed at the camp outside Vennia, his sides heaving. Falier slid off and reached up to Missy.

"Let's get you down."

Levan slid down Graydonn's opposite side in the time it took Missy to recognize Falier's offer of help. Levan patted the dragon's neck and whispered his thanks, which bolstered Graydonn. Beyond them, the other dragons of their ferrying squad began letting their own passengers off.

Missy's eyes were puffy and red, her grip like iron as Falier helped her from Graydonn's back. Setting her on her feet, Falier went to the packs now lying on the ground underneath Graydonn. He marveled at his friend. Three passengers and two bags, after a full day of similar loads. And all this after a terrible battle.

"You are incredible, Graydonn." He spoke aloud for the younger slayers' benefit. "Thank you."

Falier hauled up the packs, passing Levan's to him and taking Missy's on his shoulder. He searched the other dragons landing around them, then pointed at Saynan.

"Levan, I see your mom and brother over there. Missy, do you remember what color dragon your family flew with?" He should know this. His thoughts were so muddled.

"Black," she whispered.

Good. There was only one black dragon here—Korin. Sesína was with Alísa and the rest of Eskann. The entire village had been evacuated, its people walking toward Vennia. Only the old, infirm, or very young rode horses. Few of the animals remained after the battle this—no, *yesterday*—morning. Any free horses or mules pulled carts with people's belongings. Eskann would continue marching until the dragons could ferry everyone.

The slayers stayed with those on foot, all except the riders needed to lend a sense of safety to passengers. They and the dreki watched the skies for enemy dragons, ready to fight for the people should they return. So far, there had been no attacks.

Falier spotted Korin. "There they are. Let's go."

As they headed for Missy's family, Falier sensed Graydonn building up the energy to lumber to the water station. Large buckets and barrels had been filled from the well for the exhausted dragons. A few already lay there, taking long draughts with drooping wings. Though Alísa had established peace with Vennia a month ago, the people remained wary and stayed far back.

Just outside the village, wayfaring women and teens established their camp. Tents stood in the dim morning light. Those who weren't asleep helped the newcomers unload. Sprinkled among them were Vennia's holders, who directed villagers of Eskann to empty rooms and any homes with extra beds. At the center of the wayfarers' camp, smoke rose from cook-fires. Selene worked among them tirelessly, while Hwinn and the other young adolescents flew about hunting. There were many to feed.

Sorrow, fear, and grief shuddered underneath it all, mixing with Falier's own. The lengthy flights let him process some, but not enough. Could any amount of time be sufficient? They lost. People were dead. Rayna. Two dragons and their riders. Many slayers of Eskann. A few wayfarers. Karn.

Falier's heart ached like a chunk had been cut out. He could still hear Alísa's scream. He should be with her right now, comforting her. Instead, he was here. He passed Missy's bag off to a holder who had come to collect her family. Did being a tiern sometimes mean abandoning your chief to help your people?

"You there!"

Falier jumped, senses frayed from lack of sleep. A burly man with pale skin and red hair stalked toward him. For a moment, it looked like Karn, especially with the red dragon-scale armor over his arms and chest. But this man's hair was cropped against his scalp, and his clothing too pristine for a wayfarer. Chief T'kan.

"Who's in charge here?"

Falier stepped up. "I am."

T'kan's scowl deepened. "Aren't you that holder Alísa traded Kallar for?"

Falier ground his teeth. "Yes, but—"

"Yet another insult. Where are your chiefs? Why do they send children and dragons to give me orders?"

The holder with Missy's family spoke gently. "T'kan, I'm sure that—"

"You're sure of nothing," he snapped. "You know less of this situation than I do. The chiefs should be here taking council with me before they send their people to invade my village!"

A whimper made Falier turn. Missy. She was crying again, though she tried to hide it. Her mother whispered something to her, but Falier didn't hear it. His tired blood pounded in his ears. He looked at T'kan.

"I'm sure this must be frustrating, but—"

"Frustrating?! It's insulting! Treating me as an underling to salvage a mess I know nothing of!"

"Nothing?" Falier clenched his fist and tried—*tried*—to even his tone. "Alísa sent her seconds-in-command to you first. Surely they explained the situation to you." It had been Briek and Koriana—there was no chance they hadn't. "If you have more questions, I'd be happy to—"

"I don't want seconds and messenger boys. If we are at war, I need a proper war-council before you bring it to my doorstep!"

"You'll have one, but—"

"If Karn were alive, he would—"

"Look at these people!" Falier snapped, gesturing to Missy's family and the other refugees beyond. "Look at them! Do you see their fear and pain? These are the ones who are *safe*. Imagine the rest, still under threat of attack. What kind of chief would leave their people to face that terror alone? Karn certainly wouldn't have! So I'm sorry you won't get your precious war-conference as soon as you want it, but until everyone is safe, you'll just have to put up with the seconds. Now ask your questions and let me do my job!"

T'kan's face turned red as his hair, his jaw working. As Falier's words echoed through his mind, anxiety filled him. He'd just called out a chief. If T'kan retaliated…

"Keep the tents away from the gates. Merchants will be here soon and I can't have them turning back." T'kan pivoted toward the village, muttering. "Especially now, with twice as many mouths to feed."

Falier breathed a sigh of relief. "I'll see it done."

As Missy's family passed him, the holder nodded his thanks to Falier. Falier returned the gesture. He would be much more comfortable in that man's position. Making space, serving food and calming teas, making quiet conversation to help people forget their worries if only for a few minutes.

But that wasn't his role anymore. Falier approached the tents closest to the gates and asked that they be moved further away. One family complied quickly, the other with much grumbling, though they settled a bit when Falier helped carry their things to the new location.

His task done, he grabbed some stew from Selene at the kitchen tent and made his way to the outskirts of camp to sit with Graydonn. Around them, riders inhaled bowls of food while dragons ate chunks of deer whole. The crunching bones and snapping tendons didn't bother Falier anymore. It was simply life with dragons.

With no conversation among the exhausted warriors, Falier's thoughts drifted, the stew doing little against the fatigue pulling his body ever closer to the ground. Alísa was so strong. She, Hanah, and L'non. Before leaving Eskann, the family stood in conference with Slayer Chief N'ravi and the normal chief of the village. Together, they made decisions that affected hundreds—where to evacuate, what villages needed to be warned, who they might call on as allies. All during the meeting, Alísa remained composed. But Falier knew her. Behind the strength she exuded lived a terrible, all-consuming grief. It hurt to see her holding it at bay. She shouldn't have to do that. She should have room to grieve. But she refused all comfort from him.

"I can't stop. If I stop, people will die."

So she was there, and he was here.

Movement called Falier back from his thoughts. Riders mounted their dragon partners, ready to bring in the next batch of non-combatants. Without dragons, reaching Vennia would require eight days or more. Even ferrying, it would be two or three more days before everyone arrived.

As dragons launched, Graydonn curled on the ground beside Falier. *"We should try to sleep, so we're prepared to switch in when the next squad arrives."*

Falier nodded and set his bowl aside, too tired to return it to the kitchen tent. He reached back through the bond, easily finding Graydonn's telepathic strength on the other side.

"What happened, Graydonn? In the battle? I couldn't pull from your power."

Graydonn's eyes dimmed. *"I was—distracted. I did not keep my mind open enough for you. I am sorry."*

Falier studied the dragon. *"Are you sure that's all? It's never happened before. Can a bond weaken? We've been arguing—"*

Falier grabbed at the thoughts slipping through in his exhaustion. Graydonn clicked in his throat.

"I am sure. I won't let it happen again."

Falier held his thoughts tightly. It didn't make sense. If Graydonn had to work to keep his mind open during a battle, wouldn't that hinder his physical abilities?

Yet, Graydonn's knowledge of the bond far surpassed Falier's, and he had no reason to lie. Right?

Pushing the thoughts aside, Falier dipped under Graydonn's wing. Though much smaller than his tent back at the cave, Graydonn's wing-tent held a warmth Falier missed occasionally. He found a spot in the grass and curled on his side, his arm his only pillow. Amber eyes closed, Graydonn breathed out calm. Falier grasped the emotion, letting it push out the questions and fears until sleep took him.

"Falier. Rise."

Falier pulled in a breath as Graydonn's mental prodding pushed him from slumber. It couldn't be time yet. It didn't feel like a full rest-period. They had already taken two—a full day and night of ferry runs between each. They were getting close, only a couple more shifts and everyone would be here. This third sleep period, though, felt incredibly short. He didn't even remember dreaming.

"It is not time to leave. Just awaken."

Graydonn pulled his wing back, revealing twilight. They had only slept a couple hours, then.

Movement caught his eye. Sesína weaving between the wayfarers' tents, and at her side—

"Líse."

Falier rose, exhaustion fleeing. He hurried toward her, but slowed as he noted her tall stance and emotionless face. She was still wearing the mask. This was his chief, not his beloved.

He stopped a few feet from her. "What can I do?"

Alísa swallowed, paused, then spoke telepathically with Sesína's help. *"Hide me."*

Her grief and fear crashed over him. It clenched in his stomach and stuck in his throat. Each clawed at his heart, which beat his own desperate longing to be what she needed. To shelter her, to give her the safety to release the tide that had built inside her for the past two days.

Fighting off tears, he reached for her hand and found in it a tremble not visible anywhere else. Her grip tightened, as though to hold back the shaking. Sesína stepped up behind her, wings lifted.

"To Graydonn," Sesína ordered. *"We'll block her from view."*

Falier led her under Graydonn's wing, sitting against the dragon's side. Sesína lay at their feet and Graydonn stretched his wing over her, the dragons' bodies creating a cocoon of warm scales. There, clinging to his chest, Alísa finally allowed herself to sob, her whole body wracking.

Falier tightened his hold, one arm around her waist and the other hand stroking her hair as she released her sorrows. Her pain washed over him as their telepathic connection remained open. He could close it and spare himself the raw emotions, but that seemed like abandoning her.

He kissed the top of her head and stayed there, tears falling into her hair as her grief mingled with his own. He hadn't been close to Karn by any means, but they had connected. Now every potential for their relationship—one of his few among the wayfarers—was gone. And Alísa—she had just gotten her father back, only to have him ripped from her.

They stayed there a long time, Alísa alternately sobbing and crying softly. Holding her silently, Falier felt so inadequate. He should have the words to banish the awful anxieties mixed in with her grief, a sword with which to slay them. But he had only exhaustion and sorrow.

Eventually, Alísa's shuddering breaths slowed in a deliberate manner, only to pick back up as grief fought her efforts. Falier reached for peace. Alísa described it as a deep green feeling, though to him it was like a gentle breeze. He pushed it toward her, focusing hard to keep hold of an emotion he didn't feel. She stiffened a moment, then relaxed against him.

"I did this for Mamá," she said. *"To help her sleep. I suppose it's only right…"*

Something about that set his aching heart more at ease. He might not know his place among the clans, might have no one else he could talk to, but here he was enough. He kissed the top of her head.

"Try to rest. We're all here with you."

Graydonn and Sesína followed his lead, filling the space with peace and allowing him to relax again. They were far stronger than he was, and more skilled in empathy.

Alísa shifted. *"Can we lie down?"*

Falier nodded. They had slept sitting up against dragons before, but he wasn't keen on repeating that. The stiffness in the morning alone made it undesirable.

They lay between Graydonn and Sesína, Alísa's head on his chest. Falier shoved away thoughts of how perfectly she fit there, using the effort of pushing peace as a distraction. Darkness enveloped them as the dragons closed their eyes, and slowly Alísa's breathing evened. Finally, he ended his empathic work and allowed the dragons' continued push to lull him into slumber once again.

23

BETTER TO DIE

Pain shot through Kallar like a thousand lightning strikes as the keeper forced memory upon him. As his dagger plunged into Karn's chest, it burned through his hand, raced up his arm, and settled in his own heart, drawing a scream.

This isn't real. It already happened. It isn't real.

"It is real," the keeper hissed in his ear, the sound shivering through Kallar's bones. *"It will always be real. You killed him."*

Karn's eyes flashed in Kallar's vision. Wide. Shocked. In pain.

Flesh gave as the dagger plunged again.

"It wasn't me!"

"Yet you couldn't stop it."

Kallar strained, half in the astral realm and half in the physical, trying to break out of the keeper's grip. He could feel it under his skin, holding his muscles. The pain of his wounds still afflicted him. How long had he been like this? Hours? Days?

He threw his astral self at the dark form of the keeper, intent on wrestling it to the ground in hopes of one free breath.

The monster caught him by the throat. *"You cannot fight an eternal being. Dirt cannot defy those who walk on it."*

It hurled him down and pinned him, sending more images through Kallar's mind. Tents ablaze. Slayers fighting and dying. Triumphant cries of the an'reik. Betrayal in Karn's eyes.

Kallar shouted and writhed, trying to break free.

"Kal? Kal!"

The voice echoed through the space, drawing Kallar's gaze to the window. It was dark—his physical eyes shut—but the sound definitely came from beyond it.

"Kallar!"

R'lann.

With a shove, Kallar threw the keeper off him. It left too easily—somewhere in the back of his mind, he understood that—but the prospect of freedom overwhelmed his caution. He dove for the window, eyes opening as soon as he touched it.

Kallar gasped in a breath, sitting up. Fire flared across his side as his lungs expanded. R'lann gasped and pulled away.

"Whoa, easy!"

Kallar's stomach churned, pain clashing with the strain of his fight against the keeper. He twisted, dry-heaving away from R'lann, the motion tearing at his wound.

"Kallar, stop."

Kallar jumped as his brother touched his bare shoulder, twisting again despite the pain. The sixteen-year-old's eyes were wide with fear as he yanked his hand back.

"It's me. Just me. No one else is here."

The keeper chuckled at the irony. It sent Kallar's stomach churning again, but there was nothing to come up.

Breathe. Focus on what's around you.

He drew his legs up and laid his head on his knees. He was in a tent, dark with either night or dye. Only a small lamp lit the space, beside it a bag of medical supplies. A thin bed-mat barely cushioned him from the ground. His shirt was gone, but he wore the same pants and boots as during the battle. They smelled of blood and alcohol. R'lann's clothing was dirtier than before, and he had a tight bandage on his arm.

"You have to stop moving," R'lann said, calmer now. "You'll pull your stitches. I'm going to check your ribs and see if any need redoing, okay?"

Kallar's breath shuddered. R'lann was stitching him up. That likely meant the battle was only this morning. Focusing, Kallar could feel the wrappings around his ribcage. Funny how he hadn't noticed it before. He was off his game.

Of course I'm off my game—my body hasn't been mine for...I don't even know.

"It still isn't yours, dirt."

A new image flashed through his mind, forced by the keeper—Kallar grabbing R'lann's throat and crushing his windpipe.

"Everything is mine."

"No!" Kallar moved, throwing himself to the side as R'lann started undoing the bandage. He struck the tent's wall and the boulder that pinned it down. "Get out of here, now!"

R'lann stared at him, confused. "You need help. Let me——"

"Leave! Before it makes me kill you too!"

R'lann scooted forward. "I'm not afraid of you. You won't——"

"Flames, R'lann!" Kallar's voice hardly sounded like his own, panic pitching it higher. "It made me kill him! Get out!"

That made R'lann pause. The boy's brow wrinkled in confusion.

"Shall we show him?"

Pain lanced through Kallar's heart. Its pace quickened and his breaths became shallow. Cold sweat sprouted over his body as he tightened his muscles to try to keep control.

"Go!"

R'lann's face fell. "I can't. Even if this tent weren't guarded, I won't leave you."

More panic spiked through Kallar as the keeper grinned inside of him. "They want you alive, R'lann. Tell them I'm going to kill you and they'll let you out."

R'lann looked at his hands in his lap. "They *do* want me alive, so your keeper won't kill me. Even if they didn't care——"

Sorrow overtook his expression. "They made me watch. As they lined up the slayers who came to save me and one-by-one tried to possess them. As they burned all who wouldn't bow. As they killed Pa."

R'lann's voice cracked, and he cleared his throat. "I couldn't help him, but I can help you."

Kallar breathed through the panic. The keeper reveled in the feeling, feeding on it like it did other emotions, but it didn't take control. R'lann was safe.

"For the moment," it threatened, shoving the images through Kallar's mind again.

R'lann grabbed the bag and approached. Kallar shivered as he uncurled from his fetal position and let R'lann take off the bandage. Who was this person he had become? Pathetic. Terrified. Weak.

"Pa got the better end of the deal," Kallar mumbled as R'lann worked. "Better to die than be forced to obey them."

R'lann paused, then wiped at the blood around the ripped stitches. "Better to die than to bow. That's how it's always been with you."

Kallar winced at the sting of the alcohol. "What does that mean? You think I should let this—this *thing* have its way?"

"Maker forbid." R'lann pulled a needle and string from the bag. "But you're only here because you wouldn't bow to the Maker."

Kallar scoffed. This again. "If you're going to talk like Gia, I'd rather you not talk at all."

"There are higher powers than the Nameless Ones."

"Yet here you are, as trapped as I am."

"Indeed," a feminine voice said.

Kallar started, looking at the tent flap just as it opened. Isarra. He should have heard her footsteps outside—what was wrong with him?

"Sorry to interrupt. I simply wished to check on the heroes of the battle." Isarra knelt close by, directing her ever-smug smile at R'lann. "Your contribution worked exquisitely."

Contribution? R'lann hadn't been there…

His brother's hand went to the bandage on his opposite arm. The pain in his eyes made Kallar's heart rage. The magic that foretold when Karn would attack—she had used R'lann's blood.

Isarra gave Kallar a knowing look. "And you, first bringing us powerful allies, then crippling the enemy by killing one of their chiefs. I may just have to keep you both."

"When I'm free," Kallar snarled, "you'll be the first to die."

Isarra chuckled. "Free? Haven't you realized the true nature of a keeper?" She scooted forward, a light in her eyes like she was a young girl about to talk about her first crush. "The Nameless Ones are jealous for souls—they will literally pull themselves apart to gain them. You carry a piece of an Eldra, and you think to escape it? To dislodge its claws? You cannot."

"You cannot," the keeper said in tandem, growling its pleasure.

Kallar's stomach clenched. They were lying. There had to be a way. Every being had a weakness—dragons, humans—Eldír must have one, too. They had to be lying!

Isarra cooed in false sympathy. "I know. It's terribly uncomfortable. Frightening, even. Yet, you can relieve your suffering. I'll tell you a secret—they don't want your body. All they see is walking dirt. What they seek is your soul. Relinquish it, and your keeper will not only leave, it will fill the void with power—"

She raised a hand and dark mists seeped from it, swirling throughout the tent. R'lann stiffened, but the fear and pain had left his eyes. Now he looked like a wayfarer holding his shield at a cave's entrance, prepared for the flames coursing around him.

"—more power than you can imagine." Isarra closed her fist, and the darkness vanished. "Surely a slayer so driven can see it is a worthy trade."

Kallar stared her in the eyes. "I will die before I give it anything!"

Isarra's expression grew stony. "We'll see. Until then, you'll make a more than adequate lap dog." She stood and marched to the tent entrance. "With your power added to ours, we defeated three clans. Tomorrow morning, we march to finish the job."

Opening the flap, she looked back at him, moonlight painting her face a ghostly white. "Sleep well, my little Singer."

24

CHIEF

Alísa awoke with the knowledge her father was gone. No blissful moment of forgetfulness, no sudden lurch as she remembered her sorrows. Only a numb knowing.

She didn't want to face today. Didn't want to leave the safety of this dragon cocoon, or Falier's heartbeat under her head. She ran a finger over the seam of his tunic, letting the stitching ground her here.

"You're awake." Falier's voice was quiet in her mind. "Or did you even sleep?"

"I did, but I'm still exhausted. Is it morning?"

"I'm not sure. The dragons have us closed in tight."

Alísa listened for a moment. "It doesn't sound like there's much movement outside. And Sesína probably would have woken if the next shift came in."

Falier nodded, his short beard catching in her curls. "Don't take this the wrong way, but I thought you weren't coming until the final shift. What changed?"

Alísa shivered, and he held her tighter. "They said I needed sleep. The last refugees will arrive soon, then I must address them. Chief N'ravi sent the rest of us on ahead because—because we needed to mourn as well as rest."

Blinking back tears, Alísa pushed the grief away. She would continue to mourn, but she needed to be ready for everything that would happen today.

Falier must have caught that impression, because he didn't tell her she should let herself grieve. Instead, with a holder's grace, he pulled the topic elsewhere.

"I'm sure you've heard reports, but everyone here has done a great job keeping camp. Even Chief T'kan started helping, once he simmered down from the shock of it all. Between Vennia, Eskann, and the wayfarers' coin, we purchased enough food and supplies from the merchants to last us over a week. We have time to figure out what comes next."

"Good. Thank you—you have a good eye for such things."

Falier shrugged. *"Comes with my upbringing. Do you know how many flights remain before everyone's here?"*

"Only one or two. I'm proud of you all. Everyone pushing forward, helping each other. It would be cause for celebration, if not for…"

She swallowed. No, she couldn't start again. She needed to hold on to her courage, like they did.

"It still is worth celebrating," Falier said gently. *"Music in the storm, remember?"*

Her fingers curled against his shirt. *"I don't want the music! I want Papá!"*

Tears fell past her barrier as she buried her face in his shoulder. Falier wrapped both arms around her, regret edging in.

"I know. I'm sorry."

She stayed there, willing her breaths to steady. It was so difficult, getting back under control, especially after two days of reining everything in. Even their moments of sleep under the stars had required her and Mamá to keep up their guard. Grieving was acceptable, but heaving sobs would call to question their ability to make decisions. So they cried softly at night, then rose in stoicism.

Alísa didn't want to hold back again. She was safe here. In Falier's arms, she didn't have to think of wars, logistics, or responsibilities. She could simply feel and hurt.

But tonight would require more. She sniffed against her tears and tried to match her breaths to Sesína's. She traced the stitches in Falier's tunic again, focusing on the small bumps of thread.

"Mamá and L'non pulled me aside. They said that after Kallar supposedly died, they had to discuss the future of the wayfarers. Papá…" She breathed, willing herself to continue. *"They said he wanted me to—to be his heir again."*

Surprise flowed from Falier, though he didn't speak.

"I told Mamá I already have a clan and couldn't abandon them or split my time. That she or L'non should take over. But she said it was his hope I would unite the two clans."

She sniffled and wiped at her eyes. *"It wasn't supposed to happen this soon. But Papá knew the time of wayfarers was ending. Now that he's gone—it makes no sense to move backwards. We're telling everyone tonight."*

"And your ma and uncle agree?"

She nodded. *"They said they'd help. Between them, my current betas, and you, I know I have the support I need. I just—don't want to disappoint him."*

"You won't." Falier kissed her forehead. *"The Maker made you for this. Karn saw it, as have many others. Including me, though I'm incredibly biased."*

She forced a chuckle, but doubt still circulated within. The Maker may have designed her for this purpose, but recent events didn't seem to line up with his plans. Surely he would want the an'reik to fall. Instead, they defeated three united clans and killed her father.

By the hands of his former apprentice.

She pushed her anger aside. Now wasn't the time.

"Thank you. I'll need your help, especially with training up new riders. I spoke with N'ravi and he has agreed that dragon-rider pairs work best against this foe. Briek's men benefited greatly from your and Graydonn's teaching in Me'ran—can you do the same here?"

"Of course. I'm sure Graydonn will agree, too."

The ground shook with thuds that woke Sesína and Graydonn, who looked out with calm resignation. The next batch of refugees had arrived, just a couple of hours before sunrise. That meant Falier and Graydonn would have to leave soon, and she should check on Mamá and begin her day.

As she started rising, Falier drew her hand to his lips and kissed her knuckles.

"We're right behind you, chief."

His spoken words tickled her fingers, making them feel somehow more real in this moment than those spoken mind-to-mind or abstract thoughts of the Maker's failing plans.

"Thank you."

Growing up, Alísa had known many who perished in the war between humans and dragons. The deaths of her own clanmates—of Chrí, Sareth, Namor, and Faern—had been especially poignant. She had always taken comfort in the songweavers' words when they honored those who now resided in the Maker's halls. Their sacrifices gave others life. They were mourned, but also celebrated. To refuse to live the life someone died to protect was to dishonor their memory.

Now, as Farren sang to honor the dead, it all seemed hollow. To celebrate after her father's death was too much to ask. And yet, she did. Outside Vennia, at the edge of the wayfarers' camp, she echoed the words of blessing alongside Eskann, Vennia, and her own clans. She was not alone in feeling the difference. The ceremony was muted. Fear and strife bled into grief as slayers and villagers ate on the trampled grasses in the evening light. Wary eyes watched the dragons, who circled the gathering, silent and stoic.

They all needed hope and direction. Once Farren introduced her as chief, it would be her duty to give them that. She spent the whole day conferring with her betas, key wayfarers, and chiefs N'ravi and T'kan, developing the plan. She knew the required words, knew which emotions would rouse the warriors after such terrible defeat. But inside, she trembled.

She was supposed to bring peace, not rouse an army to war.

"You are the only human the dragons will listen to," Sesína said. Their connection hummed with the dragoness' reassurance. *"And you hold the treaties with the villages. You alone can call both races to fight."*

"But I'm not a warrior. At least, not like Papá or Bria. Who will trust a stammering eighteen-year-old to command an army?"

Sesína hummed. *"Remember what Bria herself said. The Maker made you enough for the tasks he set before you. You don't have to be Karn. You need to be you."*

Alísa shook her head, accidentally drawing her mother's eye. *"And what am I?"*

"Understanding. Compassionate. Strong-hearted. Brave. A Dragon Singer who has already brought multiple clans of multiple races together. And the only person in the entire world nearly as fabulous as me."

Alísa let out a breathy chuckle just as Hanah tapped her arm.

"It's time, love."

Fatigue lined Hanah's eyes, and the black mourning shawl over her shoulders made her appear more pale than she was.

On Alísa's other side, Falier took her hand and squeezed. "You've got this."

She returned the squeeze and stood, following her mother to the front of the gathering. L'non, Farren, Chief N'ravi, and Chief T'kan, too, pushed forward.

The people watched them, every face solemn. Alísa wiped her hands on her skirt. She knew she could lead them, but the thought of everyone's eyes on her still created a pit in her stomach. She had gained the wayfarers' respect these last months, but before that were years of dismissal. Years when she was merely the chief's daughter whose birthright was handed over to an apprentice.

An apprentice who then betrayed his master. Betrayed her. Betrayed every one of them. As she reclaimed her place, the rightness of the moment mixed with anxiety, grief, and rage.

Among the crowd, Tenza sat with Kallar's step-family. They all knew of Kallar's treachery now. Alísa wished she had words for them in their sorrow that surely matched her own, yet she did not.

Farren took the front, carrying a small bowl—the kind used to mix war-paint. The others stood side-by-side behind him, Alísa with her mother on one end, followed by L'non and the chiefs.

Farren lifted his free hand to the crowd. "Brothers and sisters. We have gathered to honor the dead. We remember them and encourage one another to live as they would have us live, even in our grief."

He paused, sorrow taking his features before he spoke again. "But a clan cannot stand on its own. The wayfarers have lost a great leader. Karn called us into a life of honor and danger, and he above all knew what it may cost. Now our beloved chief sits proudly in the Maker's halls, reunited with the warriors who went before him. Though our pain is near and our grief strong, a hole remains that must be filled. Therefore, I call Lady Hanah forward."

Hanah left her place in line to stand beside Farren as he continued.

"There is a tradition among the spouses of fallen chiefs. As a clan moves through a time of transition, the lady or tiern may choose to represent the former chief as their *anam nasctha*—their soul's voice. Lady Hanah has claimed this responsibility. Hanah" —he turned to her, eyes softening— "before the Maker and the clans, do you swear to continue serving the wayfarers in your new role?"

Nothing in Hanah wavered. "I swear it."

"Do you swear that when you claim Karn's name, you will speak for him and not yourself?"

"I swear it."

"And do you swear to guide the new chief with Karn's wisdom and strength?"

"I swear it."

Farren bowed his head, acknowledging Hanah's commitment, then dipped two fingers into the red war-paint. His tone turned lyrical. "Two souls bound by love and vow, even death cannot undo. Now, by her choice, the missing voice through her lips shall speak anew."

He placed his fingers under Hanah's bottom lip and dragged the paint down her chin in two close-knit lines. The color called to Alísa's mind the violence by which her father had been taken. Red had always been the chief's color—the color of sacrifice, a reminder of one's duty to serve their clan at any cost.

"Before these witnesses," Farren said, "I name you Karn's *anam nasctha*. For one year, you will speak on his behalf. Though the new chief shall claim ultimate authority, you will advise them, and the people will look to you for Karn's wisdom."

Hanah bowed her head, then looked to the gathered clans. "Upon what we thought the death of Karn's apprentice, the future of our clan became of utmost importance to Karn. We prayed for wisdom and sought counsel from our most trusted advisors." She indicated L'non and Farren. "In the end, only one answer satisfied us. With the war against the dragons shifting toward peace and the war against the an'reik beginning, Karn chose a slayer who knows intimately the balance of compassion and justice."

Eyes shifted to Alísa, some blank, some hopeful, and some uncertain or even confused. Some looked between her and L'non, as though expecting the former chief's second to stop this. L'non merely watched Hanah.

"Alísa Karns-daughter," Hanah said, "come forward."

Alísa breathed, envisioning the deep green of peace, and stepped up beside Hanah. She forced her head high. Confident. Assured. Ready. That was what they needed to see.

Farren approached with the bowl of war-paint. He looked on Alísa with the grandfatherly love that had always bolstered her. He had believed in her long before anyone else. With him, she discovered she didn't stammer when she sang, and learned to weave words into lyrics more easily than speech. Lyrics that eventually empowered dragons and set her on this path. She needed to tell him that one day.

Farren spoke loudly. "Alísa, daughter of Karn, Dragon Singer. Before the Maker and the clans, do you swear to claim the wayfarers as your own, welcoming them into your ranks with no partiality between them and your current clan?"

Wayfarers glanced around—some at clanmates, others to the dragons and riders. Alísa forced herself to look at them rather than at Farren. These promises were for them.

"I swear it."

"Do you swear to protect them as your family, acting for their good and never for their harm, to the best of your ability?"

"I swear it."

Farren smiled. "Do you swear to fight for them with the strength given you by the Maker and his Eldír, and guide them by the wisdom they teach?"

"Yes," she said, returning her gaze to Farren. "I swear it."

He dipped a finger into the bowl of paint, and Alísa closed her eyes as he drew a crowning mark across her brow.

"Then, by the authority the Maker has given me" —he painted a second line underneath the first— "I name you Karn's successor. Chief Alísa, born of slayers, lifted by dragons, blessed by dreki, chosen by the Maker."

Chosen. Eldra Bria's words echoed over Alísa in her mind. *The Maker has made you enough for this task.* Yet despite Farren's blessing before the battle— despite their certainty that standing against the an'reik was the Maker's will— they had failed. Where did that leave her now?

Farren backed away and placed his fist over his heart. "May you lead your peoples well."

The charge settled on Alísa's shoulders like a winter cloak—weighty, unyielding, and right. Her breath shuddered silently as she looked back out at her clan. Even if she wasn't sure she trusted the Maker's plan for her would succeed, she would do right by them.

Alísa let the clan's emotions flow to her unhindered, searching for what they needed. Even with those who opposed her chiefdom fouling the astral air, grief remained the greatest—some of it sharp and piercing, but much of it numb and lifeless.

Give them hope and direction.

"Brothers and sisters of all races, I know the p-p-pain you bear. Today carries no joy for me, for we have lost many g—g—g" —*Breathe. Redirect.*— "noble warriors. My heart bleeds with yours, for my father—"

Her voice cracked as her throat closed around the word.

Breathe. Just breathe.

"—my father is gone. K-k-k-killed by the traitor Kallar."

Tears fell as the words made the pain fresh, her chest constricting. At Kallar's name, some looked up, eyes burning with shared anger. Good. Anger would push them forward.

"But though we grieve, we must remember what our loved ones died to accomplish, and what remains for us to do. We have a p-powerful enemy that would see our world darkened. They p-p-prey on the innocent and d—devour those who dare stand against them. But we are warriors. Branni's p-p-people"—she looked at the dragons, who did not claim the Eldír as their guides—"c-called by the Maker to fight for the physical and spiritual good of our c-c-c-country. We will not back down!"

More and more gazes fixed on Alísa. For once, the attention didn't frighten her. As her chiefdom settled around her, the eyes of her people were her strength.

"T-today, the leaders before you held a war council. Faced with this threat, w—we have formed an alliance. Together, we shall draw the line against the an'reik, and we will not d—do it alone."

At this, L'non stepped forward, lending his voice and, hopefully, the confidence of the wayfarers. "Over the past couple of months, Alísa and Karn established peace treaties among both human villages and dragon clans in the area. Now we shall return to them with news of this threat. Both races have reason to hate and fear the an'reik. With the respect and trust Alísa has already gained from them, we will raise an army like none this country has seen—humans, dragons, and dreki, united."

Chief N'ravi of Eskann stepped up alongside L'non. "We are not naïve. It will require time to train and prepare. During that time, the an'reik will probably follow us, infecting villages along the way as they did L'rang. Therefore, while Chief Alísa calls to her allies, we shall send riders to warn of the danger and encourage people to evacuate."

Chief T'kan of Vennia came forward, completing the united line of leaders. "We will set up a war camp ten miles south of here, with Vennia open to take in more refugees. We will also establish other villages of safety for the evacuees heading westward."

Alísa took in a deep, low breath. It fell to her to finish. Knowing that louder volume caused more stammering, she formed her words deliberately. Though all else failed them, she would not.

"It will not be easy. B—but we are p-p-peoples forged by war. Where once we wielded sword and spear, t-tooth and flame against each other, now we shall join them against our t-t-true foes! Together, we shall make the enemy tremble!"

Taking her cue, Sesína snarled her agreement, the other dragons following her example. Many villagers cringed and looked back at the dragons, but they also witnessed the riders standing to join their dragon partners' war-cries.

"Though fire b—burns, our souls' flame shall burn brighter!"

More affirmations—dragons growling, dreki barking, men and women of the other clans now rising to their feet. Alísa latched onto her anger, knowing it would call others to action.

"Though t-t-traitors rise, we will not be moved!"

Slayers shouted against those working alongside the an'reik, and a few threw curses at Kallar. She breathed in their rage, letting it fuel her past her stammer in a final shout.

"Though darkness falls, we shall fight to see the sunrise!"

The crowd erupted in a joint battle-cry. Dragons pumped their wings and snarled. Dreki jumped into the air, swirling around each other in a dance of war. Beside Alísa, L'non thrust his fist high.

"Fight!"

Karn's men echoed his call, followed by the rest of the warriors. He called out again, the entire crowd taking up the echo this time. The air resounded with their battle-cries and the astral plane rocked with righteous anger and determination. Alísa and the other chiefs joined L'non on the shout, her voice calling the dragons' roars louder.

On the fourth call, L'non took the paint bowl from Farren. Alísa's heart thudded as he drew more lines on her face, one under her right eye and two under her left in the full battle-markings she rarely saw.

L'non thumped his fist to his chest as the shouts died out.

"We are yours to command, Chief Alísa."

25

TRAITORS, SHEEP, & WOLVES

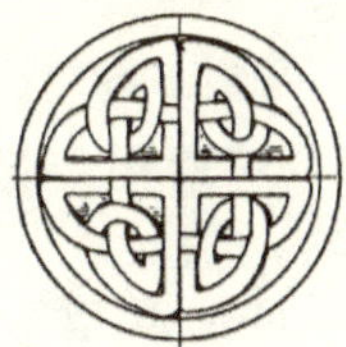

Eskann was empty. The quaint village was never as bustling as L'rang, but it had been alive. Now, with abandoned homes and fallen belongings scattered on the paths, it felt long dead. The only signs of life remaining were the abandoned livestock—some cows and sheep. Kallar would have expected the owners to take them, or at least set them free. They must have been terrified as they ran.

What was he thinking? Of course, they were terrified. He hadn't seen how many survived the battle, but the an'reik had soundly defeated Eskann's slayers, along with the now-chiefless wayfarers.

"We will rest here tonight," Isarra announced. She looked back at the an'reik and their allied slayers. "Enjoy the hospitality of the traitors who have followed the Dragon Singer. We'll continue after them in the morning."

"'Traitors'?" L'rang's slayer chief said, arms crossed. "A harsh simplification. Most of the villagers are normals. They are sheep following N'ravi, not sworn to the Dragon Witch."

Isarra considered him, face smooth in a haughty look Kallar now knew as dangerous. Then she smiled. "Of course. And we shall rescue all we can. But our army is growing. We need rest and food if we are to save them. So, as I said, enjoy their hospitality. Take what beds you will, eat your fill, and note supplies that will travel well."

"So we're to steal from them?"

Another slayer scoffed. "Calm down, old man. It's the same as if the wayfarers came through their village."

L'rang's chief narrowed his eyes. "No. The Hold manages those supplies, giving them out only once every couple of years."

"I don't see any holders."

Kallar remained silent as they bickered. Adding his opinion was pointless, even if the keeper allowed it. Speak for taking the food, and he would be on Isarra's side. Speak against it, and the others would call him out for hypocrisy. As a wayfarer, he lived off the donations of the villages.

Isarra rolled her eyes exaggeratedly. "I will not have my allies dropping dead from hunger as we march. We'll take what we need and decide how to repay Eskann after we destroy the Dragon Singer. Sleep under the stars if you must—I'm finding myself a room."

She eyed Kallar, then waved him off. "Go, make yourself useful."

Useful? As if.

"She wasn't talking to you."

Kallar shivered as though the keeper had whispered in his ear. The sudden movement set his side-wound throbbing. It didn't hurt much today, likely due to whatever nasty concoction Isarra and the keeper force-fed him this morning. He didn't want to know what such a potion might contain.

"Go," the keeper said, *"mingle with your fellow slayers."*

"Why?"

Rather than answer, the keeper moved. Kallar's body stiffened as it stretched into his limbs, leaving him conscious but controlled. This was worse than being forced back inside his psyche. He struggled to wrap a choke around the monster, but it ripped the power in two like a thin sheet. Kallar's cry of pain reverberated only within his mind.

"You will learn not to question me, dirt."

His body moved, muscles stretching and contracting in feelings both familiar and foreign. They passed into the crowd. Kallar estimated that the slayers' numbers nearly doubled the an'reik—warriors of L'rang, the deserted Karns-men and Tellas-men, and some he didn't recognize. There were perhaps thirty an'reik and over fifty slayers. If he could somehow turn the slayers against their dark allies, they might stand a chance.

"Kallar?"

The keeper spun them toward the voice. It took a second to recognize the speaker in the dark. Harrík—a Karns-man who had deserted with Tern. The moment Kallar identified him, the keeper pulled up memories. Conversations, sparring matches, battles—all raced past Kallar's eyes at a dizzying rate.

"When did you arrive?" Harrík asked, coming toward him. "I haven't seen you in camp."

The keeper thrust his arm forward to clasp his traitorous former clanmate's. Kallar tried to fight as his mouth moved to speak.

"Couple weeks ago. I've been in the an'reik camp, honing my new powers."

Harrík stiffened. "New powers?"

Kallar raged within himself. *What are you doing?! I'm not an'reik!*

The keeper ignored him. "You heard the report of the an'reik's Dragon Singer?"

That drew more eyes. Harrík released his arm.

"You?"

Kallar's face smirked. "The Nameless Ones granted me the same power as Alísa. With it, I've summoned my own army of dragons and used them against our enemies." He looked around at the others—slayers with mixtures of disgust and awe on their faces. "A useful tool as long as we need them. I trust you all will be ready to slaughter them once we're finished."

That changed some of the disgust to begrudging respect. The keeper continued to talk as it pushed them through the crowd toward a small home.

"I'm sure many of you wonder whether the trade for these powers is worth it. Watch me and see."

Slayer and an'reik alike parted for him. A torch-lit sea of traitors, sheep, and wolves—all eyes on him. The keeper took him inside the house and shut the door without another word, leaving the slayers wanting more and Kallar in utter darkness.

26

COMPROMISE

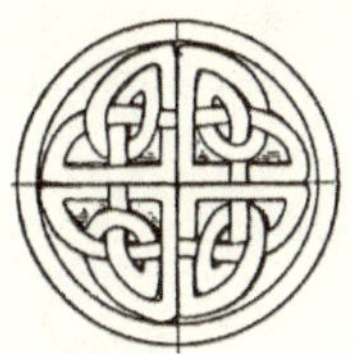

The flight to Bezin was quiet. Alísa didn't much want to chat, nor did the rest of her party. Their grief was too raw. But as Sesína, Graydonn, and Koriana landed on the hill just outside their allied village, Alísa reined in her sorrows. Though the winds played in her hair and skirts, they were not strong enough to wipe away tears as they formed. She would have to hold back her grief until the return flight.

Riders slid from the dragons' backs. L'non practically jumped from behind Briek, more than ready to touch the ground again. Koriana and Graydonn settled to their bellies, looking out over the village.

"Are you sure these are slayers you trust, Singer?" Koriana asked.

"As much as I can. They hold no love for the an'reik. Lorin is a powerful chief, and his men skilled warriors. If they accept our call to fight, others will follow."

Koriana still didn't seem convinced, but she folded one taloned paw over the other and quieted.

Alísa checked herself—clothing smoothed, sword at her side, Papá's scale on her wrist. Today, she was a slayer.

"Let's go."

Falier, Briek, L'non, and Sesína fell in behind her. Alísa wasn't ready to bring giants like Koriana into Bezin, and Graydonn always appeared ill-at-ease among strange slayers. Still, the slayers needed to adjust to dragons if they were going to ride into battle alongside her clan. Sesína's presence seemed an appropriate place to start.

Already, three warriors ran toward them with drawn weapons. Alísa felt Briek and L'non tense, ready to defend if need be, but the slayers slowed as they recognized Alísa and her people. She lifted a hand in greeting.

"P-peace, friends. The dragons are mine." She halted before reaching the village-bound slayers. "I w—would speak to Lorin. We bring d—d—d—dreadful news."

Now seven strong, the slayers exchanged looks. One at the front cleared his throat.

"Of course, Dragon Singer. We can take you to him, but your dragons must remain outside Bezin."

Alísa lifted her chin to meet his eyes. "The others will wait, but Sesína stays with me."

He shook his head as another slayer backed him up. "No dragons."

Falier came up beside her and, though his mind quaked, spoke forcefully. "Who are you to deny a chief?"

Where had that come from? Alísa placed a quieting hand on his arm and breathed, drawing strength from her memories of her father and Eldra Bria.

"Lorin has established p-p-p-peace with my c-clan. You would g—go against your chief's word and reject my lieutenant?"

The slayer's eyes narrowed. "I will not be the one to bring a beast into our home."

Alísa looked past him. "Then step aside for your chief."

He blinked and twisted to see what Alísa already had. Lorin strode from the village and into the grasses, his men parting for him. He wore his sword, but left it sheathed. He eyed Sesína, then studied the others.

"Where is Karn?"

Even expected, the words hit like a physical blow. Sesína pushed courage through their bond, helping to keep Alísa's tears at bay. Alísa's preparatory breath was too loud as sorrow grasped at her throat.

"My father is dead. K-k-k-killed by his traitorous apprentice in service to the an'reik." Her anger rose with the words, fueling her past her grief. "I am chief now, and I have much to discuss with you."

Lorin's face slackened before he caught himself. He glanced at L'non, seeking confirmation. It was an annoying habit of his, looking past her. It made Alísa want to both shrivel and fight.

"Normally, I would say fight," Sesína whispered through their bond, a growl in her tone. *"But seeing as we need allies, perhaps a middle ground is in order."*

Alísa breathed low and deep, straightening as she did. "Shall we speak here, or w—would you p-p-p-prefer within the village?"

Lorin looked at her again, eyes calculating. Then he raised his hand to his heart with an open palm. "I am sorry for your loss, Chief Alísa." He nodded to her uncle. "Slayer L'non. Karn was the greatest of us."

"Yes," L'non said, his voice gruffer than normal. "He was."

"Come." Lorin turned, gesturing toward Bezin. "I will hear what you have to say."

Alísa started forward, taking position alongside Lorin. Everyone else fell in behind them, Falier staying close. Lorin glanced back to see Sesína among them, but said nothing.

He guided them through the village to the slayers' quarter. Most villages in the west housed slayers in their own section, apart from the normals. Such separation gave the normals a sense of security. The slayers' code dictated telepathy never be used on other humans, but many normals preferred distance, regardless.

Lorin brought them inside a large stone facility built for training in the wet seasons. Weapons hung from hooks and pegs pounded into the spaces between stones. Their gleam alongside the gray rock made the space cold and impersonal, nothing like the warmer wooden buildings of the east. Here, the only wood was the benches lining the walls, where slayers would await their turn to spar.

"The dragon will be fine outside?"

Alísa met Lorin's eyes again, already drained by the constant need to show authority. "Sesína requires an open window. She is one of my seconds and we will include her in this meeting."

Sesína's eyes brightened as Lorin regarded her. Alísa caught the impression that she desperately wanted to grin with all her teeth visible, but she kept that desire at bay. With the village-bound slayers' shields up, only Alísa's people heard Sesína's sarcasm.

"If you would be so kind."

Lorin gestured to one of his men, who unlatched the panes of the largest window and opened them outward. Sesína took her place and Alísa crossed to the bench nearest the window. Every time Lorin looked at her, he would also see a dragon.

The slayers, one of whom Alísa now recognized as Lorin's second-in-command Amarr, pulled benches from the walls and brought them into a circle with hers. Falier sat beside her, Briek next to him and L'non on Alísa's opposite side. Once everyone settled, Lorin leaned forward, elbows on his knees.

"Tell me of Karn's death."

Alísa caught herself pressing her lips together against the emotions. She did not wish to speak of it, but leaving it to another would give Lorin yet another reason to look to someone else. This was a burden she must bear.

Quietly, she told of the an'reik in L'rang and of Kallar's supposed death, the story raising the ire of Lorin and his men. Their reactions emboldened her as she told of the joint assault to free L'rang, then of Kallar's betrayal.

Lorin shook his head. "But Kallar was the one to kill Tsorr while everyone else waited! How could he turn so suddenly and completely?"

Alísa fisted her hands in her lap, her own anger overcoming the pain of the memory. "I d—don't know, but I was with my father when he died, our minds t-t-touching. I felt it all. The p-pain, the betrayal, the deep sorrow. It was Kallar. And there are others, t-t-t-traitorous slayers who have aligned with the an'reik."

With a grunt, Lorin stood and paced. "So other villages have fallen to tricks similar to Tsorr's. This is grave indeed. We must send messengers to the other villagers, warning them of their lies."

"It's already done," Alísa said, "but the situation is m—more dire than mere falsehoods. The an'reik march. They have assimilated, d—driven out, or k-k-k-killed all of L'rang and Eskann's slayers. Now they come for my c-c-clan and our allies."

Lorin nodded. "It is a hard truth you bring, Karns-daughter. Many of us believe you are trying to change the world too quickly. In the ensuing chaos, evil thrives."

Alísa blinked. Had she heard that correctly?

"*Yes.*" Sesína growled, drawing the eyes of Lorin and his men. "*You did.*"

Alísa breathed, working to douse the rising flame inside of her. "It is a hard truth, but necessary to save the lives of c-countless innocent humans and dragons. With such stakes, no change can be t-too quick."

"Of course," Lorin said. "But even you must admit the an'reik kept to the shadows until you returned."

Alísa shot to her feet. "Are those who bring good t-t-t-to blame when evil retaliates? Three armies f—fight each other, and when two find peace it is their fault that the third still k-k-kills?"

Falier stood up beside her. "Right, you can't blame us for evil people doing evil things."

Again, so quick to stand and speak, though his words did little to help. Lorin's jaw tensed, eying Falier before settling on Alísa.

"It is more like you closed a gaping wound without first cleansing it. The bleeding stops, but infection festers and threatens the entire body."

"Ah yes," Briek said dryly, "metaphors make far more sense than the actual events."

"Do not forget, Lorin," L'non said, the quiet intensity of his tone silencing the room, "who it was that alerted you to the infection in your own village. You attack us, you attack him."

That gave Lorin pause. His respect for Karn collided with Alísa's grief, together cooling her rising temper. She let out a silent breath. She needed people willing to work with her, not necessarily ones who fully agreed with her. Relaxing the tension in her shoulders, she reset her stance—tall, but not aggressive.

"Regardless of why," she spoke quietly, taking a cue from L'non, "the an'reik move. I and my c-c-clan will fight them for the sakes of all *anam*, human and d—dragon alike. B—but we cannot win alone. You and your warriors are strong. P-please, join us in protecting our peoples."

Lorin frowned, scrutinizing her. Alísa tried to sense his emotions, but he and his slayers all held tight shields. Their faces gave little away.

Finally, Lorin spoke. "I must confer with my men."

"Of course."

Alísa looked at her people, who stood and followed her out. The chilly autumn air felt so much more free. Alísa hadn't realized how stifling the training building was.

"Well, I won't be sad if he says no." Sesína snorted steam as she trotted up. *"Can you believe him?"*

Briek crossed his arms. "Now, Sesína, who would we roll our eyes at without him?"

"You're not helping," L'non said, eying Briek. "We need every clan we can get. We don't have to like him to fight together."

"Enemy of my enemy," Alísa whispered half to herself. "I know he has no love for the an'reik."

Looking around the square, Alísa caught village-bound slayers watching from windows and small conversational groups. Most eyes were on Sesína, some less welcoming than others, but the dragoness didn't notice, more interested in inwardly mocking L'non's rebuke.

Falier stepped up beside her. *"You did well in there. I'm sorry I didn't add much."*

Alísa took his hand, feeling his tension through their skin-contact. He was right, his words hadn't helped either time, but he was trying hard for her.

"Your presence adds plenty."

The door to the training building opened and Lorin led his confidants out. He glanced about at the people as he strode past Alísa and her party to stand in the center of the square.

"Brothers and sisters," he said, his voice booming so even those indoors could hear. "The dark one who arrived in our village last month did not act alone. A shadow moves across our world—an army of an'reik who would see us fall to their dark arts."

As slayers filed from their homes, Lorin became more animated, fueled by his people. He pointed, sweeping his finger across the filling square.

"Many of you have asked me where we stand without dragons to fight. Now the Maker has given us a new task. Give yourselves to training with the sword, for soon we march alongside the wayfarers to war against the an'reik!"

Alísa grinned as shouts of agreement and even excitement rose from the warriors. She had allies!

Lorin turned to Alísa as one of his lieutenants walked off and began calling orders. Amarr stayed at his side.

"We will not allow the servants of the Nameless to walk freely among the villages," Lorin said. "If you need help to convince other chiefs, I offer my aid."

Alísa nodded graciously. "Thank you."

"Let us talk logistics. When do we march, and where shall we gather?"

March. Sword-training. Alísa began catching up to Lorin's words and realized he had gotten a bit too far ahead. Now she had to rein him back in without losing momentum.

"I would have you join with my c-c-clan soon—tomorrow morning, if p-possible."

"Tomorrow?" Amarr narrowed his eyes. "I understood your camp was far east of here."

Alísa nodded. "We have established a w—war-camp outside Vennia. We can fly your men easily enough." Amarr's jaw worked, so Alísa focused on Lorin. "As dragon clans ally themselves as well, I and m—my riders will train you to work with them—"

"Dragon clans." Lorin crossed his arms. "You would have us ride the beasts into battle?"

Sesína snorted beside Alísa. *"I am no mere beast."*

But Lorin's shield was still up. Alísa touched Sesína's wither.

"They are not beasts. They are souls, like you. The an'reik are your c-c-common foe."

Lorin glanced between them, then nodded. "Yes, so you've said. It may indeed be true, but I and my men have spent our lives fighting dragons. The trust required to ride won't come easily, nor can we afford to lay down our weapons in desperate times. Surely you see that taking slayers into the air only takes away a warrior."

His condescending tone again rankled her. Alísa breathed in the breeze and imagined it transforming to the deep green of peace within her. L'non was wise—showing her ire would not help.

"We have found the opposite. D—dragon-rider pairs may cover less ground at a t-t-t-time, but they are stronger together. Many an'reik p-p-powers are most dangerous on the ground, so slayers on dragonback are better protected. Likewise, the slayers' mind-shields psychically protect the dragons. Eskann and V—Vennia have both agreed to ride."

"A decent defense, I grant you," Lorin said, "but merely protecting ourselves will only get us so far. We need to wipe these demons out. By making slayers ride, you take away all weapons but their minds. No. My men will fight as they know best—boots on the ground and weapons in-hand. Some may die, but this is war. They understand the cost."

Before Alísa could respond, L'non touched her arm. "Chief. If we could speak?"

Alísa's heart squeezed. 'Chief' in L'non's voice had always meant her father, not her.

She shook off the sorrow. Later.

"Excuse us a moment, Lorin."

The chief stepped back in acquiescence, his second watching her with eyes like daggers. Alísa led her people to the training building, stopping just outside the door.

"Yes, Uncle?"

L'non rubbed his chin. "I understand what you're trying to do. But Lorin has a point—his men are proficient on the ground. I believe you could provide some training, but" —he looked to Briek— "how long did it take you before you felt comfortable on dragonback?"

Briek glanced at Alísa, a slight guilt in his eyes. "A couple weeks before I didn't constantly think I would fall. Over a month for true battle proficiency."

Falier shook his head. "We took it slowly because we could. We'll be training much faster this time."

Alísa nodded sharply. "Yes. I know this will work."

"Alísa," L'non said, his tone that of her uncle rather than her second, "maybe some can change that quickly, but not all. The wayfarers will follow you, but other clans—dragons, too, I'd wager—will protest, even to the point of staying behind."

Something within Alísa cracked—a hope perhaps too fragile to hold so tightly. The idea of dragon-rider pairs carried more for her than just the safety of her warriors. It held the possibility of true peace, of slayers and dragons having to trust each other. The camaraderie of combat would build a bridge between them. Without it, would the races return to fighting? Would she have to continue reaching villages and caves one at a time and praying the peace held?

"Much as I enjoy disagreeing with L'non," Sesína said, *"he has a point. Eskann and Vennia will ride. We can still build a bridge with them."*

Alísa nodded to herself, a new plan forming. "Maybe there's another way to recruit at least some of Lorin's slayers."

She returned to Lorin, head high. "There is w—wisdom in your words. We will present a united front, with d—dragons in the sky and slayers on the ground."

Lorin smiled. "You are wise yourself, Karns-daughter."

Karns-daughter. Her love and respect for her father collided with how Lorin said it. As though she were only a valuable ally because she held her father's clan.

She pushed the ire away. Her next words would reveal her distinction from Karn.

"However, my p-point regarding the strength of dragon-rider pairs stands. Therefore, I suggest a c-c-compromise."

Lorin raised an eyebrow, but Alísa lifted her chin, undeterred.

"We c-cannot wait for slayers to march to the war-camp. The distance is great, and we must p-p-prepare together. Therefore, you will ride dragons to c-camp, t-t-t-turning your days-long journey into hours. Then you and your men—and all other c-c-clans—will watch the riders t-t-train for two days. After that, each warrior shall m—make their own decision to work t-t-together or separately. Fair?"

She reached out a hand, distinctly feeling her betas behind her. Without looking, she knew the light quirk in L'non's lips, Briek's smug arm-cross, Falier's hidden grin, and Sesína's eye-brightening. If Lorin refused her offer and marched his men for a week instead, he would appear flippant about the evil walking their lands. And by the way his jaw clenched, he knew it.

Lorin considered her outstretched arm, then took it. His clasping was hard enough to bruise, but Alísa could only smile.

Victory.

"No!" Amarr rounded him, his jaw set. "Lorin, don't do this. Non-aggression toward certain dragons is one thing, but riding them, even for a day, is something I cannot abide!"

Lorin turned from Alísa to face him. "This is not up for debate, Amarr. We must travel quickly if we are to have any chance to prepare."

Alísa's heart stuttered as Amarr's hand fell to his sword's hilt.

"Do not make me do this, Lorin. We cannot fight for the Maker by accepting his enemies."

"We're not his enemies," Falier said, exasperated, "or yours! If you would just—"

Alísa shot him a quieting look just as Lorin held up a hand. Lorin's voice lowered to where Alísa could barely hear it.

"Alísa and her people have proven their allegiance by fighting the an'reik. I've no love for the dragons either, but though they may be *our* enemies again when this is over, they are not the Maker's. Stand down."

Amarr searched Lorin's face, then let out a breath.

"You force my hand."

Alísa backed away as Amarr drew his sword. He pulled it from its sheath quickly, its ring echoing through the square and drawing eyes. Alísa's people fell back with her, Falier beside her with wide eyes.

"Brothers!" Amarr shouted. "There's something Lorin didn't tell you. In order to fight alongside the wayfarers, we must entrust ourselves to dragons. Must ride them to camp and watch them train with the traitorous slayers who have chosen to ride them in battle! Deny it, Lorin!"

"It is interesting who you label as traitor, Amarr," Lorin said, squinting at his second. He lifted his voice. "I do not deny it."

That changed some expressions among the slayers, though Alísa couldn't tell if it was because of the dragons, or Amarr's obvious intentions.

"I will not stand for it!" Amarr spat. "The Maker will not stand for it! I challenge you, Lorin, for leadership of this clan. Because you dare to lead them astray, you are no longer fit to command them."

Lorin drew his sword. "So be it."

Amarr didn't hesitate. He lunged, the clang of steel reverberating through the village. Falier grasped Alísa's hand, the buzz of psychic connection coming with it.

"If Amarr wins—surely the clan won't just follow him, will they?"

Alísa's heart thudded as Lorin took a glancing blow on the arm. *"Those who agree with him will. Those who are indifferent too, most likely. Those who agree with Lorin might still join us."*

"Only might?"

Alísa couldn't tear her eyes from the fight. *"Slayer clans are family—in spirit, if not in blood. Some would rather die than see that family torn apart. If Amarr wins the chiefdom, we have lost this village."*

Amarr sidestepped a blow from Lorin, then pulled in close, his off-hand pulling a dagger. Karn's death flashed before Alísa's eyes, and though it was cowardly, she shut them. Metal rang and someone thudded to the ground. Tears welled. Heart pounded.

Papá.

"Yield."

Lorin's voice. Alísa opened her eyes to see the chief standing over his second, sword pointed at Amarr's throat. Amarr's weapons lay too far away to grab.

Amarr breathed heavily. "I cannot."

Lorin pushed the point closer. "Think of your children, Amarr."

"I would not have them live with the shame of a cowardly father."

"Not a coward." Lorin's tone and expression softened, revealing something that still lived despite treachery. "Take them and go. Reject what you deem heresy and start anew elsewhere. Do not harm your family by making me kill you."

Again, the tears welled. Sesína set her chin on Alísa's shoulder and breathed slowly. In. And Out. Alísa focused on the pattern. In. And Out.

Finally, Amarr relented. Lorin let him stand, then announced his banishment to the crowd. One of Lorin's other lieutenants came forward to escort Amarr to his home, refusing to let him retrieve his weapons. Lorin held his sword out, point toward the sky.

"Will anyone else challenge me?"

It seemed the village did not breathe. Lorin sheathed his blade. "As you were. Tomorrow we fly to the war-camp, from which we will *march* to war."

Alísa jumped as Lorin's eyes suddenly turned to her, hard and cold. He lowered his voice. "I have lost my best warrior and a friend today because of you. Remember that."

Alísa couldn't speak, her throat closed with emotion, but Lorin did not appear to want a reply. Taking a handkerchief from his pocket, he pressed the cloth to the wound on his arm. His tone became more pleasant as he looked to L'non.

"I expect your people at sunrise. We will be ready."

L'non did not respond as Lorin pivoted and left. Alísa let out a breath. She held no words, only a trembling heart. After a silent moment, Briek approached her.

"This is a victory, chief. The weight of this clan is Lorin's to bear, not yours."

L'non nodded sharply. "It's practically tradition that the village chiefs test the chief of the wayfarers. Lorin's predecessor made many petty demands of Karn before learning to respect him." His eyes glazed with memory before he cleared his throat and returned to her. "Ultimately, you've gained an ally, and created a chance to get those extra riders you want. I'd say you're following in his footsteps well."

This time, Alísa breathed back the tears on her own. "Thank you, Uncle."

27

ARGUMENTS

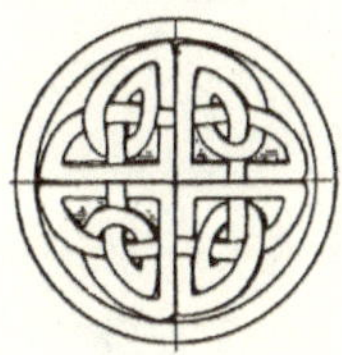

Falier had hoped that working with slayers in the sky—his domain—would be easier than on the sparring grounds. He had never been so wrong.

It had been five days since the clans started arriving at the war-camp. For the first two, Falier, Graydonn, and two other experienced dragon-rider pairs had worked with the wayfarers, Eskann, and Vennia, Alísa and Sesína supervising. After that, the dragons and slayers who completed their required days of watching could participate. However, not all who joined wanted to be there—some merely followed their chief's orders. And the wayfarers, who made up the majority of the three squads under Falier's supervision, didn't appreciate taking orders from a former holder and his pet dragon.

"Squad one," Falier said, *"ascend."*

Dezra and Rassím led the squad, the other dragons following. Unlike the slayers, most of the dragons obeyed willingly, having taken riders because they trusted the Dragon Singer. Even those here only at their alpha's command were rarely insubordinate.

Falier and Graydonn circled their trainees, banking lazily to watch them all. Falier's gaze was constantly drawn to Hwinn and Selene in squad two. They had decided they were needed in this war, and it made Falier's heart quake.

As soon as squad one flew high enough, Falier reached out again. *"Squad two, bank left and take their position."*

One slayer swore as his mount banked, not ready for the turn. Falier reached out to see if he was alright, but hit a wall. Shielded. Falier looked at Trísse and Komi at the front.

"Tern is shielded again." He sought the others in her squad. *"As are Varek and Rassi. Three out of six!"*

Falier hadn't meant for that last statement to reach her, but his frustration kept his thoughts flowing. Trísse's own ire returned to him.

"I warned you, I'm not used to this! Alísa has been teaching me to use my empathy as a weapon, but I have barely any control over Komi's telepathic connections."

Komi sent an apology. *"And I've been focusing on the dragons' physicality, not telepathy."*

Falier blew out a breath. *"I know. I didn't mean to yell. I'm not angry at you. I'll take care of the current problem, but please try to keep a better eye on them. This won't work if they don't open themselves to telepathic communication."*

Trísse and Komi sent back affirmatives.

Falier grabbed onto Graydonn's power. *"Get ready, there might be backlash."*

Falier steeled himself along with Graydonn. He didn't want to be harsh, but sometimes a situation called for it. He was a slayer now.

Shields broke with Falier's three psychic arrows, drawing cries of surprise, then indignant rage.

"What in hellflames was that?!" Varek shouted, his mental voice throbbing with pain.

"I told you," Falier said, trying to maintain an even tone, *"fighting on dragonback requires constant communication with your partner and squad-mates. You won't survive without it."*

"It's the code, holder boy," Tern hissed. *"True slayers keep their minds closed to protect others. But you know nothing about that, growing up a barkeep."*

"We're training for battle, not wandering a village!" Falier snapped. *"If you truly care about protecting people, you will connect to your partners to communicate plans and dangers. I had hoped you and Rassi would at least respect Trísse enough to listen."*

Tern's mind grew hot. *"I respect her by staying out of her head!"*

Falier pulled at the threads of the squad-link, connecting them to the others. *"Why don't you ask your squad leader what she wants?"*

Trísse sent an air of authority and reprimand. Shockingly, that quieted Tern. Rassi, meanwhile, squirmed.

"So we're supposed to just sit here while the dragons do all the work?"

"No," Trísse said with a know-it-all older sister tone, *"you're supposed to be listening to your dragon partner, leaning with their turns, and learning how not to die."*

"Once your squad gains proper flight skills and communication" —Falier emphasized that word— *"then we'll move on to telepathic combat."*

"We already understand that," Varek scoffed. *"We've been fighting psychically our whole lives."*

"Right," Falier said, *"only now you'll be flying, which takes more focus. You'll also be protecting not only yourself, but your dragon partner—more psychic ground to cover. Believe me, it's harder."*

Tern sneered. *"What do you know about what's harder?"*

Falier rolled his eyes. *"Right, you got me. I've never stormed a cave before. I have worked with other slayers, though. I know what they struggled to learn."*

"Then why isn't one of them training us?" Tern pointed up at squad one. *"Like that guy with the knives? He seems knowledgeable."*

"Oh, give it a rest," Trísse growled. *"You're just upset because the newcomer knows more than you. Your chief set him over us. Get over it."*

Falier rubbed his neck. Not the best way to win respect, but he wouldn't contradict her. Trísse's words had worked, the slayers chagrined and the dragons wisely remaining out of the conversation.

Selene and Hwinn sent peace to Falier, but it didn't help the frustration. All he could do was redirect his focus back to the training. But flames, why did Alísa have to assign him the wayfarers? Didn't she realize what a hard time he had connecting with them already?!

No, she didn't, because he acted like everything was alright. Falier took in a long breath. He could do this. He *could* do this.

The final hour brought another bout of insubordination from squad three and a save after one dragoness banked too hard and dropped her rider. Then it was finally over. Falier and Graydonn landed first, ordering the squads down one-by-one. As each pair landed and riders dismounted, Falier required the partners to thank each other. No one fought this requirement outright anymore, but many slayers' gratitude was half-hearted, and most dragons thought it ridiculous to thank those did nothing but hold on.

Falier tried to simply be glad he didn't have to fight for this, but their attitudes—it seemed hopeless. He was supposed to create a fighting force for Alísa, partners who would keep each other alive against terrible, dark powers. Unfortunately, all he had were warriors who claimed to care about the conflict, yet refused to make an effort.

Graydonn pointed with his snout. *"There are some slayers willing to bend."*

He said it like all the dragons behaved perfectly. Falier pushed away the thought and followed Graydonn's muzzle. Sure enough, Jossen faced his dragon partner, an older adolescent with dark green scales and golden eyes, and dipped his head as he gave his thanks. The dragon returned a respectful slow-blink.

Falier allowed himself a smile. *"Jossen's a good man."*

The squad leaders brought their reports—Trísse and Komi, Rassím and Dezra, and Taz and Harenn. Each had warnings about problematic trainees, but almost all bore praise reports, too. Falier grasped onto that. Some pairs *were* learning—he just had to spend his focus on those who weren't.

As the leaders dispersed, Jossen caught Falier's eye. He excused himself from a group and approached.

Falier offered his arm. "How was your ride today?"

"Can't say I love flying yet, but I'm learning." Jossen clasped his arm warmly. "Some of us planned to spar today—work off the energy we couldn't spend in the sky. Join us?"

Falier found himself smiling. Someone was asking him to join, not merely tolerating his presence! Though, looking at Jossen's group, the others wouldn't feel the same. He didn't know if he could face more scrutiny or outright hostility.

But he was a slayer now. Surely sometime soon, when he won a sparring match or came up with the perfect snarky comeback, they would see it.

Graydonn growled in his mind. *"You do not need that. If they won't accept you, seek those who do. Taz and Harenn would be enjoyable company."*

Falier pushed past his irritation at Graydonn's continued dismissal. He had spent his entire morning arguing with trainees—he did not want to argue with his mind-kin.

"You go on, Graydonn." Falier looked to Jossen, who waited with patient amusement. "Thank you, I'll come."

Jossen chuckled. "You needn't thank me, it's your right."

Graydonn hummed his irritation, but Falier ignored it, falling into step with Jossen. "It doesn't always feel like it's my right."

"Just keep getting back up," Jossen said. "They'll soon see what I do."

"And what's that?"

"That you're here to stay," Jossen clapped Falier's back hard, "so we may as well make a warrior out of you."

Jossen waved to the small group of slayers waiting for him, joining in their march to the southeastern side of camp. Many other slayers joined them, including those among the ground troops.

The war-camp held seven human camps, with the six dragon clans gathered along the outskirts. The dragons despised staying outside and so close to the slayer camps, but there were no nearby mountains for them. Alísa's dragons did their best to keep them pacified, but even they hated being stuck under an open sky. Alísa's camp—the human portion of it—was the largest, holding not just her warriors but also the women and teens. These and those of Tella's wayfarers helped sustain all the camps, as most village-bound slayers left their families at home.

Sparring lasted two hours, ending at lunchtime. Falier took his meal with Alísa, though her attention mostly stayed with the other chiefs. Still, with how busy they were, any chance to see her was a blessing.

The afternoon held another training session, during which Graydonn orchestrated the dragons' flight formations while Falier—*joy of joys*—poked and prodded the slayers until they understood shielding wasn't an option. As the day progressed, the strange resistance in his and Graydonn's bond became more prominent.

"It's nothing," Graydonn insisted as he reopened his mind.

"Please don't tell me I'll have to remind you as much as I do the trainees."

Graydonn growled. *"No. It's fine."*

By evening, all Falier wanted was his bed. No more arguments, no more dragons ignoring obvious problems, just sleep. He plodded through camp unnoticed until a familiar buzzing entered his mind.

"Hey, Uncle Falier!"

Falier stopped, looking for Hwinn. Telepathic communication did little to convey direction. He found the young dragon's nose poking out of the kitchen tent.

"Do you have a minute? Selene wants to talk to you."

Falier debated asking if it could wait until morning, then hurried to duck inside. The front of the kitchen tent had a large awning-like flap hanging over multiple serving tables. Falier passed these and the large, open space for servers, heading for the cooking area at the back. Here, Selene stood among cauldrons, dormant cook-fires, and stacks of supply crates. There were many small holes in the sides and ceiling to allow heat and smoke to escape, each with flaps to close against the elements. He'd have to be careful—someone might see him.

Falier pulled his eyes to Selene. "Hwinn said you wanted to see me?"

She nodded, smiling. She wore an apron over her dress, her hands already covered in flour. On her shoulder, Laen spread her wings for balance as Selene gestured to a tray full of balls of dough.

"These are finished proofing. Help me make flatbread for tomorrow."

Falier blinked. Baking. Two weeks ago that would have made him smile. His gaze slid to the windows.

Selene grabbed a rolling pin. "You've been working so hard recently, I figured you could use a break to do something you actually enjoy."

Falier crossed his arms. "Did Graydonn talk to you?"

Selene cocked her head. "Should he have?"

"No." He went to rub his neck, then stopped himself. Selene would recognize that. In fact, she probably already saw the tension in his voice with her flaming sound-lights. "I'm not a holder anymore, Selene."

He regretted the words as pain crossed her face. She masked it quickly, but he caught it all the same.

"Everyone helps in the war camp," she said, pulling on his arm. "Even big, burly slayer men who would rather swing swords. Did you know L'non has especially good spicing skills?"

Falier blew out a breath. "Selene, I can't be seen working here." Flames, that sounded so bad. "I mean, everyone expects me to be here instead of out there. If they see me back to my old ways…"

Selene raised an eyebrow. "So slayers can't have hobbies?"

A growl escaped his lips. "You don't understand. I'm under so much pressure here. Everyone's eyes are on me. I can't make a mistake—they'll think I'm backsliding."

"Backsliding?" Hwinn whined like a dog. *"Are you ashamed of being a holder?"*

"No! But everyone else is. Of me, not you." He winced. "I'm sorry, I don't know how to phrase it so it doesn't sound horrible."

"You're right." Selene rolled more aggressively. "It does sound horrible. I don't understand? Really? I—a holder, a newly discovered slayer, and an empath learning to fight telepaths—don't understand?"

"You aren't in command. You don't need them to respect you enough to follow orders."

"No," Hwinn growled. *"She just has to be one of the few female humans in the fighting force, worry constantly whether she can protect me, and still make meals every evening!"*

Laen barked her agreement and Falier's ears grew hot with shame. For his ever-happy nephew dragon to scold him, Selene must really be feeling the pressure, too.

"I'm sorry," he said to Selene. "I don't mean to belittle what you're going through, but I need you not to belittle what I'm dealing with, either. I don't get to be a holder anymore. If I'm going to become the slayer I'm supposed to be, I need to give up certain things."

Selene nodded slowly. "Okay. Yes, we all leave things behind as we change and grow. But what if we leave so much behind that we lose ourselves?"

He shook his head, watching as she flipped the dough over and rolled the other side. "Sometimes we have to become someone different. Growing up a holder has left me sorely unprepared. The Maker made me a slayer—I was supposed to be one all along. Now I have to catch up."

"Have you considered the Maker placed you in a family of holders for a reason?"

"Like what?"

This time, she couldn't mask the pain in her eyes. Instead, she worked more vigorously at the dough. "The clan has plenty of hardened slayers good with swords. You can bring something new and different."

Falier laughed bitterly. "They don't want new and different. I know you're trying to help, but life is about growth and change. Why can't you and Graydonn understand that?"

Selene set the rolling pin aside and grabbed the edge of the dough. She had overdone it, the way she had to peel it off the counter.

"Sure," she said, "growth requires more than sticking to your strengths or maintaining a singular focus. But spread yourself thin, pull yourself in too many directions simultaneously—"

She held up the dough for him to see—a wide, flat circle—then pulled in two directions. It went with her hands, spreading until a hole tore in the middle.

"—and even the center will break."

She stared at him meaningfully, a crease of worry between her brows. Falier didn't know what to say. Selene was wrong, but she wasn't going to hear it. He didn't want to fight anymore—not her, not Graydonn, not the flaming slayers in his training squads. He just wanted someone to hear him and understand.

"This is war, Selene. We're all tired and stressed and being twisted into shapes that are uncomfortable. Eventually, though, it will all work out."

He approached Selene and offered a hug. "Thank you for caring about me. I'll be fine."

Laen hopped off to get out of the way while Selene's shoulders slumped. His sister accepted the hug, squeezing him around the waist.

"I hope so."

He pulled back, then headed to the tent opening, rubbing Hwinn's neck scales as he passed. The adolescent clicked in his throat—a thoughtful sound rather than an appreciative rumble. Neither of them believed him.

Touching the hilt of his sword, Falier headed back out into the cold night air. Graydonn, now his sister and nephew. No one understood. Alísa would. He wanted to find her, but the hour was late. She would be in bed, resting for tomorrow. As he should be.

He sighed and marched to his tent. *Just keep moving.*

28

EMBERS

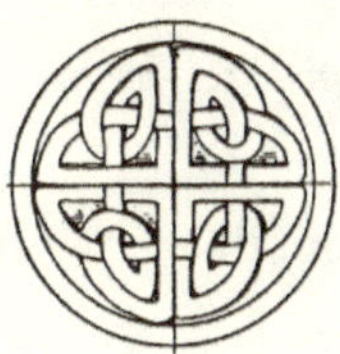

Five villages, Tella's wayfarers, and seven dragon clans. In only seven days, Alísa had raised an army worthy of pride. She met with the chiefs, alphas, and their seconds in the field north of the war-camp, away from the noises of training and sparring.

A full deer-skin map spread out between them, nailed to the ground against the winds. Large tokens marked villages, the gathered clans, and the an'reik armies based on the scouts' latest missions. Typically, dreki made the best scouts, but they still couldn't approach the enemy's camps or caves. The closer they got, the more the poor creatures complained of headaches and deep depression. Supplemented by dragon-rider scout reports, however, Alísa held a decent understanding of numbers and positions.

She fought not to shiver as the cold, damp wind cut across the field and water seeped through her skirt and wool leggings. It had rained yesterday and would likely again tonight. The chiefs would have preferred a tent, but nothing in camp could hold the alpha dragons.

Chief Lorin used a long stick with a flat end to push tokens across the map. He pushed the human an'reik token from its position at sixty miles south of them to N'moth—the final village before Vennia.

"To ensure enough time to finish preparing your riders," Lorin said, "I propose we wait to attack until they reach this position. We station our troops in N'moth, then march to meet them predawn. Their journey will have diminished their supplies. They will be sluggish and hungry—a perfect opportunity to strike."

The emerald Harazím growled softly. *"No. We should wait until their first night in N'moth. They will have feasted and will sleep soundly in your human cushionings. Then we attack in the night."*

Chief Tella, adorned with red scale bracers and the ever-present kohl around her eyes, shook her head. "Typical dragon. Such a move would burn N'moth down, depriving many of homes and livelihoods."

Harazím snapped his jaws. *"Humans are always building and rebuilding. Ridding the world of these dark vermin is the highest peak—one we must claim no matter the loss."*

Alísa let her ire at the 'us and them' wording flow through the link. With Sesína's help, she spoke to the group telepathically.

"Harazím, your point about their complacency while in the village is valid, but Tella's counter is too. A nighttime attack will also hinder visibility for our ground troops. I agree with Lorin's assessment. We should strike before the enemy reaches N'moth."

Attacking before the an'reik reached the village would also protect the villagers still there. Out of all the villages they attempted to evacuate, N'moth held the highest contingency of people who refused to move. Most families there depended on their livestock. Some evacuees had driven their herds before them, but many stayed, preferring to risk losing a few to a hungry army than risk all in a cross-country journey.

"What of the enemy dragons?" A sapphire alpha, Zarria, pointed her muzzle at the mountains—the real ones rather than those on the map. *"If they see us move, our attack will not be a surprise. And by if, I do mean when. We cannot escape their notice."*

Alísa tented her fingers. They hadn't been able to get numbers on the enemy dragons. Sightings were few and far-between. Still, to assume they weren't watching would be foolish.

She looked to Zarria, most of whose clan refused to take riders. *"I respect your decision to fight on your own, but if dragons and slayers flew together to the battlefield, that would solve many problems. We could spend the days needed for marching on preparations instead, and we can more easily attack the humans before their dragon allies realize what's happening."*

Chiefs and alphas quieted, some giving wary glances while others stared into nothingness. Sesína growled.

"Look, you're all here, aren't you? Sleeping near each other without being attacked, training without being attacked, and" —she gasped— *"sitting here without being attacked! If we can't trust each other enough to fly sixty miles to strike a common enemy,*

what in flames are we doing here?"

Zarria snapped at the air. *"Watch your tone, hatchling!"*

Alísa glared at the dragoness. *"You watch yours. I might have used different words, but my sentiments are the same. Dragons can cover the distance in an hour-and-a-half. Marching requires two-to-three days. Can you not swallow your pride to rid the country of this threat? Any of you?"*

She looked to the slayers, especially Lorin, who still adamantly opposed rider training. *"For the spiritual good and physical safety of our peoples, I ask again— will you fly together to this battle? You can fight separately as you desire, as I cannot force the deep trust that requires. But this demands no more trust than what you have already given."*

Tella joined Alísa in staring down the more stubborn chiefs. "If my men will ride, after years of hunting and being hunted, none of you have a single excuse."

Alísa fought back a smirk. Tella had surprised her by offering half of her clan as riders. More surprisingly, they had given Alísa's betas the least trouble of all the new riders. Fear of a chief and zeal to destroy the Maker's enemies made even the hardest of warriors bow.

Chief Lorin narrowed his eyes at Tella, then looked to the alphas. His words came in a low growl worthy of a dragon.

"Let it never be said that I allowed evil to thrive. If the dragons will carry us, I and my men will fly. But only to the battle. We shall fight on the ground with sword and spear" —he eyed Tella— "as the Maker intended."

Slowly, in a rare show of generosity, the other chiefs followed his example, nodding their acceptance. Harazím hummed in his throat, watching them.

"If the slayers will ride, we shall carry them."

One by one, the other alphas accepted Alísa's proposal, Zarria the last among them. Upon the clans' agreement, they talked strategy for another hour, creating plans for the ground troops, unladen dragons, and dragon-rider pairs. Based on the an'reik's current marching rate, the attack would take place in six days. So soon, yet a ready fire burned within Alísa. Her alliance was strong, the plan solid.

Only one question remained—how to handle Kallar. He would empower the an'reik dragons as surely as she would her allies. He needed to be eliminated, ensuring her army's safety and satisfying justice for her father.

I hope you're proud of me, Papá. I hope I'm leading them well.

Sesína nosed her cheek as the leaders rose to return to their clans. *"You got them to agree to a plan. If that's not effective leadership, I don't know what is."*

Alísa rubbed Sesína's neck. *"Thank you. I can always count on you to call people out."*

The dragoness tossed her head like a prancing horse. *"It's part of my charm."*

They watched the sky as they returned to camp. Falier and Graydonn led a training session for new dragon-rider pairs, apparently working on agility. L'non and other wayfarers were among them, and all were making great strides. She had been correct—they trained faster here than they had in Me'ran. Impending battle did that to warriors. Even Falier was progressing nicely in his sword-play. He rarely beat his opponent, but he held his own far better now than when he fought her father.

She shook her head as her eyes prickled. No time for tears when she was about to re-enter camp.

At the edge of the tents, Sesína's attention turned to a group of young teenagers playing kickball on a semi-flat patch of grass. The teens of Briek's slayers and the wayfarers got along well, perhaps also spurred by the coming conflict and a need for camaraderie. The sight of Levan and Taer among them made Alísa smile.

Longing rose inside Sesína. Patting her scaly neck, Alísa steered them closer. The young dragoness had few chances to be an adolescent of late.

The teens halted their play as they came near, some staring wide-eyed between Alísa and Sesína while others ducked their heads as though expecting a reprimand. Being chief changed things. Even her cousins didn't seem sure how to respond to her intruding on their playing field.

She smiled, trying to be as unthreatening as possible. "D—don't mind me, just passing through. Though, if you need another p-p-p-player, Sesína is pretty good at kickball."

"And fivers!" Sesína added a little too quickly. She shifted her wings against her back. *"I like games."*

Taer grinned. "Sesína's on my team!"

"What's fivers?" One of the wayfaring girls asked.

That launched the easterners into explaining the game, which Sesína joined readily. Alísa left her to it, continuing her march into camp. She passed women hanging laundry, men sharpening weapons, and a mixed group preparing dinner. Everyone appeared busy with a task of some sort. She should be too. If she didn't move, the grief would hit again.

What could she do? What would her father do? Join a group, most likely. After a long planning session, however, she wasn't ready for more people. Perhaps that was wrong. Perhaps she should force herself through it.

I don't have to be Papá. I'm enough as I am. The Maker said so.

That thought made the tears prickle again. Stupid.

Walk. That was something she could do. Just move. Walk out the emotions until they left her.

Circling camp toward a better field for walking, Alísa strode like she was on a mission. An excuse to avoid eye-contact as she passed clanmates. That probably wasn't the correct choice. Her father would never have—

Her goal to avoid tears altered, becoming a need to simply get somewhere safe to release them. She reined in her emotions as tightly as she could, determined not to disturb Sesína's play.

"Alísa!"

She stiffened and choked back the forming sobs. Cautiously, she turned around to see Songweaver Farren approaching.

Relief passed through her. Farren was safe.

"Y—yes?"

He didn't speak until he reached her, long legs closing the distance easily. "Would you like company?"

She swallowed, her throat closing. Was she that obvious? Had others seen through her as well?

She let out a breath. "Yes. Thank you."

Together, they continued up a hill, away from the sparring grounds and camps. Alísa's breaths came more quickly, less from exertion and more from her attempts to hold back sobs. The day was slowly becoming evening, the sun casting long shadows over the land. By the time they crested the hill, tears wet her cheeks.

Farren pulled Alísa close, letting her cry on his shoulder. If she tried, she could imagine it was her father holding her, could smell the safety of his road-weary clothing. But thinking like that helped nothing.

"You are doing so well," Farren soothed. "Your papá would be proud."

"I—I'm so t-t-tired. And I miss him."

She sniffled and pulled back. Grabbing a handkerchief from the pouch on her belt, she wiped her face clean. Farren remained silent, rubbing a hand over her back as she tried to calm herself. He had always been patient. It made asking the hard questions easier.

"W—why did the Maker allow this? Papá knew the t-t-truth now, and he was m—m—making a difference. Now, just when he gets on the right p-p-path, he's t-taken? It—it's not fair!"

Farren sighed. "No, dear one, it isn't. I've sung many a remembrance in my time and I still can't pretend to understand it. One good man dies violently while an evil one goes peacefully in his sleep at an old age. It is one of the most challenging questions for mortals."

Indeed. She could also ask why the Maker allowed the unjust war between humans and dragons to stretch on for so long. Why so many hatchlings were slaughtered or children burned alive in their homes? None of it made sense.

Farren looked out over the hills. "I do know one thing—two, I suppose. The Maker's ways are good and right and too lofty for mortals to fully comprehend, and he is big enough for our sorrows amidst it."

Alísa clutched the handkerchief to her mouth with a choked sob. Months ago, she had learned the dragon empathy the Maker cursed her with was truly a blessing—one that enabled her to bring dragons and humans together. She remembered that lesson well and knew logically the same goodness and rightness somehow applied here. But in her heart? What could fit there besides her grief?

Farren watched her. "Have you sought him since Karn's death?"

Alísa swallowed her tears and straightened, gazing at the country her father had spent years protecting. A land she must protect now—all because the Maker saw fit to let the an'reik win. To let Papá die.

"What is there to seek?" she whispered. "I know the duty he has placed on my shoulders. I know what he made me to do, and I'm doing it." People were even listening to her. She was stepping into her role and proving Bria's declaration that she was enough for the task. She just had to keep leaning into that truth.

Farren thought a long moment before responding. "What about seeking healing? Your own and the clan's?"

She shook her head. "Our healing will c-c-come with the rest of our world's. When K-Kallar and the an'reik are no longer here to wound us."

"Can you defeat them when you are not whole?"

Alísa drew back. This from one who just praised her progress?

"C-can I be made whole by the one who w——wounded me?"

Farren's brows pulled together. "I thought the an'reik were who wounded you?"

Alísa felt herself tense, but she couldn't release it. Her breaths shallow, she turned away from Farren. None of this was right. Talking to Farren was supposed to make her feel better, not fan the raging flames burning inside her.

"The Maker is big enough for your anger too, dear one." Farren's voice barely rose above the breeze. "Have you told him of it? I can help you do so, if you need."

Alísa shook her head and faced camp. "I m——must get back t-t-to my duties."

"Alísa——"

"No." She stepped past him. "Thank you for your concern, b——but I do not require your c-c-c-c-counsel at this t-time."

Farren's sorrow stuck to her like cloying mud on a wagon's wheel. "Then I will pray for you."

She paused, hating that her answer grieved him but unable to give him anything better. She returned to camp in silence, passing through without tears until she made it to her tent, where Sesína waited with the understanding Alísa had expected from Farren. She would heal in her own time. Once the enemy was vanquished and the Maker had proved his goodness to her again.

29

GROUNDED

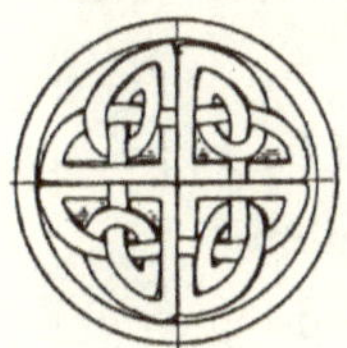

Kallar's psychic spear caused a scream of agony in the skies.

A sword slash ripped through a hatchling's wing.

A flex of his muscles sent an egg shattering down the mountainside.

And always, a dagger's thrust brought his master's betrayed eyes.

Kallar fell to his knees on the astral grasses. Twilight surrounded him, each star in the sky a memory the keeper could call down upon him. He forced himself to breathe through it. Around him, the mists turned pain-red as another star crashed down, bringing memories of a dragoness slain at the mouth of a cave.

He ground his teeth against the sword through his heart, willing himself not to scream and give the keeper satisfaction. His dragon empathy had been dormant in these memories, but now it hit him with each remembered act.

"It was war. My duty! Everything I did was to protect humanity. I am not ashamed of it!"

"So noble," the keeper said, *"killing a mother protecting her young."*

The memory focused on small eyes glowing in the darkness beyond the dragoness. The hatchling's terror assaulted Kallar, causing him to stumble back. His heart raced as the mists turned ice blue with guilt.

Damned dragon empathy. He shook his head, trying to clear his vision before it continued. Before he saw what he did.

"I didn't know then. I have nothing to feel guilty about. It wasn't my fault!"

The colors didn't change.

"Awaken."

Kallar started, as did his keeper. That was Isarra's voice. Both glanced at the darkened window, but only the monster moved. It lumbered slowly, sated by Kallar's roiling emotions. Kallar didn't try to beat it there, too exhausted to rise.

The keeper touched the window and opened the body's eyes. Gentle daylight shone through the walls of a tent—Kallar's own rather than the prison. To Kallar's relief, they took him from there days ago. The further he stayed from R'lann, the better.

The entry flap opened and Isarra peeked inside. "There is a matter with the dragons requiring your attention."

The dragons. Were they causing trouble for the camp? That was the best he could hope for, that the different factions of an'reik would fight and thin their numbers.

The keeper flew back to Kallar—the motion more like floating as its wings didn't move. It grabbed Kallar by the arm, its touch hot needles, and hoisted him up.

"Let's see how well you've learned. Follow the mistress' orders and I will allow you to stay."

Kallar yanked away as soon as his feet were under him. This was a trap of some kind. Or perhaps just an opportunity to prove what a compliant pet he was becoming. He should say no, but the keeper would force consciousness on him anyway. Better to retain as much control as possible.

Kallar limped to the window and, bracing for awareness, touched its edge.

The initial breath was always sweet, like he had been held underwater and finally surfaced. He lay there a moment, regaining his bearings, clenching and unclenching his muscles. The fatigue of the astral world remained in his mind, but his body was strong and healing quickly.

He pushed up from the bed-mat. The keeper hadn't bothered changing into sleeping clothes when it laid down last night. On went the belt, Kallar's sword on his left hip, and Karn's dagger on his right. He didn't know what happened to his own dagger, nor did he care. Even if it showed up on someone else's person, Kallar would never reclaim the weapon that had dripped with Karn's blood.

He pushed through the tent-flap into the cold autumn day. Late-morning, based on the angle of the sun behind the clouds. He was in a camp akin to Karn's wayfarers', Eskann now a week behind them. Slayers and an'reik alike walked through the now-combined camp, weaving between tents about their tasks.

Kallar's anger rose. Some slayers were surely possessed like he was, but many remained of their own volition—allying with Nameless-worshipers, which they previously believed the dragons to be.

Hypocrites.

"Ah, back in control, I see."

Kallar twisted to find Isarra waiting for him. "What's happening?"

She crossed her arms and looked to the mountains, toward the newest caves the an'reik alphas had commandeered for their growing clans. "Some of the unenlightened dragons attempted to escape last night, killing one of their betters before the alphas' compulsion smothered their rebellion."

For perhaps the first time in his life, Kallar mentally cheered for a dragon's efforts. Ideally, the an'reik would fight amongst themselves, but any dissension in the ranks was desirable. If some dragons could still resist their alphas' power, maybe Alísa and her allies had a shred of hope.

"I'm sure your keeper has a reason for giving you free rein right now," Isarra said, voice lowering, "but it certainly makes it inconvenient for me. Listen well. The rebel dragons must be punished, and our slayers need reassurance. Many of them hold themselves back because of our alliance with these dragons. They joined us to stop the dragons' rule through Alísa, not to make friends with the beasties."

Thinking of the wayfarers' alliance with Alísa's clan, Kallar understood that completely.

"The alphas are bringing their rebels to us," Isarra continued, "and you will kill them before the slayers. This will prove your claim in Eskann, that these dragons are merely tools to be destroyed upon our victory."

Movement in the sky drew Kallar's gaze to the mountain. Sure enough, dragons flew toward camp.

Kallar's hand moved to his sword. "And the dragons will just play along?"

Isarra smirked. "They'll tire of the charade eventually, but they know they cannot stand against your counterpart alone. Your power will hold them here, and it will protect us when they are through with the game."

As other slayers began noticing the shapes in the sky, Isarra strode forward, lifting her voice.

"Brothers and sisters! We have heard your fears. Come witness our authority over the dragons. See for yourselves how the Nameless have supplied the power to use them—how we rule over them!"

The slayers exchanged questioning glances. Some grabbed for their weapons, only to be halted by another slayer or an'reik. A few stared in awe and immediately followed, prompting others to do the same. How many were possessed slayers with keepers in control, and how many truly held Isarra in high esteem?

Harrík walked among them, hand on his sword until his eyes landed on Kallar. He hurried to Kallar, coming alongside.

"Is this what you spoke of? You're going to use your Singer powers over them?"

Before Kallar could even consider his response, the keeper seized his voice.

"Follow."

Harrík paused a moment, then fell in behind him.

At the crest of the hill just outside camp, Isarra ordered the slayers to halt. "Only an'reik past this point, for we alone hold true power over them."

Kallar paused with them, torn. The keeper and Isarra wanted him to continue on and pretend that he himself was an'reik. A huge part of him wanted to stop now and defy them both. But he also knew his mind was still too weak to fight the keeper—it would force him forward. If he moved of his own volition, he might control some small facet of what happened next.

Hating himself, he followed Isarra down the hill.

The dragons landed at the bottom—seven of them. Three had the presence Kallar now associated with an'reik dragons: massive bodies, brighter eye-flames, and a penchant for snapping at anything that annoyed them, which currently included the four rebels. These beasts slouched low, eyes dim. Blood dappled the scales around their wounds.

Curious, Kallar left his telepathic shield down. The rebels' pain pulsed through the air, but he could handle it. Within the pain and emotions, he searched for the alpha's power. A stormy mixture of hatred and desperation flowed from the dragons, but he couldn't sense anything abnormal—

A rebel with silvery-gray scales lurched at the an'reik dragon closest to it. It snapped at the an'reik's emerald neck like a serpent, the intended victim barely pulling back in time. Wings flaring, the rebel roared and swiped with its talons. The an'reik prepared to strike, but stopped as dark mists poured from

Isarra in droves. They twisted into ropes that surrounded the rebelling dragon, yanking it to its belly.

The silver struggled against the bindings, but then Kallar sensed pulses of authority and dominance. He raised his telepathic shield on instinct, the sensation uncomfortably close to the feeling of the keeper. It wasn't the same, but it hung heavy in the air like the dark, cloying mists of the shadowy body. The rebelling dragon stilled under the power, as did the others.

Isarra chuckled and faced the slayers. Kallar turned halfway to both watch her and monitor the dragons. Some slayers drew their swords, ready for the moment the dragons attacked.

"So you see, these beasts are under our rule. Though they rebel, they cannot overcome us or the alphas we have set over them."

The alpha dragon growled and the zing of its telepathy filled Kallar's mind. The connection expanded to include Isarra and the an'reik, but not the slayers.

"I despise this game, vermin. Be quick—my patience runs thin with your lies."

"Just a bit more." Isarra raised her arms. "Dragons who will not obey shall be slaughtered by our Dragon Singer, for we know our place above them."

The alpha snapped his jaws, but he did not move to harm any of the humans. Isarra turned to Kallar, expectant. He was supposed to kill the rebels now—to complete the lie. He looked over the cowed dragons, eyes stopping on the silver one. Its rage and desperation mingled with the alpha's empathic command, and Kallar realized his guard was down again. He shored up his shield as choices warred within him.

He couldn't help but pity the rebels, especially the silver fighter. It would be a mercy to kill them and end their suffering. But such a move would encourage the slayers to truly join with the an'reik.

There must be a way to win.

"Too slow."

Kallar's bones ached as the monster slipped under his skin as before, taking control over his muscles even though his consciousness remained in the physical world. Kallar struggled against it, but only briefly. The damage was done— better to wait for the keeper to release him again.

Kallar's sword slid from its sheath. He could feel the leather-wrapped hilt in his fingers and the air as his arm moved, but his muscles were not his own.

"A better idea," the keeper said loudly, "is to ground them."

In a swift motion, it lunged for the silver dragon's wing and slashed. The silver roared as the sword carved a long, bloody swath. The dragon's pain pierced Kallar's back, as though he, too, had a wing there.

The silver snapped at him, sharp teeth gleaming with its fury, and the keeper leapt backward and swung again. It cut the dragon's upper lip, drawing blood from the tough skin. Then the keeper shouted a battle-cry full in the silver's face. The dragon slumped under the Singer's power, just as it had with the alpha's.

Satisfied, the keeper addressed the slayers. "I will personally keep them in line. Come the next battle, they shall meet their fate on the ground against Alísa's traitorous slayers." It turned to the alpha. "Tell the others this is their future if they cross me."

The an'reik dragon stared at him, eyes burning. Then it blinked slowly, pleasure wafting from it.

"This is acceptable, Singer."

The keeper smirked and approached the next of the rebels. Its voice slid through Kallar's mind.

"Do you want the rest? You certainly have the experience."

Pain gripped Kallar as the shadow shoved memories of slashed hatchling wings into the forefront of his mind. Their terror gripped him, crushing his heart so he could hardly breathe.

The keeper laughed as it lapped up the fear. *"No?"*

"Kallar!" A slayer's shout broke through the haze. "Is it true your power comes from them? You have become an'reik?"

No!

"Yes," the keeper called back. "The time of relying on the Maker's meager gifts is over. We will protect our people with true power!" It twisted to look the alpha dragon in the eye. *"And when the rival Singer is gone, you may rule dragonkind as you please."*

It scrutinized him. *"If Isarra said that, I would call it another lie, but you…"* It rumbled in its chest. *"Keeper. A piece of the masters, I trust."*

Kallar shuddered. Behind him, the slayer declared his intent to fully join the an'reik, and others murmured their agreement.

Idiots! Can't you see all the lies? Can't you—

"Maker—" An unfamiliar voice entered Kallar's mind, feminine and proven

draconic by the name that accompanied it. Lellani. *"Maker curse you for all you have done!"*

The keeper glanced at the silver dragoness, then returned to its work, slashing the next rebel's wing and bringing Kallar more pain. Alpha dragons cast their controlling empathy over the rebels, while behind Kallar an'reik and slayers came together.

He already has.

30

LOST

"Good. Dragons return to starting positions. Let's go again."

Falier watched the astral plane as the two dragons laden with riders moved. The morning light glared through the clouds, making the dark psychic landscape not only practical but preferable. L'non's and Tern's glowing forms each sat astride a dragon, tentatively leaning as their partners banked. Only one pattern of mind-shields and spears remained before they broke for lunch.

Beneath Falier, Graydonn rumbled his approval and gave similar instructions to another practicing pair. They banked wide around the four dragon-rider pairs, allowing them each to attend to their dueling students. As the riders practiced telepathy, the dragons moved through dips and turns, adjusting to the added weight.

Falier drummed his fingers on his thigh. His and Graydonn's bond throbbed in the back of his mind like one of his old, shield-induced migraines. The dragon still stubbornly claimed nothing was wrong, even when Falier prodded him about it.

Can't they get to their spots faster?

Graydonn hummed at him, chiding his attitude toward their students. It didn't help, especially since he knew Graydonn was right—in this, if nothing else.

Falier breathed slowly. He was just tired. Tired and hungry and fed up with slayers who barely acknowledged him, mind-kin who wouldn't talk to him, and sisters who didn't understand.

As soon as the dragons were in position, Falier gave the order. *"Begin."*

Souls and powers lit up the astral plane. The dragons flew toward each other as L'non put up his shield around him and his dragon partner H'sinth—

bronze, like his eyes. Tern shot his first psychic arrow, a beam of darker brown that slammed into L'non's defense. After another blast and a twist of Tern's dragon, the two slayers switched—Tern shielding while L'non threw his own set of attacks. Everything was pre-planned. A dance with steps already called.

How long had it been since he last danced?

No. Slayers didn't care about music and dancing. Only swords and spears and attitudes as tough as their overcooked venison.

The dragons swirled together, rising high above Graydonn's students as L'non and Tern exchanged faster attacks and defenses. Falier mentally called the steps, trying to focus, careful to keep the words in his own head rather than sending them through the mind-link. After nearly a week of working together, they didn't need him coaching them step-by-step anymore.

Dragons break apart. Two arrows. Swirl. Three arrows. Charge. Two arrows—
Three?

Had he forgotten Tern's count?

No. L'non dropped his shield just before Tern's third arrow flew. H'sinth roared in angry surprise, his flight wavering as Tern sent a fourth blast. Heat filled Falier as Tern's partner trumpeted her pain, L'non's pre-planned arrow hitting her because Tern hadn't shielded.

"Stop!" Falier's mental shout caused Graydonn to falter. *"Stop, now!"*

Tern's partner shook her head hard. She and H'sinth ended their aerial dance as all four combatants looked at Falier. He clenched Graydonn's spine.

"Tern, you can't break the pattern like that! You've hurt both of the dragons!"

Tern's tone was unconcerned. *"They'll be hurt in battle. We can't avoid it."*

"So you would stab your sparring partner in the back? Because they'd be stabbed in battle anyway?!"

"They aren't bleeding! You'd know the difference if you knew anything about fighting."

Tern's ire stoked Falier's own. Tern had no right to be mad when he was the one harming his flight-partners! And why wasn't L'non jumping down Tern's throat for this too? He just sat there, watching.

"At least I know who my allies are! Your duty is to your partner. We're trusting our lives to each other—now do it right!"

"Patterns aren't like combat," Tern shot back. *"If you truly wanted us prepared, you'd let us fight for real."*

Strong. Be strong. *"If I can't trust you with patterns, what makes you think you're ready for freedom?"*

"Ready?" Tern scoffed. *"You spend your life waiting tables, then presume to tell a born slayer whether he's ready?"*

"Tern." L'non said. *"Your chief placed Falier over us for this training. That is enough."*

Tern said nothing in response. Tension pulsed in Falier's body. L'non had stepped in because he thought Falier couldn't handle the situation.

"Didn't you want his help?" Graydonn said to Falier alone.

Falier ignored him and addressed the others. *"Once more, and use the flaming pattern."*

Falier slid off Graydonn with two goals in mind—eat, then find Alísa. He had to get away from these insubordinate slayers and aloof dragons. He shivered in the cold late-autumn air, the clouds becoming grayer as the day pressed on. He hoped for rain. That might stop this afternoon's training. The sound of raindrops hitting a tent's roof couldn't rival their playing in the leaves of the trees, but it would be something.

He left Graydonn with the dragons, who one-by-one began flying back to their camps. They said nothing, Graydonn likely sensing his sour mood. Didn't the dragon understand that was partially his fault? Maybe if Graydonn actually talked to him, he wouldn't feel so—empty.

Alísa. He needed Alísa.

Falier passed through the crowd of riders-in-training and ground troops. Sparring after rider-training was routine now, and nearly all the warriors partook. Falier tried to block out the conversations flowing around him, hoping to avoid more jabs. One particularly spirited voice, however, called his attention.

"—I'm staying on the ground, as I've always done against dragons."

"But against men *and* dragons?" another said. "It's likely we'll be facing the human army while the riders focus on the sky. They can distinguish more easily between our allies and enemies, while we might hit the wrong dragons."

The first voice scoffed. "Nothing will stop me from spearing some of the enemy beasts in the sky. And if a so-called ally 'accidentally' falls, well… I doubt there'll be many tears."

Falier stopped as the other slayers laughed. Visions of Hwinn or Graydonn being choked by their own allies first chilled his blood, then brought it to a boil. He turned on the group of four.

"It's not funny."

Only one glanced at him—Tern, Falier recognized. The others paid no heed.

"Hey!" He stormed to the group, drawing a few eyes outside of it. *Be strong. Strong and loud and unafraid. I am a slayer.* "Did you hear me? You shouldn't joke about harming them any more than you would about stabbing your sword-partner in the back. It's *not* funny."

A couple of them glanced at him, then ignored him. Tern, however, smirked.

"Holders. They've got no sense of humor."

"I'm no holder," Falier growled, coming closer than he would normally dare so he could look down at Tern and his comrades. "I am Rorenth's slayer, soon to be tiern of the wayfarers, and your commander. Tern, you should know the importance of not joking about choking allied dragons to their deaths."

Tern glared right back at him, unmoved. The jokester grabbed Tern's arm as many others now looked on. "Come on. Let's go."

"No." Tern crossed his arms, still glaring at Falier. "I'm sick of him talking such a big talk when that's all it is—talk. See, I know the story. The fae killed Rorenth—you played little part in his death. And as for tiern of the wayfarers, you're nothing beside Kallar."

Flames grew hotter inside Falier. "You forget who betrayed Karn."

"And you forget your place, holder boy! Standing there telling us what to do? I don't need your patterns or your rules—I've been killing dragons all my life, as have all the other slayers in the air. Just leave us alone and let us do our jobs!"

"Your 'job' is to fly and protect your squad. And you will not disparage your allies, dragon or otherwise!"

"Make me."

"What does Trísse even see in you?!"

Tern started, then grit his teeth. "She has nothing to do with this."

That was true—the barb was childish, but Falier couldn't withdraw now.

Not with so many watching.

"She's a member of your squad—the squad that's counting on you to set aside your stupidity and fight alongside them. That starts with you respecting them and your commander."

"Or what, holder boy?"

Falier grabbed the hilt of his sword. Like with Lorin and his second, some slayers' respect only came one way.

"Or meet me on the dueling ground."

As soon as the words left his mouth, Graydonn's anxiety filled him. *What are you doing?*

Falier ignored him as Tern smirked and pulled his weapon. "This *is* the dueling ground. Let everyone else see who the true slayer is."

Tern watched, expecting Falier to back down. But he expected the holder, not the slayer. Eyes locked on Tern's, Falier drew his sword. The surrounding warriors moved away, murmurs rising from the crowd. He pushed them from his thoughts. Focus.

Tern's expression turned serious as Falier gripped his sword's hilt in two hands and began circling. Determined to take the lead, Falier made his first testing swipe at Tern's chest. Tern batted his blade with a zing no waster could create. He followed rather than continuing to circle, striking at Falier's strong side. Falier danced backward. Karn's instructions from weeks ago filled his mind.

Let's end this.

He advanced with a sequence of three slashes Darrin had taught him. Tern deflected each, though the second strike earned a look of surprise as Tern realized Falier was foregoing further testing swipes.

That's right, I can play the game too!

Falier circled to Tern's weak side and attacked, jabbing at his armored ribs. Grunting, Tern blocked, then let loose his own flurry of attacks. Falier parried frantically as his opponent proved his superior speed and tried to knock Falier off-balance. With quick, light steps, Falier managed to dodge the swipes he couldn't block.

"Are we dancing or fighting?" Tern snarled.

Falier stopped the next blow, pressing blades. It didn't give him the breathing room he hoped for. Tern pressed back with equal strength, face twisted.

"What gives you the right to command us?"

Falier shoved him away and attacked, crashing his blade down against Tern's. The blow felt good as his anger and frustration flowed. He *was* a slayer. A commander, given authority by the Dragon Singer and chief of the wayfarers. He would make Tern see it!

He circled to Tern's weak side again. Tern spun, momentum giving him a more powerful strike. Falier hopped back, barely avoiding the tip of the blade. A true, sharp blade.

Don't think about it.

Tern attacked again, never slowing as he taunted. "Even a wayfaring child would be a better commander than you, holder boy!"

Gritting his teeth, Falier batted a swipe away and advanced with his own burst of attacks.

"Not. A. Holder. Boy!"

Tern deflected each blow, his bored expression telling their audience that blocking Falier was simple. Falier fought harder, hit faster, pressed blades before swirling his sword in a harsh circle meant to wrest Tern's weapon from his hands. Tern persisted, but anger replaced his boredom. Falier matched with his own ire as Tern threw his weight behind his blade.

"Here," Tern bit out. "Let me show you how it's done."

Tern gave, and Falier fell forward a step as Tern circled their swords and forced Falier's from his grip. The weapon fell with a dull thump on the damp grass, drawing gasps from the watching crowd. Tern pointed his sword at Falier's neck.

"Yield."

Falier reached for Graydonn through their constricted bond. It wouldn't end this way.

"No."

Yanking on Graydonn's power, Falier shot a psychic spear. It shattered Tern's ever-present shield. With a cry, Tern stumbled back, holding his head. The crowd murmured as Falier went for his blade.

"You stupid—" Tern's words strangled off as Falier hit him again. By the third attack, Tern had his shield up, but he winced as Falier's attack nearly broke through again. "It's against the code!"

"Isn't respecting your commander part of the code as well? How about your squad?" Falier swung his sword, and when Tern blocked, he mind-speared him again. He advanced, forcing Tern back. "I will use everything I have to defend my people—mind and body. You stood by as another slayer threatened them. You even laughed with him! Now you face their commander. Fight me!"

Rage blazed in Tern's eyes. "Fine."

Falier shielded as Tern shot him, raising his sword to block Tern's simultaneous swipe. Tern surpassed Falier in skill, but he didn't have a mind-kin bond. Graydonn, now fully aware of the danger, forced their bond wider. Falier dodged Tern's attack, waited for his psychic spear, then shot a new blast faster than Tern could reform his defense.

Falier mind-speared him again, then hit Tern in the side with the flat of his blade. The simultaneous blows sent Tern to the ground. Falier reformed his shield, stepped on Tern's sword, and pointed his own weapon at Tern's throat.

"Yield."

Tern's face went red as his humiliation filled the astral plane. With a cry of anger, Tern shot Falier again and again, but Graydonn's power didn't budge.

"Yield, slayer."

Shouts came up from the crowd—cheers for his victory. They formed a smile on Falier's lips.

Tern glared with a newfound hatred, hot and seething. It pricked Falier's heart. Even when Tern was insubordinate, superiority lived in his eyes. Never hate.

"I yield."

A tremor ran through Falier as the adrenaline began wearing off, and he pulled back before he could accidentally nick Tern's neck.

"Get up." Flames, why was his voice so shaky? He had won.

He stepped away, allowing Tern to lift his sword as he stood. Tern sheathed the weapon and spat on the ground between them.

"Find yourself another rider. I won't fight for a man"—he looked behind Falier—"or woman with a dragon inside them."

Falier didn't have to look to know Alísa was in the crowd. For some reason, that made him feel ashamed.

Tern stomped off, calling his friends to follow. The jokester did, as did ten others—some of them new riders. Were they all refusing to ride again? Had he—

The rest stared after Tern before returning to Falier. They stood silent now, their psychic energy a mix of excitement, fear, and—curiosity, maybe?

"Show's over," Alísa said in her chief voice. "Back to your d—duties. All but you two" —she pointed at Tern's companions who hadn't moved— "and Falier."

She approached them, Sesína at her side and Rís on her shoulder, as the crowd dispersed. Alísa didn't even look at him as she passed. Falier followed, an odd numbness falling over him. He saw L'non and vaguely heard him and the others recount what had happened. Falier watched but didn't hear. His own remembered words echoed too loudly.

Not. A. Holder. Boy!

It was true in that moment. There, he had been a slayer. Strong. Confident. Able. He had turned a near-defeat into victory. Using telepathy was cheating, sure, but he didn't regret it. He meant what he said about defending his squad.

But, wasn't Tern part of his squad too? Yes, he had disrespected his squadmates and commander before other clanmates. There should be consequences for that. But was this duel, this humiliation before his clan, the right solution? The crowd seemed to like it. The tiny bits of conversation he caught from the slayers talking to Alísa revealed *they* considered it warranted. It was what a slayer would do.

But it's not what I would do.

Perhaps the duel's outcome had gained him some respect, but Tern… Tern was lost in an unfamiliar world, and Falier had just shoved him further away. Reacting in anger, hurting those entrusted to him—that wasn't who he was.

Selene was right. I'm losing my center.

Tern's friends and L'non walked away, drawing Falier's focus back to Alísa. Her eyes were hard as they took him in. His heart shriveled even smaller as Sesína connected them and he felt her fury.

"Líse, I—"

"No. You don't get to talk right now. What have I ever done to make you think this is how I want my camp managed? By the sword? If you couldn't handle him, you should have come to me. What were you even thinking, challenging a subordinate to a duel?"

Alísa waited, but before Falier could speak, he heard wing-beats overhead. He looked up as Graydonn swooped in and landed heavily. The dragon's eyes blazed, pinning on him and ignoring Alísa and Sesína entirely.

"What was that? You get mad at someone, so you draw a sword? Congratulations, you're becoming just like the slayers you've been trying so hard to emulate!"

"Graydonn, I—I'm sorry."

"Sorry for what?" Graydonn's nostrils flared. *"For scaring me half to death by dueling with true blades? Or was it for yanking on my mind to win the idiotic fight? Or how about for trying so hard to become the man who murdered my father?"* The bond constricted, muffling Graydonn's voice, though its intensity didn't waver. *"Do you know how much it hurts to watch you become like him?!"*

Something snapped in Falier's mind. For a terrible moment, he thought the mind-kin bond had broken. Then he realized the truth. Sesína had cut Alísa off from them. Graydonn's eyes dimmed as he looked at Alísa, who held a tremulous hand to her mouth.

Graydonn dipped his head low in apology and submission. *"Alísa. I—"*

"No," Sesína growled, keeping a tight hold as Alísa turned and hurried away. *"You both are complete morons."*

She snapped at the air—a warning not to follow—before turning around to escort Alísa. Graydonn, thoroughly ashamed, took to the sky without another word. Leaving Falier alone to his misery.

31

LONELINESS

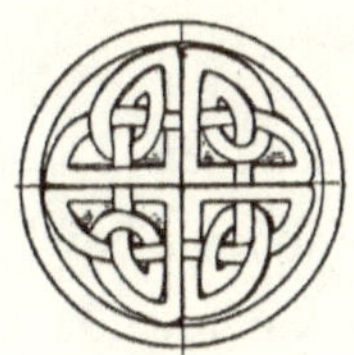

A night of fitful sleep did nothing to lighten Alísa's heart, nor did the rain pouring over the war-camp. For the humans, it was a nuisance, weighing down their clothing as they performed their tasks, or else confining them to their tents. For the dragons, it was claustrophobic. The water rolled off their scales easily and most didn't mind the constant dripping, but the amount of it made it near-impossible to see while flying, keeping them grounded. For the dreki, it was just plain cold. Rís snuggled in Alísa's hair under her cloak's hood, occasionally chirping his woes to her.

Alísa couldn't avoid the rain—not yet. As she searched about her camp, she nodded encouragement to those who had to work in it, periodically stopping to ask if they had seen her quarry.

She finally found him in the kitchen tent, working alone at a table while three women chatted at another.

Waving to the women making flatbread, Alísa approached Falier. He averted his gaze the moment he saw her, a cloud of shame covering him as he chopped potatoes for the midday meal. She stopped opposite him and spoke softly.

"It's embarrassing how long it took me to find you. It's been a month since I last found you in the k—kitchens."

"I can't hurt anyone in here."

He continued chopping as Alísa searched for words. They needed to talk about what happened, but in the midst of her fury, she had sensed his remorse. How to balance being his chief and his beloved? How to reprimand while understanding he already knew he was wrong? How to find the heartache that made him act so out-of-character?

"I'm sorry," he said quietly, eying the others. "I—I'm sorry."

Carefully, Alísa reached to rest her hand on Falier's, stilling his knife. "I know. We need to talk."

One woman looked at them. Falier shook his head, his voice entering her mind.

"Not here. Please."

Alísa let go of his hand. *"Mamá's tent. She'll give us space."*

With a tense nod, Falier grabbed a bowl and scraped the potatoes into it off the edge of the table. Leaving the bowl, he followed Alísa into the rain. Her mother's tent was on the opposite side of camp as the kitchen, providing the needed quiet for catching rest between tasks and meetings. Alísa could have brought her own tent from her caves, but right now, she and her mother desired companionship over privacy.

Ducking inside, Alísa dropped her hood and undid her cloak. Rís barked a complaint at the sudden loss of warmth and flew to Hanah. She sat in a corner of the main chamber, embroidering a royal blue cloth that might be a bodice. Hanah took in Alísa and Falier's entry as Rís landed on her shoulder, her eyes tired and her *anam nasctha* paint prominent on her chin.

Sticking her needle in the cloth's edge, Hanah rose with a knowing look. "I'll be in my chamber if you need me."

Alísa gave a small, grateful smile. Her mother had heard bits and pieces of what happened, sobbed out amid Alísa's grief. How she could be Alísa's rock even in her own grief, Alísa couldn't comprehend. Perhaps the *anam nasctha* legends were true and Papá wasn't far from her, or perhaps being a parent simply came with a special grace for one's child.

Forcing herself back to the present, she led Falier to kneel with her in the center of the chamber. There, she waited. Falier didn't meet her eyes, staring instead at his hands on his thighs.

"I made an awful mistake, Líse. I don't know what I was thinking—no. That's not true. But it's all excuses. What I did helped nothing. It went around your authority, it displayed my utter incompetence at keeping control over my charges, and, worst of all, it lost us riders. I doubt Tern and his companions will return."

He looked up, a sliver of hope in his eyes. "Maybe if you discipline me for what I did and set someone else over them, we can get them back."

"We'll talk about that. Tell me your 'excuses'. What truly happened yesterday?"

Falier's gaze flitted to her mother's chamber, a touch of fear entering his emotions. Alísa touched her temple.

"Talk here."

Falier hesitated, tension in his voice. "I don't think I'll make sense there."

Flames, Alísa had never seen him so terrified. She touched his cheek and kissed him. It was a light kiss, their lips cold from being outside, yet Falier's desperation flowed through the contact.

She looked him in the eyes. "I love you. Nothing I see will change that. Talk to me, aloud or t-telepathically. Just talk to me."

Falier reached out telepathically, the gentle buzzing of his presence overwhelmed by fear, striving, and loneliness—such aching loneliness.

"I'm trying, Líse. I'm trying so hard to be someone who can be your tiern, a slayer who can gain the respect of warriors, and—I can't do it."

Scenes flashed past Alísa's astral eyes. Slayers who mocked or ignored him. Others who loathed him for his position. Graydonn's constant pushing for him to stop becoming a slayer who might earn even an ounce of recognition. Selene tempting him to return to who he used to be. Her father's words. Fear going into battle. His and Graydonn's bond slipping. Alísa's attention constantly elsewhere. Dueling Tern.

"I just wanted to prove I belong," Falier said. *"I wanted to be a slayer. But the others don't hurt people simply by existing like I do. I hurt Graydonn, Tern, you. If I can't be a slayer, how can I be your tiern? Why did the Maker leave me with the holders instead of letting me go with Taz to learn before I was ruined?"*

That last question hit a wound within Alísa so raw that she gasped. The sound brought her back to the physical world, where tears flowed for her beloved.

"I don't want to be alone anymore," he said, wiping his eyes. *"I thought I could give up everything to become what I'm supposed to be for you, but I can't, Líse. But I don't want to lose you!"*

Alísa shook her head and lunged for him, wrapping her arms around him, pulling his head to her shoulder.

"You will never lose me," she whispered. "I fell in love with the holder. He is more than enough for me."

He didn't sob against her as she would have if their situations were reversed. She wouldn't have judged him for it—he had every right to it. Instead, he just breathed, trying to regain control.

She rubbed his back. "I'm sorry I let you think otherwise. I didn't know."

Falier squeezed her, then pulled away, wiping his face with his sleeve. He spoke aloud again, his voice tight. "I should have talked to you sooner. I let things go too far, then *I* went too far."

Alísa pressed her lips together. "You d—did go further than what I want for my c-c-clan. But, you didn't for most others."

He blinked. "What do you mean?"

Alísa shrugged. "Many say Tern deserved what he got. Now, some were upset about your use of t-t-telepathy, and others think it disgraceful for a superior to challenge a subordinate. B—but for most, you haven't lost ground. That being said" —she affected her chief persona— "don't do that again."

Falier looked down. "I won't. It doesn't really matter that others support my poor decision. I pushed Tern away. I don't want to be that man."

"Then don't."

He shook his head. "But what else can I do? They don't respect me unless I *am* that way. Strong. Unyielding. Wholly not me."

"You can be strong without shouting or beating p-p-people into submission." She allowed a smile. "B—believe me, I know."

Falier held up his hands. "I'm sorry, I didn't mean—"

"I know." She pressed a palm to his and threaded their fingers. "It t-t-t-took me a long t-time to figure it out. You will t-t-too."

He sighed. "I hate to tell you this, Líse, but time is something we're sorely lacking. I need to train dragons and riders to work together, now. But to get them to listen, I have to be—someone else."

"Are you sure they aren't listening to you?"

Falier lowered their hands and looked at her like she hadn't been listening. "Yesterday wouldn't have happened if I hadn't been so wrung out from their constant pushing and mockery."

"Falier," she said, gentling her tone, "I've watched your training sessions. The wayfarers may be less skilled than Briek and his men are, b—but they are learning. From you. Yes, Tern and a few others are being belligerent, but even they've progressed."

"It doesn't feel that way."

"Okay," she said. "Why not?"

Falier looked at their clasped hands, eyes unfocusing. Watching him, holding his hand, being close enough to breathe him in, she realized how much she missed him. Not the striving version she had seen frequently these last two weeks, but the earnest one sitting before her.

"Maybe some do listen," Falier finally admitted, "but they don't—flames, this sounds petty—they don't like me. They ignore me, or else mock me for not being one of them already, even when I'm trying hard."

"I think that's where the problem lies, love. They can feel you striving. It tells them you think you don't belong, that their standard is something that you have t-t-t-to rise to." Alísa reached up to finger her betrothal necklace. "Warriors are t-t-trained to seek weakness. Not all will attack, but some will."

Falier looked at the necklace. "You overcame that. You stand among the chiefs so confidently now. I'm trying so hard, but it's just not coming. Or when it comes, I go too far."

"Do you know why I asked you to train the dragon-rider squads, Falier?" Alísa took his hands in hers. "It wasn't your experience or skill, though Maker knows you have both. It wasn't because you needed a leadership position to gain legitimacy as my t-t-tiern. It was because you, holder Falier, understand people and how to build relationships. Yes, we need skilled pairs, but we also need an army that trusts each other. I b—believed you could make it happen. I still do. You don't need to be a sword-master or surly or have a tale of dramatic change from killing dragons to befriending them. Just bring people together, as you've always done."

Falier looked down at their hands. "So Graydonn was right, huh? I should stop all this" —he touched the hilt of his sword— "and just be who I've always been?"

Alísa smiled. "You're the man I fell in love with."

Falier sniffed a laugh. "I'm not looking for the riders to fall in love with me."

"Good to know they're no c—competition."

"Absolutely not." He paused, levity falling away. "Though your pa told me by marrying you, I was marrying the clan. Don't you think that requires some sort of change?"

Alísa ran a finger over her bracelet, taking comfort in the scale's smoothness. "Of course it does. But not losing who we are."

"I know who I don't want to be now. I guess I can start there." Falier squeezed her hand. "Thank you for listening. I needed to get it all out."

"Of course. We're a team, right?" She touched her necklace for emphasis, drawing an agreeing smile from him. "As for everything else, I want you to still t-t-train your dragon-rider squads. I want you to do it as you, d—drawing from your battle experience *and* your time as a holder. Bring them together."

He swallowed. "I'll try."

Alísa tasted the astral plane. Uncertainty still wafted from Falier, but rather than a swirling windstorm, it was like a tent pegged to the ground. The wind pulled and stretched, but there was a lifeline. It filled her to know that she had helped that happen, yet it also, strangely, made her feel empty. She had her own windstorm blowing her about like a hatchling without its—without its parent.

No. Don't cry. This is Falier's moment. Not. Yours.

"Líse?" Falier ducked to look into her downcast eyes. "I'll make it happen. I will. Somehow."

Alísa shook her head and forced calming breaths. "It's—not you."

Falier was silent for a second, then gently tilted her chin up.

"We *are* a team. Right? Let me carry you now."

She blew out a breath, more tears flowing. She did need someone to talk to. Sesína was an enormous support, but also entirely too close to the situation because of their Illumination. Farren wasn't an option. She wanted Falier.

At a finger to her temple, Falier connected them again. There in her mind, Alísa let him see her own doubts, insecurities, and fury. He had no answers, but he held her as she cried. And right here, right now, that was enough.

32

MIND-KIN

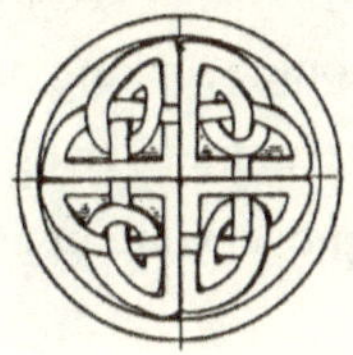

The mind-kin bond remained walled off throughout breakfast, to where Falier wasn't sure Graydonn would attend today's dragon-rider training. They had already missed yesterday because of the heavy rain. They couldn't afford to lose more, especially since Falier had plans to switch things up. He wanted to run everything past Graydonn first, but the longer the dragon remained away, the more harried their conversation would be. That wouldn't help either of them through their issues.

But Graydonn came with the dragons, all arriving from their various camps and landing with great thuds before the riders. Falier stepped forward to greet Graydonn in the same manner he always did. Within, however, he was far more cautious. With a sight-line to the dragon, or simply because Graydonn finally allowed it, Falier got through.

"Morning."

Graydonn averted his gaze, eyes dim and hints of shame in his connection. *"Morning. You—ready to fly?"*

Falier nodded. *"We should talk, after."*

"Yes. Can we act like everything's normal until then?"

"We have to. Despite everything, we're still a united front on the topic of dragons and riders, right?"

Graydonn blinked slowly. *"Right. Hop on, then."*

Falier did as he said, trying to move as normally as he could. Though everyone saw his display with Tern, none knew of the fallout between him and Graydonn. He planned to keep it that way.

"Graydonn, I spoke with Alisa about being a holder in a world of slayers, and I'd like to try something new today, if you'll help me. I kind of can't fly without you."

Graydonn didn't respond to his attempt at humor, just flexed his neck to look back at Falier. *"I'm listening."*

Falier's three squads filled the sky west of camp, two working on keeping riders during aerial maneuvers, and one working their combat patterns. Rassím, Dezra, Taz, and Harenn led the maneuvering pairs and, assuming they took Falier's instructions, would keep everyone in conversation to get to know each other better.

Falier and Graydonn flew with the third squad, ready with today's new pattern. By now, everyone knew the drill. The difference today, however, was Falier and Graydonn did not supervise.

"Today, each of you pairs will take a turn running patterns with us," Falier said. *"Now, I think most of you are ready for some unbounded combat, but you'll have to earn it by answering a question I pose at the beginning of your match. If both partners answer before we finish the pattern, you'll get five minutes of free-sparring with us."*

That sparked some fresh interest from the pairs. Hoping to start easily, Falier called L'non and H'sinth forward. As the dragons circled, Graydonn cut the four of them off from the squad.

"Here's your question," Falier said. *"What's one thing you would do on a day with no responsibilities?"*

Graydonn started the pattern, ascending quickly. Bewilderment filled the conversation link, though H'sinth did not miss a wing-beat. Falier shot his first psychic arrow, which pinged off L'non's shield. As L'non lowered his defense, his words entered Falier's mind.

"That is your question?" He sent his own two arrows as H'sinth twisted to change directions. *"Seriously?"*

"The real question is" —Falier shot another blast— *"can you answer it?"*

The dragons flew toward each other as Falier and L'non exchanged predetermined blows. H'sinth's voice rumbled in Falier's mind.

"I would hunt waterfowl for my daughter. They are her favorite."

"I don't know, Graydonn," Falier said. *"Does that sound like a responsibility to you?"*

"Have you ever seen a hatchling given their favorite food, young slayer?" H'sinth thrummed. *"It is delightful."*

"How old is she?" Graydonn asked while Falier and L'non continued their bout. Falier's shielding almost made him miss the answer.

"Hatched two months ago. She is with her mother at the cave." H'sinth's voice turned with sorrow. *"I fear I will miss much, but I cannot abide an army of an'reik in the same country as my daughter."*

One of L'non's arrows hit its mark, making Falier wince. He'd been too slow to shield. Good thing L'non aimed at him and not Graydonn. *"How about you, L'non?"*

"Climb a mountain," L'non said. *"Not to fight dragons or hunt healing herbs, just to do it. I'd probably bring my boys along, since they've never gotten to climb for any reason."*

Falier grinned. *"Congratulations, you've earned five minutes of free-sparring."*

Graydonn thrummed. *"If you can catch us."*

Graydonn speared west, away from camp and the squads practicing flight formations. H'sinth gave chase, a thrill in his end of the mind-link. They led their opponents on a wild chase, Falier constantly having to crane his neck to watch the astral plane for L'non's attacks. By the end, sweat rolled down Falier's spine and Graydonn's sides heaved.

"Well done," Falier said, waving to L'non. *"Next time, try using the astral plane to help anticipate attacks. I use it extensively when fighting."*

L'non grunted. *"I don't much like it when I cannot see where I am going."*

"I understand. But remember, H'sinth doesn't want to run into problems either, and he's controlling your flight. Worrying about something you cannot control will leave your guard down at the points you can."

L'non pondered that. *"I will try."*

Their session over, Graydonn sent L'non and H'sinth back to their squad with a request to send the next pair. As they left, Falier reached out.

"L'non, one more question for you. What's your favorite song?"

He thought for a moment. *"Bear in the Briar."*

Falier grinned. *"I know it. Great pick!"*

They flew off and Graydonn reset himself for the next match. *"Did that go as you wanted?"*

"Yes. I don't think many partners interact. Now L'non and H'sinth know they are both fathers and enjoy spending time with their kids. Hopefully, most pairs will find some common ground."

"And the song?"

"For the future." Falier saw movement among the squad—a fiery orange dragoness separating from the group.

Maker help him. Varek was the rider.

Falier sighed. Well, he had started easy so he would be ready for harder trainees. He waved. *"Varek, Mennáli, good morning."*

Mennáli rumbled a pleasant greeting. Even Varek's tone smirked.

"I must admit, I was shocked when you challenged Tern the other day, but it appears you've gained some skills. Just needed a true weapon and stakes, I suppose."

Of course, Varek would be someone to respect Falier more for his brash actions. Should he humble himself now by admitting what he did was wrong, or leave it be? Such an admission would antagonize Varek, for whom the same actions wouldn't necessarily be bad.

Better to move forward. *"Ready for a real match?"*

"I just have to answer a question?"

"Both of you do," Falier said pointedly. *"Are you ready, Mennáli?"*

"For anything, young slayer," she assured with a growl.

"Then begin. What's one thing you would do on a day with no responsibilities?"

Graydonn and Mennáli ascended rapidly, twisting and weaving. Varek's mind-shield was hot as Falier's first blast hit it.

"Get-to-know-you questions?" Varek shot two arrows in rapid succession. *"What is this?"*

"A long flight," Mennáli said. *"A few hours, at least, followed by time in the hot springs."*

"Your mountain has hot springs?" Falier sent his second arrow of the pattern. *"That's amazing!"*

"No," Varek growled, the sound almost worthy of a dragon, *"what's amazing is you acting like a holder again with these touchy-feely questions."*

Falier formed a shield against Varek's too-hard arrows. *"What, you don't know your sword-partners? Your clanmates? That's too holder-like for you?"*

Graydonn dipped low while Mennáli rushed high. Falier's stomach dropped with him and he gripped Graydonn's spine tighter.

"When you act like it's our purpose, yes," Varek said. *"We're here to fight. If not dragons, then an'reik. I almost thought you understood that now."*

Falier shielded as Varek sent more psychic arrows their way. *"You're running out of time. Answer the question if you want an actual fight. How would you spend a day with no responsibilities?"*

"I would find and berate you for this idiotic game."

That drew a loud thrum from Mennáli. Hopefully, her humor was loud enough in the mind-link to drown out Falier's uncertainties. How else would he motivate them to talk about things besides war? That was what they needed, what Alísa required, and, truthfully, what he himself wanted.

Technically, humor *was* a good way to connect people…

"Fair enough. Lose them, Graydonn!"

Varek's blows were aggressive and frequent. He often forgot to shield, which Falier took full advantage of. He even aimed a few arrows at Mennáli, so she would remind Varek to defend them both.

After five minutes, Falier called the end of the match, and Varek and Mennáli flew back to their squad. Falier didn't ask about a song this time—it wouldn't help with Varek in the slightest. As they waited for their next sparring pair, Graydonn mused.

"I think this new plan has merit, connecting with each individual pairing. As I spoke with Mennáli and felt you and Varek speaking opposite us, I sensed similarities in their psychic touch. When I asked Mennáli, she confirmed—they have mind-kin potential."

"What?" Falier twisted to find the fiery orange dragoness in the sky again. *"Seriously? Varek?"*

"Mennáli feels the same. She hasn't spoken to him about it. They barely speak at all, she says."

Falier breathed in the statement. *"That's exactly why I wanted to change this up today. I hope it facilitates more conversation between the pairs, but that isn't something I can enforce."*

"Some simply won't be swayed," Graydonn said.

"I know. But it's our duty to reach them if possible. I just need to keep trying."

Falier held back the rest of his thoughts as the next pair joined Graydonn's circling. This change had worked decently for L'non and H'sinth, but Falier couldn't help but feel that something important was missing. And that just being a holder, just being himself, might not help him identify it.

By the end of training, Graydonn panted and Falier's mind felt frayed. Two hours with only one break in-between. True, many battles went on far longer, but training lacked the adrenaline that masked fatigue. It also lacked Alísa's songs that empowered Graydonn's—and, by extension, Falier's—mind and heart to continue.

The work was not without its benefits. There were some among his squads Falier had never spoken to beyond giving orders. Many of these were indeed learning to respect each other—Falier simply hadn't noticed while handling the more difficult trainees. They weren't a cohesive unit by any means, but speaking with them lifted Falier's heart from the mire training had become.

He hoped these next two conversations wouldn't bring him back down. Searching the squads as they landed in succession, he called out two pairs. As the rest of the warriors dispersed to sparring, food, or duties, Varek stalked toward them. Behind him came Mennáli, Jossen, and his dragon partner, P'raenn.

Falier marveled as he watched them approach. He and Graydonn had missed not one, but two potential mind-kin bonds. Why Graydonn missed them, Falier didn't know, but his own neglect was stark. He would be better.

"Thank you all for coming."

Varek crossed his arms. "We had a choice?"

Jossen chuckled, shaking his head. "Any opportunity to be sour, eh?"

Falier smiled, grateful. "Graydonn and I need to tell you something. It's somewhat personal, and I apologize for having to speak it rather than you discovering it yourselves" —he paused as Mennáli growled— "but recent events make this necessary."

Graydonn slow-blinked. *"There is a dragon-rider pairing among Alísa's clan who discovered they were mind-kin suddenly and violently. Though Komi and Trísse emerged stronger and now are friends, we cannot assume this will be the result for every human-dragon pair. And today, Falier and I discovered that there are potential bonds lingering in the air between each of you pairs."*

P'raenn's head shot up. *"Mind-kin? Me and—Slayer Jossen?"*

Jossen looked first to his partner, then to Varek, then back to Falier, confusion scrunching his brow. "Like the two of you? Or Chief Alísa and Sesína?"

"Not like them," Falier said. "Their bond is Illumination and is far deeper. A mind-kin bond forms between individuals whose minds pulse at the same speed and who have aligned goals and desires. It allows for a greater sensing of thoughts and emotions, a longer range of communication that doesn't require sight-lines, and a sharing of psychic strength and power."

Varek's jaw worked. "I've already opened myself to dragons further than I'd like. I am *not* going further."

Mennáli growled. *"Which is why I said nothing when I sensed the potential. Both parties must accept it. You cannot bond if you, with your obtuse psychics, do not notice."*

"Obtuse?!"

Graydonn groaned. *"There's no need to offend, Mennáli. You are mistaken— bonds can and have formed near-spontaneously. While Komi and Trísse claim they chose to bond, it came abruptly, and they had little knowledge what was happening. Perhaps it's because it involved a human and a dragon instead of two dragons—we don't know."*

"Which is why we needed to tell you," Falier said. "Honestly, I would love it if you became our next bonded pairs. We need the power and camaraderie such bonds bring. But to not warn you simply because we hope for it is wrong. We're prepared to answer questions, as well as to either help you learn how to use the bond or else assign you new partners so it won't form accidentally."

"Reassign me," Varek snapped. "I don't want this creature in my head any more than necessary."

Mennáli thrummed. *"Finally, we have found something that scares you, slayer. I have no fear that a bond should occur—spontaneous bonding is ridiculous."*

Varek glared at the dragoness. Falier hoped Varek would see it as a challenge and remain, but the slayer shook his head.

"Reassign me. I pity the man who gets paired with her. Perhaps use it as a punishment for your worst performer."

"We'll figure out the reassignment," Falier said. "Thank you. You two are dismissed."

Mennáli huffed and leapt into the air, the wind of her wings making Varek and Jossen both flinch. Varek watched her fly away, then shook his head.

"Come on, Joss. I could use a good sparring after that infernal creature's tricks."

Jossen didn't respond, his eyes fixed on P'raenn. The way his expression changed, it seemed he and the dragon were communicating privately. Then Jossen looked at Varek.

"You go ahead. I'll try to make it before the end."

Varek blinked. "You can't be serious."

"This is a serious time."

Varek stared, first at Jossen, then P'raenn and back. He walked away with no further protests or mutterings, just long strides that said he would rather be anywhere else.

Jossen looked at Falier. "P'raenn tells me that a mind-kin bond does not require you to remain together forever. Is this true?"

Falier didn't look at Graydonn, the question bringing unease. "Yes. It's true."

"And when you separate, your minds are no longer connected?"

"If you are too far removed," Graydonn confirmed. *"About four or five miles. If you come close again, though, you will probably feel each other."*

Jossen nodded slowly while P'raenn watched. The dragon's eyes faded in and out, signaling his own conflict. Jossen looked up at him.

"It appears we have much to discuss. With our commanders' permission, I would fly with you as we consider what we must do."

Falier grinned. "You have it. Just don't stray far from camp. No one should be alone, in case of an'reik scouts."

P'raenn lowered for Jossen to mount. They flew off without another word to Falier or Graydonn, though the look in Jossen's eyes said they had already begun their discussion.

Falier rubbed a hand through his hair. "That went better than expected. Jossen's a good man, but he's hunted dragons longer than P'raenn's been alive."

Graydonn clicked thoughtfully. *"I, too, expected both pairs to split."*

Silence hung heavy between them as they watched P'raenn and Jossen disappear in the glaring white clouds. Falier let out a breath. Nothing left to keep him and Graydonn from their own private discussion.

"I'm sorry, Graydonn. I should have realized how comparing myself to Alisa's pa and other slayers affected you. To be completely honest, I don't think I could have avoided making the comparison. But I could have shown more empathy for your pain."

Graydonn rumbled in his chest. *"And I should have spoken up before it flamed out of me."* He looked across the hills. *"I do not understand why you wish to change. You are a good man. You needn't become like these ruffians. Anyone who won't respect you solely because you grew up differently isn't worth your time."*

Falier rubbed his neck. *"The whole clan has to be worth my time, if I'm going to become tiern. What if I have to change in order to lead them?"*

"The dragons are also your clanmates. Not just the slayers."

"I know." Falier sighed. *"I feel like there's no right answer. If I change, I hurt people, including myself. If I don't change, I can't take care of them."*

Graydonn looked at him, amber eyes seemingly bottomless. He stayed silent, though his mind shifted about inside of Falier's. Not a mind-reading, but a searching. For what, Falier couldn't tell, but he left himself open.

Finally, Graydonn's presence pulled back to its normal position. His eyes dimmed.

"You deeply desire to care for others, yet when you needed me, I did not care well for you. I am sorry."

Falier sniffed, glancing away momentarily. *"I forgive you. Let's both do better, okay?"*

Graydonn blinked slowly. *"Let's."*

A burden lifted from Falier's heart. Not the whole, but he could breathe a bit easier. The rest would come with time.

"Will you go sparring now?"

Falier shook his head. *"I don't think I'm ready to hold a sword again just yet. Besides, I need to speak to Farren. There are some favorite songs I have to learn."*

Graydonn's eyes brightened, and he stood. *"Then allow me to accompany you, my friend."*

Falier smiled and began the trek back into camp, though as he passed the path to the sparring grounds, his heart wavered. Surely it hadn't all been bad? He had bonded with Jossen while sparring, hadn't he?

Falier shook his head and set his eyes forward. Whatever the answer, today he had a mission. Today he was a holder again.

33

SUSTENANCE

Camp awoke with the dawn, and Kallar with it. He 'awoke' outside, shoved back into control like every morning since grounding the rebel dragons. The keeper watched them through the night, using Kallar's powers to shout them into submission if they moved. If they didn't move, it satisfied its boredom by raiding Kallar's mind for more memories to inflict.

Kallar's eyes were dry from lack of closure, his back ached from sitting up straight, his crossed legs were numb, and everywhere dew settled on him. It seemed every joint popped as he twisted to take in the camp's movements. He only caught a glimpse, though, before a dragon moved. Lellani's silvery scales reflected the morning sun as she lifted her head high above him. Her copper eyes flashed.

"One of these nights, I will catch you off-guard and kill you for all you have done."

After days of this routine, he almost wished she would.

"I should think you'd be grateful," the keeper hissed. *"I've given you complete power over your enemy. They cannot harm without your permission, every attempt to leave is thwarted, and your body is never in danger despite your proximity."*

Yet how long would his body survive without sleep? The keeper forced him to take one of Isarra's healing potions every day, but could that actually substitute? And beyond his body, Kallar's mind frayed. The final image of the night echoed like remnants of a nightmare—the door of the dragon-shelter falling shut as fire consumed a brave woman with warrior's braids in her ebony hair. The last thing he had seen was pain, an agony he learned when his arm burned. One small piece of justice in his life, to feel the pain he had caused.

Kallar stood as an'reik came to relieve him—two of fire and one of strength. All were slayers who had become an'reik after the keeper's display with the rebel dragons. They knew the truth now, that Kallar was possessed and not an'reik, but it didn't matter to them anymore. It was enough that the slayers who hadn't sold their souls believed the falsehood.

As Kallar moved through the morning routine of changing clothes and getting breakfast, he saw many more turned slayers. More than half of the an'reik's allies had now become them. It twisted his stomach how the keeper used him to this end, but he forced himself to eat, regardless. There was still a chance for rescue. If he couldn't sleep, he sure as flames would ensure he got sustenance. Anything to give him an edge.

Movement drew Kallar's eyes from his food. Marizarr, a fire-manipulator and Isarra's second, stalked toward him. It might have been intimidating if he didn't hold a small bowl of gruel in his giant, dark hand. The keeper stirred to attention inside Kallar's mind.

Marizarr shoved the bowl at Kallar. "It's your turn to feed the prisoner."

R'lann. Kallar stared at the gruel. He had never been allowed to serve R'lann before. That had mostly been a blessing, as it kept the keeper from taunting Kallar with thoughts of harming him. But he also hadn't seen his brother since the day R'lann stitched him up, except for small glances while moving camps.

"Take it," Marizarr said. "Eat it yourself for all I care, but that's all the boy's getting today."

Kallar dropped his own bowl and grabbed the one in the an'reik's hands. Emotions collided within him, but he began the march to the prison tent.

"Well," the keeper purred, *"this is an unexpected pleasure."*

The first of what Kallar presumed would be many images filled his senses— a dagger covered in blood. Kallar pushed on, his sword-belt heavy at his waist.

"You can't kill him," Kallar said quietly. "Isarra needs him."

The keeper growled. *"Isarra isn't the only authority."*

Kallar kept going, willing his heart to settle. There were two guards at the black tent's entrance. They would hear if the keeper tried anything. They would stop it, because they *did* follow Isarra.

The guards let him through easily, expecting him. Inside, the tent was rank with sweat and other odors. It was also dark, with no lamp and barely any light shining through the crack in the flap. Rage pulsed in Kallar's veins for R'lann's treatment, and the keeper lapped it up greedily.

"R'lann?"

Further in, a shadow stirred. "Kal?"

Kallar went to him. "It's me. Not the keeper"—he paused as it growled—"not yet."

Kneeling, Kallar passed the bowl off, which R'lann took and began wolfing down. A new violent image surfaced, spiking fear in Kallar. He should leave, right now. He stood and turned toward the door.

"Wait!" R'lann said through a mouthful of food. "Don't go."

"I have to." Another vision and a growl of pleasure. "It will kill you."

"The Maker is with me," R'lann said. "I'm not afraid."

The growl became more violent, raging. Kallar felt the keeper's breath on his neck.

"Karn believed in the Maker, too. Look how he ended up."

R'lann stood, abandoning his bowl and grabbing Kallar's sleeve. His hands were clammy. "They can't touch what belongs to him—"

Kallar's arm shot out without his consent, grabbing R'lann's neck and squeezing. Kallar panicked and fought the control, struggled with all of his might, but he couldn't stop it. The keeper took hold of his voice.

"But I can."

R'lann grabbed at Kallar's hand, trying to claw it away, but the boy was too weak. Kallar screamed in his own head, but no one would hear him. None but the monster feasting on his terror.

Light flooded the tent. "Hey!"

In an instant, the keeper retreated, leaving Kallar in control. Kallar let go of R'lann just as the guards grabbed for his wrists. He trembled as they pulled him away.

"I'm sorry, R'lann. Don't trust me again."

He could see R'lann's face now, dirty with dark circles under his eyes. He rubbed at his neck, brow creased.

"Call to him, Kal. He'll help you!"

The keeper lunged, but the guards drew Kallar out of the tent completely. When it realized it couldn't finish its attack, the keeper made Kallar walk away. Its snarls filled his ears until it brought him to a tight space between two tents. There it sat and pulled Kallar fully into the mind-world, where it unleashed its fury.

34

PUSH & PULL

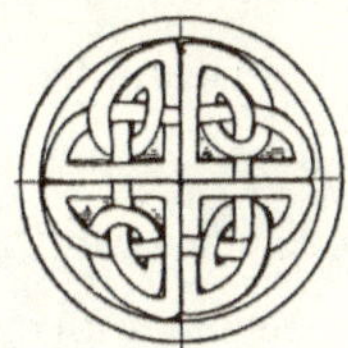

Falier ate his dinner with Selene, Taz, and Farren, all the while thanking Eldra Aeba that it did not rain tonight. He had invited Alísa to join them, but she wasn't ready to face Farren. Her pain was still too raw, so she sat instead with her family, enjoying her young cousins' antics and, hopefully, being distracted from her woes.

He and his crew finished their food quickly, then approached one of the large fires lighting the camp. Falier carried with him Farren's bodhrán. He had left his in Alísa's caves—after all, it was useless to a slayer. Thankfully, Farren brought more instruments than there were in all of Me'ran. Why didn't slayers deride Farren for being so holder-like?

Farren plucked at the strings of his lute, tuning them quietly as people chatted over their meals. "This is a good idea, Falier. Something to raise people's hearts in troubled times."

Falier glanced at the sky. "I just hope Graydonn comes through. The dragons don't know what they're missing out on, not having music in their culture."

Beside them, Selene warmed up her fingers with patterns over her flute— she had brought one of her own to camp, because she was perfect like that. Taz, meanwhile, meticulously cleaned the mouthpiece of Farren's low-fife. The flutter of wings announced Ska and Laen's presence, as well as that of an orange-highlighted drek who favored Taz.

Soon all were ready and waited for Falier. Here went nothing.

He chose an instrumental song first, something light to ease the people in. Eyes turned to them—some appreciative, others indifferent. He picked the next piece by scanning the crowd for a rider who had finished eating. L'non. That made it easy, as Alísa would be sure to sing along, hopefully drawing in the whole family.

It worked perfectly. Soon more slayers joined—some as they continued shoveling food in their mouth, to Falier's amusement. A couple, including Varek, shook their heads and walked off, presumably to their tents. That was about what Falier had expected. Graydonn led a group of dragons in at the end of the last verse, about thirty settling to listen just outside camp.

Falier and the rest of the musicians ran through more songs on the list of riders' favorites he had gained yesterday morning. A part of him basked in the fact that it was working—the clan was singing together, even drawing curious slayers from other camps. This wouldn't facilitate human-dragon relationships necessarily, but hopefully the dragons would sense a piece of the humans' camaraderie. The dreki certainly did, dancing about and weaving between the singers.

Despite everything, however, another part of Falier felt hollow. Yes, it was fun and he loved playing, but a sense of wrongness persisted, much like yesterday. He should be happy. He was a holder again. Alísa didn't need him to change, and Graydonn and Selene didn't want him to either. But Karn's words haunted him. This—what he was doing—wasn't wrong, but it wasn't right either.

As the final notes faded and the clan applauded the musicians, Falier passed the bodhrán off to Farren with a word of thanks. He wandered in a daze, half-heartedly accepting words of gratitude and encouragement.

"This is war-time, holder boy," a familiar voice snapped him from his reverie. "Not an occasion for music, cheer, and drinks."

"Tern." Falier hadn't seen him since the duel. Alísa said he had deserted to a clan of ground troops. Falier rubbed his neck. "I'm sorry. I was wrong to fight you. I should have handled things differently."

Tern shook his head. "I'm not sorry. Now I know what you truly are—a coward and traitor to your race."

Falier's shoulders slumped. "I'm sorry you feel that way."

Tern scoffed and shouldered past him. "Mousey holder."

Falier couldn't find the energy to be angry. Numbness covered him again. He needed Alísa.

No, not Alísa. The realization took hold in his heart. He needed Hanah.

He searched the crowd for her to no avail, then found her and Alísa's tent.

He stopped at the entry flap embroidered with symbols of chiefdom, honor, and strength.

"Lady Hanah?"

After a few seconds, Hanah lifted the flap. "Yes, Falier?"

He caught himself rubbing his neck and blew out a breath. "I need guidance. From you, and perhaps Karn?"

Her brow smoothed as she smiled gently. It reminded him of his mother, a smile that promised help no matter what it required.

"Enter."

He followed her inside, obeying her prompt to sit on the ground in the center of the main chamber. It was lit by a single candle in an elegant stand on the kneeling table where the family took non-communal meals. Hanah sat across from him, her *anam nasctha* paint stark against her pale skin.

"Speak your mind, Falier. How can we help you?"

'We.' So odd. Falier had never heard of this slayer tradition before seeing Hanah take it on. Could she actually communicate with Karn? Or, at least, feel his thoughts on matters? Or did she simply know him best?

Falier cleared his throat. "I'm lost. I tried to do what Karn said. Learn the sword, speak and be heard, become a slayer. But when I did, I became harsh. I hurt people and lost myself. So I tried just being me again. It's what Alísa said to do, it's what Graydonn's constantly telling me to be. And it partially worked! But I still feel like I'm failing Karn and, through that, failing his clan and daughter. I don't know what to do."

Hanah hummed thoughtfully, then closed her eyes and sat in silence. The long quiet was like a widening hole in Falier's chest. Was she disappointed? Had she known this would happen all along? Was she thinking, or communicating with Karn somehow?

She opened her eyes. "Tell me, Falier, when did you lose your way? When you started learning the sword, or when you started emulating other slayers?"

He saw where she was trying to take this, but her logic was faulty. "Karn didn't just want me to learn sword-play. He said a holder can't have the respect of a slayer clan. That I needed to become more. And I've learned it's true."

"You hear with ears tuned to your failings, much like a certain daughter of ours." Hanah shook her head. "Karn did not say a holder cannot gain their respect. He said they will not *easily* give it. He wanted you to develop new skills to build your confidence among warriors." She placed a gentle hand on his. "Hear me, Falier. Karn and I spoke of you frequently. He never sought to douse the flame our daughter so loves."

Falier closed his eyes, thoughts whirling. "And if a holder can't gain their respect? If they don't give me a second look when I am that version of me?"

"Is that who you want to be?"

"I want to be who the clan needs me to be."

"That's a lovely answer, dear, but not a good one."

At Hanah's blunt tone, Falier opened his eyes again. Her gaze was at once scrutinizing and caring.

"You have the heart of a servant," she continued. "But if your aim is solely to please everyone else, you will cave in from the weight of their expectations, real and perceived. You feel it now, I can see. So you must set your sights elsewhere. Who do you, Falier, want to be?"

"I don't know."

"I think you do. Otherwise, going back to your former ways would not leave you hollow." She took his hand and pressed it to his chest. "Who were you created to be?"

"I was made a slayer."

"Is that all?" She pressed so that he felt his heartbeat. "Don't just spout words. Search. Where do you thrive?"

Falier thought back. When was the last time he thrived? On the mountaintop with Alísa. Finally earning a smile from Jossen in sparring. Making music among the clans when Karn was still alive. Eating stew surrounded by friends of all races after winning a terrible battle. The answer to Hanah's question was simple, and yet so complicated.

"I want to be both. Holder and slayer in the right balance. I want to be hard when I need to be hard, and soft when I need to be soft. I want to dance and make music *and* learn the sword."

He removed his hand from his chest and looked away, thinking now of all the times he hadn't thrived these past few striving weeks. "But that seems impossible. I constantly go too far in one direction or the other."

"I'm afraid that's just life, Falier," Hanah said. "It's push and pull, hard and soft, give and take. Each situation is unique, and you won't always find the correct balance. But that does not mean it's the wrong answer."

"Can't it just be a recipe? Two parts slayer, two parts holder, and one part sheer dumb luck?"

Hanah laughed, a musical sound much like her daughter's. "If only it were that simple. I do have a suggestion, though, if you'll take some unsolicited advice."

"Consider it solicited, please."

Hanah scooted so she sat side-by-side with him. "A tiern leads differently than his chief. Alísa, by necessity, must stand apart from her clan in many ways. Not every way—they must know and trust her—but she handles the big picture and cannot get bogged down by details, lest the clan stagnate."

She held two fists before her. "This is where we fill in the gap. The chief must stand at the front" —she held one fist in front of the other and pushed outward— "giving orders, making the hard choices, and leading the way."

Hanah pulled her forward fist back, so the two pressed side-by-side. "A lady or tiern, however, stands among the people. We lead by showing them the way rather than telling it. We struggle alongside our clanmates and guide them in following our chief. As in everything, we may not always move correctly. We may fall. But every time we rise shows our commitment to chief and clan."

Falier leaned forward to better see her. "And I can't skip the falling part?"

Hanah shook her head. "Without it, we cannot have the continued return, and the learning that comes with it. That is what will earn the respect you seek—not your title, not defeating someone in a duel or lifting their spirits through song. Just you stubbornly persevering, no matter how many times you fall."

Falier breathed in her words, one standing out. Stubborn. That was a quality both dragons and slayers possessed. If nothing else, it might at least prove he belonged. He wanted to ask more questions, to try to find a recipe that would help more practically despite Hanah's advice that it would change from situation to situation. Instead, he dipped his head.

"Thank you, Hanah. I'll—well, I'll do my best."

"That's all we ask." She touched his shoulder. "You *can* be both, son. We know it to be true."

With another word of thanks, Falier stood and left the tent, Hanah's last words echoing through his mind in Karn's voice.

35

OVERWHELMED

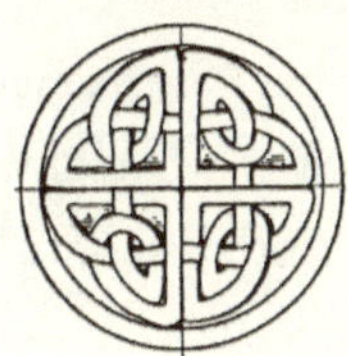

The entire army spread out before Alísa outside the war-camp. To the east, the dragon clans stood in squads according to their alphas' orders—sixty-six strong. To the west, sixty-four slayers split into two divisions, one led by Tella and the other by Lorin. And in the center, ninety-one dragon-rider pairs stood together, with the dreki collective flying overhead. Over half of the gathered dragons and slayers chose to fight this way. Despite the drizzling mists dampening her clothing, seeing them sent warmth through Alísa's heart.

They were ready. Today, they practiced maneuvers to ensure their plan was solid. In four days, the an'reik would face their combined might and pay for the lives they had stolen.

Alísa glanced at Sesína. *"Connect me to them."*

Growling her readiness, Sesína reached out to the army. She pulled in each squad commander among the dragon and dragon-rider sections, bringing with them the warriors already connected to them, then reached for Lorin and Tella. The rest of the slayer section likely held their telepathic shields tight around themselves, but Lorin and Tella would relay instructions to them.

Alísa shuddered as so many minds met within hers, the dragons the loudest among them. Their emotions rang through her—battle-readiness, excitement, fear, anger, boredom—every one its own pitch and rhythm that pounded like it wanted to escape. She had never connected to such a large group. Breathing low, she grasped at her own undercurrent of righteous anger to hold herself together.

"Slayers, mix among yourselves as though the dragons have just dropped you off. Dragon squads"—she winced as their attention came fully on her, the discordant pounding now a steady, harsh beat against her skull—*"strafe the camp."*

The dragons did as she said, launching in squads of seven and flying toward the war-camp. The non-combatants gathered a few hills away at a large tent, some facing the elements to watch while others waited inside. This test-run wouldn't involve flames or weapons, but Alísa felt it prudent to send the women and young teens away, just in case.

Alísa's legs quaked beneath her. She leaned against Sesína as the dragoness shook her head hard, feeling much of what Alísa was.

"I don't know if I'll be able to fly like this," Sesína whispered to her. The admission weakened Alísa's resolve. If even Sesína didn't think she could push through it—

Alísa forced herself straight again. *"Dragon-rider squads, you'll fly in behind them. If you spot the an'reik dragons, they are your target, but watch for any non-an'reik among them who turn to our side at my song. If they aren't nearby, strafe the camp after the others. For this"*—she wrapped her arms around herself as nausea ran through her— *"pretend you've sighted them. Dreki, you'll—"*

"Singer!"

Rís' cry gave way to many as he rushed to her. *"Singer!" "Singer!" "Singer!"*

As one, the dreki followed him. Alísa tried to scold them, but another wave of nausea hit as the dragons' emotions shifted toward concern and fear. The fae were moving. Despite their larger size and greater numbers, dragons were always uneasy around them.

Koriana's voice rose above the others. *"Alísa, what is—"*

Her question cut off along with all of Alísa's connections as the dreki surrounded her. Rís landed on her shoulder and rubbed his muzzle against her cheek.

"Safe."

Alísa drew in a deep breath, realizing now how quickly and shallowly she was breathing. She shivered with each inhale, exhausted. Sesína wasn't faring much better, her wings slumping from her back.

Rís' father Rann flew to Alísa, his glowing ruby eyes searching her face. *"Overwhelm."*

Laen flew up beside him, little Chrí following. *"Dangerous."*

Alísa shook her head. *"No, I can do this."*

A roar drew her attention from the dreki. Koriana rushed to her, Briek on her back and Graydonn and Falier behind them. The rest of the army had halted, the dragons circling above the war-camp while the slayers stood in ranks.

Rís pointed to Koriana with his muzzle. *"Speak?"*

Alísa nodded.

Her mind instantly lit up with Koriana and her companions, the dragoness hot with worry. *"—singe each one of your tails if you don't let me though!"*

"I'm okay," Alísa said.

Koriana landed just outside the circle of dreki. *"What happened? Why did they cut you off?"*

Alísa looked between her and the dreki. *"Too many dragons in my head. They think I was in danger."*

Rís and Laen both barked their displeasure at the word 'think.' Alísa rubbed her temples and ignored them.

"Koriana, have you ever fought in a large army like this? How do we deal with the telepathic crowding?"

Koriana snorted a negative. *"The largest gathering of dragons I've fought with wasn't even a sixth this size. But I felt no 'crowding' just now."*

Falier slid to the ground as Graydonn landed, eyes full of concern. *"It's your empathy, isn't it? How did we not consider that?"*

She shrugged. *"We've had a lot to keep track of. But strengthening dragons requires connecting to them."*

Falier slipped past the dreki and took her hand. *"What if we share it, like we've done before? Two probably won't be enough, but if we grab more—"*

Alísa shook her head. *"Unacceptable. We need everyone on the battlefield, not sitting on a hill coddling me. We'll try again. I know what to expect now—I can get used to it."*

"Chief, if I may." Briek leaned down from Koriana's back, brow furrowed. "Merely speaking to everyone was overwhelming. When we're all fighting to stay alive... I doubt expecting it will help."

"I agree." Koriana lowered her head to look Alísa in the eye, a motherly tenderness pouring from her. *"I know you want to strengthen everyone at once, but overextending yourself will hinder us all. Your strength songs last for a time after you finish singing. Perhaps if you focus on a few squads at once, switching as needed, we can gain the same effect without harming you."*

"If you think a squad leader's name to me, I should be able to find them for you," Sesína said, though her words held an undercurrent of uncertainty.

"No." Rann barked, landing on Sesína's head between her horns. He sent a flurry of images of dreki on people's shoulders. *"Dreki."*

"Dreki!" Rís flapped his wings excitedly, making Alísa wince and Falier pull back a step.

The dreki glowed, eyes and wing-baubles lighting up all together as their minds joined as one. Then they dimmed and scattered with a chorus of barks. Only three remained—Rís on Alísa's shoulder, Ska fluttering to Falier's, and Rann to Briek's.

Falier looked from Ska to Alísa. *"What's happening?"*

"Twerps," Sesína muttered. *"Always flying off without explaining."*

"To be fair," Graydonn said, *"I think they think they communicated clearly."*

Rís purred, glowing. *"Saynan."*

With the name, everyone but Sesína and Rís left Alísa's mind, replaced by the white dragon, the members of his squad, and Laen.

"—not understand. Did Alísa tell you to—oh? Singer, what's happening?"

Rís trilled. *"Koriana."*

Suddenly, Saynan was gone and Koriana was back, along with Briek and Rann.

"L'non."

Now the telepathic signatures of L'non, his squad, and Chrí filled Alísa's mind.

Alísa looked at Rís, dumbfounded. That was so smooth and quick. She knew dreki telepathy worked differently from other races, but the tight control Rís just displayed was astounding.

"But I thought you can only relay dreki words and thoughts?"

Rís trilled low as though apologizing. He sent two images, one of Laen with Saynan nearby, then another of the vast hill country that held a speck Alísa knew was Chrí on L'non's shoulder.

"Close."

So, distance played a role in how the dreki's messages worked. *"What about the other dragon clans? Can we send a drek to each squad leader among them?"*

Rís bristled and barked once. *"Strangers."*

Sesína growled at him. *"They need her songs too, twerp."*

Rís swished his tail across Alísa's back. He sent an image of the seventeen dreki, then one of the many squads.

Alísa nodded slowly. *"We'll have to combine some squads, but this should work!"*

Koriana rumbled in her chest. *"We shall test this theory."* She looked at Rann. *"Tell everyone to return to starting positions. The Singer will start us again when she is ready."*

As Koriana took off, Falier rubbed a hand over Alísa's arm. *"You sure you're okay?"*

"Positive. This is why we practice." She gave him a peck on the cheek. *"Thank you for coming to check."*

"I'll take any excuse to see you." He walked backward towards Graydonn. *"Maybe supper together tonight?"*

Alísa smiled coyly. *"No chiefs, alphas, squads, or gagging dragons?"*

Sesína rolled her eyes. *"Thank you for releasing me. Get out of here, lover boy, we've got an imaginary battle to win."*

Falier thumped his fist to his chest in a mocking salute to Sesína, then hopped onto Graydonn. Ska nearly fell off Falier's shoulder as they took off. The dreki would struggle to stay with their squads, but practice would help.

"Okay," Alísa said, petting Rís. *"Let's try again."*

The rest of the exercise went well. Alísa and the leaders identified as many problems as they could and discussed them afterward. With the dreki's help, Alísa also practiced strengthening only a few squads at once. She could aid five with a manageable headache—though once wounds and heightened emotions entered the mix, she would likely only be able to handle four. By the time the chiefs and alphas dispersed, their plan of attack was refined and ready to practice tomorrow afternoon.

However, there was one item Alísa still needed to attend to.

"Rís, get me Graydonn. And Dezra, if you can."

As before, the drek cut Alísa off from her prior telepathic connections and brought the two requested dragons into her mind through Ska. Falier was still with his squad—though he trained three, he would only lead one in the battle— a team comprised mostly of the bonded pairs.

"I need to speak with you," Alísa said. *"North end of camp."*

They gave affirmatives and began walking toward her. As she searched the crowd for them, she caught sight of Farren speaking with some wayfarers.

Today, he sang a blessing over the warriors and would repeat the act before the battle.

Like it had helped last time.

Alísa shook her head at herself. She didn't know how it might have gone without Farren's blessing. They may not have survived at all.

Yet Karn, her most important ally and one she loved the most, had fallen. Why?

As though sensing her gaze, Farren met her eyes. Alísa looked away casually, trying not to appear angry. Her anger wasn't at him. And if his prayers gave the warriors hope? That alone might be worth something.

"Might be?" Sesína nudged her shoulder with her snout. *"Hope is worth a lot. As is faith. I know you still have that."*

"I do. It's just hard right now. Tell me we'll make it."

Sesína's chest rumbled. *"The Maker knows."*

"And shares nothing."

The thought ran through her unbidden, but they disregarded it as Falier and the others neared. There were no answers.

Falier came straight to Alísa's side and kissed her cheek. "How did it go?"

"Well. The alphas and chiefs are relaying the changes to their c-c-clans. We are as ready as we can be, except for one thing." She glanced at Rassím. "I need to steal Rassím and D—Dezra from you, at least for part of the battle."

Rassím's brows raised. "Us? What for?"

Alísa met his eyes. They were so different from their first meeting. He had held a knife to her throat, and though he immediately switched sides upon learning the truth, she had remembered the hatred of a killer for days after. Now she knew him for who he truly was—kind, slightly awkward, a medic.

And highly trained in an unusual weapon. One which required deadly accuracy and few slayers ever prepared to face.

Rage and grief collided within her. She couldn't aim her anger at the Maker—that accomplished nothing. But here... Here she could pour out her wrath.

"I need you to kill Kallar."

36

TO REACH A SLAYER

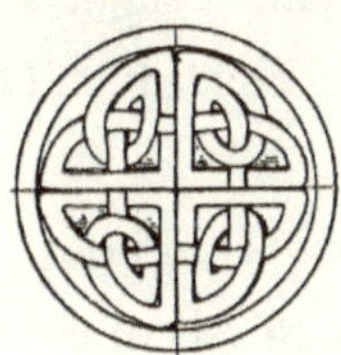

The next morning, Falier didn't train all of his squads. They knew patterns and formations and now even had war-game experience. With this afternoon bringing a rehashing of the battle-plan, Falier left it to his squad-leaders to decide whether to practice or rest. His own squad, made up mostly of bonded pairs, practiced their push-and-pulls and worked on strategies to use Selene and Trísse's empathic clouds in combat.

Falier kept up a constant push-and-pull with Graydonn, feeling out their bond. Though their connection occasionally felt strained, it had improved significantly. As Graydonn focused on leading the squad in formation, Falier reached out to Jossen and P'raenn.

"How are you two doing with your push-and-pulls?"

"Decently," Jossen said. *"Though it's hard to remember not to close off sometimes."*

P'raenn thrummed good-naturedly. *"You slayers cave in on yourselves so easily. It's like you expect to be attacked every moment."*

"It's not so much our fear as others'," Jossen explained. *"If we don't hold ourselves back, we might accidentally read someone else's mind. That would violate the code."*

P'raenn looked at him. *"Even when you're only among slayers?"*

"Even so."

"That seems awfully lonely."

Graydonn, who listened with half an ear, clicked in his throat. *"You forget, though, that humans can speak vocally. They don't need opened minds to talk."*

"Speaking without openness seems like encroaching storm-clouds."

Graydonn thrummed. *"Perhaps."*

Falier let the dragons thrum about their metaphor, then set back about his purpose. *"Now that you can share power, it's time to practice using it. With the an'reik arriving in three days"* —Maker above, that was frightening— *"let's prepare you to attack an abnormally powerful dragon."*

They practiced, Falier watching the astral plane as Jossen drew psychic energy from P'raenn and blasted it into the sky. A lifelong slayer, Jossen took hold of the concept quickly. Falier caught some unease from P'raenn, but Graydonn assured him that was normal. It had felt odd when Falier first started drawing off of him too.

They continued like this for half-an-hour. While simulating chasing enemy dragons into Selene and Trísse's clouds of confusion or terror, Falier assigned Jossen to shielding teammates as they flew amid the overwhelming empathic power. Graydonn advised Jossen to change his shields from walls to interlocking scales, which better absorbed the impact of a psychic attack. For a short time, Falier even had everyone mind-spear the newly bonded pair at once, giving Jossen more confidence in his shields and helping P'raenn grow in trust.

At the end of the session, Falier and Graydonn dismissed their squad until the afternoon's battle-simulation. Falier slid off Graydonn to the ground, realizing too late that he picked the wrong side. His sheathed sword hit Graydonn's spines and scraped across his scales, making Falier stumble as he landed.

"Do you really need that?"

Falier sighed. *"Yes."*

"I thought you weren't trying to be a slayer anymore."

Falier looked away. Graydonn had been distracted during Falier's conversation with Hanah, and he hadn't talked to the dragon about it yet. How could he explain what he didn't fully understand? Dare he risk wounding their bond again so close to battle?

"We're at war. It's wise to be prepared."

Graydonn hummed, but dropped the subject. *"What will you do until this afternoon?"*

Falier looked into the camp. *"I don't know. Check on Alisa? See if the kitchens need extra hands?"*

Those answers set Graydonn at ease. *"Perhaps I'll accompany you."*

Falier shrugged. *"Fine."*

He started walking, but found uncertainty in the bond. He looked backed at Graydonn, whose eyes dimmed.

"You okay?"

Graydonn hesitated. *"You don't feel like it's fine. Are you angry with me?"*

"No. Why would I be angry?" Falier cringed at his tone. Mind-speak was too revealing. *"Okay, maybe a little. I wish you'd stop telling me I don't need the sword."*

"You're always striving. I simply want you to understand you needn't."

"And you simply don't like slayers."

Graydonn hummed, irritated. *"I don't like certain slayers, just as I don't like certain dragons."*

Falier shook his head. *"You only like noncombatants and riders. And even when riders spar, you cringe and groan as though it's a travesty. Carrying a sword and enjoying learning it isn't the same as hunting dragons!"*

Graydonn jerked his head back as though Falier had slapped him. So much for not starting another fight.

Falier sighed. *"I'm sorry I yelled. But I'm not just a holder anymore. I won't leave that fully behind again, but I can't ignore the rest. I'm also a slayer, and I'm trying to find the balance. Is our bond so strained you can't see that?"*

"Can't you see the Maker made you a holder for a reason? That it's the reason we're mind-kin? We were able to bond because you didn't grow up killing dragons."

Falier gestured at Jossen, who headed for the sparring grounds with P'raenn. *"What about him? He's bonded to a dragon, and he spent his life hunting you."*

Graydonn snorted steam. *"Perhaps his crimes weren't as bad as the others."*

"And Rassím? He grew up a slayer—a flaming good one, to use knives instead of a sword—and Dezra chose him!"

Graydonn looked away, silent.

"I made mistakes while forcing myself to fit their mold. I'm not doing that again, but I can't go back either. Life itself requires we grow and change. I can't stay stagnant just to avoid hurting you. We"—Falier pointed between them—*"need to grow, too."*

Graydonn rumbled in his throat, a strained sound. Falier sighed and turned away from camp.

"Where are you going?"

"The sparring grounds."

"Just to spite me?

"No. To take my own advice." He looked back. *"Come with me, if you want. P'raenn is there too."*

Falier continued, walking a considerable distance before Graydonn finally followed. The dragon didn't catch up, just plodded with shocks of worry in his stride. Anticipating Graydonn would stay close to his fellow dragon, Falier stopped a few spectators beyond Jossen and P'raenn. He needed some distance. Somehow, he found himself next to Varek.

He watched the sparring in silence, his mind only halfway in the activity. The other part flitted from half-thought to uncertain half-thought. Varek might never accept him—it was his right to choose—but Falier wasn't ready to give up yet.

"How are you and your new partner doing?"

Varek side-eyed him. "She flies."

"I would be concerned otherwise…"

"Then you needn't concern yourself."

Falier crossed his arms. "Do you talk this way with L'non?"

"L'non doesn't ask stupid questions."

The crowd cheered as the sparring pair nearest Falier's section finished their bout, one man on the ground with a waster at his neck.

Falier let out a single mirthless laugh as he applauded. "Knowing whether sword-partners work well together is far from stupid."

"That's different."

"Really? That's what you're going with?"

Varek stepped forward, toward the chest of wasters. Falier clenched his fists and followed.

"Dragon-rider pairs entrust their lives to each other in the same way. Want to tell me what's different?"

"What I want" —Varek selected his weapon— "is to fight. It's why we're all here, besides you. Leave us to it."

Falier let out a quiet breath, then reached for his own waster. "Fine, if it's the only way I'll get more than five seconds with you, let's fight."

Graydonn immediately came to attention at the back of Falier's mind. *"What are you doing? You said—"*

"This isn't like with Tern, I promise. Trust me." Falier lifted out the practice weapon and marched into the cleared space.

Varek scoffed as he passed. "I wanted a challenge."

Falier shrugged. "I don't know—sparring while talking and doing your best not to kill me… I'd call that a challenge."

That drew some chuckles from the crowd. People from each clan gathered here. Some were riders, others completely unfamiliar. L'non was there, as was Trísse. Further on, Tern stood with other former riders. Why hadn't Varek left with them? Just honor, since Alísa, his chief, had ordered all her slayers to ride? Did any piece of him care about the dragons?

There had to be something. He was mind-kin to one, despite not accepting it.

Varek let out a loud sigh. "I suppose I can give you a charity bout."

Falier bowed like he would after a performance, flourishing with the practice weapon. "You are too kind. You've trained enough to handle telepathic attacks as well, but I'll let you choose—psychic hits allowed, or no?"

Varek hesitated. Then, to Falier's delight, he fell for it.

"Fine. Allowed."

"I am not aiding you in this," Graydonn said. *"You are making a mistake, again."*

Falier sent back acceptance. He swung his waster in a few wide arcs, warming up his muscles. Movement and weight felt good, releasing some of his built-up tension. He set himself.

"Ready?"

"Falier, please, stop," Graydonn said, anxious. *"He's not worth it."*

In response, Varek slid forward. His testing blows were powerful, as though he hoped to knock Falier's sword from his hands before the bout even began.

Falier circled. *"No, he* is *worth it. Everyone here, especially our own clanmates, is worth fighting for. Maybe I'll never earn his friendship, but I won't leave him floundering when there's still something I can do."*

Dancing forward, Falier tested Varek's strong side, Karn's voice in his ear. He feared dropping his blade, but forced himself to keep the loose grip L'non had taught him. Too tight a grip made it easier to drop the weapon at a hard blow.

"And 'something you can do' is fighting?"

"It's not about the fight. Slayers are free in the sparring ring—laughing even as they hit each other, talking about things they won't anywhere else. There is camaraderie here, and I will find it!"

Varek tested again, ending in a press. He grinned as his greater strength became evident.

"Too occupied to talk?"

Falier reached out telepathically. *"Not here."*

Varek's eyes widened. He backed off and shielded himself. Falier's power alone was too weak to break a shield. He had counted on Graydonn's help with this...

Falier went in for his final test swipes, all the while processing the emotions he had caught while connected to Varek. Their connection had been too brief. Anger reigned, but something lived beyond it. Falier had entertained too many people at the bar of his family's Hold to be fooled by a mask of anger.

"So? Who's a better fit?" Swipe. "Menálli?" Slash. "Or Alanti?"

Varek easily deflected Falier's attacks and, rather than disengage, attacked in earnest. "Either is fine! I'm a slayer—I have no preference between the beasts."

"Not beasts." Block. Swipe. Dodge. "And if you don't care, I might want you back with Menálli. Alanti and her previous rider worked well together."

Varek growled. "Fine, then I have a preference. Do not send me back to that dragoness."

Ah. There was something there. Falier formed a mind-spear, the strongest he could without Graydonn's power behind it, and hit Varek's shield. Varek winced—Maker above, Falier had never made someone wince on his own before!—then did exactly as Falier wanted. He shot his own psychic arrow.

Falier didn't shield, only braced for the pain. The hit *hurt!* He stumbled back, struggling to keep his waster up lest Varek win here. He held onto the sensation of the strike. Anger coursed through it, making it strong. And underneath it...

Fear.

That was something he could work with. Fear was a tricky beast. It carried no hint of what caused it. It might be the dragons in general, the mind-kin bond, the looming battle, or simply looking a fool before his fellows. Falier picked which he thought the most likely and treaded carefully forward.

"All right." Advance. Retreat. Like a dance. "I meant what I said about not wanting a bond to form accidentally." Bat. Parry. Duck. Not a dance. "I know this is hard, dealing with the dragons as allies. Perhaps especially knowing that you have the potential to bond with one."

Varek grit his teeth and circled to Falier's weak side. "You know nothing, holder." He stabbed, Falier barely dodging in time. "You can't understand what it's like to learn your entire life has been a lie—don't you dare pretend otherwise!"

Match or de-escalate?

Slayer.

Sparring.

Match him.

"You're right," Falier grunted out as he attacked. "I don't know your pain, but this isn't easy for me, either!"

Slash. Parry. Parry. Parry!

"I didn't grow up fighting dragons, just fearing them and knowing I couldn't do anything against them. Graydonn told me we were mind-kin the day we met. Do you know how terrifying that was?"

Varek struck high and Falier blocked, pressing weapons with one hand on the hilt, the other on the flat.

"I didn't" —Falier grunted as Varek tried to push him to the ground— "I didn't accept the bond until I fought alongside many dragons and learned—"

Either his arms or legs were going to give out. Falier chose his legs, dropping to his knees on the damp grass as Varek continued to press.

"Learned what?" Varek bit out.

Falier rolled, Varek's waster hitting the dirt with a thump. Falier got to his knees just in time to block with a loud crack.

"That I could trust them, at least as far as I can trust humanity. Each dragon is as different from another as I am from you, and we can still—"

A roar split the sky, drawing Falier's eyes south.

"Mother?"

Through Graydonn, Falier heard Koriana's response, as did all other squad leaders with unshielded minds.

"Singer! The an'reik army bypassed N'moth."

Briek joined her report. *"I don't know how—they weren't to reach it until tomorrow. But they're ten miles past. They'll be here in mere hours!"*

A rush of panic ran through the line, a mixture of Falier and the others, but was swiftly quashed as Alísa forced calm to saturate it. Her empathic strength was incredible.

"Everyone, to arms," she said, her tone reminiscent of Karn's. *"We must meet*

them as soon as possible. We can't let the an'reik dragons get close to camp or Vennia. Go!"

Koriana and Briek cut themselves off, banking toward camp. Falier's heart pounded, now separated from Alísa's calm. It was too early. They needed more time!

As the crowd scattered to their respective camps for their gear, Falier looked to Varek. Their eyes met, and this time Varek held no defiance, only dazed resignation. Behind Falier, Graydonn trotted up with similar emotions. Each needed something from him. He forced himself to show only confidence, much like the holder's mask he wore all growing up.

"You don't have to accept the bond, Varek, but know this—the possibility of it shows you are kindred spirits. You and a dragon. They are not unknowable monsters any more than you or I." Falier looked at Graydonn. "You might fight, might even hurt each other, but when battle comes, you can trust your partner."

Graydonn rumbled in his chest and sent affirmation, lowering for Falier to mount. He did so, looking back at Varek.

"Trust Alanti, and fight well."

Graydonn launched, returning to their squad's designated area. Battle was upon them. Maker help them all.

37

ENTHRALLED ARMY

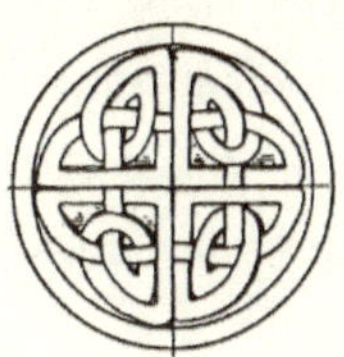

The an'reik army surrounded Kallar, standing in ranks just outside their camp. Every faction had grown during the last two weeks' march. Though Alísa had evacuated most dragons in the nearby mountains, dissenters had surrendered themselves to the an'reik alphas, some becoming an'reik themselves. Two village-bound slayer clans had also joined, led by an'reik who had warned them of 'the Dragon Singer's lies', much as Tsorr had attempted.

And, of course, certain humans had surrendered themselves to the Nameless Ones. Not only slayers, but also normals who wouldn't evacuate because they feared Alísa's dragons came to conquer. The offer of power in a powerless situation was too great to refuse.

Kallar stood at the center of the ground troops, Isarra, Marizarr, and one other an'reik beside him. The third was newly made, her powers unknown to Kallar. The grounded dragons stood in a square around them, wings drooped and eyes glazed with the alphas' compulsion. The other dragons were nearby, waiting for whatever Isarra had planned. She told everyone to be prepared to fight today, that they were going to take Alísa's war-camp by surprise. But they were still two days out. Three, if they wanted daylight.

What horrors did she have in store?

Isarra turned to the new an'reik woman. "It is time. The masters have assured me we can reach the enemy with my power amplifying yours. You are ready?"

The new an'reik nodded, her blonde hair falling over fair features. She appeared to be in her early twenties, perhaps only a couple of years older than Kallar. She offered her hands to Isarra.

"I am."

Isarra pulled a vial from her belt-pouch and uncorked it, chanting some gibberish Kallar couldn't understand. She drained the reddish-brown liquid into her hand and threw the empty glass away before rubbing her palms together. Then Isarra clasped the blond's hands. She continued chanting as mists flowed from between them, tinted with shocks of green. They gushed out, coating the ground at the speed of a river in flood season. They whisked over Kallar's boots, swirled between the dragons' legs, and spread into the rest of the army.

The keeper purred in Kallar's mind, making his stomach clench. What was this?

The blonde whimpered as more mist poured out and rose higher. Isarra held her hands tighter, keeping her from pulling away as the darkness engulfed them. Soon Kallar couldn't see anything—all obscured by the green-tinted mists. He batted at the thick blackness, but it accomplished nothing.

The world shuddered around him, the air pressure fluctuating and making his ears pop. The blonde an'reik screamed as Isarra's chant grew louder, the two battling for Kallar's attention. His stomach roiled and his head throbbed with the pressure until, finally, everything stopped. The blonde's scream died out into a low moan, and Isarra's incantation ended. The mists dissipated seconds later, leaving Kallar blinking in the glaring white of the cloud-covered morning.

Exclamations of awe came from the army. *What the—*

Kallar glanced between the guard dragons. Those mountains. They were different.

They had moved north. Somehow, that blonde's power had—

Something thumped on the ground behind Kallar. He whirled to look. The blonde had fallen, sightless eyes staring up at the sky.

Isarra tsked. "Pity. It would have been nice to use her again. She could have at least lived long enough to complete the trip." She stepped over the body and spoke, her voice unnaturally loud. "The enemy lies ahead. Onward!"

Other an'reik, commanders of divisions, shouted orders and the army marched. Kallar's breaths came heavily. How close were they?

"You too," the keeper growled, sending a shock through Kallar's system. *"March."*

Another jolt, this one bringing forth a memory. Him and R'lann, far younger, hiding behind a stone bench to watch a woman with ebony warrior's braids face down a dragon.

Kallar shuddered. Not that memory again.

"Then march."

A third shock and the woman turned and saw him, her righteous warrior's anger melting into a mother's fear.

Kallar stepped forward, hating himself. How would Ma react to seeing him in this state? At the mercy of this dark power, unable to keep it at bay. Would she feel pride for what fight he *could* put up? Or disappointment in his efforts?

"You think her a saint?" The keeper scoffed. *"You desire her approval? She was just as wicked as you!"*

Kallar stumbled as flashes of hatchling-killings filled his vision, as he remembered dashing eggs against the mountainside.

The keeper's voice was like oil. *"More so, for she already knew the truth of the dragons' souls when she began killing."*

Kallar shouted with rage and pain, speaking aloud where it could not get lost in the mire of memories. "She was a hero!"

"She was a murderer, just like you."

"She saved hundreds!"

"And destroyed hundreds more to do it." The keeper grinned. *"How we cheered as she kept the war going strong. It was a dreadful day indeed when you led her to her death. We raged against you and longed for you or your brother to replace her."*

Kallar's stomach churned with grief and rage. He halted his march and threw all of his energy into a mind-choke, wrestling it around the keeper. The monster ripped it apart as it always did, sending agony through his mind. He fell to his knees, screaming.

"You should know better by now, dirt."

Abruptly, the keeper took hold of his body again, rolling to the side, drawing his sword, and slicing the neck of a grounded dragon as it snapped at him. Hot blood poured from it, drops flecking Kallar's scale armor as the keeper made him rise and sing to bring the other dragons back under control. The hate in their eyes dimmed as the keeper's alpha song invaded their minds. They continued their march, leaving their fallen companion behind.

The keeper pulled away, and Kallar gasped for free air. He fought to keep his breakfast down, half-wondering what the point was. He needed to die. Die and rob these thrice-damned an'reik of their tool. He tried to stop marching, but white-hot pain seized him as memories of dragon-killings ran through his mind. Exhausted and tormented, he was too weak to resist.

A slow clapping rose to his left. Isarra.

"Surely the masters smiled the day you came to me." Isarra placed a finger under Kallar's chin and he couldn't help but shudder. "Your skill is as legendary as your mother's."

"Burn in hellflames."

She grinned. "Still testy, I see. Makes this all the more fun, eh, keeper?"

The thing inside him purred.

Isarra turned back to Marizarr. "Look at us. Near a hundred an'reik, twenty possessed slayers, fifty more allied of their own accord, and over sixty dragons waiting for our Singer's call. With dear little Alísa soon to be gone, consider the possibilities."

Marizarr grunted. "You run too far ahead. The masters don't just want her dead, they want to rekindle the war she's dousing. That, unfortunately, won't simply build back up with her death. We'll need more careful planning, more—"

"You think too small." She glanced at Kallar. "Tell me, keeper, which do you desire more? A world where we solely operate in shadow? Or one that knows your power and fears it? Where souls come to you daily and your army grows large enough that your servants can fight even Eldír?"

Kallar struggled as the keeper stretched through his body. His muscles moved without his consent in a smile. "Your ambition, as always, is impressive. We would hear your ideas, *after* we accomplish our goal here."

A shout came from the front, followed by a battle-horn. They had spotted one of Alísa's scouts. The keeper shifted, grabbing Kallar's voice to call the an'reik dragons and their enthralled clans to fly. Kallar fought it, his body convulsing until he fell to a knee. He wrestled with the keeper, which slashed at him with astral claws until he collapsed into his mind, bleeding mists the colors of fear and dread.

Through the window, his voice called out the keeper's song. With it came connection. He sensed the an'reik dragons' pleasure and the panic of the compelled, then felt all terror dull as the alphas worked their dark magics over their clanmates.

Control, power, and blood—the way of the an'reik, the keepers, the 'masters.'

Kallar faced the window. Alísa's army wasn't yet visible, but a few dragons dotted the sky. Her and Karn's ranks were decimated in the last battle, and it had been only sixteen days since. Without Karn, how many could she possibly rally? As Kallar considered the dragons under his keeper's strength-song, he despaired.

Alísa had no chance.

38

CHAOS

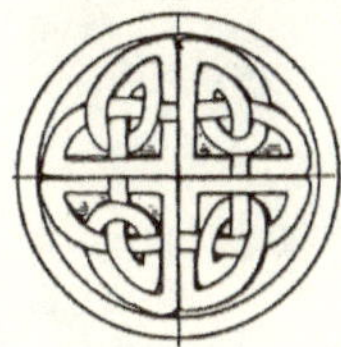

Falier's heart pounded in his chest as his squad took flight. Hwinn stayed on Graydonn's right, and Dezra on his left. Behind them, Komi and P'raenn flew as partners and Harenn flew with a brown dragon named Renegal. Harenn, Renegal, and their riders were the only unbonded pairs in this squad.

A lump over Falier's chest moved. Fitted snuggly between shirt and tunic, Ska placed a paw over Falier's heart.

"Drum."

"Yeah, don't need you to tell me that."

The sensation of the drek in his tunic was odd. With the dreki being assigned to squads only two days ago, they hadn't found many solutions for not losing the creatures during flight. A few squad leaders carried packs strapped across their chests, allowing the dreki to ride. One had fashioned a shoulder pad for his drek to cling to. But most of the commanders, including Falier, had to carry them between layers of clothing. What dreki assigned to dragons without riders would do, Falier could not guess.

Ska trilled low. *"Strong."*

Falier wasn't sure whether the drek meant that his drumming heartbeat was strong, or that Falier should *be* strong.

"Strong," Ska repeated, pushing empathic courage.

Falier breathed, trying to grasp the feeling. He could do this. He had done it before, and he would do it again to protect those he loved. Tamping down his fear, Falier pushed Ska's courage to the others. The power scraped and pulled against the walls of the mind-kin bond.

"Graydonn, I need you to keep things open for me."

"I'm trying!"

The an'reik dragons were all airborne now, speeding toward their forces. Graydonn gave instructions to the dragons.

"We must give our dragon allies room to drop off the ground troops. No enemy dragon gets past us!"

Falier copied Graydonn's confident tone. *"Riders, keep your eyes closed to watch the astral plane. Target any dragon without a shield with your heaviest blast. If you can, team up with your wing-rider."*

"Falier," came Taz's voice, *"are there dragons down there, among the human an'reik?"*

"I have better eyesight, idiot," Harenn said, his tone an eye-roll. *"Ask me, not another human. And yes, there are three of them."*

"They'll be guarding my target, unless I'm mistaken," Rassím said. *"Dez and I will wait a bit before slipping away—make it less obvious we're going after their Singer."*

Ahead, Koriana's squad speared forward and Saynan's went right. Graydonn veered left while other squads spread out above and below them, creating a wall of dragon-rider pairs to protect the dragons dropping off slayers.

Ska trilled as Alísa's strength song came to him. Lyrics and power passed through the drek, first to Falier and Graydonn, then through them into the squad's link. Strength, courage, and the woman he loved—the three combined to quiet Falier's heart. Dragons roared with fresh energy, and the riders shouted their battle-cries along with them.

A chorus of frightful roars answered, a squad of enemy dragons spearing for them. A monstrous copper dragon flew at the head, veering toward them with eerily bright eyes. Every dragon in that squad was bigger than Graydonn. Only Komi and Renegal could match them. Grappling would be deadly for the rest.

Thoughts raced between Falier and Graydonn faster than words until a plan formed. Graydonn addressed Komi and Renegal.

"Take out the dragons at the back. We smaller dragons will keep the rest of them from piling on you. All riders, find any enemies without shields and choke them!"

Graydonn charged. Falier glanced at Hwinn and Selene, swallowing his fear.

Maker, shield them.

Graydonn swerved around the lead dragon, gravity pulling at Falier's stomach. When the next dragon back-flapped to grapple, Falier threw a telepathic net to choke it as Graydonn dodged. Graydonn's power was sluggish, however, leaving Falier unable to encase the enemy dragon's mind.

The dragon roared a challenge and snapped after Hwinn, but the smaller dragon easily evaded. They bypassed the remaining dragons and banked to attack from behind, but the enemy squad broke up to engage. Komi already had her talons in a dragon's wing, pulling them into a fall. As another dragon dove after them, Graydonn led Hwinn and Dezra down to keep it off Komi's back. Ska barked in surprise as Graydonn slammed into the dragon's wing and pushed off to knock it off-course.

"Shield the dragons," Selene ordered.

Falier and Rassím complied as she pulled energy from Hwinn and blasted it around the enemy dragon. Confusion tickled at the edges of Falier's wavering shield. Sparks dripped from the dragon's mouth as it looked about in a daze.

Graydonn struck. He lunged for the neck from above, keeping far from the terrible talons. He clamped down, drawing a pained cry, though the scales on top of the neck were stronger than those underneath, keeping Graydonn from dealing a deadly blow.

Falier drew his sword, ready to plunge it into the dragon's skull, but the brute twisted. Scales and blood flew as it yanked from Graydonn's grip. Its wing slapped Graydonn in the side and sent him and Falier tumbling away. Graydonn nearly collided with another enemy, but he righted himself just before. He shook his head to clear it, then dodged swiping talons. It was chaos, but every dragon chasing them was one unable to pile on Komi or—

A trumpet of pain rose and was quickly silenced. Falier's heart clenched as Renegal and his rider dropped from the sky, flames covering them both. Regular fire didn't burn dragon scales—it had to have come from an an'reik. Falier could only watch as his squad-mates burned and broke against the hillside.

His charges. He couldn't protect them all.

Rattling drew Falier's eyes up, and Graydonn dove just before flames could engulf them. Falier shook off the grief grasping at his heart. Now was not the time for mourning. Instead, he took hold of the horror pounding through him, formed it into a psychic spear, and searched for his next target.

INTERLUDE

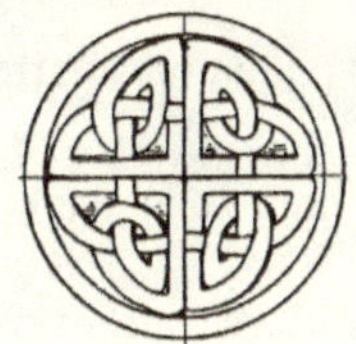

The darkness glowed.

Rassím had almost forgotten the sight. An abyss that surrounded a human and dampened everything around them. Dark mists barely contained, desiring to engulf the world. Rips in the fabric of the physical, with humans as the conduit through which something *else* could claw. This wasn't the mere dozen that had walked his home village in the deserts of the Southlands. Not a gathering in the night for bloody sacrifices to malevolent powers. This was darkness parading itself across the land and shining to beckon the unsuspecting into its maw.

And indeed, the unsuspecting were drawn. The proud an'reik led the horde, displaying their horrid might, while Rassím's brothers and sisters stood at the back. Slayers who, blinded by their determination to protect their world, ignored the monsters directly before them.

Dezra flew low and fast around the perimeter until she could duck behind a hill where the watching army couldn't see them. But lack of sight could not stop Rassím from thinking about those slayers. He had been like them once. He had snuck into the dark room of his supposed enemy, caught her as she slept, and held a knife to her throat. Alísa's lack of glow had surprised him, but that didn't still his blade. Only when his former chief ordered the slaughter of villagers had Rassím realized the enemy wasn't the Dragon Singer and her dragons, but his allies before him.

If only he could rescue them. Bring the truth to them so they would understand. But this was war, and they had picked their allegiance. He had another mission—one of blood, not salvation.

"Yet this Singer's blood will *save our clanmates,"* Dezra said, landing at the lowest point behind the hill nearest the slayers. *"Less contemplation. More action."*

Rassím sighed. *"Right as usual, Dez."*

He swung to the ground. Most of their dragon allies fought at the head of the battle, defending the war-camp and Vennia from the enemy dragons. This eased his anxieties. Here, at the rear, Dezra should be safe while he completed his mission. His paternal instinct toward the dragoness had nearly overwhelmed him as they charged into the fray. This was better.

"Keep thinking like that, and I'll sneak in alongside you." Dezra snapped her jaws in the air. *"I am not a hatchling."*

"You're also not sneaky. At least, not in that crowd."

Rassím crept to the crest of the hill. The dampness of the grasses seeped into his clothing as he crouched to peer over. The fighting wasn't far. He should be able to infiltrate the slayers. The only problem would be those dragons. His throwing distance was excellent, but even he had a limit. To hit the enemy Singer, he would need to get right next to one.

"So? What's the problem?"

"Everyone else is staying back. Getting close will reveal me. They'll attack."

Dezra rumbled in her throat. *"You're a slayer. So go slay."*

"You know, most dragons would feel conflicted by that order." Rassím glanced at the slayers, ensured their focus was forward or otherwise away from him, and moved.

"Your Illumination ensured I would never be normal. Some dragons have to die— even ones who aren't an'reik. It's just the way it is."

Rassím drew his telepathy inward. Passing the space most telepaths would hold their shield, he held his powers tight against themselves, like a tiny ball of power within his head. He knew few who could accomplish this. As a telepath, his mind wanted to venture beyond the boundaries of his body. Even normal minds had a tiny aspect of them that sat outside themselves—the part that told them when someone was watching them. Pulled in like this, he walked invisible to anyone's sixth senses. No one would notice him unless he drew their attention by speaking or bumping into them.

Or killing a dragon beside them, then flinging knives at their face.

The sensation was uncomfortable—claustrophobic, even—and he had to remind himself to breathe as he entered the ranks. Fighting had not yet reached the rear. Most of the slayers kept their eyes on the aerial battle, likely sending psychic arrows in hopes of a lucky shot.

Trumpets of pain strengthened his resolve. Falier and the others were up there, facing monstrous glowing beasts and their allies, all bolstered by the dark Singer. Rassím slipped between slayers, steering clear of the few an'reik in their midst. The three dragons defending Kallar were large, but none glowed with the darkness. All tricked into service.

Were those tears in that black one's wings? That explained why they weren't in the sky. Perhaps wounded by in-fighting. An'reik weren't known for their kindness, even toward allies.

He slunk to the edge of the space between the slayers and the grounded dragon. What now? Sneak in and kill the Singer, then deal with a raging dragon? Or kill the dragon and use its body as a shield between him and an angry Singer?

Kallar had to be the priority. If Rassím stayed behind the dragon, it shouldn't spot him until it was too late. So long as no one raised the alarm simply because he left the ranks.

He pulled knives from their sheaths, three in his off-hand.

Here goes.

Mind held tight, he crossed the space between the slayers and the dragons. He moved in close to the black dragon's hind legs. These talons were as sharp as those in front, but the limbs lacked dexterity. The dragon would also have a hard time hitting him with its bone-crushing tail.

He kept pace until he could see his target. Kallar strode in the middle of the dragons, chanting words Rassím could not hear. Two other an'reik marched with him. Rassím pulled one knife into his throwing hand and focused on Kallar.

His heart twinged, a tiny prickle that made him pause. Something wasn't right.

Of course, something wasn't right. He was staring at three an'reik, closer than he thought he would ever get again after fleeing his home village. An'reik with their glows that sought to engulf the world in darkness.

"What are you doing, slayer?"

The barked question came from behind. He had taken too long.

The dragon looked at him. In the last few months, Rassím had learned to read some draconic expressions. This one he knew especially. Dezra held it often when she was younger. A seeking curiosity, searching not for something to crush or fear, but for light. A hope he should not have seen in his enemy.

Kallar's chant changed to a single, shouted word.

"Fight!"

The dragon blinked and shook its massive head. When its eyes opened again, the curiosity was gone, replaced by malice.

Flame it all.

The dragon's ebony scales shimmered as it whirled on him with open jaws alight with fire. Rassím released his telepathy and bolted under the dragon. As flames erupted, he rolled to emerge on the other side.

Acutely aware of the three an'reik watching him, he forced himself to wait. When the great black head appeared, Rassím threw. The knife struck below the dragon's jaw, where the scales were smaller and the artery pulsed. The dragon screamed and shook to rid itself of the blade. That would be its undoing. The knife fell and Rassím turned away. The dragon would bleed out in seconds, and his true target was behind him.

Pulling another knife into his throwing hand, Rassím aimed for Kallar. That nagging feeling came again, biting at his heart and skewing his aim. Kallar ducked to the side, pulled his broadsword, and ran toward him. Rassím had only one throw left before needing to pull his own sword and defend.

He breathed, time slowing as he took aim. One hit through the skull and the enemy would lose their greatest weapon.

The glow. That's what was off. Kallar's glow differed from the others. It didn't reach as though trying to claw its way out. It pulled inward.

Rassím hesitated. *Not an'reik. Possessed!*

He threw. The knife passed by Kallar's ear as he ran, making the young slayer flinch to the side and giving Rassím more time to draw his sword.

"What was that?" Dezra near-shouted in his mind. *"You had him!"*

Rassím ignored her, parrying Kallar's first swing. "Kallar, can you hear me?"

Kallar lunged, offering no sign he heard the question. Rassím dodged, hoping he wasn't too close to the dead dragon to be trapped against it, but not daring to look and confirm. The sword wasn't his preferred weapon, and he had watched Kallar spar.

"An'reik or possessed, it doesn't matter," Dezra said. *"He's strengthening the enemy. Kill him and get out of there!"*

"If you can, fight it! We'll help you." That was a half-truth. Killing him might be the only solution. Rassím sidestepped and blocked. "Fight it!"

Beyond Kallar, the other two dragons turned toward them, their eyes on Rassím and ablaze with ill-intent.

"Alísa commanded it, Rassím!"

"But she didn't know." Parry. Step. Dodge. *"I made this mistake once, taking Alísa before Segenn. I can't do it again!"*

Rassím blocked, pressing blades with Kallar. The boy was strong, but not enhanced. He shoved Kallar back and bolted, dodging around the dead dragon's body to gain some distance. The marching slayers continued, and as Rassím looked them over a second time, the truth spilled over him. Some were indeed an'reik, but there were possessed among them. Souls with no control over their actions, no chance to enter the light.

"This isn't right, Dez. Alísa wouldn't want this. We must tell her!"

A rattling inhalation pushed Rassím forward. He dodged left, only to realize the dragon wasn't targeting him, but his escape route. Fire gushed from the silver dragon's maw and ignited the grass in a long line in front of him. Rassím turned to see Kallar stalking toward him, looking every bit an an'reik.

But he wasn't. He was a victim. Not simply lied to, but a prisoner.

Great Maker, save him.

Raising his sword, Rassím strode forward, giving himself more space from the flames. He glanced at the silver dragon and the green one beyond it. They made no move, statuesque as they watched him and Kallar.

"Come on, Kallar, fight it. I know you're stronger than this."

Kallar smirked. "The only thing here to fight is you." He stopped six feet away and took a ready stance. "I suppose I should thank you—I was getting bored just singing."

Which, Rassím supposed, Kallar had at least been distracted from now. Perhaps he could still give his clanmates time without killing the victim.

But meanwhile, others will perish. I have to——

Kallar moved, striking at Rassím's face. Rassím deflected the blow and dodged from the next. He tried to circle away from the fire, but Kallar didn't let up. He forced Rassím back against the flames. Dezra's fear rose in his mind and, in desperation, Rassím grabbed one of his knives for his off-hand. Kallar pressed blades, perhaps thinking Rassím would have to drop the knife in order to hold him off. Rassím instead let himself be pushed down, then slammed the blade into Kallar's arm. Kallar didn't even flinch, inhuman in his resolve. Rassím gripped the sword with his second hand, trying to keep Kallar at bay. Sweat beaded as the heat became oppressive.

I can't die and leave Dezra alone.

"No, you can't."

With a roar reminiscent of a battle-cry, Dezra swooped down. She collided with Kallar from the side, releasing Rassím from the press. Sensing her plan, Rassím ran from Kallar while Dezra leapt back into the air. He lifted his arms and jumped as high as he could, cringing as talons scraped through leather armor and against his ribs.

Dezra beat her wings furiously to keep from being pulled down by his sudden weight, then faltered as Kallar shouted a battle-cry. She trumpeted in pain before Rassím locked a psychic shield around her. Kallar's shout battered against him, but his defense held until they were out of sight.

Dezra set him down none too gently. *"What are you thinking?! It doesn't matter that he's possessed—our friends are dying by the talons of dragons he's strengthening! You are so soft, I can't even—"*

"There are more, Dez," Rassím said. *"More humans being forced to fight, and likely some dragons as well. This is different than Alísa thought. As chief, she must know before we take further action."*

"We aren't even sure they can be saved." A slight dimming of Dezra's eyes softened the statement, though her tone still held frustration.

"We don't. Before today, I thought the possessed were mere stories to scare children." Rassím shook his head and jogged to her side to mount up. *"Whatever the answer, we must find Alísa and tell her what's going on."*

Dezra let steam drop from her mouth. *"Okay. Keep me shielded until you see her—I don't want that Singer anywhere near my mind again."*

Rassím firmed up his shield and gripped her spine. *"Let's go."*

39

FIRE & ICE

Falier fought not to cough as Graydonn dipped low to evade the clutches of an enemy dragon. Between the initial strafing of the an'reik army and the an'reik's fire-manipulators, the air was thick with smoke. Even the dampness of yesterday's rain and this morning's dew wasn't enough to keep the field from catching. Watching the astral plane allowed him to keep his eyes closed, but he could do nothing for his lungs.

A trumpet of pain seized Falier's ear. His heart pounded. The dragon's voice was familiar. Not from his immediate squad, but——

Graydonn banked hard, rushing for a sapphire dragoness caught between two enemies. Alanti. Blood sprayed from her neck. On her back, Varek swung his sword, shouting war-cries at the dragon trying to snap him up. Falier braced himself as Graydonn slammed into the dragon at Alanti's neck. Falier pulled his weapon while Graydonn grappled, carving a hole in the enemy's wing. When Graydonn dislodged, the dragon fell.

They turned around to head back for Alanti, but her wounds had already taken their toll. She fell, and her second attacker flew off to find another opponent. Varek leapt from her, spreading his limbs to slow his fall, as Falier had taught.

"Catch him, Graydonn!"

Graydonn pushed peace and pointed his muzzle at a large, orange dragoness who was closer. With a trumpet of victory, Mennáli snatched Varek from the air and descended, likely to deposit him on the ground.

Falier released a breath of relief, then sucked in as Graydonn veered to avoid an attack. Falier needed both hands. And they needed their squad-mates.

Sheathing his sword, Falier reached out through the link. *"Regroup! Selene, send up a cloud so we can find you. Everyone, get to her and Hwinn!"*

A burst of bright orange erupted north of them. Graydonn bolted for it as another dragon shot toward them. Its lack of shield would make it easy prey for Falier. He pulled at Graydonn's power, but it resisted.

"Open the bond, Graydonn!"

The power came quickly as Graydonn asserted his will over it, but his flight slowed. Falier hit his target with a mind-spear, then spread his power to choke it. The dragon wrestled against him, struggling and scratching with telepathic talons.

Ska chirped, and Alísa's song rushed into the squad, renewing their strength again. Energized by it, Falier sealed the choke and watched the dragon tumble from the sky. He held firm against the dragon's struggling mind until it hit the ground. Pain shocked through Falier and he pulled away. It wasn't dead, but its wing was broken. He left it to the slayers.

They were almost to Selene. Taz, Jossen, and their dragon partners were already there. Once everyone was together, Falier would split them into two groups and—

"Left, Graydonn!" Hwinn's voice shrieked through the squad-link.

Falier saw it coming before it happened. Time slowed, yet even with Hwinn's warning, he could do nothing.

Nothing but watch an incoming dragon body-slam Graydonn.

The impact sent Falier tumbling through the air. Panic gripped him as he flailed, his terror amplified by Graydonn's. He spread his limbs, but the ground still rushed toward him, all smoke and flames and flashing steel.

Talons dug into his side and Falier cried out in pain. They pulled him against a warm underbelly and he tumbled more with his rescuer until—

Impact. The air left Falier's lungs as Graydonn hit back-first. It softened the blow for Falier, but Graydonn's claws dug deeper as he curled around him. They rolled across the battlefield, through flames and over bodies of the dead. Finally, after an eternity, they stopped.

Falier's ears rang. He couldn't make himself move. Even his telepathy wouldn't respond as he lay in Graydonn's clutches. The dragon breathed heavily beneath him, panting for air. Metal clashed around them and smoke caked Falier's throat. He coughed and choked, only finding the ability to move once the fit ended.

He gripped the paw holding him against Graydonn's underbelly, wincing at the talons digging into his shoulder and side.

"Graydonn. I'm alright. Are you?"

Graydonn's panting continued, but he loosened his grip. *"I—am alive."*

It sounded more a question than a statement.

"Ska? Ska!" With horror, Falier felt at his chest under the dragon's paw, but there was no drek there. He breathed a sigh of relief—Ska must have fallen or phased out. Falier couldn't sense him, nor the rest of the squad. Head ringing, he was barely aware of Graydonn.

Falier shimmied from under the paw and took in their surroundings. He thought the battle in the air was chaos, but here… Fire glowed as it caught in the grasses, white smoke lifting into the sky as last night's rain burned away. Dragons roared above as the ground troops fought. Flames flashed off swords and bronze shields. Strewn about were the colors of Alísa's allies. Dead.

Falier drew his sword with a trembling hand. *"Get up, Graydonn."*

The dragon groaned, rolling to his belly. Falier searched the bond for where Graydonn's pain radiated. A lot of it settled in his back.

"I think I broke some of my spines." Graydonn twisted his neck to look, then bleated with pain. *"Agh. No. Shouldn't turn my head like that. Can you look?"*

Falier backed up against Graydonn, searching for signs of the enemy coming after them. Nothing so far. He cringed as he looked at Graydonn's back. Three spines in the middle were, indeed, broken. Two were reduced to mere stumps a few inches tall. The third had lost only a piece of the tip, the remaining spine now razor-sharp.

Spines were bone. If those were inside the body, that would be a terrible problem, but Graydonn's pain didn't seem quite that level.

"Three broken. How are your wings?"

Graydonn stretched them and Falier saw some tears.

"In one piece. It will hurt to fly with the tears, but I should—watch out!"

Falier whirled, catching sight of a man charging them, broadsword raised. Graydonn twisted and breathed fire at him, the pain in his neck drawing a roar with the torrent. The slayer dodged and raised his shield to block the flames. As soon as Graydonn's fire ended, Falier moved, crossing between the swordsman and dragon to parry the first blow. The man attacked and Falier defended, blocking repeatedly as his opponent unleashed a series of strikes.

"You call yourself a slayer, riding these beasts?" The man pressed swords with Falier and spoke through his teeth. "Traitor!"

Falier pressed back, traumatized muscles protesting. Graydonn tried to stand, then bleated as the slayer hit him with a psychic spear. Pain and terror radiated through the mind-kin bond and made Falier's blood boil.

No one hurt Graydonn.

He shot his own psychic spear at the slayer. The man stumbled, shocked. Falier didn't let him recover, spearing him again while slashing across his chest. His scale armor deflected the attack. Falier swiped again, knowing it would fail but using the time to pull more power from Graydonn. It came with difficulty, but when the slayer parried and lunged, Falier released a lightning bolt of energy. It crackled over the slayer's shield and overwhelmed it, wrenching a scream from him as he fell to his knees. Falier acted instantly, running the man through. It was only when their eyes met that Falier felt sorrow.

He pulled his blade free, nearly dropping it as the slayer's body flopped to the ground. He had killed multiple dragons earlier, but it felt different with humans. Especially one who, as far as Falier could tell, wasn't an'reik. One who, in other circumstances, Falier might have talked with and tried to persuade. He would never have that chance now.

Yet Graydonn was alive. Falier gripped his sword tighter and scanned the battlefield. *"Are you able to contact the others?"*

Graydonn struggled to his feet. *"I'm trying, but my mind is so foggy. I can barely hold on to our connection."*

"Can you fly?"

"Soon." He looked around. *"People are running."*

"Running?" Sure enough, people were disengaging, but smoke obscured the details. *"Which side?"*

Graydonn's eyes dimmed. *"I think ours."*

A flash of flames drew Falier's gaze as it consumed two retreating slayers. His heart stuttered. The fire came from ground-level, not the sky.

Hellflames.

"We have to move, Graydonn!"

Falier ran for him, sliding his sword into its sheath. Graydonn crouched, but when Falier tried to pull himself up by a spine, the dragon roared with pain. A crack in the bone sliced into Falier's palm and he let go, clutching his hand to his chest. Graydonn's spines were more damaged than he had realized.

"*I'm sorry,*" Graydonn said. "*I don't think I can carry you. You must run, now!*"

"*I can't leave you!*"

"*I can fly, just not with you.*" Graydonn stretched his wings, then yelped. "*Duck!*"

Without hesitation, Falier dove to the ground. Graydonn jumped over him and Falier heard the rush of fire flying past. Someone screamed as flames consumed them.

"*Go! Run!*" Graydonn ordered, standing and pushing at Falier with his snout.

"What a noble, stupid dragon," a woman said, her voice high and giddy. "My flames burn scales, and you think you'll be able to protect your rider?"

"*Run, Falier!*"

Falier scrambled to his feet, but he couldn't make himself leave. In desperation, he shot the an'reik with a psychic arrow—if he hurt her, they could both escape—but it ricochetted back into him. His knees gave out and he slumped against Graydonn.

"Hmm, nice try." The woman's hands glowed, her sadistic grin lighting with her growing fire. "But you're no match."

She thrust her hands forward and flames roared from them. Falier turned his face into Graydonn, bracing for death.

It never came—only a roar, high and familiar. Falier looked back and saw white scales standing between him and the an'reik. A plume of bright steam rose where fire met icy breath.

"*Saynan? You can...*"

From Saynan's back, Darrin gave orders. "*We are in retreat, as are the war-camp and Vennia. Get to your squad. We must cover the civilians and our slayers as long as we can.*"

Ska leapt from Darrin's shoulder and flew to Falier, rubbing his muzzle against Falier's cheek. With his psychic connection came Alísa's song again. It surged through him and Graydonn, lightening the dragon's pain.

"*Fly?*"

Beyond Saynan, the fire manipulator screamed with rage, but the plume of steam continued to rise.

Graydonn lowered to his belly. "*I think so. I'll carry you as far as I can.*"

Falier carefully pulled himself up. He winced as Graydonn's back twinged with pain, but it wasn't as bad as before, thanks to Alísa. Avoiding the spines, he gripped with his legs as Graydonn rose on bruised wings. Falier looked below just in time to see Saynan's ice breath overwhelm the fire manipulator, covering her with a glowing sheen of burning ice. The dragon turned, snapping his tail against her and shattering her body over the already blood-strewn ground. Then Saynan launched after them.

"I see. You're hurt more badly than I realized," Saynan's voice was soft and fatigued. *"Head for the war-camp. Cover the civilians' retreat alongside the slayers. If you can carry one more person, even a single child, do so. I will watch over you until you're out of range. Fly strong, Graydonn."*

Graydonn sent back an exhausted affirmative and Falier pushed as much of Alísa's song as he was able out of himself and into his friend. Ska clung to Falier's shoulder, but the pain of his tiny talons was nothing compared to the comfort of his returned presence.

Falier looked over the smoky battlefield and saw dragons flaming an'reik as they chased the few retreating slayers. Dragons still battled in the air above, but Alísa's army formed a tight protective formation as they slowly pulled into retreat. Their numbers had dwindled, as had the an'reik's, but it was nothing compared to the devastation on the ground.

A second retreat. A second terrible loss.

Could they ever defeat this monster?

40

AFTERMATH

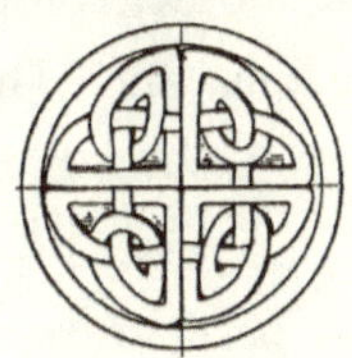

The enemy army advanced, slowing but never stopping. Alísa had little voice left, her strength songs barely whispers. In the air, dragon-rider pairs held back the dragons from the retreating villagers and refugees. On the ground, slayers formed ranks before the war-camp and shot psychic bolts at enemy dragons as they waited for the human army to arrive. She intended them to be gone long before.

Sesína swooped down upon an enemy dragon chasing a wounded ally, slashing at its wings before vaulting back into the air. She roared defiantly, dodging another enemy's talons and breathing fire into its eyes before returning to cover the wounded dragon's escape.

How had this happened? Their alliance was strong, but the an'reik army had grown more quickly than Alísa thought possible. With so many at her side, she hadn't considered defeat.

What have you done, Maker? I did everything I'm supposed to do! Why have you abandoned us?

Too many allies had died today. Paired with Rassím's news of the possessed who were forced to fight, she had no choice but to call this retreat before she lost every ally she had. The pain throbbing in her skull told her she might still lose them all. She needed to get them out.

"Sesína, I'm entrusting command to you. My thoughts are about to become muddled."

Sesína didn't object. With a thought to Rís, the drek released her, opening her mind to her full army of dragons. Alísa gasped as agony, terror, grief, and confusion converged within her. She let out a wordless cry, pushing what strength she had as it flowed to every dragon in her ranks. Her song lessened the pain of their wounds and brought courage, and Alísa tried to feed off that courage to keep herself going.

Distantly, she felt Sesína swerve after an enemy dragon. Behind her, Tora and Q'rill batted back those seeking to destroy the Singer. They had been a constant for her in this mess, the mother-son pair brilliant in their teamwork and dedicated to keeping their alpha safe. The rest of her squad was near, fighting off dragons and strafing the ground to create room for those picking up refugees from Eskann and Vennia.

Alísa gripped Sesína's spine hard, tears dripping with her exertion and pain. Her father's words came back to her. *Get our people to safety.*

Just a little more. She could do this. Even with knives slicing through her mind and heart. Just a little more.

Soon it became Alísa's squad's turn to pick up slayers and villagers. Alísa barely felt Varek mounting behind her—had he lost his dragon partner?

"Watch the sky," Sesína ordered Varek. *"Spear any dragon who gets too close."*

But as they made their retreat, the an'reik dragons and their allies did not come close. While Sesína led their army away, the enemy circled back. Apparently, they didn't think it wise to pursue without the support of their human allies and Singer.

Singer.

Kallar.

It wasn't him.

The thought swam through Alísa's muddled mind with so many emotions attached. Guilt for aiming her anger at the wrong person. Rage at the an'reik who could bend someone so strong-willed to their whims. Grief for what he must have felt, forced to hold the dagger.

Too much.

It was—too much...

Sesína prodded her mind. *"Wake up, Alísa. We need you."*

Alísa sucked in a breath and opened her eyes. She had fallen asleep? The night was dark, cloud-cover obscuring moon and stars. Small fires within a grove of trees showed people either hurrying about or otherwise huddled for warmth in the chilly night. Dragon and dreki eye-lights revealed that her entire army was here. What remained of it.

Varek loosened his grip on her. "You alright, Chief?"

"Yes," Alísa said, voice hoarse. "Thank you for keeping me upright."

He nodded, then slid off Sesína's back and offered her a hand. She must look dreadful for him to act so gently. Alísa accepted the help, sure she would fall on her face if she tried alone.

Entering the grove, she looked over her army, walking in a daze with Rís on her shoulder and Sesína behind. Around them, dragons cauterized each other's wounds while human medics checked on person after person. Villagers huddled in the darkness, unwounded but afraid. Tears and dimmed eyes abounded.

As more fires lit the space, Alísa saw exactly what she had feared. The clans that accepted dragon-rider pairings fared relatively well. Many were wounded, some gravely, but their partnership provided the strength and protection they needed to make it through with few losses. The clans that worked alone, however, had sustained much higher casualties. By a quick estimation, the dragon-rider pairs had lost about one in five of their numbers, while those working on their own had lost nearly twice that.

So many deaths.

Would it never end?

"Karns-daughter." Alísa turned to see Lorin rise from among his people. His voice held accusation. "What are we to do now? Where are we to go?"

"Home," said another chief. "We should never have come. Better to defend our villages as we always have rather than embark on this fool's errand."

"You really think you could face the an'reik if they came against your village?" Tella rose to her feet from wrapping a man's leg-wound. "Retreat is not the answer. We must gather more. Stop this damned army before it comes to your door next!"

The sound of wings caused Alísa to turn around. A clan of dragons taking off. She forced her legs to move, running to the last of them.

"D—don't leave!" They needed to stay together, come up with a new plan.

One dragon turned to her, his voice grave and sorrowful. *"I am sorry, Singer, but with our numbers now dwindling, we cannot do more than defend our own cave. We must protect our little ones from this evil."*

"You c-c-c-cannot stand on your own," Alísa pleaded aloud so that others could hear. "Call to your alpha—t-t-tell Zarria I m—must speak with her."

"I am sorry." With that, the dragon followed his clan.

"She cannot even command the dragons," T'kan of Vennia said. "The one thing that brought us under her banner."

Alísa whirled on him, sending a dizzy spell over herself. "W—wasn't stopping this evil the c-c-c-cause that united us? They are still out there—"

"Then why did we run and leave my village to them?"

"Tactical retreat was the only sensible option," a second said. "Half my clan perished, but she got us out before the rest were lost. We should stay together and create a new plan."

Alísa blew out a sigh, relieved someone else said it first. "P-please. Emotions are high and the c-c-c-cost has been grave. Care for your wounded, then come back with me to my mountain." She turned to the remaining dragon clans. "There are c-c-c-caves enough for all of you. T-tomorrow we shall have council and decide what to do."

"Your mountain?" Lorin looked at her incredulously. "After this debacle, you think I will bring my men anywhere near your cave?" He gestured at her. "Why should we follow her? Karns-daughter is a far cry from the man himself."

That hit her like a slap in the face, stinging with its truth. Thankfully, she didn't have to respond, as N'ravi of Eskann scoffed.

"I trust her dragons not to attack more than I trust the an'reik not to find this grove." He placed a hand over his heart and nodded to Alísa. "I am with you, Dragon Singer."

"As am I," Tella said. "It is true we suffered defeat today, but the only one who can prove the good dragons and bring them to our aid is Alísa. Like it or not, humanity cannot oppose this monstrosity alone." She looked between the chiefs. "I suggest we rest here tonight and seek guidance from the Maker and Eldír. Tomorrow we will decide our direction."

All, even Lorin, agreed Tella's plan was correct, but the thought of seeking guidance sent a pang through Alísa's heart. Twice the Maker had failed her. Twice the darkness had won. Did he not care? Did his Eldír sleep? What of the possessed he had abandoned?

No, she couldn't seek. Perhaps the Maker would deign to show his will to another chief.

Alísa took her leave, following Sesína to their clan's section of the grove. Her betas had already taken command, cauterizing dragon wounds and checking on their people.

Her heart clenched as she caught sight of Tenza, Gia, and Tobin speaking with Rassím. Gia covered her mouth in shock while Tobin laid a comforting hand on her shoulder. Tenza just stared with only the slightest hint of sorrow. Perhaps it was cowardly, but relief filled Alísa that Rassím was the one to tell them of Kallar's true state.

Alísa found Falier and Graydonn among the bonded pairs, gathered around a small fire. Graydonn lay on his belly as Koriana looked him over. Several of his spines were missing, while she had a gash along her underbelly that had been cauterized and now oozed. Falier sat on the ground near Graydonn, holding the side of his shirt up while Trísse dabbed him with a cloth.

Falier gave a tired smile that didn't reach his eyes. "Líse."

She jogged the last few steps and fell to her knees in front of him. Mud caked his pant legs and mixed with blood. She couldn't tell whether the blood was his or someone else's. Bandages already wrapped his shoulder underneath his tunic, and then there was the gash Trísse was cleaning.

"Graydonn's worse off than I am," he said.

Alísa studied the broken spines along the dragon's back. Pushing herself to her feet, she touched Graydonn's cheek.

"W—what happened?"

"Took a tumble. Mother says I'll be fine."

Koriana growled. *"'Fine' is not the word I used. You have three broken spines and two cracked ones. It's a miracle none of the cracks extended down past your scales."* She sniffed at the base of his neck. *"And you will not be able to turn your head without pain for days."*

"Hear that? Only days." Graydonn held the bridge of his nose to Alísa's cheek and she pressed back with her hands under his jaw. *"I'm fine. And I saved your mate."*

Sesína sniffed at Falier. *"If you can call puncturing him rescue."*

"I'd like to see you do better."

"I have. Remember Rorenth?"

Graydonn paused. *"I'd like to see you do better only a few hundred feet from the ground."*

Alísa fought not to shudder as she pictured Falier free-falling in an aerial war-zone. She kissed Graydonn's nose. "Thank you."

"He gets a kiss for nearly skewering me?" Falier scoffed lightly. "I demand at least two."

"Not until I'm finished," Trísse mumbled, not looking up.

Alísa looked to the others. Harenn slept against an enormous tree trunk, Iila at his side and Rassi—Trísse's brother and Iila's rider—nearby. All appeared unhurt. Taz and Selene sat on the ground together, leaning back against Hwinn.

"Everyone else okay?" Alísa asked. All gave quiet affirmations, but the astral plane held tension and leftover terrors. She glanced at Hwinn. This was his and Selene's first battle, and a terrible one at that.

"You were very brave, Hwinn. Were you hurt at all?"

Hwinn shook his head, his body wobbling with the large motion. *"We were too fast for anyone to catch. Too small to deal much damage, though."*

"You did great," Falier assured. "You and Selene worked well with the squad. I'm proud of you."

Hwinn's eyes brightened. His contentment joined the cacophony in Alísa's mind, lightening the tones of exhaustion and echoes of terror.

Trísse let Falier's shirt fall back down over his side. "There. Take it easy for a while, okay?"

"I'll try." He watched as Trísse stood and began walking away. "Where are you going?"

She hesitated. "The ground troops sustained heavy losses. I—have to know."

Alísa pressed her lips together. Tern had been among the ground troops.

"I'll go with her, Singer," Komi said, standing. The dragoness limped slightly, but shuffled after her mind-kin.

Alísa returned her attention to Falier, who leaned back against Graydonn, eyes shut. He seemed so frail in this moment—wounded and tired and full of tremulous emotions Alísa couldn't untangle. She went to his uninjured side and sat beside him. His tension relaxed as he leaned into her, his gentle telepathy entering her mind.

"What about you? Are you alright?"

Alísa swallowed. *"Physically, yes. Everything else?"* She pressed into him. *"I'm so glad you're safe. I couldn't bear it if—"*

He put his arm around her. *"We're okay, Lise. We'll find the way forward."*

She didn't respond. She had done everything she knew to do, had raised an army like none the country had seen. Given all she had.

And she had failed.

41

USELESS

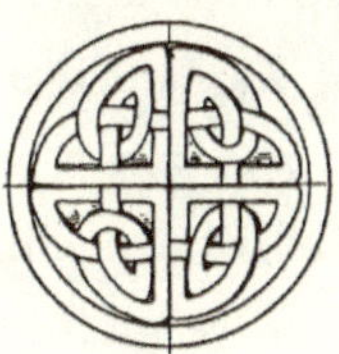

Despite the darkness of night, Kallar could tell the impressive size of Alísa's abandoned war-camp. Seven sections of tents with Karn's people at the center. He recognized each of the wayfarers' tents with bitterness as the an'reik raided supplies and prized possessions. Surprisingly, his own tent was here, as was his trunk of personal effects. Who would keep these?

Three bed-mats cramped the space. A barely familiar black mourning shawl draped the foot of one. Next to another, he discovered a whittling knife and a small piece of wood shaping into a dragon.

So Tenza had found Tobin and Gia. And they had kept his things.

He left the tent, chest and throat aching. He couldn't reclaim what they'd saved, anyway. Not with the keeper inside him.

That flaming assassin should have killed me. He had watched Alísa's knife-thrower practice. By all rights, Kallar should be dead. Yet somehow the southlander had seen through the possession and, rather than end the nightmare, allowed Kallar to continue strengthening the enemy. Idiot.

He studied the camp, unsure what to do now. Some an'reik who fancied themselves cooks were doing something in the kitchen tent. Others made piles of abandoned weapons and gear. Isarra stood nearby, grinning as she spoke to all within earshot.

"Didn't I say we needn't raid N'moth or bring our supplies? Between this and Vennia, we'll have enough to last us weeks. Enough to finish what we've started."

Marizarr spoke to her, but Kallar ignored him. Far behind Isarra, two men dragged R'lann toward a tent. R'lann pulled and twisted against them, earning a fist to the gut. Rage flooded Kallar, and he made to run toward them.

"Please, try," the keeper chuckled. *"I would love to make you join in."*

Kallar froze, fists clenching.

"Slayers!" Isarra called out. "You have seen us face a larger army and win, watched as the powers of the Nameless Ones broke the enemy before you! Some of your own clanmates held the power and can testify to its efficacy. Will you hold yourselves back while Alísa Karns-daughter still draws breath? Come to me, champions of humanity, and gain power over your enemies!"

As slayers turned to her, Kallar opened his mouth to shout down her lies. Instead, the keeper took hold of his tongue.

"We will rid this land of all dragons who do not bow, finally bringing peace to our people!"

Kallar pushed against the keeper, writhing and shoving until he felt he might break out of his skin. Nothing happened. Nothing but more of his slayer brothers and sisters converging on Isarra to take her up on her offer. They would need the last of someone's lifeblood for the sacrifice. Hopefully, Vennia was evacuated.

Then again, they might just give up on R'lann and use him.

What a terrible thought, hoping a stranger would die so his brother could live. R'lann would probably prefer death to this nightmare, regardless of how they used his blood.

Kallar stopped his struggle. Useless. He was useless to all except the enemy.

The idiot assassin should have killed him.

42

STAY

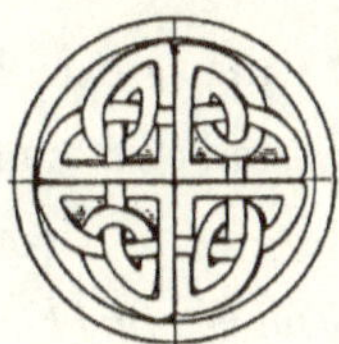

Battle consumed Falier's dreams. He flew through fire and smoke, Graydonn nowhere in sight as their squad died around him. He had no talons, no inner flame, no tail-spines, and his telepathy was near-inert. There was nothing he could do as they fell one-by-one.

Then he stood on the ground, men and dragons surrounding him, each someone he had killed or been unable to save. They rose from the smoke, their swords piercing him in the shoulder and side with a sluggish pain, their flames a thousand tiny needles.

The an'reik fire-wielder appeared before him, the contours of her face shadowed like a ghoul.

"You are no match."

Falier awoke with her flames, gasping in a breath. Darkness surrounded him, suffocated him, and he could not move.

He could *not* move!

He struggled with muscles heavier than the mountains, finally managing to twist to the side. He hit a wall of tough skin. Graydonn's belly. He was in the grove with Alísa's army.

Shuddering with remnants of terror, he tested his control over his body. His toes flexed at his command, his knees bent, his arms moved despite the soreness permeating them. He was alive.

I need to get out of here.

Careful not to wake the exhausted dragon, Falier crawled out from under Graydonn's wing. The earth was soft under his hands and knees, and when he hit the outside air, he realized just how damp his clothes were from sleeping on the ground. He shivered and wished for his cloak. Like everything else, it was left behind at the war-camp.

Around him, humans were slowly waking while most dragons continued their slumber. Dragons required far more sleep than humans, especially after a day-long battle. They would also need a ton of food to recover from their injuries.

One awake dragon caught Falier's eye. Komi lay at the edge of Alísa's portion of the grove, legs tucked, head alert, and a wing splayed over her curled tail to create a tent for Trísse.

Falier reached out to her. *"Did you find him? Tern?"*

Komi turned her neck to regard him, eyes dim. *"He never made it here. With the ground troops' numbers... Trísse is certain he was killed."*

Sorrow rippled through Falier for Trísse. If it had been him and Alísa—

The thought was too heavy to consider.

"How is she?"

Komi clicked in her throat. *"Her relationship with Tern is—was—complicated. She grieves, but it differs from the grief for her father."* Komi's eyes unfocused for a moment, and Falier knew she was thinking of her own father, Faern. She returned quickly. *"I will tell her you asked after her. I know you will have many responsibilities today."*

Falier nodded his thanks, adding a slow eye-blink before returning to his walk. He passed the last of Alísa's clan and looked over the others. He saw mostly humans, the majority of the dragons too large to navigate the trees. Many slept, and those awake were covered in mud, blood, and sweat, like him.

Movement drew Falier's gaze to a gathering. What colors he could see indicated their village—Vennia, both their warriors and villagers. They stood in small groups, whispering and glancing at the edge of the grove.

What's going on there?

Falier headed for a small group of riders. "Morning."

The slayers paused, eyeing him. Falier drummed his fingers on his thigh. "Your clan is certainly organized. Most others are asleep."

One slayer crossed his arms. "And?"

Falier raised hands in peace. "Just curious. I don't remember T'kan being so strict with morning drills."

Another man, one Falier knew to have a more pleasant demeanor, sighed. "We're leaving. Taking our people far from the an'reik's path."

The first slayer growled. "He doesn't need to know that."

Falier blinked. "All of you?"

The informant nodded. "We will stay together, with our families and those we've sworn to protect."

Falier's mind raced. Even the warriors would flee? That couldn't happen. They needed everyone to defeat the an'reik. Questions rose inside and fell just as quickly. These men might give him information, but they couldn't change anything.

"Where is your chief?"

"T'kan doesn't need your—"

"At the fire." The pleasant slayer jerked his head back. "But you won't convince him to stay."

Falier nodded his thanks and pushed past them. Perhaps he should get Alísa or L'non, but this clan was geared to move. They might be gone before he could find an actual authority figure.

T'kan and his second sat with palms toward their fire, speaking in hushed tones. Falier approached them, fist to his heart. Here went nothing.

"Eldra Branni strengthen your hands."

T'kan eyed him. "What do you want, Alísas-man?"

Straight to the point, then. "I hear you plan to leave us."

T'kan glanced at his second, then sighed. "We must protect our people."

Falier let concern fill his features. "I understand that, but Alísa offered sanctuary within her caves. You can still stay together and help bolster our forces. We need everyone we can muster."

"This army" —T'kan looked about and shook his head— "it cannot stand. We've seen it with our own eyes now."

"And what will you do when the an'reik approach your new village? You saw their forces—two clans alone can't face them."

"They will not march against us," the second said. "Their vendetta is against the Dragon Singer. They have only harmed villages between her and them, never deviating from their path."

T'kan watched the fire. "Vennia is who the Maker entrusted to us. We will do what we must for their sake."

Falier drummed his fingers on his thigh. Fear lived in both men's eyes, a strange sight after weeks of training with them. Their arguments were easily dismantled, but emotions and fatigue ran high. Experience taught Falier it was sometimes better to sit and wait for people to reach their own conclusions rather than straight-up tell them they were wrong. Typically, that happened over a mug of ale or hot mead in the Hold's warmth. He would have to settle for a campfire and, well, nothing else.

"When do you leave?" he asked.

T'kan glanced at the grove's edge. "One of my men rode out with his dragon partner to speak with Chief N'lan of Perrin and see if he will take us."

Falier nodded and sat on the ground across from them. "You have time for a story, then?"

T'kan squinted. "A story?"

Please, Eldra Nahne, help this work. "A true one, from when I met an an'reik who wasn't trying to kill me." Falier smirked. "At least, not directly."

The second's face smoothed with interest, while T'kan looked on with scrutiny. He glanced to the border again, perhaps hoping his scout would return that moment. Falier waited.

"Very well, but we are leaving as soon as my man returns."

Falier smiled. "Of course."

Sending up a prayer of thanks, he launched into the story of finding a village under attack by an'reik dragons. Remembering Namor and other storytellers of Me'ran, Falier embellished the recounting with vivid descriptions and wide gestures. He unintentionally gained others' attention, drawing in the weary, sodden Vennians. He told of how Sesína and Graydonn fought eight dragons, then of facing Moraggan. After a moment's hesitation, Falier mentioned the name of the slayer chief who had fallen under Moraggan's influence, making T'kan start.

"Even R'gan gave in to them?"

Falier nodded solemnly. "Moraggan didn't have to lift a finger against us. The chief raised his sword and ordered his men to do the same, trapping me and Alísa at the center. Obviously, we escaped, but the village remains under an'reik influence. They welcomed him as their savior even as they tried to kill others who helped rescue them."

Falier clasped his hands, his story through. The chief hadn't checked the edge of the grove for the last half of the telling, his expression changing from tolerance to interest. Now he focused on the campfire before him, contemplative.

Finally, T'kan looked up. "You wish me to understand it does not take an army to harm a village. Merely the willing welcome of darkness. Your story is not so subtle as you think."

Falier shook his head. "I never claimed to be subtle. Every word is true, though. Your people will never be safe when an'reik are tolerated in our lands." He opened his hands in supplication. "Don't leave, chief. Help us fight them, for Vennia and all of Arran."

Footsteps approached, drawing all eyes. A slayer with clothing dried by the winds looked over the gathering, his gaze questioning until he found T'kan.

"Chief," he said, fist to his heart. "Perrin will accept us."

T'kan nodded. "Good. Then I shall speak with the villagers and learn whether they would rather go into N'lan's care or stay with us in the Dragon Singer's mountain."

Tension fled Falier's body at the words. T'kan stood and held out his hand, hauling Falier to his feet.

"Tell Alísa we shall remain."

Falier grinned and let out an exaggerated sigh of relief. "Good. Do you know what a pain it is to train new riders?"

T'kan barked a laugh, clapping Falier on the back. "We'll see you in the air."

The chief returned to his people, prompting Falier to leave. He pointed his boots toward Alísa's clan, and found himself face-to-face with Hanah. She still bore the red chin marks of Karn's *anam nasctha*, though the paint was flecking away.

"You got here before I did." She grinned. "I'm impressed."

Falier blinked. "You knew Vennia would try to run?"

"Not Vennia specifically" —she motioned for him to walk with her— "but after yesterday's defeat, someone was bound to try. I mean to check in with each clan before we move, to prepare them to follow Alísa back to her mountain."

Hanah smiled up at him. "I should have asked for your help. We can cover more ground together."

Falier nodded, purpose rising in his chest. "You have it. We have a few hours before the dragons awaken. You take the west side, I'll take the east, then we'll go to the alphas together?"

Hanah chuckled.

"What? Did you have a different—"

"No, you just continue to surprise me." Hanah veered toward her end of the grove. "Our daughter chose well."

Falier breathed in the words and smiled, feeling for the first time like a tiern.

43

QUESTIONS

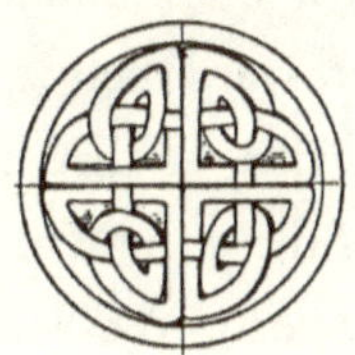

Alísa walked through the main cave, surveying her allied slayers and refugees from Eskann and Vennia. What food she hadn't carted off to the war-camp before—mostly salted meats and dried fruits—was given to the wounded and few children. Medics doled out salves and fresh bandages. Flattened tents and blankets were spread throughout to help shield sleepers from the cold stone floor.

Most of her own clanmates were off doing various tasks, whether helping their dragon allies settle, trading Rorenth's old hoard for supplies, or hunting. T'kan had secured refuge for Eskann's and Vennia's villagers, but only a third had gone. The rest either desired to serve the army, or else thought themselves safer here than on the ground.

Briek and Sesína escorted Alísa through the cave. She acutely sensed the eyes of all studying her, filled with questions.

Where do we go from here? How can we proceed with such loss? What allies can we find who we haven't already led to their doom?

She didn't know. She had done everything she knew to do. Brought the races together, gained their trust, created a fighting force—and it was all for nought. She had failed them. All she wanted was to locate a tiny, dark cave and disappear. But her sense of duty was stronger than her fear. The clans needed reassurance she wouldn't abandon them and that she had a plan, even though she most certainly did not.

Now, walking among them, fear was steadily overtaking her sense of duty. Even Sesína's empathic calm wasn't helping. Alísa felt the undercurrents of the dragoness' own uncertainties. If someone so confident as Sesína doubted—

"I'm not doubtful!" Sesína protested. *"We'll figure it out. We just—have to*

figure it out."

"Karns-daughter."

Alísa drew in a sharp breath, drawn from her contemplation. The chiefs gathered with some of their seconds at a nearby fire. She wanted to move closer to Briek for protection from their questioning eyes. Somehow, she kept that desire at bay and instead turned toward them.

"We were discussing the villages that need to evacuate," N'ravi said. "Getting them out of the path of the ground army is one thing, but the an'reik dragons may attack them on the road. We hope to send dragon-rider pairs to escort them."

There was a question in that statement, as though asking her council or permission. They still counted her as an equal.

She nodded. "It's a g—good idea. An adult dragon can c-c-c-carry four slayers. We can send t-two or three dragons to each village, laden with riders—"

"*And a drek,*" Sesína added.

"—and a drek, who can relay news of an attack and c-c-call reinforcements in q-quickly. Sesína, would you ask K-K-Koriana—"

"*On it!*" With that, Sesína trotted for the cave entrance. Koriana was organizing one of the high caves. She could identify the best individuals for the mission.

Lorin squinted. "Do you truly think dragon-rider pairs are the correct move? These people have lost much to dragon attacks."

"And what do you suggest instead?" Tella crossed her arms. "Horseback will take days, dragons will take hours. Villagers will respect the riders."

She looked to her second and tiern. "Gather the most fit of our men. If Lorin won't fly, we wayfarers will send as many as we can."

"I never said I *wouldn't* help! Only that thinking people will trust a dragon's call to evacuate is foolish." Lorin eyed Alísa. "I should very much like to know how you plan to fix this flaming mess."

So would I.

"You mentioned a war council," T'kan said. "Shall we have it now?"

The thought sent a pulse of panic through her. Fortunately, she had an excuse to decline.

"We must see our p-p-p-people t-taken care of first. W—we will also need the dragon alphas present."

Lorin scoffed. "We're already doing all we can at this moment. Best to call the creatures now so we may move forward." His expression turned predatory. "Unless, of course, the great Karns-daughter is merely stalling because the best she had failed yesterday." He looked to his fellow chiefs. "Her plan decimated our clans. With these numbers, we can't even defend our own villages."

"You already couldn't defend your villages against that army alone," Briek snapped. "We *all* put forth our best plan, and we *all* failed."

"Yet you treat her like the world's savior," Lorin snarled. "She saved no one yesterday—in fact, she sent many to their deaths. Without her insistence on riders, our ground force would have been stronger, potentially overwhelming the enemy."

Alísa shrank. She hadn't considered that.

"But the pairs fared better than the loners," Sesína protested, apparently still listening through Alísa.

"The dragons fared better because of my song," Alísa said, heart thumping as her thoughts raced. *"It's impossible to determine whether they would have been just as fine without riders. If I hadn't convinced Eskann and Vennia's slayers to train with us, if I'd left Papá's men alone instead of insisting they train with Briek's..."*

"—if she has no plan, perhaps someone else should step up."

Tella leaned forward. "I haven't heard any useful ideas from *your* mouth."

"And the dreki," Alísa continued as they argued. *"I had them split up to help me. If I'd been stronger, they could have taken down dragons together."*

"Chief?"

Her eyes snapped up to meet Briek's. The concern there made her go cold. He noticed her rising panic, and—she looked to the fire—so did the chiefs. They had ceased arguing and now waited on her, Lorin's expression smug. Had they asked her something? She wracked her brain for the information.

"How soon?" Tella prompted, none too gently. "When will the alphas be ready to meet?"

Alísa's mind raced with her pounding heart.

She didn't know.

Why did they think she knew anything?

What could she say?

"Breathe, Alísa," Sesína soothed. *"I'm coming back. Just breathe."*

Alísa tried, but every attempt was shallow.

She couldn't make herself slow.

She had nothing.

Nothing.

Everything was for nothing.

Lorin huffed. "Just what we get, trusting a teenager to lead us."

"We have all been through terrible loss," Briek said, stepping to Alísa's side. "The Dragon Singer perhaps most of all. If we are to devise a solid strategy, we must first prioritize healing our wounded, protecting evacuees, and taking time to grieve. We will check in tomorrow and discern whether the time is right."

He spoke with a finality that allowed no objections, a tone that Alísa envied. Then he stepped in front of Alísa and across, subtly prompting her to come with him.

Alísa complied. She needed to get away, to breathe. Everyone looked to her for hope, but she had none. Briek fell in behind her, blocking off the chiefs' gazes. They headed for the landing platform above the slayers' camp, pushing forward—ever forward—and out of view of the people below.

I did this. We fell because of me.

"No." The sound of flapping wings spread from the landing platform as Sesína reentered the cave. She hurried down the ramp toward Alísa. *"You did the best you could."*

"And my best wasn't enough!"

"You have three races willing to follow you."

"And I can give them nothing!" Her legs shook underneath her. *"Who am I to lead mortals against demons?"*

"Chief."

Alísa stopped, but she couldn't look at Briek. He had stood up for her, and she was going to disappoint him. He should have stayed in the east, where he would be safe from her and her stupid plans.

"Stop it!" Sesína skidded to a stop in front of her. Despite the sharpness of her tone, her eyes were dim with concern. *"We underestimated the enemy, but a loss does not make you stupid or weak or anything else your mind is telling you!"*

Alísa stared at her. Sesína was right, her thoughts were spinning out of control. But knowing didn't matter—she still felt every bit. She pulled in a breath. It hurt to expand her lungs. Everything inside was so tight.

"Alísa."

She breathed again. She didn't want Briek to see her panic. But Sesína's anger cooled as she looked past her at him. She indicated Briek with her muzzle.

"Look at him."

Another breath. Then Alísa turned. His compassionate eyes made her avert her gaze to avoid tears.

"I'm s—sorry. I sh—shouldn't have g—g—g—" *gotten so emotional. Say it!*

But she couldn't. Her throat was closed. She could barely breathe.

"Chief, I— Would you—" He stopped as though searching for words. Then, tentatively, he opened his arms.

Alísa choked back a sob. She was his chief. She shouldn't allow herself to be weak in front of him. Yet, Briek was one of the safest people she knew. Loyal. Unwavering. Kind. So, when Sesína gave her the tiniest nudge, Alísa stepped into his embrace.

She had meant to hug and release, but his arms enclosing her brought memories of her father to life. How she wanted a hug from Papá. She hugged Briek tighter and let her tears flow silently.

"I meant what I said, Alísa. You've suffered a terrible loss and have barely taken the space to grieve. The Maker made you for this age. I know you'll find a path for us. So if you need time, I'll provide it."

Alísa sniffled and pulled back. She swallowed against the tightness in her throat and whispered. "Thank you for being someone I can count on."

Briek placed a hand on her shoulder. "Maker shield you. Branni strengthen your hands."

The tiny traditional prayer threatened to send her tears overflowing again. She didn't feel strong or protected. She hadn't even prayed for it—hadn't prayed a single word since her father's death, not even for someone else.

Another failure.

"Go," Briek said. "I will take care of things here. You take care of yourself, then return to take care of us."

Alísa blew out a breath, then nodded. She couldn't say anything, her throat still too tight. She merely turned to Sesína and mounted. Neither had a destination, only the desperate need to think, to plan, and to grieve.

44

SERVICE

The wind from Sesína's wings ruffled Falier's hair. He glanced up from his work on the landing platform to watch her and Alísa fly away. Perhaps they were going to check on the dragons in other caves. He returned to the crates before him—supplies from Bezin. Hopefully, other villages would send more soon. Until then, he would manage with what he had.

He hefted a crate full of fruits and vegetables, passing it off to the next hauler. "Kitchens."

The man, a slayer bound to Eskann, looked out over the cave, searching. Falier pointed out the area filled with tables and stacked crates. The next box held potatoes and days-old bread. He hauled it up to pass to a man from among the ground troops.

"Let me guess," the slayer rolled his eyes. "Kitchens."

Falier chose not to rise to this comment. "The potatoes, yes. Distribute the loaves among the medics first, then give the leftovers to haulers, including yourself. You" —Falier pointed to the next hauler in line, a rider from Tella's clan— "go with him and bring a bucket of water and cloths for the medics to wash their hands."

The first slayer huffed, taking the ramp down to the main floor. The Tellas-man gave a quick nod before following. Falier returned to the crates, using the motion to hide a sigh. Should he have been harder with that man, rather than keeping a neutral tone and offering him food? Perhaps. Perhaps not. Balances and unknown recipes.

Falier's eye caught on Graydonn as he twisted to hand off a crate of blankets to a normal of Vennia. Overnight, Graydonn's neck and back had become so sore that he could barely lift his head. He'd needed to be carried to the mountain. Other wounded dragons were in the higher caves, but Graydonn had insisted he be near Falier. He was small enough not to impede incoming dragons, so Koriana had agreed to leave him on the landing platform. After receiving the first of the hunting parties' catches, he now slept soundly.

Falier took up the final crate, another of blankets and other soft materials. "I've got this one. Take a break. I'll signal when more arrives."

The three remaining haulers appeared all too happy for a break. Truthfully, Falier was too. After moving everyone into the caves, he had toiled to create some semblance of order amid the chaos. The physical labor was one thing. Add to it hundreds of hungry, grieving people, and Falier was exhausted.

He plodded toward a clan at the back of the cave that hadn't yet received sleeping materials. This area was especially cold with the mountain stream so near. He didn't recognize most of the slayers here. The few he *did* recognize were once riders—those who had abandoned their dragon partners alongside Tern. The one who had joked about spearing allied dragons from the sky smirked as Falier passed his companion a deerskin.

"How the mighty have fallen. Seems you've remembered your place, holder boy."

Really? Must he do this now? Falier considered ignoring him, but dismissed the idea. He handed out another blanket.

"I didn't realize feeding the hungry and clothing the cold was weak. Good to know it's so beneath you—I won't ask for your help when more supplies arrive."

The man narrowed his eyes. "I never said it wasn't necessary, only that it's all you're good for."

So, basically, what Falier claimed he had said. He didn't have the patience for this today. Yanking the next blanket free, he shoved it at the slayer.

"Look, you need this, and I'm going to give it to you whether you mock me or not. I'd rather skip that part, but if helps you feel better about yourself, then get it over with."

Another former rider snickered. "Oh, that sure showed us."

A few laughed, continuing their mockery. Falier almost felt sorry for them. Almost. He passed out the remaining blankets, accepting the apologetic looks some gave him. At least they weren't all against him.

He left the crate in case they could use it, then ambled back through the cave. All around him, family and friends grieved, the wounded moaned, and the healthy whispered harshly of many woes. Falier lowered his telepathic shield. He breathed in their pain, each one matching with something inside him. Loss. Anger. Frustration. Loneliness. It festered inside them as they could only wait for whatever might come next. They needed a release.

As Falier's wandering brought him near the kitchen, Selene waved him down. She, Taz, and five women—mostly wayfarers—were hard at work chopping vegetables and potatoes for tonight's supper and slicing up chunks of fruit to distribute. Fresh meat went to the dragons first, as both the wounded and exhausted needed it for healing. The humans probably wouldn't have much meat for a couple of days.

He approached the stone platform where Hwinn watched Selene about her work. This counter was the first item the dreki carved when Alísa's clan moved in, made from a lengthy boulder. Their repeated phasing shaved the rock sliver-by-sliver until the top became remarkably flat.

"How are things over here?" Falier asked, scratching behind Hwinn's jaw.

"Selene's cutting everything too small." Hwinn leaned in. *"I told her having more pieces won't trick stomachs into thinking they're more full."*

"Ah," Falier said, "but the eye is more important to convince than the stomach."

"Thank you." Selene looked pointedly at Hwinn. "Will you believe me now that your uncle agrees?"

Hwinn snorted a negative. *"Dragon sensibilities are far more, err, sensible."*

Falier laughed, drawing questioning eyes from a few of the other cooks. Partially telepathic conversations often left others confused.

"Did you need something from me, Selene?"

"Just a truthful answer." She pinned him with a stare. "Have you eaten anything?"

Falier couldn't even consider lying, not with Hwinn in his head and Selene awaiting confirmation from her sound-lights. "No. There's someone passing out bread—I'll try to find him."

"No need." Selene set down her knife and squatted behind the counter. When she stood back up, she held a small basket containing a few slices of bread and pieces of dried, salted meat.

Falier quirked an eyebrow at her. "The meat is for the wounded."

"And most of it went to them." She pushed the basket toward him. "But I know certain medics—and tierns—will refuse food until they drop dead. I saved these in case I caught them. One piece of each, and you should grab some fruit from Taz as well."

For a moment, Falier meant to refuse, but his eyes and stomach alike agreed with Selene's logic. He took a slice of bread and the smallest hunk of meat.

"Happy?"

"Very. If you catch Rassím anywhere, send him my way for some of the same."

"Will do. Anything else?"

She shook her head. "Thanks for not fighting me."

"It's not you I'm worried about. If I refused, Hwinn would have sat on me until I complied."

Hwinn gave a Sesína-like grin. *"Oo, that's a great idea for next time!"*

With one last scratch for Hwinn, Falier grabbed a couple of apple slices from Taz. After checking in with him, Falier returned to the landing platform. He would be ready when more supplies arrived.

Graydonn's eyes opened as Falier approached, brightening with recognition. Falier reached out telepathically.

"How are you feeling?"

"Terrible," Graydonn responded with an almost cheery tone. *"But it got me out of hunting duty, so I suppose I can't complain. How are you? What have I missed?"*

Falier sat next to him, placing himself so that Graydonn could see him without moving his neck. He took a bite of his salted meat—sheep or goat, he was pretty sure.

"I'm alright. Hoping the other village-bound slayers we sent to their villages have more luck than Lorin's men did. Alísa and Sesína are off on some mission, and I haven't seen any other dragons. I can only assume they're figuring out the cave situation."

Graydonn rumbled, his head still on the ground. *"That answers my second question sufficiently, but not the first. How are you?"*

Falier let out a breath. *"Worried. Tired. Constantly second-guessing myself. This morning I felt competent, helping Hanah talk to the clans and ensuring we all stay together. Now... I just wish I knew a better way to help everyone."*

Graydonn clicked in his throat, his eyes wandering. *"I think you're doing a good job."*

Falier didn't scoff, though he wanted to. *"You don't have to lie to me. We both know you don't agree with everything I'm doing."*

Pain ached through the bond, flavored with shame. Graydonn started lifting his head, and Falier held up a stalling hand.

"Don't hurt yourself. It's okay. We can disagree."

"I know," Graydonn said, squinting with his efforts. *"But I've done more than that. You need to know"*—he winced as he fully faced Falier— *"I was wrong."*

"Graydonn, lay back down. Aree will come after me if I'm the reason you're disobeying her orders."

"This should *pain me. I mistreated you, and I'm sorry. Truly. I apologized before, but I didn't fully realize what I was doing then. Now I do."* Graydonn groaned, closing his eyes for a moment before reopening them. Resolve glowed within. *"I was so scared you would become one of them. That somehow your personality and beliefs would change because you wanted to be friends with slayers and learn to use their blades."*

Falier deflated a bit, looking down. *"I did change. I went too far and validated your fears."*

"Do not interrupt," Graydonn growled. *"You've already apologized for your mistakes and have become better. Let* me *speak now."*

Falier winced. *"Sorry. Go on."*

Graydonn blinked slowly, this time in acceptance rather than pain. *"I allowed my fear to weaken our bond. I would not listen to your reasons for learning what you wanted to learn, and when you would not accept my warnings, I pulled away. I did not trust that you would remain the compassionate friend of dragons I first met. Maker forgive me, it took nearly dying to see how wrong I was."*

Graydonn paused, breathing a moment before settling his head back to the floor. Falier's shoulders loosened. He hadn't realized how much he was cringing at the thought of Graydonn's muscle strain. Or perhaps it was simply due to the growing emotions at Graydonn's words.

"On the battlefield, you saved my life with a sword in your hands." Graydonn's eyes turned distant. *"You can't fully realize what it's like for a dragon to not have access to telepathy or wings. I was terrified, but there you were. Sword in hand, telepathy honed, anger under control. A slayer, yet still wholly yourself."*

Graydonn clicked in his throat. *"I understand now, even why you had to fight Varek. You want to use the slayer part of you to serve them just as you've always used the holder part to serve others. Forgive me, for taking so long to see."*

"*Of course I forgive you.*" Falier grasped onto his relief and care, sending it with his words. "*You really think I can do this? Balance the holder and the slayer?*"

Graydonn blinked slowly. "*You are already doing it.*"

Falier glanced back at the cave and its occupants. He remembered their grief, their pain, their anger, all of it festering in their separate spaces.

"*There's something I'm missing here. Help me find it?*"

Falier and Graydonn talked—*really* talked—for the first time in weeks. By the time the next group of dragon-rider pairs returned with supplies, Falier knew what he needed to do. He wanted to speak with Alísa beforehand, but Briek didn't know when she would return. Falier went instead to Songweaver Farren.

This time, when Falier stood before the clans with Farren, he didn't try to bring joy into the midst of pain. There were certainly times for that, but not tonight. Tonight was for grief released, for remembering the lost, and for bonds forged by shared sorrow. As Falier led the clans in mournful song, Farren's authority behind him, he prayed for Alísa and her grief, and that she might find release as well.

45

NEVER ALONE

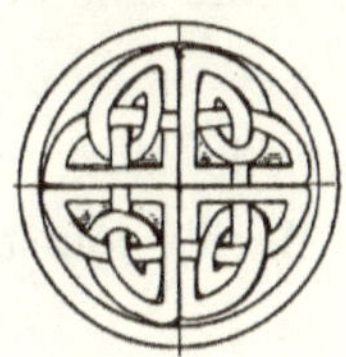

Alísa shivered in the breeze and scooted closer to Sesína. The dragoness' warmth was just enough to combat the night's chill, though Alísa kept her fingers lodged under her arms. They had flown for hours, ultimately returning to their mountain to huddle outside, far from any entrances or prying eyes.

Stars peeked out through gaps in the cloud-cover. Alísa could relate to their soft, flickering lights easily silenced behind foreboding clouds. Though she had ideas for next steps, she couldn't solve the problem of the possessed. And nothing she held made her ready to face the chiefs and alphas she had previously led astray.

Alísa wrapped her arms tighter around herself. It seemed impossible to both defeat the dark forces invading Arran and somehow rescue captives from their clutches. They were too strong for her. They had already defeated her army twice. Killed so many.

Sesína's warm muzzle brushed her cheek, but even she was full of anxiety. The an'reik were too powerful with their fire that burned scales, their oppressive waves of empathic power, their inhuman strength and speed!

"This isn't what I was called to," Alísa whimpered. "I was supposed to bring peace between slayers and dragons, not fight the Nameless!"

Sesína coiled tighter—neck, tail, and legs curling around Alísa. *"I wish I could make it better. Devise some crazy plan to win the day. I just know the Maker placed you here, so somehow you can do it. I believe in you. Remember Bria's words?"*

You are enough.

It didn't feel like that anymore, not with the sorrow smothering her soul. She wasn't enough. Not for this. Not for the darkness that oppressed her, for the anger and grief suffocating her. Her breaths came shallow and quick around the gaping hole in her heart.

"You're supposed to be here" —a sob choked her prayer, but she pushed on anyway— "so where are you? Don't you care? Why would you let them die?"

The words flamed to life the embers of rage within. She shouldn't cry out against her Maker like this. He could smother her with a thought. But she couldn't hold back anymore.

"Rayna. Paern. Alanti. Tern. My father! And so many more! Why would you let your enemies kill them? Aren't you stronger than them?! Or do you cower?!"

The accusation sent a shock of guilt coursing through her. It should have been lightning, striking her for her insolence. Instead, only silence met her, wide and gaping. As sobs wracked her, she curled into a ball, rocking as Sesína wrapped more tightly around her.

"Forgive me," Alísa whispered. "I'm so lost. Help me."

Another shock pierced her heart, this time hot and overpowering as it ran through her entire body. For a moment, she was sure it was punishment—the Maker smiting her for her words—and she gasped in a terrified breath. Sesína jerked her head upright, eyes dimming with fear.

Then Alísa felt it. Not punishment, not anger, but a love and compassion that speared through her with its intensity. The sweet tang of familial love sharpened to a point where she both wanted to clutch it closer and pull away. She had felt this once before.

Bria.

As though summoned by the thought, a piercing light manifested before Alísa and Sesína. They winced as the brightness sent pain spiking through their skulls. Alísa shielded her eyes until they adjusted just enough to see the source.

Eldra Bria wore the same red battle-dress as she had their last meeting, one with a long skirt slit up both sides to reveal tight brown leggings. Her forearms and shins bore leather armor carved in the shape of dragon scales. Her hair formed a halo of fiery curls around her head, and her skin was dark as rich soil.

But this Bria differed from before, for sprouting from her were a pair of glorious silver wings, large as a dragon's yet with a drek's wing-baubles. Through the back of her dress, with no visible hemming or holes, thrashed a tail with silver scales and the sharpest spines Alísa had seen. The spines continued up her back until the last short ones hid underneath her hair.

In her taloned hands, she grasped a shining broadsword, which she swung at an enemy Alísa could not see.

"B—Bria?"

The Eldra did not respond, instead slashing her sword in one direction while breathing fire in another. Alísa scooted back against Sesína as the Eldra's profile came into view. Her face held a fierce battle-rage as the flames spewed from her mouth, and her eyes glowed red with a dragon's eye-lights.

"Do you see that?" Sesína pointed her muzzle. *"She's burning something!"*

Alísa peeled her gaze from the warrior to search the air as Bria continued to fight. Smoke rose from nowhere until Alísa saw stars she hadn't noticed before. Once she recognized them, the scene became clear—darkness pressed in around them, but Bria opposed it like a mighty wind scattering smoke.

Alísa's heart beat harder inside her chest. Darkness. Had the enemy sent this to harm her?

It didn't matter. Bria was here. All would be well.

With two more puffs of fire, the darkness fled, leaving Alísa and Sesína under a cold, starry sky. Somehow, the twinkling pinpricks were still visible, despite the light of the Eldra in front of them. Alísa only saw them in her periphery, however, as her eyes fixed on Bria.

Bria stood guard a moment longer, her free hand flexing its talons. Then she sighed, and her sword disappeared. Alísa braced herself as Bria faced her, but when Bria's gaze lighted on her, the ferocity vanished, as did her draconic features. The blazing light fell to a candle's flicker, and the emotions that pierced Alísa's heart softened around the edges.

"Little one." With two steps and a fall to her knees, Bria enfolded Alísa in a tight embrace. "You finally called."

Alísa shivered as she held back a sob. "I'm sorry."

"I forgive you." The words rippled over Alísa like cooling waters. When Bria pulled back, her eyes were soft. Then she looked at Sesína and brushed her muzzle. "Hello again."

Sesína's mind raced with excitement and nerves. *"Hi! Uh, sorry I called you a serpent that one time. I promise I wouldn't have if I'd known who you were, and I— oh, flames!—I threatened you, too!"*

Bria laughed, the sound melodious. "I take it as a compliment to my acting skills. I am glad my Alísa has someone so fierce at her side."

Sesína closed her eyes as Bria scratched under her chin, a deep happiness flowing from her. Alísa smiled and let the moment sit. Bria, too, seemed joyful here. Perhaps the former Singer missed interacting with dragons.

When Bria removed her hand, she sat back on her heels and folded her hands in her lap. Her eyes met Alísa's with the intensity of an eagle, not unkind but seeing all.

"The darkness about you was great."

Alísa shivered, wrapping her arms around herself. "W—what was it? Some weapon of the an'reik?"

Bria shook her head. "There are many sources of darkness. Sometimes the worst lives in our own minds."

Alísa paused, pressing her lips together. "So—that was me?"

"A glimpse of the emotions hanging over you—grief, anger, fear, confusion. Such feelings are not wrong, but they have a tendency to bog us down."

Alísa swallowed. "I t-tried to hold on to the t-t-t-truth you told me and k-keep moving. I thought I was doing well, but—"

"You are," Bria said. "I'm proud of you."

"B—but I failed."

"You did. I am still proud of you. You have brought together clans once at war and united them under your banner." Humor filled her eyes. "Even those who give you trouble are pulled into your current."

At least someone could laugh at Lorin's contrariness. Alísa shook her head. "Yet it hasn't worked. I d—don't understand, I've been doing everything I know to do, and it isn't" —she sighed and looked away— "it isn't enough. Who am I that I should be p-p-p-pitted against the Nameless? I am nothing."

Alísa didn't meet Bria's eyes. She knew Bria would remind her of the truth she had spoken before—*you are enough*—but Alísa wasn't ready to believe again. She felt like a leaf tossed by autumn winds.

"You're right."

Even Sesína started at the words. Alísa looked up. Bria was supposed to refute her—build her back up so she would have the strength for whatever came next. Bria just waited.

Alísa swallowed. "B—but you said I was enough."

"Oh, little one." Bria reached and took one of Alísa's hands in hers. "I said you do not have to become someone else to fulfill the Maker's plans for you. In that, you are indeed enough. You don't have to conform to other leaders or be 'fixed' to answer his call. This is the truth you needed, but you require a deeper truth now."

Bria searched Alísa's eyes. "You are not enough. Not on your own. No one is—not even the Eldír. Each of us may win battles in our own strength, but if we try to follow the Maker's calling on our own, we will eventually fail. Especially when our fight overlaps into the spiritual realm."

Bria squeezed Alísa's hand. "You cannot fully follow the Maker without the Maker himself at your side. He alone can rescue those lost to the Nameless, and he alone can convince some hearts to join the fight."

Alísa stared at nothing. Not enough. The thought wasn't ground-shattering. Alísa had felt it ever since losing her father. The inadequacy came in waves, sometimes overwhelming, other times hidden beneath everything else. The truly ground-shattering revelation was the Maker needing to be at her side. She knew she shouldn't have neglected her prayers, but this—this sounded different. Like a sword-partner or wing-dragon.

But such a position required trust, and he had let her father die. How could she walk her path with him when she didn't trust him anymore?

That wasn't quite true. He had led her to the dragons, to her clan. She never would have left her father's tent to find Graydonn if not for the pieces the Maker brought together inside her. She never would have fought for both dragons and humans without the empathic powers he gave her. Even the arguments she used for peace were steeped in him—that both races bore souls that could choose between good and evil. His touch was on everything good in her life.

But it was also on everything bad. Her father's death, and the deaths of so many others. People like Lorin or Yarlan who opposed her. Kallar and the other possessed. If the Maker was truly in control, then he had allowed these terrible things.

How could she reconcile the two?

Sesína shifted behind her and touched her snout to Alísa's arm. *"You have an Eldra before you. Who better to ask?"*

Alísa fingered the folds of her skirt. It seemed too sacrilegious to speak.

"You say I n—need his help t-t-to follow his calling, b—but how? How can I come before him when I'm so angry? When I'm g—grieving what he has allowed?" Her eyes stung fiercely. "If he's so p-p-p-powerful, he could have kept Papá alive. He c—could fix all the wrongs, if he wanted. D—doesn't he want to? Doesn't he c-c-care?"

Her voice hitched as the first of many tears fell down her cheek. Sobs rolled through her, the grief Briek had told her to release finally coming to bear. Grief over the loss of her father, for her fallen warriors, for the possessed, for her broken relationship with her Maker.

Strong arms wrapped around her. Bria rubbed a hand over her back and kissed the top of her head. "He cares more than you can know, little Singer."

"Then why?" Alísa choked out.

Bria shifted, looking up at the sky. She remained silent as the worst of Alísa's sobs spent themselves. When the tears quieted, the Eldra spoke again.

"You ask a question of the ages, one even Eldír do not fully understand. I've caught glimpses here and there, but no answer that definitively explains why evil persists. Some say the world's wrongs are simply consequences of existence. Some claim they are punishment for evils done. Others that everything bad that happens is in the service of some greater good. I have witnessed each."

Bria put a finger under Alísa's chin and lifted her head. Her dark eyes were soft and steady. Though it hurt, Alísa held her gaze like a drowning woman grasping for rope.

"The only true answers are that the Maker is the greatest good, and that he is wisdom itself. Even the worst evils can be twisted—or, I suppose, untwisted—to serve his purposes."

Alísa sniffled. "I can't see how P-Papá's death could ever be good."

"I know, little one. But if we understood all the Maker's ways, wouldn't he be too small? Every *anam* eventually reaches a crossroads where they must choose: hold fast to truth in the darkness, or forsake it to pursue something else. Perhaps this is your crossroads."

Alísa wiped her face on her sleeve. "I don't want to let go. B—but I'm still angry and hurt."

Bria smiled softly. "He is big enough for that, too. He won't let go of you."

That nearly started the tears again. Alísa breathed through them. She didn't feel better, exactly. Emotions still rattled within, but it was like she could place them inside a crate rather than letting them run wild. Once she was sure she had her sobbing in check, she straightened out of Bria's arms and asked what had plagued her since Rassím's report.

"What about the p-possessed? Has he let go of them?"

Bria had responded to Alísa's sorrows in many ways before—anger, sympathy, patience—but for the first time, Alísa saw the Eldra's own grief. The gentle light coming off her revealed a new shine to her eyes. She swallowed before speaking quietly.

"No. None who cling to him or his Eldír can be possessed. Only those who have rejected our protection. The Maker has not let go—they never gave themselves to him to hold."

Alísa rubbed her arms. "Then is there no hope for rescue? Are they even still alive?"

"There is, and they are, but it is a difficult road." Bria's eyes hardened past her sorrow. "The Nameless Ones always seek control—it is why they left the Maker. When he made commands they didn't like, they rebelled. Now they seek to dominate mortals through any means possible, creating both the an'reik and the possessed."

Bria held her palms up and some of the gentle light surrounding her coalesced over them to create two small balls of fire.

"An an'reik's soul is gone completely. As the name suggests, they have sold their soul to the Nameless Ones and it cannot be reclaimed. Dead, though they live."

The fire in one hand extinguished. A circle with the dimmest of glows replaced it, suggesting a ball of darkness or emptiness within.

"The possessed are those who refuse to sell their soul yet are not protected. The Maker has given mortals full autonomy over their souls, so they cannot be taken by force. Physical bodies, however, are a different story."

Another dim circle formed to float beside the second flame, crowding close until it surrounded the flame but did not snuff it.

"Some of the Nameless so desire dominion over mortals that they literally pull themselves apart so pieces of them may be placed inside an unprotected mortal's body. These 'keepers' effectively own the body they inhabit, but the soul is what they truly want. The keeper will torture the mortal in hopes of them giving up and becoming an'reik. But if the possessed instead calls to the Maker for help, the soul's shield is created."

A new circle of light formed around the ball of fire, this one bright and burning. The keeper hissed like a drenched campfire, yanking away. The two circles sat on top of Bria's hand, close but not touching.

"This will protect the soul from the keeper's tortures. The shield will never fall or dim, and when the body dies, Eldra D'tohm will pluck the soul unharmed and carry it to the Maker's halls. Before then, however, the keeper retains the body."

Sesína, enthralled by the shining lights, shook her head. *"So, the only thing we can do to stop their body is kill them?"*

"No," Bria said. "An Eldra can regain it by killing the keeper. Before the soul's shield, the keeper and the mortal soul are too entwined to untangle. If we attack, the mortal will be killed alongside the keeper. If, however, the mortal's soul is shielded, the mortal can regain their body once the keeper is dead."

A new ball of light collided with the keeper, both tumbling from the image. Then the mortal soul's fire grew back to its normal size, the shield remaining around it.

"That's wonderful news!" Alísa said, hope rising. "C-can you go there now? Identify those with the soul's shield and fight for them?"

Sesína picked up her excitement. *"That will thin the an'reik's numbers—make it easier for us to oppose them!"*

Bria sighed. "I love your enthusiasm, but I cannot enter the enemy camp. The dark forces within have created a barrier too strong for me to penetrate. Even the older, greater Eldír cannot enter. But flesh" —Bria poked Sesína's muzzle, which had gotten quite close as she watched the lights— "can pass through it."

Sesína pulled back sheepishly. *"Sorry."*

Alísa turned over Bria's words in her mind. "W—what are you saying?"

"Where our people are, there we are. Branni, in his great strength, will move with the warriors, and I, in my smaller strength, will move with you. From there, you must touch the possessed body and call on your Eldra. Then, if the person has accepted the soul's shield, we can fight to free them."

Alísa worried her skirt. "That's a lot of variables."

"Yes," Bria said, sadness tilting her eyes. "It is a valiant thing you wish to do, working to rescue the possessed. I applaud it, even hope my lost one might return, but you must know this is not required of you. Your mission is to bring the mortal races together to defeat the army threatening your lands, nothing more."

"B—but what about the Eldír?" Alísa gestured toward the hills. "Couldn't you all go together? P-push through the darkness and t-t-t-t-take care of it?"

Bria turned slightly, looking over the land. "There is much you cannot see, little Singer. War is upon you, yes, but every day battles rage over A'dem. Should Lochi abandon her rivers, knowing what might taint them in her absence? Should A'fir leave the sun unchecked, allowing the blood of men and animals to boil while he fights on your ground? Even the comparably few Eldír whose charges are mortals have souls to fight for. No. You have Branni and me. Perhaps Nahne, who has deep connections to a few of your clanmates. Your world must continue, even amidst such troubles."

"And the Maker?" Alísa whispered as her earlier fears returned. "You say he is stronger than all the dark forces combined. Can't he simply snap his fingers and fix it all right now?"

Bria cupped Alísa's cheek. "One day he will. Until that time, he works not through snapped fingers and lightning strikes, but through his people—Eldra and mortal alike—moving in the way he has called them. As you must."

Bria leaned in and kissed Alísa's forehead, sending a wave of warmth through her. Then she looked at Sesína and caressed her scaly cheek.

"And you, good dragon. Thank you for caring for my Alísa. I couldn't ask for a better match for her. As always, the Maker knows."

A twinkle shone in Bria's body, and for a moment, Alísa thought she was conjuring another image of light. Then she realized it was a star. She saw many now. Bria was fading out of the physical realm.

Alísa's heart raced. "B—Bria, wait! W—what if the d-d-darkness c-c-comes back to me?"

"The Eldír and the Maker are always present, seen or unseen. Call on us—call on *him*—and we will answer you."

Clouds and distant mountains were now visible through Bria's rapidly disappearing body, but Alísa still caught her eyes softening. "Maker's wings lift you, dear ones, his hands a shield about you."

With that, she vanished, leaving Alísa and Sesína in the icy darkness of the mountain air. Tears welled at the emptiness. She shook them away and reached out to touch Sesína's neck and breathed out a truth.

"We are not alone." The words curled in the air.

"Never." Sesína prodded her cheek, sending comfort through their bond. *"Are you ready to go inside now?"*

Alísa shivered. *"Yes. But, not for sleep yet. I—I'll need help."*

She immediately second-guessed herself. It was late. Farren wouldn't want to be woken up, and she needed sleep before the war-council.

"He would absolutely want you to wake him," Sesína said, standing. *"Your father would do the same."*

The words put a hitch in Alísa's breath, yet also firmed her plan in her mind. As Karn's songweaver, Farren had always been there to guide his chief in the histories and spiritual matters of their people. If anyone could help her speak to her Maker for the first time in weeks, it would be Farren.

Standing, she climbed onto Sesína's back, and the two of them launched into the chilly sky. Oddly, they found quite a few dragons perched just outside the main entrance, and even more on the landing platform. Thankfully, Sesína was small. With a few mental nudges, she found a spot to land. Once the wind and flapping of Sesína's wings no longer filled Alísa's ears, she heard what must have called the dragons.

Singing.

It was a song she recognized, one of grief and loss. This final verse, however, spoke of hope for the future—for the day the Maker renewed all and death became only memory. Tears overflowed Alísa's eyes as she and Sesína wove through the dragons.

> And when it finally comes my time
> When troubles cease and body falls
> My soul's flame will still burn bright
> As bright as yours in Maker's Halls
>
> When D'tohm's breath takes up my own
> And carries me into the sky
> The Maker's heart will call me home
> And you'll be standing at his side

Only a few watched Alísa as she descended the ramp. Most closed their eyes, or else stared at the ceiling or floor. All the clans stood together in a sea of grief and hope. Dreki perched on shoulders, stalagmites, or small crevices in the walls. The smaller dragons stood among the people as well. Not every dragon attended, but there were perhaps fifty—half of those who remained.

Alísa's eyes lighted on the musicians. Selene and Taz sat off to the side with their wind instruments, and Tella's songweaver played somber tones on a fiddle. Surprisingly, Farren sat among these rather than taking the lead, eyes closed as he plucked the strings of his lute.

Falier stood at the front, doing as chiefs and their tierns should—honoring the lost and allowing their people to grieve. Pride and gratitude swelled within Alísa. Here, when she couldn't, he took the lead.

The song ended in a moment of reverent silence. There, Falier caught sight of her. The gentle buzz of connection filled her mind.

"Do you want to speak to them?"

"No. Not yet." She looked around. *"How long have you all been here?"*

"About an hour. I was about to open a time for sharing memories."

Alísa pressed her lips together. *"Good. I—"* She searched for words, letting her pride in him fill their connection. *"Thank you, for taking care of my people."*

Falier smiled softly. *"Always."*

He returned to the clans, calling for stories and sharing his own about a dragon and rider from his squad who had fallen. Alísa took that moment to approach Farren, calling him away with her. It was finally time to be afraid and angry, and choose to trust anyway.

46

ABANDONED

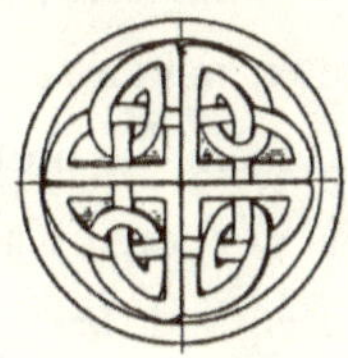

Kallar lay in the astral grasses, exhausted after yet another night of torturous memories. It felt like he hadn't slept in months. The keeper filled his nights with pain as his body watched the two remaining grounded dragons, while his days were spent either in the body following Isarra's commands or in the mind-world watching the keeper control him. He tried to rest during the latter, but his constant worry over what it might do made it difficult.

Currently, the keeper walked among the grounded dragons. Kallar had expected them to die in the battle, but Alísa's army had pulled back before anyone could reach them. All except that assassin.

The green dragon snarled as the keeper took its slashed wing in its hands, but it did not attempt to bite him as on previous days. It and the silver Lellani were learning it was wiser to save energy until the perfect moment.

The keeper moved on to Lellani, tugging her wing to look at the damaged leather. Both dragons' wings were mending. The wounds still kept them grounded, but they would fly soon. That was the keeper's plan all along—make them fight on the ground, then return any lucky enough to survive to their alphas.

Lucky wasn't the word Kallar would use. Life under someone else's control, whether a keeper's or an alpha's, wasn't living.

"There is a way out." The keeper turned to him, voice oozing. *"And I don't mean that trick you tried to pull with Karn's dagger."*

The memories hit like a shock of cold water—first the kill, then the attempted suicide. The panic he had felt, so foreign and raw.

"Isarra isn't controlled," the keeper continued. *"All an'reik move as they please, for all self-service ultimately serves the Nameless. The lust for power, the will to govern*

oneself, the strong ruling over the weak. True freedom."

Freedom was the only piece Kallar cared about. It latched onto his heart with a dragon's talons. To regain his life, uncontrolled and unfettered—

The keeper bent and pressed a claw into the astral dirt. "*Your delusions of yourself amuse me, but only so far. You want more than mere freedom.*"

When it pulled its claw out, it held a tendril of white mists. The keeper examined it like a treasure mined from the mountains, then tossed the rope at Kallar. Remembering the tendrils of agony, Kallar rolled out of its way and to his feet. He staggered as dizziness rushed through him, and in that misstep, the rope ensnared his leg.

No pain rose when it touched Kallar. Instead, his senses flooded with images, sounds, and emotions. His first dragon kill and the pride of his accomplishment. The trust of his men as they followed him on the battlefield. The release when he killed Paili, his mother's murderer.

"*You want to continue your mission, do you not? Ridding the world of the dragons, unhindered by your Singer's empathy, bolstered by warriors who believe in you.*"

Kallar stumbled as the tendril released him. "*It's what I was made for.*"

"*You can do it again, of your own volition. Just bow, and I'll leave.*"

"*That's all, is it?*" Kallar spat at the keeper's feet. "*I will defeat you without giving up what's mine. No one touches my soul.*"

He braced himself, expecting the keeper to attack him for his insolence, but the creature of shadows merely stared with what Kallar might call a thoughtful expression. It was hard to tell based solely off of burning eyes.

It returned to the window and the morning routine, heading toward the kitchen tent for breakfast. But then the keeper strode past, focused on the center of camp.

"*Where are you taking me?*"

The thing didn't reply. It glanced, lingering on slayers who had given themselves to the Nameless after the last battle's success. Two sparred with their newly enhanced speed. Another stuck her hand into a cooking fire and drew out a ball of flames balanced in her palm. One carried eight dead hares strung up on a pole he carried with a partner. An animal-manipulator, no doubt.

"*Combined with the power you already hold,*" the keeper said, "*your an'reik powers could be the greatest of all. A Singer who could overpower that whelp of a girl's charms. Every dragon would lie at your feet and offer their heads. Perhaps we could even grant control over more than just dragons. Dreki. Humanity."*

Kallar remained silent. Greater power was tempting, but it wouldn't truly be his. He would merely be a tool in the Nameless Ones' schemes.

The keeper chuckled. *"You are already a tool, dirt. The question is whether you'd rather be my blunt instrument, or your own sword."*

The keeper's attention shifted away from the new an'reik and fixed on a black tent.

R'lann's tent.

The keeper smiled as fear colored the mind-world's mists. Damn this world's inability to hide his emotions! Kallar forced himself not to move, not to expend energy until the moment he needed to.

In Kallar's voice, the keeper spoke to the guards outside the prison—two of the newly changed—and the fools let it inside. Kallar tensed as the keeper lifted the flap, but again, he held himself back.

Not yet.

Sunlight illuminated the tent, revealing a space with a bed-mat, an oil lamp, and a dirty dish from breakfast. R'lann sat up from the mat, his cheeks sunken. The hope in his eyes pained Kallar.

Don't be fooled, Kallar willed. *It's not me.*

"I've no intention of hiding that fact," the keeper told him, smirking. The flap shut behind them, leaving only the flickering glow of the lamp's light.

"Have you finally realized there is no escape?" The keeper said to R'lann in Kallar's voice. "Are you ready to surrender?"

R'lann didn't answer right away, his hopeful expression shifting into revulsion. "Let me talk to my brother."

"You're angry. I don't blame you." The scene lowered as the keeper sat on the ground. "I know abandonment. To believe in someone, blindly following until one day you realize they aren't who you thought they were. The Maker has forsaken us both."

"Shut up." R'lann looked away. "You don't know what you're talking about."

"Don't I?" The body leaned forward. "We were gods. We held worlds in our hands. Mountains rose and fell at our whim. Waters raged at our call. The deep blackness of space that kills mortals invigorated us. And then the Maker squandered his favor on creatures whose lifespans are a drop of rain in an ocean.

Creatures given their own will, who we were not to touch except by his command."

The keeper's growl echoed in the mind-world. "Dreki. Dragons. Humans. All mortal and weak. It was our right to rule them, but the Maker took that from us. Betrayed and abandoned us, just as he has betrayed and abandoned you."

"I'm not abandoned," R'lann said, his voice barely above a whisper.

The keeper looked about the tent. "Then where is your rescue? You trust so deeply in him and the puppet Eldír who remained with him, yet has he sent any to pull you from our clutches?"

At R'lann's silence, the keeper straightened. "I will admit, there was a folly in our thinking. Mortals are not as weak as we once believed. With help, you could be great. So we abandoned the Abandoner and worked with mortals to create a grand alliance. Born from the pain of loss, the an'reik are our children—ones we, unlike the Maker, would never abandon."

The keeper reached and touched R'lann's shoulder. "We take care of our own."

R'lann pulled out from under the hand. "I highly doubt that. I've seen what you do to Kallar. The agony you cause when he fights you."

The window shifted as the keeper shook its head. "This is different. You wouldn't require a keeper. An an'reik keeps their mind and body—"

"Just not their soul."

Kallar tensed, ready to move as a huff of anger came off the keeper. Physically, however, it kept its tone civil. "And in the hole left behind, we pour our power into you. A mortal soul for the power of an eternal being is more than a fair trade."

The keeper leaned in, its voice lowering. "Perhaps this will also free Kallar from his torment. He doesn't have to fight this constant struggle for control. He simply must make the right choice. If you showed him the truth, he might finally save himself."

Kallar seethed. *You thrice-damned serpent! Playing us off each other!*

The keeper eyed him. *"Oh, I haven't begun playing yet."*

R'lann's eyes turned down with sorrow. "I pray every day for his rescue, but *you* won't bring it."

The boy's jaw tightened as he locked eyes with Kallar, but it felt like

R'lann was truly seeing the keeper and not the body they both occupied. "And I will not bow to you. Even if it means I'm stuck here until I die, I won't trade the Maker for a counterfeit."

This time, the keeper's rage flowed past the mind-world. The window's view grew smaller as eyes narrowed. Kallar could almost feel hands becoming fists.

"*He* is the counterfeit—leaving you here to suffer!"

"I'm done talking to you. Let me talk to my brother, or get out."

No, no, no, idiot!

"Dirt cannot command me!"

The keeper threw Kallar's body at R'lann. The boy yelped in surprise, falling back too late to escape. He was pinned beneath Kallar, clawing for release as the keeper wrapped Kallar's hands around R'lann's neck.

No! Kallar lurched forward, calling the emotion mists to his aid. With a thought, they formed around him, reinforcing his arms and chest and turning the ends of his fingers to claws the color of rage. He threw himself onto the keeper, but as soon as he touched it, he was thrown into the scene at the window. His hands were at R'lann's neck, his body holding the boy down as he thrashed.

Kallar couldn't move. He wasn't strong enough. The only one possibly strong enough was—

No. The guards would come. They would stop this so long as Kallar stalled.

Reaching back into his mind, Kallar pulled at his telepathy to form a net to trap the keeper and regain control. The net twisted around its prey, then ripped apart as the keeper shredded it with talons and dagger-sharp wings. Even stalling didn't work!

R'lann clawed at Kallar's arms, drawing blood, a desperate fear in his eyes.

Sunlight poured into the tent. "Hey! Stop!"

Suddenly, R'lann's two guards grabbed Kallar. The keeper let go of R'lann then, leaving him to cough and clutch at his throat.

"Isarra wants him alive," one guard near-shouted. "You know that!"

The keeper didn't reply, though it threw off the guards' hands. It looked back at R'lann and growled, then marched from the tent.

As soon as they were outside and the guards at their posts, Kallar stopped fighting. He slumped inside himself as the keeper controlled every muscle.

Nothing had worked. R'lann had been completely at the keeper's mercy, no matter where Kallar fought it. He had saved his energy, used the mists in a new way, threw a choke strong enough to drop any dragon. Yet at this dire point, when adrenaline and fear should strengthen him, nothing made any difference.

The keeper purred. *"Yes. Now you finally see."*

Kallar grasped to stay in his body, but the keeper's talons yanked and hurled him down. Astral mists swirled in the golden orange of fear and a brownish-gray color. The color of true defeat, of hopelessness, of knowing one could only accept their fate. He would never be free, or be able to protect anyone from himself.

Perhaps I should *take the deal—give in and become an'reik. At least I would have some control over my actions. And the keeper couldn't make me hurt R'lann.*

The thought disgusted him, as did the keeper's pleasure in it. But when fighting truly did nothing? His only remaining options were variations on surrender.

Taking in the physical world, Kallar watched those who had already become an'reik. Some were slayers he had known before, and they were no longer themselves. They still had some individuality, but they were harder, colder, harsher now. And Kallar knew himself. He already was all of those things. If he, too, gave up his soul for control and power, what might he become? Someone who would hurt innocents—hurt R'lann—of his own volition?

As awful as what just happened with R'lann—as awful as Karn's death—a willing murder would be infinitely worse.

The keeper spoke, its purrs turning suddenly to a fiery rage. Sitting Kallar's body down on the outskirts of camp, the keeper faced him.

"I have the rest of your pitiful life to convince you. And there is nothing worse than what I will do to, and through, you!"

Talons extended, the keeper leapt at him. Kallar scrambled back, pulling the mists to him on instinct, but his hasty shield shattered on the keeper's impact. It raked its claws across Kallar's astral chest, and with the pain rose memories. His mother's death, slaughtering hatchlings, killing Paili—each a moment full of the same white-hot rage he now saw in the keeper's eyes.

And again, Kallar wished for death.

47

NEW ASSIGNMENT

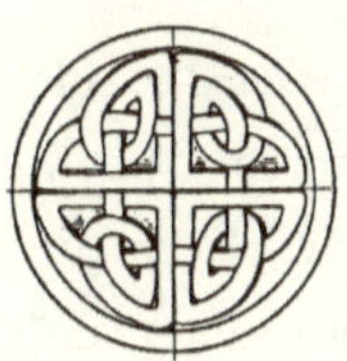

Even with the longer nights of winter creeping upon them, sleep seemed in short supply for Falier. He woke before dawn and laid under Graydonn's wing for a while longer. The dragon did not wake up, his body taking every ounce of energy it could to heal.

While silence was nice for a time, Falier soon left the wing-tent. He relieved a medic for a while, changing bandages and bringing water and tea to the wounded. As the cave awoke, many others did likewise. By the time someone relieved Falier, the sun shone through the entrance, the scent of hash filled the air, and Saynan's family ministered to Graydonn's injuries.

Falier wove through the mess of people, unable to avoid bumping into some as he passed. Perhaps Hanah could help him move some clans into another cave. There was one humans could reach without draconic assistance. Of course, that path was outside. With the increasing rain, the trek was less than ideal. A way to travel between the two caves indoors did exist, but that tunnel sat forty feet up the wall. Maybe they could build a platform to lift and lower people? He had seen one in a Hold before. But that wouldn't help their immediate need. Perhaps a clan could fit in the sparring cave?

"Hey," a voice said. "Falier."

Falier stopped. Varek? He turned to see the man rising from the folded blanket he used to separate himself from the cold stone floor. Like everyone else, his clothing was stained with sweat, mud, and blood—all extra clothing left behind in the war-camp.

"Yes?"

Varek stood. He seemed uncomfortable, looking at those nearby who were also awake. "Walk with me."

He walked past Falier, not waiting to see if he followed. With a sigh, Falier went after him. Varek took the ramp to the landing platform, silent until they were halfway up.

"I lost my dragon partner. Alanti. Does that disqualify me from riding again?"

That—sounded like Varek *wanted* to ride. "No. I haven't spoken with Alísa yet about how we'll do reassignments, but we need all the dragon-rider pairs we can get. It wasn't your fault…" Even after grieving and speaking of Alanti last night, it was hard to finish that sentence. "It wasn't your fault."

Varek grunted. "Good. I" —he paused, tension in his tone— "I want Mennáli. I've already spoken with her current rider. He's willing to let me switch back to her."

Hope rose in Falier's chest, but before he could speak, Varek continued.

"I'm not committing to bonding with her. I don't know that I'll ever be ready for that. But after she caught me…" Varek shook his head and hardened his stance. "We can't have dragons distracted by riders who aren't their own. If the fool of a dragoness is going to watch me, better for all that I ride her."

Falier hid his rising smile. "You're absolutely right. I'll make sure you're reassigned to her. I have some pull with the chief."

That was supposed to help ease the tension, draw out a laugh, but of course Varek didn't take the bait. He nodded sharply, muttered his thanks, then marched back down the ramp.

Falier shook his head, chuckling to himself. Perhaps he would get Varek and Mennáli reassigned to his squad so that Jossen could influence him.

Not wanting to follow Varek, Falier watched Saynan and his family work on Graydonn's sprained neck and back. Graydonn's nighttime rest had clearly helped, as he could now lift his head with far less pain. Falier shivered as Saynan breathed burning cold over a thick blanket draping Graydonn. Graydonn's relief was palpable.

Saynan's voice was gentle. *"Once your pain settles, perhaps Falier can grate down the sharp edges of your broken spines."*

"They will grow back, right?" Graydonn worried.

"Yes," Aree said. *"But they will always be shorter than others, unless you grind those down too."*

Aravi, their now four-foot tall adolescent, jumped in. *"But how else would anyone know he survived a terrible battle? I would keep them."*

Falier chuckled. *"You barely have spines yourself. Wait until they grow in, then tell us you don't mind if they're uneven."*

"I've known dragons to wear such scars with pride," Aree said. *"Others work for weeks, patiently grating them down with tooth and stone to match."*

"Yes," Saynan said, *"I merely meant that humans would speed up the process. They possess greater dexterity and have invented tools for such purposes."*

"I'll think about it," Graydonn said. His thoughts brightened as wing-flaps sounded outside. *"Sesína is coming."*

Líse. Falier stood back as Sesína landed, then offered Alísa a hand down. She looked like she needed it, especially with those dark circles under her eyes. Her smile was bright, however, as she accepted his help. Rather than let go once she touched the floor, she clung to him.

"Hold me forever," she said groggily. Belying her words, she pulled back. "Or don't—I'd probably fall asleep."

"Did you sleep at all?"

She nodded. "A few hours. There was something more important."

Sesína went to check on Graydonn while Alísa took Falier's hand. She poked her temple, and Falier connected them telepathically in response.

"Thank you," she said. *"This is easier, and more private."* She walked them to the ramp. *"I saw Bria again."*

Falier looked down at her. *"What? Really?"*

Alísa relayed last night's events as they grabbed breakfast. When her story was through, they lingered on the revelation of the possessed among the an'reik.

"I'm still working out how we can help them." She played with her necklace, as she usually did when she was nervous or thinking. *"We'd have to find them and perhaps immobilize them as we fight the true enemy."*

Falier remained silent. The possibility was dangerously slim. Rassím might locate a few, but he couldn't search the entire army. Working to immobilize them would also risk their warriors—all to rescue people who might be beyond saving.

Still, to die simply because something evil was forcing you to fight for the wrong side sounded horrific.

"But there's hope. I had lost that before Bria showed up." Alísa leaned against his

shoulder. *"I want you and Graydonn there among the betas as we figure out next steps. We'll meet in an hour in one of the high caves."*

"I'll be there," Falier focused on his bond to Graydonn, trying to feel the dragon. *"I think Graydonn will be able to fly there, but he can't carry me yet."*

"Right," Alísa said. *"I'm so glad you have each other and that you're alright."*

Falier kissed the top of her head. *"Me too."*

Falier rarely noticed when Alísa was doing well speaking to a large group anymore. It only occurred when she got stuck on a word and had to either pause or change the word entirely. Then he would remember the girl hesitant to sing for eager ears at a céilí. It filled his heart to see her talking as an equal among the leaders.

He sat cross-legged only two places away from her, Hanah between them as Karn's *anam nasctha*. Graydonn lay behind him, alternately holding his head up and taking a break with his chin on the stone floor. The rest of Alísa's betas sat in the circle near her, with the other leaders completing the circle.

The first priority was supporting the warriors and refugees, ensuring their basic needs and ongoing training for the next confrontation. Alísa asked Falier and Graydonn to continue helping the dragon-rider pairs train alongside Koriana and Saynan, a task they happily accepted.

From there, the council posited potential allies. They would need every warrior they could find to face the growing an'reik army. As they listed caves and villages in the area, Farren recorded them in three categories—clans to approach a second time, clans they'd never spoken to that would likely give favorable responses, and clans that would be hostile. Alísa assigned the agreeable ones to others and claimed the rest for herself. Falier didn't miss the spike of anxiety when Azron, Alísa's old home village, came up. Farren put it on the hostile list.

"There is one other clan we should c-c-call, but they live much farther away," Alísa said. "You all witnessed the t-terrors of the an'reik's hellflames, but few saw the p-p-power that can match it." She looked at Saynan. "Your ice breath saved lives. Could your former c-c-c-clan be convinced to help us?"

Saynan blinked slowly. *"It is worth an attempt, though they are—apathetic. They will take much convincing. They are two days' flight from here, however. Four days of travel, plus a couple to speak with them—can you afford such time away?"*

Alísa shook her head. "That's why I assigned you and D—Darrin to a larger t-team, so others can c-c-cover your duties. I would send you p-plus whoever you deem necessary. I c-c-c-c—" She stopped and breathed. "I must be here."

Saynan tapped his talons on the stone. *"Though my former clan is complacent, they are also prideful. I fear your absence may offend them into refusal. They might even take offense at my leading the squad being sent to them, considering I abandoned their ways years ago. If you cannot go, I recommend sending your mate in your stead."*

A shock ran through Falier as Saynan looked at him. He glanced at Alísa, who blushed.

"Uh, Saynan," Falier said, rubbing his neck, "we're betrothed, not mates."

He blinked slowly. *"By human customs perhaps, but by dragon standards, you are. Your commitment before your clan is sufficient. Where the Singer's absence may offend the ice dragons, the honor of sending her beloved mate might gain their welcome."*

Falier's mind still tripped over the word 'mate,' as well as this new development. Just when he started discovering where he belonged in this clan, he would be sent away?

Alísa blew out her breath and looked at Falier. The buzz of telepathy shifted as Sesína maneuvered her into a private link between the three of them and Graydonn.

"You don't have to go," Alísa said, sorrow in her tone. *"We can figure something else out, something that doesn't involve you leaving for a week to meet a strange dragon clan."*

Alísa's sadness sparked his own. They already saw each other too little. Yet, as he considered Saynan's rationale, Falier realized the dragon was correct. He had been looking for opportunities to prove he would be a worthy tiern. Gaining allies where the chief couldn't go certainly qualified.

Graydonn caught his eye and blinked slowly. He was willing, pained though he was.

Falier gave Alísa what he hoped was a reassuring smile. *"We'll go."*

Alísa's shoulders rose and fell with her breath, and the telepathic link returned to normal. "Very well, it is decided. Saynan, you will still accompany them. They'll need you, even if you aren't allowed into the c-c-c-caves."

Saynan's tail thumped in agreement. *"I believe if I am a mere guide rather than an authority, we should not have trouble."*

"Good." Alísa paused. "Now for the last part."

Lifting her eyes, she told everyone of the possessed. Her explanation included Rassím's ability to soul-see, as well as an outline of how to set souls free. Touch the person, call on your Eldra, then hope the Eldra wins the struggle.

The chiefs and alphas remained silent as she explained, the cavern going still. When she finished, the quiet persisted until Chief N'ravi finally spoke.

"This is, of course, dreadful news. To think of our brothers and sisters compelled to fight—well, it's distressing. But you realize this task will more likely get our warriors killed than free the possessed?"

"I do." Alísa rubbed her arm. "If we marched today, it would be a lost cause. I almost d—didn't tell you because I don't have a true p-p-plan. But now we can all consider ways we might help them. Until then, this c-c-council is dismissed. We all have our assignments—we move to find new allies at dawn."

The next few minutes were an organized chaos of humans and dragons leaving the cave, while a few approached Alísa. Graydonn stood and stretched out the aches in his neck and back. Falier winced as he heard the pops and creaks.

"How are you feeling?"

Graydonn yawned. *"It still hurts, but my muscles are looser after Aree's poking and prodding."*

That had been fascinating to watch, almost a draconic massage, but focused on pressure points rather than rubbing. *"Should we ask her to join us? Or do you think another dragon could learn it?"*

"Aree needs to stay with Aravi because of their Illumination, *and Aravi needs more training with her rider. Perhaps Saynan knows how."* Graydonn shivered at the memory of ice breath. *"Who else should accompany us? Selene and Hwinn?"*

Falier nodded. *"The ice dragons should see an* Illuminated *pair. We'll already be there as mind-kin. And Taz and Harenn can represent the unbonded partners."*

"I'm sure your sister will appreciate her mate being there."

Falier shuddered. *"Not mates. They aren't even betrothed!"*

"Yes, and why not? They seem committed enough."

"Don't ask me. And, for the sake of my stomach, don't call them mates again."

The dragon thrummed, eyes bright with humor. Then he pointed his muzzle behind Falier, making him turn around. Alísa approached. The dark circles under her eyes had worsened, and as he took her hand, her sorrow flowed into him.

"W—would you stay here for a bit? I'd like to see you b—before…"

"Of course." He twisted to look back at Graydonn. *"Finish planning later?"*

Graydonn blinked slowly and padded toward the exit. Sesína came alongside him, but not before throwing a wink in Alísa's direction. The last of the stragglers followed them out, leaving Falier and Alísa alone in the cavern. Caves pocked the sides, some on the ground level and others higher up. Were all mountains just mounds of stone and dirt hiding undiscovered tunnels and caverns?

Alísa pulled him further into the cave, out of the glaring daylight. There, she yanked him to her and pressed a desperate kiss to his lips. Her sorrow was potent in their skin-contact, and for a millisecond Falier thought of pulling away and asking what was wrong. The notion fled instantly, and he pressed closer, wrapping his arms tight around her. She returned his grip, nearly squeezing the air out of him, then left little kisses across his mouth to his cheek before laying her head on his shoulder.

"W—why do you have to b—b—be so perfect?" She sniffled. "It makes sense to be you—has to be you—but I don't want you to leave. I want you here, with me."

Falier rubbed a hand over her back. "I want that, too."

She turned her head in. "Stay with me?"

Falier swallowed as her breath skimmed his neck. How could something make him want to both tense and relax so badly?

"I d—don't mean don't go," she clarified, looking up at him. "Just for now."

He kissed her forehead. "Of course."

Pulling her to the wall, they sat against it, his arm around her back and her head on his chest. They stayed there for a time, Falier getting the impression she was listening to his heartbeat. That sounded nice, having her heartbeat in his ear. But that brought thoughts of—other things. He looked up and tried to count the stalactites in the darkness.

"I thought having a plan would bring me peace."

Falier waited, unsure how to respond.

"B—but I'm just as scared, even with the others' support." Alísa swallowed and tucked closer. "I'm running headlong into the d—darkest of caves where my nightmares lurk. I'm going to chiefs who know me only as K-K-K-Karn's scared little girl who then became a t—t—tool of the dragons. I'm going to T-T-Toronn."

A sob escaped her, and Falier wrapped his other arm around her. He remembered when Yarlan's accusations had broken through to her core and Namor had to help her release some deep-seated emotions. Toronn was associated with her fear, her feelings of worthlessness, her deepest insecurities. And Falier couldn't stand beside her as she asked for alliance.

He kissed the top of her head. "You are amazing. You are brave and capable and a leader in your own right. You've created friendship and family where there was once only war. And if I had to choose to hear only one sound forever, it would be your voice."

A sob wracked her body and her arms tightened around his ribs. The reaction brought tears to his own eyes. That anyone had told her otherwise—he couldn't fathom it.

He kissed her hair again, letting a tear disappear into her curls. "Even if I'm not there, you are not alone."

She gasped in a breath past her sobs, her second bringing them under control. "N—no. We are never alone."

He meant the clan was with her, but her echo held a certainty she lacked before last night's visitation. Somehow, Alísa's declaration was a reassurance he hadn't known he needed. The darkness couldn't isolate them; they were never truly alone.

Alísa shifted so that her head rested over his heart again. Soon her breaths were deep and smooth with sleep. Though the stone was hard against his back, Falier refused to move and slowly, slowly drifted off, too. Tomorrow, they would part. Today, he would stay.

48

LIMITATIONS

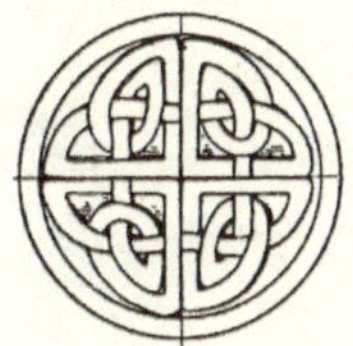

Memories swirled in the wind—Secrets revealed. Mockery. The pain of two hatchlings. The path that led her to Graydonn.

Alísa swung off Sesína's back. One hand on her wither, she watched the other dragons landing around them. Azron lay just south of them. The last time she crested this hill, she was running from the ceremony where everyone learned about her dragon empathy. Three slayer boys her age had jeered her for feeling the dragons' pain, a new low after years of mocking her stammer. She questioned everything as she ran to camp that night—her sanity, her value, the Maker's goodness.

Now she was back again, clinging hard to all three lest she lose herself.

Sesína pressed her cheek to Alísa's. *"You just tell me who to bite and I'll do it."*

"You hate blood."

"Some people are worth biting. Or at least worth biting for."

Alísa kissed her snout. *"You're sweet."*

"Bite!"

Rís leapt from her bag and settled on Alísa's shoulder. He gave a growl that would surely have terrified a mouse. Alísa patted his head.

"You're sweet too. Let's hold off on biting, okay?"

They turned their attention to the others. L'non and Farren dismounted H'sinth while Chief N'ravi slid from the back of Alpha Harazím. On her other side, Briek helped Hanah down from Koriana. Hanah's chin still bore the stripes of the chief's widow, displaying her authority. It should have given Alísa comfort, but at this moment, it only reminded her that her father was gone. As Toronn's former apprentice, he would have easily tamed the village-bound chief's scorn.

And today, even Falier was gone. She longed for his hand to hold and his quiet voice in her mind. It would be a long, difficult week without him.

Farren caught her eye and approached her. "Are you ready for this?"

Alísa swallowed against her tightening throat. "I have to be."

He considered her words a moment, wise green eyes searching her face. "Would you like me to pray with you?"

Alísa pressed her lips together. Her trembling could be taken as shivers against the chilly, misting breeze, but she knew the truth.

She nodded. "Thank you."

Pride wafted from Farren as he placed a hand on her shoulder and prayed aloud. His prayer wasn't a song, yet the words took on a melodic quality.

"In this place of chaos, bring the peace of Eldra Landera's gentle waters. In this place of death, bring Líla's green life. Where past and present may meld, stealing thought and word, bring Veni's wisdom and truth."

He breathed in the silence, then finished. "Branni's strength, and Maker's hand to guide all things to right."

Farren began pulling away, but Alísa reached up and held his arm. She wasn't sure she could speak her own prayer aloud, but she wanted him still with her. Farren, ever patient, waited.

You've seen everything. You know I am nothing to Toronn. He is powerful and respected—I will need his help to gain more slayers to my side. I don't think he'll listen to me, but Bria says only you can convince certain hearts. Please, bring him to us.

Alísa blew out a breath and released Farren's hand. "Thank you."

He squeezed her shoulder. "Of course."

As one, Alísa, Farren, and Sesína turned to the others. Alísa contemplated speaking, but everyone knew the purpose of their presence. Best to save her energy for Toronn.

"Let's go."

Together, they marched toward Azron. Rís leapt into the air to flutter in the breeze with Chrí. Out of the corner of her eye, Alísa saw N'ravi give Harazím a friendly pat on the leg. The alpha's eyes brightened in response, and Alísa smiled. Battle had formed a bond of camaraderie between them, as it had for many other dragon-rider pairs. This was what she was made to achieve, and the sight filled her heart.

She should only accept slayers willing to ride dragons.

Alísa stopped walking. Where had *that* thought come from? That would be highly foolish. She had hoped for it once, but that strategy would significantly reduce her army's size. So many slayers—and dragons—weren't ready for that step.

"Don't worry," Sesína said. *"We'll get through to them someday."*

Alísa nodded and continued down the hill, watching the *anam* before her. Walking together because she brought them together. As the Maker called her to do.

Only slayers willing to ride, and dragons willing to bear.

No. That was illogical and unwise. Toronn would never accept it. He would have a hard time as it was, and she needed his support.

But couldn't the Maker change his heart, anyway? Wasn't that what Bria said? She was enough for her calling, and yet, without the Maker beside her, she also wasn't. She still didn't quite know what it meant to walk with him as her sword-partner, but—

Is this from you?

No. It couldn't be. Forget the question of Toronn—this would severely limit her numbers. Lorin would leave for certain, perhaps others. The Maker wouldn't tell her to do something completely against reason, would he?

No audible voice followed. No Eldra's visage or whisper in the breeze. Only a lake's cool peace, the deep green of life, and the inner assurance of truth.

Sesína's eyes dimmed. *"Oh."*

"Holy Maker."

Farren looked back at her. "Alísa?"

She hurried to his side, Sesína on her heels. "Farren, has the Maker ever asked you t-t-t-t-to d—do something stupid?"

"Practically idiotic," Sesína agreed, shifting her weight from paw to paw with eager energy. Alísa didn't feel nearly as energized by the thought.

Farren's brow wrinkled. "I would never call his plans idiotic, young dragon. Yet, he has been known to go against conventional wisdom at times. He sees the entire journey, while we see only the next hill before us." He half-closed an eye. "Why?"

Alísa hugged herself as tiny pieces fell into place. Her calling. The impossibility of it. Bria's message. The impression of a plan she had just conceived, or been given.

"I—I think he just t-told me to change my p-p-p-plans."

But they weren't solely *her* plans—the other leaders helped craft them. What right did she possess to alter them so drastically?

"You? Little." Sesína wrapped a wing over her shoulders. *"The Maker, however, has every right."*

Alísa shivered despite the warmth of the dragon's hug. *"Why am I called to the impossible? Why me, with all my fears, insecurities, and weaknesses?"*

"Company is coming."

Alísa looked toward Azron. Sure enough, slayers emerged—the whole clan, by the look of it. And at their front, a tall man dressed for war. His cloak was made of wolf's fur, and he used his spear like a walking staff. The dreki broke off from their frolic in the air and fluttered to shoulders, Rís hooking his tail around Alísa's neck.

"Alísa," Farren called her eyes to his. "I don't know what the Maker has told you, but sometimes he calls us to move solely based on faith that his perspective is greater than our own. Now you have a choice."

She had already made the choice. By Landera's waters, Líla's life, and Veni's wisdom, she knew what she must do.

Alísa blew out a breath and straightened out of Sesína's embrace. "By Maker's wings."

Sesína growled a low agreement and together they walked. Past Farren, past the others who now held questions in their eyes, and toward Toronn.

The chief watched her with a hawk-like glare, stopping at the boundary line of the village. Alísa trembled under his gaze and she fought not to look back and ensure her lieutenants were with her.

Why do I feel so weak even as I commit to the Maker's path? I should be strong. Immovable.

'Lift your eyes' came the memory of her father's voice. She did as he said. Chin up, shoulders back, arms at her sides. She was just as much a chief as her father. Just as much a chief as Toronn.

She stopped twenty feet away and held up a hand to signal the others to stop behind her, praying that Toronn wouldn't notice the tremor in her arm.

"They told me you were marching across your father's territory to force us to make peace with demons." Toronn looked past her. "Where is your traitorous father? I would speak with one who can communicate in a *timely* fashion."

Rís growled on her shoulder. The words were meant to cow her. She already felt her throat grabbing at her voice. But his accusation of her father—that sparked anger. And anger was easier to talk through than fear.

"You must not have had messengers recently, else you w—would know that my father was k-k-k-killed, in a battle against *t-true* demons. An'reik walk our land."

Toronn stared at her, then looked behind her again. His eyes widened, and she knew he saw Hanah's paint.

"Karn—is dead?"

His voice was low and muted. She recognized that tone, a rare display of humanity he showed when mourning the fallen. Despite his accusation of treachery, he still loved her father. Karn had been Toronn's pride. Even when Karn left to join the wayfarers rather than staying as Azron's future slayer chief, Toronn had gloried in his ability and been his loudest supporter.

This was her opening—his love for her father.

"Yes. He died honorably in battle against an army that m—marches across our land. They have already t-t-t-t—"

"I know this," Toronn said blankly. "Azron will not bow as L'rang did. Even if the an'reik somehow make it here without first being wiped out by another village's slayers, we are prepared to handle their tricks, be they physical or spiritual." He lifted his spear and pointed the tip at Sesína. "We are also prepared for yours."

Maternal instinct flared in Alísa, adding to her anger. She stepped in front of Sesína, holding herself tall while Rís spread his wings.

"You think K-K-Karn, greatest of chiefs, was k-killed by a band weak enough for you to 'handle'? The wayfarers live in war. If they could not stop them, even allied with my c-c-clan, do you truly believe Azron will stand alone?"

Toronn didn't lower his spear, now pointed at Alísa's chest. "I think I am done trading words with a child who cannot say her own father's name. L'non" —he glanced past Alísa— "I would speak to the wayfarers, not this dragon whelp. Since the apprentice is not here, I assume you are the successor."

"Karn has made *Alísa* his successor," Hanah said, voice deep with authority. "As she always should have been."

The spear wavered. "Have the dragons that much power? To strip Karn of his senses? Even if she could speak, she possesses no telepathy for battle, and I see no tiern. The girl weeps at the ceremonies, and you would follow her into war?!"

"What has gotten into you, Toronn, that you talk this way?" Hanah stepped up to Alísa's side. "If Karn were here, you would be dangerously close to a duel. She is our daughter, and you will respect her."

Alísa fought the urge to glance at her mother. Hanah spoke as if Toronn's behavior was a surprise. Perhaps to her it was. Toronn's venom had always been more subtle or saved for times when her parents weren't around to witness it. This was exactly what Alísa had expected.

Great Maker, what do I do? We need his aid, but I'm so angry, and he wants nothing to do with me. How can I salvage this? Help me.

"All respect fled the moment she ran to the dragons," Toronn spat. "Now I see everyone else has done the same. Give me one reason I shouldn't kill every dragon here."

"Because you want Azron to survive," Alísa said, stepping forward. The tip of his spear was a mere foot away—striking distance. "You c-c-cannot stand against the enemy alone. Slayers from many c-c-clans have banded with them, g—giving their souls for p-powers greater than the strongest telepath's. An'reik dragons, too, have joined them. No lone clan can face them."

Toronn studied her, then looked behind her for confirmation from the others, his spear still held at the ready. She didn't wait for him to form a response.

"Only an alliance of slayers, dragons, and fae-kind will stop this army." She paused, considering the best route to her destination. "W—will you help avenge my father and p-p-protect your p-people?"

Toronn looked her up and down. "You ask me to consider the lesser of two evils." The word 'lesser' held more meaning than the idiom. "Ally with one monster to defeat another."

"*Bite?*" Rís hissed.

"*No.*" Alísa forced herself to hold the chief's gaze and remain silent.

Finally, the spear lowered. "I would speak to my seconds."

Alísa was sure he noticed her relief, but for the moment, she didn't care. She nodded and stepped back. As Toronn left, five men swiftly took his spot, armed with spears and unyielding stares. When Alísa came to stand between Sesína and her mother, Hanah touched her arm.

"You don't seem surprised Toronn treats you this way."

The statement held questions Alísa didn't know how to answer, so she simply said, "No."

Sorrow flowed from Hanah in the silence as Toronn spoke with two men. Alísa watched, silently running through what needed to happen next. She should have stopped Toronn before he turned to confer, because there was one crucial piece of information he was missing.

Five minutes later, Toronn returned to stand at the front, his spear held vertically. Looking past Alísa to her companions, he spoke.

"We will not ally with demons. The dragon scourge has taken too much from us. We will not train with them, nor will we take any orders from this traitor to her race. However, to protect our country from this dark army, we will march to fight them on a different front simultaneously."

"No." The word passed through her lips before she could think.

Toronn glared at her. "No?"

Maker, give me strength.

"The task the Maker has given me is to c-create a true, full alliance between the races to stand against this threat. He has told me to accept only those w— willing to lay down their p-p-pride and work as a unit. Slayers who will ride dragons, dragons who will b—bear riders, and dreki who will bind us together." *Where did that last part come from?* "I will accept nothing less."

Behind her, her allies' surprise filled the air. Rís flapped his wings and barked, startling several of Azron's slayers.

Toronn's face was red with rage. "You stupid, stupid girl! You can't afford to turn down my help—without me, the villages in this area will never join you. Your forces will only thin out the an'reik as you fall! Do you even think you could stop me if I ordered the march?"

His shouts made her heart stutter in her chest, but his last statement sparked even more fear. She needed allies, but something deep within her said that disaster would befall any who didn't listen.

"P-please, do not go alone! If you go into battle on foot, you will die. P-p-please, don't do this to your men."

Toronn spat on the ground. "You claim the Maker's hand in this? Knowledge of the future?! It is the Dark One you follow, like these dragons of yours, and he leads you to your doom!"

The Dark One? He thought that in her quest to stop the an'reik she followed the greatest of the Nameless, the one who created the first an'reik? It almost made her laugh. In that moment, the imposing chief of her memories vanished, replaced by a small, petty man more willing to craft ridiculous falsehoods than hear truth from an unwelcome source.

No, Toronn would not come with her. He would not help her gain more alliances in this region. But he was not the sole warrior standing before her.

Alísa lifted her voice. "Slayers of Azron, my brothers—my offer of alliance stands n—not just with your chief, but with each one of you."

Toronn crossed his arms. For a second, Alísa expected him to shout over her. Instead, he merely smirked and waited.

"If any of you would humble yourselves and c-c-c-c-come together with the good dragons and d—dreki of my clan and allies, c-come forward now. We will p-protect you from retaliation."

Behind her, L'non, Briek, and N'ravi stepped up, emotions like static rising from them as they prepared for a fight. But no slayer of Azron moved.

So be it.

Alísa turned away, grabbing onto Sesína's spines to pull herself up. Still, none moved. She should have felt a heaviness because of it, yet her heart cooled like Eldra Landera's peaceful lakes. Though numbers were important, they had never been her clan's priority. When she called five dragons from Tsamen's clan and when Briek's men decided one-by-one whether to return to Me'ran or stay and fight with her, she had believed the right ones had come to her. Now she chose to believe those who refused were the right ones to stay behind.

Her companions mounted and still Azron made no move. Toronn spat on the ground, his dark, hawkish eyes glaring at her.

"I always knew you had a dragon inside of you."

Alísa smiled softly as Sesína spread her wings. "So you did. I should have gleaned that bit of wisdom from you much sooner, chief."

She placed her hand over her heart, a salute from one chief to another. Toronn did not return the gesture, and somehow that made Alísa grin even wider. Though it may take a lifetime to overcome the feelings of shame and worthlessness he instilled in her, she could see Toronn for what he truly was now. In that, she was free.

As Sesína rose into the air, Alísa's heart rose with her and found the room to laugh.

49

TRAPPED

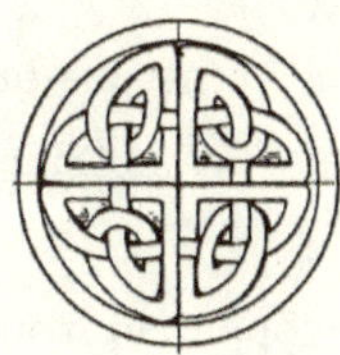

Kallar ate. Not because he was hungry. Not because he needed the energy to resist his captors. Simply because the keeper told him to. Every minute free of the mind-world was one free from torment.

Yet even here, his mind frayed and throbbed like blood pulsing from a wound. Ever since being forcibly dragged off R'lann, the keeper had been crueler, harsher, and more violent.

Kallar caught himself slouching with sleep and forced himself upright. He couldn't sleep in the mind-world, and as soon as he physically fell asleep, the keeper would seize control and the torture would resume. In the meantime, the monster growled at the back of his skull, each change in tone making Kallar flinch.

Somewhere within still lurked the slayer who loathed this newfound fear. That Kallar shouted and raged that they had faced worse pain before and always triumphed. That slayer thought he knew everything, but he was a fool. The keeper used those worse pains, piling them on and enhancing them with every terrible act he had ever committed. There was no escape. None but death, which the keeper would not allow.

A shriek of laughter jolted Kallar from staring through his food. He had almost fallen asleep again. He stood, setting aside the nearly empty bowl and running his hands through his hair. The shorn side had grown half an inch since his capture.

Why had he stood?

That's right. Laughter. It sounded like Isarra. A part of him didn't care. Another, stronger part needed to know what was happening. Searching camp with his eyes, he caught sight of movement at the prison tent. Though no longer shrieking, Isarra continued to chuckle as she exited and clapped a guard's shoulder.

Anxiety clutched at Kallar's stomach. What was she doing there? He kept himself still, not willing to bring the keeper anywhere near R'lann again, until he saw Isarra cleaning a dagger with a cloth.

He ran, dodging an'reik and tents, his brother's name the only thought pounding in his skull. Isarra smirked as she caught sight of him.

"Like a dog to his master."

"What did you do?" Kallar stopped in front of her, all his strength focused on not attacking her. Not until he knew exactly what happened.

"Oh, relax, my little Singer. I only took enough blood for a divining spell." She laughed again. "And oh, what a result!"

Kallar had to stop himself from diving through the tent-flap to see his brother. Despite wanting to ensure R'lann's well-being, bringing the keeper anywhere near him might be disastrous.

"Not even a hint of curiosity?" Isarra tsked, then snapped her finger at her side. "Follow."

Kallar didn't move on principle.

"You'd rather I do it?"

He shuddered at the voice so oily he felt it on his skin. He didn't know which was worse, letting Isarra treat him like a dog, or purposefully giving the keeper control. Which did he want—his pride, or his body?

What pride remains here? Kallar stepped forward, staying in Isarra's wake. Her smirk almost made him change his mind. She led him to the middle of camp and raised her arms and voice.

"The masters have spoken!"

Throughout camp, people paused in their tasks and looked at her, curious.

"Our defeat of the Dragon Singer was great, but not complete. With ten days' march between Vennia and her mountain, I sought insight to her plan. Past visions have shown small clues—a date of attack, the number of warriors. Today, however, the masters granted I witness her speaking with her allies as though sitting among them!"

Isarra began chuckling again, unable to contain herself. "The girl is so devoted to the dragons that she will not allow any human to join or remain with her unless they agree to ride one. She has already rejected the strongest chief in the west because he would not stoop so low, and some of her previous allies have abandoned her."

Kallar caught his jaw dropping. Alísa wasn't well-versed in war and leadership, but this? How stupid did she have to be? Didn't she realize the country's fate rested on her inexperienced shoulders?

Isarra pointed at a crew of people packing up the kitchen tent. "Hold off on that. We've no need to rush after her."

Marizarr shook his head. "This is the perfect time to press forward, while she's weak! We can't stop simply because the girl is making it easy for us."

Isarra rolled her eyes. "We're not stopping, we're resting. Regaining our strength to better crush her pitiful army." She looked at her nails. "Besides, with her mandate, all who rally to her are those who would bow to the dragons—slayers we absolutely want dead. We should let her gather them all into one place for us."

She raised a brow at the gathered crowd. "Why are you all standing here? Go play! We move out tomorrow, at a gentler pace."

Pivoting toward Kallar, she took his chin in her hand. "Your old girlfriend is an idiot, you know that?"

Kallar pulled away, giving her nothing. Inside, however, his last vestiges of hope crumbled to dust. He remained motionless as she sauntered off and camp came back to life. So, there was no rescue for him or R'lann. He had nearly resigned himself to dying with the keeper inside already, but R'lann—R'lann could have had a chance.

I can't count on Alísa. Can't get near him for fear of hurting him. What am I supposed to do now?

The sounds of sparring rose from across camp. Kallar considered a moment before turning toward the clanging swords. He had previously refused to spar because it would help the an'reik he sparred with become stronger. But they trained whether or not he joined, and they used true weapons in order to better display their power. It wasn't uncommon for someone to come away with serious wounds that needed a healing potion. A couple of men had even died. If they trained anyway, he might as well try to kill a few.

And if he died instead, no loss.

"You think I'll let you go so easily?"

Kallar did his best to ignore the fear that shocked through him, pushing forward. Camp was far too large, too full of slayers and an'reik. More slayers traded their souls by the day, leaving few untainted. The an'reik dragons, too, grew stronger as more dragons made the deal for power.

He came upon the grounded dragons lying near the sparring field, docile under the influence of Moraggan—an an'reik with pulsing empathy. It was nearly as effective against them as his weakening song.

Who was I kidding? Even if Alísa weren't limiting her army, she couldn't defeat us.

The keeper purred in his mind. "Yes. 'Us.'"

Kallar fought back panic as the voice reverberated through him. *"That isn't what I meant."*

"Mortals lie to themselves all the time, but the subconscious doesn't. You've finally accepted your fate."

Kallar gritted his teeth. *"The only thing I've 'accepted' is that I will use every breath I have to sabotage this camp while I'm trapped in it!"*

A burning pulse shocked from his head to his feet, and he bit back a cry.

"I see your thoughts. Even your foolish hope to wound your sparring partners." The keeper shifted until its taloned hand rested on Kallar's shoulder. *"You are mine."*

Kallar twisted away, realizing too late that he dodged from nothing. The dragons and Moraggan stared at him. The green dragon held a predatory gaze Kallar knew all too well. The keeper kept its hold on him, claws pricking at his skin.

His heart pounded. It was going to draw him back inside.

"Don't the slayers have a phrase?" The keeper's other hand reached for a memory. *"The stronger will shape the weaker?"*

Fire. Fire burning his arm at his first cave-storming, crossed with the blaze that consumed his mother. The flames covered his body, biting at skin, muscle, and bone. Kallar fell to the ground with a scream of agony.

It's just in my head. It's just in my head! Yet he couldn't help but roll, trying desperately to stop the feeling, to put it out!

Finally, the torment ended. He lay curled on his side, heaving breaths through shredded lungs.

Movement in his periphery activated instinct. He rolled out of the way just as the green dragon snapped at him.

Moraggan shouted something and his power pulsed through the astral plane in droves. Though the nausea he sent was only directed at the dragons, Kallar's damned Singer empathy felt every bit. The green slumped on its side, puffing. It glared at Kallar with a look that spoke of future attempts.

Lellani, too, fell. Her eyes, however, held something besides hatred. Her words echoed in his mind before he could shield against her.

"You're just as trapped as we are. Maker, have mercy."

Kallar shivered. He didn't want her pity. He grabbed the memories the keeper had been shoving at him for weeks—flashing swords and dead hatchlings—and threw them at her. The dragoness flinched, closing her eyes as though that might block out the images.

"There is no mercy for what I've done," he said. *"Save your pity."*

Lellani growled, saying no more. The keeper, too, stayed silent, but it was a smug silence. One that spoke of the victory Kallar had just given it. It lifted its hands from his shoulders.

On shaking arms, Kallar pushed up to continue his march to the sparring ground. It was all he could do.

50

AWAKENING

Darkness and dragons surrounded Alísa in a cave only slightly familiar. With dragon and human clanmates behind her and Rís on her shoulder, she did not fear. She did, however, flinch as the massive black alpha dragon before her manifested his anger in an astral shout.

"Why have you come to me again?!"

Sesína growled in annoyance at her father's display. Alísa exuded as much authority as she could muster.

"The situation has changed, Crakil. My message isn't regarding peace with slayers, but war against the an'reik. If you value the security of your caves, I suggest you listen."

Crakil's talons scraped the stone. *"My caves are sufficiently secure, aside from a couple of scouts allowing certain clans inside."* He huffed smoke toward the dragons who led Alísa here. *"We have no an'reik within our borders. We kill all we catch."*

Alísa squinted at him. *"Then you don't know of the an'reik army marching across the land? Both humans and dragons have banded together, terrorizing caves and villages in their wake."*

Crakil was silent in both words and emotions, which meant he purposefully held his emotions back. A sign that Alísa's news surprised him.

"None of us can defeat this army alone," she continued. *"Already I have fought them twice and failed, despite having allies. Warriors from all clans must unite against this threat."*

Above her, dragons growled and slapped their tails against stone. Their agreement filled her with the courage she needed to speak her next words— they never became easier, no matter how many chiefs and alphas she spoke to. Toronn wasn't the only one to reject them. Lorin and most of his slayers had abandoned her when she brought back the change in plans, as had a dragon clan.

"We need both dragons and humans willing to embrace the Maker's call to fight them on his terms. He has spoken to my clan—we are to attack as a unit. Every dragon who commits must carry a rider. Together, we will—"

Crakil roared, his inner flame burning in his eyes and mouth. *"I see through your guise, vermin! You speak of a threat too strong to ignore, then demand conformity?"* He looked up at his clan. *"If the situation were truly so grave, she would accept any help offered, not force us to become beasts of burden. The Maker granted the skies as our domain—we will not give it to slayer vermin!"*

He snapped at the air. *"I see no need for my dragons to accompany you. Only fools who follow D'lann's teaching would stoop so low. We all know what happened to him, don't we, Koriana?"*

Alísa didn't bother trying to quell Koriana's anger, not with Crakil speaking so haughtily against her mate. Graydonn once told Alísa how his father taught that peace with humans was possible, and that such teachings harmed his position in the clan.

Koriana's tail slashed through the air in defiance. *"Maker judge between you and him."*

"He shall, and true dragons will be revealed. Dragons as he intended—strong and unhindered by humanity."

Crakil took a step forward, wings spreading as a dangerous hatred rippled through the astral plane. Rís flared his own wings as Alísa fought her prey instinct. She couldn't cower if she was to be respected as Crakil's equal.

He came closer, glowing eyes pinned on her. *"Even if the Singer offered herself as my rider, I would not bow."*

"Stop!" With a snarl, Sesína pushed forward, wings raised in challenge. *"I can't believe half of me comes from you! Prideful and selfish, staying in your precious sky while the world burns beneath you, simply because you refuse to admit humans are as good as we are! Well, guess what? Some of them say they won't stoop so low as to accept alliance with dragons!"*

Her tail swished behind her. *"We are all stupid and stubborn and prideful, and it takes courage of heroic proportions to admit when we need help. Your refusal is not strength, father. It is cowardice. We fly with heroes. Show them, Alísa."*

Crakil snarled, but Alísa already knew Sesína's wishes. She raised her voice in the song she had used in Tsamen and Paili's caves—one to entrance dragons and prove their hearts as she called them to fight.

Who will seek wisdom in an age of violence?
Only the quiet, who stand by nothing else.
Who will listen to the quiet in a time of chaos?
Only the ones who tire of the noise.
Who will stand with the weak through the storms?
Only the ones who too are affected.

None will listen. None will stand. None will seek the truth,
Until fire meets fire, and sword meets sword,
Until man gives life for dragon,
And dragon gives life for man.
Woe to the ones who will not stand!

Every dragon held in place like time stopped, eyes either on Alísa or closed. Crakil still loomed above Sesína, his snarl now merely a dropped jaw. Alísa pressed on the Illumination bond to awaken Sesína from the trance.

"Wake the others."

Sesína sent an affirmative, pressing the bridge of her snout to Alísa's cheek before prancing to rouse Koriana. Alísa breathed low and deep, then spoke aloud to the entranced dragons.

"I will not use force to bring you to my aid, though the need is dire. Instead, I c-call to all who would set aside their p-p-pride to embrace a better way. One of peace between former enemies and justice against those who would crush the weak. If that c-c-calling is yours, awaken and follow me."

Alísa left Crakil and approached Sesína. The last of their clanmates had woken with Alísa's command and now prepared to fly. Rís leapt from her shoulder and phased into her pack as Alísa pulled herself onto Sesína's back.

At Alísa's command, Sesína led them out. The two scouts who allowed them access leapt into the air behind them, followed by more. Eleven dragons out of a clan of twenty-five.

Koriana clicked in her throat as she flew beside Sesína. *"I never expected so many to join us. Given the years of hate for D'lann's teachings, I wouldn't have been surprised if none awoke."*

"Sometimes ideas require time to take root," Alísa said. *"I wish I could have known him."*

Koriana blinked slowly, silent with lingering grief before returning to clan business. *"Back to the cave?"*

Alísa surveyed the dragons behind them, smiling as an idea formed. *"No. First, we head to Kannin. I told their slayers we would pick them up today."*

Briek squinted at her. *"Then you'll have the dreki send more dragons to help?"*

"We have plenty here."

Koriana thrummed. *"A bold move, Singer."*

"Wait." Briek looked at the new dragons, then returned to her. *"You're going to force dragons who just decided to work with us to carry riders who also just decided?"*

Alísa grinned as Sesína snickered beneath her. She had caught on.

"Certainly not, Briek. The dragons who are already used to riders will carry the new slayers. Crakil's dragons will carry us."

The emotional equivalent of a grimace ran through the mind-link. *"And here I'd hoped I would never again ride an untrained dragon…"*

"Trained?!" Koriana snapped at the air. *"I am not your pet, Slayer Briek."*

"I'm well aware of that, Dragon Koriana."

Sesína continued snickering while Alísa shook her head.

"There are many to train—dragons and riders. I assume you and the others will use this opportunity to teach Crakil's dragons what flying with a rider is supposed to feel like?"

He sighed with swollen exasperation. *"We'll do our best, chief."*

"And Koriana…?"

The dragoness huffed smoke. *"So long as the slayers do not choke us with their meaty legs, we can 'train' them to lean into turns and not fall."*

Briek chuckled and patted Koriana's neck, which earned him another huff of smoke that Koriana sent over her back and into his face.

"Good." Alísa said. *"This is their first test, so monitor everyone. I will take anyone willing to fly together, but I need to know who needs extra attention."*

Affirmatives flew from both Briek and Koriana and the mind-link quieted. All except for Sesína, who whispered through the Illumination bond.

"Smart move. The faster they get comfortable with each other, the faster we can teach the fancy moves. I like teaching the fancy moves!"

Alísa patted Sesína's neck. *"Me too."*

She looked at the dragons again, counting them up and making eye-contact with the riders. There was one man missing. Not truly missing—none were still in Crakil's cave—but the hole in her heart grew every time she caught herself searching for a certain face.

Alísa reached into her pack and petted Rís' mane. The drek connected to her.

"Sad?" The question came with confusion.

Alísa pressed her lips together. *"I'm happy for what we just accomplished. I just miss Falier."*

Rís cooed and nuzzled her fingers. An image entered her mind—one of her and Falier dancing in the bonfire's light at Me'ran. She spun at his lead while he grinned like the rest of the world didn't exist.

"He'll return soon," Sesína said softly. A bit of mischief rose in her. *"Then you can get back to purposefully grossing me out with your mushy stuff."*

Alísa chuckled and set her eyes forward. The village was in view now. Falier was doing his part, and she was doing hers. They were a team, even apart.

"Right. Let's go."

51

BEFORE THE ICE DRAGONS

Falier didn't like riding dragons as a mere passenger. With Graydonn's injuries, however, the dragon couldn't carry a rider for a few more days. So instead, Falier rode Komi one spine behind Trísse.

On a map, the ice dragons seemed a reasonable distance away. As the hawk flew, it was a bit further than the trip from Me'ran to Tsamen and Paili's old caves. That flight lasted a day and a half.

Unfortunately, Falier's squad of envoys had to travel as the dragon flew, which included skirting other dragons' territories. Though, a longer flight had its benefits. It gave him more time to plan his approach to the alphas, and to develop Jossen and P'raenn's bond with Varek and Mennáli close enough to witness. Varek remained as resistant as ever, though his belligerence was less now that his only human companions were bonded riders, Taz, and Darrin.

On the third day, the squad entered the ice dragons' territory. All dragons but Graydonn bore a truce-boulder to signal that their squad wasn't entering for violence. Ska peaked from the flap of Falier's pack to take in the view. The Prilune mountain range filled their vision, the colossal peaks reaching up beyond the low clouds.

"*Inside,*" Saynan said, pointing his muzzle, "*there is a vast network of tunnels, caves, and underground lakes and streams. They entwine throughout the range, like the hollow roots of a massive tree. Dragons block many branches with stones to keep clans from each other's territory.*"

"*How do they avoid getting lost?*" Jossen asked.

"*Talon-scoring in the stone portions. The caves have a numbering system that hatchlings memorize with the help of Illumination. The ice caves are a bit more—elaborate. Each tunnel and cave is named for an animal or story, and matching images are carved throughout by talon and breath.*"

"*Whoa!*" Hwinn exclaimed, his wing-beats speeding up briefly. "*That sounds incredible!*"

"*I'm eager to see it,*" Selene agreed. "*Are the ice tunnels as vast as the stone ones?*"

"*Yes. You should not traverse them without a guide. Dragons on pilgrimage always struggle to navigate initially.*"

"*Pilgrimage?*" Varek asked.

"*Did I not mention? The ice dragons are the keepers of legends and arts. Many clans—*"

A trumpet interrupted him, making Falier jump. He twisted to locate its source.

Saynan responded with a high, extended note. As his call faded, a white dragon descended from the clouds. She was large and imposing, her spines longer than Falier was used to, which likely meant she was quite older than Saynan.

"*Hail, B'thrial!*" Saynan called.

"*Saynan,*" a female voice growled back. "*Why have you returned with such— companions?*"

"*I bring a message from Alísa-Dragon-Singer, borne by her mate, Falier.*"

Mate. It still felt odd being called that. Wonderful, but odd.

Oh, and that was his cue. Falier straightened. "*Hail, B'thrial. We have traveled far to seek a parley with your alphas.*"

The scout dragoness circled and Saynan kept pace, keeping her in sight while the others followed.

B'thrial let out a spray of ice. "*We want no part in your war. Go home, little slayer.*"

Saynan's instructions over the last few days ran through Falier's brain. The ice dragons lived lives of isolation. Intrigue them with something new.

"*It is true I bring news of the war. I also bear news of Arran's first dragon-human clan and the bonds within.*"

B'thrial's emotions felt like an eye-roll. "*We have already heard of the Singer's Illumination of a hatchling.*"

"*And what of mind-kin bonds? Dragons and slayers with minds aligned? Surely you can feel it in me.*"

Falier focused on his connection to Graydonn for B'thrial to sense more easily. The scout's curiosity rose.

"*A dragon and a slayer? How did this come to be?*"

"*Take us to your alphas and you will learn.*"

B'thrial growled, eyes brightening. "*I know what you are doing, Singer's mate.*"

"*I figured you would.*" Falier displayed open palms. "*The Dragon Singer and I have no guile, but much is happening within our clan and we would have our neighbors know. Let us pass, and we will discuss these matters and beyond.*"

B'thrial squinted at him as they continued circling. Her horns looked like icicles, white and vaguely transparent. Besides the usual two long horns, she had many smaller ones on her head and cheeks, plus one on her snout pointing skyward.

With a huff of ice, B'thrial veered toward the mountains. "*Follow.*"

Falier let out a breath. His plan had worked. Komi's spine pressed against his back as she followed B'thrial up the mountain into the clouds. He shivered as they ascended, pulling his cloak closer around him. The double-layer of clothing was definitely a good idea. He also had fur-lined gloves in his pack, but it was challenging to grasp a dragon's spine with cloth over his fingers.

They rose above the lowest set of clouds, but Falier still couldn't see the mountain peaks. "*Just how high up are the ice dragons' caves, Saynan?*"

"*You'll be able to breathe, don't worry.*"

Falier straightened. "*That's a concern?*"

"*No, I just said it wasn't.*" The dragon's humor was less comforting than he seemed to hope it would be. "*You may get short of breath or dizzy for the first couple of days, but you'll acclimate.*"

They passed into another layer of clouds and, for a moment, the mountain disappeared. Then Falier saw the snow. It blanketed the mountains, blending their contours in with the clouds. He couldn't even see B'thrial against the blinding white, but Saynan didn't hesitate. He followed the curve of the mountain, then circled over a large opening in the snow and ice.

"*This is it.*" Saynan waited as everyone reached his altitude. "*Stay close.*"

Saynan dove for the cave, the others following behind. The entry tunnel was long and wide, with multiple offshoots. B'thrial was already out of sight, but Saynan didn't hesitate. He sent an image of the wall carving they rushed past. The art depicted a dragon fighting an enormous stag with fangs and a snake for a tail. Saynan gave it a name, but Falier didn't recognize it.

Droplets fell from the ceiling as a roar echoed through. Falier was fairly certain it was a call to attention rather than to arms, but he tested Graydonn's emotions just in case. No anxiety—must be okay. He marveled at how effortlessly he could feel Graydonn now. It seemed even easier than before their troubles.

The next tunnel came with an image of stars falling from the sky and water spewing from underground.

"The creation of the oceans," Saynan supplied. The third tunnel displayed a dragon's paw holding a glowing orb. *"Eldra A'fir."*

Ah, so the orb was the sun.

"Do dragons perceive the Eldír as their own kind, then?" Trísse asked.

"What else would they be?" Harenn said. *"You can't think of them as—as humans, can you?"*

"Of course they're humans!" Taz hesitated for a second. *"Or, human-shaped, anyway. Like the Maker."*

Mennáli growled. *"The Maker is* not *a human!"*

"Drek," Ska agreed. Laen confirmed it from Selene's pack with a bark.

"No!" Komi sounded scandalized. *"He has wings, yes, but he forged the world with fire. He is a dragon."*

"Young ones," Saynan said, *"do you truly think the Maker can be contained in only one form? Perhaps he and the Eldír change shape depending on who they speak to."*

"That's what Alísa said," Falier confirmed. *"Eldra Bria appears mostly human, but once she also had wings and—"*

A sense of bafflement entered the link. Too late he realized that Bria becoming an Eldra was *not* common knowledge, nor was the fact that Alísa had seen her—twice.

"—never mind."

"No," Trísse said, *"I'm definitely* not *forgetting that."*

"Nor am I." Komi glanced back. *"Alísa-Dragon-Singer has seen an Eldra?"*

Varek crossed his arms. *"There is no Eldra Bria in lore."*

"Later," Saynan quieted them. *"We're here."*

At the end of the third tunnel, the floor dropped out from under them in a sharp, thirty-foot slope. Then the sides fell away, becoming a massive cave with many other icy entrances. At least forty dragons already lounged in the crevices and side-caves, almost all of them larger than Saynan. Also among them were a few fire dragons of different hues.

Falier pointed to them. *"Pilgrimage?"*

"Ah, yes," Saynan said. *"Many clans send representatives every few years to learn history and lore. Think of it as dragons training to become songweavers, but without the human art of music."*

"The alphas approach," B'thrial said, leaving them to fly up to a vacant side-cave.

Saynan descended to the stone floor and Komi landed in front of him, displaying that she carried the leader of the squad. The rest touched down behind them.

Falier slid to the ground just as the ice alphas entered the cave. They landed on the ledge of a lower tunnel wide enough for them to stand together. Lowering to their bellies, they studied their guests.

The alphas reached at least twelve feet at the withers, large and imposing. Yet, they were also leaner than Falier was used to—with long, slender legs and necks rather than the battle-honed muscles of most dragons he knew. Thinking back to Saynan's comments on his old clan literally living above the dragon-human war, it made sense. These dragons lived longer and did not find it necessary to train for combat. Would this be the future of all dragons once Alísa brought peace?

One alpha rumbled a growl and a deep male voice entered Falier's mind. Shironn.

"Singer's mate. We have not envied an audience with the Dragon Singer. We had hoped, however, that upon her inevitable call she would have the courtesy to appear herself."

"Alísa sends her regrets," Falier said. He stood tall, exuding as much alpha-ness as he could. *"She hopes to come in-person someday, but the current situation keeps her with the army. In the meantime, she sent me, along with one of her most trusted betas"* —he gestured to Saynan— *"and bonded dragon-rider pairs, both Illuminated and mind-kin."*

The alpha female, Riantha, crossed a paw over the other. *"So, there is another hatchling robbed of their culture through unnatural Illumination. A human girl with a dragon soul made a modicum of sense. What makes this other girl so special?"*

"Everything!" Hwinn jumped in, talons clicking on the ground. *"She's kind and smart and brave and makes the best meat pies ever except for Grandma's—sorry,*

Selene, I won't lie to the alphas—and she sees sounds, which I thought was normal until she told me because apparently Illumination meant I see them too, but mine are different colors than hers, and—"

"Hwinn." Selene patted his neck. *"That's plenty."*

"But I didn't tell them about—"

"Plenty."

Falier took back the conversation. *"When we defeated Rorenth, there were two eggs left behind without parents. The dragons of our clan kept them, even made sure humans didn't touch them. But in the end, neither chose a dragon. Hwinn chose my sister and the other a former slayer who repented of his dragon-killing. And that is not all."*

Graydonn stepped up alongside him and Falier placed a hand on his neck. He found it hard not to lean on the dragon, then noticed his breaths felt shallow. That thing about altitude Saynan warned him about, he supposed. No matter, he had to keep going.

"When Graydonn and I met, we were terrified of each other. I wasn't trained in telepathy or swordplay to defend myself from him, and he feared I might tell slayers of his whereabouts. Yet, thanks to Alísa, we discovered we are mind-kin. As are Trísse and Komi, and Jossen and P'raenn."

Shironn and Riantha both looked on with interest, the alpha male's head high and alert while his mate cocked her head.

"Fascinating." Riantha clicked in her throat. *"I have cherished my bond to my mind-sister. I never would have considered humans capable."*

"Bonded to a slayer," Shironn mused, shaking his head as though clearing water from his ears. *"A fascinating idea. Would it affect thought, like Illumination?"*

"And who would be the more affected?" Riantha looked at the dragons with mind-kin bonds. *"Tell me, why did you choose to bond with humans rather than wait for another dragon?"*

Graydonn's talons scraped against the stone. *"The Maker brought us together. It did not occur to me that something 'better' could be waiting."*

Komi's tail hit the ground in agreement as a growl rose in her throat. Above, Riantha thrummed her amusement.

"Of course. The idea is novel—I meant no offense to your mind-kin. If a bond was possible, they must surely be worthy."

Falier drummed his fingers against his leg and ignored the implication that all other humans weren't worthy. Time to get to the point.

"The Dragon Singer has shown us much about each other, breaking down images of monsters and vermin with the simple truth that we—humans, dragons, and dreki alike— are all soul-bearers. We have already learned, grown, and helped each other in many ways, including the fight against—"

"Ah, yes. I've noticed your fae friends." Shironn growled thoughtfully. *"Dreki? Is that what they call themselves? If the Singer has brokered peace between them and dragonkind, that is indeed a feat."*

A bigger feat than peace between humans and dragons? *"Yes, we've allied with two dreki clans in battle."* Though whatever happened to the second clan that fought Rorenth with them was anyone's guess. They had disappeared after the fight, likely heading back to their territory in the forests.

"And none of your dragons have gone missing?"

Missing? Legends of fae luring humans into the forest were common, but the idea of luring dragons was strange. Ska and Laen barked their offense, and Falier hurried to talk over them.

"None. They have proven valuable allies in and out of battle. Their telepathy is partic—"

"Out of battle?" Riantha's eyes brightened. *"How so?"*

Falier took a deep breath. That was the second time they cut him off when he turned the conversation toward war. He needed to be stronger.

"They raise morale, help to shape the caves for easier human access, and bear messages faster than any scout. Messages which warned us of a rising evil—"

"Shaping caves? How—"

"There are an'reik on the move," Falier finished, adding a growl for good measure. *"Humans and dragons. They are marching across the hill country. They've taken over villages and caves, and they have the support of non-an'reik members of both races. An unprecedented threat. That's why—"*

"It is indeed unprecedented," Shironn said, looking at his mate. *"I suppose they have learned to work together from the Singer's ways."*

"Perhaps," Riantha said. *"Though I doubt they are so altruistic as to seek each other's good. Make no mistake, they use each other."*

"Yes, but to what end?"

Falier allowed himself to relax a bit and let the alphas discuss. After their topic-changing attempts, he thought he would need to work harder to reach this point.

"The dragons' goals are evident, I would think. Physical dominance—gaining dragons, killing those who won't bow, eating anam *as blood sacrifice. The humans' army would help them in this."*

"Ah, but you forget, human an'reik want followers. They would fight to keep the dragons from killing."

"An interesting point." Riantha looked into the cave above Falier's head. *"Ideas?"*

Another dragon speculated about the human an'reik's desire to gain dragon followers. Gentle growls and tail-slaps followed as others agreed or disagreed.

Falier searched about, jaw dropping. He had expected debate, but not—this. They weren't discussing whether they should help, but why the problem existed and how the an'reik planned to sustain it. He glanced at Saynan, who growled and bowed his head. The mind-link changed to include only their clanmates before Saynan spoke.

"I warned you. You will need to press the issue, likely many times, before they deign to answer your question."

"To be fair, he hasn't even gotten to ask," Harenn said.

That was true. The ice dragons moved their heads and wings, their eyes brightening and dimming as they continued to discuss.

"Graydonn, I need help to pull them back."

Graydonn assented. As dragons exchanged questions and theories, Falier's quieter voice would surely be lost. Pulling on Graydonn's strength, Falier chose his words.

"THEIR END-GOAL IS TO DOMINATE AND KILL." Falier drew in a breath as the dragons quieted and glowered at him. He almost smiled as he sensed approval from both Jossen and Varek, but it faded quickly as he released Graydonn's power and his head started swimming. The telepathic shout had sapped more from him and Graydonn than it should have. *Just a bit more.*

"Whether by physical, psychic, or other means is not the issue. Their army is growing, gaining power. They have possessed another Singer, bringing him under their control. Their darkness is spreading across the country. We are fighting them, but we need more allies. Saynan has proven that your kind's ice breath can defeat the an'reik's hellflames—a weapon we have no other defense against. We can offer psychic protection with riders and the Singer's strength in battle." Falier paused, opening his hands in

entreaty. *"Please, help us."*

The dragons continued to stare, some growling their displeasure.

"An'reik are always moving, little slayer," Shironn said. *"The Southlands are full of them and their schemes. Every time they rise, it eventually falls apart, for they are selfish by nature and feed on each other when they cannot feed on others. A'dem will remain—you need only be patient."*

Falier scoffed. *"Patient? People are dying—humans* and *dragons. What about those who can't fight or flee while we're 'being patient'?"*

Riantha lowered her head past the ledge to look him more closely in the eye. *"Death is a part of life. It is tragic, but it is how the Maker designed it. He will stop it at the appropriate time. We have seen this many times."*

Falier looked between the alphas, cold running through him. *"So if they were to ascend this mountain and storm your caves, you would do nothing? You'd just let it happen?"*

Riantha pulled back, affronted. *"Absolutely not! We have been charged with our clan's well-being—protecting our family. This we will do to our dying breath."*

"But they'll come here eventually," Falier said. *"They're too strong for any one clan to handle, and when they've finished with us, they'll look to your mountain!"*

Shironn huffed icy mist. *"You do not know that, little slayer. An'reik have moved in the open on the south side of our mountain since before my mother hatched. Never once have they tried. Even the slayers do not come here."*

"They are too busy fighting the an'reik to come here," Saynan said. *"So here you stay."*

Shironn regarded him coldly. *"I am glad you found a life that suits you, Saynan. But do not presume the battle you disappeared to fight is ours. We have been given the gift of safety in our mountains—safety which allows us to maintain our sacred duties. We cannot squander it on the unlikely chance that war will gain large enough lungs to sustain itself here."*

Falier caught his eyes drooping. Large enough lungs. Yeah, that's what was needed here.

Riantha's eyes softened. *"I see the altitude is affecting you, Singer's mate. I have more questions regarding mind-kin and dreki, but for now you may rest. B'thrial will show you to your cave. Tomorrow, we shall speak again."*

Falier fought not to slump as both relief and disappointment ran through him. These secluded dragons only cared to talk, disregarding the threat that would one day arrive at their door. He would have to keep refocusing their conversations on the war against the an'reik and hope they eventually saw reason.

For now, though, his head and stomach both hurt, and he sensed a similar aching throughout the squad-link. They would rest and try again tomorrow. He wouldn't return to Alísa empty-handed.

52

SHIELD

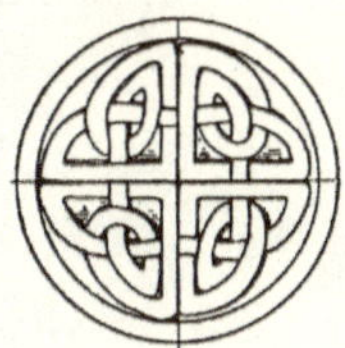

Exhaustion weighed down Kallar's legs as he crossed the trampled, empty streets of Annakím. Once thriving with a bustling textiles trade, the village had been evacuated before the an'reik army arrived.

I guess that's one thing Alísa's doing right.

Only about twenty-five people remained—some slayers wanting to fight Alísa's dragons, an an'reik who had been in Annakím already, and two stubborn but non-combative families. The latter gave up some of their livestock to feed the army, attempting to protect the remaining animals. Once, Kallar might have thought them cowards for giving this darkness free rein in their town. Now, however, he couldn't make himself believe they should do any differently. Resistance would only yield death.

A few slayers—two an'reik and one unturned—crossed in front of Kallar to enter the Hold. The opening door released sounds of coarse laughter and utensils clinking against dishes. A few self-proclaimed cooks had taken control of the kitchen.

Kallar's stomach growled. He hadn't eaten since this morning, and afternoon was quickly becoming evening. Among Karn's wayfarers, he would sit with his fellow warriors at dinner. They would swap stories that became more ridiculous with each retelling or goad each other further in their training. He would watch as two competed to talk through the most turkey, or as some poor fool worked up his nerve to approach a village-bound woman. There Kallar would feel—full. Complete.

It wouldn't be like that here—not among sold-souls and fellow possessed. He couldn't pretend, and his keeper wasn't interested in forcing that, so he would wait until the crowd died down and eat alone.

Turning away, Kallar marched back toward the carts left just within the village boundary. Many planned to occupy emptied homes tonight, but that didn't sit well with Kallar. He would set up his tent instead.

Kallar stopped as the keeper came to attention. He had no sign why it became alert so suddenly, but the hair on his neck and arms stood on end.

"Go left."

The sound shuddered through him, and his inner self flinched at the window to the outside. Fear coiled around his stomach. He shouldn't listen to the monster. Shouldn't give in, no matter what it wanted. But he was so tired of fighting. Of pain. Of horrific memories.

Kallar obeyed. Skirting the carts, he searched for what the keeper wanted. Food boxes, trunks of weapons, picketed horses, a tree.

He stopped, heart catching. There was a figure tethered to the tree, like one might tie a horse.

R'lann.

And he was alone.

Kallar attempted to spin away, to distance himself from his brother, but it was too late. Sharp talons gripped him, yanking him into the mind-world. The keeper threw him down with a force that sent him rolling fifty feet. A week ago, Kallar could have stopped himself sooner, but everything within him was exhaustion and open wounds. Long gashes ripped through his astral body from night upon night of attacks, each hemorrhaging pain and fear.

As he lifted his head, the keeper pinned burning eyes on him. He froze. It was going to attack. Shaking off the panic, Kallar reached out to the mists, knowing that facing the keeper would take its focus off R'lann.

The shadow turned back to the window. Kallar struggled to rise, astral arms and legs giving out multiple times. R'lann filled the view, just as disheveled and sallow as the last time Kallar saw him, plus a black eye and bruised cheekbone. His hands were bound with a long rope, the opposite end tied high in a tree. His guards must have deemed it sufficient and departed to dine at the Hold.

Damn them. Damn them all!

The keeper laughed with Kallar's voice. "Here is what becomes of the Maker's prisoners. You follow his ways, refuse to turn even when abandoned, then are left at the mercy of your tormentors."

R'lann, eyes wide with fear, pulled at the ropes. His fingers were already bloody around the nails from picking at the knot.

"Will you claim his protection still?"

Kallar's approach to the keeper was like walking on the edge of a sword, slow and painful. The keeper focused entirely on R'lann. If Kallar surprised it and took control for just a moment, he could seize Karn's dagger, cut the rope, and grant R'lann a chance to escape. A slim chance, but he would give anything for it.

R'lann grunted as he pulled. "He never guaranteed our bodies protection, only our souls. I know which is more important."

"Do you now?" Another step.

R'lann backed further away. "I do, and I bet Kallar does as well. Let me talk to him."

"I am Kallar," the thing said.

"No. He wouldn't give in. Not to you."

"I'm free now. You can be too. Free from this prison, free from the Maker's code, free to be whatever you will."

Kallar leapt for the window, jamming his elbow into the keeper's side. He reached for the glowing frame, grabbed hold, and—

Nothing.

The window didn't react to his touch. There wasn't even a struggle, it just—wasn't his anymore.

The keeper tossed him aside. Kallar braced for its attack, but it only stared outside and used Kallar's stolen voice.

"True freedom is yours for the taking."

"I want to talk to my brother."

Kallar made for the window again. It had to work. It had to!

"I'm here, R'lann!"

Talons dug into his side as the keeper yanked him away. Each claw was Karn's dagger against his ribs.

"The Maker has abandoned you," the keeper told R'lann. "With the Nameless, you will never be alone again."

"I'm not alone." R'lann stood straighter. "Let me talk to Kallar!"

Kallar pushed to rise, but collapsed as memories of fire coursed over his body. He cried out, but no one could hear but himself, the keeper, and their silent Maker.

The keeper loomed over R'lann now, blackness pouring into the mind-world as its rage grew stronger. "The Maker and the Eldír have done nothing for you! It's the Nameless who want you!"

R'lann swallowed but stood his ground. "Even if all you say is true, I would rather die holding on than give in to the creatures who've worked all the evil I've seen these past weeks."

Kallar looked up at the portal, panting. Why? He understood holding out against the Nameless. He'd fight and die against this keeper, but never for a Maker who didn't care. Who permitted atrocities in this broken world. Who let a young boy's mistake lead to his mother's death, or a warrior's pride kill the chief who meant more to him than his own father. Why did R'lann hold on like this?

The keeper roared with Kallar's voice. It grabbed R'lann by the throat and hoisted him off the ground.

"Why do you hold on?!"

Nausea hit Kallar as the keeper's question matched his own, as its anger matched the next memory, this of a slaughtered hatchling. Kallar attempted to reach the keeper but could only curl inward with pain and loathing.

"Stop! Don't!"

The keeper threw R'lann down and leapt on him. "Even Kallar, who hates me, knows better than to call to someone who won't answer!"

Slowly, R'lann's expression turned from wide-eyed fear to resignation. His voice was hoarse. "He doesn't have to answer. He has never left me. Even if he stays his hand, I will not leave him."

The keeper roared with the same roar Kallar used as he stormed caves. It punched R'lann in the face once, twice, again. R'lann pulled against the rope to block the beating, but Kallar's muscles were stronger and the keeper was full of rage.

"NO!" Kallar clawed at the astral grasses and tried to pull himself forward as memory's sword sliced at hatchlings' wings and legs.

He was trapped.

Useless.

Alone.

Do something, Kallar cried inwardly. *Anything!*

The monster closed its hands around R'lann's throat and squeezed. R'lann's desperate clawing at the body's arms sent more pain through Kallar until he felt he couldn't breathe.

Please. Not again. If you love him like he claims, help him!

Kallar collapsed. He was just as helpless as R'lann. More, for R'lann still held the strength to fight while Kallar was utterly spent. The rope tethering his soul to life seemed only a blade of grass.

I know you can. Help him. Help—

Kallar curled in on himself as despair took him.

—help me.

Shouts rose beyond the window, simultaneously close and so, so far away. The tether snapped and Kallar fell. Air thick as water and warm as light surrounded him, so it felt both like falling and floating. In an eternal second, pain ebbed into nothingness and dark memory slipped away…

He awoke on a bear-skin rug. It smelled of wood-smoke and long, quiet evenings. Not of home, but something like it. Running his hand over the fur, he let it catch between his calloused fingers. How long since he had experienced such warmth and softness? All he could remember was dirt and grass in the chill of twilight.

Pushing up, memory stirred. Fire crackling in the fireplace. Embroidery on the stone walls. Finely crafted chairs. A table with fresh roses in a vase. Gia's house, yet not quite. A familiar black mourning shawl draped one chair, a blue wool blanket over another. The few windows were boarded shut against what sounded like a thunderstorm raging outside. The door was also barred from within. Its panels were covered in carvings—swirls symbolizing honor, hope, and protection. Around him, mists of fear and dread swirled and sent his mind racing.

What happened? How did I get here? Why—

"R'lann!"

Kallar bolted upright, sending throbbing pain through his skull. Where was R'lann? Why wasn't he here too? The last image of his brother's face as the keeper choked him ran through Kallar's whole body like a punch to the gut.

Something touched his shoulder and Kallar whirled, hand going to his empty knife belt. An older man waited for him there, one with a salt-and-pepper ponytail, wise green eyes, and a gentle smile.

"Peace, Kallar," Farren said. The songweaver knelt in front of him. *"Remember the final thing you saw."*

All Kallar could recall was R'lann's face as the keeper choked him.

"You saw more than that." Farren's tone was far too gentle for the situation. *"Breathe it in."*

Kallar met his eyes and forced a breath. It came heavily, like the first taken in ages. Farren's gaze grounded him, allowing him to rein in his breaths until they became calmer.

"What did you see?"

Slowly, memory surfaced. *"There was shouting. Then someone pulled my body off of R'lann. The an'reik must have found us and stopped me—stopped it from killing him."*

Farren nodded. *"R'lann is fine. His guards have been disciplined and will not leave him again. As for the piece of the Nameless in your mind—it will have less impetus to harm him since it can no longer torture you by it."*

Kallar ran a hand over the shorn side of his hair. Something wasn't adding up.

"Am I dead?"

Farren chuckled, pulling back. *"If this is your image of the Maker's halls, you have far less imagination than I'd realized."*

Kallar shook his head. *"I'm not going there. People like R'lann go there. Those who care about the Maker, who follow him no matter the cost. Who haven't murdered innocents and tortured children."* Kallar looked around the house. *"I hoped I would still see Ma again, but this isn't Ma's home. It's Gia's."*

"So it is." Farren glanced about with fondness. *"This is the home she and others built in the hope you would return."*

"Built?" Kallar shook his head. *"Why are you here? Where is here?"*

Farren's gaze lingered on the walls a moment more. *"This is the help you asked for. A place where the keeper can no longer touch your soul."*

Kallar's first instinct was to slump in relief, but the second came immediately after. Storm winds hit the boarded windows as anger turned the mists white.

"No! I asked the Maker to help R'lann, not me. He's alone out there—captive and tortured, and he doesn't deserve it! I—"

Kallar's breath shuddered, and he stopped before his voice could crack.

"R'lann has everything he needs." Farren's voice held an ocean of compassion. *"And now you do as well. Your call may have started as a plea for R'lann, but you also cried out for yourself at the end. Evil cannot touch anyone who calls."*

"Lies." Kallar looked away. *"R'lann claims the Maker's presence, yet the an'reik have mistreated him for weeks. Even if my soul is safe, the keeper still holds my body. You can't say evil can't touch us."*

"Are you a body, Kallar? Or are you a soul? Which has proven true this last month?"

Kallar looked down at his astral body. At the mist-leaking gashes from the keeper's tortures. At the scars far older.

Above the sounds of the thunderstorm came a shrill roar. Kallar fell back as panic gripped him. The keeper. It was right outside. It had found him again. Memories of pain and anguish flowed into him, choking his heart.

"Look at me."

Farren's voice seemed so far away. The keeper would get in. The torture would continue, and for the first time, Kallar questioned his ability to survive. This tiny reprieve had only been a false hope.

"It cannot touch you here," Farren said. *"Its only power is what you give it."*

Kallar swallowed against his fear. He wished he could believe it, but the keeper's might overshadowed his, and its every weakness had been a lie. He hated himself for fearing what he deserved—he should be able to take it, bear it, and die knowing he had never given in.

"Son. Look at me."

Farren leaned close, but talons scraped at the wall to Kallar's left. Kallar's heart beat wildly in his chest, and he couldn't tear his eyes away.

Farren sighed, and again Kallar felt depths of compassion he did not deserve. *"I will distract it for a time. You must rest and regain your strength."*

Farren stood and walked toward the door. Only then did Kallar turn his gaze from the shadow outside the window.

"What are you doing?" His voice trembled, so unlike the warrior he should be. *"How do you know all of this? Farren can't project himself here, and you can't be imagined because you know things I don't. Who are you?"*

Farren smiled sadly, his answer barely audible with the keeper's railings. *"I am help."*

The songweaver's visage touched the door, then slipped through the oak panels as though they were nothing. A yowl rose from the keeper, followed by the diminishing sounds of a man running and a beast giving chase. Soon all Kallar heard was rain beating against the roof, fire in the hearth, and his own ragged heartbeat.

In the absence of both the keeper and Farren, exhaustion fell over Kallar. It had been weeks since his mind had slept—weeks that felt like years. Pushing to his knees, he grabbed the blanket off the closest chair. Its blue was what R'lann's tunic was when clean.

Save him. You protected me. Why not him?

Kallar laid back down on the bear-skin rug before the fire and pulled the blanket over himself. As his tired eyes finally closed, a memory rose, one of R'lann looking Isarra full in the face with defiance worthy of a wayfarer.

'I am not alone.'

Kallar clutched the blanket tighter until the patter of the rain lulled him to sleep.

53

FIGHT & FLIGHT

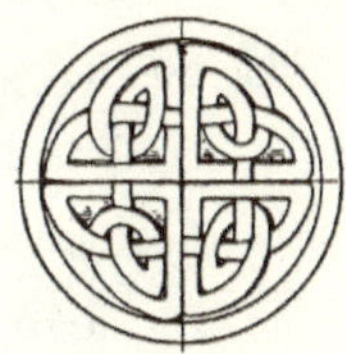

Falier's dizziness and nausea were nearly gone by the end of the second day among the ice dragons, as was Graydonn's pain. After pushing through sickness to address the clan again—and failing to gain more than off-topic debates—Falier and his squad were exhausted. All except Saynan. Even after living in the lowlands, he apparently didn't need to re-acclimate. After today's audience with the alphas, Saynan had taken the squad to his family's caverns, where his parents and his sister and her mate all resided.

Now they sat at the end of a tunnel looking over a vast cavern—one tall as the mighty pines of the eastern forests and twice as wide. Ice and fire dragons alike occupied the many side-caves and tunnels, all watching an aerial performance led by Saynan's father in celebration of Saynan's return. The dancers swirled, dove, and twisted in patterns that told favorite legends. They also used their breath to create wafting patterns of mist and snow as they flew, occasionally consuming various plants to color their next plume of ice.

Beside Falier, Selene shivered and leaned into Taz, who extracted his arm from the warmth of his cloak to wrap it around her shoulders. Behind them, Hwinn let out a gentle stream of hot air that covered them both. Falier caught the edge, which made the rest of him shiver with the contrast. He pressed back into Graydonn's warm scales, careful not to disrupt Ska, Laen, and Darrin's drek under his cloak. The dreki didn't seem to care they were missing the performance. The poor creatures weren't built for the cold.

Saynan's sister turned loops with her mate, her ice breath a dusty blue and his a bright red. The colors mixed as the two swirled together, making a hazy purple through which another dragon flew.

Saynan's voice entered the minds of the squad, explaining the story few of them knew. *"And so, the exiled prince took back his mountain and claimed his rightful position as alpha."*

"Purple is the color of alphas," Graydonn whispered to Falier through the mind-kin bond. *"It is rare, and so symbolizes a role few dragons ever get to play."*

Falier let gratitude flow. *"I don't think Alísa owns anything purple. Maybe we should get her a dress with it for special occasions."*

Graydonn clicked thoughtfully, though added nothing as Falier's thoughts turned melancholy. Alísa would love these performances, the beauty and skill. She could sing for them and introduce music to the dancers. Perhaps she would also have ideas for getting the alphas to move. He had already employed every trick he knew, but they were content here in the mountains.

Dragons trumpeted and thumped their tails in their version of applause as Saynan's family finished the story with colorful flurries swept by the wind of their wings. Falier slipped his hands out of his cloak to add his own appreciation, his thick gloves muting the sound. The other humans clapped as well, though Varek and Jossen held long-suffering expressions.

Falier reached out to them. *"Don't tell me you're bored."*

He kept his tone jocular, though he only earned a raised eyebrow from Varek.

"Bored is a strong word," Jossen said. *"It's only——is this all they do? Tell stories and fly for fun?"*

P'raenn clicked in his throat. *"It isn't mere fun. The control they display is a trove of skill built over years of training. I couldn't do half of what they do——a quarter, even."*

"But athletic ability for its own sake?"

"Haven't you been paying attention?" Graydonn asked. *"The sake is that of keeping the stories of our race alive. It's a noble cause."*

Varek scoffed. *"Histories are well and good, but this?"* He gestured to the dancers preparing for the next telling. *"You don't need dancing to keep them alive, and certainly not as one's sole profession. It's a waste of time and talent——not that I mind they aren't using their aerobatics against humanity. With their size and ice, fighting them is one of the few challenges I would gladly pass up."*

Jossen chuckled. *"Don't tell me you're afraid of a little frostbite!"*

Falier shook his head and turned his attention to the dreki. Their minds shifted against his, showing they were awake, just refusing to come out into the cold.

"What do you do in the forests?" Falier asked. *"It snows every winter. A lot."*

An image of a tree with a large hole in its trunk and many dreki piled inside filled Falier's mind.

"Sleep," Ska said.

"So that's where you always spent the winters. I assumed you were elsewhere in your territory, like wayfarers."

Ska sent a negative. *"Small."* That came with an overhead view of a forest with a glowing oblong circle. The circle encompassed two villages and the area surrounding, all near a mountain. Falier was fairly certain they were Me'ran and Soren.

"That's your territory?"

An affirmative.

"It's smaller than I'd thought. Are there more dreki in that area?"

This time Laen sent the image, one with a wider view. The previous territory held a blue glow, and three adjacent territories glowed in other colors. Between each was a space about a couple of miles wide.

"Spread."

Falier blinked the image away. *"Is it the same throughout the forests? Dreki territories scattered about with spaces in-between?"*

Another affirmative.

Interesting. *"Do you remember the other clan that helped us against Rorenth?"*

All three dreki sent back a feeling that spoke, '*Of course we do. We know everything, puny human.*'

"What if we asked them for help?" As it stood, they couldn't afford to waste much more time here. *"They would probably be easier to convince than this clan."*

Ska considered for a moment, then chirped. *"Yes."*

"It's not a bad idea," Graydonn agreed. *"Spreading them out between squad leaders, we lose the dreki unit, which is one of our most powerful."*

A self-satisfied feeling came from Ska. Falier grinned to himself. The powerful warrior, hiding from the cold in his cloak.

The next performance began. Again, Saynan's voice entered their minds, narrating the story and translating the movements and colors that humans didn't understand. This tale was about the creation of mountain elk. When the ice dragons grew too large for deer to sustain them, the Maker put thousands of deer to sleep under trees shedding their leaves. To illustrate, a few performers lowered to the floor and laid down as the others blew green-tinted ice over them.

"The leaves did not decay that year," Saynan supplied, *"sheltering the deer from the dreadful winter. When spring came, the hibernating deer awakened larger, hardier, and more agile upon the mountainside."*

Here the dragons on the floor awakened and, in a simultaneous burst, jumped into the air while breathing brown-tinted ice. The dragons branched off from each other until the streaking remnants of their breath created a giant antler.

"Since then, no ice dragon has starved," Saynan finished, *"for there are always sufficient elk to sustain us."*

"Praise the Maker," Komi said, closing her eyes reverently as the 'applause' began.

When the sounds died down, Saynan's father—an enormous dragon with a beard of icicle-like horns and bright green eyes—flew higher than the rest of the performers. He rumbled a low note and his voice resonated in everyone's minds.

"Thank you. For our last performance, I was hoping my son would join us for a dance that was once his favorite—Adne's Ascendancy."

Saynan perked up at this. *"I believe I remember my part. I would be honored to fly with you again."*

Cold air rushed over Falier and the others as the dragon beat his wings and flew out into the center to fly beside his sister.

Varek leaned closer to Jossen. "He said 'last', right?"

Jossen chuckled. "I believe so."

Mennáli growled. *"Uncultured. They could go far longer and I would be happy."*

"Just how are we potentially mind-kin, again?" Varek shook his head. "There is a war raging beneath us, one our clans are training for—are *counting* on us for—and you want to waste time on dancing?"

"You seemed willing enough to sing with the clans a few nights ago," Falier said, eyeing him. "You can't truly think art is worth nothing."

Varek scowled. "That was different. We were honoring fallen warriors, not flitting about telling myths and legends while the rest of the world burns."

"So if we weren't at war, you would allow yourself to enjoy it?"

"If we weren't at war, we wouldn't be here." Varek gestured at the dancers. "This? The carvings in the walls? The endless philosophical debates? These do nothing but fill idle time. And we shouldn't be idle, not with the current state of the land."

Falier glanced at Saynan as he masterfully wove in and out with the others. He used that same prowess in battle, but his bright eyes as he flew here spoke to his joy in simply creating something beautiful. And not just beautiful, but meaningful. Some stories were history, some myth, some had teachings and others simple enjoyment. But all of it was meaningful because it touched another *anam*.

Yet, Varek wasn't without a point.

"I'm as frustrated by their apathy about the war as you are," Falier said. "But what they do here? I see the value. Dance, carvings, the keeping of culture and legends—all of it is how we express the deepness within us. It's so human, and so beyond."

Falier looked between Varek and Jossen. "If we fight to protect all *anam*, then we fight to protect this too. We aren't *anam* without it."

"We aren't *anam* if we're all either dead or soul-sold," Varek said.

Technically, the dead were still souls. Falier ignored that argument and inclined his head. "Still, I respect this, even if I don't agree with their conclusions."

Mennáli rumbled her agreement, which soured Varek's expression. He didn't push back again, however—just returned to the performance. Falier came back as well. They were like him, these dragons, but with one crucial difference. Falier had found a reason to fight. Somehow, he needed to help them find theirs, too.

Falier came before the ice dragons for the third and final time. Three days wasn't much, but with battle looming and the new possibility of finding dreki clans, they couldn't spare more. So today when they stood before the alphas, the dragons were laden with packs, ready to leave when Falier gave the word.

Of course, the sight of dragons bearing human packs instigated a debate on whether it was more logical or demeaning to carry things for humans. Or to carry humans, for that matter.

Falier allowed it for a moment, gathering his thoughts. One final argument, based in the one thing Falier, Graydonn, and Saynan agreed these teachers of wisdom and legends might fight for. With a steeling breath, Falier snapped up the next pause.

"Great Shironn and Riantha, our remaining time is short, so I must interrupt this debate. Over the last few days, we have seen much of your clan. We have admired your masterful artwork and experienced a mere portion of the legends you keep. Your openness in inviting members of other clans to glean from your wisdom has impressed me and would awe Alísa."

He paused a moment, allowing the compliments to sit. Before he could continue, Riantha spoke.

"Then you understand why we cannot accompany you. We cannot maintain the peace of our mountain, which allows others to sojourn here, if we involve ourselves in the conflicts of the lowlands. Nor can we risk the lives of our people, who hold the stories and wisdom of the Maker to shape future generations of dragons."

She waited, expectant. Falier drummed his fingers on his thigh and came a step further into the main floor of the cave.

"I see your concerns, yet I wonder. If an'reik conquer the lowlands, will dragons still seek your counsel? With all who dare to oppose the an'reik gone, who will you teach? The an'reik do not seem the types to tolerate teachings of the Maker's wisdom."

A few dragons above growled or clicked thoughtfully. Falier braced himself for another turn toward debate, but Riantha responded first.

"The Maker will ensure we can continue working our sacred calling." She puffed out a plume of swirling ice. *"I do not fear the future you see."*

"We are not called to battle, young Singer's-mate," Shironn growled. *"Our responsibility is safeguarding that which the Maker has entrusted to us. Nothing more."*

"But hasn't he entrusted you with them?" Falier gestured to the fire dragons above. *"Your students, who come to you for guidance? How can you instruct them if they're dead, or else under the influence of an'reik who teach their own 'wisdom'?"*

Falier lifted his hands in entreaty. *"Your people are not only learned, you also have physical abilities none can match. Your dances have made you the most agile dragons in the world, able to evade like none I've ever seen. And your ice can combat one of the enemy's most dangerous weapons, something we have no other defense against."*

He let out a puff of air. *"I know you are peaceful, as is your work. I'm from a similar background. My family harbored travelers needing a place to stay, provided for them and for our village, arbitrated meetings, and brought them together with stories and songs. Although I was unfamiliar with war, I was forced to fight when my people were attacked. I even left to push the battle further from them. I know what I ask of you."*

He gestured to the dragons around the cave, eyes passing from dragon to dragon as he hoped that even if the alphas wouldn't hear him, others might.

"I once thought that joining the fight meant I had to leave everything else behind, but that isn't true. We fight so that our callings may live on, so that those we serve through them live on. There are anam *who need your help—yours specifically. Without it, many will die or fall to the an'reiks' lies. Ensure future generations know the truth by standing for this one. Stand with us."*

Shironn growled so low that the sound shook droplets from the icicles in the ceiling. *"We will not dishonor the Maker's provision of safety by leaving it. Nor will we risk our dragons and their knowledge in a war that is not ours."*

Falier looked the alpha in the eye, letting its chilling glow pierce him before looking away. *"I suppose that is between you and the Maker, then."* He addressed the rest of the ice clan. *"Between each one of you and him."*

Turning around, Falier marched to Komi's side and hoisted himself up behind Trísse. Talons scraped and wings shifted as surprise filled the cavern.

"We did not dismiss you," Riantha said. *"There are more matters to discuss."*

"No." Falier sat tall. *"I have other clans to approach. If anyone here would fight, look to Rorenth's former mountain."*

He felt for his squad-mates in the link. Those newer to Alísa's clan held questions, but the others understood his abrupt exit.

"We've done all we can here," Falier said. *"More argument will do nothing. If any follow, they are who we need."*

Graydonn thumped his tail on the ground. *"The Maker knows."*

The rest of the dragons repeated the phrase and readied themselves for flight.

"So we admit defeat?" Jossen asked.

Falier shook his head. *"We strategically retreat, and we move to another front where we might actually win. Let's go."*

With a growl of resolve, Komi leapt into the open air of the cavern. She circled up toward the exit, the squad behind her. As they went, Falier tried to catch as many glowing eyes as possible. Some watched him, while others looked at the ground or left the main chamber. Then the ice tunnel surrounded him, and his clanmates flew from the caves.

"*Where to now?*" Graydonn asked as they descended.

The others, too, waited on the answer, hanging on to the clan-link as to a tent's support rope. Falier looked east.

"*Once we hit the space between territories, we head to the forests. Ska, can you find the dreki who helped us against Rorenth?*"

Ska chirped, peeking out of the bag. "*Dragons.*"

Falier shook his head. "*No, dreki. The——*"

Ska growled and pointed his muzzle behind them. "*Dragons!*"

A dragon trumpeted as Falier searched the sky. Komi turned as well, flapping hard to stall her momentum and face the mountain. Clouds obscured the cave entrance, but soon ten glittering white dragons and two fire dragons dropped through the canopy. Saynan trumpeted back at them, familial love washing through the mind-link. He flew for them, dipping below one and back-flipping over another. The other ice dragons banked, twisted, and flipped around them, each trumpeting long, melodious notes.

A sharp tang of awe rushed through the link.

"*But without the alphas?*" Varek asked. "*How could you know some would follow?*"

Falier grinned. "*Haven't you heard the histories of Alísa's clan——of Tsamen and Paili and how Alísa called out the dragons whose hearts aligned with her mission? They aren't just stories, you know.*"

Falier sent the last phrase with humor, which he hoped Varek caught. Jossen did, chuckling.

"*Singer's mate indeed. You didn't even need a song.*"

"*The song was more to keep the alphas asleep so they wouldn't retaliate. I don't think we need to fear attack here, though.*"

Wry humor rose from Varek. "*No, I suppose not.*"

Saynan led the newcomers to Graydonn and the others. Falier recognized Saynan's family among them. Once Saynan introduced everyone, he spoke to Falier.

"*What is your plan now that we have dragons to deliver?*"

"*You and Darrin lead these back to our mountain. They'll all need to train with riders as soon as possible. The rest of us will find that dreki clan.*"

Darrin glanced at him. "*Are there any messages you would have me deliver?*"

Falier hesitated. He didn't know Darrin well, but the offer was thoughtful.

"Just—tell Alísa I miss her and I'll return as quickly as I can."

The slayer nodded once and faced front again as Saynan led their new allies north. As they grew smaller in the distance, Falier set his eyes on the east. He blew out a breath, stealing himself for the unknowns ahead.

"Let's go."

54

SIGNS & SIGNALS

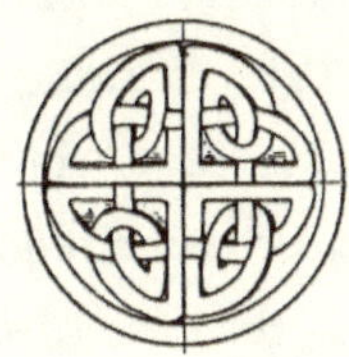

The skies around Alísa's mountain were full of dragons. Squads of eleven or twelve spread out on all sides for training maneuvers. Soon they would join for war-games, but many were still learning how to keep their riders from sliding off when they banked.

"Do you think we should split up the ice dragons so there's one per squad?" Sesína asked, emerald eyes shining. *"Or should we have an ice squad?"*

Saynan had come back into dreki communication range only a few hours ago. It had taken work to decipher their message, but her and Sesína's ability to understand Rís had improved significantly in the last few weeks.

Alísa leaned into Sesína's turn. *"I'm not sure. It makes some sense to place them in a single squad to focus on fire an'reik, but Saynan might have different thoughts."*

"I can't wait to see them tomorrow! The images from Darrin's drek made the ice dragons look huge!" She pondered a moment. *"Though, I suppose any dragon would seem huge to a drek."*

Rís chirped from his spot on Alísa's shoulder. Over the past few days, those skilled with a needle sewed leather pads for the squad leaders and their assigned dreki. These teardrop-shaped pads curved over each shoulder with points that jutted out. They went on over the rider's head with arm-loops to stabilize the pads during flight. They weren't perfect yet—the leather straps in Alísa's armpits were rather uncomfortable—but they presented a better option than riding in bags, stuffing between layers of clothing, or tearing apart a rider's arm.

Giving a mental command to Rís, Alísa reached out to the squad leaders. *"Time to switch out. Koriana and Briek first, then everyone else in a circle."*

Affirmatives flowed to her, and a few dragons trumpeted acknowledgements. As each squad moved to the mountain, Alísa checked in with them. How did the riders fare? Did they need a break before hopping onto the next dragon? There were fewer slayers than dragons, so many riders pulled double training shifts to give all dragons the opportunity to learn to bear a rider.

The nature of Alísa's powers caused the imbalance. If an alpha refused her, she could silence them and still call out some of their clanmates. This didn't work for slayers, however. Some of Lorin's warriors remained after his departure, and one chief who rejected her request allowed his men to come if they wished. Beyond those two, the rest of the clans stayed behind simply because of their chief's stubbornness. All told, twenty-three of her allied dragons were without riders—thirty-five, counting Saynan's newcomers.

For the dozenth time, Alísa questioned the charge to only accept slayers willing to ride and dragons willing to carry. What if the call wasn't truly the Maker's but her own? What if by turning away those warriors, she led everyone else to their deaths? As it stood, the an'reik army outnumbered her forces by more than double if a dragon-rider pair counted as one unit.

Sesína nudged her mind. *"You're stuck in your thoughts again. I also thought the charge was from the Maker. Farren agrees."*

"And the rest of my questions?"

Sesína let out a steamy breath. *"I don't know. If the point is humility, I think the dragons without riders should also fight. They've proven themselves by showing up. And you're right, our numbers are—not great."*

"But they won't have a rider for psychic protection. We'll have to figure out a different strategy for them." Alísa checked the sun's position. *"You ready for the next training phase? We need to finish before dark."*

Sesína snorted. *"You humans and your terrible night-vision."*

For the following hour, Alísa alternated between strength songs and songs to weaken the dragons, forcing riders to focus to know when to block. She had never tried a weakening song before. It felt contrary to her very purpose to take from her allies rather than give. But if Kallar sang to hurt her people, they needed to be ready.

During all of this, Rís helped her transfer the songs from squad to squad. The tiny drek switched between his clanmates with incredible ease, always sure where they were. Would other dreki be similar if Falier found them?

Alísa rubbed her arm against the growing chill. It had been nearly a week since Falier left. That wasn't long—she understood that—yet they had hardly been apart for a day for the past three months. Compared to that, a week was forever. And now it would be longer. Falier's idea of finding more dreki was excellent, and she was proud of him for taking it on. Still, what she wouldn't give to have him flying on Graydonn beside Sesína right now.

She shook her head and forced herself back to the present, switching to a weakness song. She knew her strength songs like she knew Sesína. Weakness songs required effort.

If Kallar sang a weakening song, could she cancel his powers by singing for strength? He was strong already, and she didn't know if possession strengthened him further.

A dragon trumpeted behind her, the call high with anxiety. It shocked her singing to a stop.

"Was that—?"

"One of our scouts!" Sesína twisted and speared toward a blue dragoness. Alísa shivered. What if the an'reik had somehow moved faster than expected? They had done so before. She couldn't afford an attack now.

"Hail!" Alísa called to the scout once they were in range. *"What news?"*

"Singer! Slayers approach from multiple directions south and west." The dragoness' worry and fatigue washed over Alísa. *"Some troops as large as twenty. I think the villages that rejected you are rallying against us!"*

Alísa clenched her skirt in her fists. They wouldn't be so shortsighted, would they? Toronn said he expected her to fail, but she would at least weaken the an'reik before they reached his village. Attacking her at this point only hurt everyone.

"How far?"

"The closest is twenty miles out."

"Chrí," Alísa ordered Rís. Once she felt her uncle's squad, she spoke again. *"L'non, slayers approach our mountain. You and your squad will accompany me to find out what they want."* Another mental command brought all the squad leaders into her mind-link. *"Halt training and remain on standby. We might have trouble."*

As L'non's squad sped toward them, Alísa returned to the scout. *"Show us."*

"By Maker's wings."

The dragoness headed for the setting sun, Sesína behind her. Trusting L'non to catch up, they followed for miles, crossing more territory in a half-hour than the wayfarers could cross in a day.

Then Alísa saw them. Two squads on separate but converging paths through the hills, the south-most only five strong, the other perhaps twelve. Both groups carried the same standard, one that made Alísa's heart skip a beat.

White flag. And the group of twelve was waving theirs.

"See, Singer?" The scout said, still anxious. *"According to other scouts, there are more of them approaching the southern perimeter!"*

"Peace," Alísa said. *"The white flag is like your truce boulders. They aren't here for war."*

Her heart pounded. There were no villages nearby, no reasons to hold a standard of any kind while marching, unless they were trying to signal someone who could show up suddenly. Someone like her.

Telling L'non to stand by, Alísa and Sesína descended toward the twisting flag. Alísa waved her arms in the air, signaling that this dragon bore a rider. If only she carried something white to confirm peace. When one slayer waved back, Sesína landed.

Rís flapped his wings from Alísa's shoulder. *"Azron!"*

Alísa studied the slayers. He was correct. She recognized about half of these men from her home village. There was the slayer who trained her father and uncle, and behind him a young man who used to mock her stammer.

"Hail, Azron!" She raised a hand of truce. "W—what brings you here?"

The trainer—the oldest of the group—came forward. He placed his fist over his heart. "Praise the Maker, you found us. We weren't sure which mountain your clan claimed, but hoped your scouts would recognize the white flag."

Alísa cringed inwardly. She needed to explain that to the dragons.

The trainer continued. "Toronn was a fool. We will not stand by as this dark army ravages other villages, even if fighting means having to trust dragons. If you have proven them, Karns-daughter, it will be enough."

Something softened inside Alísa, the edges of her anxiety easing back as a memory of Bria rushed through her. *'The Maker alone can convince some hearts to join the fight.'*

Is this of you, Maker?

Behind him, more slayers placed their fists over their hearts. Another man in his forties stepped forward and dipped his head.

"When our brothers of Azron stopped in Perrin, Chief N'lan sent them away immediately. I, however, rallied a few men."

A slayer from a different village said something similar. Only two from his village, yet Alísa grinned like a fool.

"You are all most welcome. I will send d—dragons and riders to retrieve you. The lead dragon will c-c-carry a white flag." She reached for Sesína's spines and hauled herself up. "I shall see you on the mountain."

From there, Alísa and Sesína traveled south to meet the other marching slayers, one group after another. All bore white flags and similar stories. From some villages, only one man had disobeyed his chief's orders. From others, like Azron, six or seven had defied their chief to fight the an'reik. With Farren's help, Alísa totaled her troops that evening.

"Well," he said, lowering the graphite. "We've now got the opposite problem, though not as bad. We've twelve more slayers than dragons."

Twelve. Alísa's hand flew to her mouth. She heaved a sob, drawing a concerned look from Farren. She hadn't told him—in the excitement of the slayers, she had forgotten.

Sesína clawed the ground. *We heard from Saynan. He's returning tomorrow, with twelve new dragons.*

Another sob. It felt wrong to cry at this. She should shout for joy. Instead, awe overpowered her, drenching her in confirmation that the call to limit her forces was indeed the Maker's and not her own misguided hopes.

The an'reik's army still outnumbered them over two-to-one, counting each dragon-rider pair as a unit. She didn't know how to fight such odds, but maybe that wasn't her charge. Her fingers landed on her betrothal necklace and the twisting symbols in the tree's roots. Perhaps all the Maker required of her was to train those he provided and trust.

55

RAGE

Kallar opened his eyes. The world smelled of wood-smoke, fresh flowers, and a hint of cinnamon. Gia's house.

Memory stirred Kallar to full wakefulness. He pushed up from the bear-skin rug and found his astral muscles less sore than when he had fallen asleep. Same with the ever-present weight in his chest. How long had he slept? Fire still crackled in the hearth, and he certainly hadn't woken up to stoke it. Rain fell outside, though not as hard as before. No sounds of the keeper.

He let out a breath and stretched. He hadn't slept this well in ages. Honestly, he wasn't sure he had ever slept like this. Part of him resented that.

Something shifted to his left. Kallar whirled and pushed up into a crouch, reaching for his knife belt. He stopped before he could remember he carried no weapons, blinking at the figure in the chair.

R'lann. Except, it wasn't R'lann. This figure was older than his brother—perhaps in his early thirties. His tunic was the same blue one R'lann wore in his prison, but whole and spotless. In his soft smile, Kallar found their father, even though both R'lann and Kallar looked more like their mother. R'lann's glossy black hair was pulled back at the top and loose at the bottom aside from a few small warrior's braids.

"How was your rest?"

The voice was also R'lann's, but deeper and more mature. A kind voice, one that called to let one's guard down.

Kallar settled, but kept his eyes pinned on the strange visage. *"Fine."*

R'lann nodded. *"Good. I see you're in better shape."*

Kallar followed his gaze to the exposed skin of his arms. Sure enough, the gashes from the keeper's tortures were closing. A few of the smaller cuts were light scars now, while the deeper ones only trickled emotion mists rather than hemorrhaging.

He looked back up. *"Are you going to say anything useful, or just state the obvious? What is this place? Is the real R'lann alright? Where is the keeper?"*

"R'lann is fine," not-R'lann said. *"And, as I said before, the keeper cannot harm you here. You are safe within this space."*

As *he'd* said before. Same visitor, different face. Kallar realized too late that his mists were orange-gold. Nothing was hidden here, not even the fear he had spent his life keeping at bay. That realization turned the mists an angry white.

"I don't want to be 'safe'. Not while R'lann is out there, imprisoned by those thrice-damned an'reik! I should be fighting for him, not cowering here."

"You cannot defeat the keeper. You know this. You tried for a month with no success."

"I don't care." Kallar clenched his teeth, but the fear mists still came sprinkled throughout the anger. *"At least I hadn't abandoned him. He's alone now— that thing is torturing him with my body!"*

"R'lann is not alone." Not-R'lann looked Kallar in the eyes. *"He has never been alone. He has told you as much."*

Kallar scoffed, breaking their eye-contact.

"Do you believe your brother a liar? Or delusional?"

"Then why would the Maker forsake one of his devoted servants, giving him to those monsters?" Kallar clenched his fists against his thighs. *"What about the an'reik's army? The people they've lied to, or possessed? Those they killed because they couldn't possess them, like Pa? What about them? How can you say the Maker cares when he allows all this?"*

Kallar pinned not-R'lann with a stare, waiting for an answer. Not-R'lann said nothing, but his eyes held the same compassion the visage of Farren held. One that spoke of things he, in all his mistakes, did not deserve.

"Save your pity." Kallar straightened, white rage mists rising higher around him. *"What about those dragons Alísa claims are* anam? *Soul-bearers—the Maker's children—yet he allows people like me to slaughter them, and all for a lie! Do you know how many I've killed? How many I've tortured because I believed them monsters?"*

Sorrow laced the edges of R'lann's gaze, but the compassion didn't leave. His hands moved into his lap, fingers laced. And he remained infuriatingly silent.

"Of course, some are monsters," Kallar said, memories running through his mind. *"My mother may have slain innocent dragons like I have, but she did good for the world too—protected humanity. Yet it wasn't an innocent dragon that killed her! She died at the flames of a terror attacking our village, and only because—"*

Kallar's breath shuddered. He clenched his fists in an attempt to stave off the ice blue guilt now swirling amidst the rage and fear. *"She didn't deserve to die, not for my mistake. The Maker should have protected her! Isn't he big enough to fix the mistakes of a child who simply wanted to watch his revered mother singing dragons from the sky?!"*

The keeper roared outside, and with its call the painful memories resurfaced. In his mind's eye, the red dragoness Paili dove toward him. He should have been in the dragon shelter under the house. Should have gotten himself and R'lann to safety. But nothing could hurt him while Mamá was near.

And nothing did. Allara, in her full battle gear of blue scales and bronze, blocked Paili's flames with her shield. She let out a war cry that sapped even Kallar of strength. As the red dragoness passed overhead, his mother turned angry, fearful eyes on him. Urged him and R'lann into the shelter as the monster bore down on them. Closed the stone door just as the fire reached her.

"Kallar."

Kallar jumped as a hand on his shoulder yanked him from the memories. R'lann locked eyes with him as the keeper pounded against the door.

"It cannot harm you here."

The compassion was still there, unbearable in its tenderness. Kallar twisted away.

"No! Don't you understand? By all rights, it should have me!" Kallar growled against the keeper's howling. *"What about Karn? He didn't deserve to die! He was actually becoming better. He changed where I, in my flaming arrogance and anger, wouldn't. Can't your Maker so full of wisdom and justice do anything right?! Why can't he overrule my mistakes?"*

The keeper's shrieks grew louder, and the winds grew higher, each shattering against the house with a force that would kill any creature unfortunate enough to be outside. He should be there, dashed to pieces against the stone. Even inside, Kallar fought not to shudder with the weight of it. He grasped onto the anger swirling between him and not-R'lann and shouted.

"The Maker has never cared—why should he now?" The white mists built up

around him in a terrible pulsing mass he couldn't hold. *"Answer me! Why should he shield me from it when he didn't shield Karn from me?! I didn't care, didn't change, didn't do anything. I belong out there!"*

The mist exploded from his grip. Their raging torrent upended the chairs. Shattered the flower vase. Blew out the fire in the hearth. It swirled through the house, mirroring the terrible winds outside. In an instant, every bit of white rage exposed its true colors of fear, guilt, and dread. Wall-hangings tore free in his storm, one whipping across his face to draw more mist. The pile of wood toppled and collided with walls and furniture.

The shrieking scrapes against the walls became unbearable, grating against Kallar's ears till they felt like they bled. He covered them and shut his eyes tight, trying to block it all out. When that didn't work, he screamed, but even that couldn't drown out the keeper's claims on his mind, his soul.

This was what he deserved. He should be able to take it.

Idiot.

Coward.

Murderer!

Hands covered Kallar's ears, and the cacophony silenced. Startled, he looked up. The mists still swirled, ripping apart the interior of Gia's house, yet he heard nothing except R'lann's breaths. R'lann locked eyes with him and breathed slowly, prompting Kallar to follow his lead. Silently, Kallar did.

In. And out.

In. And out.

"You're right. You deserve to be out there," R'lann said. *"But you called for me, and I always come when my* anam *call."*

Kallar's heart stopped. Breath ceased, and the raging mists paused.

He hadn't heard that correctly.

He couldn't have.

Not-R'lann lifted his hands from Kallar's ears. As he did, the room stilled, though the wind continued to howl outside. Rage turned to fear as Kallar glanced between the window and not-R'lann. The keeper screamed its terrible lust for his blood. After all he had just said, surely it would be allowed to claim its prize.

Not-R'lann stood. *"It cannot harm you, but you are not yet ready to stop listening to it. I will distract it again."*

"You're—not going to send me out there? After everything I just accused you of?"

Not-R'lann was silent, his compassion seemingly the only thing remaining in the room. For a moment, staring at him, the keeper's cries quieted. But the winds came again and drew Kallar's gaze to the boarded window. The roars resumed.

Not-R'lann approached the door and ran a hand over its carvings. *"I am big enough for your anger."*

He passed through the oak panels into the storm. As with Farren, the keeper howled and gave chase as not-R'lann led it from the house.

Kallar's breaths came in shudders as the orange-gold mists faded into the gentle yellow of relief. He leaned forward, pressing his fists into his thighs, then startled straight as a hot tear fell to the back of his hand.

Swiping the remnants away, he considered the room. Everything was in shambles and cast into darkness. Needing to do something, he searched the wreckage for the logs previously stacked by the fireplace. He also managed to find the iron and flint for the fire.

Exhaustion spread over him, but he slowly cleared the bear-skin rug of broken pieces and fallen items. As rain pattered against the roof, he tried to puzzle out what just happened. Was this all imagined—his tortured mind desperate for comfort? Or was it exactly as it appeared?

By the time he cleared the rug of debris, he was too tired to continue. He grabbed the black mourning shawl and the blue blanket from the chair, folding the shawl into a pillow. Laying down, he covered himself with the blanket, though he still shivered as thoughts swirled in his head.

This must all be a dream. Who could scream and spit in the Maker's face and live?

56

THE SEARCH

Without the dragons and dreki, Falier was sure he would be lost. Logically, he knew they could simply fly above the canopy and see their exact location. But in the forest's darkness, being led along the space between dreki territories, the squad seemed hopelessly lost. It didn't help that Ska and Laen had an annoying habit of flying off and expecting everyone to keep up.

It took a day and a half to reach the spot Ska considered their best chance for finding the other dreki clan—a few miles northeast of Russig Lake. Initially, Falier assumed they could simply land in the other clan's territory and have Ska reach out to them. Easy. Except, upon further discussion, he discovered that entering another clan's territory without a direct invitation would almost certainly mean death for the dreki and dragons. Humans might enter unharmed, but Falier wasn't willing to split up.

The setting sun cast further darkness on the forest and they began setting up camp. As with previous nights, the humans gathered firewood while the dragons hunted, each with an image from Ska that would keep them from stumbling into dreki territories. They had skirted a couple for two days now and were nearing a third. Ska was certain the correct clan was near, but unsure which side of the safe-zone they owned.

As Falier and Trísse searched for wood, he sang a strength song—one Alísa used during the fight against Rorenth. He shook his head as his voice cracked at the end of the verse.

"I don't know how Alísa manages it, singing all the time for training and battle." He pointed at a fallen log. "Think we can use swords like an ax?"

Trísse considered. "We'll need to be careful not to damage the blades. This end looks more decayed."

Falier looked where Trísse indicated. Slightly wet, but with the dragons' fire, it would probably work. He drew his sword and started hacking.

Trísse crossed her arms. "You've been singing from sunrise until now. Alísa takes breaks when she can."

Falier pulled back and wiped his brow. "I take breaks."

"Five-minute intervals over eight hours. I think you've seared it into my brain. Don't you know any other songs?"

He swung again, the impact reverberating up his arm. "I know plenty" — *thwack*— "but none that I'm sure she used" —*thwack*— "during the battle when these dreki" —*thwack*— "allied with us."

As the section came apart, Falier stepped away for Trísse to take a turn. "I just hope we're in the right place. I'm beginning to think Ska knows less about this other clan than he let on."

"They *are* rather overconfident creatures." Trísse hacked at her section. "You really believe they'll recognize the song?"

"Considering how long Alísa was singing it, *without breaks*, yeah. Dreki have an ear for music."

After another ten minutes, they had the decaying log split up fairly well. Falier grabbed four sections and returned to camp, Trísse following. Selene and Taz were already back with a nice pile of kindling and larger fallen branches.

Back, and kissing.

"Ugh, at least hide behind a tree or something." Falier took his duty as a younger brother very seriously. "You're going to ruin my appetite."

"I'm with him," Trísse said. "Next time, we're splitting you two up."

Taz grinned. "Seems we have no choice but to get our kisses in now, right, love?"

It seemed Selene took her duty to gross him out seriously too, because she planted an exaggeratedly large kiss on her pursuer's lips in response. Falier rolled his eyes and shook his head.

"I'm so glad there's more wood to go back for."

He turned around and hurried away, though it was mostly for show. He was happy for them. Still, he had to get in his quota of annoying little brother moments wherever possible.

Trísse walked alongside him, silent. Her expression was neutral, but sorrow wafted from her. Falier's heart folded in on itself. He hadn't spoken with her about Tern yet, unsure how. But remaining quiet didn't sit well anymore.

"Trísse," he ventured, "about Tern—"

"You think you killed him."

Falier stopped, mouth opening and shutting twice as words abandoned him. Trísse continued a few paces, then faced him.

"It wasn't hard to figure out. I know what happened between you, you've been suspiciously silent around me, and, while I may not be as strong as Alísa, I *am* an empath."

Falier blew out a breath. Of course. "I'm sorry. I shouldn't have stayed quiet. You deserve better, I just—didn't know how to tell you. But I did push him away. I made him join the ground troops."

Trísse crossed her arms. "You couldn't *make* him do anything. That *was* the problem, yes?"

Falier drummed his fingers on his thigh. "Still, what I did destroyed any chances he might have given me."

"He already wanted to leave the riders."

"But I—"

"Look, do you *want* me to hate you?" Trísse's eyes flashed. "Because I'd really rather not. Tern was a fool."

Her voice hitched, and she looked away. After a moment, she returned.

"Tern was a fool who couldn't see what he didn't want to. Every day, he told me Komi was keeping me captive, despite all the evidence against it. He didn't try in training. He hurt his dragon partner. Honestly, he would probably still be dead if he had flown, only his partner would have died too."

She shook her head, speaking more quietly. "And through it all, I still loved him. Guess I'm a fool, too."

Falier remained silent. He wanted to tell her it wasn't foolish to wish for someone to become better, but words, especially his words, wouldn't help this. He waited for her to speak again.

Finally, her eyes returned to him. "He chose to fight on the ground, and he was good with a sword. So, if it's all the same to you, I'd rather hate the an'reik who killed him, not you. Alright?"

Falier nodded once, not sure if her statements brought relief or more guilt. But this wasn't about him. He took a cautious step forward.

"I don't think I ever said—I'm sorry for your loss, Trísse."

She swallowed. "Thank you." Turning around, she finished the march back to the firewood and began picking up logs. "By the way, if I blamed you, you'd know. I can be—abrasive when I want."

Falier forced a smile. "You?"

Trísse shot a glare at him, one that melted into a good-natured chuckle. "Come on, fearless leader. Don't make me do all the work."

Silence fell as they gathered, and as they walked, Falier sang again. Trísse was right—this song was getting tiresome. But he didn't know another method of telling the dreki that the Dragon Singer needed them.

Soon, Jossen and Varek returned with more wood, and the dragons with meat. Hwinn brought back a wild turkey, while Harenn dragged a young buck in his jaws. Mennáli complained, yet again, that forests were too cramped for dragons to hunt properly.

Selene and Falier prepared the bird while the dragons split the deer. Adult dragons only required one large meal a week and adolescents needed one every three-to-four days. They had shared a deer almost every day since leaving the ice caves, so they were keeping up their strength, but they would need a more substantial meal soon. How much longer could he devote to this search before calling it a lost cause and getting his clanmates to a more stable environment?

Soon the turkey roasted on a spit Taz and Jossen fashioned from stripped branches. Trísse cautioned it would catch fire with how close the bases were to the flames, but they managed to roast the bird without incident.

Falier ate quickly, then went to work on Graydonn's spines. He could sit on Graydonn's back now, and they would most likely be able to fly together. Pulling out a file he had packed for this purpose, Falier hoisted himself up and began filing the third and final broken spine.

Soon the forest came alive with sounds of night. Creatures tramped through the underbrush, owls hooted, and wolves howled in the far distance.

Harenn growled as the wind rustled the trees. *"I don't understand how anything can sleep outside a cave. It's too—open."*

Taz chuckled, elbowing the dragon's chest. "Worried something might try to eat you?"

"I might." Hwinn crouched like he was about to pounce. *"I'm still hungry!"*

Harenn snorted at the smaller adolescent. *"You joke, but there are stories. I've said it before, I don't like this mission. Dreki hate dragons, and we're right in the middle of three clans. Who's to say none of them will cross the barrier and attack us?"*

Ska barked his indignation. *"Law!"*

"Dragons and humans break laws—why not dreki?" Harenn shuddered. *"Dragons who enter the forests vanish, and most tales blame the fae."*

P'raenn growled softly, glancing into the darkness. *"Do humans have legends about them, too?"*

Selene sidled closer to Taz. "Yes, but they vary widely. Some say they are malevolent and lure people so deep into the forest they get lost forever. Others claim they're mischief-makers who steal things from people's homes—"

"I'm fairly certain they've stolen at least ten of my socks," Taz said, poking Laen on Selene's shoulder. "Do they make good nests or something?"

The drek chomped at his finger playfully. *"Toys."*

Taz and Selene chuckled, and Falier took up the conversation. "But these are the only ones we've ever met. They're harmless—friendly allies and dance partners."

Ska growled. *"No."* The word came with the image of a large animal's skeleton, one with sharp teeth and claws. A mountain bear, perhaps?

Harenn half-stood, wings flaring. *"See? They're more powerful than they look."*

Ska chittered a laugh and Laen joined in. Mennáli huffed.

"They're just trying to scare you. 'Mischief-makers' seems to be the most accurate legend."

Trísse offered her last piece of turkey to Ska, who eagerly fluttered to her shoulder. "Who says they're a monolith? Can't they differ from clan to clan as they do drek to drek?"

"I dunno." Taz grinned and poked Laen again. "They all seem the same to me."

Laen leapt onto his head and arched her neck to look Taz in the eye upside-down. She hissed, wings rattling.

Selene reached up from under Taz's arm and stroked the drek's mane. "Now, now, teasing just means he likes you."

Laen leaned into her touch and purred, meanwhile slapping Taz's face with her fuzzy tail. Taz laughed and brushed it away.

"Okay, okay, you are your own drek. I give."

Laen hopped down onto Selene's lap, curling up like a cat.

Taz kissed Selene's temple. "You always were a drek whisperer."

"You'd think they'd have flocked to her already," Falier muttered, looking off into the forest. "Ska, is there any other way to get their attention that doesn't involve entering their territory uninvited?"

Ska chirped apologetically. *"Sing."*

Falier sighed, looking at the others. "One more time before bed, then?"

Varek groaned. "I'm never going to get that song out of my head."

"At least be glad it's the former holder singing," Jossen said. "He stays in tune, unlike some of us."

Varek snorted a laugh. "Small blessings."

Falier grinned and began.

That blasted song stayed in Falier's dreams, constantly in the background as he fought through a nightmare full of an'reik and dying squad-mates. When he finally figured out it was a dream, he tried to alter it. Perhaps make Alísa's song give them all strength so they wouldn't fall.

It didn't work. The an'reik swept Graydonn out from under him, leaving Falier flying alone, without wings to bank. A dragon swooped down at him, its gaping maw alight with fire.

Time to wake up.

Wake up!

He woke just before the flames hit and shivered at the unexpected cold. He attempted to roll over, but his body wasn't quite awake yet. Breathing slowly, he listened to the song and waited for his limbs to work. A few stars peered at him through the canopy.

That was odd. Normally, Graydonn kept his wing over him. That was why he felt so cold.

With the song as his impetus, Falier pushed himself up as the chorus began.

Wait. Song?

Yes, the one from his dream. The one he'd been singing for the past few days. Someone sang it nearby.

No, not *someone.*

"Líse?"

He scanned the forest, his heartbeat quickening. That was definitely her.

And she was close.

Standing, he stepped away from the fire and toward the voice. His eyesight should become better quickly, then he would find her.

The song stopped.

"Líse?"

A soft giggle rose from the direction of the song. "I hoped you'd wake."

Finally, he found her. Her hair fell around her shoulders, loose and perfectly curled. Her dress swished as she emerged from behind a tree, an off-the-shoulder white chemise with a green overdress embroidered with gold thread. With a smile that would compel anyone to fall over themselves to please her, she beckoned.

Falier released a breath and came closer. "What are you doing here?"

She stepped further back into the shadows. "You've been gone so long, I wanted to see how you fared." She bit her lip. "To see you."

The ache he had felt earlier that evening lifted, replaced by a warm calm. "Can't say I'm disappointed. But shouldn't you be training new recruits?"

"Yes, I must return soon, but first" —she smiled coyly— "a private moment would be nice, don't you think?"

Before he could respond, she spun and pushed deeper into the forest. Heart thumping, Falier followed, only for her to quicken her pace with a teasing chuckle. He laughed as he tried to catch her, weaving through the trunks. He lost her at one point, but she took up the song again. Breathless, he continued, relying more on sound than sight in the thick darkness. The fire's light was far behind him now, but that didn't matter. Alísa would know the way back.

"Líse?"

Her voice rose to his left, and he turned to follow. Then came a giggle to his right.

"Where are you?"

"Here."

He whirled and saw her shadowy silhouette. Holding out his hands in a plea for her to stay, he stepped toward her.

A sharp pain stabbed at his earlobe, causing him to gasp. He swiped at the space beside his ear and searched for the source.

"Falier?" Alísa said, concerned.

Another pain, this one at his arm. Something bit him.

"What—?"

A loud bark sounded in his injured ear. Falier twisted to find two sapphire eyes staring at him in the darkness.

"Wake!" Ska ordered. *"Wake! Wake! Wake!"*

The drek's words pushed at Falier's mind like a mop at a nasty stain. Falier struggled to breathe as a deep sense of danger replaced his previous calm.

Ska chirped in fright and dove away as a green light rushed after him. Falier searched for Ska but caught many other lights in the trees instead. They cast an eerie glow on the landscape.

Heart pounding, Falier looked for Alísa but only found Graydonn a few feet away. The dragon followed a glowing purple light, steps slow and amber eyes dim.

Falier's hand went to the empty spot where his sword should have been. He left it back at camp! That realization snapped him fully into the present.

Dreki. And not nice ones.

He shored up his telepathic shield and started for Graydonn, then saw Selene, Taz, and the rest all around him. Most followed an unfamiliar drek, eyes locked as though mesmerized. Selene and Hwinn, however, appeared awake. Hwinn bit and clawed at a thick briar that held Selene's skirts captive, the dragon's fearful whines now plain to Falier's freed ears.

Movement in his periphery sent Falier into a panicked sprint as three glowing dreki speared straight for Selene.

57

OUT OF TIME

Alísa started awake in the eerie red glow of Rís' wing-baubles. The drek's urgent barks echoed off the cave floor.

"Attack! Scouts!"

Alísa sat up, hitting her head on Sesína's wing and startling the dragoness. *"Who, and where?"*

Rís sent one of Alísa's scouting pair's names and the image of a mountain two hours away.

Alísa grabbed her overdress. *"Sesína, send someone to wake the other caves. We'll wake the slayers here. We're going into battle."*

Sesína trumpeted an alarm as Alísa pulled her overdress over her nightdress and tied it together. She looked to Rís while strapping on her shoulder pads. *"Were our scouts attacked, or did they find a cave under attack?"*

"Found."

"Who is attacking?"

An image of dragons. *"An'reik."*

"Just the dragons?"

Affirmative.

Alísa's heart pounded. Two hours away. A single clan wouldn't last that long against the numbers Rís showed her. They might all be dead before she arrived.

"Rís, call the other scouts." Praise the Maker, she had thought to send a drek with every scouting pair. *"Some are close. They may be able to help. Tell them to try to get the attacked clan to retreat. If they come toward us, we can meet them and push back their pursuers."*

"Dreki."

Rís glowed in front of her, wing-baubles lighting in the way his kind did when they all connected. Anticipation flowed from him, like he was waiting for her to give him a command. She just had, but he apparently wanted something else.

"I don't understand."

"Dreki." He sent an image of all of their dreki—sixteen in total. *"Fast."*

"You're—saying you can get there faster than we can."

Rís gave a growling chirp, one that spoke of his readiness to fight. *"Help."*

Alísa pressed her lips together. The dreki were powerful, but sixteen was a tiny clan. Their former clan had been thirty or forty strong. Still, if they could help the defending dragons escape…

"Yes. Go."

Rís chirped, swooped around her in a circle, then trilled a long, loud call, his wing-baubles fully aglow. The rest of the dreki dove toward him and together they sped for the cave entrance. If Alísa had blinked, she would have missed them.

"They became insubstantial," Sesína said, awed. *"Do you think they can phase through the air itself, flying without resistance?"*

"They do that when it's windy and they want the wind to pass through them," Alísa said, grabbing onto Sesína's spines and hauling herself up. *"I've never thought to apply it to plain flying. What's our status?"*

Sesína trotted, heading for the entrance. *"Dezra and Rassím are waking the other dragons."*

"Good. Have Briek and L'non get the slayers organized. We have little time."

An hour into the flight, Alísa saw glowing eyes ahead.

"Dragons approaching," Alísa said. *"Ready yourselves."*

She scanned the astral plane. The dragons became fully visible there, each a bright outline. The lead dragon carried a hatchling on its back.

Relief flooded Alísa. *"They got some out! Keep the attackers off their backs. Slayers, watch for shields. Don't mind-spear unless you're certain it's safe. Go!"*

Roars and trumpets sounded from the squads behind her, each group breaking off to approach from a different direction. Sesína speared forward as well, falling into Koriana's squad. They went high, and as they rose, Alísa sang to call the dreki to her. Without them, the dragons' emotions would overwhelm her.

> Dreki, dreki, shining bright
> Dreki, come in winged flight
> Dreki, dreki, hear my plight
> Dreki, arm us for our fight

Her mind flooded with the dreki collective's consciousness, a swirling river of anger and determination. They separated. As Rís fluttered to her shoulder, Alísa sang, trusting him to direct her strength as he did in training. The night was a mess of shadows blocking out the stars, slivers of moonlight glinting off scales, and eye-lights burning with battle.

A man screamed to Alísa's left, and she twisted to see a shock of fire crash into one of her dragons. It coursed over the dragon's scales, catching in them as it consumed the rider. Hellflames! The dragon roared its agony and fell, its cry lodging in Alísa's heart as its pain crashed over her.

Koriana's commanding tone entered the squad-link. *"Ice, now!"*

She banked after the an'reik with super-heated breath, the squad following. Saynan's father rushed to the front, his anxiety shuddering through the astral plane. Alísa changed her lyrics to push courage to him. None of the ice dragons had seen battle before.

Koriana at his side, Saynan's father twisted after the enemy, somehow propelling his massive body through the air with ease. A volley of burning cold rushed from his mouth, catching in the an'reik's tail and yanking a screech from its jaws.

"Duck!"

Alísa followed Sesína's command as another an'reik dove at them, its wicked talons spread. Sesína pulled her wings in and dropped out of reach while their wing-dragon slammed into their attacker. The dragons grappled above them and Sesína swirled back up to help, catching another enemy's wing in her talons. It pulled away before she could rip it through. Rather than give chase, Sesína dove to help their grappling wing-dragon. The an'reik dragon retreated and Sesína flew back to the squad. Breaking apart would only make them more vulnerable.

Rís shifted Alísa's song to the next few squads, and the battle continued. By the time they switched to the third group, the enemy was retreating. Alísa ordered her army to chase them down, but kept her gaze on the ground. The human an'reik camp would be near, and though they could challenge the an'reik dragons, they weren't ready to face them all.

Too soon, the watch-fires of the enemy camp came into view. Five fires, and the astral plane revealed many people out and awake.

"Fall back!" Alísa ordered. *"Now!"*

A dragon roared in pain as a psychic spear hit it. Another hit to her right, and then the riders put up their psychic shields. Koriana pulled up and away, leading her squad back north. Sesína twisted after her while Alísa watched to make sure everyone else retreated. She shuddered as her eyes fell on the an'reik camp again.

There's more of them now. Holy Maker, what do we do?

"This isn't the only cave between us and them," Sesína whispered. *"We need to evacuate them."*

Alísa shook her head. *"We're out of time."*

"We can stop along the way and warn them. They'll fit in the high caves if we squeeze."

Alísa worried the folds of her skirt. *"I mean to prepare. We need to speak to the squad leaders as soon as we get back."*

She reached out to Koriana and asked her to send scouts to the nearby caves, then went silent.

Great Maker, give us strength and wisdom.

Alísa directed Saynan and Aree to settle the rescued dragons. Only six of a clan of twenty escaped—one adult, two adolescents, and three hatchlings. Besides those deaths, a scout pair and a rider had perished, along with three other dragon-rider pairs and two dreki. The losses shuddered through Alísa and made her question the Maker's call again. If these warriors were handpicked to support her, why did the Maker let them die? If their lives were not guaranteed, what of victory against the an'reik?

These were questions she couldn't afford to worry about. She pushed them away as the truth of what they needed to do settled over her. The an'reik dragons had just proved they were within easy striking distance of her caves, which were full of human and dragon refugees. Her clan could likely keep those at bay, but the an'reik camp was also close. They had somehow moved two days' worth of foot travel in a single day before their last battle. If they did that again, they would arrive at her doorstep in two days. With so many cave entrances to guard and the non-combatants housed here, she couldn't wait any longer.

None of her caves were large enough for the near two-hundred dragons to congregate, so Alísa kept her warriors in the air. They circled just outside the mountain in a swirl of color, each eye aglow. A sight to behold, the full army flying together in the breaking of dawn.

When Saynan and Aree returned, Alísa reached out to everyone. Their emotions churned inside of her—sorrow, camaraderie, and curiosity chief among them. Tears trickled down her cheeks, but the sadness that would have choked her voice had no grip on her telepathy.

"You did well tonight, brothers and sisters. You fought bravely and rescued all we could. Having trained courageously with former enemies, you now bleed together for a common cause. Thanks to you, our world has changed forever."

Alísa let her words sink in and wondered if this was why the Maker had her gather these brave souls. Not to defeat the an'reik, but simply to bring humans and dragons together. Perhaps her band could not defeat the an'reik's staggering numbers, but the survivors might carry tales of alliance and awaken the rest of the country to fight.

Was this beautiful army mere kindling, meant to be burned up in order to spark something larger?

Sesína's presence wrapped around her mind like an embrace. *"That wouldn't be a terrible ending. To die for a cause and watch from the Maker's halls how our actions are ultimately used. An end worthy of remembrance."*

Hadn't her calling always been to bring the races together? Not to fight demons, but to broker peace among those falsely labeled as such.

A wash of peace came over Alísa, and she pressed her mind against Sesína's. *"A worthy end indeed."*

She reached out to the warriors again, strengthened by a calm assurance she could only attribute to Eldra Bria or the Maker himself.

"Tonight, you saw the enemy's strength and numbers. They will only grow as they gain others who refuse to evacuate. We are all who answered the call to stop them, and we

cannot afford to wait any longer. Each one of you chose to rise. Now it is time to fight!"

Sesína roared, and the dragons echoed her, the sound cracking through the air like thunder unleashed. With them rose the men, Briek and L'non leading them in a chant of "Fight!"

"We are with you, Singer!" Koriana declared, the authority in her tone prompting more roars and trumpets.

The clan's rising emotions filled Alísa to the brim, crashing against her questions and doubts. This was her calling, and no matter the outcome, she would be proud to fight alongside every one of these brave *anam.*

"Take what rest you can," Alísa said. *"We attack tomorrow at dawn. Until then, two scouting pairs and a drek will watch the enemy, switching frequently. All dragons must eat. Rassím and Dezra, L'non and H'sinth's squad, and dreki, to me. Everyone else, get some sleep."*

The swirling column of dragons dispersed, taking their riders to their cave before heading for their own.

The dreki reached her first, and her message for them was the quickest. *"Send your fastest flier to the Nissen River and fly south. Try to contact Ska and Laen and tell Falier his squad must return."*

Rís and Rann both barked acknowledgement. With a quick shared glow, they made their choice and a single blue drek speared into the distance, fast as the wind. Alísa dismissed the dreki and looked to the summoned dragons and riders. Despite multiple talks with Rassím and Farren, all of Alísa's ideas for finding and rescuing the possessed were severely lacking.

But now there was no more time. Her best plan would save some, but certainly not all. It was a necessary sacrifice to stop the advancing army.

She only hoped Kallar would not be one of those sacrifices.

58

A SHINING CHAOS

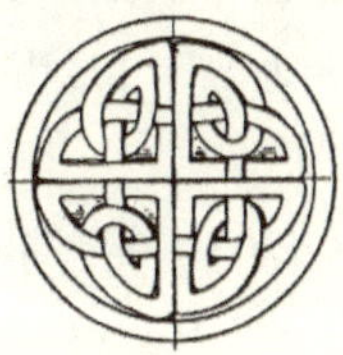

Kallar should have been used to finding another person in the room, but his heart raced all the same when he woke to someone occupying Pa's chair. Or perhaps he shouldn't be used to it—the idea of the Maker being in the same room was pure madness. Either way, he shot up, reaching for an absent dagger. Someday he would learn. Though that thought only reminded him he was stuck.

Here.

Forever.

Anger rose within him, and the person in the chair only exacerbated it.

"I thought you weren't like the keeper," Kallar growled, looking away. *"Why would you take this shape and remind me of what I've done? What you refused to stop?"*

"I did not choose this form, nor the others. You did. First a sage to give you peace in an unfamiliar situation, then a trusted family member with whom you could be angry. Now Karn."

Kallar waited, but the visage was silent. *"You won't explain why?"*

"What do you think?"

Kallar didn't want to think. Not about Karn. He stood and surveyed the mess his emotions had made. He spotted pieces of pottery—Gia's flower vase— and went to put them together in a pile.

"What happens now?" He kept his eyes fixed on his task. *"Do I just stay here forever?"*

"That is one option. You will have a chance to reclaim your body, but whether you'll take it depends entirely upon you."

Months ago, Kallar would have found hope in that. The old Kallar would have trusted he was strong and skilled enough for whatever task lay before him. Today, however, it only made him angry again.

"Why?" He yanked a red wall-covering off the floor. *"You're the Maker, aren't you? The songweavers claim you're stronger than any Eldra, and a keeper is only a piece of one. Why can't you just force it out?"*

Kallar shoved one end of the wall-covering onto its hook, then grabbed for another portion as its weight threatened to pull the decoration apart. Gia had spent months making this, and even his dislike of his stepmother couldn't cause him not to care.

As he struggled with the hanging, the Maker stood. Kallar pinned his gaze to the next hook and pulled the decoration up. He moved to grab another section, but found his unwanted companion already held it. Lifting it reverently, the Maker set the last two sections into their hooks. Oddly, his arms bore scars which Karn's hadn't.

"It's true," the Maker said, taking in the artwork. *"I am stronger, and in my strength, I created the natural order. I wrote the laws by which each realm works, and I gave certain strengths and abilities to humans, others to dragons, to dreki, and to the Eldír. Amidst it all, though Eldír can possess a mortal body that hasn't been given to me for protection, I made a way for my children to reclaim it."*

Kallar forced himself to look at the visage of Karn. *"But you're right here, right now. Yet you do nothing."*

"I am not here for your body, Kallar. I am here to rescue something far more precious, something I don't entrust even to my faithful Eldír—you."

The Maker met Kallar's eyes, and it seemed the depths of love and compassion they held sought to pour into him. Kallar looked away, grabbing a chair tipped over in the winds of yesterday's emotions and forcefully righting it.

"And what I fail to reclaim my body? You'll just let that thing keep working evil with it? It could be taking control over more dragons, or hurting R'lann or someone else. Why are you letting it go unchecked?"

He moved on to the next fallen wall-hanging. *"Better yet, why allow the an'reik to roam free in the first place, terrorizing villages and lodging keepers in people's heads?"*

"Would you prefer I were like the keepers? That I take control every time someone makes a choice I disapprove of?"

That thought stopped Kallar with a fear he had never known before the keeper killed Karn. Here, he found safety for the past two 'days', regardless of their actual length. But now, memory made Kallar shiver as though the dark, misty tendrils enclosed him again. Outside, he heard scratching against the stone walls.

A hand on his shoulder snapped him out of his stupefied fear. *"Eyes on me, son."*

Slowly, Kallar lifted his gaze to the face of his master. To the man who had been more a father to him than his biological father.

"It cannot harm you here," the Maker said, each word building around Kallar like interlocking shields, *"and I am nothing like it. I will not take control because choice is one of the most precious gifts I have given* iompróir anam. *Without choice, there cannot be love."*

Kallar breathed a little easier as the words sank in. If the mere notion of the Maker taking over inspired such a reaction within him, he wouldn't want it for anyone. Perhaps Isarra or Paili—but even that idea twisted his stomach. If the Maker had forced Paili not to kill Allara, then surely he would have taken over Kallar long ago to protect the hatchlings he had slaughtered.

However, A'dem contained more evil than what soul-bearers caused. Kallar stepped out of reach.

"And the other horrors in this world? Villages flooded by heavy rains? Sailors drowned in storms at sea? The great mountains in the Southlands that erupted so violently they killed thousands?" His hands became fists at his sides. *"You've done nothing to stop these things either! Why?"*

The Maker nodded slowly. *"The answer is harder than you know. Even the Eldír struggle to ponder the infinite."*

The Maker extended his hand, palm upward, and a multitude of tiny lights reminiscent of colored stars formed above it. They spun around a central point, some close to the center, others reaching beyond the outstretched hand. Each spun at its own pace, weaving between each other perfectly.

"The world wasn't always broken. Love cannot exist without choice, yet choice carries the potential for disaster, and the choices of some bore consequences for all. But I will tell you the great secret—love is always worth the risk. And through my *love, the pieces hold together."*

Two stars collided, making Kallar jump as sparks flew apart. They hit other stars, nudging them into new orbits and slightly changing their colors as they continued to dance.

"None of you see the true picture, the tapestry that contains the lives of every human,

dragon, drek, and Eldra. I take every thread your choices give me—every color, every knot—and I weave them into a grand story in which each wonder, disaster, and choice is both everything and nothing."

Another two crashed together, but instead of bursting into sparks, they combined into a new, single star with its own color. The Maker smiled as he observed. *"And every thread in that story, including the choices for evil, I place where it magnifies the good."*

"Tell that to those experiencing the evil."

This time, three stars collided, setting off a chain reaction of sparks and new lights birthing from them. The image spread further into the room, past the Maker's fingertips to where Kallar could touch them if he wanted. The collisions created a sphere of movement rather than the ring it started as. A shining chaos.

"I have told them. It is a hard truth, and not everyone listens, but I will never stop speaking it. This truth flies on the wings of the birds, stands in the strength of the mountains, and sings among the stars. It is whispered by the widow who comforts a fearful new bride, and shouted by the family that finds a greener land across the treacherous sea. It is found in the peacemaker who stands between armies—"

Kallar looked away. Alísa. Of course he would bring her up.

"—as well as the warrior who fights for the helpless." The Maker paused, and when Kallar glanced up, his eyes held pride. *"For it is what created them both."*

For a moment, Kallar felt his resolve slipping. Then he noticed another collision—a large star against a small one. The larger tipped into a new orbit, but the little light shattered completely. That collision was him. He knew it in his bones. But whether he was the careless smasher, or else the one shattered by greater forces, he could not decide. Either way, he didn't deserve the pride in Karn's eyes, much less the eyes of his Maker.

The lights disappeared, leaving them back in the living space's chaos. Kallar shivered, feeling more like the broken pieces now that the wondrous imagery was gone. He was aimless. He had a purpose once, but Alísa had taken it away. And when he tried to find new meaning, all he found was a prison of his own making.

Kallar shook his head. *"I will never understand how this can be spun toward good."*

"Perhaps not," the Maker said. *"You are not infinite. You cannot see all the*

threads, nor take in the grand tapestry. Sometimes mortals will catch glimpses, but never the whole. That, my son, is where faith comes in." The Maker's face lit up as he looked past Kallar to something invisible. *"Faith like R'lann's. It's not that he doesn't recognize the surrounding evil. In some ways, he sees it better than you do. But even in his lack of understanding, he chooses to believe that I see the full picture and that I weave others' evil choices toward a greater good."*

His eyes came back to Kallar. *"That is the choice all* anam *must make. Each will encounter in their lifetime a darkness they cannot understand, and each must there decide whether to cling to me or turn away."*

"I've had more than my share of these choices," Kallar muttered, picking up another wall-hanging. Gia's wall-hanging. They were all hers—Kallar only remembered one from when his mother was alive. It had burned four years after her death, when a dragon got a lucky shot of flames through the window.

That loss was like losing her all over again. He had lost her, lost his father to his stepfamily, lost his purpose, lost Karn, lost his body, and he was going to lose R'lann. And the Maker would just stand by and claim it was all for a good cause? How could Mamá's death bring any good? Or Karn's? R'lann's torture?

Kallar felt his hands turn into fists, then forced himself to loosen them. He couldn't blow up this time. The keeper was still out there—was that a howl in the distance?—and he wasn't ready to be thrown out.

"You can be angry, Kallar. Anger is a correct response to the world's wrongs. And I will not abandon you for directing it at me any more than a mother would throw her child before a charging bull." Kallar cringed at the comparison, but the Maker continued. *"There is nothing you can do to make me cast you out."*

This time Kallar knew he heard the monster outside, distant but distinct. Memories of torture made him shudder. Then he looked back at the Maker.

"What if you're lying? What if you're not good and those who depend on you only see what they wish to see? Or if your goodness has a limit, and once we hit it, you'll abandon us?"

The Maker traced one of his scars with a finger. *"That's faith too, though it eventually becomes experience. R'lann started calling to me because he believed Gia. Now he knows me for himself. I reveal myself to all so they can understand, as I am presently making myself known to you."*

Kallar raised an eyebrow and looked around the cramped living space. *"Some revelation."*

Strangely, that drew a chuckle from his companion. Kallar ignored it, backing up against the wall and sliding down to sit.

"Am I stuck in here, then? Forever, since the keeper is—out there?"

"No," the Maker said, taking his own spot against the wall. *"This house is for your healing, where you can overcome your fear of the keeper. Once that fear is gone, you will no longer see or hear it and you may venture outside again. Your mind-world holds much more than it allowed you to experience."*

"And—my body?"

"The keeper owns it now. If you touch the window to the physical world, nothing will happen. But a chance is coming, if you would reclaim it."

Kallar looked at him. *"When?"*

The Maker smiled. *"I won't let you miss it. When the time comes, you need only stretch out your hand to your rescuer."*

"That's it?"

"That's it. You do not need me to move heaven and earth for you—I have already provided." The Maker met his eyes, and Kallar thought he saw something beyond Karn's visage—something vast and terrifyingly soul-seeing. *"Only be ready."*

59

A HOLDER'S STRENGTH

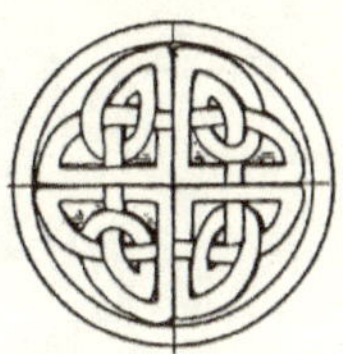

Falier had never run so quickly in his life, but the dreki were faster. Glowing in the darkness, they dove straight through Selene and Hwinn. Selene gave a strangled gasp as one drek phased out through her back, and Hwinn stiffened without a sound, his teeth still in the briars holding Selene captive.

Ska's panicked voice flew through Falier's head. *"Shield!"*

As the attacking dreki returned, Falier pulled at Graydonn's sleepy mind and threw a psychic shield around Selene. The drek aiming for her swerved, and Laen tackled another, leaving only one to crash through Hwinn. This time, the young dragon released the brambles and bleated in pain.

Falier ran to Selene's side and helped yank away the briars. "Hwinn, can you shield yourself and Selene?"

Hwinn wobbled, blinking hard. As Selene's skirt finally came free, she stroked Hwinn where the drek passed through.

"He'll cover me," she declared, glaring furiously at the malevolent dreki. "Wake the others. You go left, we'll go right."

Left suited Falier just fine. Graydonn was there, so entranced he didn't react as two dreki flew through him. Falier threw a shield around him, but as he tried to snap it shut, he hit something as immovable as an oak—a line from Graydonn's mind to the drek in front of him. Falier winced as an attacking drek crashed into a different portion of the shield like it was a solid object. The individual drek's strength nearly matched Falier's own. If they combined into a collective…

"Graydonn!" Falier shoved at their bond. "Wake up!"

On the other end, Falier sensed the dragon's deep joy and longing. It held his attention completely, like he wanted nothing more in the world than whatever the drek was showing him.

"*Pain!*" Ska yelled from somewhere nearby.

That's right. Ska had woken him with pain.

Falier pulled at Graydonn's power and sharpened it into a psychic arrow. "*Sorry about this.*"

He let the arrow loose. Pain flared up in Graydonn a second later, which traveled back to Falier through their bond and made him stumble.

Graydonn spit sparks, shaking his head hard before looking at Falier. "*Did you just—throw a mind-spear at me?!*"

"*Slayer, remember?*"

The drek in front of him barked madly and swooped forward. Falier formed a shield just in time to stop it from phasing through Graydonn. The crack of the impact reverberated through Falier's whole body. He couldn't handle many more hits like that.

Graydonn looked about in shock. "*What—*"

"*Keep your shield up,*" Falier said, searching the darkness of the forest. "*Can you see the others?*"

"*Jossen is behind us, and Taz and Komi are over there.*" Graydonn pointed with his muzzle, growling. "*Taz is awake, but Komi—*"

Another drek dove at them, talons extended. Falier threw his hands up to protect his face, swatting at the creature. Pain sliced through his hand as a claw scored him. Graydonn spewed fire after it, but the flames only hit branches as the drek veered off.

"*Careful,*" Falier warned as the wet wood tried to catch. "*Go wake Komi and bring her and Taz. We need to stick together.*"

Graydonn snorted steam. "*Come with me.*"

"Falier!" Selene's voice rose behind him. "We can't find Trísse!"

"*I'm going to find the others.*" Falier grabbed a large branch off the ground. Never had he longed so greatly for his sword. "*Wake Komi so we can find Trísse!*"

Graydonn grumbled but complied, rushing for Taz and Komi. Another drek joined the first, diving at Falier. He swung his club at one, but the drek was too clever. It phased through the improvised weapon, forcing Falier to dodge. The other drek swooped past him, came back around, and lodged its talons in his arm. It bit his fingers with wickedly sharp teeth. Falier slapped it away, wincing as claws ripped free. He ran for Jossen. A trumpet of pain split the air.

"P'raenn!" Jossen shouted, slashing at a drek with his dagger. "I'm coming!"

"*We're* coming," Falier said, heart ablaze at the dragon's cry. He swung at an incoming drek and joined Jossen in a run. The green dragon was spitting sparks as four dreki attacked his face. Harenn was with him, trying to bat the dreki away with his wings with little success.

Falier threw a shield around P'raenn. It stopped one drek from phasing through, but pain rocked Falier as the others shattered his defense. Crying out, he stumbled and failed to protect himself. Lightning froze his muscles as a drek dove through him. He fell to a knee, his heart skipping two beats. The drek came back, but he couldn't raise his shield in time.

The drek phased, but hit something. Its momentum carried it off to the side, sliding against someone else's shield.

"Up, fearless leader," Varek called. "This isn't a time to rest."

Falier twisted to see Varek atop Mennáli, sword in hand. If he had his weapon, he must have woken up back at camp. That or he slept with it strapped on. Trísse sat behind him, slumping against him as she barely held on.

Falier rose as Varek slid off the dragoness to aid Jossen and P'raenn. Mennáli snapped her tail in a rage, cracking it against a young tree and toppling it. Her eyes and mouth glowed with fire, but she didn't release it until a drek flew toward her. With incredible control, she sent out a thin burst of flame, burning the drek mid-flight and sending it hurtling to the ground. Five more took its place, the creatures seeming to materialize from nothing.

Behind Falier, Graydonn and the others tramped through the underbrush. Selene, Hwinn, and Taz faced him, Selene with a dagger and Taz with a large tree-branch. Graydonn and Komi covered their backs. About twelve dreki whirled around them. He didn't see Ska or Laen anywhere. Falier waved Graydonn down, but though the group saw him, they couldn't rush to his position with the dreki diving at them.

"*I told you!*" Harenn snapped at a circling drek. "*But no. No one ever listens to the sensible dragon!*"

"*What do we do?*" Selene said, holding the dagger high. The shake in her tone ignited rage in Falier. Not even fighting the an'reik army had scared her like this.

"*Everyone, get together,*" he ordered, swinging at a drek and putting his shield back up. *"I'm going to talk to them."*

"Talk?!" Harenn growled. *"What good will that do? They're trying to kill us!"*

Falier changed to a two-handed grip on the branch as blood slicked his dominant hand. *"The canopy is too thick to fly. Fighting isn't working so well, and you dragons can't run fast enough to escape. So yes, I'm going to try talking."*

Falier cleared his throat and sent up a quick prayer to Eldra Nahne for the right words. "My name is Falier. We mean you no harm. We came seeking aid. An'reik have invaded our land, bringing chaos and pain. My mate, Alísa-Dragon-Singer, once gained aid from—"

Something changed. The dreki's glow became eerier—brighter, but without brightening their surroundings. Many hissed or barked a warning. Then one dove straight for him. He swung his branch and hit it, sending it to the ground. Then came another and another.

Jossen, Varek, and the dragons stood with him now, the slayers standing back-to-back. Trísse slid from Mennáli's back and stumbled, but Varek caught her and pushed her to the center. She had cuts all over her arms and a large gash on her forehead, and she appeared dazed. P'raenn, though alert, looked worse, blood dripping from a darkened eye. Falier's heart pounded. They needed to get out, now!

Ska appeared at his shoulder, barking an alarm. *"Unite!"*

The word screeched through Falier's mind and pulled at the edges, as though compelling him.

"We're trying." Falier swung at another drek but missed, catching its talons in his arm. Jossen swiped his dagger at it, but the creature phased and flew away. *"Everyone, move toward the others."*

They moved slowly, dreki diving at them from every side. Ska circled a few inches above him.

"No!" Ska said, sending an image of a dreki clan together, eyes all aglow. *"Unite!"*

More dreki joined the attack, ten swarming as Falier's two groups converged. Selene cried out, the sound ramming against Falier's heart.

Graydonn snarled and snapped at a diving drek. *"Humans in the middle!"*

They moved, humans standing back-to-back within the circle of dragons. Jossen held Trísse up with one arm and wielded his dagger in the other hand. Harenn breathed fire at a descending drek. Flames caught in the branches directly above the dragon's head, but they burned out before they could travel down the branch.

"*Unite!*" Ska screamed at Falier now. It raked over his mind just as two dreki dove toward Trísse and Jossen.

"*We're together,*" Falier said, swinging at the attackers. They veered away. "*What more do you want?!*"

Each time Ska spoke, he tugged Falier's mind. Then Laen joined.

"*Minds!*"

What? "*Humans and dragons can't!*"

The attacking dreki glowed fully, connecting in the way Ska wanted their own group to. Their presence grew in the astral plane, becoming a hulking singular entity full of hatred and menace. The next diving attack focused on the dragons. Falier shored up his defense around Graydonn, adding to the dragon's strength, but it wasn't enough. The shield shattered on impact, sending Falier reeling back into Varek. Graydonn was silent, unable to voice his pain as five dreki passed through him at once, tearing at his mind.

"*Unite!*" Laen joined Ska this time, the two of them pressing images of Selene and Hwinn, then Trísse and Komi, Jossen and P'raenn, and finally Falier and Graydonn. "*Now!*"

The dreki yanked at the clan-link, barking with the effort. Another drek speared through Graydonn before Falier could rebuild the shield. The dragon wobbled, and to Falier's right, Hwinn trumpeted his pain. Anger pulsed through Falier and he gripped his weapon tighter.

"*Selene, Hwinn, join minds. Komi, try to do likewise with Trísse. You too, P'raenn. The dreki are stronger together—maybe we are too.*"

He reached out to Graydonn as the dragon reached back. As each bonded pair pulled together, Ska and Laen drew all of their minds closer until it seemed they all—even the unbonded—tried to occupy the same space. The sensation prickled over Falier's mind like static. Each mind's melody clashed against the others—warbling, vibrating, and sawing at each other like instruments failing to tune. Or dancing partners tripping over each other's feet. Two drummers insisting on their own tempo.

"*Yes!*" Ska's voice rang in Falier's ear as the drek threw an image into his mind. Falier standing at the bonfire in Me'ran at a céilí. Then another of him leading the slayers in song a week ago. "*Unite!*"

Falier bent double as pain rushed through the mind-link. Graydonn's legs buckled and he fell to his side. Falier rushed to stand over him, weapon high, but the dreki weren't attacking physically anymore, and there were more of them—forty at least. Taz stumbled, and Jossen nearly dropped Trísse as the dreki broke through their shields. The pain affected all of them and sent their close-knit minds apart again.

"*Sing!*" Ska ordered, yelping as two attackers chased him. "*Unite!*"

Falier's whole body seized as a drek flew through him. For a second, he couldn't breathe, couldn't think beyond the pain. When he came out, his clanmates' fear and pain shuddered through him. Mennáli roared as four dreki passed through her at once. Though Ska's command made little sense, the situation couldn't get any worse.

Falier sang Alísa's song, only getting through a line before another drek slashed through him. He nearly dropped his weapon, then sang again. Ska and Laen purred in his mind as he did, urging him forward.

"*Unite!*"

"*Everyone, sing with me.*"

Varek coughed. "What in hellflames—"

"*Just do it!*" Falier shouted in everyone's minds as he continued.

Selene took up the song next, her airy tone harmonizing above him. She placed a hand on Hwinn, and Falier sensed them merging minds again. As they did, Hwinn spoke the lyrics, elongating them in the closest approximation to singing Falier had ever heard from a dragon.

Ska and Laen continued to pull, drawing them toward each other. The warbling dissonance wasn't as cacophonous now. Selene and Hwinn no longer pulled against him. Ska sent him more images—memories of Me'ran joined in song, following Falier's drumming.

Unite. Bring people together. That was something music did.

Something *he* did.

Falier chanced a moment to speak. "Come on, dragons too. Sing!"

Graydonn followed next. Falier could feel the dragon's mind bleeding from multiple wounds, but as he sang, their minds came into alignment. Falier nearly toppled at the shock of new sensations running through him. He felt limbs that were not his, including two glorious wings. If he focused, he could also see their surroundings better—everything illuminated with a slight amber tint.

The others sang now—even Varek, though with incredulity. Ska and Laen sped around them, both glowing in the joined ways of their people. Falier's mind expanded outward, like the others were pulling him toward them, even though he was still firmly rooted within his own body. His night-vision tinted in other colors as he recognized each dragon attached to him. When he reached Hwinn and Selene, flashes of colored lights lit up his periphery in time with every sound.

"Unite!"

Ska trilled victoriously, then barked a challenge from Falier's shoulder. The other dreki's attacks had stopped, but every eye pinned on them. Falier, through both his own mind and the others', felt their seething hatred. He felt his strength working to uphold his clanmates through their physical and psychic wounds, even as they worked to mend him. Even Trísse stood on her own now and pressed courageous empathy alongside Selene.

They were strong together. Mighty. United.

The Mennáli part of them called an alarm as their enemy moved together, turning from a swirling cyclone into a single mass of coordinated dreki. The enemy speared toward them. Their Komi part breathed fire in the same controlled blast Mennáli had used earlier. The dreki phased through the flames, heading for them as Falier's squad raised their shield.

The impact sent all parties reeling, the attackers scattering while humans and dragons staggered. Their minds nearly fell apart, but the Falier part of them sang in their minds again, drawing them back into alignment. Their Taz part pulled at the clan's strength and threw psychic lightning at the dreki, who raised their defense fast enough to block a portion of the attack.

Dreki barked and dove, alternating between attacking en masse and in smaller groups. Falier's squad met them with sword, club, fire, and psychic shield, all perfectly coordinated as the dreki attacked them from all sides. At one point, the enemy swarmed Trísse, but the squad anticipated it through her eyes, each knowing which drek to grab, hit, or mind-spear without getting in each other's way.

Multiple parts told them to go on the offensive. Dragon parts prepared to breathe fire, but human parts pulled against that thought with terrible anxiety, especially the Taz part, who drew up memories of forest fires. The mixed thoughts vibrated and warbled against each other. Ska and Laen tried to yank their minds together again. Their Falier part sang aloud to help them focus, then choked as the sounds of ferocious dreki barks came from deeper in the forest.

More of them.

Ska shrieked at Falier as the drek pulled at his mind. *"Unite!"*

Falier sang, but the damage was done. The squad had separated and he was alone again. Just him, a tiny human in a vast world.

Graydonn growled toward the barking. *"We are all small individually, but you brought us together. You have always sought this, whether as a holder or a slayer. Let me join you now."*

Graydonn sang, each word perfect from days of hearing the song. He threw his voice into Falier's mind like a man reaching down to help his brother to his feet and, with a joy that belied their situation, Falier grabbed hold.

Their clanmates joined more easily this time, fearful but determined. Again, their connection shored up each other's minds and bodies, a little like how Alísa's songs strengthened dragons to fight beyond their normal means. As one, they raised their shield. Their dragon parts drew rattling breaths through snarling fangs. Their human parts gripped their weapons, accessing the night-vision of their dragon parts.

Ready.

Like ghosts on the wind, the new group of dreki swooped into view. Their Harenn part called up his fire, but halted suddenly as their dreki parts chittered with joy. A split-second later, the rest of them felt what Ska and Laen did—a familiarity.

The new dreki swerved past them to strike the enemy, creating a tumultuous collision in both the physical and astral planes. One drek stayed back, watching the fight as he hovered beside Ska and Laen. Fen-foraging-green-beetle. Their dreki parts knew him as the leader of the clan they had been searching for, who had helped them against Rorenth!

The fight lasted only a minute longer. Their enemy was tired and wounded—they could not stand against two allied clans. Their leader—who their dreki parts knew as Naam-jay-feathers-by-moonlight—growled and spat in protest of the clans being in her territory, but she could do nothing about it. With a low bark, she retreated into the forest, her glowing clan following behind her.

Ska-sunlight-through-water and Laen-rain-dripping-from-trees let go of their grip on the squad-link. Without their dreki abilities and knowledge, the rest of them fell apart into individuals once more. Falier breathed a sigh of relief, his branch thumping to the ground. Dawn's light filtered through the canopy, allowing him to see his clanmates and rescuers without the dragons' night-vision.

"Whatever that was," Harenn said, shaking his head, *"I am* never *doing it again. I'd rather be eaten."*

Taz snorted, then laughed. The rest followed as pure relief washed through them, even Harenn thrumming with bright eyes. Falier grabbed Selene and hugged her tightly, his sister returning his grip while Hwinn wrapped a wing over both of their shoulders. Varek slapped Jossen's back, then Mennáli's scaly leg. All were tired, their minds taxed by the exertion, yet all reveled in their accomplishment—they were alive!

Falier pulled back from Hwinn's embrace and glanced at the others. "Was it just me, or did you guys see Selene and Hwinn's sound-lights?"

"Is that what the flashes were?" Graydonn asked. *"I kept thinking there was a drek when there wasn't. It was highly distracting."*

"You're telling me," Selene said, pressing a hand to Hwinn's neck. "They disappeared for me a few times, too. It might have been peaceful if it weren't for the imminent doom."

Falier laughed, but stopped at an abrupt elbow to the ribs. He looked back at Varek. "What was that for?"

"Your stupid song. I now have an annoying dragoness lingering in my mind."

Mennáli snorted. *"That's nothing to the obstinate, abrasive, condescending slayer in mine."*

Falier smiled as Varek matched her glare, finding only a begrudging respect in the astral plane. Somewhere during the battle, they must have accepted the mind-kin bond.

His happiness faded as his gaze landed on the group's injuries. Trísse would need stitches, as would he. A pulse of pain ran up his arm from his gnawed hand. And what about P'raenn's gashed eye? Hopefully, someone knew how to help.

"We should return to camp," Falier said. He looked up at Fen. "Thank you. Your clan saved our lives."

The green drek trilled back, but before Falier could continue, Ska fluttered to his shoulder. He anchored his tail around Falier's neck with an anxious whine.

"Message."

Falier turned his head. *"What message?"*

Images flashed through him, rapid and disjointed. A battle in the sky. Fires on the ground. Mind-spears. Circling dragons and riders. Alísa and Sesína. Hellflames meeting ice breath.

"Tomorrow."

Falier's heartbeat quickened. *"Where?"*

Another progression of images, these more cohesive. They started at the Serpent's Fangs, then traveled north one after the other until they reached a mountain only a couple of hours from home.

Tomorrow. It would normally take a day-and-a-half to reach home. They could try flying through the night, but his squad was tired and injured. If they got to the battle in their current condition, they wouldn't be much help.

The dreki, however, could fly faster than anyone.

"Fen, I come bearing a message from the Singer. We face a great threat and humbly ask your clan to ally with us once again." Falier gestured at the squad. "My people are wounded and need to care for our injuries. Would you take us to your territory so we can speak?"

Fen sent an affirmative and barked a command. Flashes of silver and jewel tones flew past Falier as the dreki surrounded him and the others. Fen landed on his shoulder opposite Ska, while the other dreki took positions on Falier's squad-mates—a guard as they walked back through enemy territory.

Falier sent up a prayer for Alísa and the clan, hoping whatever he accomplished would be enough.

60

A RED DAWN

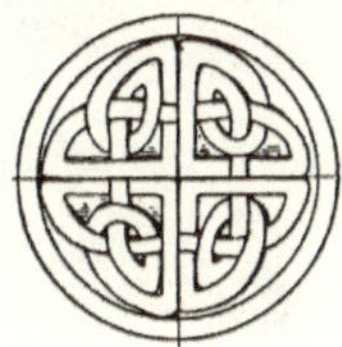

In the dark chill of pre-dawn, Alísa's army flew in solemn silence. Dragon and dreki eye-lights filled Alísa's vision in every direction from her and Sesína's spot in L'non's squad. Winds buffeted them as they traveled only fifty feet above the hills. The low altitude would keep them hidden from the night watchmen longer, though an'reik dragons would likely remove that advantage soon. They were out there, somewhere.

Alísa rubbed her hands together and blew on them while Rís hid in the hood of her cloak. Normally, he would also snuggle into her hair, but today she wore it pinned up, hoping to keep the enemy from recognizing her right away. Between her pinned hair, new squad, and trousers that felt distinctly different from the slip-pants she typically wore under her skirts, she could hide for a time.

In the astral plane, the clan-link Rís held for her was more wobbly than normal. He and the rest of her dreki worked hard to hold the newcomers. Dreki excelled at sightless connections to their own clans, but working with other clans was challenging. But Alísa's squads needed more dreki, and Fen was gracious enough to lend out the seven she requested. The rest of his clanmates flew in a group, prepared to fight as a unit.

For the hundredth time since Fen arrived, Alísa prayed for Falier and the others. Fen brought the message that they were on their way, but the images showed injuries and exhaustion that brought her to tears. That other dreki clan had nearly killed them. She almost wished they wouldn't make it in time—they would be at far greater risk than her rested, well-fed army. But if this was their last stand, she needed all able warriors.

Give them strength and courage, Branni. Protect them, Maker. If—if there's any way we can survive this, please.

Perhaps she should be more eloquent, but she could only repeat the same prayer. In her caves, Farren, Hanah, and Kallar's step-mother Gia led the families who stayed behind in prayers, both spoken and sung. They would be at it for hours as the warriors fought.

Sesína rumbled underneath her. *"We're almost there. We should see the camp in ten minutes."*

Alísa sent back gratitude, then contacted Rís. *"How far away is Falier's squad?"*

He shared a picture of the mountains from the east, but Alísa wasn't familiar with that view.

"How many hours?"

An image of the sun, its position in the sky three hours away.

Alísa sighed. It would be dawn soon, and she needed the element of surprise. If she stopped to wait for them, more an'reik would be awake.

"Rís, connect me to everyone."

Her mind filled with dragons, humans, and dreki. Determination and battle-readiness dominated their emotions, though fear and sorrow were present as well. She breathed everything in, then latched onto anticipation and courage, letting the rest flow out with her exhale. While practice made it less overwhelming, speaking to the entire army still made her head swim. With Sesína's help, however, she delivered her call to arms.

"Brothers and sisters. You know the thrill of battle. You are no strangers to the pain of defeat and the glory of victory. Now we come upon the fight of our lives. Our enemy is powerful. They will show no mercy. For the good of our families, our clans, our world, we must be fierce.

"But this battle isn't different only because we face the an'reik. It is different because we are united. Dragons, slayers, and dreki—together. Each one of you came despite hatred and fear because you believed we could be stronger together. And that is what we are!"

Alísa paused, grasping Sesína's spine tighter as her world wobbled. She wanted to hurry through the rest, but she needed to let her words sink in. They couldn't react aloud, not without giving away their positions to the enemy, but she sensed the fires being stoked inside them.

"Alone, we are mere candles against the dark, but like our dreki brothers and sisters, together we blaze brighter than our single flames combined. United, we fight and bleed for all our peoples! United, we show them a way through the darkness! United, we bring

the light once again!"

Around her, dragons growled, unable to contain themselves fully, though they did not roar. Alísa turned her eyes forward.

"You know what to do. Let's teach the winds what speed is."

Sesína rumbled and pushed herself faster, as did the others. Rís anchored his tail around Alísa's neck while cutting off all but a few squads. The world blurred beneath them, the barely lit hills passing with a swiftness that threatened to turn Alísa's stomach. She focused ahead.

A roar sounded in the distance, then a second. They had been spotted.

"Dezra, go!"

The sky-blue dragoness speared toward the camp, Rassím crouching low on her back. A single squad followed, ready to cover her as she circled the camp.

Rís switched to different squads at Alísa's command.

"Sky team, into position."

Half of the army rose higher into the air. They would keep the enemy dragons off of the ground team.

"Ah, Chief," Rassím said, *"I think they knew we were coming."*

Sesína crested a hill and the an'reik army came into view. Over two hundred strong, armored and standing in ranks.

"Do what you can, but stay safe."

"Safe will not find the possessed," Dezra countered. *"We shall become the wind, but stick to the plan."*

Alísa pressed her lips together. *"Eldra D'tohm under your wings."*

Fierce determination was all that returned. Alísa focused on the sky team, singing her strength song for them. The an'reik's dragon army flooded from their caves, perhaps a hundred dragons strong. They outnumbered the sky team pairs by about thirty. Hopefully, the riders' mind-spears would even the odds.

An image of a man filled Alísa's thoughts, one in green scale armor with yellow war-paint and a full beard that reached his chest. One of the possessed. His picture passed from the drek with Rassím to the ground team. Alísa and Sesína both tried to burn his face into their minds. Saving every possessed warrior would be impossible, but they would help any they could. Getting close enough to touch was a dangerous venture this early. Their best hope was to avoid harming the possessed until the an'reik's ranks thinned. Assuming they survived that long, then the warriors could attempt to free them.

The first wave of their army strafed the ground troops. Enemy slayers lifted their shields in interlocking patterns, while in other places the dragons' fire flew back into the sky. Hellflame manipulators. Alísa glanced at Saynan's ice dragon squad. They would stay together for now and work to silence the flame-bearers.

Alísa felt flames rattle in Sesína's throat and lungs. She switched to her shielding song just before they reached the front lines. Fire gushed from Sesína, the heat almost unbearable on Alísa's legs. Curling tighter, she crouched as the dragoness twisted from arrows and spears. Alísa tried to scan the faces for Kallar, but everything moved too quickly.

H'sinth trumpeted an alarm and banked hard as a tendril of dark mists grabbed for him. Alísa clutched to Sesína as they followed with the rest of the squad, dodging two more of the grasping appendages. One dragon didn't turn fast enough, flying straight into one's grip. The tendril slammed the dragon to the ground. The pain of broken bones flooded Alísa, and she bit back a cry. A second later, she burned with the flames of a fire manipulator as it consumed the fallen pair. The pain cleared, leaving a piece of her numb with death. That would happen a lot today.

Sesína warned the other squads through Rís. *"Watch for dark mists on the south end! We don't know what it is—stay clear!"*

H'sinth and L'non led their squad back into the air and out of reach of weapons and mists. As they rose, Rassím sent another image, this time a woman with blond braids and a quiver full of arrows. Alísa shook herself into wakefulness and tried to commit the face to memory. Sesína growled a negative.

"I'll worry about who we're flaming. You sing and try to sense the other Singer."

Alísa agreed, switching back to a strength song and trusting Rís to get it to the proper squads.

"Heads up," L'non ordered.

Sesína roared a challenge as they saw the source of L'non's warning—a squad of six enemy dragons had made it past the sky team and headed for them. Sesína stayed directly behind H'sinth's wing as he moved to engage.

"Break!" H'sinth commanded.

As practiced, Sesína followed him to the right while other pairs from their squad veered in other directions. H'sinth flapped hard and raised his talons to grapple, while Sesína meant to go for a wing. The enemy dragon did not take the bait, however, instead diving toward the ground army. Others did the same, forcing L'non's squad to follow them.

Sesína trumpeted a warning as the enemy descended on the ice dragon squad. Alísa's stomach pressed against her heart as Sesína pulled her wings in and dove. She braced for impact as Sesína slammed into an enemy dragon to knock it off-course from an ice dragon. The dragon roared its outrage as Sesína's talons ripped through a wing's edge. Smoke pouring from its nostrils, it broke off its attack and chased Sesína instead.

Clutching Sesína's spine, Alísa glanced back at the pursuing dragon, the hood of her cloak long since removed. She pulled hard at Sesína's power and sang a prolonged "Bind!"

Their combined power sealed around the enemy, making it drop. It bit and clawed at her choke with its telepathy, but couldn't trumpet in alarm or spread its wings. Its inner struggle clashed against her like a song played in two different keys simultaneously—warbling and piercing in its dissonance. She shut her eyes as she fought to keep her choke clamped down, checking the astral plane as she did.

Alísa gasped with pain as the dragon finally hit the ground. She yanked her power away. The dragon was alive, but judging by where the pain settled in Alísa's body, a wing was broken. More importantly, it had shown her what she was looking for. The inner clashing song wasn't the dragon—it was the other Singer strengthening it. Now aware of the sensation, she could trace it back to the source.

"Get me one of the other leaders." Alísa told Rís. *"We'll need them to cover the ice dragons while we go after Kallar. We're joining the sky team."*

The sky battle reached wide and high, spreading out as dragons chased one another with murderous intent. Flames flashed, dragons fell as they grappled, and blood sprayed into the air. Alísa ducked as Sesína twisted from the talons of an enemy dragon. Another dragon met them, jaws wide with brewing fire. The terrible heat sent sweat dripping down Alísa's neck. H'sinth descended on their flaming enemy and L'non shouted a war-cry as he slammed a mind-spear into the creature.

Again, Sesína circled toward their target—a cave entrance barely large enough to fit a dragon of Graydonn's size. Alísa couldn't hear anything over the rushing winds and warriors' shouts, but the pulsing song strengthening the enemy originated there.

Unfortunately, the cave was heavily guarded. They had been trying for half an hour and still couldn't get close. Two squads of large dragons zipped around the entrance, keeping them from entering. Perhaps one dragon could evade long enough to drop off their rider and hurry away, but that would leave a single slayer against a possessed Kallar. As much as Alísa desired to free him, she wouldn't risk her men like that. She needed at least two with her.

"And if we call more dragons to aid us," Sesína said, growling as she ripped at the wings of another dragon, *"they'll just send more to stop us! Are you sure we shouldn't just blast the cave with fire? Stop Kallar and hope his soul is shielded?"*

Alísa shouted her binding tone to choke a dragon from the sky. *"I can't kill him for what isn't his fault."*

"But his strength is killing us."

Alísa released the choke as the enemy dragon hit the mountainside and rolled down the steep embankment. Three of her dragon-rider pairs were already down there. More would fall before the day's end.

Still, they were warriors who had chosen this fight. Kallar had no choice.

"He did, at one point," Sesína said, rushing after another dragon's tail. *"He knew what this life might mean."*

All Alísa could see were her father's tears upon Kallar's supposed death. *"I can't give up on him. Not yet."*

Sesína went quiet, focusing on the enemy before her. In a burst of speed that yanked at Alísa's cloak, she latched her talons into the dragon's tail. The bigger dragon whipped the appendage, making Sesína wobble as she struggled to keep herself upright. With a deep push of resolve, she bit down hard. The taste of blood sent a wave of disgust through her and, by extension, Alísa, but the move worked. Tail broken, their enemy screamed in pain. When Sesína released it, it tried to bank to attack her, but its tail made movement sloppy and slow. In an instant, another of L'non's squad was upon it—a dragon large enough to grapple and win.

Sesína rushed away to find her next target, then yelped as a much larger dragon appeared. Alísa clung as Sesína rolled, catching the dragoness' instinctual thought just in time to avoid being flung off. Giving chase, their enemy rattled an inhale. Alísa tensed and Sesína pulled her wings in to dip under the coming flames, only to see another dragon spearing toward them, jaws ablaze. Sesína twisted to put her body between Alísa and the fire, trumpeting a cry for help. Alísa cringed as heat poured over her legs and through her mind as the flames touched the less-protected underside of Sesína's wings.

"Are you——"

"Not good, not good, not good!"

Flapping vigorously, Sesína stabilized herself and extinguished the fire on her left wing, then dove. Thank the Maker, it hadn't been hellflames.

Both enemy dragons gave chase. Alísa pushed more of her strength through their bond, fatigue growing inside her. With a growling bark, Rís spread his wings and let go of Alísa's shoulder-pad, the wind whisking him toward their attackers. Panicked, Alísa glanced back and saw the tiny speck of a drek phase through the closest dragon's face. The dragon twitched and faltered, its eye-lights flickering as Rís came out the other side. His attack gave Sesína just enough room to avoid the two dragons.

"Why did we have to give the ice dragons their own squad?" Sesína said, her voice strained. *"I could use some freezing breath right now!"*

Alísa agreed. Her boots and trousers had protected her legs from full-on burns, but she still felt the heat. She added words for pushing through pain, then searched the sky for Rís. She needn't have worried, for he appeared on her shoulder a moment later, huffing and brimming with pride.

"Good job," Alísa said, *"both of you. Let's find some squad-mates."*

She glanced back at the cave. Two giant an'reik dragons latched onto the rocky slopes on either side of the entrance, roaring and flaring their massive wings in challenge.

Great Maker, how will we ever get inside?

Alísa switched her song to a plea for enemy dragons to join her. The an'reik alphas had their awful ability to hold unwilling dragons under their thrall, but her call had worked when she fought Rorenth. As she wove her song, she came against warbling dissonance. Kallar's power, slashing and stabbing to keep her out.

We have to stop him. One way or another, we must.

Sesína speared for two grappling dragons. A quick check of the astral plane showed Alísa the enemy dragon was shielded, making it impossible for the rider to help with mind-spears. The shield combined with the taxing physicality of grappling also made it likely this was one of the an'reik dragons.

The combatants twisted through the air, the slayer holding desperately to his mount while trying to avoid the talons of the enemy. Sesína dove for them and Alísa pulled her short-sword from its sheath.

"*You sure?*" Sesína asked.

In response, Alísa did her best to bury herself within the squad-link as a shield. Sesína latched onto the base of the dragon's head, and Alísa slashed her sword across the spot Rassím had shown her—behind the jaw, where the artery lay. Pain sliced across Alísa's neck, but with her own clan at the forefront of her mind, it felt more like a paper cut than a deadly blow. Sesína launched off the dragon as blood sprayed into the air. Alísa replaced her sword, nausea bubbling inside her.

"*I hate this.*"

"*I know,*" Sesína said.

Rís trilled an encouraging note, then showed an image of the now-dead an'reik dragon. "*Alpha.*"

Hope filled Alísa. She sang to call to the dragons previously under that alpha's control, but all she found was a wall of another alpha's power, reinforced by Kallar.

Alísa shouted her frustration and rage. These dragons deserved the chance to make their own choices. They shouldn't have to die because an alpha forced them to fight for a cause they didn't believe in!

Her cry echoed through the battlefield, drawing roars from her allies as her righteous anger filled them. Fires burned hotter and extra strength flowed in their veins as they gave their next blows. And many enemy eyes fell on her.

"*Uh-oh,*" Sesína said, adrenaline filling her.

Alísa cursed. "*Move!*"

Sesína twisted and dove, three dragons already in pursuit. "*You think they figured out who we are?*"

"*Less sass, more flying!*"

Fire crossed their path. Sesína ducked under it and spun from another dragon's talons. She moved with a frantic grace—dodging, flipping, and twisting as every dragon in the two squads took their best shot at her. Behind them, Alísa's squads worked to pick them off, the astral plane displaying a myriad of chokes and spears.

Enemy dragons fell, but more arrived, pursued by some of Alísa's own. H'sinth and another of their squad-mates fell in behind Sesína to guard her rear. They flew a mere hundred feet above the ground and were running out of room to dodge. Sesína looked up, wanting to ascend, but too many enemies waited there.

If they all dive at once...

As though prompted by her thought, dragons descended. Sesína yelped and swerved as fire crashed around her. H'sinth moved in over her, L'non holding his bronze shield high against the flames. Sweat covered Alísa's face and plastered her clothing to her back. Another allied squad dove into the mass, targeting enemy wings and faces while the riders shot mind-spears.

Seven enemy dragons fell in the space of a minute, giving Sesína room to ascend out of her trapped position against the ground. With all the squads who came to their rescue, Alísa formed a plan. Rís connected her to the leaders of each squad.

"L'non, you and your chosen swordsmen get ready to follow me in. Everyone else, we need to get inside that cave. I need two squads at the front to grapple with the guardians. The rest of you, keep the enemy off our back. We're making a break for the cave."

L'non responded with his team's readiness as Rís redirected her song to the aiding squads. Alísa firmed her jaw.

"Go."

The dragons moved as she directed, breaking off their grappling and pursuits to spear for the cave. Enemy dragons pursued, raging eyes fixed on Alísa. Around her, L'non's squad and two others rushed in to intercept. Alísa's heart fell into her throat as Sesína twisted upside-down to dodge one that made it past them.

Ahead, the two lead squads hammered into the dragons guarding the cave. Dragons roared and screamed, allies' pain sending bolts of lightning through Alísa. But a hole opened.

"Go, L'non!"

H'sinth and the others dove toward the mountainside and grasped the rock on either side of the entrance. Riders slid down, drew their swords, and rushed inside. As soon as the path was clear, Sesína followed behind, she and Rís lighting the way with their eye-lights, ready to face the possessed Singer within.

61

FIGHT

Swords clashed before Alísa could take in the situation.

"Take him down!" L'non yelled.

"He's shielded," another slayer called. "No telepathy!"

Alísa gripped Sesína's spine with whitening knuckles. Kallar's sword moved in an unending blur as he fought the first of the slayers. He struck with a serpent's speed, keeping her warrior on the defensive. His ice-blue eyes, usually so cold and calculating, were crazed with battle-lust. The long side of his hair flew unbraided, and the shorn side had grown. It made him appear savage and wild—something to be put down rather than rescued.

L'non circled behind the combatants while the second slayer stayed back to guard Alísa. Her uncle, too, seemed to change. He had always been steady and sure, the rock her father leaned on. Here, in battle against the thing that killed his brother, steadiness took on the quality of stone—unblinking, unyielding, uncaring.

He lunged. Kallar spun to meet his blow, pushing the sword away in an arc and swiping at the legs. L'non danced back and Kallar slashed at the first slayer. His speed was inhuman, not with an an'reik's power, but like he cared nothing for fatigue or pain. The slayer blocked once, twice, a third time, but Kallar had already swung around to confront L'non.

Alísa slid from Sesína, legs wobbling from hours of clinging. Sesína lifted her wings, prepared to shield Alísa if needed.

Alísa shuddered as Kallar fended off both men. *"How am I going to get close?"*

Rís curled his tail around her neck and whimpered.

Sesína growled. *"You're sure it has to be you?"*

"Bria moves with me."

Alísa jumped as the first slayer took a glancing blow on the arm, Kallar's blade sliding up the dragon-scale bracer to cut his bicep. Her guard tensed as though holding himself back. L'non moved in to cover while the wounded man recovered his wits, matching Kallar's every frenzied strike.

"We're here to save you, Kallar," the injured slayer said, adjusting his grip on his sword. "If you can help from your end, do it now!"

Kallar made no response except to look straight at Sesína and shout a feral, elongated battle-cry.

PAIN!

Sesína yelped a trumpet and Alísa bent double as the possessed Singer's cry lanced through the dragoness. White-hot flames pierced their minds, biting and burning with hatred. Sesína wobbled, and Alísa's stomach churned.

Swords clashed beyond the veil of pain. Kallar shouted again. Sesína stumbled, a rare surge of fright running through her. Alísa slumped against her, groaning. Kallar was strong. *It* was strong. The shout pulled up memories of past injuries and knifing griefs. Burning muscles. A serpent's bite. Abandonment.

Maternal instinct spiked. Alísa reached for lyrics and, finding none, sent up another cry of pain. She drew out the sound, letting it warble until it batted back the attack just enough for her to weave a simple shielding song.

Maker's wings
Bria's song
Branni's steel
Make me strong

Maker's hand
Bria's spark
Branni's fight
Hold back the dark

Sesína let out a moan, shaking her head to clear it. Kallar shouted again, but this time, the attack hit Alísa's shield. His ice-blue eyes glared at her with a new hatred. Alísa fell back a step, but did not falter. She would not leave Sesína vulnerable.

Roars and grasping talons turned Alísa's head. Outside, dragons struggled for the cave. Riders screamed battle-cries and dragons trumpeted their pain. One dragon guarding the entrance slid down to cover the opening as another dragon spewed fire. Sesína spread her wings wide to block the few flames that snaked inside. Her tail swung in agitation.

"This isn't good. Tell the slayers to push further inside, where fire can't reach us."

Alísa returned her eyes to the fight, stopping her shield song to call to L'non. "G—g—get—"

"Fire!" her guard yelled, understanding her intent. "Push forward!"

"Little busy here!" L'non barked.

L'non and the wounded slayer both fought between Alísa and Kallar, trying to press him back with little success. As they clashed, Kallar's hateful eyes found Alísa, sending a shiver over her. She sang her shielding song again and drew her sword.

A flash swept light over the cave, followed by heat and a moan from Sesína as flames burned the less-protected edges of her wings.

"Seriously, move! If one of those hellflamers gets close, we're dead!"

"Move, L'non!" Alísa ordered.

L'non and his partner pressed harder, spreading apart so Kallar had to fight at two different angles. Finally, Kallar stepped back, teeth gritted in a permanent growl. Alísa's guard joined them, and the three slayers pushed Kallar further into the cave. Sesína walked forward, wings still spread to protect as she and Alísa moved into the darkness. The dragoness drew in a rattling breath and opened her mouth, her inner flame lighting the cavern.

L'non and the others kept Kallar occupied, the possessed slayer moving at the same incredible speed with no signs of fatigue. Perhaps in a normal fight, they would have already taken him down, but Alísa's order not to kill or seriously injure held them back.

Kallar had no such fetter. With a snarl, he threw himself at the slayer with the wounded arm, batting aside the slayer's sword and punching him in the face. With a crunch of cartilage, the slayer fell and Kallar lifted his blade to plunge it through his heart.

L'non bowled into Kallar, throwing off his strike. Kallar went down but rolled to his feet as though he had expected that, weapon high to swipe at Alísa's guard. The guarding slayer blocked and Kallar wrenched his sword around in an arc, throwing the slayer off-balance, then sending him to the ground with a kick.

Kallar ran for Alísa, eyes locked on her with murderous intent. Sesína's rage scorched Alísa's mind as the dragoness let loose her fire. Kallar dodged, rolled, and came up on the far side, swinging for Sesína's outstretched wing. Alísa tried to parry, but Kallar pivoted. With a roar, he stabbed Sesína's side through the leather of her wing.

Alísa's cry joined Sesína's as pain cut through her ribcage and arm. Shocked, scared, and enraged, she pushed all of her psychic might into her scream. Kallar faltered, his limbs seizing in her power. His weapon slipped from his grasp and Sesína's side, his hand going to his head.

"*Go,*" Sesína said, voice shaky. "*Now.*"

Rís leapt off as Alísa dropped her sword and lunged for Kallar. Her heart beat like a thousand drums. She collided with him, knocking him to the ground. Grabbing his arm, she called out.

"B—Bria! Help—"

Kallar's other hand shot up, grabbed her throat, and squeezed.

62

EYES ON ME

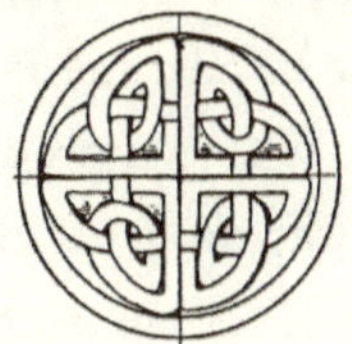

"It's time."

The words pulled Kallar from his slumber, as though his *anam* knew their intention instinctively. Once his thoughts caught up, they latched onto the voice. Simultaneously new and known, it held the strength of mountains and the life of their streams.

Kallar looked toward the door, where the Maker stood. No longer in the form of Farren, R'lann, or Karn, this visage was strange. Try as he might, Kallar couldn't focus on it. Whenever he tried to grab hold of detail, things shifted and changed like light through a prism. The colors of skin, eyes, and hair were elusive, and each time Kallar thought he grasped the body's shape, it seemed to change.

If his form is determined by my subconscious, what does this tell me?

"Kallar."

His name, soft with a mother's love and hard with a trainer's instruction, made Kallar stand. He hurried to the door. Even closer proximity did not help him discern the Maker's form.

"You said I just have to reach out my hand to my rescuer." Kallar stopped before him. *"Do I wait here until he comes?"*

"No. We must return to the portal."

Tension seized Kallar as the keeper howled in the distance. *"I have to go back? Out there?"*

His emotion mists turned the orange-gold of fear. He cursed his weakness. He had endured the keeper's torture before. He should be able to face it again, especially with the promise of his body waiting. But those hateful eyes pierced through his memories, and the pain they caused stole his breath.

"Yes."

The Maker's tone held a compassion Kallar didn't deserve. Every torment the keeper had sent him, every emotion it had wrested from him, every terrible thing it had done—*that* he deserved. Kallar was a murderer. A stubborn, arrogant, spiteful slayer who had only ever accomplished evil even when he tried to bring good. Each human life he saved came at innocent dragons' expense, and he hadn't been able to save those who mattered most. Mamá. Pa. Karn.

The keeper screeched at the walls of the house. Its talons raked the boarded windows. Kallar watched, certain the monster would break through.

"Eyes on me."

Kallar tried. The boards rattled harder as he turned his face toward the ever-shifting yet unmoved form of the Maker.

"It cannot get inside. Keep your eyes on me."

It took all Kallar's strength to turn those last few inches and stare into eyes both soft and strong. The Maker's voice soothed like a parent holding their child who was afraid of the dark.

"You are right, son. You have done terrible things to your fellow anam, *whom I love—"*

The keeper's rage called at the door again, but before Kallar turned, the Maker's hand settled on his cheek, guiding him to stay. The touch was soft, one he could easily break free of, but within it was the reminder to keep his eyes fixed here. Kallar stayed.

"—but I also love you." The Maker smiled. *"And just as I weave every thread of the universe to accent and uplift the good, I can do the same for the tapestry of your life. Your story doesn't have to end with mistakes and shame. All you need do is hand over the tools and let me complete the work."*

The steady hand on his cheek accented Kallar's shaking. It seemed wrong to voice what he was thinking, but he couldn't help himself.

"You're saying I need to trust you with me." He shook his head, but didn't look away. He wouldn't cower. *"But I don't."*

The Maker's expression betrayed no anger. *"Only days ago, you feared I would throw you back to the keeper, yet you hold none of that fear now."* The Maker's hand dropped from Kallar's cheek and extended in offering, the scars on his arm the only clear feature Kallar could see. *"Time is short. You do not have to go, but if you wish the chance to regain your body, we must leave."*

Kallar glanced at the door. He hadn't heard the keeper in a while. *"Is it gone?"*

"No. But it cannot touch you when your focus is on me."

Kallar's heart raced. He needed his life back. If he didn't try, would he ever get another chance?

He clasped the Maker's proffered arm before he could change his mind. His companion returned his grip and with his free hand lifted the bar from across the door. Then the Maker led him outside.

The same twilight Kallar had lived in for weeks met them, the sky a deep indigo and the grasses of the wide hill country tinted with dusky blues. Mountains encircled them as before, but the safe-house sat at the edge of the circle. The land stretched for miles, the floating window to the physical world nowhere in sight. The only unnatural thing Kallar saw was a long, dark tendril of solid mists stretching from somewhere nearby into the distance ahead.

Snarling rose to Kallar's left. His heart stuttered. The keeper. Only a few feet away. Every nerve in his body screamed to turn and face it, lest it take him from behind.

"Eyes on me," the Maker said.

But that thing. It would—

No. Eyes ahead. *"Where are we going?"*

"Forward. Time is closing fast" —the Maker changed his grip to take Kallar's hand— *"we're going to run."*

That suited Kallar just fine.

The Maker moved and Kallar ran with him, traversing the astral world faster than should have been possible. They passed a grove of bare trees, then a lake. They leapt over a river in a single bound and wove through another grove with ease. The wayfarer in Kallar wondered about these landmarks. All he had seen before was a vast, plain grassland. Here lived streams and brush and distant lights that looked like animals' astral forms. The land held a strange beauty now that he beheld it without threat of torture. Not that he wanted to stay.

He chanced a peek and saw the black form of the keeper flying directly behind them. Its blazing white eyes speared into his heart, and he stumbled. The Maker's grip on his hand tightened, keeping him upright.

"Its only power over you is what you give it. It cannot harm you when your focus is on me."

The monster yowled over the Maker's words, nearly drowning them out. Kallar tried to push himself harder, faster, but couldn't affect their speed. His heart pounded like it might burst any moment. The sound of wings behind him was so loud he wondered why he hadn't heard it before.

Portal. Just get to the portal. Reach for help.

As though in answer to his thoughts, the glowing window appeared as they crested a hill. The wide plains Kallar remembered stretched out around it. Again he tried to push faster, but his speed seemed dependent on the Maker's. Though their pace ate up the plains beneath them, they didn't outrun the keeper. He felt its breath on his neck. Gathering his strength, he pulled at the astral mists and formed them into a shield behind him. The keeper shattered it with the same ease as before, sending echoes of pain pulsing through Kallar's head and tearing at his scars. Kallar gritted his teeth against the cry threatening to wrench from his lips.

"Look at me, son."

Kallar tried to speak but failed. His astral muscles trembled and faltered. He stumbled, again held upright by the Maker's hand, but his pace slowed. The Maker pulled him, beckoning him forward, but Kallar spent his strength on his shield, bracing for the keeper's attack. It slashed his defense to pieces. Kallar fell to his knees. He wouldn't make it. He trembled, first with fear, then rage.

"You can stop this!" he shouted at the Maker. *"You can send it away!"*

Kallar's eyes shot to the keeper. It prowled like a panther, growling its murderous intent with indecipherable words.

The Maker lowered to the ground, but Kallar couldn't tear his gaze from the thing waiting to devour him.

"Talk to me."

"Why should I?" Kallar snarled. *"Why don't you take it away?! You said it has no power, but it—"*

He stopped as the keeper crouched, ready to pounce. Its limbs coiled beneath it.

"Eyes on me!"

The ground quaked with the force of the order. Nearly everything within Kallar screamed not to turn from the creature about to attack, but one tiny portion knew nothing else had ever worked against his tormentor.

Kallar tore his gaze from the keeper and braced himself for whatever the

Maker had for him. Yet the anger he expected wasn't there. It was closer to desperation—except, on the Maker's face, the expression held no fear or need. Not a drowning man gasping for air, but one with a longing so deep it physically hurt. And that longing was for Kallar himself.

Kallar stayed. The keeper leapt for him—and passed through, insubstantial.

The Maker's eyes shone. *"Well done."*

The Maker's form shimmered and shifted before Kallar as though it contained too much to understand. But although the features were incomprehensible, the emotions they conveyed were not. Joy. Peace. Love. All so pure and true that they bit at Kallar's impure, untrue self. He deserved none of it, yet all he wanted was to accept it. To be accepted, even in his wretched state.

The Maker took Kallar's hands in his. *"Come, son. There isn't much time left."*

Kallar rose, legs shaking, the Maker's grip keeping him steady. They walked, the Maker going backwards and never breaking eye-contact. Kallar stayed. Somewhere in the back of his thoughts, he realized he didn't hear the keeper. Whether it had slunk off or Kallar simply couldn't perceive it anymore, he didn't know until they made it to the window. There, a translucent version of the keeper stood like a shadow, everything behind it visible but darkened.

The Maker stepped aside so Kallar could see the portal. Kallar followed him with his eyes, unwilling to accidentally give the keeper power again.

"You can look," the Maker said. *"Just do not fear. I am with you."*

Kallar intended only a quick glance to test what he'd been told. Then he saw the scene. A cave, dimly lit. L'non and two other slayers. Alísa and Sesína. His body ran at the keeper's will, disarming the slayer between him and Alísa, then charging. It dodged Sesína's flames, twisting to slash her wing and get to Alísa. Sesína pulled away, but the keeper charged forward. It stabbed the dragoness in the side, the depth unclear because of her wing.

No. No, no, no, no!

When Alísa screamed, her power pierced the window. Kallar stumbled back as astral mists flew away in the terrible wind. The outside world turned lopsided as his body fell to her voice's psychic grasp.

In an instant, Alísa was on top of him. Pain filled her eyes with tears, but her resolve was firm.

"B—Bria—"

Kallar froze. *Bria?*

The moment Alísa said the name, the image shifted. A second form overlapped Alísa's, as if two bodies occupied the same space. One was pale, with pinned mahogany curls and eyes that held a lifetime of sorrows. The other had dark skin, orange curls that formed a halo around her head, and penetrating brown eyes. She glared at the keeper, somehow seeing through the portal, then softened as she turned to Kallar. Her hand stretched toward him.

Reach out your hand.

He was supposed to, but—it should have been Eldra Branni! Not the slayer who forsook her people. Not the human-turned-Eldra who failed his mother. He was a slayer. It was supposed to be Branni!

The keeper moved Kallar's body, catching Alísa's throat and silencing the rest of her call to the wrong Eldra. Her eyes widened with fear while Bria's remained steady on Kallar with a love that said he was hers.

Reach out.

A taloned hand landed on Kallar's shoulder, the one opposite the Maker. Kallar flinched, shaking as the keeper's eyes burned into him from behind.

"Now you see," it hissed, *"even your Eldra has abandoned you, leaving you to this traitorous weakling."*

Kallar fell to his knees as the whispers filled him. Beyond the window, Sesína roared while Alísa clutched at the hand around her neck. Alísa let go of her hold on his other arm to fight it. That was a mistake. Kallar's body was stronger than hers. The keeper rolled them away from Sesína, pinning Alísa down.

"Rejected as a warrior," the keeper said, its breath hot on Kallar's neck, *"and you are no Dragon Singer."*

It was right. He wasn't Alísa, who loved the brutes like she loved humanity.

This was wrong, everything was wrong!

Reach.

He couldn't.

Alísa clutched at the choking hand. At the keeper's command, his other hand went for Karn's dagger at his belt. Bria's eyes stayed steady.

"You don't need them controlling your life, who you are," the keeper said. *"With*

us, you can be whatever you will.” Its hand slipped down over his heart. *“Relinquish this, and your life shall be yours again.”*

Shadows told of Sesína moving. Shouts rose from the slayers behind them. Alísa's eyes implored.

Where was the Maker in this?

The keeper's talons tightened, puncturing Kallar's astral skin, pulling him away from the window and into its haze. He couldn't fight it. His breaths came in short bursts. It was going to claim him. All because the wrong Eldra stood before him.

I can't do it. I'm not strong enough.

Beyond the pleased growl of the keeper, a quiet voice echoed in Kallar's mind.

“I am.”

Kallar looked to the Maker as the keeper's haze surrounded him, his voice barely a whisper.

“Help me.”

A flash of light pierced his eyes and heart. The pain and heat of it was like scrubbing away the crust of blood and mud after a days-long battle—rough, vigorous, biting. But with it all, the keeper's hand again became translucent. It grasped at Kallar's chest, but its talons only passed through harmlessly.

Through the window, Karn's dagger slid loose.

Kallar clenched his fists as the Maker's light pulsed through his astral body. *Slayer or Singer, what does it matter? I won't let any more die by my hand.*

With a growl of effort, Kallar pushed up and reached for Bria. He hit the portal's barrier, its touch sending the burn of fire up his arm, but he pressed on until he felt someone grasp his forearm. He yanked and Bria's form beyond the window shifted, coming closer. She broke through in a burst of light.

Through the portal, Bria had appeared human. She emerged into the mind-world, however, with silver wings sprouting from her back. A sword of light manifested in her free hand, and the fingers grasping Kallar's arm turned sharper. She let go of him, revealing talons at the end of each digit. Her curls flowed down her back like the mane of one of Alísa's dreki and continued down a powerful dragon's tail. Spines protruded all along the mane, ending in three wicked-looking barbs at the end of the tail. Bria's eyes fixed on the keeper.

“You will never touch him again.”

With a blast of fire-breath, Bria leapt at the keeper. It jumped back from the window, only a wavering tendril still connected until Bria's sword slashed through it. The outside world went black.

Kallar glanced at the Maker. *"Alísa. Did I—"*

"She is alive. Your body is unconscious." The Maker's eyes softened. *"I love that you are a protector, willing to sacrifice for others. I would grow that in you, if you let me."*

Kallar looked away, unsure how to answer. Instead, his gaze fell on Bria and the keeper. Their battle had moved from the window. Bria growled, slashing with sword and talon. For a moment, the keeper seemed helpless. Then the monster's eyes flashed from white to red. In an instant, its shape changed into a giant, serpentine creature with wings. It struck Bria with fangs dripping stringy saliva, biting into her dominant shoulder.

Bria screamed, a guttural sound that rocked the mind-world. The bite would have taken off a man's arm, but Eldír were apparently crafted of tougher substance than humans. The monster's teeth remained lodged in her shoulder as she transformed, her form stretching and growing until a great silver dragoness stood in her place. Extra spines and horns spiked from her leg joints, head, and chin. Her talons raked her opponent and she jabbed the horns on top of her head into the creature's neck. The keeper didn't cry out, instead biting down harder. Its long body lashed over Bria's back and under her belly to constrict around her.

Bria roared and chomped at the keeper, but the serpent kept a tight grip. Her tail lashed in its coils. When the keeper dislodged from her shoulder, it left giant, bloody holes in her scales. It pulled back and struck again, aiming for her neck.

Suddenly, Bria wasn't there. The keeper bit down on air, then took a face-full of fire as Bria's winged human form flew from the rapidly constricting coils. The monster lurched back with a hiss as Bria passed it, twisted midair, and manifested her sword in her uninjured hand. In a flash of light, she dove at the keeper's neck and slashed straight through it.

Kallar stood, hope surging. Then dark mists poured from the keeper's wounds and flew at Bria. She breathed fire, spinning in a circle as the dark power surrounded her. Her flames burned it, but not quickly enough as the whole of the keeper stretched to reinforce itself. Soon an orb of mists enclosed her, translucent but solid. She struggled, filling the space with yellow flame.

Kallar glanced back at the Maker. *"Why don't you help her?"*

The Maker's eyes remained on the battle. *"I am with her as surely as I am now with you. As I am with Alísa. As I am with Karn."*

Kallar shook his head. *"Karn died."*

The Maker gave a small smile. *"Karn is more alive than he ever was on A'dem. The keeper meant his death for evil, but it brought my son home to be who he was always meant to be. It shaped others who are still in the physical realm as well. It can shape you into something better, too. Something whole."*

Bria roared desperately behind him, but Kallar couldn't bring himself to look. He hadn't known wholeness in a long time. Perhaps ever.

"I still don't understand."

"I know," the Maker said. *"Can you trust anyway? Trust that your soul is safe with me, no matter what else happens?"*

Kallar let out a tremulous breath, his mind turning to R'lann. His little brother, who had grieved their Mamá alongside Kallar but had never given up. Who had allowed himself to heal where Kallar clung fiercely to his wounds. Who held hope and strength amid the an'reik's torture. Kallar had thought himself strong once. He wanted to be strong again, but how could he after discovering his complete inability in the face of A'dem's darkness?

Perhaps R'lann was right. In this darkened world, perhaps the greatest strength was to cling to the light and refuse to let go.

Kallar looked down. *"I can try."*

A hand found his shoulder. *"One day, you will run without stumbling. Today, you take your first step. Now, look to your Eldra."*

Kallar started, realizing he no longer heard the struggle behind him. He turned to see the dark orb filled with fire so dense he couldn't see Bria anymore. The orb constricted, trembling with effort, then exploded as claws made of flame ripped through it on all sides. A piece flew at Kallar, but the fire consumed it before it reached him. All pieces burned away except for one. Bria held this foot-long piece between two talons. It squirmed and wriggled, now more worm than serpent. The Eldra spread her wings and lowered to the ground.

"It's over," she breathed out. She pressed her fist to her chest upon seeing the Maker, then looked to Kallar. *"Come. There is one last matter to settle."*

Kallar glanced at the Maker, who nodded him forward. With a breath of trepidation, Kallar stepped toward Bria. In her talons, the worm gave tiny growls and groans. She smirked at it, amused.

"Yeah, yeah, we're dirt and all that nonsense. What should we call something defeated by dirt, hmm?"

She stretched out her free hand, manifesting a dagger of light. Deftly, she flipped the blade around and offered the handle to Kallar. When he hesitated, she pushed it closer.

"The kill is yours." She threw the keeper on the ground and stepped on its tail, keeping it from slithering away.

Kallar stared at the thing as it writhed, uncomprehending. *"You defeated it."*

"I did. But I would see my charges freed completely. You still fear it. No more."

Kallar slowly reached for the dagger, eyes fixed on the keeper. Its growling and groaning seemed like words just beyond his ability to understand.

"Place your foot on its neck."

The keeper writhed more violently, little fangs gleaming in warning. With a glare, Eldra Bria spoke.

"Cease."

The command resonated through the mind-world. The creature stopped moving and fell limp. Silent. Pathetic.

Kallar stepped closer, and when the keeper didn't move again, he placed his foot on its neck. It felt—good. Right. He pressed harder, drawing renewed growls and wriggling, but the creature could do nothing. Not with Bria standing over it, too.

Eldra Bria grinned, pulling a handkerchief from a pocket in her battle-skirt to press against her shoulder wound. *"You were always meant to be more than mere dirt, little warrior. Finish it."*

Kallar drew a breath, stooped, and severed the keeper's head from its body. It was such a small thing, like killing a worm. No grandness, no gravitas or ceremony. His enemy was reduced to something low beneath his boot.

Kallar straightened and the knife of light vanished as the keeper's remains dusted away.

"It's yours again." Eldra Bria nodded to the portal. *"Go. Tell your sister the Maker is your sword-partner."*

Kallar blinked. *"Sister?"*

But Bria was gone. The Maker, too, was nowhere in sight. All that remained were the darkened window and the vast, now sunlit landscape. When had that happened?

No time to ponder. Kallar pivoted and sprinted for the portal and his body waiting outside.

63

TWO SINGERS

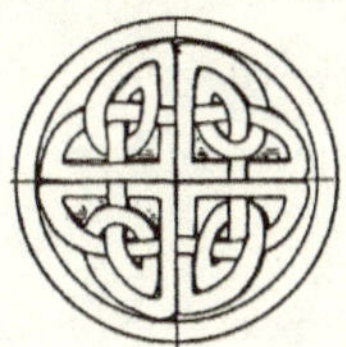

Alísa coughed, rubbing her neck as L'non and the others pulled an unconscious Kallar off of her. What happened? She had called for Bria, but nothing changed. Then, just as she thought Kallar would kill her, he collapsed. And he had yet to wake up.

But that wasn't the worst part.

Alísa pushed to her feet. "Hold him."

She ran to Sesína, her ribs pounding with fiery pain on each of the dragoness' inhales. Rís fluttered around her head, trilling nervously. Sesína moaned.

"Am I dead? I don't feel dead."

Alísa dropped to her knees beside Sesína. *"Let me see."*

Growling with effort, Sesína flexed her wing out above Alísa. A hole in the leather revealed where the blade pierced through to her side. Under the base of the wing, four of her interlocking scales were missing, having cracked and fallen off at Kallar's blade. Blood oozed from the wound, sliding down her scales to drip in a puddle on the stone floor.

Alísa forced her breathing to slow. Remain calm. She looked at Sesína's face. No blood dripping from her mouth.

"Do you taste blood?"

"No, praise the Maker." Sesína's voice remained soft, but with a hint of humor. *"I know what happens when I taste blood in my food—I don't want to know what happens when it's my own."*

"Nausea?"

"That's probably what would happen."

Alísa glared at her. *"Do you feel any nausea right now?"*

"No. A little?" Sesína looked at the wound. *"Koriana told me that if I'm bleeding, I need to flame it."*

"But if he punctured an organ?"

"He stabbed hard, but I don't think the sword made it past my ribs." Sesína flexed her wing, the movement not creating any extra pain. *"It hurts when I breathe, though, like a rib or two might be cracked."*

Alísa would have to take her word for it. All she knew was Kallar had stabbed her mind-sister.

No, not Kallar. The thing possessing him.

"I'm going to flame now. You should step back."

Alísa did as she said, scooting on her knees to avoid being singed. Rís followed, landing on her shoulder. Sesína let out a narrow stream of fire and aimed it at the bloody gash. The pain of the flames made Alísa grit her teeth.

A loud gasp pulled her gaze to Kallar. L'non stood over him while the other slayers each held an arm so that Kallar lay flat on the cave floor. Kallar coughed like he had been drowning. The men tightened their grip as he came awake. L'non pointed the tip of his sword at him.

"Don't let go until we're sure who's in control."

Kallar looked around, panting. His eyes were wide and his shock dripped through the astral plane like sweat.

"I'm—back."

L'non looked at Alísa. "How do we know it worked?"

Alísa glanced at Sesína. The dragoness eyed her, keeping her flames steady.

"I'm okay. Do your thing."

Pulling herself away, Alísa stood. In truth, Eldra Bria hadn't given her anything to test whether she had won the battle for Kallar's body.

You'll tell me, right Bria?

Kallar swallowed, his gaze moving over each person. He settled on Alísa.

"The—the Maker is my sword-partner."

Alísa blinked as the words echoed in memory. She exhaled.

"It worked. Let him go."

The slayers complied carefully, as though expecting him to jump them. Kallar only sat up and took in shuddering breaths. His emotions filled the astral plane in alternating waves of fear and relief. Knowing that Kallar never lowered his telepathic shield like this made their force stronger. They pulled at Alísa, prompting her to step closer. As she knelt before him, his shield went up.

"You came for me," he mumbled, looking down. "Why?"

"B—because you needed help, and I was the only one who could g—g—give it."

"I killed him."

Alísa shook her head. "It wasn't you. I know that now."

"But I made it possible." He forced his pained eyes to her. "I killed him."

Alísa pressed her lips together, then whispered. "What do you want me to say? That I hate you? That I wish he were here instead?" She blew out a breath, fighting tears. "He wouldn't have wanted that. And as much as I miss him, I am glad you're free."

A flash of fire illuminated the cave entrance, followed by roars Alísa had previously blocked out. The battle outside was still going strong, and by this point both sides would have lost the lingering effects of their Singer's strength song. This was their chance to turn the tide.

"We fought together once, combining our p-p-powers to k-kill our enemy. Fight with me again, this time to strengthen our dragon allies."

She reached a hand for Kallar's, prepared to stand together. He stared at it, then looked toward the cave entrance.

"I just got that thing out of my head." His fist clenched against the ground. "I can't open myself up again. I'm not like you."

Alísa didn't know how to respond. Compassion and ire met within her. She couldn't understand his experience, but it must have been terrifying to leave the ever-confident Kallar so cowed. But dragons and slayers were dying, in need of their Singers.

She pet Rís' mane thoughtfully before speaking again. "Men, g—go back to your dragon partners. Fight well—I'll follow shortly."

She didn't look at them as she gave the order, trusting they would obey. As they left, Rís connected her to the clan-link and Alísa sang her strength song. One verse made her head spin, and she steadied herself with her hands on the ground. That would renew the power for five minutes, if they were lucky. For now, it would have to suffice.

Kallar watched her the whole time, mental shield up and legs curled to his chest. She had never seen him so shaken before. It allowed her compassion to win the fight within herself.

"I know you've been horribly wounded and used. P-p-probably tortured. It's n—not fair to ask this of you so soon. You should have t-t-t-time to heal. To mourn. I'm sorry."

Alísa looked him in the eye. "B—but we are outnumbered. Our enemy carries too much power and though we have a good d—d—defensive strategy, we're b—barely making a dent in their ranks. I can only strengthen so many dragons at once. W—we need your help."

Kallar shook his head. "I never wanted this. Put me on the ground and I'll fight whatever man, dragon, or monster comes my way. Opening up to pour my strength into dragons—that's not how I was made."

Alísa paused, thinking. *Eldra Bria, give me words.*

"What about rescue? Weren't you made for that? To p-protect? Isn't that what you've t-t-t-tried to do your whole life?"

That gained a reaction beyond a head-shake. Kallar met her eyes and straightened a little. She pressed forward.

"There are d—dragons experiencing a piece of what you've gone through. An'reik alphas hold them in their c-clutches. I can sing to c-call them out, b—b—but the alphas will fight me."

Alísa looked him in the eye. "But since you've disconnected from them, they p-probably don't know you're free. They'll let you in to d—d—d" — *breathe*— "deliver your strength song. Instead, you'll call the compelled dragons out. Then they'll be yours to strengthen and command."

Kallar's brows knit in calculation. "Have you seen R'lann anywhere? A prison tent?"

Alísa blinked, startled by the shift. "No. I can ask my c-commanders, but—"

Kallar stood. "Do it. But first" —he paused a moment, gathering courage. He helped her to her feet— "I'll need your help. I don't know how to do this Dragon Singer thing."

Alísa nodded sharply, then turned to Sesína. She still felt the dragoness' pain, but cauterization made it more a constant ache than a rhythmic stabbing.

"She okay?" Kallar asked, startling Alísa.

"She will be."

"Good." Kallar sighed, running a hand over the normally shorn side of his hair. "I'm—sorry. Sesína."

Sesína clicked in her throat. *"Tell him I'll forgive him if he lets down his shield so he can hear me properly."*

"She says it wasn't your fault, b—but she forgives you anyway."

Sesína huffed and crossed one paw over the other. *"Fine. Just get him singing. We're faltering."*

"Right." Alísa nodded toward the entrance. "Let's get you a sight-line."

They hurried from the darkness to where they could see outside. Dragons shot back and forth across their view, roaring and spewing fire. Kallar visibly tensed.

"What do I do? Quickly, before I change my mind."

"Enter their clan-link and I'll feed you the words. Unless you want t-to find your own—"

"No. I'm no songweaver."

He closed his eyes and took a slow, deep breath. When he opened them again, they were hard. He was the cold, dispassionate warrior again. After a moment, he winced.

"I'm in."

"Okay. Repeat after me." Alísa paused, searching. A song to make the alphas think their Singer was back, only for it to free the dragons in their thrall. "In darkest hell and raging fight—"

Kallar repeated, his tone more a drawling speech than a song, as though he couldn't believe he had to stoop so low. Alísa stopped and got in front of him.

"You have to feel it" —she tapped the blue scale armor above his heart— "here."

Kallar sighed, exasperated. "I don't—"

"The words aren't the important thing," she interrupted. They had to be quick, before the an'reik realized what was happening. "You can b—blunder through them, not rhyme, whatever. But our songs are attuned to a dragon's heart. If the intent isn't there, it won't work."

Kallar's fists clenched. "Which is why I can't do it! Just leave me here. I'm useless."

Alísa shook her head. "No, you aren't. You may not hold any love for them, b—but you are a p-p-p-p-passionate person. You're angry about what was done to you, yes?"

He stared at her blankly, as if her question were idiotic.

"C-c-can you be angry that they're experiencing the same thing?" She pointed out the entrance. "Angry and wanting to end it? Even if you don't love them?"

Kallar stared outside. His breaths came heavily, as though he was already in battle. He shook his head with a growl.

"Again. Let's try again."

With his mind open and reaching out to the an'reik dragons, his frustration and determination flowed in the astral plane. Alísa sang again, feeding him one line at a time.

In darkest hell and raging fight
My strength I give to you
To power you amidst your plight
Arise, awake, push through

Kallar winced and gritted his teeth between each line, but the emotion was there. His anger grew as he sang, blossoming into a righteous rage.

I see your hearts, I know your pains
And so I come to you
To free the captives from their chains
Come out and live anew

A commotion rose outside, a mixture of victorious trumpets and indignant roars. Kallar flinched. A drop of fear cooled rage to anger.

"They're free, but they" —he grunted with pain— "they're being attacked by both sides now."

Alísa's eyes widened. Of course, her clanmates wouldn't know these were freed.

"C-c-c-c-cut off the an'reik dragons, b—but—"

"Already done," he said. "It's only me and the freed dragons now."

"Good. Rís, bring Kallar into our c-c-clan-link."

Rís barked, obeying while Kallar protested. His objection halted abruptly as Rís brought everyone together. All the dragons at once overwhelmed the Singers—anger, pain, fear, thrill, and sorrow crashing down on them.

Alísa breathed through her swimming head and nausea as slashes, bites, and burns manifested in her mind. With a snap, Kallar cut himself off, shield firm as he put his hands on his knees and dry-heaved. For a second, Alísa panicked—had the freed dragons been cut off too?—but Rís trilled reassuringly.

"Safe."

He closed off the link, returning it to the deadened version where it was only Alísa, Sesína, and Rís. Sesína was beside her now, offering the shoulder on her unwounded side. Alísa leaned against her, breaths shuddering as she looked at Kallar.

"I'm sorry. I know that was a lot. We'll g—get you a drek—that will help when we reconnect."

"No," he said, voice edged with panic. "I'm not doing that again."

"I p-p-p-promise, it's b—better. They—"

Kallar whirled on her and she saw the fear he was trying to hide. "I said no. Put me on the ground. I'll fight the an'reik and traitorous slayers. Find R'lann myself."

Alísa kept her tone low and gentle. "I have no ground forces for you to join, and I'm not sending you in alone. You don't have t-t-to fight alone anymore. You n—need help."

Kallar shook his head, fists clenched. "Do you have any idea what I've gone through? What opening my mind has done to me?"

"That wasn't you opening your mind. That was something evil t-t-t-taking from you. These are warriors who have united t-t-t-to fight that evil. We're on the same side. Help us, and let us help you."

Kallar's breath shuddered. "I'm not you, Alísa. I will never be you. I can fight, but I can't do this."

Alísa could only stare. The Kallar before her was so foreign. He was supposed to be arrogant and always ready to fight. To charge forward, knowing that he would make it work.

And he was supposed to help strengthen their allies. Based on their brief connection, they were in trouble. They needed two Dragon Singers, and she had been so sure Kallar would help.

Eldra Bria, Maker, what do I do?

"Kallar doing something small is better than Kallar doing nothing," Sesína whispered. *"Turn him back to his brother. Get him moving, then we'll do what we always*

do. Pull strength out of a hopeless situation."

Alísa sighed. "What about R'lann? How are you going to find him?"

"I'm willing to bet the human portion of the an'reik army still doesn't know I'm free. I should be able to move about without them giving me too much notice. Just get me down."

Alísa pointed outside. "How on A'dem will you find him in that chaos?"

"I'll make it work."

She shook her head. "Let us help you. I have humans, dragons, and d— dreki everywhere. If he's here, someone has likely seen him."

He considered a moment. "Fine. Ask them."

"You need to do it—"

"No!"

"Would you listen?" Alísa went to rub her skirt, but only found those stupid trousers. "I haven't seen R'lann in over a year, and if he's been imprisoned for w—weeks, I bet he doesn't look the same as I remember him."

That made Kallar's eyes soften with pain. Alísa gentled her tone.

"If they're going t-t-to find him quickly, they need your vision of him. Just this, then you can go. N—no more arguments." Alísa lifted empty hands. "I can't force you to be a Dragon Singer."

Kallar stared out the cave entrance, over the field of fallen dragons to the battle with the ground troops. He gritted his teeth and cursed.

"Fine. Hurry."

Alísa came back to him and knelt. "Sit."

He followed her down, unblinking eyes fixed on her. She reached up to pet Rís, who purred gently.

"I'm g—going to have Rís help you. He'll guide you to only a few squads at a t-t-time. Give them the image of R'lann, then move on to the next group. If someone recognizes him, their squad's drek will reach back out. This will be easier than t-taking in the entire army."

He eyed her. "Why didn't you do that before?"

"Because your d—dragons were in dang—"

"Not *my* dragons."

Alísa rolled her eyes. "Just lower your shield and let Rís guide you."

At that, Rís hopped to Kallar's shoulder. Kallar tensed like he expected the drek to bite him.

The clan-link opened. Alísa and Kallar both breathed in sharply as sensations flowed to them. Dragons' battle-thrill quickened Alísa's heart and their pain pounded through her, but with only three squads—four, counting the newly freed dragons Rís also pulled in—she kept it in check.

"We need to find someone," Alísa said. *"A teenager the an'reik have captured. Show them."*

The last command she directed at Kallar, who sent an image of R'lann. His hair was matted and tangled, his clothing dirty, his cheeks sallow. His eyes, however, held the same gentle strength Alísa remembered.

Without immediate recognition from the squads, they moved on to the next group. Again and again they showed R'lann's image. Kallar tensed with each change, but he never shut himself off.

"See! See!"

A drek chittered excitedly. Before Alísa could respond, Kallar straightened.

"Where?"

Images flooded the link—the south side of the battle, near twisting dark mists, a boy tied to a tree. Kallar's anger spiked and he cut himself off from Rís and the army. He looked at Alísa.

"I need to get there. Can you take me down?"

Alísa opened her mouth to protest—Sesína's injury wouldn't allow her to carry two people—but a loud trumpet stopped her. Alísa tensed as a silver-gray dragon dove toward the cave, then realized this was one of the new dragons in the link. Kallar stared at it, disbelieving.

"Lellani?"

She landed on the mountainside and snaked her neck through the entrance. She looked at Kallar, grunted, then turned to Alísa.

"Remind this brute of a Singer that he must lower his shield for me to speak to him."

Sesína hissed a laugh, and Alísa tapped Kallar's arm. "She needs to speak with you."

Kallar blinked and dropped his shield. Still connected to Lellani, Alísa could hear their conversation.

"Kallar-Dragon-Singer, we are here to offer our wings."

Kallar looked past her. "We?"

"Yes." Lellani snapped her jaws in triumph, her copper eyes lighting the

cave. *"Some dragons you freed are cowards and fled, but the rest of us are ready. We will help you free the boy."*

Kallar stared, trepidation flowing. Then something changed. His stance hardened and his eyes took on a warrior's focus.

"I accept."

Alísa gaped as he ran forward and grabbed Lellani's neck-spines with the confidence of a man who had been riding dragons all his life. Was it really that simple? He just needed the dragons who understood his pain to offer their support?

Actually, that made perfect sense. Alísa lifted a hand.

"Wait. I'll get you a drek so you can——"

"We're flying solo," he said, looking back at her. "I told you, I'm not like you. I can't do hundreds of dragons. But I will do twenty, for R'lann."

He slid between two spines at the base of Lellani's neck. Eyes meeting Alísa's, he deflated slightly.

"Thank you."

Letting out a harsh cry, he bid Lellani forward like a horse into battle. The dragoness pulled from the cave, joining him with a ready snarl.

"A pleasure to meet you, Alísa-Dragon-Singer. Fight well."

With that, Lellani leapt into the air with a roar, leaving Alísa, Sesína, and Rís alone. Alísa let out a sigh that was part relief, part resignation. Kallar was on his own path, whatever it might be. That left her to strengthen the army. By herself.

"Eldra Bria sing over you," she whispered.

Sesína's eyes dimmed. *"And us."*

Alísa shuddered as Rís reconnected her to the clan. *"And us."*

64

THE FUNERAL PYRE

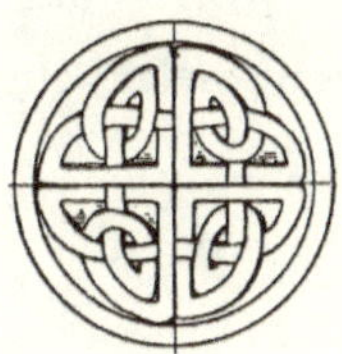

There were dragons in his head. Dragons with wounds that throbbed in his skull and emotions that rushed through him. But, for once, the emotions didn't feel foreign. The two most prominent were completely familiar.

First, a terrible fear—one Kallar understood in the depths of his being. The residual terror of being used, forced to do another's bidding. Part of it wasn't even residual. Some of his squad actively feared he would do what their alphas had. These dragons pulled at the edges of his mind, wanting to leave but also needing to exact vengeance on those who had held them captive.

That raging fire was the other familiar emotion. A deep, gnawing need for justice. An all-consuming ache to ensure no one experienced what they had again.

If I can't relate to that, I can't relate to anything.

Lellani rumbled beneath him. *"Where are we headed, Singer?"*

Kallar scanned the battlefield, searching for—

"There." He sent an image through his link to the dragons. *"The grove in the mountain's shadow."*

Lellani led the charge, seventeen dragons in their wake. They swooped and twisted through the battle as enemy dragons dove at them. The power in Lellani's muscles, the way she pushed through air and gravity like they were nothing, sent a thrill through him. It almost made him forget the irritation of having no control over their movement.

Pain slammed into Kallar as one of the freed dragons trumpeted. It throbbed in his mind and settled in his back.

Wings. An enemy had attacked the dragon's wings. Before Kallar could think to command, another of his squad veered off to help. His heartbeat raced as their battle raged, as though he were the one grappling.

"The song, Singer," Lellani prompted. *"We need your song."*

Kallar tensed. Singer. Meant to fight with his voice just as much as his body, like his mother. Allara had no strength songs, but he could remember one Alísa used. He didn't know the words, but the gist of it still lived in his memories. All he needed was intention and emotion, right?

Feeling foolish, he elongated his words so that his speech would become song-like. "Dragons, hear me now. May this song give you speed. To fly and save a boy in chains. And strength to make them pay."

Lellani snorted steam. *"You call that a song?"*

"It's working, isn't it?" Kallar growled back at her.

Sure enough, Lellani and the others flew faster. Only two stayed behind— the one with torn wings and its helper. At the back of Kallar's mind, he sensed the latter helping the injured dragon to the mountainside.

We're not losing any more.

Kallar continued his speech-singing, eyes fixed on the nearing grove. His stomach clenched as power flowed out from him to the dragons. It seemed like his soul was being poured out. Emptied. He was vulnerable, and with dragons— *dragons!*—he didn't know or trust. Maybe he could trust Lellani to use it well. The others…

It didn't matter. R'lann needed rescue, and these dragons were the only way to reach him. If any an'reik guarded him, Kallar was certain he would need help.

"Like wind under wings, may this song lift you. Like strength inside your limbs to fight for what is true."

"Aha!" Lellani made a guttural sound Kallar felt more than heard. *"So you can* rhyme.*"*

"Shut up."

He pushed out more words as they skirted the ground-based portion of the battle, avoiding the mess of fire, screams, and death above it. They were close now. So close. He recalled the tree R'lann was tied to. It stood amid the grove, but not in a thick patch. It was likely near the edge, able to be seen from outside.

He caught movement in his periphery just before Lellani swerved. Clenching legs and fists, Kallar twisted to shoot a mind-spear into the dragon attacking them.

It wasn't a dragon.

A tendril of solid mist grabbed for Lellani. With a frightful trumpet, she rolled out of the way, Kallar's stomach dropping as she did. Another dragon roared its outrage as a second rope caught it and yanked it to the ground with bone-shattering force. Kallar barely registered the pain before it ceased, the dragon dead.

Rage burned hot in Kallar and the dragons. Isarra. The tendrils led his eyes straight to her. She stood a ways outside the grove, Marizarr at her side. In the trees just beyond them, a figure slumped against ropes binding it to a trunk. He only caught a glimpse as Lellani twisted to avoid another of Isarra's attacks, but it was definitely R'lann.

"Go!" Kallar shouted to his squad. *"Get between her and R'lann."*

Marizarr shot his hellflames into the air, chasing down a dragon while Isarra sent up another rope of mist.

Lellani veered away from the deadly appendage. *"And how do you suggest we get close without dying?"*

Before Kallar could answer, Isarra's voice resonated with power. "You may have defeated your keeper, little Singer, but you are still mortal!"

Kallar shook his head to clear the ringing in his ears. Of course, she would use her dark magic just to taunt him.

Isarra pulled a vial from her belt pouch and downed the contents. Immediately, her two tendrils of mist split into four, then six, one snatching a dragon as it tried to escape the hellflames. A cry silenced Kallar's song as fire coursed through his mind. The dragon and the mists that held it burned away, leaving behind only ash tossed by the wind.

Isarra's voice again cut through the battle. "You cannot stand against the power of the Nameless Ones!"

"Attack!" Kallar ordered.

Lellani swooped, her speed aided by his strength, and breathed fire at Isarra. The tendrils of mist retracted to form a shield around her. Behind them, two dragons dove at Isarra, also flaming, but nothing made it past the barrier. The flames splashed over the ground outside the shield instead.

Marizarr, too, was unharmed as a fourth dragon came after him. He pulled the fire from the surrounding grasses and shot it in two bursts, the first burning a hole in a dragon's wing. The unfortunate creature crashed, rolling toward the grove until it hit a tree with enough force to split the trunk. It didn't move, but its pain continued to pulse in Kallar's arm and back. Alive, but unconscious.

Kallar clenched Lellani's spine as the dragoness twisted away from another tendril. He did not like someone else controlling his position! She swerved and dove, trumpeting as a shot of hellflames nearly caught her.

"What do we do, Singer?"

Kallar's heart thudded in his throat. Dragon-fire didn't work against the mists, but Isarra did have to block it. Perhaps if Lellani dropped him off, he could fight on the ground while the dragons distracted her—

No, he wouldn't make it. He'd probably be killed by his own allies' fire, and he hadn't seen anything ever beat the mists.

What do I do?

The pain of another dragon's body breaking against the ground roiled in Kallar's stomach and blacked out his vision. Only, it wasn't completely black. In the center of pain's harsh darkness, he remembered Bria trapped within the keeper's orb, and the way she spun her fire until it overwhelmed the darkness.

Were Isarra's mists the same as the keeper's? Her mists were how it had entered his head, so perhaps—

But again, her misty shield held back dragon-fire.

But not hellflames. Her misty tendrils had burned away in Marizarr's flames a moment ago. But the chances of getting the flame-manipulator to hit Isarra accidentally were slim.

Vision returned as Lellani flew out over the grove. *Maybe I should fight on my own two feet.*

"Your strength is waning within me," Lellani prodded. *"You must sing again."*

Kallar growled mentally. There was a solution in his thoughts, if he could only pull it free.

"Hold on. I need to think. I can't sing for you at the same time."

"Seems like something you should work on." Lellani's tone turned serious. *"What are you planning?"*

Kallar shook his head. *"I'll figure it out. You keep flying."*

"Unlike some, I can multitask."

It took everything within Kallar not to mind-spear her. Or so he told himself.

"Some Dragon Singer the great Allaras-son is," Isarra's voice returned, sneering. "Do you finally see? Your Eldír leave you helpless—you cannot defeat those the Nameless have empowered!"

Kallar had no words to combat hers. He still didn't understand why the Maker and the Eldír didn't help their people like the Nameless helped theirs.

But no, they did. Just not with flashy powers. Kallar couldn't deny their presence anymore.

So where are you?!

In a dizzying moment, the memory of Bria's fire destroying the keeper's mists flashed through his mind again. This time, another memory accompanied it—that of the Maker's words in Karn's voice.

'You do not need me to move heaven and earth for you—I have already provided.'

What was provided? Dragon-fire wouldn't work. Only hellflames and whatever fire Bria used had worked.

"Talk to me, Singer!"

Kallar let out a frustrated snarl. *"I need to figure out how to use hellflames against Isarra. They can burn her mists away. So unless you're an'reik yourself or have some—"*

"What are hellflames?"

He rolled his eyes. *"The an'reik fire that burns through everything. Demonically powered flames."*

"The ability for a single dragon or human to wield such fire is indeed a gift of the Nameless, but they are not special flames—just extremely hot."

"How can you possibly know—"

Lellani snapped her jaws. *"My former alpha's gift was in his flames. A dragon's funeral pyre is also hot enough to burn through scales. Perhaps through the witch's magic, too."*

"What?" Kallar leaned closer. *"Are you sure?"*

She looked back. *"Dragons know fire. Trust me, Singer."*

Lellani veered from the safety of the grove, heading for the enemy. Kallar's breaths came fast. He didn't know what she meant by a funeral pyre, but whatever it was, he wouldn't have any control. No chance to adjust if it didn't work. No knowledge to give orders as the dragons maneuvered.

But he had nothing better. And R'lann needed them.

He let out a breath. *"Okay. I don't understand your idea, so you take command.*

I'll strengthen you through it."

Lellani roared a battle-cry. *"By Maker's wings!"*

Kallar clenched and unclenched his fist. *I sure hope this is the provision you were talking about, Maker.*

Lellani's instructions flew through the clan-link as she neared Isarra's position. Kallar resisted listening, allowing the dragons to act while he focused on his song.

"Like wind under your wings, may my songs lift you. Like strength within your limbs to fight for what is true."

When no more words came, Kallar simply repeated as Lellani circled high above their enemies. Marizarr shot a bout of flames at them, but they dissipated before they could reach. Isarra's tendrils, however, could stretch just high enough to snatch them. Dragons dipped and spun to escape as their spirits strengthened under his song and Lellani's instructions.

At Lellani's command, they dove. Twisting, spiraling, circling down in a tight pattern that had Kallar clutching hard to hang on. Ropes of mist and spurts of hellflames came at them, sending dragons dodging out and back in, single-minded in their mission.

They opened their jaws. Their rattling inhalations made Kallar flinch, the sound typically heralding death. Then fire burst, aimed at the center as the dragons twisted toward the ground. One fell from the pattern to avoid hellflames and flew into the grasp of Isarra's tendrils, but despite its panicked trumpet, the others remained focused.

Down, down they flew, the heat of their flames making Kallar sweat faster than the wind could whisk the moisture away. His throat dried, leaving him barely able to croak out a word. Another tendril grabbed onto a dragon, but the concentrated fire in the center of their circle burned away a portion and set the dragon free.

"We're landing hard," Lellani said. *"Brace yourself!"*

"How?!"

He took a blow to his stomach as he slammed against Lellani's spine. He sucked in a new breath as Marizarr turned to Lellani. Kallar tensed—there wasn't time to escape. But his dragons continued pumping their wings. As they surrounded the two an'reik, the wind of their wings and continuous fire created a swirling column of flame. Marizarr's blast was swept up with the dragon-fire.

The heat became too much. Kallar slid down Lellani and got behind her, clothes and hair plastered to him. A scream raked over Kallar's ears and mind—one of effort and sheer will. Ropes of dark mist reached, retracted, and reached again, two of them making it through to grab the necks of Lellani and another dragon. Their panic flooded Kallar's thoughts, but he twisted their fear within him into rage. He shout-sang a battle-cry, falling to a knee as he pushed every ounce of his strength into it. The dragons responded with greater flames and faster wings, incinerating the tendrils that choked Lellani and the other dragon.

Isarra screamed again as the fire became too bright for Kallar to see her. Then, in a flash of light, something within the flames collapsed. As one, the twelve remaining dragons stopped flaming, some shaking their heads, others stumbling. In the center, there remained only a circle of ground red with heat. No sign of Marizarr or Isarra.

Kallar breathed heavily as silence overtook them all. It was over. Isarra was dead and would no longer torment him or R'lann.

Coughing with the effort, Kallar rose and turned toward the grove. As quickly as his body would allow, he went to the barely conscious figure slumped in his bonds. Kallar pulled Karn's dagger from its sheath and sawed through the ropes at R'lann's legs, then at his torso. R'lann fell forward into his arms, and Kallar slowly lowered him to the ground. He looked terrible and his arm bled from a fresh cut, but as he lay in Kallar's arms, he gave the smallest of smiles.

"It's you."

Kallar's eyes prickled fiercely, but he had no strength left to restrain his weakness. He turned his back to the dragons and tugged R'lann closer as his body betrayed him and tears fell.

65

THE MAKER'S PLAN

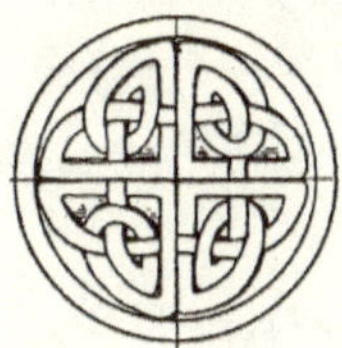

Dragon pain closed around Alísa. Even with Rís limiting her connection, it was becoming too much. Gouged legs, torn wings, bitten tails, cauterized wounds. Though they were holding on, they had started this fight outnumbered.

Alísa and Sesína remained in the cave, three of their squad-mates guarding the entrance while L'non and the rest followed the enemy. Now that the an'reik dragons no longer guarded Kallar, the sky battle moved closer to the ground troops. Sesína hated staying, but L'non rightly pointed out that the fighting was fierce, her wound would slow her, and losing Alísa would cost them the war.

Alísa leaned on Sesína at the mouth of the cave, gazing at the chaos as she sang. Rís moved her from squad to squad at a dizzying rate, each bringing with it new flashes of agony until they all blended together. Sesína carried as much as their bond allowed, but the fear, rage, sorrow, and pain threatened to overwhelm them both.

Flames coated Alísa's mind as a fire-manipulator burned a dragon-rider pair to death. Tears streamed from her eyes.

Keep them alive. Keep. Them. Alive.

She grasped for the strands of courage and camaraderie as despair tried to consume her. Her army was brave. At the very least, all would die honorable deaths and enter the Maker's halls together.

What a sight to behold.

"Don't give up yet, dragon-heart," Sesína said, nosing her shoulder hard. *"We have more within us. Keep going."*

Alísa blinked, dazed. Had she been falling asleep? She was so exhausted. How long had they fought? Pulling up more strength was like gouging out the bottom of her heart. But her people faced exhaustion, physical pain, and death.

How could she hold anything back?

A rider's terror as he fell from his mount.

Is this truly how it ends, Maker?

A slash across a belly.

Are we only meant to delay the an'reik?

Fire to cauterize.

A spark to ignite those too stubborn to listen before?

Anguish as a mate died.

Will you abandon us, like you did Papá?

No. Not abandon. She knew that. The Maker was here, as were Bria and Branni. Bria promised she would fight. And she had, for Kallar. She was here. Wasn't she?

"B—Bria," Alísa breathed out, "please. Help me."

She searched the darkness of the cave, hoping for a piercing light to appear and give her strength, but none manifested. A sob escaped Alísa's lips, and she pressed forward in her song again, her body shaking. Sesína curled around her, and Rís whimpered his sorrow as another pair died. Their enemies surely fell too, but all Alísa felt were her own warriors.

Their pain.

Their fear.

Their despair.

No. Anything but despair. She had been there before, seen it as Bria snuffed it with her sword of light. Alísa wouldn't abandon her people to it.

"Make sure they *all* hear this, Rís," she whispered.

The clan-link shifted, more pain and emotion pouring through it. Tears in her eyes, Alísa changed her song.

Branni's strength within you all, to carry through your pain
To heal your wounds, may Líla's life flood into every vein
Bria's song fill all your hearts, to learn our sacred call
And if death comes, D'tohm to carry us to Maker's halls

In darkest night, may Maker's light shine bright upon the land
In his anam who fight and die, who chose to take a stand

For if we live or if we fall, the victory is sure
Though mortal plans may wash away, the Maker's will endure

Alísa sensed the change as she prayed over her army. No measure of extra power or healing, but a shift in emotions. In place of despair, she found purpose. In place of fear, courage. She grasped onto both and sang again, sending every ounce of strength their emotions gave her back to them. It wasn't enough, but she gave it anyway.

Use it as you will, Maker.

Rís perked up on her shoulder, craning his neck as though to look out the cave entrance. He chirped questioningly, then excitedly, flapping his wing against Alísa's head.

"Ska! Close!"

Alísa opened her eyes, hopeful as Rís brought Ska into the communication line and, with him, Falier's squad. At least she could say goodbye.

"Líse! What's happening?"

She could feel the injuries within his squad, but also their readiness. She wished she held the same rather than this numb loneliness.

"We're outnumbered. I'm trying to give as much strength as I can, but I'm wrung out." She paused. *"I don't think we can win this, love."*

"Talk to me."

She relayed the situation, pausing her song for a breath to better feel his presence. His mind was warm and steady, like sunlight. Even his terrible worry for her couldn't cloud it.

"It's okay," she told him. *"We came knowing this might happen. We're united within the Maker's plan, and he will use it, even if we die. That's all that matters."*

"United." The word sounded ethereal, as though Falier rolled it over in his thoughts rather than speaking it. *"Líse, I have an idea."*

66

ALPHA

With one final push, Falier's squad crested the interlocking mountains of the range. The battlefield spread out before them. Dragons clashed in the air while others breathed fire and ice against the human an'reik on the ground. Bodies littered the field while smoke rose from whatever fires could catch in the wintery-wet grasses. Through Ska, Falier searched for Koriana and Briek, finding them in command as expected.

"Graydonn," Koriana said, her voice tired, *"praise the Maker, you are alive."*

"For you too, Mother. We have a plan, but what's the situation?"

"At present, our attention is on the dragons, while a few squads target the ground troops. We also have multiple squads dedicated to protecting the ice dragons, who are constantly under attack. They are most effective when they land and can apply all their strength to their breath, but landing is impossible with so many human enemies."

Koriana stopped, the fierceness of her thoughts telling Falier she was grappling. He felt Briek build up and release power in the astral plane, then they returned.

"We are also avoiding the southern end for now," Briek said. *"There is an an'reik there who controls strange dark mists. Three pairs have already fallen to her, and one dragon came back possessed, according to Rassím."*

"What's the plan to help the possessed?" Falier asked.

Briek sighed. *"Rassím is sending us images of those he finds. We are doing our best to avoid harming them, but we can only remember so much in this sea of enemy faces."*

"Alísa's plan is not working," Koriana growled. *"Avoiding them prevents us from using our full firepower on the ground. We would be much further along if they weren't an issue."*

"At the risk of sounding treasonous," Briek said, *"please tell me you have a better*

plan."

Falier relayed his idea as Graydonn dove down the mountainside. Each of his squad-mates held a mixture of exhaustion and readiness. They had joined minds a few times throughout their journey, boosting their strength through their connection. It only worked for short bursts, though, as it was extremely taxing for non-dreki to hold for long periods of time. Right now, however, the perfect coordination and stronger telepathy might give their army a chance to defeat the larger enemy.

Koriana's skepticism filled the link. *"Your squad is filled with those already bonded—no one else here has that except Rassím and Dezra."*

Harenn let out a steamy sigh. *"A bond isn't necessary. I can't say I love it, but Taz and I joined as well. It can work."*

"It will *work,"* Taz said, a grin in his telepathic voice. *"Trust binds us to this squad. I'm willing to bet many feel the same after training and fighting together."*

Koriana's emotions turned thoughtful. *"All right, then."* The mind-link opened to include the other leaders. *"Alísa's tiern has returned with a plan. I cede leadership to him. Go ahead, Falier-Dragon-Friend."*

For a moment, Falier hesitated. The entire army waited—dragons he only partly knew, slayers who knew him as the holder striving to become a slayer, and clans who didn't know him at all. Would they even listen?

"Some will," Graydonn whispered through their bond, *"and others will follow their example. Speak with certainty. You are Alísa's tiern, and you have what they need. Show them."*

Falier breathed out his anxiety. Their squad was closing in on the battle quickly. Drudging up every ounce of confidence he had, he spoke.

"The an'reik have cornered us into fighting defensively. We need to take back control, so we're going to redefine the squads. Don't move until I say—we'll hopefully be able to use the confusion of the sudden change to our advantage."

He outlined the plan for them as quickly as he could as his allies continued to fight before him. Many hesitated at the prospect of a dreki mind-share, but others grew curious, even eager.

"You ready, Rassím, Dezra?"

"As we'll ever be," Rassím acknowledged. *"Prepare yourselves—this isn't the prettiest of sights."*

Falier wasn't sure what that meant, but it was too late to hesitate. As

Graydonn dodged an attacking dragon, Falier reached out to the mountain.

"Are you ready, Líse?"

"Yes." Her psychic voice was so weak it made his heart shudder with worry. Hopefully, the joining would help her, too.

She shifted to her simplest strength song—one everyone knew. Falier sang aloud as well as in his mind, using the physical act to anchor the music inside himself. Immediately, Ska pulled him and Graydonn together. The others of his squad came next, followed by Alísa, Sesína, and Rís. As they joined, a burst of power shot through the link. It flowed from drek to drek and latched onto each dragon and human in their army, calling them to join.

The call settled deep within the dragons' hearts and minds. They had trusted the Singer thus far and now, though fiercely independent, they chose to trust her still. If she believed this would get them through the battle, they would follow her.

With the dreki and dragons pulling the clan-link to merge, slayers began to accept it. Falier instantly recognized some minds, those he had trained as riders. Others he didn't know, but they came with memories of provisions in dark caves and of warriors honored in song. Still others pulled away from him, full of skepticism and fear. As Falier's squad aligned, however, their Jossen and Varek parts reached out to these, Jossen coaxing and Varek demanding.

Minds grasped the melody—not all, but enough. Their Alísa part basked in wonder as each additional *anam* joined her song, her spirit lifting and drawing others into her hope. Alongside it, Falier felt the collective's fear of connection, excitement that it was working, and readiness to fight and rescue.

Falier grasped onto battle-readiness and, by unspoken consensus, the collective followed him. Somehow, in the immense collection of personalities, motives, and knowledge, he held the reins just a tad more than the others.

Alpha.

"Now!"

Dragons scattered in a swirl of colors, releasing their grapples and squad patterns to form the new groups Falier had outlined. One team to cover the skies, one to find the possessed, one to defeat hellflame-manipulators, and one to strafe the remaining ground troops with fire.

Falier's team dove toward the ground. He searched through the myriad of minds for Rassím and his view of the world, pushing aside dragons' intense focus and Selene's sound-lights. Nothing seemed to change at first. Everything looked normal, perhaps tinted a bit differently than Falier's own sight, but—

Then Rassím's sight revealed the enemy army for what it was. Darkness surrounded the warriors, four out of every five, its black glow reaching out as though trying to claw its way into the world.

Everyone the Nameless had touched. Falier knew it like Rassím did. The distance prevented him from distinguishing between those who willingly embraced the darkness and those being consumed by it. Hopefully, when he got closer, he could find the latter.

Enemy slayers launched mind-spears at them, but the rider parts held a shield firm around the collective, sending the astral projectiles ricocheting back. Arrows and javelins flew, as did hellflames. Graydonn spiraled left to avoid a spout of flames while Falier warned another dragon of an archer just below them. All the while, Falier kept Alísa's song firmly in his mind—insistent, like a drummer beating loud patterns to keep unpracticed musicians together.

Their Rassím part spotted a possessed woman first, the information instantly reaching the others. He saw her too late for Dezra to do anything, but their Iila part flew just behind them. Iila's rider Rassi drew power from the collective and threw a mind-choke around the woman. She fought it unsuccessfully, dropping unconscious after a couple of seconds.

Iila dove, employing her small body's speed and dexterity to avoid jabbing spears and swords. She landed on her hind feet beside the choked woman and grabbed her. Behind her, a slayer moved to stab through her wing, but Harenn blasted him with fire. Iila launched back into the air unscathed, the possessed woman dangling unconscious in her front paws until Komi flew under her to take the burden.

Uncertain but hopeful, their Trísse part touched the woman's arm and whispered. "Eldra Branni, help her."

The swirling inhale of darkness did not leave. None knew whether it was because she had to be conscious, she wasn't within the soul's shield, or it simply took time to defeat a keeper.

Whatever the answer, Falier spotted another possessed. While Komi flew off to deposit the unconscious woman outside the battlefield, Graydonn dove in to repeat Iila's actions. Simultaneously, a different team pursued a third possessed human. As Falier choked his target, searing pain lanced through the mind-share. Graydonn wobbled and Falier lost his choke as grief replaced pain. The other dragon had dived straight into the hellflames of a fire an'reik.

Clanmates roared their anger at the death. Falier channeled his rage into a choke, knocking out multiple people around his possessed target. Another dragon-rider pair followed behind and captured the man.

Again and again, Falier's squad snatched up possessed individuals while the other squads fulfilled their roles. He showed the fire-strafers areas cleared of possessed, where they could burn without fear, while the ice dragon squad worked to keep the hellflamers away from them all.

When they were sure they had captured all the possessed, Falier's squad joined the sky team. They twisted through the air, ripping past an'reik dragons at a speed granted by both the collective and Alísa's strength song. Her energy was returning, thanks to the bonds tying them all together. Falier drew his sword and slashed upward as Graydonn flew dangerously close to an enemy dragon, slicing through a wing and allowing Komi and Harenn to kill it.

A trumpet of alarm sounded among the an'reik dragons—a cry the dragon parts of the collective recognized as a call to retreat. Graydonn and Koriana led the charge, chasing down the fleeing dragons as they headed for their caves. Their assigned dreki streamed forward to phase through enemy bodies, cutting through their minds again and again until they fell. Between them and the rest of the sky team, not one enemy dragon made it to the mountain.

"Back," Falier ordered. *"Time to end this."*

Together, the two squads banked back toward the human an'reik army. It looked so small now, surrounded by flames and walls of ice. The teams remaining with the ground troops had scoured the battlefield, rescuing fallen clanmates who might still be alive. Several slayers who were merely allied with the an'reik surrendered and were taken away. Only an'reik and their loyal slayer allies remained.

By Falier's order, the army encircled the enemy, letting out streams of fire to cut off escape, then pushing inward until the last of the darkness burned away.

Falier let go of the song, letting Rassím's vision fade back into his own as the collective split apart. The war was over.

67

TOGETHER

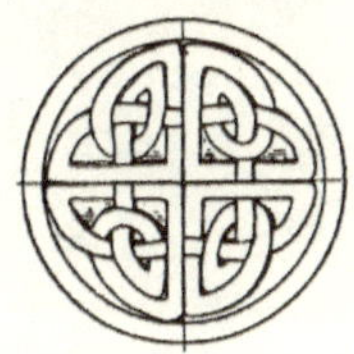

Alísa's mind twitched with overuse. Humans were not designed to share minds like that. Nor, apparently, were dragons. As Sesína landed on the battlefield, she shook her head as though covered in flies.

"Let's not repeat that," Sesína said. *"Ever."*

Alísa's hands trembled as she took them off Sesína's spine. She agreed, but couldn't deny the effectiveness of Falier's unconventional plan. And, despite the itching mind-fatigue, the collective had restored enough of her strength to stand and move.

Alísa slid from Sesína's back and checked the wound in the dragoness' side. It oozed clear liquid, but hadn't reopened, Maker be praised.

Looking up, Alísa forced herself to survey the battlefield. Two camps were forming, the first a small one for their prisoners. A couple of her allied chiefs hailed from villages with prisons and were placed in charge of the slayers who surrendered. When Alísa asked about dragons in a similar situation, she discovered none had survived. Dragons did not have prisons and instead killed their worst criminals. Siding with the an'reik and wiping out other clans certainly qualified.

The other, far larger camp held the injured. As Alísa's eyes skimmed over to that camp, they caught on the many bodies littering the battlefield. Nearly half of Alísa's army was dead or had severe injuries. Slayers moved about on the ground, checking for wounded they might help. Dragons followed behind, cremating human bodies and noting dragons who would need a funeral pyre. Rís and the dreki, too, searched for their dead, transforming flesh into glowing specks that floated up into the sky.

A breeze rippled through Alísa's hair. She closed her eyes. *Eldra D'tohm guide you all safely to the Maker's halls.*

A shadow passed overhead. She and Sesína looked up to see Graydonn circling back to land. The muted buzz of Falier and Graydonn's telepathy entered their minds—no words, only their presence. Alísa and Sesína hurried to them as they landed, Sesína to nuzzle Graydonn's cheek and Alísa to wrap her arms around Falier.

Falier's grip was fierce and comforting, and she sensed his own need for comfort. He stooped to kiss her, but as soon as their lips touched, he jerked back with a wince.

Alísa grimaced. "Sorry. Dragon p-p-pain. I should have thought of that."

"It's okay. I should have too. I'm expecting it now." He pulled her close and, rather than kiss her, laid his head against her temple. He let out a breath. "We made it."

"We did."

They stayed there for a moment, basking in each other's presence and safety. Alísa felt the wounds pulsing in Falier's body, most acutely the one on his bandaged hand. She would have to ask what happened later. They had duties to attend to.

Alísa looked Falier in the eyes. "How are the possessed? Were you able to help them?"

He jerked his head back toward the prison camp. "We've laid hands on all of them. Some were freed, but more are unchanged. We even called to multiple Eldír, in case some of them weren't warriors who answer to Branni. They're tied up and the others are watching them."

Alísa thought for a moment. "I w—wonder if K-K-K-Kallar might have an idea how to help them." Assuming he had made it. Last she had seen him was on the south side fighting whatever controlled the dark mists.

"Let's head there," Sesína said, lowering to her belly.

Alísa went to her, addressing Falier as she climbed on. "Come with us?"

Falier didn't answer right away, staring at her. He opened his mouth, closed it, then opened again. "Are you—wearing trousers?"

His shock was adorable, and Alísa couldn't help but laugh.

Sesína stood, thrumming. *"You should see a medic, Falier. If you can't tell what she's wearing, that dreki mind-share might have damaged your brain."*

With that, Sesína headed south, Graydonn and Falier following. They stayed under the smoke as best they could. Ice dragons had extinguished the worst fires, but some still smoldered in the wet grass.

As they flew, Alísa looked on the destruction and death with a heavy heart. She regretted nothing, yet she expected the eradication of the an'reik army would make the world seem—lighter. With smoke overhead, a burnt-out field below, and many dead or wounded, the world seemed anything but light.

They found Kallar and some of his dragons at the edge of a grove. The dragons, including Lellani, stood around one of the fallen and breathed out their funeral pyre. Two piles of ash nearby told of other dragons already honored.

Kallar knelt a ways back from them, R'lann in his arms. He seemed quiet rather than grieved. That likely meant R'lann was alive, yet Alísa hesitated. After everything Kallar had been through, he deserved time to process. Still, there was work to be done. As a warrior apprenticed to a chief, he should understand. Perhaps offering something first would be prudent.

Alísa approached quietly. "Is he—"

"Asleep." Kallar didn't look at her. "I think he'll be okay."

Alísa nodded, though he wouldn't see it. "Shall we fetch a medic?"

Kallar hesitated. "That would be good. Thank you."

Alísa looked back at Falier, who returned to Graydonn. As they flew off to find someone, Alísa came closer.

"I'm glad you found him." When he didn't react, she added. "I saw the p-p-pillar of fire."

"Why are you really here?"

Alísa sighed, kneeling in front of him. "We captured as many p-p-p-possessed as p-possible, but prayer only freed a few. I w—wondered if you have insight for how to help them."

Kallar met her eyes briefly, then looked down again. "Maybe. I'll go see them once R'lann is safe."

Alísa smiled. "Thank you."

"No one should be trapped that way. A captive in their own mind. Tortured by those—those things."

Alísa stayed silent, leaving room for Kallar to talk more if he wanted. He didn't. After a few minutes, Graydonn returned with another dragon whose rider bore a pack filled with medical supplies. The medic asked about R'lann's experiences and condition. After a not-so-subtle threat from Kallar, the rider carried R'lann to the dragon, who flew them to the medic camp.

Kallar watched them go with anxiety in his eyes. Then he hardened and glanced at his dragons, who had just finished the last of their funeral pyres. Lellani pulled away from the group and came to him, pulling Alísa into communication. Kallar asked her to bear him again, which she readily agreed to.

"What shall the others do?"

Kallar shook his head. "Whatever they want. They're free."

Lellani hummed. *"You are not used to command, are you?"*

Kallar shot a glare at the dragoness while Alísa fought back a wry smile.

"If they're looking for ways to help," Alísa offered, *"they should find Koriana or Saynan. They'll give them tasks. Otherwise, like Kallar said, they are free and may leave if they choose."*

Lellani snorted a negative. *"Our an'reik alphas are dead, our clans scattered or destroyed. We have nowhere to go. Therefore, we shall help as we can until we decide how to proceed."*

Alísa blinked slowly, then went to Sesína.

Once at the prison camp, Alísa and Kallar followed Falier to the area with the possessed. There, Rassím, Trísse, and Taz watched thirteen bound men and women. Some bore bandaged wounds, and some were gagged.

"A few of them got mouthy since you left." Rassím gestured to the captives. "Figured we'd spare Trísse."

Trísse crossed her arms. "You know I grew up among wayfarers, right?"

Taz mimicked her stance and pouted. "Rassím doesn't care about *my* delicate ears, apparently."

"Not a joking matter," Kallar muttered. He passed by the guards to stand in front of the captured possessed. "Let me talk to them. Alone."

When no one moved, Kallar faced them with an exasperated look. "Well?"

"Sorry, friend, but you're not the chief here." Taz looked at Falier and Alísa.

"Do as he says," Alísa said. "He's their best chance."

"Chief," Rassím said, looking at the captives, "I should stay. Who knows what tricks those things might use to deceive us?"

"They can't fool me," Kallar said. "Not anymore."

Rassím squinted at him, unconvinced. "Be that as it may, it's important that we're certain."

Alísa nodded. "You'll stay, then."

Kallar glared at her. A buzz that felt like a static charge entered her mind and cut off everyone else except Sesína.

"I need to be alone. I don't want this stranger here while I basically beg people to accept what I refused all my life."

Shame and desperation wafted through the connection. Each seemed so wrong coming from Kallar, sparking pity in Alísa. She would grant his request if she could, but he wouldn't know for sure whether someone was free or still under a keeper's control. Only Rassím could be certain.

"I don't want your pity," Kallar said. *"I want your respect."*

"Respect has nothing to do with this. Whether you admit it or not, you need help." Alísa sighed. *"Rassím is a good man. He won't judge you for caring for these lost souls."*

Kallar cast him a sidelong glance. *"I don't like it."*

"I know. Do it anyway."

Kallar paused a long while, pulling his telepathy back. Everyone was staring at them now, waiting.

He let out a breath. "Check on R'lann for me while you're gone."

Alísa nodded firmly. "I will."

Leaving Taz and Trísse with their dragon partners and Dezra a short distance away, Alísa and Falier flew to the medic camp. Warriors lay on soft grass untainted by battle, guarded by dragons as those with medical training made their rounds. Within an hour, the pairs Alísa had sent back to her caves would arrive with additional medics.

The wounded dragons who could be transported were also here. Saynan's mate Aree walked among these, helping as she could, and informed Alísa of a few humans helping dragons still on the field. Those with deep wounds might be better served by a medic's needle and thread than simple cauterization.

Falier left to assist with less critical wounds, Graydonn at his side. Alísa walked among the wounded, offering the reassurance and honor only a commander could give. She found R'lann conversing with a couple of bandaged slayers. When he saw her, he sat up straighter, wincing at the movement.

"Kal?"

"He's alright," she said. "He's talking with the p-p-p-possessed we captured, hoping they'll accept the help of the Maker and his Eldír and be freed."

R'lann's brow creased. "You left him alone among keepers?"

"My *radharc anam* is with him," she assured. "He'll be okay."

That seemed to ease R'lann's mind. "And Kal sent you away because he was embarrassed?"

Alísa nodded. How well he knew his brother.

"He needs to get over that if he's going to marry you."

Alísa flushed. Sesína coughed beside her.

"Awkward."

Indeed. But, of course, R'lann wouldn't know. Last time they spoke, Alísa and Kallar were essentially betrothed.

"That's, uh, not going to happen anymore. I c-called it off. We—finally figured out we don't work." Not that she had ever expected them to.

The slayers with R'lann suddenly appeared highly interested in the clouds, or perhaps on the hill to their left. R'lann, however, grinned.

"Took you long enough."

Alísa smirked. "Like you knew. We were always p-p-perfectly civil at your parents' home. Gia and T-Tobin are fine, by the way. They've been staying with my c-c-c-clan."

R'lann glanced at Sesína. "Your clan of humans and dragons?"

Alísa nodded. "They're safe. T-Tobin flew back to get Gia. They'll be here soon."

"Flew." R'lann's eyes wandered, taking in Aree, the wounded dragons in camp, and those on the battlefield. "I can hardly believe it. The an'reik dragons and humans marched in the same direction, but this... Your army truly worked together."

Alísa followed his gaze. She watched a man kneel beside a dragon lying on its side, fumbling about in his bag for something to help it. She observed a dragoness carrying her rider and two wounded slayers to the medic camp. She smiled as dreki danced among the injured and brought hope to their pain-creased faces.

"Yes," she said. "Together."

68

JUSTICE

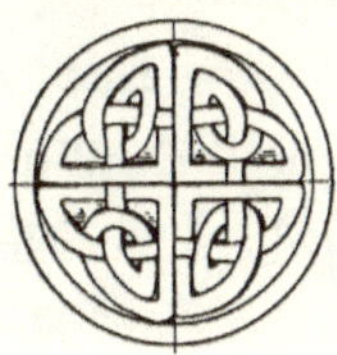

Exhaustion didn't even begin to cover how Kallar felt. The day held both victory and defeat. Defeat in finally admitting his need for the Maker and Eldra Bria. Victory in regaining his body. Defeat in giving up his strength to empower dragons. Victory in rescuing R'lann from the monsters that tortured them both. Defeat in humbling himself before the possessed warriors and Alísa's assassin. Partial victory as six of them regained their bodies when he and the assassin called for Eldra Branni's rescue.

He had thought it finished then. That he would return to the medic camp, see R'lann, and somehow will himself to sleep surrounded by strangers.

He had been wrong. The eyes of Karn's people caught him the moment he arrived.

"What is he doing here?"

Kallar squared his shoulders. No weakness. If they saw it, they would fall on him like wolves. But the wayfarers and others who loved Karn were not easily avoided. Alísa's efforts to intermix the allied clans and races had worked too well.

"Traitor."

He walked past them as their voices brought to mind memories of the keeper. Accusations that were truth. Pain he wished he could forget.

Where was R'lann? If he could see his brother, it would be okay.

"Murderer."

The word was a dagger to his heart. Distantly, he heard Alísa scolding the voices. He walked away from her. He didn't need her protection or deserve it.

So many wounded. Where was R'lann?

Kallar tensed as dragons approached from the north. He gathered his telepathy on instinct, then let it go. No one else looked on with anxiety or battle-readiness. Still, he waited and watched as they landed, unwilling to be caught off-guard. Each dragon was at least eight feet tall and carried multiple people. All passengers carried bags or large packs, presumably medical supplies and shelters for those unable to be moved.

Kallar's heart lurched as he recognized Tobin in the rider's position on a copper dragon, with Gia and Tenza behind him. R'lann called to them from somewhere close by. Kallar turned around. He wanted to see his brother, but the others—how would they receive him? How did he *want* them to receive him?

He didn't know, and the pain it caused rivaled that of his former clan's glares.

On the other side of the camp, another dragon landed near Alísa. On its back, immediately behind its rider, sat Hanah. Tall and proud, Karn's wife surveyed everything. Her chin bore red war-paint. *Anam nasctha*—the sign of her grief and authority as Karn's voice.

A decision settled in Kallar's mind. A duty, really. One that meant he wouldn't need to face his family after all.

Forcing himself forward, Kallar wove back through camp. Again, murmurs and discontent rose around him as he passed former clanmates. He kept his gaze on Hanah until Varek barred the way.

"Where do you think you're going?"

Perhaps pinning his eyes on Karn's widow hadn't been the best choice. People often said his stare was too intense.

"Let me pass."

"If you think I'm letting you near Lady Hanah—"

"That's enough." Alísa's voice rose from beyond Varek. She strode forward, her tone more sure and authoritative than Kallar had ever heard it. "I t-t-told you all, it wasn't his fault. He's free now. Let him be."

"All due respect, chief, letting him roam is a mistake. Whether he meant it or not, Karn is dead by his hand."

Alísa's eyes narrowed. "If you truly respect your chief, you will stand down."

"Kal!"

Kallar stiffened. Gia had spotted him.

Sidestepping Varek, he hastened toward Hanah. Many noticed him now, but he didn't stop. This was necessary. Honor and duty demanded it. As Hanah's emotionless eyes met his, he looked down. It should have been purposeful—a deference to the lady of his clan—but it was involuntary. He couldn't look at her, especially not with the reminder of Karn's death painted on her chin.

He stopped five feet from her, and in one smooth motion, fell to his knees and drew Karn's dagger. Holding the weapon in open palms above his head, he turned his face to the ground and waited.

The world went silent. A breeze swept over him, carrying the stench of smoke, sweat, and blood—a combination he knew all too well from slaughtering dragons in their caves. Perhaps he should have offered this to Lellani instead, but though he had committed terrible crimes against her kind, he hadn't betrayed her as he had Hanah.

"Was my husband killed, then, by his own blade?"

Kallar flinched at her stern tone. "No, Lady Hanah. When I saw what I did, I threw my dagger away. I seized his blade to end my life, so no one else would die by my hand. That action was denied to me by my keeper." He lifted the weapon higher. "Justice now belongs to you, or whoever you choose to deal it."

After a moment's pause, Hanah took the dagger from his hands. Kallar set his fists on his thighs, head still bowed.

"Then," she said, "you do not claim that it was your keeper who killed him?"

"I would never have hurt Karn, nor any of our clan. But my actions led to his death, as well as others. I brought my men to a slaughter. I refused to call to the Maker for help, thinking I was strong enough to face the Nameless myself. And when the keeper took hold of me, I blinded myself to its power and entered the battle where Karn ultimately died."

He forced his eyes up to take in Hanah's stoic anger. "The keeper is dead by Eldra Bria's hand. I am all that remains."

Hanah regarded the blade, turning it over in her hands. "Justice for the death of one chief belongs to his successor. However, as Karn's *anam nasctha*, I request the right to mete it out as he would have."

Alísa hesitated a long moment before she spoke. "You have it."

Relief washed over Kallar. Alísa's compassion was too great to deal justice.

She would leave him alive, but remaining among a clan who saw her choice as a mistake would be a living death.

Hanah returned to him. "Then, for acting against Karn's orders and leading his men into battle unprepared, I strip Kallar of his authority. I remove the right of succession his apprenticeship granted, and all who fought under his leadership shall remain under their new commanders rather than return to him. He now holds the lowest position in this clan."

Kallar looked down as she spoke. The words were deserved, but unnecessary. She could have simply killed him, but instead humbled him in everyone's eyes first.

"As for Karn's death" —she paused gravely— "he would never have held the keeper's actions against Kallar. He would declare there is no blame, nor anything to forgive. However, since Kallar claims guilt in the death of his chief, blood is required."

Hanah knelt before Kallar, remaining tall and sure. "Stretch out your hand."

He did as she said, turning his inner wrist toward the sky. He had expected a dagger to his heart, but there were more ways to bleed someone to death. This was less visceral and perhaps allowed Hanah the satisfaction of killing him herself without feeling bone and cartilage breaking under her hand.

She held Karn's weapon over his wrist for a long moment. Then, in a motion too quick to comprehend, she grabbed the blade with her free hand and pulled it across her own palm. Kallar's heart skipped a beat as her blood dripped over his wrist.

Hanah's face screwed up in an attempt not to show the pain as she spoke to the gathered crowd. "The death of a chief requires blood. And a chief has the authority to take the punishment upon themselves."

She squeezed her wounded hand shut, dripping more hot blood onto Kallar. Then she stood and displayed her palm.

"You have all trusted my voice as Karn's. Hear, then, what my husband declares from the Maker's halls. His death was for Kallar. He died so Kallar's eyes would be opened, leading to his rescue from the grasp of the Nameless Ones. My blood now flows as a symbol of this. Every action or inaction of Kallar's that led to Karn's death has been justified by that same death. Any who dare to act otherwise shall answer to Karn's authority and mine."

She may have said more, but Kallar didn't hear it. His blood pounded in his ears as he struggled. He had wanted justice, but instead received mercy. Not the mercy Alísa would have given, with kind words and gentle sentiment, but harsh and exacting mercy that Hanah claimed was still just. Would Karn truly declare Kallar's rescue worth his own death? How could anyone judge the value of one person's life against another's?

Hanah placed the dagger back into Kallar's hand, drawing him from his thoughts, then closed his fingers around the handle.

"You must keep this," she said, her voice soft. "Use it as Karn would have. Defend the defenseless, right the wrongs, and never harm that which he loves."

Her eyes held meaning, an order to never repeat the action for which he first took up Karn's dagger. Amazingly, depths of compassion flowed from her, this woman whose husband he had taken from this world. The emotion struck him like a spear through the heart, its sharpness reminiscent of the Maker's.

"Swear it," she ordered.

Kallar's breath left him, and it took great effort to pull in another. "I swear."

Hanah searched his eyes for a lie, then nodded firmly. She glanced behind him, then stood and walked away. Her form was quickly replaced as Gia knelt in front of him. She looked him up and down, remnants of fear on her face.

"Let's get you back to R'lann."

Her gaze landed on Kallar's hand and the dagger. Brow furrowing, she reached to take the weapon. Kallar didn't know whether to let her have it or tighten his grip and refuse. He opted to wipe it off in the grass beside him and slide it into its sheath. Gia merely watched.

When he brought his hand back, he saw the blood covering him. He stared at it, still trying to comprehend Hanah's actions.

"Here." Gia held out a handkerchief and, when Kallar didn't move, she gently took his hand and wiped away Hanah's blood. Depths of love flowed from her and hit like another dagger in his chest.

She focused on her work. "We never stopped praying for you, especially when we learned—your true situation."

Her voice cracked with emotion and she went silent, as though afraid she would scare him away. Her fear wasn't unfounded. Yet her statement brought to memory something the Maker had said.

"This is the home Gia and others built in the hope you would return."

Kallar swallowed as understanding dawned. His past self clutched at the words that tried to exit his mouth, and it wasn't until they walked together that he finally won the battle.

"Your prayers shielded me."

A tiny gasp escaped Gia's lips, and she met his eyes. He nodded once, assuring her he told the truth.

"When I finally called to the Maker for help, I found myself in your home. The keeper tried to get in and harm me, but the walls held firm. The Maker said it was you" —he remembered certain items within the house— "and R'lann, and Tobin, and Tenza. All of you. But the house itself was yours."

Gia blinked back tears. "I have prayed for you since the day your father brought me to meet you."

So many years. He hadn't deserved it.

"Thank you."

Gia inhaled, but apparently decided against speaking as tears filled her eyes once more. They finished the walk in silence, coming to the spot where Tobin and Tenza cared for R'lann. Kallar needed to tell them, too. A huge part of him urged to wait, but he would never speak if he put it off, so he fought the battle for gentle words once more. It was easier the second time, helped by R'lann sitting beside him. Exhaustion crept over him at the end.

"You both need rest," Gia said as R'lann yawned.

Tenza nodded her agreement, looking to Kallar briefly before returning her eyes to R'lann, as though afraid to spook Kallar. "We will watch over you both."

And so, amid strangers, dragons, and Karns-men, Kallar laid down beside his brother. The grasses felt soft as a bear-skin rug as he drifted into sleep.

69

DRAGONS & RIDERS

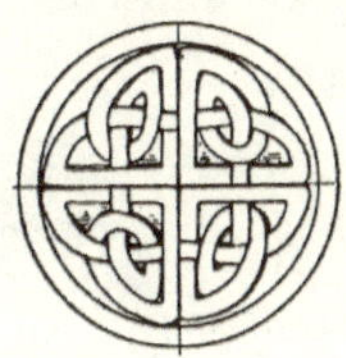

The days following the battle were long and full—keeping the medics supplied, hunting to feed the recovering dragons, sending messengers with news of the victory, scouting for any remaining contingencies of an'reik. The tasks seemed endless.

Alísa remained in the medic camp, where she could easily be found as she gave the wounded hope through presence, song, and prayer. The dead were honored and mourned, and the recovered were celebrated. And amid it all, relationships between members of each race grew as they relied on each other for shelter, sustenance, and comfort. Camp's quiet provided much time for contemplation while the winds and rains cleared away the stench of war.

Five days after the battle, they cleared the medic camp. Dragons who could not fly were carried back to their clans or, if their clan was no longer safe for them, to Alísa's caves. Slayers, too, went home, borne by dragons carrying white banners.

Ten days later, however, the chiefs and alphas returned to Alísa's mountain.

Alísa observed the leadership from the landing platform above the main cave. As hoped, even some who hadn't fought the an'reik attended, reassured by her allies among their race. There was Crakil alongside one of his betas and another dragon alpha he trusted. Far from the dragons, Lorin stood with his new second, their sharp eyes scrutinizing. Toronn had refused her invitation.

Behind the leaders, Alísa's clan watched the proceedings. All knew the proposal she brought and many had given counsel, refining her plan until it became its own living, breathing entity.

Alísa took Falier's hand and squeezed it for reassurance. The last of their messengers had returned fifteen minutes ago. The only delay remaining was her.

She looked to her betas and leadership behind her, her eyes fixing for a moment on her mother and uncle. If she squinted just right, she could imagine her father there instead of L'non. The thought brought both pain and courage. This meeting was for him, based on a discussion what felt like eons ago. The future of the wayfarers.

She turned to Falier and grasped onto his connection. *"You're sure all the slayer chiefs will allow telepathy?"*

He nodded once. *"The riders informed them it would be expected. Some of their seconds won't be listening, instead ready to fight if we try anything, but every chief has agreed."*

"Good. Thank you for taking care of that."

"My pleasure." He kissed her temple. *"You've got this."*

With that, Falier stepped back. Sesína lifted her wings, her wounds healed but for a small hole remaining in the leather near the base. At her movement, the alphas and chiefs gave their attention. Sesína connected Alísa to them.

"All present are in the link," she whispered. *"Including the grumps like Lorin."*

Alísa raised her hands in welcome. *"Thank you all for returning. I know recovery demands much of you. Even in victory, there is loss, and with that loss comes change. With that in mind, I wish to speak to you about my father and the change he and I spoke of before his passing."*

She met each leader's eyes. *"You are all familiar with Karn's wayfarers. They were a product of war, a fighting force that defended one race and fought the other. But all of that ended three months ago, when Karn learned the truth about dragon souls and, together, we began a mission of peace."*

Memory washed through Alísa's mind of villages she and her father had entered side-by-side. Of his support as she brought her message, and the pride in his eyes as she spoke before crowds.

She swallowed back tears. *"Upon his death, I took command of the wayfarers and, united with many of you, we fought for the future of all races. In so doing, we proved we needn't be enemies. That we can, in fact, work together to bring light against the forces of darkness, and perhaps even build friendship between us. My aim is to continue—to not only keep the peace, but to establish lasting alliances and friendships. But to accomplish this, I must ask for your help once more."*

A buzz of thoughts filled the link, occasional words breaking through, but

Alísa continued before anyone could take over. *"When I established peace treaties with you, I pledged to come to your aid should a clan of the opposite race attack your homes. Dragons and humans alike trusted that we would protect them and help keep the peace. Now, I propose a melding of these alliances with the wayfarers' original mandate."*

This was the hard part. Alísa began walking to one side of the platform, pacing out her nervous energy as she outlined her desire for her clan.

"Allow my scouts to roam freely within your territories, watching for trouble and lending aid where needed. We will watch for highwaymen, keep vigil against the return of the an'reik, and assist in peacefully resolving disputes between clans."

Crakil growled and his voice came through powerfully. *"You wish to set yourself over us! To take our resources and force your will upon us!"*

"Ask any of the alphas who have worked with me," Alísa countered. *"I seek no greater authority than that which the villages gave my father—to pass through, lend aid, and interact without fear of attack. As to resources, I would indeed request my scouts be allowed to hunt for themselves, but never for my full clan. I will restrict those hunting rights to my own territory."*

A slayer spoke up next. "What guarantee do we have that your scouts won't harm our villages? We may trust that your heart is in the right place, Dragon Singer, but with a clan so spread out, you cannot hope to keep track of them all."

Rather than pace the other way, Alísa descended the ramp toward the leadership. *"Scouting teams will consist of two dragon-rider pairs and at least one drek, so that they can stay in contact with me and each other throughout their tours. The presence of each race will provide accountability."*

Reaching the main floor, she stepped in front of them again. *"In addition, I invite members of your clans to join me—not to lessen your strength or undermine your authority, but to provide you with representation. Yes, these warriors will be under my command, but they will also be free to return to their original clans as they desire, without fear of retribution from me."*

Alísa extended her hands to them. *"My calling is to establish and keep peace between the races, not to rule. I know this is new and strange, but it ensures the peace you shed your blood to find. Do not let our peoples backslide into old ways of fear, hatred, and death. Allow my wayfarers to continue patrolling this land, not for the sake of one race, but for all of us. I also welcome your ideas to make this arrangement lasting and beneficial to all of you. I do not wish my clan to be merely a fighting force"*—she looked back up at Falier and smiled— *"but also one of service and camaraderie."*

Lorin shook his head. "A lovely sentiment, but what happens to the villages that disagree?"

Alísa fought back a sigh as she faced him. *"Nothing. We will leave any clan that does not wish our help alone. But if they attack our allies, our wrath against their warriors will be swift and fierce. We won't touch civilians."*

The buzz of thoughts continued, though none formed words for her to respond to. Alísa lifted her hands in entreaty once more.

"We wish to be a force for peace, not violence. Let us work together to ensure our hatchlings and children can grow up in a land without war. Send representatives to fly with me, if only to keep watch on me. Prove my sincerity if you haven't already. Let the war cease."

The chiefs and alphas stood silent before her, the astral plane fluctuating with their emotions. Then Chief N'ravi stepped to the front, an open hand over his heart.

"I would speak with you more on the specifics, but Eskann will keep our alliance and allow dragon-rider pairs within our borders. I already know several of my men would be eager to continue as riders if you'll accept them."

Alísa grinned. *"Yes, let us talk further on the matter."*

Then came Harazím, unwilling that a human clan be the only one to accept her offer. Quickly, more chiefs and alphas accepted, the show convincing even Crakil to agree to further talks, lest his clan be left behind.

Heart full, Alísa looked back at her betas, who took their cue to move out among the leaders of the clans and hear their ideas and concerns. Today would be filled with talk and negotiation, but the first and hardest step was behind them. Now they marched forward, perhaps out of step, but together toward a better tomorrow.

Alísa lifted her eyes to the sky and smiled.

70

DREAMS & REALITIES

Kallar's body was heavy as hot winds raced past him. His breaths were shallow, his nostrils clogged with ashy sand. He could barely see his surroundings. There were no landmarks nearby, no plants or hills or rivers or lakes. Only a dark, misty form hiding within the sandstorm. The wind screamed with the voices of men, women, and children. Somehow, Kallar knew the shadow was their tormentor.

Anger rose inside of him, hotter than the friction of the sand against his lungs. His hand went for his sword and found only Karn's dagger. His heart pounded as the dark form turned toward him. Its eyes…

Keeper!

Gasping in a breath, Kallar shot up from his pillow. Cold sweat covered his body, making him shiver. He reached for his cloak.

I've got to get out of here.

Quietly, to not disturb his family, he pushed through the curtain of his chamber, across their tent, and out the flap. A fire lit the cave, sending shadows of tents crawling in all directions. He turned from it, lest anyone spot the terror still pounding in his chest.

I thought you said it wouldn't have any power over me, Bria. That's why you let me kill it.

He pressed out the entrance and walked a short distance over the stony mountainside. There he sat, looking up at a starless sky under late autumn's cloud-cover. The sounds of screaming still echoed in his ears.

Kallar watched from the shadows as riders helped the last of the still-possessed warriors onto a dragon's back. The prisoner was gagged, his hands bound, his person checked for anything he might use against the dragon and its riders. He sat between the other two men, one the dragon's rider from Alísa's clan, the other a slayer chief who had come for her announcement. The chief would keep the man in prison, and the village songweaver would visit occasionally to try to free him from his bondage to his keeper.

Kallar shivered. That could have been him.

No. He was too dangerous to keep alive with his Singer's abilities.

I'm not sure which is worse. To live in prison with a keeper's torture, or to die unshielded and be done with it.

He had suggested the second to Alísa, a mercy for the remaining five. She gave it thought, but ultimately decided the potential for future life was better. This was one instance where, though Kallar didn't fully agree, he couldn't disdain her tendency toward mercy.

"I wish we could do more," Rassím said quietly at Kallar's side. "Poor souls."

"They have to make the choice. No one can make it for them."

Kallar's stomach tightened as the man settled between the spines. Helping the possessed was his one remaining task. Hanah's proclamation had been true—he was the lowest in this clan now. And though her decision to cover his guilt with Karn's blood had convinced some clanmates, others still swore they would never forgive him. Nor should they.

Not only that, but Alísa had transformed the wayfarers, their purpose now for peace. Kallar was a warrior. He needed to fight, to strategize, to defend and attack—not fly here and there looking to solve conflict before it happened. Most seemed ready for their new mission. He was not. He still had R'lann and their reunited family, but who was he without a purpose?

"In my home village in the Southlands," Rassím said, obviously uncomfortable with the silence, "many an'reik passed through. Some even lived among the people while practicing their dark arts. I had heard of possession, but didn't know it was real. Now that I've seen the difference in how an'reik and possessed look, I wonder how many I missed as a child."

Kallar waited a beat as the dragon and its riders took off. Rassím had always accompanied him to talk to and care for the possessed. He wouldn't call the assassin a friend, but he respected both his battle prowess and his compassion for those who hadn't escaped their keepers.

"How old were you when you left?"

"Seven. We hopped from village to village after that until we finally made our way past the Prilunes. I was twelve then." Rassím gave a sad chuckle. "If I'd known what trouble I was causing my parents, I might have kept my mouth shut about the dark ones."

Rassím gazed out the entrance. "I'm glad I could help here, but I wonder if I would have served better if my family hadn't run. They need *radharc* in the Southlands."

Kallar eyed him. "You make it sound like every other person there is an'reik."

Rassím turned to the tunnel to the main cave, prompting Kallar to follow. "Not so many. But here, they typically lurk in the shadows. There, they walk freely and ensnare people more easily. It's not uncommon for a chief to employ one as a counselor, much like a songweaver. Some even have one of each."

Kallar kept pace, thoughts forming. "What about dragons? Did you see an'reik dragons there?"

"Actually, no. I didn't see many dragons in my childhood, and those I saw didn't glow. I assumed it was just how their race was, them being damned and all. Now, I suppose it's just because none came near enough. They likely exist, though." Rassím narrowed his eyes. "Why?"

Kallar shrugged. "Curious."

They continued the walk in silence, Rassím occasionally glancing Kallar's way as though to say something further. Kallar let him squirm in the quiet as thoughts built on dreams. A sandstorm filled with dark mists, fears he needed to face, people crying for help, and both humans and dragons oppressing them. An enemy he could fight without shame.

71

THE BRIDGE

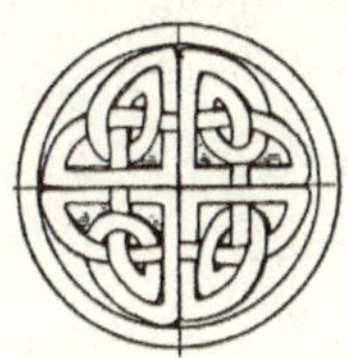

"Steady…" Falier backed away from the rising wooden platform. He observed as Jossen operated the crank connected to the intricate pulley system. Slowly, the platform, and Jossen on it, began rising.

Falier didn't fully understand how the pulleys worked, but after a few days of planning with more mechanically minded slayers, they designed and built the elevating platform. Once it worked, it would allow humans to move freely between the two caves without traversing the rocky slopes outside.

The platform could carry four and had railing for safety, plus lockable gates on opposite ends. Watching Jossen test the crank, it was apparently still hard work to make the platform rise. A lone teen might operate it, but if it was at full capacity, it would likely require a well-built man.

Falier voiced this to the engineers, who began discussing the merits of adding another pulley. The platform reached the desired tunnel, about forty feet above the main cave floor, and Jossen pulled the lever to secure its position there. Then he opened the gate, stepped onto the stone, and raised a victorious fist.

Falier cheered along with the others, applauding and slapping the nearest engineer on the back.

When the noise subsided, Jossen glanced up and down the distance exaggeratedly and shouted, "A bit premature, don't you think?"

That drew laughter as he returned to the platform, locked the gate, and began the process of descent. Again, it appeared doable for any single person, but less so if the platform was full.

Graydonn trumpeted just outside the main cave entrance. Falier grinned. *"Be right there!"*

He watched the platform traverse the last few feet and land with a solid thud. Falier joined the clapping, then turned to the engineers.

"You have ideas?"

They nodded, and one looked about to explain. Falier held up a hand.

"I'll leave you to it. My guests have arrived."

With that, Falier spun to jog up the ramp to the landing platform. Graydonn stood at the edge, wings lifted in excitement.

"They're close enough that Laen and Ska can relay voices."

Falier jumped onto Graydonn's back and suddenly found Ska on his shoulder. Thankfully, Falier already wore the pads to keep his arm intact.

"Let's go!"

Graydonn launched with as much enthusiasm as Falier felt, pushing them into the frigid sky. It seemed it might snow any moment.

As soon as they faced east, Falier reached out through Ska. *"Pa didn't fall off, did he?"*

Hwinn laughed in his mind. *"He's holding onto Saynan too tight for that. Grandpa's afraid of heights."*

"Afraid implies I think he'll drop me," Parsen said. *"I'm just a bit, uh, dizzy."*

"Uh-huh," Selene smirked.

Falier grinned as he caught sight of the four approaching dragons. *"Saynan, he hasn't choked you to death, has he?"*

"Not at all," Saynan said. *"Though I wouldn't let him ride Aravi just yet."*

"I fought an'reik with a rider," Aravi retorted. *"I can take any human and their tight squeezes."*

"It's good to hear your voice, Falier."

His heart warmed. *"You too, Ma. Aree taking care of you?"*

"Yes. I am very glad for her inner fire—something your father is mighty jealous of."

Falier laughed. Saynan's ice breath thankfully didn't translate to cold scales, but his riders missed out on the extra warmth of a fire dragon.

Graydonn sped toward the incoming dragons and dipped low as he reached them. Ascending as they passed, he back-flipped over them with a happy trumpet. Falier's own joy flew with him, bursting through the astral plane with a force that surely even his normal parents could feel. His family was here, and all to witness his marriage to the woman he loved!

Hwinn and Aravi spun after Graydonn, the adolescents catching Graydonn's enthusiasm. They played the rest of the way while Saynan and Aree flew steadily behind them.

Falier slid off Graydonn the moment they landed, hurrying to help his mother down. Ska screeched and took off as Kat embraced Falier. He relaxed against her, letting her presence melt away any pieces of tension lingering within his body and mind.

"I'm so glad you came."

"You don't think I'd miss my favorite son's wedding?" She pulled back and looked him over. "You have a beard."

"Alísa likes it."

"I'm surprised you can grow one," Parsen said, coming up from behind. "Mine was always patchy. It's why I married your mother, and took her vocation rather than her taking mine."

"Oh hush, you," Kat said, slapping his arm.

"What? Holders are traditionally clean-shaven."

Falier turned around and hugged his father, holding on longer than Parsen's back slaps told him to. Parsen chuckled and squeezed him back.

"I missed you too, son."

When Falier tried to pull away, he found himself caught as Hwinn crowded close to get his own fill of affection. Soon Selene was in on the embrace and Graydonn closed the circle opposite Hwinn. Parsen glanced up at Graydonn as the dragon's neck stretched over his shoulder.

"I think you've been around my son too long. You've learned to hug without a human's Illumination."

Graydonn thrummed. *Between him and Alísa, I have needed to adapt.*

The hug relaxed, and Kat looked over the rest of the cave. "Speaking of Alísa, where is she? And Taz?"

"Taz has been on scouting duty this week," Selene supplied. "He'll return tomorrow."

Parsen squinted at her. "And you're sure you won't spring a second wedding on us before we leave?"

"Not yet." Selene smiled sweetly. "How else would we persuade you to visit again?"

"Grandchildren."

"Duh!" Hwinn agreed. *"Of course they'll come to see me!"*

Selene slapped a hand over her eyes. *"I don't think they were talking about you.*"

"Yes, we'll visit you, dear." Kat rubbed the adolescent's neck and grinned at her children. "Along with any other little ones that come along."

Falier looked over the main cave. "As for Alísa, she could be anywhere. If we can find Sesína—aha!"

He pointed to the small black dragoness near the back of the cave and the redhead standing next to her. They spoke with someone he couldn't recognize this far away.

"Let's go," he said, grabbing Kat's bag from where Aree's rider had placed it. "We'll show you the space on the way."

He, Selene, and Hwinn led them to the ramp, Graydonn bringing up the rear. Ska flew overhead, flitting in and out of the group as they walked. Falier explained the function of this cave as a place of gathering, whether it be for food, play, training, or meetings. Only a few tents remained, housing those unable to travel to the other cave.

"Essentially, this is our Hold."

Hwinn charged past him toward the kitchen area, talons skittering on the hard floor. *"You two will help cook while you're here, right? You can teach everyone how to season my deer properly!"*

"He's decided that my cooking isn't sufficient." Selene gave an exaggerated eye-roll. "Be sure to do it wrong, otherwise I'll never be able to make him happy."

Hwinn snorted. *"Your food is fine. Grandma's is just better."*

Selene indicated the dragon to Kat. "See?"

One woman chopping vegetables for dinner looked up at them. "Welcome back, Selene. Falier, was that a working platform I saw?"

"It was." He remembered her warrior husband, whose leg had been badly wounded. "It's not quite ready for full usage yet, but as soon as it is, your tent is the first we move."

"I'll hold you to it."

He nodded sharply, and the family continued. Proudly, he showed them the elevating platform—or, as much as he could with the builders and engineers crowding around it for the next iteration. Iila lay nearby, feigning disinterest while awaiting instructions for who needed to be taken up to the pulley system. Falier pointed to the contraption on the ceiling.

"We figured out that dreki can phase anchors into the ceiling for us. Once they're set, though, adjustments are limited. Each time a drek flies through rock, it becomes a little more unstable. But one placement of four anchors makes a sturdy system."

"Should be ready after this adjustment," Varek said, barely glancing up. Apparently, his true choice of how to spend a free day was building.

"You said that last time," Falier quipped.

"You're just impatient to finish this project and return to the sparring cave."

Falier chuckled. "Yeah, I'm really eager for you to trounce me again."

One engineer turned to him. "Just sing in his head. That should be sufficiently distracting."

Ska swooped over their heads and chittered grumpily. *"No."*

"My sentiments exactly, Ska. I'll save that headache of a move for special occasions." Falier smirked at the slayers. "Though, good to know you find me distracting."

"You're just pitchy," Varek grumbled.

The engineer chuckled. "The warrior said to the musician."

Falier grinned. "On that 'note,' I'll take my leave."

That earned him multiple groans, making him laugh. He returned to his family, pointing out a side-cave on the ground.

"That's the sparring cave he referred to."

"You fight with swords often?" Kat asked, eying the weapon on his hip.

Falier tapped the hilt, carefully framing his answer. "I train with it and have learned a lot. I'm rarely on the ground in battle, but it has happened. Graydonn and I watch each other's backs."

"And what of you?" she asked Selene.

Selene shook her head. "Hwinn and I will fight when necessary, but we're holders through and through."

Soon they reached the back wall of the cave and Falier met eyes with Kallar—the person Alísa was speaking with. Kallar said a brief goodbye to Alísa and departed without another look.

Alísa regarded him only a moment more before her gaze caught on Falier's family. In an instant, her countenance brightened and she ran to meet them.

"I'm so glad you're here!" She hugged Kat and Parsen, her grin never faltering. "I m—must introduce you to Mamá. Or do you need rest first?"

Sesína shoved her nose in front of Kat to nuzzle her cheek. *"Did Saynan and Aree take care of you? I warned them I would get a full report."*

Kat assured her all was well while Parsen made up some complaint. Falier grabbed Alísa's hand and reached out with telepathy.

"Everything okay with Kallar?"

She nodded almost imperceptibly. *"He's leaving."*

Falier blinked. *"Leaving leaving?"*

Another nod. *"I'll tell you everything later."*

Kat returned to Alísa. "As for meeting your ma, I am more than ready. The sooner we meet, the sooner we can get the ceremony in order. Of course, I'll need to learn the intricacies of slayer weddings. I've never been involved in one."

Alísa grinned. "I'm sure Mamá would love the help. She's been so focused on embroidering my d—dress, she's overwhelmed with everything else."

"And the less Aunt Elani plans the wedding, the better," Sesína said, thrumming.

"Will you be cooking for the wedding, Grandma?"

Selene sighed. "The things I deal with."

Alísa smirked. "At least he doesn't challenge every new acquaintance to a c-c-contest of strength and p-prowess, unlike some dragonesses I know."

Sesína tossed her head. *"Guilty."*

The group began walking away, following Sesína to wherever Hanah might be. Falier took up the rear with Graydonn, but halted at Parsen's thoughtful chuckle.

"Pa?"

"I knew you would do it. I just wasn't sure how."

"Do—what?"

Parsen gestured to the cave. "This. Bridging your holder and slayer halves. I've been here fifteen minutes and already see it. You have the trust of these slayers, and they don't just give away their confidence."

He grasped Falier's shoulder, his eyes bright. "You will make a fine tiern."

Falier's chest swelled. "Thanks, Pa."

Parsen nodded, pulling back. Then he cleared his throat and screwed up his face in the manner of one of his 'serious' talks.

"Now, while they discuss wedding organization, you and I need to talk about being a husband." He threw an arm around Falier's shoulders and began guiding him after the others. "Rule number one—your wife is always right."

72

THE NEXT STEP

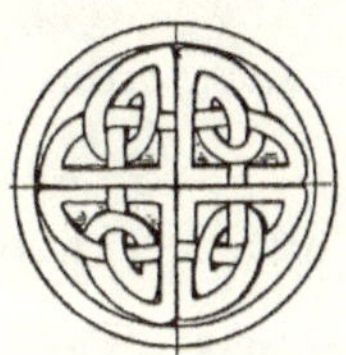

Kallar looked up the slope, shivering in the beginnings of snow. Alísa's mountain held too many caves, and too few that humans could access. It made finding dragons annoying. It was too much to hope Lellani would simply show up again.

He gazed at the hill country, standing on the outside path between the main cave and the cavern where he and his family, among others, stayed. Further out, the land was blanketed in white—the snowfall keeping the distant Prilune mountain range from sight. Soon he would see them up close before entering an unfamiliar land. How soon depended on Lellani's answer.

He pushed a strand of wet hair from his face. *Let's get this over with.*

Taking a breath, Kallar sang Lellani's name. He elongated the vowels like a mother calling her child for dinner across the hills, singing it three times before a trumpet announced the success of his summons. The dragoness appeared around the curve of the mountain, her silvery scales somehow shimmering even in the gray.

"I wondered if I would ever hear your voice again." Lellani alighted on the mountainside beneath Kallar. *"What do you want, Singer? Actually, hold that thought. You look like your tail might freeze off."*

Kallar didn't give her the satisfaction of a chuckle, merely indicated the main cave with his head and walked down the path. Lellani watched him as he went. His skin prickled to feel her eyes on him, to give his back to a dragon. But what he was about to ask required trust—he may as well start now.

Just before he reached the cave, Lellani dipped inside. The space was quieter than normal, a fact Kallar attributed to both the frigid weather and the preparations for the wedding ceremony.

Below the landing platform, he saw Alísa and Falier walking with hands clasped. A pang of something ran through him, as it always did upon seeing them together. He wasn't sure what it was. Anger over a stolen bride? Jealousy for the joy Falier brought her that Kallar never had? Self-loathing because the weakling holder boy was a better man than he? Perhaps a mixture of all three.

I have to get out of here.

"Now" —Lellani shook the snow from her scales, making Kallar duck away— *"why did you call for me?"*

Kallar wiped the water off his face. "I have a favor to ask. I'm heading for the Southlands and—I don't want the journey to take months."

"Months?" Lellani cocked her head. *"How slowly do humans walk? It takes me little more than two days to reach the Prilunes!"*

"Exactly. If I'm walking, it would take me two months. Less on horseback, but Alísa apparently got rid of the clan's horses, and I don't have the funds to buy one."

Why was he explaining all this? He should just ask and get it done. "Would you carry me there? Preferably past the mountains, but if you only bring me to where the Nissen hits their base, I can use the river."

Lellani stared at him a moment, copper eye-lights fading in and out like a breath. *"You are truly leaving?"*

Kallar nodded sharply. "You have Alísa. You don't need another Singer."

"And what will you do there?"

He should tell her it was none of her business, but something compelled him to speak.

"Find an'reik who are harming villagers and destroy them."

"And how, exactly, do you plan to recognize the difference between an'reik and possessed?"

Kallar whirled, hand instinctively going to his sword's hilt. Rassím leaned against the cave wall behind him, arms crossed and one eyebrow arched. How had he gotten that close without Kallar noticing?

He looked away. "Not your concern."

"Ah, yes." Rassím pushed off the wall to come closer. "You ask about my homeland, steal my ideas, then claim it's none of my concern. Makes perfect sense."

"His ideas?"

"Your ideas?" Kallar said simultaneously.

Rassím nodded. "I told you I thought my leaving the Southlands was a mistake. That they needed people like me. I've been thinking of returning for some time, especially since Dezra makes it easy to come back occasionally. Now you take my plan up and claim it as your own?"

With a flutter of wings, a sky-blue adolescent landed on the platform behind Lellani. *"So rude. What should we do to punish him?"*

The southerner appeared to consider, then gave an exaggerated shrug. "Only idea I have is to accompany him. Does that sound like sufficient punishment, Dez?"

The adolescent's eyes brightened. *"I'm sure we'll think of something better along the way."*

"What?" Kallar looked between them, unable to keep his surprise at bay. Go with him? Why would an Illuminated pair want that? And Alísa's assassin, no less. "No. Look, this is my mission. You can do your own thing—"

"I ask again" —Rassím crossed his arms— "how are you going to know that you're fighting an'reik and not poor souls who are trapped like you were?" His eyes softened slightly. "You needn't fight alone."

"Speaking of stealing ideas" —Lellani made a vibrating sound in her chest— *"I will indeed bear you, Singer, but only on the condition that I remain with you as well."*

Kallar shook his head. "You don't want this. You don't know what kind of person I am."

"I do."

Kallar tensed and turned to see Trísse ascending the ramp. Her dark eyes held a cold, emotionless certainty.

"Which is why I'm coming too. Someone has to call you on your posturing."

"Do you even know what we're discussing?"

Trísse looked disappointed in him. "You told my best friend."

Kallar shook his head and growled. "You hate me. Why on A'dem would you come?"

Her coldness didn't waver. "They killed Tern."

Grief clamped over Kallar's stomach. He had hoped Tern simply ran off with another clan. This confirmation of his death, as well as the hardness it brought to Trísse's manner, made something start to settle inside him.

"I, too, know who you were," Lellani said, snapping him from his thoughts. *"If*

you'll recall, you yourself showed me what crimes you have committed against my race. I also know you aren't the same now."

He looked at the great dragoness, taking in the soft glow of her eyes. Did she really see a difference? He was trying, but it was so hard. Why couldn't the Maker just make him a different person? But no, he didn't actually want that either. That was too close to control.

But if the Maker wouldn't force change, Kallar would have to fight for it. Starting here.

"This wasn't supposed to be a group mission," he said, letting the sharp edge drop from his tone. "I meant to go alone. But if you're sure" —he breathed, mustering words he felt but didn't want to say— "I wouldn't mind having company."

A buzz of telepathy entered his head, different from the dragons. Kallar started to shield himself, but heard Rassím's voice and stopped.

"I don't know about Trísse," the southlander said. *"Seems all she wants out of this is revenge."*

"Yes. I've been there," Kallar said. *"And if she wants to quench her blade with their blood, I won't stop her."*

Meanwhile, Trísse allowed a small smile. "When do we leave?"

"Tomorrow," Kallar said.

Trísse shook her head. "Alísa is getting married in two days. We'll leave in three."

Kallar sighed. He wanted to skip the wedding. He could insist on leaving tomorrow and tell Trísse that if she wasn't there, she wouldn't be coming. But that would reveal just how much he dreaded attending.

He had suffered through being possessed. He could make it through a wedding. Technically, he didn't have to be at the ceremony, anyway.

"Fine. Dawn in three days."

Trísse's self-satisfied smirk almost made him change his mind right then, but Rassím drew his attention with a clap on the back.

"Good man. Now, what say we head to the sparring cave? I'm dying for a rematch now that you're, ah, better."

Kallar stared at him a moment, trying to comprehend this man who was an odd mixture of collected assurance and friendly awkwardness. He let out a breath.

"Sure."

Rassím grinned and descended the ramp to the main floor. Kallar watched him for a second, then allowed himself to smile. So, he wouldn't be alone. He had resigned himself to that fate—one he deserved after leading his men into slaughter and realizing just how hateful a man he was.

But maybe that wasn't the end.

What did the Maker say? One day, I will run. Today, I take a step.

Kallar followed Rassím.

73

HAND-FASTING

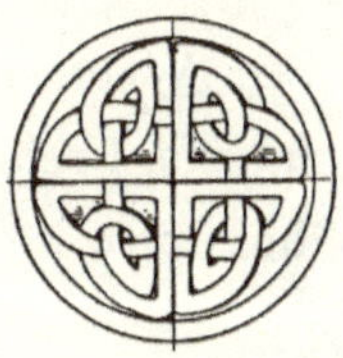

Dreki danced through Alísa's insides as she waited in the dimly lit passage to the empty sparring cave. Hanah stood with her while Sesína guarded the exit into the main cave. A curtain of white gauzy material draped over the exit, allowing Alísa to see without being seen herself.

She felt ethereal in her wedding dress, like she might leave the ground as she stepped forward. Its royal blue color drew attention to her eyes and beautifully contrasted her red curls. The bodice was a masterpiece of embroidery and beadwork, most of it completed by her mother, whose family's trade was weaving and embroidery. The swirling patterns held knotted symbols within—those of love, hope, honor, and trust.

The sleeves and top layer of the skirt were of the same white gauze as the curtain, making them shimmer. Her white belt sat comfortably on her waist in a V-shape, ending in a long strip hanging down the front of her skirt. Finally, more gauzy material cascaded from under her arms and across her back, creating a flowing cape that kissed the ground. Everything about the dress made Alísa want to spin and dance.

In the cave, humans, dragons, and dreki formed a ring facing the center, where the hand-fasting would occur. Some dragons watched from the landing platform, a bit too large for the circle. Dreki fluttered from shoulder to shoulder with an energy Alísa keenly felt. The humans were all dressed in their best, non-armored clothing, some men even wearing their ceremonial kilts. Alísa smoothed her skirt for the hundredth time, making her mother reach out for her hands.

"It's plenty straight, love." She squeezed Alísa's fingers, silvery-blue eyes meeting hers. "Are you truly so nervous?"

Alísa shook her head. "Only a little. It's also a bit of everything else. Excited. Happy." Her gaze landed on the red paint on her mother's chin. "Sad."

Hanah stepped closer and pulled Alísa into a hug. "He is here."

"Do you really believe that?" Alísa murmured against her mother's shoulder. "*Anam nasctha?*"

Hanah hummed an affirmative. "Whether some true spiritual connection or merely my knowledge of my husband, I believe his spirit is with me, even as it is in the Maker's halls. I know he is proud of you and wishes you and Falier every happiness."

Alísa sniffled, but shoved back her tears. Today was for celebration. Papá wouldn't wish her to cry for him now. She pulled away from Hanah and returned her gaze to the curtain. Sesína looked toward her, eye-lights bright.

"Koriana says everyone is here. The ferrying dragons have returned with reports of caves being empty. Also, Falier looks far more nervous than you. Help me think of a good barb to tease him!"

Alísa just smiled. The mention of Falier and his nerves turned her mind to mush.

"Ugh, you're no help." Sesína grinned mentally. *"I'm glad you're happy. Hanah, it's time for you to get into position."*

Hanah gave Alísa's hand one more squeeze, then grabbed two red-and-brown plaid sashes from the ground. She draped them over her arm and carefully slipped out the curtain, leaving Alísa alone in the tunnel. A few minutes later, the sounds of the crowd died down. Then the music began—Selene's soaring flute and Taz's soothing low-fife. Falier would begin his journey around the outside of the ring now, the circle a symbol of his eternal soul.

Alísa rubbed her arms to let out some of her nervous energy. She wanted to rub her face too, but didn't dare lest she smear the chief's paint on her forehead. She couldn't see Falier, but she knew the musical cue to begin her journey, when he would be directly across from her.

Sesína stood and slipped a wing through the curtain, pulling it back. As the flute fluttered high, Alísa stepped out to walk her soul's circle. Smiles abounded, as did brightening eyes and fluttering wings. Behind her, Sesína entered the crowd for her next part in the ceremony.

Alísa had to resist the urge to rush. It seemed an eternity as she walked the ring. Her gaze flitted from the ground to faces of loved ones to the rain falling outside. That in itself was a blessing. Though snow was beautiful, rain spoke of joy amid sadness, pressing through the darkness, and choosing the good over the bad. Her and Falier's courtship hadn't been long, but it had been full of those moments, revealing their true character to each other throughout their journey.

When Alísa finally completed her circle, the ring of clanmates parted at her position and Falier's, allowing them into the center. Falier's grin was wide and genuine as she met his gaze. His hair and beard were freshly trimmed, his midnight eyes bright. His kilt was a royal blue plaid that matched her dress and his shirt a complimentary dark brown.

Before she saw him, Alísa thought to forego dignity and hurry to meet him. Now, with his loving gaze on her and his appreciation of her beauty evident, she found it easier to do everything correctly. She wanted to give them both every moment to savor, though her heart pounded in anticipation as their paths converged—two eternal *anam* coming together.

Their families waited in the center. Selene played her flute beside Parsen and Kat, while Farren and Sesína stood with Hanah at Alísa's request. The songweaver would officiate, but Alísa thought it only right that he should also stand as her family. Hanah still carried the two sashes draped over one arm. With her other hand, she held one end of the white hand-fasting cord while Kat took the other.

Alísa's grin could not diminish as she and Falier reached the center. His eyes trailed over her dress before settling on her face again.

"You are so beautiful."

She blushed. *"You know we're not supposed to talk until our vows, right?"*

His expression turned a bit mischievous, but he said no more as their mothers pulled the cord taut between them. Memories filled Alísa's mind—the kind holder who helped her integrate into a new life. The scared yet brave young man who pressed onward no matter how difficult. The leader beginning to emerge.

The music ended with a long, warbling note from Selene's flute. Its echo rang through the cavern like the voice of an Eldra. Then Farren spoke, a smile in his voice, though Alísa didn't see it. Raging dragons couldn't turn her eyes from her beloved.

"Alísa Karns-daughter, Falier Parsens-son, this day your clan has gathered to witness your pledge. Before those you love and who love you most, what are your vows? Before the Maker, who knows your hearts, how will one join to another?"

Alísa forced her breaths to stay low and steady. It was her and Falier's turn to speak. Experience told her she didn't stammer when speaking in tandem with someone, but nerves still fluttered. As Farren asked the last question, Falier's eyes softened from delight to assurance. She held onto his gaze, breathed with him as though they were about to sing together, and spoke the vows she had practiced for days.

> Though all is in the Maker's hands,
> What once was mine, I freely give.
> My body, heart, possessions, all,
> In humble service, I will live.
> I pledge to you the best of me,
> And humbly know you'll see the worst.
> So may the Maker give us strength
> To live and put each other first.

Falier turned toward Farren and held out his arm to Alísa, the palm of his hand facing the ceiling. She turned similarly, laying her hand in his so their wrists touched. His warm fingers interlocked with hers as they finished.

> Sure as the sun,
> Two become one,
> A marriage of equals is never undone.

A relieved sigh escaped Alísa, making multiple family members chuckle through their bright smiles. Alísa laughed with them, her heart too full for anything else as Hanah and Kat bound her and Falier's wrists together. Farren took up the words again.

"Your vows spoken before your clan and Maker are accepted." He looked at Falier. "But this marriage goes beyond even the wonder of joining two souls. Falier Parsens-son, as you marry this clan's chief, do you vow to claim them as your own, protecting them as your family?"

Falier nodded solemnly. "I will."

"Will you fight for them with the strength given you by the Maker and his Eldír, and guide them with the wisdom given you?"

"I will."

"Will you serve your chief, encouraging her strengths and covering her weaknesses?"

Falier turned a smile to her. "Yes. I will."

At this, Hanah passed one sash to Farren. She fastened the second across Alísa's chest, over a shoulder and under the cape at her back. Though the garment bore the chief's red, Hanah had chosen a plaid with blue also woven in to help tie the colors together with the wedding dress. As Hanah fastened the garment, Farren draped Falier with the other.

Farren accepted a bowl of red paint from L'non, who had emerged from the crowd. Dipping his fingers in the bowl, he painted a line on each side of Falier's forehead, leaving a gap in the middle where Alísa's own crowning paint sat.

"Then, by the authority the Maker has given me, I present to the clan Chief Alísa and her tiern, Falier. May souls bound before all never be separated."

Alísa squeezed Falier's hand and faced him again. Wearing his sash and crowning marks, he looked every bit the tiern he now was. Lifting his free hand to her cheek, Falier leaned in and kissed her, garnering whoops, rumbles, and trills. He started pulling back, but Alísa hooked her free arm around his neck and deepened the kiss, soaking in his love, desire, and joy.

When they finished, they found their families had backed into the crowd, leaving them alone in the center as a fiddler started a reel. Grinning, Falier led Alísa into a simple dance. Tied together as they were, he couldn't embellish the basic steps with spins or separations and returns, but their dance held energy, nonetheless. After a short while alone, Parsen and Kat re-entered the circle. L'non offered his hand to Hanah, and a few other couples danced as well. Farren, Selene, and Taz joined in the music-making, and the audience clapped along. Soon, dreki flew among them too, lending their wonder to the mix.

As the song ended, Falier pulled Alísa close and pressed his forehead to hers. *"Have I told you you're beautiful?"*

"You wanted to, but tradition dictated you be silent."

"Well then." He kissed her, then spoke aloud. "You are beautiful. We'll have to find another occasion for you to wear this."

Alísa nodded toward her mother. "Mamá believes in both p-p-practicality and beauty. She fashioned it so the gauze c-comes off, leaving a dress suitable for ceremonies and d—diplomatic functions."

Falier released her and moved into position as a new dance began. "Please tell me you'll keep the cape at least. You can claim it represents dragon and dreki wings and is necessary for your role as the Dragon Singer."

Alísa smiled. "I like that."

More dances ensued, the after-ceremony leaning hard into the holders' céilí traditions. After a couple, Falier and Alísa forewent tradition and undid the hand-fasting cord. A few older women gave them raised eyebrows, but the opportunity to dance more elaborately and participate in partner-switching dances was well worth it.

One switching dance ended with Alísa and Falier on opposite sides of the cave, and Alísa found herself surrounded by well-wishers and unsolicited marriage advisors. Sesína quickly rescued her, the dragoness' size and sass allowing her breathing room. Alísa looked at her clan with a fondness she had never imagined she could feel for a crowd.

"I think we're going to be alright," Alísa said, leaning against Sesína.

"Don't get too mushy—you're bad enough with Falier. They still need some work." Sesína thrummed. *"Of course, with a beta as fabulous as me to help them along, I suppose they'll get there soon."*

"Yes. They will."

Alísa's eyes landed on the platform where multiple dragons still lay watching the proceedings. One of them was Lellani, and beside her—

"I haven't seen Kallar since he spoke to me about leaving," Alísa said, torn. *"He chooses now to emerge? Should I go see him—say goodbye?"*

Sesína clicked. *"Up to you. I'll accompany you."*

That settled it for Alísa. That and the eye-contact they just made. His expression was impassive, and he didn't look away until she did. Weaving through the crowd with Sesína, she ascended the platform. She stopped to take the congratulations of the dragons as she passed, but her mental distraction told them not to hold her for long. The closer she came, the more Kallar tensed, though he didn't leave his spot beside Lellani.

Lellani's connection came with Kallar in the background. *"Alísa-Dragon-Singer, congratulations on your marriage. I have found your kind's mating rituals most fascinating."*

Alísa smiled politely. "We humans love our ceremonies and symbolism."

"Indeed. Kallar has been answering my questions. Very symbolic. My favorite is the wings on your dress."

Alísa looked at Kallar. "You c-caught that, huh?"

Kallar shrugged. "It's obvious."

Alísa fought back a chuckle. "Trísse t-t-t-tells me you're leaving t-tomorrow?"

Kallar nodded once. His ice-blue eyes watched her unblinkingly, just like they always did. Even after two weeks without him causing any trouble, it unnerved her. A vigilance that saw and judged all.

"Take care of them," she said.

"I will."

The conviction in his answer transformed his uncomfortable gaze into something more earnest. Something that said he had already promised himself that. Alísa looked up at Lellani.

"And you take care of him."

Lellani blinked slowly. *"I will watch his back."*

Kallar eyed the dragoness, but didn't respond. His attention turned to the crowd below.

"You don't have to stay up here," Alísa ventured. "You could—"

"No."

Alísa held up her hands in surrender. "Okay. Thank you for c-coming. I hope you find what you're looking for." She offered an arm of friendship. "Eldra Bria sing over you."

Kallar stared at her for a moment, then clasped her forearm. "And you."

They released each other and, with a final slow blink to Lellani, Alísa descended back to the main floor, Sesína behind. Falier met them at the bottom, arm extended for Alísa.

"Did that go well?"

"I think so."

"Good. Thanks for going with her, Sesína."

Sesína huffed steam. *"Of course. Who do you think I am?"*

He walked Alísa along the outside of the chamber, the dragoness following. "The Southlands won't know what hit them, with that group invading."

Alísa laughed. "It won't be able to contain them."

"And you're really okay with our people going? Trísse?"

"If this is their p-p-path, how can I hold them back?" She looked out over the clan. "They aren't the only ones who needed t—t-to leave to become whole."

Falier kissed her head. "Well, I know my place is here." He kissed her temple. "With them" —her cheek— "and with you."

Sesína fake-gagged. *"Ugh. I'm going to find Graydonn. Maybe he'll gag with me."* Sesína shoved Alísa in the back with her snout, pushing her closer to Falier. *"Have fun, you two."*

She trotted away and Falier tugged Alísa tight against him, leaning down to murmur an inch from her lips. "Beta's orders."

Alísa giggled. "You're tiern now—you outrank her."

He shrugged and kissed her, an arm at her waist, a hand in her hair, and the buzz of his telepathy in her mind. Happiness swept through her, and when the next dance began, Falier whisked her away to join their clanmates, their hearts full.

EPILOGUE

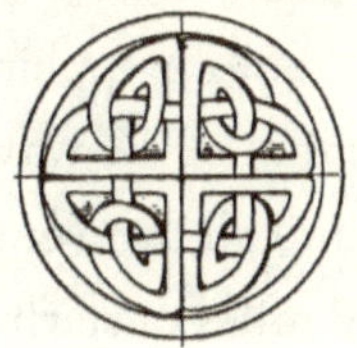

"—and Alísa continued her work for harmony between the races, Falier and Sesína ever at her side."

Songweaver Imáre paused, letting the last words breathe as the fire crackled. Lowering her hands, she bowed her head as she had the prior two nights of storytelling. Her audience showed their appreciation with applause and soft growls that rumbled through the air. When she lifted her eyes again, she smiled.

"Thank you, I'm glad you enjoyed this telling. It is a particular favorite of mine and F'gian's."

She looked back at the dragon lying behind her, grateful beyond words for what he contributed to her storytelling. F'gian, his scales a tawny orange, slowly blinked his light-green eyes.

"But, but!"

Imáre returned to her audience, where a small girl lifted her hand into the air.

"Yes?"

"Did Alísa and Falier have kids?"

The buzz of telepathy entered Imáre's mind as a male hatchling spoke up. *"Enough of the mushy stuff! What about Lellani, Kallar, and their crew? Did they succeed?"*

"Were they all still alive during the slayer wars?" An older teen asked.

A dry female voice ran through their heads. *"Did Kallar ever learn to songweave properly?"*

Imáre laughed. "All excellent questions, and all stories for another time."

Young children continued raising hands while hatchlings pawed the ground, but F'gian stood to silence them all with a deep, purring rumble.

"*Hush now. Songweaver Imáre is tired, as are many of you, I'd wager.*"

Parents took their cue and gathered their little ones. As dragons nudged their hatchlings with their muzzles, they gave slow-blinks to both Imáre and F'gian. Some young ones climbed onto their parents' backs, wings spread to practice flying. One man climbed onto a sapphire dragon and saluted her before taking off. His cloak bore the symbol of the wayfarers.

The space cleared slowly until all that remained to Imáre and F'gian were the sleepy town behind them and miles of starlit hills before.

"*That took longer than expected.*" F'gian stretched his forelegs, pawing at the ground. "*Do you wish to spend another night, or to return home as intended?*"

Imáre began her own series of stretches, fatigued from sitting so long. It was three hours' flight to the cave where their dragon-rider clan resided. One last sleep in the Hold wasn't a terrible idea, but her own bed also appealed. In the end, F'gian's needs swayed her—he had slept under the stars for weeks now as they made their rounds. Her mind-kin deserved the assurance of a stone ceiling.

"I think I can stay awake a few more hours."

"*Good.*" He lowered to his belly as she snapped up her pack. "*Then we can discuss the errors in your storytelling.*"

Imáre scoffed. "Errors? I've been telling this story for years now!"

"*Yes,*" he rumbled, "*and I've told you before that many of Alísa's songs were not nearly so polished on her first try.*"

"I'm a songweaver. Of course, I want to use the final versions!"

"*And your timing doesn't line up correctly as you jump between Alísa's and Kallar's portions of the story.*"

Imáre threw the loop of her pack over F'gian's spine and hauled herself up. "Small poetic licenses. I get them close enough. Otherwise, we'd go too long without hearing from one. After all our time together, you should understand story-elements like these."

She slapped his shoulder for emphasis, making her palm sting.

F'gian thrummed, standing. "*Careful. Your 'story-elements' may overtake great-great-grandmother's memories. Then where will you be, unable to trust the details of my Illumination?*"

Imáre shook her head, grinning. "Keep telling me I'm wrong, my friend, and I'm sure Sesína's memories will stay intact. Your will is as strong as hers."

With a trumpet, F'gian launched into the night sky and turned his muzzle toward the Sisters constellation in the north. There, Alísa and Sesína continued their noble mission, guiding each generation as they had their own so many years ago.

ACKNOWLEDGMENTS

We made it! Thank you so much to everyone who helped make this journey so amazing. For every up and down, every bout with imposter syndrome, every excruciating change and cut, there have been wonderful people there to encourage me along the way.

To my alpha readers and best friends Bethea and Serianna—our ways of seeing the world are so gloriously different, and I owe so much to you two for seeing *Soulflame* at its messiest and giving me pointers for making it better and more *real*. Thank you for everything.

Thank you to my fantastic teams of beta and gamma readers—Audrey, Claire, Emily, Ericka, Isaac, Kaitlyn, Kayla, Kelly, Liz, Maegan, and Rachel! Your enthusiastic reactions made my heart soar, and your questions and concerns made this book better. You all rock!

To my editor Katie Phillips—amid my deep bout of insecurity you knew nothing about, you called this book a triumph. Those words have carried me through the rest of this book's journey. Thank you!

To the Unsanctioned Saints—now you know why I lobbied hard for one of our studies to be on spiritual beings! Thank you for your prayers; our long, messy, "this may sound heretical" conversations; and for constantly reminding me that God is bigger than my boxes.

Thank you to my parents for always asking how the next book is coming along, how sales are going, and what I'm learning. Thank you especially for encouraging me to ask questions and think deeply—these books would not exist without that.

To Meeko, Pidge, Liddy, and Jace—thank you for all the ideas for how dragons and dreki act. The slow-blinks, swishing tails, cheek rubs, and excited trills make them all just a bit more believable.

Thank you to my readers for sticking with me and my messy characters this long. Your emails, comments, and reviews keep me going.

Finally, to Jehovah-Rapha—the LORD my Healer. Thank You for being big enough for my anger, my sadness, my insecurities, and for the healing You continue to work in me. May the truth shine amidst the fiction and bring glory to You.

ABOUT THE AUTHOR

Michelle M. Bruhn is a YA fantasy author whose stories focus on outcasts, hard questions, and hope. She is passionate about seeing through others' eyes and helping others to do the same, especially through characters with diverse life experiences. She finds joy in understanding others, knows far too much about personality theories, and binge-watches TED Talks on a regular basis. She spends the rest of her free time making and listening to music, walking, reading, and snuggling with her cats.

www.michellembruhn.com
News & Musings: michellembruhn.substack.com